The
Mabinogion
Tetralogy

The Mabinogion Tetralogy

Prince of Annwn
The Children of Llyr
The Song of Rhiannon
The Island of the Mighty

EVANGELINE WALTON

Introduction by Betty Ballantine

THE OVERLOOK PRESS
WOODSTOCK & NEW YORK

First published paperback in the United States in 2004 by
The Overlook Press, Peter Mayer Publishers, Inc.
Woodstock & New York

WOODSTOCK:
One Overlook Drive
Woodstock, NY 12498
www.overlookpress.com
[for individual orders, bulk and special sales, contact our Woodstock office]

NEW YORK:
141 Wooster Street
New York, NY 10012

Library of Congress Cataloging-in-Publication Data

Walton, Evangeline.
The Mabinogion tetralogly / Evangeline Walton.
      p. cm.
1. Mabinogion—Adaptations. 2. Tales, Medieval—Adaptations. 3. Tales—Wales—
Adaptations. 4. Mythology, Welsh—Fiction. 5. Wales—Fiction. I. Title
     PS3545.A6296 M33   2002   813'.52—dc21   2001055430

Book design and type formatting by Bernard Schleifer
Printed in the United States of America
ISBN 1-58567-504-0
3 5 7 9 8 6 4 2

Contents

The Third Branch: The Song of Rhiannon

The Fourth Branch: The Island of the Mighty

Introduction

Betty Ballantine

ROOTED IN THE oral myths and legends of Wales, the Mabinogion, which scholars believe was first set down, possibly by a single hand, before the mid-twelfth century, is the backbone and masterwork of Welsh medieval literature.

The original title, *Pedair Cuine y Mabinogi*, refers to the four Branches that appear in this volume, comprised of the loosely connected tales of Pwyll, Branwen, Manawyddan, and Mâth. The work was first translated by Lady Charlotte Guest in 1834–49, but perhaps the most prestigious translation, of more recent times, is that of Gwyn and Thomas Jones, published in 1949, just a century after the first English chronicle. Since then, various articles, monographs, commentaries, and papers of many kinds have analyzed, dissected, and ruminated over this monumental work, a rich source and subject for scholarly debate. (Indeed, it is evident from her footnotes that Miss Walton was herself a scholar of some note.) One side effect of this academic interest is that the form "Mabinogion" became commonly used for the Four Branches, rather than the contraction "Mabinogi."

Be that as it may, until Miss Walton elected to do so, apparently no one had undertaken to tell the stories of the Four Branches in the form in which they must have originated, as fiery, passionate, and very immediate accounts of real men and women, historic figures set in a time when belief in the gods of air and earth, of fire and water, were vast, inexplicable realities in a world pregnant with magic, a world of marvels and wonders, teeming with strange creatures who might well be denizens of strange other landscapes, and who almost certainly would have monstrous arcane powers. One of the great gifts of magic is mystery.

Unfortunately, by the arrival of the nineteenth century, such a world of magic evoked Victorian images of fairies at the bottom of the garden, pure fantasy, a playground for children (and scholars, of course . . .). In fact, even in 1936, when Evangeline Walton's magnificent Fourth Branch first appeared, it was ignored, its brilliant execution never recognized, and its author quickly relegated to obscurity.

In the mid-sixties, Ballantine Books, which had at last won literary recognition for the superb authors of its ground-breaking science fiction list, decided to embark on fantasy by publishing J.R.R. Tolkien's *The Lord of the Rings*, long available in England as a "juvenile." The welter of publicity that attended the appearance of *The Hobbit* and *The Lord of the Rings* in paperback reprint form spearheaded attention on what would become the equally famous Ballantine adult fantasy classics, including Mervyn Peake's *The Gormenghast Trilogy*, the works of Ernest Bramah, Lord Dunsany, James Branch Cabell, George MacDonald, E. R. Eddison, and many more. It was inevitable that research would eventually turn up the name of Evangeline Walton. But it was a long time before much more was known than just her name and the title of her first publication, that unforgettable, but nevertheless forgotten, *The Virgin and the Swine*. Where did it come from? Could there possibly be a link to the Mabinogion? Who was the author?

Evangeline Walton Ensley was born on November 24th, 1907, in Indianapolis, Indiana. She was a so-called "blue" baby and never enjoyed really good health. All her life, both as a child and as an adult, she had to cope with the after effects of silver nitrate treatments which left her with a ghostly blue-grey skin condition. Her odd appearance, no less than her frail health, necessitated a home education, beginning a lifelong reclusive habit.

She was taught largely by her great-aunt, Calista Fellows. Growing up in an adult household, and requiring to be "kept quiet" inevitably resulted in a heavy reliance on books; reading became the solace and joy of a lonely and imaginative girl. Her early reading included the popular fantasy writers of the time: characters from Rider Haggard, Edgar Rice Burroughs, L. Frank Baum, Lord Dunsany, and the like, were her daily companions. As she matured she read the romantic poets and her interests expanded to medieval and ancient history with their heavy emphasis on witchcraft and fantasy. She became precociously well-informed and was encouraged to write, not only about the friends she made in books, but about those she created from her own vivid and active mind. Writing, too, became a habit.

Her bent was toward the magic and the fantastical but her burgeoning imagination was truly captured when she encountered the heroic myths of the ancient Welsh in the body of work known as the Mabinogion. Here was richness, not only powerful enough to rivet her interest, but a major work to treasure, explore, mull over, and savor. The myths, with a matter-of-fact acceptance of magic in the everyday lives of humankind, together with the fierce, tempestuous stories of the early Celts, the titanic imagery, the blending of gods and men—all proved to be an irresistible lure. The young woman determined to one day re-write the legends of the Mabinogion as historic fiction.

We do not know when she actually began to write what would become her major work, but in 1936, when she was twenty-nine, the firm of Willett

Clark published the Fourth Branch of the Mabinogion by Evangeline Walton under the title *The Virgin and the Swine*. An America just climbing out of a worldclass Depression was notably uninterested in fantastic legend, still the stuff of children's books. Next, three loosely linked short stories appeared, based on the Breton legend of the submerged city, Ys. Nothing more was heard from Evangeline Walton until 1945, when August Derleth started his "Library of Arkham House Novels of Fantasy and Terror" with her gothic mystery *Witch House*. Eleven years later, Beuregy published *The Cross and the Sword*, a re-creation of the violent world of the Norse sagas.

After that, silence. Until the early 1970's when Lin Carter, free-lancing for Ballantine Books, found a copy of *The Virgin and the Swine*—an entry for their now firmly established adult fantasy line. I began a search for the author. The original publisher was long defunct. The British publisher had no idea where she was. Ballantine Books advertised in the science fiction and fantasy media for several weeks, with no result. In response to my enquiries the Library of Congress reported no address for the author, and moreover, that copyright on this title had never been renewed. But I was in love with the work and determined to see it back in print.

Having tried all public avenues for discovery without success, I proceeded with plans for publication under a much more suitable title: *The Island of the Mighty*. The weeks and months went by and we were on the verge of publication, the books already printed, when the Library of Congress informed me that—so sorry—they had made an error: the copyright *had* been renewed, but they still had no address . . . A publisher's nightmare. In the same week, we received a casual postcard from August Derleth mentioning that he had just come across one of our ads and felt he might as well supply us with a 20-year-old address which, he noted, was probably not still valid.

We wrote anyway to the address in Tucson, explaining the circumstances—and bingo! We had found Evangeline Walton.

I fired off a contract, accompanying it with a letter remarking that Miss Walton could not possibly have produced such a book and *not* have written anything else. (I was well aware that this Fourth Branch covered only a part of the original twelve-branched Mabinogion.) What had happened? Where was the body of her work? What else had she written?

At which point, nightmare metamorphosed into a dream come true. Miss Walton replied that indeed she had continued to write her version of the Mabinogion (she could not bear not to . . .) but had stored the unpublished manuscripts when her first publisher had not even wanted to *see* any more material on the subject. She had assumed there was simply no interest in fantasy.

I was virtually overcome with excitement at being able to read three more manuscripts in this incomparable work, to say nothing of the pride in bringing them into print. And so, in due course, and after Miss Walton had checked and revised her early work, *Prince of Annwn*, *The Children of Llyr*, and *The Song of Rhiannon* were published to the delight of the many dedicated fans by now familiar with the Ballantine adult fantasy series.

I tell this tale of a publishing triumph in some detail because it gave me such joy, and in its own way, materially affected the personal life of a writer I admire enormously. For Evangeline Walton, so long ignored, had found her home in the science fiction and fantasy world. As a result of this belated recognition of her talents, she was persuaded to attend (face, neck and even hands heavily made-up) various fantasy and science fiction conventions. Although at first bemused, she was eventually delighted by the adulation of the fans who, well accustomed to the differences that constitute one of the most intelligent reading audiences in the world, were completely unfazed by the mask-like appearance of this extraordinary lady. She proved to be a merry and highly erudite companion, and as she became more accustomed to acceptance, abandoned the nuisance of much of the make-up to appear, comfortably, as herself. She even took to traveling, and visited the birthplaces of the legendary characters she had so admired all her life. So Evangeline Walton came into her own, winning awards and accolades in the fantasy world she had adopted as a small girl.

Recognition of her immense writing talents followed rapidly in the mainstream media. The prestigious *Saturday Review of Literature*, in a broad and definitive article on the phenomenal popularity of fantasy writing, acknowledged her work (along with those of T.H. White and C.S. Lewis) as ". . . not only the best fantasies of the twentieth century . . . they are great works of fiction. Walton succeeds in creating an imaginary world that we believe *actually existed* [their italics] in this world's history." And in *Fantastic Literature*, the editors describe the Walton tetralogy quite simply as "a work of genius."

Evangeline Walton's re-creation of the Mabinogion covers the Four Branches, the first being *Prince of Annwn*, a lucid, dramatic, and powerful narrative in which Pwyll, Prince of Dyved, encounters the Grey Man, King Arawn (Death) of Annwn, and undertakes to descend to his world to do battle with the monster Havgan whom even Death cannot conquer. Epic battle scenes are followed by a tender wooing of Rhiannon in a landscape magically transformed to the Bright World of Faery, which the lady proves willing to abandon in order to become Pwyll's bride, at least for a "time." Time in the Bright World has a very strange way with mortals . . .

The second Branch, *The Children of Llyr*, deals with the drama and tragedy of Llyr's five offspring—great Bran the Blessed, beloved ruler over all the Island of the Mighty; Manawyddan, his wise, thoughtful and magically gifted younger brother; their sister Branwen and half-brothers Nissyen and Evnissyen. The latter two, born of rape, are destined to be the force behind the tragic events that will destroy Bran and all his people. Evnissyen's wicked malice carries the plot to Ireland to witness Branwen's bitter humiliation at the hands of King Matholoch, and the terror of the great Cauldron of Life in the battles that follow. This is a tale drenched in blood and horror "permeated with raw emotion, brute violence and human savagery, laying bare the evil in humanity." In the symbolic, but very real, persons of the twins Nissyen and Evnissyen, Walton makes brilliant and ghastly use of the age-old conflict between Good and Evil. Horror and high courage march hand-in-hand, each feeding the powerful impact of the other.

The Song of Rhiannon, the Third Branch, is a perfect counterpoint to the violence and rage of *The Children of Llyr*, from which only Manawyddan and Pryderi, the new Prince of Dyved, survive. This Branch explores the heart-wrenching pact between Manawyddan and Prince Pwyll, the Grey Man of the First Branch. The main themes here are the enduring strength of love and respect between partners, and the dignity of humans whether noble or humble. *The Song of Rhiannon* is perhaps the most human of the Four Branches, despite being set largely in the Bright World of Faery. There is even some wry comic relief in the person of a bogey whom Kigva, Pryderi's wife, regularly placates with bowls of milk.

Finally, in *The Island of the Mighty*, the Fourth Branch, Walton reaches the apex of her re-creation of the Mabinogion. This Branch, the longest in the tetralogy, is divided into three Books. The chief protagonists who motivate the driving narrative are Gwydion and his feckless brother Gilvaethwy, together with their sister Arianrhod, a gifted sorceress, and their endlessly patient sire, Mâth the Ancient. Book I tells of the use of illusion to steal a number of the strange new beasts called "pigs," and of the seduction of the virgin Goewyn, both of which deceptions have long and dire consequences. Here, too, is the tender and bitter love between Gwydion and his sister, Arianrhod, who is certainly not the virgin she claims to be.

Book II deals with Arianrhod's son, Llew, and with the strange way in which Gwydion is forced to raise the boy in order to protect him from his mother. Book III is the poignant tale of an exquisite creature created out of flowers by Mâth the Ancient, to serve as wife to Llew and thereby to frustrate at least one of his mother's curses.

Each of the Books of the Fourth Branch is rich in detail. In this climax to the tetralogy Evangeline Walton pulls together the threads of prophecy, the tangled emotional cross-currents of her characters, the web of plot and sub-plot, and the long reach of narrative—all of which, woven together in a vibrant tapestry of words, place her Mabinogion among the greatest of mythic works. Throughout the Four Branches runs the fundamental theme of great change, of the conflict between the beliefs of the Old Tribes whose women were powerful and free, respected by all and "blessed of the Gods," for only they were the creators of life. For millenia mankind worshiped female gods; inheritance was always through the maternal line—a man's only sure blood-line was through his sister, hence his heir would have to be his nephew. The connection of one man in particular to birth was not recognized until the growing sophistication of the New Tribes raised a revolutionary possibility about conception. Like all revolutions, the new thinking brought major problems.

Old and sacred beliefs were not easily relinquished. But the new idea was driven by a deep need for acknowledgment of paternity, by the promise of dominance inherent in such a shift in power—and sometimes by simple greed. Much of mythology grew from the massive changes in culture that took place over the generations when mankind first began to suspect the truth about the origin of birth and combined their suspicions with a continuing reliance on magic, faery and sorcerous powers. Add to this the universal theme of Good versus Evil in the art of story-telling—for eons the mainstay of conveyed information—and you have a roiling broth of imaginative explosion.

Evangeline Walton's skills do not lie merely in retelling old tales, no matter how charged with excitement; her enormous gift is in creating completely credible god-like beings whose huge vitalities, wondrous powers, and tragic weaknesses are, in the end, terribly human. Through the talent of this remarkable woman, the myths are made real, and the people who live through the titanic events of their time speak to us, very personally, with poignancy and warning, over the centuries.

Evangeline Walton was in love with the charismatic figures who moved through the high, historic drama of great change in a world of arcane power precisely because she was very much a woman of our time who recognized prophecy in these magnificent legends and—a sorceress in her own right —converted the ancient prophecies into the brilliant reality of her own words. In the end, this retelling of the Mabinogion is a great work because these are people and times she enables us to touch. We are enriched, and forever grateful.

Bearsville, 2001

Prince of Annwn

BOOK ONE

DESCENT INTO THE ABYSS

*In memory of a girl who loved all things Celtic and magical;
I hope that she would have enjoyed this book.*

1

The Hunter and the Hunted

THAT DAY Pwyll, Prince of Dyved, who thought he was going out to hunt, was in reality going out to be hunted, and by no beast or man of earth.

The night before he had slept at Llyn Diarwya, that lay halfway between royal Arberth, his chief seat, and the deep woods of Glen Cuch. And at moonset, in the last thick darkness before dawn, he woke there.

He woke suddenly, as if a bell had been rung in his ear. Startled, he peered round him, but saw only sight-swallowing blackness that soon thinned to a darkness full of things yet darker. Of half-shaped, constantly reshaping somethings such as always haunt the lightless depths of night, and make it seem mysterious and terrible. He saw nothing that meant anything, and if he had heard anything he did not hear it again.

Then, sharp as an order, came memory: *"You have come to hunt in Glen Cuch, so why not get to it?"*

"By the God my people swear by, I will do that!" said Pwyll, and he jumped out of bed.

He rousted out men, dogs, and horses, he drove them forth with their breakfast only half eaten.

"I wish he would get married," grumbled one man, looking sorrowfully back at his food as he made for the door. "Then he would get up later in the morning."

"He would have here if our host's wife had been young and pretty," mumbled a second man, still chewing. "Then he might have stayed in bed till noon." Which was true, for Pwyll was of the New Tribes, among whom hospitality included the use of one's wife as well as of one's best food and bed. It was different with the Old Tribes, who did not know marriage and whose women slept with men only when it pleased them, although they often pleased.

But that morning Pwyll would not have stayed in bed if the loveliest woman in the world had been there with him. The *Mabinogi* says that it pleased him to go hunting, but the fact is that it pleased somebody else. The idea had been planted in his brain by another, one far older, more subtle, and mightier. Pwyll, who liked to do as he pleased, whose wont it was to give orders, not to take them, never dreamed that he was being as obedient as one of his own hounds.

Out into the first feeble grey of dawn he rode, his hungry, sulky men with him. Soon the forest of Glen Cuch loomed before them, still black as night, mighty with the mystery and darkness that fill all deep forests. At its edge the men dismounted, for horses, like the sun, never could have pierced far into those depths.

Pwyll's horn sounded, and the dogs were loosed. For a space the huge beasts stood sniffing, red eyed, the hair on their backs rising. Then, with a great wild bellowing they were off. The black woods closed over them like gigantic jaws.

One man, looking after them, said uneasily: "I never saw them act quite like that before."

Pwyll laughed. "They have scented something. Let us go find out what!" And he charged into that darkness after the dogs.

For a little while he could not see anything. He pushed and broke his way through dense undergrowth, snapping off branches, and getting switched by branches that he had not snapped off. He knew that his men were all around him, for he heard them lumbering as clumsily as he through the undergrowth, and swearing when they too got switched. But ahead of them all still rang the wild being of the hounds.

This wood has always been thick, Pwyll thought, puzzled. *But the last time I was here it was not nearly this thick.*

Yet the belling of the hounds drew him irresistibly, that being which is wilder and more eerily sweet than any other sound on earth. He pressed on, heedless of torn clothes, and of the skin that was going with them. He listened so hard to the dogs that for some time he did not notice he had ceased to hear any sound from his men. *Well,* he thought, when he did realize his aloneness, *sooner or later we will all catch up with the dogs.*

But the way grew no easier and the belling no nearer, and presently it came to Pwyll that he had been fighting that slashing underbrush for far too long a time. Long ago sunlight should have begun to fall in bright patches through the green leaves above his head; daylight of some kind, at least. He began to wish that he could hear some of his men, no matter how far off, and to be ashamed of how much he wished it.

This forest must be thicker than any other forest in the world. It is certainly too thick. But She cast much rain last winter; that must be why.

The Welsh say, "She is casting rain," not "it is raining," and in Pwyll's day men still knew why. Rain and sun, crops and the wombs of beasts and women, all were ruled by that old, mysterious Goddess from whose own womb all things had come in the beginning. The wild places were Hers, and the wild things were Her children. Men of the New Tribes, Pwyll's proud golden warrior-kind, left Her worship to women, made offerings only to their Man-Gods, who brought them battle and loot. But now Pwyll began to wonder if those hunters were right who said that all who went into the woods to slay Her horned and furry children should first make offerings to Her, and promise not to kill too many. So folk of the Old Tribes had always done.

I do not know what You like, Lady, but whatever it is, You shall have it. Only get me out of here.

When he got home he would ask several women what She liked, all young ones. This plan cheered him, evoking pleasant images, but in that gloomy wood they soon faded.

Of a sudden the belling rang out fiercely, with the savage joy of dogs who are almost upon their quarry. But it was coming from the west, and the belling of Pwyll's dogs had always come from the east. Also it was not their cry. But swiftly the excited baying of Pwyll's hounds followed it; they too had turned west. The quarry must have changed its course; soon the two packs would meet! And that meeting could be bloody.

Pwyll could not run through those lashing brambles, but he crashed through them, losing more skin. His leaping feet flew above stones and roots that tried to trip him.

Ahead of him the forest seemed to open like a door. He saw a green glade, flat and open beneath a leaden sky. He stopped.

This place never has been here before. It cannot be a right place. Ought a man to go into it?

But then his own dogs came running into the far end of that glade, and his heart leapt. His mouth opened to call to them, but before any noise could come out of it a huge stag leapt out of the forest just ahead of him. Its tongue was hanging out, its eyes were mad with fear, and the strange hounds ran just behind it!

Their baying filled earth and heaven; it seemed to split Pwyll's eardrums. Before his swimming eyes flashed whiteness, whiteness that blazed like flame and shone like snow. Many bodies struck him; swifter than the wind, colder than snow, they knocked him down and leapt over him, they rushed on after the stag. In the middle of the glade they caught it, and they pulled it down.

As he stumbled to his feet Pwyll heard its tortured death cry. He stood dazed, watching those white shapes tear at the brown body that still twitched upon the ground, the long legs that a moment before had been so swift and powerful jerking feebly as the fierce fangs gnawed its flesh.

The eyes and ears and the blood-dripping teeth of those strange dogs glowed red, red as fire, but their white bodies glittered more savagely, with an unnatural, deathlike brilliance of paleness. Blackness terrifies; it is sightlessness, it blinds a man and hides his enemies; yet the darkness within the earth is warm and life giving, the womb of the Mother, the source of all growth. But in snow or in white-hot flame nothing can grow. Whiteness means annihilation, that end from which can come no beginning.

How long he might have watched that dreadful feeding Pwyll never knew. Silence roused him; deep silence that was broken only by the joyous, yet still savage growling of the victors.

His own dogs were not making any noise at all.

They were still there; at the far end of the clearing they crouched shivering. Every hair on their bodies stood up as still and straight as grass.

They were picked fighters; never before had they been known to turn tail before any foe. Always before they would have leapt light-swift, an ecstasy of rending fangs and claws, upon any other pack caught daring to hunt in any forest where Pwyll hunted. But now they cowered and shivered, afraid to tackle those unnatural, death-white dogs.

Pwyll saw that, and he could not bear it. He was young—not quite three winters had he been Lord in Dyved—and pride was still stronger in him than discretion. Also he was a little afraid himself, and what afflicts ourselves is often what we most despise in others.

He looked sternly at his dogs. "Take that stag!"

They looked at him beseechingly; they wagged their tails, begging him to change his mind. Their eyes said pitifully: *"Lord, we have always done your bidding. Anything we can do for you we will always do. But this . . . Do not ask it of us, Lord; do not . . ."*

And because he himself was afraid that they could not do it Pwyll was miserable; also their misery hurt him. And because he felt guilty he glared at them harder than ever.

"I said: take that stag!"

They cowered yet lower; they whined.

He never had struck any of them. They were his darlings and his heart's pride. Yet now he stooped and picked up a stick.

They could not bear that; death was less dreadful to them than his wrath. They moved, they advanced, tails down, bodies trembling.

Pwyll dropped the stick and drew his sword. He would not let them fight alone.

But when the stranger dogs saw them coming they backed away. With their nostrils full of the scent of blood, with their terrible, fanged mouths full of the meat and its good taste, they backed away from the hot, steaming flesh of their kill. Silently they went, their eyes gleaming redder than their bloodstained fangs, and to the watching man it seemed that those red eyes were mocking.

Pwyll did not like that retreat. No right dogs would have behaved like that. They should have fought; even if they knew that they were trespassing and were afraid, they should have shown disappointment.

Gingerly his own dogs approached the stag, but once they tasted its blood they began to tear it joyfully, growling deep in their throats. Though from time to time they stole wary glances at those pale, shining strangers, who stood off and watched, silent at the trees.

Pwyll never took his eyes off the strange dogs. Their red eyes stared back at him with a most undoggish straightness, with a glowing fierceness, an almost intolerable brightness; it took all his will not to look away.

"They are waiting for something," thought Pwyll. He glanced over his shoulder toward the west from which they had come. But there was nothing there; only trees.

His heart leapt, then sank; there was Something!

A namelessness, a far-off greyness, not solid enough to be a beast, too thin to be fog . . .

It was moving! It was coming, neither swiftly nor slowly, but with an awful, steady sureness. What shape was on it, man, beast or cloud, Pwyll could not tell; he knew only that, whatever it was, when it got there he would wish it was something else.

The bole of one enormous old tree hid it; for a breath's space Pwyll could not see it, and then a Grey Man on a Grey Horse rode out into the glade. And Pwyll's hand, that had leapt to his sword-hilt, froze there, and his eyes stared as if frozen in his head.

Both horse and rider were solid now. They looked bigger than they should have, and every part of them, hair and hide, hoof, clothing, and skin, was of precisely the same color. The same terrible, corpselike grey.

All but the Man's eyes.

Pwyll did not want to meet those eyes, but he could not escape them. Through their shining blackness cold seemed to stream through his blood and bones. Knowledge streamed with it, knowledge that he could neither understand nor keep. His brain reeled away from that awful wisdom, that poured into it as into a cup, and overturned it, and was spilled again.

He could not close his eyes; he shuddered and covered them with his hands, to shut out those other eyes. He was glad, blessedly glad, that he could still move his hands.

The Horseman spoke then, and his voice had a note of the wind in it, of a wind blowing through great space; in that it was like the baying of his dogs. But his words were ordinary enough.

"Prince," he said, "I know who you are, and it is not a good day I give you."

Nothing seems likelier, thought Pwyll, *than that you will give me a bad one. But I am a man, and I will not shame my manhood.* He threw back his head and looked at the stranger, and was delighted to find that now he could do it. Words or blows, these he could trade with any foe.

"Well, Lord," he said dryly, "perhaps your dignity is so great that it is beneath it to greet me." That was irony; these were his lands, and he was Lord of them, and the stranger had entered them unbidden.

But the other was unabashed. "By the Gods, it is not my dignity that stops me!"

"Then what is it?"

"By all the Gods,"—and Pwyll wondered if he were one of them and were swearing by himself—"it is your own ignorance and bad manners!"

Pwyll stiffened. His grey eyes had the glint of ice. "What bad manners have you seen in me, stranger?"

"Never have I seen worse manners than to drive away the dogs that had made the kill, and to set your own pack on the carcass!" Thunder rolled in the deep voice.

"If I have done you wrong," said Pwyll quietly, "I will pay you whatever face-price is due your rank. I do not know what this is for I do not know you."

Suddenly all became very still. No leaf moved, no wind stirred, the birds of the air hung motionless, and the snakes ceased to slither in the deep grasses. Even the dogs stopped chewing, though their mouths were full of meat.

"I am a crowned King in the land whence I come." The stranger's voice was low, yet the wild vastness of the wind was in it, and something within Pwyll shrank.

"Good day to you then, Lord King." He kept his voice and eyes steady. "What land is that?"

"Annwn. Arawn, a King in Annwn, I am named."

Then indeed did great cold pour through Pwyll again, freezing him, blood and bone. For he understood.

Our world is one of many. The uninstructed group them all together in the lovely, capricious, ever-perilous realm of Faery, but Pwyll, being of kingly blood, had had some druidic instruction forced upon him. He knew that the Otherworld nearest earth was Annwn, the Abyss; that primal womb in which all things first took shape. There a horde of nameless beings had struggled up, through form after form, until after untold ages, they were ready to be born upon earth as men. There most men returned at death, only a few being able to go on to a higher, brighter place. "Every world has its Grey Man," his cousin Pendaran Dyved, the only druid he trusted, once had told Pwyll. "Only among us of earth none dwells, because we are afraid to look upon his face. So he that dwells in Annwn is our Lord also. He is the gardener who tends every garden. He gathers the flowers and the ripe fruit, to make room for the new to grow. He fells the old trees, that the young trees may have room to grow."

And Arawn was the Grey Man of Annwn, the Master of the hounds of the Mother: Arawn, whose other name was Death.

Dizzily Pwyll thought: *Am I dying? But what happened to me? I am young and strong; I do not remember being killed.*

If he had been, surely he would have noticed something. But then why was Death here? He would not meet those awful eyes, he turned his head away, he looked hard and hungrily at the trees and grasses. Things he always had taken for granted, but that now seemed very precious, very dear.

Yet he felt those eyes. They burned through the side of his head, through his flesh, into his skull. Until at last he turned and faced Arawn.

"I promised you whatever face-price was your due. Take it, Lord King." He swallowed, but he said it.

2

The Meeting in the Forest

ARAWN SAID quietly: "No man may flee long from my hounds and me; we need no tricks to run him down. I do not seek your life, Lord of Dyved."

"Then what do you want?" Pwyll felt dizzier than ever, but with relief now.

"All men's lives are mine to claim when the time comes, so all men may be called my subjects. Yet that one service is all I have the right to claim. So, needing another from you, I arranged this meeting."

As lightning flashes upon a man in darkness, unseen hills and valleys blazing out of blackness into fiery splendor before his eyes, so Pwyll saw. He understood. Not by chance had he wakened and wished to go forth into the dawn; into that twilit dimness which is neither night nor day, and when, as at dusk, Beings without our gross flesh find it easiest to show themselves to men. He had walked into a trap, and here was the trapper.

"You are right," said Arawn, "I planned all." And Pwyll knew that to this mighty Being thoughts were as loud as words; no secret could be hidden from him.

He said, "I should have known! When I saw this glade where no glade ever was before, I should have known that I had ridden out of my world into yours!"

"That is so. Nothing in your world but mirrors something that was first in Annwn. You walk now in Glen Cuch as the Mother first dreamed it, not as it is on earth."

"But why bring me here? What on earth—or off it— can a man do for a God?"

"There is a Lord whose lands lie opposite mine; Havgan, another King in Annwn. Once he ruled the dead of the Eastern World as I rule the dead of the West, but now he moves westward. He sits in Anghar the Loveless, he wars on me always, he would be master of all. To spare my people I agreed that both realms should be staked on single combat, to be fought again in a year and a day, if we both lived. So we fought, and I slew him."

"But then it is all over! You won, and he is dead." Then Pwyll remembered that everybody in Arawn's world was dead, and scratched his head. "I never have believed those old wives' tales about people who died on earth going to the moon, and people who died on the moon going to the sun, yet anybody who dies in your world, Lord, must have to go on to one that is even deader."

Arawn smiled. "True. Those tales of sun and moon are for children, yet some truth is in them, even as something of a man, though little of him is in his likeness in a mirror. It is not good to lie to children."

Pwyll groaned. "You mean that although Annwn is not the moon, it is the moon?"

"It is the World of Middle Light, not the hard, bright place that earth is. My people are still much like your people; they know neither age nor sickness, but they still fight and slay one another, though not nearly so often as you do on earth. They may have many births on Annwn, but when they learn enough they are born into the Bright World, of which your sun is but the shadow. Where another Grey Man sits as Lord, where no man lifts hand against another, though he may know other, subtler perils."

"That other Grey Man—is he your kin?"

"There are Beings who cast shadows in many worlds. We Grey Men may all be shadows of One beyond your imagining; Havgan may be one of the Shadows of Another."

"I hope," said Pwyll simply, "that whatever it is you want me to do for you is something I can do without understanding what it is."

"The first part is only killing, which you have done often, whether you fully understood the deed or not. A year ago today I fought Havgan, and tomorrow you must meet him in my place. Meet him at the ford where warriors meet, and slay him if you can."

"Lord, how can I kill him if you could not?"

"Against him I no longer have any power, and no champion of mine can do what I cannot. All the might of Annwn is powerless against him now. But you are called a bull of battle and a woe to your enemies— the savage, rough strength of earth may do what we cannot."

"You think well of earth," said Pwyll, a trifle stiffly.

Arawn smiled again. "Every rung has its place in the ladder. But I meant no offense."

"There is certainly one good thing about earth," said Pwyll. "When you kill a man there he stays dead. You have no more trouble with him, though his friends and kin may try to make some."

"It is not Havgan's friends or kin that will come against me tomorrow," said Arawn, "but himself, and him none can slay a second time."

"That last is not queer. What I cannot understand is why he did not stay dead the first time." Pwyll spoke lightly, but his head swam. What help could Death need in killing? And what would happen to men if—inconceivable thought!—Death himself should die?

"Build no hopes on that." Again Arawn had read his thoughts. "Havgan too is Death, and if I fall he will slay as I never slew. All the worlds he can reach he will burn and tear and wreck. He will over-turn the order that I have maintained throughout the ages, I the Firstborn and Servant of the Mother."

For a breath's space there was silence. Then Pwyll said quietly: "Tell me what to do and I will do it."

Arawn looked at him, and in the measureless depths of his strange, sun-bright black eyes were sorrow and pity beyond man's understanding: the pity of a man for a child's sorrow, and the pity of a God for his suffering creation. For the misery that he has caused all creatures by creating them, and must share, or be less than God or man.

"You rode into Annwn unknowingly, you took only what you thought was your right. Though your heedlessness made your entrapment possible, yet a generous host would claim no face-price. The deed, if you do it, must be freely done."

"I pay my debts." Pwyll's chin rose proudly.

"You are too proud a warrior to fear Death. Yet you risk what you might think worse than dying. You ride into perils you cannot dream of."

"Whatever must be paid I will pay it," said Pwyll, "not for a stag's carcass—that I think you should forgive me for—but because my world, as well as yours, is at stake. That much I think I understand."

"Then let us swear friendship together," said Arawn. "Make ourselves close as brothers. No man born ever has sworn that oath with Death."

So they swore the oath, and Pwyll felt both awe and pride, he who now was Death's sworn brother. Oaths had great power then; ages after the Welsh country-folk still knew of one so powerful that he whose lips took it might wither away and perish, however well he kept it.

"Now I will send you to my own place," said Arawn. Pwyll started and once more the Grey Man smiled. "Fear nothing. Tonight you shall sit in my seat and sleep in my bed, and the loveliest lady you have ever seen will sleep with you there. For my shape will be on you, and neither my Queen nor the officer of our bedchamber—not a man of all the men that follow me—will know your face from my face. So it shall be until we meet again, in this same spot. After you have slain Havgan."

Pwyll could not help drawing a deep breath of relief. *So I will get back to earth.* This going down into the Abyss was to be only a visit, not a polite way of killing him, after all.

"Guard yourself well," said Arawn. "Havgan is the mightiest of warriors and the wiliest. He has arts and skills such as I have never seen in all the ages, I who have been present at all the battles of men, being Death."

"Yet you killed him?" Pwyll began to wonder if he could.

"With one great blow. As you must. Your true ordeal will come afterwards; when he lies broken at your feet."

"How can that be?" Pwyll was bewildered. "I will simply cut his head off then and make an end of it. Never have I dragged out any foe's death agonies."

His voice died, frozen in his throat by the awfulness of Arawn's face.

"Then indeed you will be lost. Whatever happens—and your heart will bleed for him as for your brother, born of one mother—strike him no second blow. So I, a God, was beguiled. I saw only him, heard only him; his agony seemed to tear my own flesh. So I yielded my will to his will, and he who does that has no more power against him forever."

"What happened?" Pwyll stared in wonder.

"When he begged me to cut off his head and put him out of his pain I did it—and the head jumped straight back onto his shoulders and grew fast there. He leapt up and fought again as well as ever. Barely did I escape from him."

Pwyll whistled. "That one," said he, "is a bad enemy to have."

"I have him," said Arawn grimly, "and if he slays you he will have my people and my world. And soon, yours."

"Well"—Pwyll's grin flashed again and he shrugged—"some day an enemy who is on his feet may get my head, but I think that when dealing with one who lies at my feet I will always be able to keep it."

"May that be true, Lord of Dyved! May your will be as strong as your arm—and both will need strength." Arawn's eyes were deeper than the sea, his voice had the rolling majesty of deep waters; of that ocean which, more than anything else that man can feel or touch, wears the likeness of infinity. "For my sake, and for your sake, and for the sake of all Gods and men."

So Pwyll rode down into Annwn to kill the man whom Death himself could not kill. He rode the Grey Horse, and when he looked down he saw grey hands on the bridle, hands that were not shaped like his hands. He did not look down often, because the sight disconcerted him. He told himself uneasily: *Down underneath it is the same old stuff—the stuff that is me. It must be!*

But was it? In that wild moment when his whole self had spun round and round—when his skin had seemed but a heaving, whirling cover over Chaos—anything might have happened. His soul might have been torn loose and blown into Arawn's body, and Arawn's soul might have been blown into his. Few earth-born men of illusion and fantasy could reshape matter, they could only throw a false appearance, cloaklike, upon what they bewitched. But the King of the Dead must be a mightier magician than any born on earth.

I have my own soul, anyway, Pwyll comforted himself. *The druids would say that was the real me.*

He did not like the druids, he never had understood their Mysteries, which he believed they often used to gain their own ends, but now that bit of their lore warmed his heart.

He had not understood at first that there was to be an exchange of shapes—something that would give Arawn the chance to take his body. He had said, troubled: "But my people—great fear and worry will be on everybody when I do not return from the hunt." And the Other had smiled. "No, for I shall be there in your place. Not a man or woman in Dyved will know my face from your face."

"But how will I find your palace?" Pwyll had scrambled wildly for objections. "And how would I know who was who if I got there? A King should know his people—"

"Give the Grey his head, and he will bear you where you should go. And when your people sleep I will be with you again. I myself will be your guide, and the way to my palace shall be clear before you."

And so it had been done, though at first Pwyll had felt as outraged as if some strange man had borrowed his horse or his hounds or his sword without leave, all the best of their kind in Dyved, and all cherished like beloved children.

My body too is the best of its kind in Dyved, he reflected. *Many men have told me so, watching me practicing my battle feats. And so have many women, when I was practicing other kinds of feats.*

There, with the drear mists of the Underworld rising about him, he grinned, remembering old prowess, old delights. But not for long. He had his soul, but he wanted his body too, the strong, warm young flesh he was used to and proud of. It had been a bad moment when Arawn had whistled, and Pwyll's dogs had followed him without a backward glance at Pwyll. It is a queer thing to watch yourself walking away from yourself.

Well, I will have his things too, just as he has mine . . . What will she be like, Arawn's Queen? I have the better of him there, for I have no wife for him to sleep with.

Not that he really meant to touch Arawn's Queen. Courtesy had compelled Death to offer her, just as courtesy would compel Pwyll to refrain from her. A man was expected to sleep with his own men's wives; that was the best way to keep a tribe strong, filling it with the sons of its leaders, of its mightiest men. Pwyll deflowered every wellborn bride in Dyved on her wedding night, and some that were not wellborn if they were pretty. If ever the High King of the Island of the Mighty visited Pwyll he would sleep with Pwyll's Queen—if there was such a person then. But Arawn was not Pwyll's man, but his equal and more. To take advantage of his generosity would be an ungentlemanly act.

And if the lady is the same color as her Lord it will be easy to be a gentleman, he thought. *Though of course I will be seeing her through Arawn's eyes . . .*

Or through eyes made over to look like Arawn's. There it was again. He would have liked to be sure that he still had his real self, all of himself. Also in battle a man does best with his own familiar weapons, and Pwyll would have liked to be sure that he had his own good, well-trained muscles. He sighed.

He had hoped soon to use those muscles in profitable earthly combat. Great Bell the High King was failing, and with him might die the peace that for many winters his strength and his justice had kept between Old Tribes and New. Bell was of the Old Tribes, so his heirs would be his sister's sons, the Children of Llyr, but in secret his own son, Caswallon, was already wooing the Lords of the New Tribes with questionable promises. "Help me to seize my father's throne before Bran, son of Llyr, has planted his big behind there long enough to grow strong. Then you shall be as the King's brothers, you shall lord it over the Old Tribes. Over those weaklings who think themselves mightier than you, though when your fore-bears swooped down like eagles upon the Island of the Mighty, they were not strong enough to drive them back into the sea." To Pwyll, Caswallon smelled like a traitor; a man's own people were his people, he should always think them the best of all, whatever they were. Yet son should follow father, and Dyved was a little land now; the New Tribes never had been able to take all of it. Pwyll wanted seven more cantrevs, and he could get them out of Caswallon the Cunning if he moved quickly, before the new King grew strong enough to forget his promises.

But will I get back now in time to help Caswallon? Earthly time is different from Otherworld time; I wish I had asked Arawn about that. I wish Arawn would get back . . .

The mists about him were growing ever more chill and drear. He had given the Grey his head, and any horse should know the way home to his own feeding trough. Yet if this was the way to Arawn's palace it was not a pleasant way.

Then it seemed to Pwyll that he heard something. A sound so far off, so eerily mighty, that he could not give it a name.

3

The Meeting on the Moors

IT WAS no right sound. Pwyll stopped his Horse, he listened, straining his ears, but now the cloudy greyness smothered all sound.
Nothing broke it, none of the myriad tiny sounds that weave themselves into a living tapestry to cover the forests and fields of earth.
To fill the houses of men at night. Pwyll strained his eyes, but he
might as well have been blind. He opened his mouth to call out in
challenge, but the mists rushed into it, cold and slimy, like half-solid
hands trying to claw their way down into the warm solidity that was
himself. He shut his mouth again, rather fast. Something might
indeed come at his call, but would that something be good to see?

He shook himself; such feelings were unworthy of a bull of battle. "Am I the Lord of Dyved? Soon I will be calling for my mother
like a little girl waking up in the middle of the night with a belly-
ache." He did not say "bad dreams"; somehow they did not seem like
things that should be mentioned, here. "Well, go ahead again, Grey."

The Grey of Arawn went; this time he sped forward. Quickly, purposefully, he galloped through the mists. Pwyll felt the hard, powerful
body under his knees, but there was none of the warm comradeship
he had always enjoyed with his own chestnut stallion, his dear Kein
Galed, that Arawn had now. He had always told his chestnut where to
go; now he was going wherever this strange Grey Horse chose to carry
him. And it seemed to him that they were heading toward the place
from which that mysterious sound had come.

There was no sound now. They galloped on and on through grey
sightlessness and grey soundlessness. Until Pwyll began to feel that
he would be glad to hear anything, any kind of a noise at all. And
then he heard it.

It was a great chopping noise that struck the deathly silence as a blow strikes flesh, and several great grinding noises followed it. Soon there was another crashing chop, then more grinding. Many carpenters and woodcutters working together, Pwyll told himself firmly, might make such noises.

Though if those were saws—he cringed as another grinding noise seemed to drive through both his ears and down into his stomach—*I never have heard saws I liked the sound of less . . . Ow! That must have been a great tree!* For there had been another mighty chop.

On earth carpenters and woodcutters seldom worked together, but this was not earth, and where people were Arawn's palace might be. These could be his workmen: Death's workmen.

They sound like it. The noises were setting Pwyll's teeth on edge, though he would not admit to himself that they made his flesh crawl. He listened intently as the Grey sped on. *They are keeping time like musicians, but they certainly do not sound like palace musicians. I do not believe any King, dead or alive, would have them in his hall . . . They are not only keeping time, all those noises sound as if they were being made by one Thing!*

For a breath's space he wavered, his hands tightened on the bridle. But the Grey clearly wanted to go on, and the Grey was the guide Arawn had given him. Also, whatever the Thing was, it was solid enough to make a noise, and Pwyll was longing for solid things.

If it is friendly I will make friends with it, and if it is not friendly I will fight with it.

Either course would be a good, manly occupation, something that Pwyll understood and knew how to do.

The mists were thinning now; floating backward and spiraling almost swiftly, as if anxious to get away from whatever lay ahead. Pwyll began to see again, though the greyness around him was nothing he would have called light on earth. Treading down discomfort, he told himself, *Well, soon I shall have a good look at this Noisemaker. And whatever it is, after all these endless mists it will look beautiful.*

Then he saw it, and it did not.

It was huge. Its flat black head pierced the grey sky, the mighty, hilllike width of the black-scaled chest and shoulders towered above the mists that swirled palely round tremendous scaly legs and massive clawed feet. It had three sets of jaws, and the fangs of all three dripped blood. From the two lower jaws protruded a human leg.

Pwyll's hand flew to his sword, yet he knew well that neither it nor his hunting spears would be any more use against that vast scaled might than would a woman's sewing needle against a charging bull. Quickly, hoping that the mist still hid them, he checked the Grey. He sat still and stared, and the Grey stood still beneath him.

Pwyll saw two immense forepaws, he saw a human head dangling from each, its hair caught in the great, glittering claws. Blood still dripped from the severed necks. There might be one uneaten body lying in the mists, at the Monster's feet, but Pwyll could not be sure.

"Nor does it matter, for he must have plenty of room in his belly for a third. It would take a whole war band to fill . . . Horse, let us get away from here as fast and as quietly as we can! What were you thinking of to bring me here?"

But he was too late. Even as they turned the Monster caught their scent. He threw back his dreadful head and bellowed, and that bellow filled heaven and earth. The severed heads swung and bobbed as in a mighty wind; the mists shook and churned like a storm-battered sea. Those red, fierce eyes burned through the fog; Pwyll felt their scorching glare when they found him.

Another bellow rose, hungry and triumphant. The earth shook.

Pwyll dug his knees into the Grey's sides, the stallion ran as he never had known any horse to run, but the Monster lumbered after them, still bellowing. His clumsiness, against the Grey's quick light grace, gave Pwyll a faint hope.

The Monster bellowed louder, angered by their speed. The half-eaten leg fell from his jaws, got to its one foot, and fled, hopping madly through the mists.

That is a wise leg, Pwyll thought. *But it will not be much good, without a man on top of it.* Then he shuddered. Men fought hard to get heads and bring them home from battle; nowadays to most warriors of the New Tribes such a trophy meant only, "I am a better man than him I got this from." But old men whispered that he who held a man's head also held some unseen part of that man; enslaved his ghost. Dreadful indeed would it be to be carried off to this Monster's den; to dwell with him in its foul darkness forever and ever . . .

He tried to make the Grey go faster, but could not. Those swift, lithe horse legs were giving all they had to give, but the clumsy, pursuing giant legs were gaining. With each stride they made a black, overlapping arch high as a hill.

Pwyll kicked off his fine, speckled shoes; he rose and stood upright in his saddle, his toes clinging hard to the edges. Often, on the practice fields of Arberth, that feat had made men applaud him and women squeal with wonder and delight. He freed one of his two hunting spears, raised and aimed it. Carefully, carefully he aimed;

with all the strength and skill he had in him he made his throw; that was a mighty cast.

It missed. The spear glanced off a great black scale beside one huge, wicked eye, fell to the ground.

Pwyll's teeth set. Swaying in the saddle, he aimed the second spear. He took his time, though it seemed that he had hardly any time left. This throw must be sure. . .

Like a flash of light the second spear cleft the air above him. It turned that awful bellowing to a screech that almost knocked Pwyll from the saddle. Quickly, joyously he straightened; was his task half done?

The spear had landed in one red, glaring eye. A lifted claw tore it out; the Monster howled with pain, then stooped to pick up a head he had dropped and lumbered on. Blood dripped from his eye now, the earth quaked harder than ever beneath his furious roars.

Pwyll still had his dagger; he had never used his sword in hurling games. Half blind, the Monster was as dangerous as ever, but there would be a chance to evade the terrible gropings of the wholly blind. The dagger was much smaller and lighter than the spear, which had not been able to go deep enough to kill. It might not even be able to blind, but if it could hit the other great pupil squarely, squarely . . .

"God of my people, be with me! Mothers, be with me!"

Like a bird the dagger flew through the air. For one glorious, sun-bright second Pwyll thought he had succeeded. But the dagger pierced only the outer covering of that huge, rolling eyeball. The Monster howled again, but this time with more rage than anguish; the dagger too was plucked out and fell to earth.

Pwyll too fell. His tortured toes lost their grip, he barely managed to get one arm round the Grey's neck. They sped on, the reins hanging loose. Then darkness fell upon them: a shadow that was indeed as black as night and death.

Pwyll felt the fiery heat of the Monster's breath, smelled its fetid stink, then the mighty tug at his cloak, the five searing pains that stabbed his back.

But then with a burst that outdid speed the Grey leapt forward. The cloak was ripped from Pwyll's back, five clawfuls of flesh went with it, but from behind him he heard the Monster's bellow of foiled rage. They had escaped, they were free! But Pwyll felt a warm tide gushing out where the cloak had been; those giant claws had raked him to the bone.

His back was a stinging agony. He saw blood splashing down beside him, he felt it spurt out, taking his strength with it. He saw the black shadow above them again, knew that again the Monster was gaining; he heard the Grey panting; there could be no second escape. Faint and sick as he was, he set his teeth again.

I will not fall at that Thing's feet. Or be plucked from the horse's back like a fruit. I will die as a man should die, facing him who takes my head.

For the space of a few more breaths he lay as still as he could on that tossing bed, gathering all the strength that was left in him. Bracing his trained warrior muscles to do their last deed, he loosened his sword in its sheath, the one weapon he had left him. Then, with a poor clumsy travesty of that lovely spring that had brought him to his feet before, he rose again. Stood erect in the saddle once more, desperate toes gripping it, his sword in his right hand. His rising placed him once again within striking range of his foe.

With an ear-splitting bellow of triumph the Monster pounced. But even as those giant claws, still dripping with his own blood, flashed down, Pwyll leapt. To one side and upward, straight at the Monster. He hoped to land on the nearest of those huge shoulders bent low to seize him. Weak as he was, had the vast, monstrous body been covered with hair instead of scales, he might have made it. His will and his warrior heart did not fail him, but his clutching hands slid vainly over those smooth scales; he fell. Scrabbling like a wounded beast, his body aching with fresh hurts, he tried to roll away through the mists that curled about those tremendous knees. But a great groping paw found him; agony tore through him again as mighty claws sank into his shoulder and into his already torn back.

He was being lifted; lifted toward those terrible triple jaws! He looked into a chamber of blazing fire; a chamber the red floor of which heaved and rolled forward.

The great red tongue, eager to taste him!

Like huge rocks a row of bloodstained teeth gleamed above him, descending. Another row glittered below him, rising. In less than a breath's space they would come together and bite off his head!

Then, far below it seemed, he heard the shrill scream of a fighting stallion, the thudding of hoofs against scales. The Grey was trying to help him! Not knowingly had he led his new master into a trap. The Monster roared again; even that black bulk felt the hoofs of the steed of Death.

That loyalty warmed Pwyll, stirred him to one last effort. Even as the deafening sound of that mighty roar beat upon him, surged over him like the waves of the sea, squirmed free of that momentarily loosened grip. He could no longer hope to clamber up to the great eyes, as he had planned. Probably his sword would have accomplished even less than his spears had, even if he had reached the dread shoulder. But at least he would hurt that tongue before it enjoyed him!

He squirmed forward and plunged his sword deep into the huge, wriggling redness. Into it and through it!

The bellow that followed seemed to shatter his head and to split all the bones of his body apart. To split the earth beneath and bring the heavens crashing down upon them!

Pain woke Pwyll. A massive scaly leg, thicker than the thickest tree trunk, was shooting back and forth through the air above him. *Soon it will fall and crush whatever is left of me. Then I shall rest.* So Pwyll thought and did not care, so great were his weakness and pain.

Then he saw the Grey again, lightning swift, darting in and out of the path of those stupendous kicks, still attacking. And the roaring still shook the earth; Pwyll's ears woke too, and he heard it. Both huge forepaws must be tearing at the sword in that terrible tongue; a cow's feet might as well have tried to grasp a splinter.

He must have spat me out, thought Pwyll, *and the Grey is holding him off. But he cannot do it long. Death, will you come for your own horse?*

If Arawn really had tried to trick Havgan, he had been outtricked. But Pwyll was tired, too tried and hurt to do anything now but lie still. And yet . . . a man should help his friends, and the Grey was his friend . . .

He tried to get to his hands and knees, crumpled, tried again, staggered to his feet, and fell back into the ever-widening pool of his own blood. His eyes closed . . .

Through the mists within and without him a cry came. Two cries. Pwyll opened his eyes.

Out of the mist the two severed human heads were rising, flying through the air like balls. As that tree-thick leg swung low to kick at the Grey they leapt upon it, perched there like birds. Again Pwyll heard those two shouts, knew them for war cries. He thought weakly: *You must have grown on the necks of brave men to come back to the fight now. Good luck, little fellows; you will need it!*

But he did not see how they could have it, and his eyes closed again. Soon there would be an end of them all, horse and heads and man.

Something made him open his eyes again. The heads must have jumped from the Monster's leg to his side. They were hopping round to his back now, leaping from scale to scale, always going up, up, up.

Pwyll wished he had strength enough to cheer them. Brave heads, clever heads!

Also, for some unimaginable reason, it seemed important that he should keep his eyes open and watch them. Although nothing could be important now. And being awake hurt . . .

The Grey was still fighting, and the heads had reached the huge neck. For a moment they rested, one perched on each giant shoulder. Then they made one last leap—the greatest leap of all. They reached what Pwyll had hoped to reach, the top of that horrible, flat head. They rolled across its gruesome plain, bared teeth flashing, and each landed in one great, red, savage eye.

Then indeed did the roaring outdo all the roaring that had gone before. Beneath Pwyll the earth rocked and heaved; he was sure his eardrums were smashed, but he still could see. He saw the heads dart from side to side like wasps, the great claws reaching for them; saw how their teeth gave up one hold only to sink into another. Saw the claws that reached for them slash down again and again, piercing, raking the very eyes they meant to guard. Blood began to roll out of the giant eyeballs, black, monstrous blood . . .

At last the Monster threw off the heads, and they lay where they fell. Still bellowing and bleeding, he lumbered away through the mists. These were rising again now; Pwyll felt their soft greyness closing over him, cool and sweet and healing . . .

Something was prodding him, pushing him, clumsily yet gently. He felt how sore his back was, then heard a whinny and opened his eyes, looked up into brown, troubled horse eyes, and knew the Grey of Arawn. He tried to raise a hand to caress the stallion's muzzle, but could not get it up that far. He said, "You are not hurt, boy?" And the stallion whinnied again, eagerly and gladly, as if he understood.

The Grey went away. He came back and somehow Pwyll understood that there was water in his mouth, and that he, Pwyll, was to open his mouth and let that water be poured into it. He did so, and nothing he had ever tasted before had been so fresh and sweet and cool. It must be wine, Pwyll thought; some said that wine, not water, ran in the streams of the Otherworld. But no! Wine was heady. Again blackness rolled over him, this time a pleasant soothing blackness, and he slept.

He woke in a soft grey light, with the Grey grazing beside him. He lay on a vast moor; the mist had thinned so that he could see clearly all things near him, but in the distance it still made undulating, silvery walls.

But one evil thing he still could see and smell. The black, dried,

yet stinking trail of the Monster's blood. Even the grasses that surrounded each foul drop looked charred and burnt.

Pwyll sprang up, then gasped, remembering his hurts; then
gasped again, realizing that they did not hurt. He looked down. His
clothes hung in tatters, but not a mark showed on the bronze
smoothness of his skin. While he slept his wounds had vanished.

But that Thing had been real; no dream foe had left that blood
trail. Pwyll sprang upon the Grey's back, and followed those dread
tracks. Soon a sickening stench smote his nostrils; the foulest smell
that ever he had smelled. But he pushed on; ahead of him something
glistened evilly.

It was a great deep pit of black, squirming slime; it hissed and
smoked and bubbled. The Monster lay there, already more than half
dissolved. The awful poison of his blood had burned deep into the
earth, making that pit about him, burning up soil and rock even as it
was burning up monstrous flesh and bone and scales . . .

As rapidly as he could Pwyll turned and rode away from that pit.
He found a stream and rode the Grey through it, then bathed there.
He would have liked to wash all memory of that stinking horror off
both of them. But he wanted to find again the spot where the fight
had taken place. He searched until he found the two heads lying
together in the deep grasses, their bloodstained faces peaceful now
as those of sleeping children. He heaped earth and stones over them;
for each he made as fine a mound as he could. Then he stood up and
bade them farewell.

"Sad it is that the rest of you had to rot with the Monster. They
must have been fine fellows who once wore you on their shoulders;
good comrades for any man to have. May we meet again some day,
and fight side by side in some world where all of us are whole."

Then he rode away and left them. He gave the Grey his head
again; he did not know what else to do.

From their fine new-made cairns the heads watched him go, they
whose sight no walls now could hinder. Then they looked at each
other and grinned. One said, "There goes a fine man, brother. I too
hope that some day we may fight by his side."

The other head said soberly: "Too soon he will need all his
strength and bravery again. I wish we had not had to drain quite so
much of that strength out of him, brother."

"Yet only with his eyes upon us, and his strength in us, the eyes
and strength of a living man, could we have done the deed, brother.
That vile flesh was too gross for any man of this world to kill."

4

The Maker of Birds

PWYLL RODE on and on, and all he could think of was breakfast. Of those steaming platters of good things that he had made his men leave, half-eaten, to go down into Glen Cuch. He saw the tempting viands, he smelled them, his stomach ached for them, and his mouth watered.

Never again will I drag man or beast from his food to serve my sport, he told himself. And pitied his horses and hounds and men until he remembered that they had probably eaten since he had; then he pitied only himself.

How long had he been in Annwn? Where was Arawn's palace? And where was Arawn? Save for his growing trust in the Grey, great trouble would have been on him. Yet something was wrong; of that there could be no doubt.

Well, it is Arawn's business to see that I get to the ford in time to kill his precious Havgan, he thought. *What I need now is breakfast.*

Then suddenly a scent came to him, as marvelous in its delicacy and sweetness as the stench had been in its frightfulness. A scent like that of earthly apple blossoms, only far sweeter than the fragrance of any flower of earth.

One of those silvery, undulating walls of mist loomed up before him. Until the Grey galloped into it it looked solid, and then Pwyll had to put his hand to shield his eyes, for all about him sparkled like fire; without heat, but jewel bright, as dewdrops sparkled beneath the morning sun. Then they came out on the other side, into a gentle golden light that came from no sun that Pwyll could see.

They were in a wood, no wood of gold and crystal such as his nurse had told of in her tales of Otherworldly wonders, but an orchard of living green. Its fragrance made breathing a delight; its tender green leaves and masses of yet more tender, rosy-white blossoms hid the sky.

As he rode beneath the first tree a marvel happened. For its blossoms fell about him like snowflakes and in a breath's space the tiny green fruit grew and swelled and ripened into great apples as round as the sun and rosier than any woman's cheek.

Pwyll stared, then dismounted. "Maybe this is Illusion, yet I am hungry enough to eat a rotten apple with a worm in it, and find the worm a tasty bit of meat. And these apples do not look rotten; let us try them, boy."

He half expected the first bite to turn into something else in his mouth, but it did not; that apple was sweet and sound and ripe and juicy, everything that an apple should be, and so were its fellows. Pwyll and the Grey munched happily until they were full.

At last Pwyll smacked his lips and said, "Those were good, boy. But you need water, and I could use some too. After those apples, a man could not need wine."

They went on until they found a well beneath a tree, a well as blue as a sunlit sky, and beside it was a golden cup. Again Pwyll dismounted; while the Grey lapped eagerly he drank from the cup, and the water of that well was sweet and pure beyond any waters of the world he knew.

Then he dropped the cup, and stared in awe and wonder. Before he drank there had been nothing on the far side of the well, but now. . .

A woman sat there, and it was from her that the light in that place came. Her body shone like the sun; her one thin garment hid it no more than water would. Her hair shone, it streamed red gold to her noble, high-arched feet, which were tender and rosy white as the apple blossoms. But when Pwyll tried to look at her face, he could not, his eyes fell, so he knew that She was no woman but a Goddess, and that that place lived through the living Glory that was Herself.

Three birds flew round Her head, and their song was sweet. One was as tenderly green as the leaves, one shone white as snow, and the third flashed like a sunbeam. She sat there whittling at an ordinary piece of applewood, and She was making images of birds. Whenever one was finished the wood quivered, turned to feathered flesh, and the new bird flew away singing for joy of life and wings. How long he watched Her Pwyll never knew, but at last She raised Her eyes and saw him.

"My welcome to you, Pwyll of Dyved. You do not laugh at Me

now, as you did on earth. Now that you have drunk from My cup, and behold My true shape."

He said: "Lady, no man could ever laugh at You. Only for joy of You."

"So? I have been Queen in Dyved from of old. No man before you ever has called himself King there save by right of Me. Only you have mocked Me, and sworn that you could hold the land by your own strength—without help from an ancient hag whose people yours had conquered."

Pwyll knew Her then, and stiffened. "Great Queen, it was not in this form that You were offered to me as a bride."

"This Shape no man may touch. Mortal flesh cannot house it."

"No. Only parts of You can dwell on earth—even I know that— and if even the least bit of You could become a mortal woman, then her man would be the happiest of all men forever." Pwyll's voice had been deep with longing; now his eyes grew hard. "But the druids keep part of You in a great White Mare. When my father died and I took the kingship, they said I must go down on all fours and seek her like a stallion in heat! *You* never could come to a man like that!"

"Man, had you done their will—gone on all fours and given your seed to a beast—you never could have drunk from My cup! The mare would have been as defiled as you. I would take no shame in putting on her flesh to meet any stallion in your fields, for all that lives and breathes in Dyved is part of Me. But man and mare—bah!"

"I knew it, Lady." Pwyll's eyes were soft again and shining. "Never could You so blaspheme against Yourself."

"Only your druids of the New Tribes could have devised such sacrilege, they who reject the Ancient Harmonies and twist what little wisdom they can gain into foul foolishness—seeking their own ends!"

Again Pwyll stiffened. "Lady, I too am of the New Tribes." Then his inner sight cleared. "Forgive me, You can see farther than men. And I am glad to think that their curses meant nothing. When I would have no part in their holy horseplay they said that no son of mine would reign after me—that I would bring the worst of ill luck upon Dyved, and upon myself. Had my warriors loved me less I never could have become King. Only one druid of them all stood by me and would not join their curses—my kinsman, Pendaran Dyved."

"He has a little wisdom. He may gain more, but not much. Even among the true druids, those of the Old Tribes, wise men grow few. For darkness must come upon your world—only if you slay Havgan can Chaos be prevented and thrown back."

Pwyll laughed joyously. "Lady, before I met You I swore to kill Havgan, and now for You I will chop him into as many pieces as there are stars in the sky!"

"In that fight I cannot help you. You take warnings lightly, but be warned: bitter strife awaits you here, and it also awaits the earth."

He looked straight at Her; as straight as he could look, since he could not meet Her eyes.

"Lady, I am drunk now. On Your beauty. And neither from God nor man will I ever ask help against any foe that has two arms and two legs. But tell me what to do for Dyved, and I will do it."

"I will do better than that. If I can I will come to earth and be your wife there, as I was wife to Dyved's Kings of old."

Pwyll's heart leapt in amazement and joy. His arms almost leapt too, but something kept them at his sides. Then a black thought smote him and he groaned. "Lady, if I must wait for You to be born a mortal maid and to grow up I shall have a long wait. I shall be grey bearded and perhaps balding—too old to do You justice."

"Too old to enjoy Me, you mean." She laughed. "Have no fear. If we two come together it will be as young man and young woman. Your loins will still be mighty."

He laughed too. His eyes shone. "Say not 'if,' Lady. Nothing can keep me from killing Havgan now."

"Yet before we can lie together you must conquer fearful foes—yourself among them. You have passed through one great ordeal, but another draws near."

"Havgan, Lady?"

"No. In this peril I can help you, if you can understand and use My help."

"What peril, Lady? What help?" He tried to say those words, but never said them. The singing of Her birds had grown louder; it was all about them, lapping them like the waves of a sunny sea. From far off Her voice came: ". . . a Bird that is not Mine . . ."

Trees and well were gone. They stood in a green plain, and She raised Her white arms, and from beneath each arm a white horse came. The horses met, they pranced and curveted, they became many horses and danced, light as leaves upon the wind. Their manes and tails glittered like foam. Pwyll's heart ached for joy; always upon earth he had loved the sight of white horses playing in a field. Nothing else, until he got there, had ever come so near to making the glories of an Otherworld seem real.

The dancing ceased. The horses came back to Her, now only two again; they nuzzled Her hands. She fondled their gleaming snowy heads, and beside Pwyll the Grey whinnied, like a child seeking its share of love.

She called to him; he sped to Her, and over the three shining heads She looked at Pwyll. "These are among the fairest of My children. Was it not partly because you loved that you hated to do your druids' bidding? To befoul such loveliness?"

He tried to answer, but the birds were still singing, their song was sweeping him away like the shimmering, many-hued floods of a rainbow river. Once more Her voice came: "Sleep and rest. Wake and wonder if you have only dreamed Me, man that I hope will be My man."

Pwyll woke after what seemed long absence from himself. He lay upon the open moor, in treeless, rocky desolation lit only by the grey twilight that in Annwn seemed to be both night and day. The Grey grazed beside him; he reached out a hand and touched that good, solid horsehide. Its warmth eased his sudden deep pain of loss—loss of what? A garden place of delicious apples—a blue well with a golden cup? White horses dancing? He must have dreamed that wild whirl of wonders. No—she had been real, that true bride who had walked with him beneath the apple trees. Woman or Goddess, she had been real. He shut his eyes, his heart aching for the golden warmth of her. But the greyness outside him soaked through his closed eyelids, into his soul, dimming memory . . . He mounted the Grey again.

"We must go on, boy. We have business to do."

The draught of kingship! He had found the cup, yet truly she had given him that drink, as the Goddess gave Her chosen to drink when She walked in woman's shape, not mare's. More dreams. Even here it was not likely that he had met Her who had been Dyved's Goddess of old, and that She had pledged Herself to him. Most likely some lady out of Faery had been playing her tricks on him, using that great ancient name. Though no name had been spoken. . . That was the kind of thing you could expect in a world like this. He would be glad to get out of it and go home, but first he must kill Havgan.

He rode on, but uneasiness rode with him. In old tales people who had seen the Fair Folk dancing in the moonlight and been drawn into that dance, had returned from what seemed a night's frolic to find all their friends and kin long dead. What if he, Pwyll, should return to find another Lord of Dyved, and himself but dimly remembered, a young prince who had ridden out and vanished a hundred years ago?

But Arawn had promised to sit in his seat until his return. "And the good folk of Dyved will get a surprise if I live to be a hundred years old!" Pwyll chuckled uneasily. Surely Arawn would never allow such a breach in the established order of things. Order was what Death had avowed himself sworn to uphold. No, when Pwyll came home everything would be the same; his homes, dogs, and men would all be there. Nothing would be changed.

"If you ever get home. What if Arawn too is playing with you? If he has tricked you all along, and there never was any Havgan? If he took your life there in the forest, and—"

Fiercely Pwyll crushed down those hissing worm thoughts. He looked about him, trying to find something else to think of. The way had grown suddenly forbidding. Rocky hills towered above him, rugged crags that he had not dreamed could be anywhere near. Mists had blotted out the moors behind him, were creeping after him. Mists that moved softly and ceaselessly, as the sea moves. There was continual coiling and uncoiling and recoiling within them, as if Something were trying to shape itself a body. A shape that would not be good to see . . .

Pwyll began to look behind him oftener than a brave warrior should. "You have already passed through one great ordeal, but another is near." Who had said that? Maybe he had only dreamed it, but in this world dreams might come true.

He was unarmed now, his spears and dagger lost somewhere on those endless misty moors, his good sword drowned and probably melted in that stinking lake that had been the Monster. Against any foe he met now he would have only his hands.

"Arawn promised that the way to his palace would be clear before you. He has broken that promise."

The worm within him spat that in his face. Suddenly it coiled up like the mists, it reared itself upon those coils, its hissing head spitting more thoughts at him. "Art and design lured you here. He tricked you and deceived you."

"But why play with me?" Pwyll demanded. "Why fright me with bogeys, as a bad nurse scares a child at night? He could have destroyed me, long ago."

But now the hissing serpent face had flat, evil eyes. "What is your pin-sized head, mortal, to grasp the designs of him who since time began has been Master of Life? Maybe he wants to taste mortal joys. The delight of the cat in the mouse, of the torturer in the man or woman he tortures? Those games that so often have brought him to mop up their spent, broken prey—why should he not grow curious as to how they feel?"

Wisdom rose in Pwyll; maybe some small leavings of that which had flowed into him from Arawn's eyes, maybe something born only of his own human faithfulness. "Folly, snake! What Being who has tasted all the unimaginable glories and wonders and delights he knows could stoop to the basest follies of men and beasts?"

But the worm said: "Boredom is mighty. In that Land of the Ever-Young where men and women clasp each other in unageing beauty, where my kind never come to coil within the sweet fruit, or to crawl into the places where the golden grain is stored—there boredom must come at last. Boredom the begetter of strange offspring."

"He cannot beget upon the Mighty anything so small as you," said Pwyll between his teeth.

"Am I small?" the snake reared high and laughed in his face, strange, hissing laughter. "I who have grown great, and shall grow greater, out of the very stuff of your being?"

"You shall grow no greater," said Pwyll grimly. "If Arawn my brother has smallnesses they are those of his world, not mine."

Again the snake laughed. "Maybe smallness is the same every-where."

"And maybe not," said Pwyll. In that inner space where they talked, he set his heel upon the snake's head. Crushed, it sank back into the depths of him, where it coiled again, waiting. . .

Pwyll and the Grey went on, through land that grew ever more forbidding. Cliffs and grim grey stones reared through the fog, stupendous, half-seen shapes that seemed alive and threatening. Once Pwyll looked back, down into the mists that hid the moors. These were steaming now, like a vast cauldron in which evil things were brewing.

Well, Pwyll told himself, *it is never a brave man's part to turn back, and I do not know where I could turn back to, anyhow. And we are going up. Maybe we will finally come out into the light.*

Never in this world had he seen true darkness. Never, unless in that wondrous Place of Apples, had he seen true light; and he was hungry and thirsty again; it was getting easier and easier to believe that he had dreamed those apples. "Your luck is out too, now," he told the Grey. "For I cannot see any grass growing among these stones, and surely even Death's horse cannot eat stones."

Indeed, he could not see anything growing anywhere. In those ever-thickening mists he soon could see practically nothing at all, and it grew constantly harder to see that. He yawned. Sleep was coming on him again, and though forgetfulness would be good, this did not seem like the right place to sleep in. It seemed like a very wrong place.

5

The Guardian of the Gate

SUDDENLY THE Grey stopped, and Pwyll took that for a Sign, and put away his misgivings. Dismounting, he lay down in the least stony place he could find. He was cold, he wished he had his cloak to cover him, but any respite from this endless, aimless journey was good. The Grey, he thought, must be lost too.

Yet, as he sank through the grey mists without into the grey mists within, he suddenly longed for his sword . . . Then he knew nothing, and wished for nothing.

He woke, cramped and shivering. Beside him stood the Grey, his head down, seemingly asleep. The mists were gone, and night had come at last. A cold moon shone grimly in the black starless sky. She grinned down at him like a glided skull.

His eyes followed her grin, and he saw a shadow blacker than night.

An immense, three-columned gateway towered above him. If walls were behind it the black shadow of the cliff hid them, but Pwyll thought there were none. Something told him that that gateway led into everlasting darkness . . .

A massive stone lintel topped those three pillars. Squarely in its center sat a giant Bird. And Pwyll looked at that Bird, and his heart became as ice within him. He strove to rise and flee, but he could not move so much as a finger. He strove to close his eyes, but the shining of the Bird held them. Its beak shone palely, cruelly, terribly: a hooked mightiness that easily could have snapped off a man's head or arm. Its eyes shone red, as had the Monster's eyes, but with a far different evil; evil as cold as ice.

But hardest of all to look away from were the feathers: the myriad shimmering, ever-changing feathers . . . red-shot, green-shot, purple-shot darknesses that all melted together into one blackness: a blackness that seized and transformed and conquered all light.

With a mighty effort Pwyll managed to move his eyes before they were caught forever; else his soul might have wandered for eons through that unwholesomely gleaming labyrinth of feathers. But he could not move his eyes far; just far enough to see the pillars below the Bird.

In the huge central pillar above which it perched were three niches, and the lowest was empty, but from each of two above grinned a fleshless human skull. Each side column held only one niche, but in each of these sat a freshly severed human head. Their glazed eyes still stared in astonishment, the blood upon the stumps of their necks was wet and red.

They saw Pwyll; they looked back at him. Even the skulls looked, their black, emptied eye sockets probing him with a gaze that was keen and searching and malevolent.

The head on the left said: "Brothers, here is Arawn himself, lying at our feet. Or where our feet ought to be. I did not know that Death ever rested."

But the topmost skull laughed, opening wide its flesh-less jaws. "Fool, have you already forgotten the face of Death? You, who met him only this morning?"

The second skull laughed too. "If the blood were not still fresh on your neck, little brother, you would know better than to think that Death never rests."

The head on the right said, "But how can he? Night and day, summer and winter, he is busier than any man ever born."

Both skulls laughed together, then answered as one. "Peace, little brothers; do not question the wisdom of your elders and betters. For ages we two have sat here and watched Death come and go. Time and space do not bind him. He kills and kills and kills, yet always finds time to sit down to meat in his own hall. To sleep with his woman, the Corpse-Devourer, into whose belly we all must go at last."

In the frozen prison that was his body Pwyll shuddered. Was this ogress that fairest of women whom Arawn had promised him for bedmate?

The head on the left said stubbornly: "I still say that it is Arawn lying there. I know his great horse; I know his face; that face is stamped upon my eyes forever."

The skulls laughed again. "Your eyes! Soon they will fall out and run down your face like blobs of grease. Ours did."

Yet once more the topmost skull laughed. "And those lips that chatter so much nonsense-soon they too will rot and fall away and leave your teeth naked to the wind. Like ours."

The head on the right said: "You two still seem to have plenty to talk with. How is that? Your tongues should have rotted out long ago."

The first skull made a sound remarkably like a snort, but the second said: "That is a fair question, and deserves a fair answer. Man's head is among the Mysteries. It sees, it hears, it thinks, it speaks. Man has only one other power that matters: movement, and its pleasantest seat is in a soft thing that rots away quickly; it does not endure, like a skull. We dead cannot hope to keep that."

"We cannot indeed," said the two heads, shaking sorrowfully. "The love of women is gone from us forever."

The second skull jeered at them. "So? Your memories are still fresh, like your blood. You will have to get used to your lack, little brothers. I have heard of a skull that spat upon a woman and got her pregnant, but there would not be much fun in that."

"There would not indeed," said the heads sadly.

"Yet there is great power in a head, the Seat of the Four Powers. Our old folk used to keep the heads of their dead as honored guardians, who could see farther than men. They cherished them as loving kinsmen and good councilors."

The topmost skull said gloomily: "Yes. Once heads were honored; they were tended, they were given offerings of milk and meat and honey. They were listened to and obeyed. But now men ride with heads tied to their saddle bows; they scoop out our brains and give us to the goldsmiths to make pretty cups with. We have fallen upon evil days."

The head on the right said: "Brave men still honor brave men. I thought the man who killed me yesterday would be proud of me and never sit down to meat without giving me my fair share. I had done as much for his brother. But instead darkness came upon me and I woke in this place. Why was that, brother skulls?"

"She summoned you. She chose you, as once she did us."

"Who is she? The old Goddess, the Queen of All?"

The skulls looked up toward the stone above them, where the Bird sat, and it seemed to Pwyll that they would have shivered if they had had anything left to shiver with.

Then the topmost skull said: "Brothers, we lied. Our eyes did not fall out and our lips did not fall off. She ate them, she who sits above us here, even as she will eat yours. She waited until they were rotten, and so tasty meat for her, who can bear nothing that is fresh and clean."

"But why? Why did Arawn give us up to her?"

"Did you not die in despair, cursing the man who betrayed you, and the Gods who did not help you? Believing no longer in anything good? Such are her portion, brother; her share of Death's spoils."

"Do not be ashamed to admit it, brother." The second skull spoke. "So it befell us, and will befall others. She has eaten up our very essence; our power to think and to do."

"But you still speak—you still have power to put words together—" The head stammered, its voice shook.

"We think what we used to think, say what once we would have said. We will sit here echoing our lost selves until she gets new heads to feed on and throws us out of our niches to roll around the dark moors forever."

"But the Cauldron of Rebirth—all whom Arawn takes come to that at last—" The head on the left stammered that.

"We will not, we four. Never will we get back into the wombs of women and be born again upon earth. If we did it would be as gabbling fools without wit enough to feed ourselves—we have lost too much. No hope is left us. We will be only our own ghosts forever."

The heads shrank farther back into their niches. Their faces, that could not turn paler, yet looked pinched with fear. "But the Mothers—will they let this be?"

"The Man-Gods from the east are draining their strength, even as She of the Dark Wings drained ours."

"But when the Son comes back—He that at three nights old was stolen from the Mother?"

"This time the Son will not come back. He has joined the Man-Gods." Again both skulls laughed together.

"The Son would not betray the Mother! He loves Her."

The two heads still spoke as one.

"He loves the Father now. The Father who claims all power, and soon will overturn and break the Cauldron of Rebirth itself. For the Cauldron is the way of the Teacher, the long slow way, by which all learn at last, and if the Father promises eternal life to His friends, He also promises eternal death to His foes. That is the gift that comes out of the Eastern World to the West—eternal torment, eternal death."

"You lie—you lie for your Mistress up there! The winter may be long and hard, it may bury the Mother in snow, it may lash Her with whips of ice, but in the end She always rises again, young and strong and beautiful."

"And you think you will rise with Her? Look at this man here. Yesterday he ate apples in a garden, and talked with a fair woman there. He did not know that in that same hour the Bird's beak pushed the skull out of the niche below us, and that now it waits for him."

Horror such as he never had known washed over Pwyll, horror deeper than the depths of the sea. *So this is why I was brought here! There is no Havgan—Arawn lied. He trapped me here for this death beyond all deaths.*

Then the heads and the skulls all laughed at him together, in a burst of sound that seemed to tear and lash and saw at his ears in a discord beyond all discords. "Yes, you are trapped! Trapped by him that swore himself your friend and brother; by Her that fed you Her apples of Illusion. What else are friends and brothers for? Was not Death himself born when brother slew brother?"

Again Pwyll tried to rise. As a man upon whose belly great stones have been piled might strive to move, so he strove. His muscles strained and cracked, his heart almost burst against that immovable, agonizing weight that was not there. And again the heads and the skulls laughed.

"You know now what Arawn is. Will you still call on Her that fashioned the birds and the steeds? She is part of the Mother—of Her who brings forth only in order to destroy! Call not on the Mother, or on any daughter of the Mother. She brings forth only that She may feed. We warned you: from Her belly we all come—and back into the darkness of Her belly we all go!"

"We rise again from that darkness," said Pwyll, stubbornly. "Even as the good grain rises, from which we bake our bread."

"For what? To be eaten again—and yet again? To struggle through endless lives for wealth and power—or only for life to keep on struggling with? It is well to lose what we have lost, what you are about to lose. Why love women, only to beget more food for death?"

Now Pwyll laughed. "Love is good. So are youth and strength. They make up for many troubles along the way."

"And how long do they last? Better to die in battle, bloody and maimed, than to live on while age slowly dismembers, piece by piece. We fare better. The Bird eats us but once. Then we sit quietly and wait for the darkness and the silence. For that endless rolling on the moor in which even memory dies."

Somehow Pwyll got one hand free. He caught at the Grey's reins, and tugged. "Horse, help me! If I can get on your back we can make a run for it—maybe hide among rocks where there is no room for the swooping of her dark wings."

But the thought of that swooping came over him like something blacker than blackness, and his hand fell. He lay helpless again. The Grey neither stirred nor opened his eyes. All four, skulls and heads, cackled in triumph.

"He will not help you this time! None can help you against her, whose beak waits. And it will not wait much longer—brother!"

Despair came on Pwyll. It took his body, that had striven as hard as flesh and bone may strive, and in vain. It took his brave heart. Even if he could escape, what would he escape to? Only to bleed and sweat to stave off for a little longer the inevitable end. What was the use?

Yet he had loved life. He raised his eyes for one last look at the heavens, at the vast freedom of them, darkened even as they were now. He wished that he could have had one more good gallop through the fields of earth, upon his own Kein Galed.

A good ride, with the wind and sun in his face! That was worth living for, whatever waited at the end of the ride. No matter; nothing mattered. Before this grinning moon was much higher the Bird would swoop down and peck off his head; set it in that lowest niche to rot. Then when it was foul enough that dreadful beak would eat out his innermost self.

She was watching him now. With the last of his strength he tried to look away from those cold red eyes.

What was she waiting for? To enjoy his helplessness? Could deathless greatness be so small? Once before he had said something like that— then set his heel upon an evil-eyed head. A head not too unlike this bird head . . . Could such a creature really have power to eat his soul?

Doubt sprang again within him, no worm this time, but a serpent of golden flame. It freed his entranced limbs. Awkwardly he rose upon one elbow; his free hand, groping in the dust beside him, found a stone. A poor, pitiful weapon against the thrashing of those mighty wings, the thrust of that cruel beak, but a man should die fighting. Maybe if he died unsubmitting his soul would go free. Hope sang within him like a bird's song.

The song of a bird . . . *Her birds!*

Beauty sprang vivid before his eyes, in his heart, justifying its own existence, all existence. He staggered erect, stone in hand.

The skulls and the heads cried out together, startled and angry. The Bird gave no cry. Huge wings outspread, red eyes blazing like cold flames, she swooped.

The wind of those great wings almost knocked Pwyll down, their stench sickened him, yet somehow he managed to stand. To raise the stone. For an awful second he thought that hand and stone would go together, before he could use them—first they would go, and then his head. Already he could see into the fiery cavern in the great, open beak. He thought with a kind of sick quietness, *This is the end,* but still his arm moved to strike. Useless as that blow must be, he would do his best to deal it; he would not die cowering.

The singing was sweet. It filled his ears with beauty, it flowed like cool, delicious water into and over every part of his tired, aching body. Words of his old nurse came back to him: "The Birds of Rhiannon . . . they wake the dead and lull the living to sleep."

He was dead, and they were waking him. The Bird had got only his head—he himself had gone free.

But no! His opening eyes saw the great beak still yawning to destroy him, the crimson eyes still blazing—then saw the fear in them. She that by existing blasphemed the name of bird hung there powerless, helpless. Entranced, as he had been.

A great road of light cleft the dark sky, fell in purifying brilliance upon the lintel where that monstrous Bird had sat, enthroned. Down that glorious pathway flew three singing birds, and one was white, and one was green, and one was gold as morning.

On they came, still singing, and all the captive lights seemed to go out of the feathers of that Bird that had been the Un-Manner of men. The brilliant plumage grew dull, it crumbled like ashes, and fell to earth. There seemed to be no body to fall after it. For a breath's space the fierce red eyes hung alone in the air, still savagely glaring, and then were gone, like snuffed-out torch flames.

The three pillars of that awful gateway buckled and quivered. Quietly, softly as snowflakes fall, they fell to the ground, their fall revealing only down-sloping hillside and bare moors behind them. The great stone lintel that had been the throne of darkness toppled as soundlessly and lay broken upon their brokenness. Pwyll caught one last glimpse of the falling heads and skulls, the skulls grinning emptily, the glazed eyes of the heads staring with equal emptiness. Their evil shadow life was gone. Then the earth covered them, and they too were gone.

Where the lintel had been the light still was. In its tender radiance the Birds of Rhiannon hovered and sang. In thankfulness and worship Pwyll raised his arms toward them, then himself crumpled to the earth, and the Grey of Arawn, wide awake now, came and nuzzled his face.

6

The Moonlit Land

"YOU HAVE done well," said Arawn's voice above him. "Eat now and drink."

He was holding out a cup of fragrant wine and a huge hunk of steaming meat, and their good smells woke Pwyll fully. He sat up.

Then he stared in wonder, for before him was the fairest land he had ever seen: the greenest woods and meadows, the loveliest flowers, and upon all the moon shining down, her brightness only a little gentler than that of day. Color that was a wonder of tenderness bloomed everywhere, in hues sweeter and far more delicate than those of earth. The Grey's coat shone like silver, and his mane sparkled like foam, and Pwyll himself—for a dizzy moment the Lord of Dyved wondered how he could be looking at himself—squatted over a fire that burned yet did not burn, only glowed like a great red flower.

Pwyll said softly: "So this is the true Annwn."

His own shape that held Arawn smiled. "Annwn is many places. As a man is, so his sight is. But this is the true World of Middle Light. Here neither your blazing sun nor your black night ever comes. Here in this gentle light, in the all-healing womb of the Mother, the battered and misshapen may find new shape."

"And here too She shapes the unborn?"

"The dead and the unborn are one. Even your druids of the New Tribes must have told you that."

Someone else—Pwyll could not remember who, but someone he had not wanted to be angry with—had mocked at the wise men of his people. Now the mocker was Arawn, and though Pwyll himself did not think much of their wisdom, yet they were his people; outsiders should not mock them. Also—what else had Arawn done? A great many questions suddenly buzzed in Pwyll's mind. Delicious as his food and wine smelled, he pushed them away and looked very hard into that familiar face that was—unbelievably—no longer his own.

"You say I have done well. But what of yourself, Lord? You promised that the way should be clear before me, yet you yourself left me to die the worst of deaths alone."

Arawn said, unmoved: "I promised that the way would be clear before you, and that I myself would be your guide. And clear it will be, now that I am here. Yet there are ways a man must find for himself, and in finding yours you have gained strength to face Havgan. The blade must be tempered before it goes into battle."

For a long moment Pwyll was silent, then he said, a trifle grimly: "So those monsters were ordeals such as initiates undergo? I had thought those mostly druids' tricks." He reached for the meat and the wine again, took a great swig of the one and several mouthfuls of the other before he said wryly: "Well, Lord, you are a master of a pretty pack."

Arawn said quietly, "Only of my hounds am I master. The foes you met every man must master for himself."

Pwyll's jaw dropped. "But I killed them!"

"For yourself alone. Every man in his time must slay or be slain by them. Fear—the uttermost, sickening fear and loathing that flesh can know—these are the Beast. Sickness of all things, doubt and despair that are worse than any fear of the flesh—"

". . . are the Bird." Pwyll shuddered. "She must be mother to the Three Birds of Midir—they that suck out a man's courage on the way to baffle. But those birds who saved me were three also—did you send them?"

"No. In time you will remember who did." Arawn's faint wise smile made Pwyll's own face strange to him. "But that winged darkness is terrible because she always mixes truth with lies; twists and blackens all. Hard indeed it is to rise up out of her slough of darkness and realize that life is worth all its long, bitter battles. Worth even me."

There was a brief, grim silence. Pwyll swallowed twice before he could make himself ask, dreading the answer: "Those skulls. Was their manhood truly lost forever?"

"No. Freeing yourself you freed them—broke their illusion and proved her power a lie."

Pwyll drew a deep breath of relief. "I am glad of that. But it was rough learning and rough teaching."

"You have my friendship," said Arawn. "All else that I can give you will have."

Pwyll laughed. "What if I should ask you never to let me see your face again? To let me live forever?"

Arawn said simply: "You would lie blind and deaf and helpless through lifetime after lifetime. Not all things are Death's to give; I cannot make you forever young."

Again, for a breath's space, there was silence. Then Pwyll laughed again, somewhat shakily: "I have no desire to outlive my own strength and manhood. Come for me before they are gone, Lord Death—but not too long before. Let me enjoy them as long as I can."

"Unless you go to that one place on earth where another Grey Man rules, that will be so," said Arawn. And for a second icy cold took Pwyll, who knew, like all Kings of Dyved, what place he meant. He said only, "My thanks, Lord."

"For a little gift. One other boon only Death, of his very nature, cannot grant; may you never need to ask that of me." Suddenly Arawn's look made the young face of Pwyll seem wise and old. Pity was in it, the awful, farseeing pity of a God, and something else also, something that in a mortal man might have been guilt or regret.

Pwyll said in wonder: "What is the matter? I thought you said I had gained strength to fight your precious Havgan with."

"Strength of the spirit, not the body."

"My body never felt better!" Pwyll spoke indignantly. "You still have strength enough to kill . . . Eat your food now, Lord of Dyved, while it is hot." And under those strange, compelling eyes that again were like black suns Pwyll forgot all else and ate.

He was barely through when Arawn whistled and a great black stallion came galloping up. Pwyll jumped; he could have sworn that no beast but the Grey was near them. Had that whistle conjured up this one, saddle, bridle, and all?

Then the Grey came up to him, whinnying, and Arawn turned to the black. But Pwyll led the Grey to him. "For he is yours, Lord. You need not let me have him yet."

"My folk soon will see us passing," said Arawn. "They would think it strange to see another ride my horse."

So Pwyll took the Grey and was glad, for since their fight with the Monster he loved him as well as his own Kein Galed. Yet as he mounted another thought struck him. "Will not your folk think it strange to see you ride unarmed, Lord? My weapons are all lost."

"Are they?" Yet again Arawn smiled. "Look."

And Pwyll looked down, and saw his own sword at his side, and his two spears back in their places. He seized them, he stared at them, he fingered every inch of them. They were bright and clean and freshly burnished, yet here was an old nick, there was a tiny scratch he knew. They looked the same, they felt the same; yet how could they be?

"They are your own," said Arawn. "I brought them out of the wilderness and the slime."

Pwyll laughed with delight. "Never will you give me better gifts, Lord. Weapons of your world may be finer and more magical, but these I know."

"All knowledge is good. Yet no man's strength lies outside himself. No sword or spear ever had the magic to fight on alone, when all effort seemed useless and all hope a lie."

"I see. It takes a man to carry them." Pwyll beamed. This was the first time he had been able to read one of Arawn's riddles, and his success made him like Arawn better.

They rode on in good fellowship, and Arawn told him much of Annwn and its Lords. So much that Pwyll hoped he could remember one quarter of it, and said so.

"That is easily remedied," said Arawn. "I can arrange your memory."

Pwyll stiffened. If every man's house is his castle, his mind is a stronghold far greater, his very self, or all the self he knows. To think that its unspeakably precious privacy can be invaded, altered, even by a wise and beneficent Power, is a terrifying thought.

Arawn read that feeling. He said quietly: "We have sworn friendship together. It would be beneath my own dignity to intrude upon yours more than I must. But tonight you sit in my seat in Annwn, with only your own will, your own wit to help you. Master of all that is mine."

". . . *all that is mine!*" Memory rushed over Pwyll. The Queen! She would be beautiful, after all; the Lady of a land like this. . . He shied away from that thought, for his own sake as well as because Arawn could read it. He said, "Do what you must, Lord. But surely no king ever got such a face-price for one stag before . . . By the way, who was that stag, Lord? He had been a man, I suppose, for your hounds hunt only the dead."

Arawn told him, and Pwyll whistled. "I had thought it hard on any man to have to die twice so close together, but if half the tales told of that one are true he deserves all he gets."

"He thought he had good cause to flee my hounds," said Arawn, "for his wanderings in the wildernesses of Annwn will be hard. Long and long will it take him to find these pleasant places. For only those who have beauty within them can see beauty."

"Yet he was a fool," said Pwyll, "and a coward. A man should face at once what he has to face. All know that your hounds cannot be outrun."

"There are worse things than the fangs of my hounds," said Arawn.

"There are indeed," said Pwyll with sudden heat. "There are the monsters that dwell in your wilderness. I pity even that fellow if he has to meet the ones I met!"

"He will meet worse. Yet I am merciful; I only help a man to cleanse himself. Already, in the Eastern World, in those hot desert lands where Gods are rising who will drive out us Gods of the West, many men believe that death will plunge them into a sea of fire where they must burn forever. So burn they will, until at last they realize that even that fire is illusion, bred of their own guilty fears.

Pwyll stared. "But I thought you said that by killing Havgan I could save our world. Gods! What kind of weakling fools does the Eastern World breed to worship torturing monsters such as those?"

Arawn said: "Brave men even, who worship one God only, and call Him the loving Father of all men."

"Loving!" Pwyll snorted. "Sooner than be loved like that I would be like the Old Tribes—too simple-minded to know that children have fathers. Worship no Creator but my mother's womb!"

Arawn said: "No man has yet truly worshipped any God. In essence all Gods are the same, and One; but few mortals have glimpsed that Untellable Glory, and no human mind may hold it. So around the little they can remember those seers fashion poor clumsy unlikenesses in their own image, and preach of these to men."

"But if all you Gods are really One, how can You fight each other?" Again Pwyll stared.

"Belief breeds reality; demons seek homes. And those Shapes built by men in their own image—Shapes in which, as in man himself, and in all created things, a spark of true Godhood yet burns, imprisoned—all differ greatly and battle greatly."

"Then let them baffle somewhere else!"

"They will battle here. For Havgan has come here."

"Then what do we gain by killing him?"

"Time, and time means much. Every God comes at last to the Cauldron of Rebirth; is reshaped there even as men are reshaped. A day when dawn when Gods of the East and Gods of the West will embrace and know their Oneness."

"And Havgan's death will hasten that dawn?"

"At least it will prevent the coming of too deep a darkness. His strength is all fire, and all fires that are lit in Annwn spread to earth, where you mortals have less power to put them out. You do not worship your mother's womb, but you loved her. Would you see men born who love nothing? Know no light but the light of burning fire?"

"Lord, I do not understand."

"Men who despise other men's mothers will learn to despise their own. Havgan has entered Annwn—and already, in green lovely Ireland, where your New Tribes have conquered the Old, no warrior can bring home a prouder trophy than a woman's two severed breasts! The same spoil that Havgan's warriors bear to him where he sits in his dread seat in Anghar the Loveless."*

Deep and painful was the silence then. Pwyll said at last, heavily: "My own people came into Dyved from Ireland. We men of the New Tribes are many, too many not to have evil men among us. But woe to any man of mine who dared to bring such a trophy before me—as woe it would have been to him who dared bring it before my father, or my father's father! We of Dyved are proud to be our fathers' sons; we know that our women's wombs could not quicken without our good seed to fill them. But never could we forget that our mothers' breasts were the first cups we drank from: the givers of life."

"If Havgan lives your sons will forget it."

"They shall not! He will die!"

"They must not. The Father must not become altogether a Being of wrath and fire. The Son must remain what He always has been: the Friend and Helper of all living."

Awe took Pwyll; he looked in wonder at that face that was his own, yet not his own. At those eyes, deeper than the sea, that seemed to gaze through all the ages, through time that had been and time yet to be. At the set mouth of a God who unflinchingly faced perils man could never dream of, and with endurance more everlasting than that of the grey cliffs battered through countless winters by the lashing sea.

And then, as he gazed, the face changed. Became full of warmth and gentleness and an almost human pride.

"Look, man of earth." Once again that deep voice of a God boomed forth, through Pwyll's own lips. "Behold that palace where tonight you will sit in my stead. Where no other man ever has entered save as my subject, at my call."

---

*St. Adamnan deplores this custom, practiced by the Christians (!) of his day. It must have dated back to much earlier times.

Pwyll looked, and thought at first that the moon had fallen from the sky, such round glory shimmered and glimmered there, in the plain ahead. Then he looked up and saw that bright Queen herself still safe in heaven, upon her age-old throne. He looked down again, and knew that shimmering wonder for a great round palace, shining like a star.

"Behold. My palace, and my court, and my kingdom, all are in your power. Enter." The deep voice of Arawn no longer seemed to come from the small cell of any throat; quiet as the twilight, it yet seemed to fill all space. Pwyll jerked round in his saddle, but saw nothing. Grey Man and black home, both were gone as utterly as though they had melted into that soft air.

Pwyll rode on alone through the sweet dusk, and awe and delight and dread were on him, altogether. What would it be like, this wonderful place to which he was going, all this unearthly splendor of which he would be Lord?

A breeze was rising, and the Grey's streaming mane shone like a woman's pale hair.

Arawn's Queen!

Pwyll willed himself not to think of her. He tried hard to think of other things. This Mother and Son he had heard so much about—who were they?

His coat shone silver white, and Pwyll, looking down, saw that the hands on the bridle were not grey either. They were still differently shaped from his own, not sun-bronzed like an earthly warrior's, but their pallor was clean and healthy.

If here in his own world the Grey Man was not grey, then she might be beautiful—Arawn's Queen!

"You will soon know . . ."

He closed his ears to that voice. He tried to think of other things. This Mother and Son he had heard so much talk of—who were they? The Mother must be She he had called on in the forest, She whom the Old Tribes believed to be the Goddess behind all Gods. They called Her Modron, "Mother," and the son She bore every year was Mabon ab Modron, "Son, son of Mother." On the third night after birth He was always stolen from Her side, but always She regained Him. If ever She did not, summer would not come, neither grass nor crops would grow, all living things would die. But so far She always had won Him back, though some years She was rather late about it. A wild tale. Yet Arawn had spoken of Her with reverence, though plainly he now ruled in this world that the Old Tribes sometimes spoke of as Her womb. This Moonlit Land was a proper world now, a man's world, the battleground of fighting Kings.

"And tomorrow I will fight!" He joyed in that thought; it cut knifelike through all the puzzling webs of strangeness. Fighting he understood.

"But first will come the night. Here darkness never comes, but the time for sleep will. The time for love."

That voice came not only from within himself. It spoke in the song of the birds, song soft as sleep itself yet somehow warming in its softness, a melody that moved in a man's blood.

The palace was very near now. Its walls were indeed of the pale gold of the moon; but where were all those birds?

And then he saw—the roof of that shining place was all one vast mass of living birds!

A great cry rose suddenly, drowning their song: "Hail, Arawn! Hail, Lord!" Folk were all about him, swarming as ants swarm, but full of loving joy. Folk-like, yet unlike the folk of earth. Their eyes shone brighter than mortal eyes, their clothes, even the lowest stableboy's, were all fine and of many colors. Not a face among them but was beautiful, not a head among them was grey. Pwyll sat as if caught in the middle of a rainbow, yet suddenly he shivered. What if, in the light of day all these fine smiling people would be only rotting corpses? Skeletons even, with grinning skulls. He shook off those frightful images. The beauty was here before his eyes. A sensible man would enjoy it.

He dismounted. Two scarlet-clad grooms, fine enough to be Kings' sons, led away the Grey. Pwyll himself passed through crystal doors, set between golden pillars. The vast hall within needed no torches; the shining splendor of its own walls lit it. Men fine to look at came and led him to a little chamber where they helped him off with his hunting clothes, brought him a golden basin to wash in and feasting garments that, where they did not glitter with gold and precious stones, were of stuff soft as flower petals.

Tables were being laid. Servants who looked like princes and princesses were carrying in mead and wine and steaming platters; the smells made Pwyll's mouth water. But the time to eat was not yet; first he had to greet great Lords, Arawn's liegemen and underkings. All were noble and majestic, and some made his heart leap in thrilled awe, for they were heroes of his boyhood, mighty men of old, whose deeds upon earth had been great, and grew ever greater in the songs of the bards and in the tales folk told round their hearth fires. He thought, *Who am I to be receiving the homage of such as these?*

But whoever came, Pwyll always knew his name, and greeted him as was his due. Arawn had arranged his memory well.

And then *she* came, her ladies around her, like the moon among stars. Her face was like nothing but itself; it was the one face she could have had, tenderly, sweetly colored as the dawn. Through her golden robe her flesh glowed, pale yet rosy, sweetly warm as only woman's flesh can be.

Pwyll saw her and knew her. His heart cried out to her, his lips opened, but no name came. Should her hair have been red gold, should singing birds have crowned her head? No—he did not know this woman. He knew only beauty, and only in dreams could he have seen beauty such as this. But he was awake now, and this Queen was flesh and blood.

She was smiling, she was coming toward him . . . How could Arawn bear to let any other man have her, even for one night?

Tonight she was his. That had been part of the bargain; Arawn had promised. *Yet we two swore friendship. He thought he dealt with an honorable man.*

They met, they kissed, and that kiss was stronger than any wine that Pwyll had ever drunk. Fire danced before his eyes, and leapt and sang in his blood.

No man whose manhood had not been cut away could lie in one bed with her, yet forego her. Arawn must know that.

King and Queen, they sat down together in all their beauty and splendor, and the servants served them. They ate and drank, they laughed and talked together.

7

Arawn's Queen

NEVER HAD Pwyll been more easy and comfortable with any Lady on earth. But never on earth had the warmth of laughter and talk filled the air around two people with a glow of rose and gold. He had been a flame, an ache, a straining agony; he had not known how he could bear to wait for the feast to end, for folk to lead them to their chamber. But every moment with her was good, however it was spent. Delight should unfold slowly, petal by petal. For the first time the Lord of Dyved learned that, he who always had been flame-quick in his loves.

When the time came to listen to the bards he hated for the sweet speech of her mouth to stop. But it was a new joy to watch the quiet loveliness of her face as she listened. To feel her hand, that had slipped, warm and firm, into his own He told himself: *She is life. The very blood and sap of life. It is not right, it is against all right and fitness, for Death to have such a woman. For his coldness to enter her warmth.*

Tonight—tonight! For this one night at least he would love her as she should be loved . . .

Then again he heard the deep voice of Arawn, as it had filled the soft twilight about them. "Behold. My kingdom, and my court, and my palace, all are in your power." Had he only stated a fact, or made the plea he could not speak?

Death the unconquerable was not unconquerable. He could not conquer Havgan. To buy a champion who might, he had himself proposed this outrage against his own majesty. No red-blooded live man could have done that; no husband worthy of her.

"Yet he could not do otherwise, knowing that you must bed her. As you must, or else shame her before all folk."

"Courtesy—courtesy. He offered what he must offer, hoping that you

would be content with the gifts he could give honorably."

To the voices that spoke coldly within him Pwyll answered sturdily: *No. It is my right. He did not come to me fairly and ask for my help. He demanded it as face-price for an insult that he himself had arranged. He tricked me and trapped me and ever since he has played with me like a cat with a mouse. Let him keep his bargain now.*

"Yet you two did wear friendship. Friendship close as brotherhood . . ."

Beside him the Queen said softly: "It is the time for sleep, Lord. Should we not get to bed swiftly, since you must rise at dawn?"

Pwyll's heart leapt as if trying to break through his ribs. Now! Now! He rose. No more time, no more need to seek justification for what he had always known he would do. For what flesh and blood must do . . .

She rose with him. Her ladies joined them, and the King's chamberlain. Together they moved toward the *ystafell,* the bedchamber of King and Queen. Toward its doors that some smith of the Ever-Young had forged from those brilliant deep lights that firelight finds in a woman's dark hair, inexplicable flaming gorgeousness now trapped in solidity, to flash and flicker there forever.

As the two neared them, the doors blazed like sunrise. No hands touching them, they swung wide to admit their Lady and her Lord. Pwyll must have hidden his eyes had not flame as fierce burned within him.

But the chamber within was all gentleness and tenderness. It had no true walls, only tiny little crystal doors set between bars of moon-gold. Most of them were open, and through them poured the cool night breeze, sweet with the scent of unearthly flowers. A wide golden bed waited, covered with stuffs that glowed with all the colors of the rainbow, but colors that were forever changing, rippling in their changes like the waves of the sea. When he saw that bed Pwyll forgot all else.

"Go!" His voice was thick and harsh. "Leave us." And as birds fly those lovely ladies fled. But the chamberlain grinned as he went.

The Queen stood and smiled. "You are right, Lord. Tonight you will be my tirewoman, and I your chamberlain. We will miss no least touch of each other, no least delight."

Her hands rose, she moved forward as if to undo the brooches that clasped his mantle. His muscles tensed to spring.

And then her smile went, and her mouth quivered. "Oh, my beloved, it is brave a woman of earth would be tonight. She would give you only ease and joy before you left her. But we women of the Moonlit Land are not used to war and battles. In the hall I could bear myself as a Queen should, but here alone with you I cannot hide my trouble. Forgive me, Lord. Soon I will give you joy."

Her hands hid her face now, her shining head was bowed. Long hard sobs tore her body, she shivered, but made no sound. Before her mute grief Pwyll stood dumb, amazed. In that silence he heard again the soft singing of the birds above them; those birds who had watched over all her nights with Arawn.

Arawn. Death had been man enough for her. She had loved him.

The sobs ceased; her hands fell. She looked up at him, and her eyes were like pools into which the sun shines. "Long have we been together, Lord. No other man's head ever has lain beside my head; no other man's hand ever has found the smooth white path between my breasts, nor fondled the twin rosy globes of them. No other man's ever shall."

But mine will! Pwyll's heart cried that; his fists clenched, his teeth set. *It is I you will love tonight, Lady. I you will sleep with, I that will enter you!*

He said aloud, roughly: "Get to bed, woman."

She showed no surprise, no hurt. Obediently her hands moved to those golden brooches that clasped her own garment. "You are right again, Lord. We should waste no more of this night. You are also my first man and my only man, and if your body should never again lie beside my body I will not live long after you. No other shall befoul your bed and me."

The golden robe fell; bared the rose white glory of her . . .

Pwyll did not know why he did not spring upon her. Why he bent his head and looked down while his shaking hands, fumbling at first, then growing wild, tore off his clothes. Then he had to look.

She lay on the great bed. Her face smiled up at him in welcome, her arms rose. Her legs were already parting . . .

As some huge fierce beast of the forest springs, so Pwyll sprang. Across her and beyond her, to lie with his face to the wall, as many folds of that glowing, wondrous stuff as he could clutch hunched up between them so that he could not feel her flesh.

He had heard the breath whistle and catch in her throat. He could not bear to think of the welcome dying in her face, of the hurt coming into it. Yet how much deeper must be her shame, her hurt, if later she should learn that the husband she loved had handed her over to another man! If only her pride would keep her silent now; the pride of a great Queen. He prayed desperately to Her who sends both sun and rain: *Mother, let her not speak again—let her not move.*

Her hand moved; its soft warmth somehow found his naked

shoulder. "Forgive me, Lord. I spoke words of ill omen, evil words. I will speak them no more. Love me."

He lay like stone. No—like wood; wood being eaten by devouring fire. Her hand moved on, steadily, thrillingly, inexorably working downward. Her other hand touched his neck, lay softly against his cheek. "Much joy have we had together, Lord. Our nights have been full of delight, and by day we have always been friends. Let it be between us as it has always been."

Still he lay like stone.

Her hands still fondled him. She spoke again, a quiver in her voice now. "Lord, love me."

He did not speak or move.

"Lord—" Her voice broke; she sobbed aloud.

Her arms were round him, her face was pressed against his neck, her breasts drove into his back. Her legs wound round him, he must have been lost save for those silky thicknesses of coverlet bunched between them, those folds that finally had stopped her downward-seeking hand. "Lord, do not deny me—not tonight. I said I would speak no more words of ill omen, but tonight of all nights let us be together. Let it be sweet."

Pwyll thought: *Sooner than this would I face the Monster again with no heads to help me. Face the Bird again with no birds to help me . . ."*

The three birds! Someone had sent them to help him. He did not remember who, but he remembered them. He could see their feathers shining on that path of light, almost he could hear their singing. If he could hear it . . .

She sobbed on and on. So a child sobs in its heartbreak that seems so world filling, yet ends so quickly, though it may leave scars that are not of the flesh: scars that twist the self within. So a woman sobs when her world ends; when her man's love dies.

Still Pwyll lay like stone beside her, and tried to hear the singing of those birds that were not there.

At last she gave up. Her clinging limbs fell away and she lay spent. He too lay spent and sick beside her.

Above him the little crystal doors gleamed. The sky flamed with stars. Its vast quiet soothed him and he thought: *Here no man can ever say that he has lost his way in the darkness.* Yet he had. Almost he had betrayed a friend. Suddenly and deeply, and with all of himself, Pwyll pitied Arawn. Knew somehow that Arawn, too, had had no choice.

Then, as suddenly and deeply, he slept. . .

The woman beside him sat up. She cast off that rainbow coverlet, and Her flesh shone like the moon. Breast and thigh and leg, all the noble length of Her glowed softly in the quiet dark. Her face was no longer a young lover's; its beauty was ageless, tender and majestic.

Her own birds in the roof above hailed Her, "Brenhines-y-nef! Queen! Lady who loves and makes all things. Modron—Mother!"

She smiled and they were silent. She looked upon the sleeping man, and Her eyes were proud and tender, truly a mother's.

"You have passed the third test, the test of My devising. Hail to you, child of Mine, born of Me as all the sons of women are born of Me."

"We too," sang the birds. "We, and the fledglings in our nests."

"You, and all that lives. Rhiannon shapes you, but she too is born of Me. Even Havgan is born of Me, he that would rend My veil and ravage this land that is My womb, this land where all things first were shaped."

Havgan! At that dread name all the shadows shuddered, came running from all parts of that lovely chamber, to huddle like scared children about Her shining knees. She laughed and caressed their black, vaporous heads.

"Have no fear, little ones. Though fire should burn both you and the shapes that cast you, yet all of you will come again. All that die are born again of Me. Light and darkness, both have their times, their places; both are Me."

The shadows were silent, comforted, but the birds said: "So You say, Lady, whom nothing can destroy. But we are little and afraid."

"Only by courage can you grow great. I gave My children freedom, and the price of freedom is hard. It is mistake after mistake, pain after pain. Yet if My care surrounded you always, you would be as caged birds forever. Men and women never could grow up, whatever their bodies did. To make all of you sharers in My wisdom and My strength I long ago yielded up My supreme power and let evil come into the world."

"But it will take lives and lives for us to learn that wisdom, Lady and Mother! Lives and lives even for men and women, who have learned enough to win birth on a higher rung of Your ladder, than that one where we perch. And now we fear the pain."

She said sadly: "I know. To Me Time is not terrible; he is only another of My children. Though My forest burn, always I will raise up green shoots from the ashes, new trees and birds to sing upon them. Yet My heart sorrows to hear My children crying in the flames. Whatever each of you suffers, I suffer. But I have the strength to bear it."

The birds said: "Lady, who suffers for so many, we will try to be strong."

"I thank you. Out of the trying—the many times repeated trying—comes strength. As out of darkness comes light. But do not
fear: hope. This man may send Havgan out of Annwn."

"That would be good, Lady. It is not good to see one's fledglings
burn. We too—we fear the flames."

"Which do not yet burn here. But if they come, remember:
Death, My son and My servant, is only the Reaper who brings home
My sheaves. Through him I free the old and tired, I make them
young and strong again. I give the maimed and torn new bodies that
are fresh and whole. That is what men who live near the sunrise call
the Wheel of Life, and no brave heart fears that Wheel. Life is a
thing to rejoice in, with laughter and pride."

Then the birds too were comforted; they fell silent, put their
heads beneath their wings, and slept. She looked down at Pwyll, and
in Her glorious face was both love and sorrow. "Rest well, son of
Mine. My blessing goes with you, and though if you return to earth
you may think it has failed you, yet in another turn of the Wheel you
shall have your reward. We have wronged you, My son and I. Yet how
can even Gods be stainless, They who let evil be?"

In the red dawn Pwyll woke alone. He thought, "She could not
bear to stay, after the hurt and shame I put upon her." Pity pierced
him like a sword.

Then he wondered at that red light, here where no sun was. He
sat up, looked through the little crystal doors, and saw that the moon
was red as blood. Black clouds boiled in the east, grim and terrible;
scarlet flames licked through them like hungry, seeking tongues.

The birds above him twittered in fear: "Havgan rises. Havgan
rises in Anghar the Loveless. To ride to the ford."

Pwyll sprang from that golden bed; he reached for his clothes and
weapons.

In the vast hall men milled like ants in a threatened anthill. Only
the Queen was calm, her face a beautiful, smiling mask. Pwyll
thought with relief, but without comfort: "She is too proud to show
her hurt before the folk."

He was glad to get out of that lovely place. When he strode forth
to find the Grey of Arawn waiting between his grooms, it was like
meeting an old friend. Joyfully he swung onto the great steed's back.
He called to Arawn's men, and Arawn's Lords called to their men.
Mighty was that host; tall fine men all, splendidly armed and
mounted. Pwyll's heart leapt for joy in them; no lack of valor among

these, their fine living had not made them soft. *Beware of us, Lord of Loveless Anghar, you whose so-called men cut off women's breasts. If, when I am cutting your head off, they break faith and try to help you, these men of mine will cut some things off them.*

With one blow he would chop off that proud head—then let Havgan plead for mercy! Though maybe his head still could, being so full of tricks. Certainly it would be as well to pick the thing up before it could roll away. Safe on a spear, it could not get back onto the rest of him.

Havgan: "Summer-White"! A ridiculous name for this awful foe of men. Pwyll remembered words that once he had heard spoken by Mâth the Ancient, Gwynedd's wise old druid-king (in Gwynedd, among the Old Tribes, druids did have wisdom, whether a man could make sense of it or not). "Here in the cool and cloudy West we worship the sun as one of the fairest forms of the Mother. As the Bringer of light and warmth; without Her love we could not live. But the folk of Sumer, near the Sunrise, where the hot summers burn earth and men like fever, fear the sun as a fierce warrior. As Him who withers crops and blasts living flesh." Havgan's whiteness must be the whiteness of charred earth, yet it was still a foolish name.

Pwyll rode on, and the host of Arawn with him. Eastward they rode, toward those flame-shot clouds that waited for them like a living, angry darkness, and the wind that blew in their faces was not cool and sweet, as dawn-wind should be. It bore the stench of burning, a stench that grew ever stronger. Presently Pwyll made out the shimmer of water gleaming under that curiously soiled red light.

The ford. The meeting place of warriors!

He quickened his pace. The Grey's white, flying mane took on a rosy sheen. They came to the ford. Green trees and flower-spangled grass grew down to the western edge of its waters; waters so deeply shadowed that they looked stained. Now the stench from the east was like a blow in the face, fire-hot and bitter. Smoke veiled the far side of the ford, smoke and the shadow of that massed blackness that filled the heavens above it. Dimly Pwyll could see the skeletons of trees, still seemingly writhing in the agony that had burned out their lives. This time words of Arawn's came back to him: *"Where Havgan treads, nothing grows again. Where he rides, the earth is burnt black beneath his horse's hoofs. He sears the breast of the Mother; all his land is a barren waste. His people live by raiding mine."*

Something moved in that murk; like a great, oncoming wave, crested with fire, not foam. For a moment Pwyll was puzzled, then knew it for the unfriendly twinkling of a host of brazen helmets. The host of Havgan! Quickly he ordered his own men well back from the ford. No sense in letting the two armies get too close together, brisk though the fun might be if they did. It would have been grand sport, chopping up these choppers-off of women's breasts. But he was there to fight one foe only, and so to save all other men.

He sent his herald forward—Arawn's herald. The man was tall and lean; in his hair night's black mingled with the grey of twilight. When he reached the ford that hair turned to hawk's feathers; he raised his arms, and his black cloak became wings that lifted him high above the waters. For a moment the whole head became a hawk's; its fierce beak gleamed in the red light, the eyes in it were no man's eyes.

Yet it was a man's voice that thundered across the waters. "Men, hear well! Lords, listen well! It is between two Kings this meeting is. He that would help or hinder either shall lose nothing but his life."

As a great bird descends from the sky so he descended then. He lit upon his own side of the ford, and his head was a man's head, his hair was hair again, his cloak was only a cloak. He had no feathers at all.

But out of the smoky murk beyond came another herald, and Pwyll and all his men gasped, for on this man was a cloak of living fire! All over his mighty frame it flared and flickered, now red, now yellow, yet always gleaming evilly. He stood there and spoke, and his voice was like a great hiss. All the men of the West shrank, feeling heat like little tongues of flame lick their faces, though the whole width of the ford was between.

"Hail, men of grey Arawn! My master comes, the Golden One, he who is ancient yet ever young. He whom no bird's wings can outstrip, whose flame shrivels all feathers, consumes all flesh. Do you hear me, men of the Western World?"

Arawn's herald said: "We have heard you."

"Then tremble. Nergal comes, the Lord of the Abyss, the Lord of the burning summer sun! He that rises out of Meslam, the Underworld, to blast every green and growing thing. He that of old dragged Ereshkigal, Queen of the Eastern Dead, from her ancient throne by the hair of her terrible head. He that turned her pride to cringing fear and made her the meek receiver of his seed. Even so will he deal with your Brenhines-y-nef, with your Modron, the Mother. Too long has She queened it here, over you gelded weaklings of the West. She shall learn Her place, the woman's place! East and west the Dead shall know but one Lord: Havgan the Destroyer!"

From Pwyll's host came a roar of wrath. Like the waves of the sea they surged forward, mighty and terrible. But Pwyll's lifted hand stopped them. "Break not the word of Arawn, men of Arawn. Loud-mouth from the East, go back and bid your woman-fighting master to come forth and fight a man!"

There was no answer. The shadows swallowed that man of flame.

Smiling, Pwyll rode down to the ford. Smiling, he thought: *Now at last I shall see him, this terrible, wonder fid Havgan. He for whom Bird and Beast were meant to prepare me. Well, he at least is man-shaped and can die.*

Then he did indeed see his enemy and the smile froze on his jaws, and his breath caught as if already his throat were shriveling in the grasp of a gigantic hand of fire.

8

The Battle at the Ford

YOUNG WAS Havgan, young and beautiful as morning: a boy who looked scarcely old enough to go into battle. His red lips smiled like a happy, teasing child's, his dancing eyes shone blue as earthly skies, his hair had the red gold of sunlight. It came to Pwyll that he had forgotten how bright and clean sunlight was: how beautiful.

Am I fighting him who should win? Like a spear the thought stabbed him; like icy water it flooded his vitals. *How could any land be laid waste by this youth's footsteps? How could the golden Sun-Lord be anything but a friend to men?*

What did he know of Havgan, after all, save what Arawn had told him, Arawn, who had tricked him always? All heralds bluster before their Lords go into battle; in war all lands are likely to be ravaged by fire. Never would this boy use a woman's breasts by cutting them off; that tale, at least, was sheer folly . . .

Then he thought no more, for Havgan was upon him.

Fierce and terrible was that fight. Pwyll swerved just in time to save his right eye from that first spear thrust. Blood crimsoned his ripped cheek. The cast of his own spear went wild. They dismounted then and fought with swords. They hewed and hacked at each other; lightning swift were their lunge and their parry. Yet always each just managed to leap aside or to turn with his own blade the blow that must have finished him.

Time after time Pwyll was pierced; his blood flowed from many wounds. He thought, *Soon my strength will go.* Yet more fiercely he hurled himself upon his foe, he lunged and he leapt and he struck, but Havgan was everywhere but where those blows fell. Always, after each vain attack, that lovely bright face would be there, smiling into Pwyll's, the white teeth shining as bright as the blue eyes. He was glorious, he was terrible, he was untouchable. He seemed, incredibly, to be growing constantly quicker, lighter, stronger. *That is because I am bleeding and he is not,* thought Pwyll, and leapt upon him more savagely than ever, but he might as well have beaten at the air. His lunges, growing ever wilder, brought him fresh hurts.

"This is not the way." As he saved himself, by a hairsbreadth, from a stab that must have cut his throat, Pwyll heard that; coldly and surely as if a voice had spoken in his ear. He began to fight as he never had fought before, covering himself with his shield as best he could, striving only to guard himself. He took prick after prick from Havgan's leaping sword, but no more deep cuts. He waited, watching for his chance.

But his eyes, his brain, were kept busy watching for, warding off, the ceaseless bright flashings of Havgan's blade. They wove a web of dazzling, whirling lights; a web that for a second covered all things . . . Pwyll dodged, but on his side a new red furrow widened. He knew then that, unless some God should help him, there could be only one end.

To win a warrior must attack; advance. I shame Dyved standing still here, fighting to live just a little longer. But I am standing, and as long as I can stand, I will.

He set his teeth and stood.

On and on and on it went—lunge, stab, parry, lunge, prick, parry. Havgan's lunge, Havgan's stab, Pwyll's parry. And then—were those light-leaping legs of Havgan leaping just a little less lightly? Had that last thrust been just a little easier to parry? No; such dreams came when a man's lifeblood was oozing away. Parry, parry, parry—thrust—parry. By all the Gods, it was true! That last thrust had been Pwyll's own; the first he had made in a long time. Havgan was weakening!

Joy leapt in Pwyll; a last flare of strength. Then, black and bleak, came understanding. *On earth is sunset near? Does his strength grow until noon, then ebb as the light ebbs? As the shadows rise to become Lords of the earth?*

If he could hold out until sunset Havgan would be at his mercy, but—if he killed Havgan, would the sun ever rise again? Death would have a full meal then; Pwyll's world would indeed be safe from all foes forever, for it would be a frozen wasteland lost in the darkness, emptied of life . . .

Havgan saw his chance. Like a striking snake his sword darted in past Pwyll's shield. The Lord of Dyved's warrior-trained body saved him, not his wandering wits. It swerved, but blood spurted from his already wounded side.

He fought then, stubbornly, savagely, doggedly, knowing that soon he could fight no more. Knowing of nothing, thinking of nothing, but his enemy. Only they two had being, locked together in that awesome flame of oneness that lovers may know, fused in the act of giving life, or two men who strive with all the strength of their flesh and wills to give each other death.

From the green bank the host of Arawn watched, white and stiff faced. In the hot foul gloom of the other bank the dark men from the East stood grinning, cheering Havgan on, but their faces too were tense. Like red, sluggish snakes the blood of both Kings crept through the waters now.

Great anger came suddenly upon Havgan. His golden hair stood up around his face; each hair turned flame red, and fire darted from it. The round boss of his shield flamed also, red as the sun that must have been setting upon earth. With a roar that filled all space he charged at Pwyll, and all his own men shouted with triumph while the men of Arawn groaned. To none did it seem possible that God or man could withstand that charge.

But the great stroke that was meant to sheer Pwyll's head from his shoulders only shore through the skin of his neck. His own blade flashed upward. With one last burst of strength he drove it straight through that fiery, glowing boss—and on, deep into Havgan's body.

With a great cry the bright King fell. His sword and pierced shield fell with him, into the engulfing waters. But magically, inexplicably, strength came back to Pwyll. He caught up his enemy in his arms, staggered toward the shore. With great shouts of glee Arawn's men ran to help him, but no triumph, only grief and pity were in Pwyll's face when, safe ashore, he looked down into that other's. It seemed very young again now, boyish and innocently fair.

The blue eyes opened; looked into his. Anguish filled them, and wonder: the bewilderment of a child who does not know why it has been hurt.

"What right had you to seek my death, Lord? I never harmed you; I do not know why you sought my life. But since you have begun to kill me, end it—put me out of this pain."

Deeper than his blade had, those eyes pierced Pwyll.

Wise in death they knew him; knew him for himself and not Arawn. Again in the whole universe they two seemed alone, the man who lay dying in pain, and the man who had dealt him that pain. The agony that tore the other's flesh tore Pwyll's heart.

Havgan gasped, "Take my head—end it."

Of itself Pwyll's arm rose. His sword flashed up, then down.

But a finger's breadth from Havgan's throat it halted. Arawn too had heard this plea; Death had done his ancient, merciful office. And the slain man had risen, his slayer powerless against him forever.

But why fear that? Such a rising would be radiant as sunrise; it would *be* sunrise. His whole being ached to see this boy stand up, whole and beautiful again. And yet . . .

Arawn. His oath. But Arawn had tricked him from the beginning, played with him, left him to fight monsters alone. Always he had had some excuse, some wordy subtlety that Pwyll had not known how to answer, but those were the facts. All the smothered resentments and distrust suddenly broke free, sprang tree-high within him. Maybe Havgan's victory over Arawn would mean that the sun would rise here too, over the world of the dead. Make dead and living one again, in the glory of that light . . .

The man at his feet moaned pitifully. "Do—not—play with—me. End it."

Again Pwyll's arm rose. The blue eyes lit with hope.

They were engulfing him, those sky-hued seas of beauty and longing, those eyes that promised a new universe. And then something— the cold feel of bonds coiling snakewise round his will—made Pwyll tear his eyes away, held his arm rigid. He looked up, seeking something else to look at, trying to clear his head, and he saw the darkness beyond the ford.

It covered all now. From the water's edge to the half-swallowed heavens that smoky blackness boiled. Through it came the wailing of the Eastern men, keening for their Lord. And with that wailing came the stench, the heat . . .

If Havgan rose, his men would cross the ford. Would that hot, reeking darkness cross with them?

Agony rocked Pwyll. The moaning at his feet stabbed him like swords. Doubts tore at him like the beaks of savage birds. Might not darkness, stench and heat be only more of Arawn's illusions? Much that he had seen, much that he heard, since he had entered this world, had not been real. Colder than ice, deeper than the sea, that knowledge poured through him; he knew that he had known it long, though he had refused to face it. How could a man know what to do in a world where his own eyes and ears were made liars?

"You can never know." Deep within him a voice answered, quietly and terribly, a strange voice that yet was his own, though it belonged to no self he knew. *"Never, until you return here a dead man, one of Arawn's own people. But this you know, this springs from your own heart: the loathing you feel for that foul wilderness beyond the waters."*

Pwyll looked at the men pressing around him; at faces that had been triumphant and now were troubled. Faces in which fear was dawning. All this host here, all those people waiting at home in their own fields and houses, waiting in dread to hear the outcome of this battle—even that shining Queen herself—all looked to him, Pwyll, to protect them. As he had promised . . .

They were his people now, even as on earth the folk of Dyved had been his people. Could he risk loosing this darkness upon them?

He dropped his sword; it had taken a long fight to lower his arm without using it. He turned his eyes away from those blue eyes in which hope was dying. He said, forcing his voice to steadiness: "Lord, I may yet repent what I have done to you. Let him who has the heart for it kill you. I will have no more blood of yours on my hands."

Havgan gave a great sigh. He said only, "Let my men come to me. The captains of my host."

They came, those black-bearded men from the East. Out of that looming shadow, into and through those bloodied waters. They crowded round their Lord, and Havgan took the hand of each and pressed it. A faint glow of the old beauty warmed his face.

"Too soon we left the ancient temples of Cuthah, in Sumer near the Sunrise. Gods from the East shall indeed rule in the West, but not yet. Bear me hence now, faithful men of mine. I can lead you no farther."

Keening, they made a bed of their cloaks and lifted him and bore him away, back into that Shadow they had made. Pwyll and his men, watching them go, saw how, even as they crossed the ford, that darkness quivered and thinned and shrank downwards. Like a cloak it fell from the heavens it had blackened, and they shone clear again, vast and unstained. What had been so huge and monstrous, seeming to challenge infinity itself, dwindled down into a little darkness that wrapped the mourners and their burden. Through its blackness came their woeful keening, until distance devoured both. Then all was still; the moon shone down upon the two sides of the ford again, tranquil as in the unremembered Beginning. Gentle as a mother's hands upon a sick child, her light caressed that scarred wasteland.

And Pwyll thought simply, happily, *Now I can go home.* Then remembered, with an inward groan, what any King must do before he went home to his victory feast. "Lords of mine, let us follow them, and see what must be done for these lands that are now my lands again. Also what people should be my vassals."

As with one voice they answered: "Lord, all men should be your vassals, for now once again there is no King over all Annwn save yourself."

9

Homecoming

ON THE back of the Grey of Arawn Pwyll, Prince of Dyved, rode down again into that green clearing in Glen Cuch: that clearing in which the stag had ended, and so much else had begun. This time the hounds of Annwn ran before him, as that other time they had run before Arawn. He looked at the place and knew it, yet felt as if he had not seen it for a thousand years. Surely, he thought, he had been in Annwn more than two days and two nights; Arawn must have a way of arranging time as he had of arranging memory. Yet how could that be?

No matter. Time does not matter, only what happens in it. Time can burn like fire, or it can pass as quietly as grass grows. For me it has been like fire. Things have been burned into me, and things have been burned out; but what things?

He was still wondering when it happened: when, with a sudden great quake and shudder, all that grassy clearing heaved and whirled and was gone. He was back again in the Glen Cuch of his boyhood. Trees covered him like a roof, into his nostrils the wind was blowing the good, woodsy smells of earth, and through the leaves the sun was shining.

The sun!

Pwyll's eyes were still drinking in that dear brightness when a voice behind him said dryly: "Were you still afraid that the golden, Crop-Bringing Mother might never rise again, my brother?"

What seemed to be himself rode up beside him, on what was certainly his horse. Pwyll looked into his own grey eyes, and out of them Arawn looked back at him.

Pwyll said slowly: "Part of me must have been afraid but not the part that matters. I trust you now, Death my brother."

"That is well. Death is the one friend who never fails any man. The child in you was afraid, Lord of Dyved, the child that used to fear the dark. But the man was not. He has grown since we two took the Oath together."

Pwyll said yet more slowly: "I know only that I have kept my bargain with you, brother."

"That I too know, and may That Which is above all the Gods men know reward you, brother. Better than I can."

Yet his eyes were sad. Briefly Pwyll was puzzled, then he remembered that golden bed. Well, what had not happened there was for the Queen to tell her Lord. When Arawn knew that, he would know that a man's generosity could match a God's. *He would know it already, if he were reading my thoughts. But he is a gentleman; he will not intrude on those again.*

He said aloud: "Lord, I led your host across the waters. I sat in Anghar the Loveless, and all those who had done homage to Havgan, paid it to you. To the semblance of you, not knowing that another sat in your place. Then as we rode home a mist came upon us—as most likely you know—and I slipped away. You may sit at your victory feast; it awaits you."

Arawn said: "Truly I sent that mist, and I thank you for your strength that won the victory."

"My crude earth strength?" For a breath's space the old resentment flashed up in Pwyll.

"That was needed, yet without another kind of strength you could not have won the victory."

Silence fell between them. A bird flew across the sky above them; in the golden light that poured between the leaves they saw the shadow of its wings; heard the beat of them, though that should have been inaudible on earth.

Then Pwyll said quietly: "I have seen what he did in Anghar the Loveless. I thank all the Gods that he did not get to my world, to do such deeds here. Yet he was beautiful—so beautiful that I could not help loving him. How could such deeds and such beauty go together?"

Arawn said: "Is a star less beautiful as it falls than when it shines in heaven? Gods must grow as well as men; grow in evil if they turn away from good. Havgan never will burn up your green earth now. Many men and women still will burn at wooden stakes because of the fiery power that he brought westward; many more will cringe in fear of what they pretend to love. For only evil should be feared; Gods should be loved. But he cannot wreak utter havoc now, turn all kinds of love to hate and fear."

"Then when he comes again he will be gentler?"

"Yes, yet he or whoever comes in his place will still bring that devil dream of everlasting fire, to be the torment of men."

Again there was silence. Then Pwyll said: "Was he truly a God? What is a God? A real God?"

Arawn said: "None can tell another what God is. The One behind the Many, the Power beyond such little words as 'he' and 'she'. Not even I, who am Death."

"Then what good are druids and their teachings?"

"True teachers set a man's feet on the path. That each may seek what each must find for himself."

Pwyll sighed. "I think I have learned nothing, Lord, except that I know nothing. And understand less."

"Then you have gained wisdom, brother."

"If it is wisdom to know that I do not know the truth."

Death said quietly: "I am one step on all men's way to it. Yet most fear me as a tormentor. They do not understand that I come only to relieve man or beast of suffering. Of the torments that others or even themselves inflict upon their flesh until it can bear no more."

Pwyll said as quietly: "Yes, I see that now. I should have known that it is never you yourself who are cruel."

Arawn smiled then; his strange, still smile. "It is hard for warm young blood not to shrink from any pact with me. You did only what I expected . . . Well, now it is time for each of us to go back to his own. Farewell for a time, brother."

A wand suddenly appeared in his hand—Pwyll's hand. He waved it.

Another great shake and shudder, but this time it was not the earth that rocked but their two selves, twisting, whirling, coming together and reshaping even as they unshaped and flew apart. When Pwyll's head cleared there before him sat the Grey Man on his Grey Horse. Pwyll looked down and saw his own hands, holding his own bridle, shaped and colored as they always had been. Blessedly, happily, he knew that they were his own hands, every part of them. He was himself again, all Pwyll.

But when he looked up to say farewell, Grey Man and Grey Horse and the hounds of Annwn, all were gone. Pwyll was sorry; he particularly would have liked to have made his farewell to the horse.

"Not that I love you less than I did, my Kein Galed"—he patted the chestnut's glossy neck, somewhat guiltily—"but that Grey One and I have been through much together. Such things as I hope you will never have to go through, my darling."

He rode home then, and his people welcomed him; gladly, as the beloved are always welcomed, but without surprise, for they did not know that he had been away. He entered his own palace, there at Arberth, and everything looked just as it always had, dear and good, if less splendid than the wonders of Arawn's glorious hall. Yet the smoke and the smells bothered him a little. He thought, *I wonder if the craftsmen of Dyved could learn to make those little doors. Even if we could not afford many crystal ones, wooden ones could be opened whenever the weather was good. They make a house bright and sweet smelling.*

Just before the evening meal was served his cousin Pendaran Dyved came in. When he saw Pwyll joy lit his face like the sun. He came and laid both hands on his shoulders. He said softly, so that no other might hear: "Welcome home, Pwyll. It is good to have you back."

Pwyll stared. "Then you knew I was not here?"

"From the beginning. We druids all knew it, but we dared not question him who sat here in your place."

"'From the beginning'? Then how long—?"

"You have been gone a year and a day. But do not worry; the crops have been good, and though a few people have died, no great friend of yours has left us—though you must know that, who would have met him where you were. And I will tell you all that has happened, and keep close to you meanwhile, so that you will make no mistakes."

"By my hand," said Pwyll, "I never have been one to sneak and hide." And he called all his people together and questioned them. "Has all gone well with you this last year? Have I treated you well? Have I been as good to you as I was in the winters before?" And many jaws dropped and many eyes popped, but all made much the same answer.

"All has gone well with us. Never have you been so wise or so kind, Lord; never, when you sat in judgment, have you seen so deeply into men's hearts. Never have you been so lovable a man, or so good a Lord."

Pwyll's old nurse beamed and said, "Truly, Lord, you have shut them up at last, the mouths of all those fools who said that the Lady, your mother, was wrong to name you Pwyll, 'Wisdom.' And indeed there were several of them."

For the space of several breaths Pwyll was silent. Then he thought: *I would not steal another man's battle honors. Is this different?* He squared his shoulders; he looked straight at them all. "Then by the sun and the moon, folk of Dyved, and by the air we all breathe, you should thank him who has been with you here. Not me." And he told them his story.

Jaws that had risen dropped again, and eyes that had settled back into their sockets popped again, but all believed him. Indeed many thought, *It is good to know that madness has not come on him, as all those foolish questions made us fear.* For in those days the walls between the worlds were thinner and visits to strange, shining places more believable than they would be now. Also, all these people had heard of the wisdom of the Old Tribes, and most of them had in their veins some of that ancient, knowing blood.

At last the oldest and most honored of Pwyll's chieftains made answer: "Lord, we thank all the Gods that you are safe at home again, and have won for yourself and Dyved the friendship of him who was here in your stead—of him who, maybe, had better not be named. Also we hope"—and here his eye fixed Pwyll's eye—"that you yourself will keep on giving us the same kind of rule he gave us."

"I will do my best," said Pwyll. And all cheered.

Until dawn they feasted and were glad. Pwyll sat by Pendaran Dyved; as boys they had been as two fingers on one hand, and Pwyll's heart had been sore when his cousin had left him to seek wisdom among the druids. Now he could not help feeling a little pleased when he saw how his kinsman longed to know what he had seen while he was away. He thought, *Yes, I the warrior, the unwise one, have been where you have never been, seen what you have never seen, my Pendaran, even when you lay blindfolded in a dark place, with a stone upon your belly.* For so the druids of the New Tribes sought concentration, and the road to wisdom.

But in that deepest darkness that comes just before the death of darkness, when wine had taken the wits of all about them, and their own talk flagged, he said musingly: "Cousin, why did Havgan's herald not threaten Arawn's own fair Queen with rape? She, and not the Brenhines-y-nef? He spoke as if that ancient Mother were still Queen in the World of Middle Light."

"She is. She is Arawn's Mother."

Pwyll stared. "But I saw no old woman there!"

Pendaran Dyved smiled. "You yourself have said that none grow old there."

"But if She is still Queen why did Arawn's wife get all the honors? Sit alone beside the King? And I never heard of any son of Hers but Mabon. . ."

"Mabon ab Modron—Son, son of Mother. That is a child's name, Pwyll. A baby name. No God is bound to one name, or even to one face. Back in Ireland, whence our folk came, some poets worship Him who has two faces: one that of a rotting corpse, the other that of a fair young lad. Poetry comes from the Land of the Dead."

"But—but I saw only one Queen. Arawn's young, fair Lady." Pwyll protested, sure of that much. But Pendaran Dyved still smiled, and the wine in Pwyll's head helped it go round and round.

Yet when at last he tumbled into his own bed peace came to him; all things settled into their proper places. Were they in bed too, he wondered, Arawn and his fair Queen? No, time moved more slowly in the Moonlit Land. All must still be making merry at the victory feast, the true King home again and his people proud of him, and that lovely Queen smiling beside him, proud too, yet still hurt and wondering.

But they would go to bed, they would go from that hall that was more splendid than sun or moon, they would go to that place of crystal doors. As a hawk falls upon a dove so the King would fall upon her—what husband would not, after a year away from such a wife? He would hold her in his mighty arms and take his pleasure, but she would lie still, still as some carved, painted image of a fair woman. He would speak to her twice, maybe thrice, but she would not answer, any more than an image would answer.

He would say at last, "Lady, what welcome is this for your Lord?"

As the moon rises, so would rise her golden head. "By the Power the Gods Themselves worship, this is a change indeed, Lord! The night before you rode away to battle you had no word or look for me. You turned your face to the wall and your back upon me!"

He would smile and say: "Lady, before going into battle the lustiest warrior needs some rest. Very sure am I that I did not keep that stern back of mine turned upon you the whole night long."

"You did, Lord, you did! All night long you lay beside me like this wall. Cold and hard as stone is, so were you to me. You laid no hand upon me, not the least finger of one hand—let alone anything else!"

Then her pride would break and she would weep, that beautiful Goddess, even as mortal women weep. And for a space even Arawn would be silent; even from that wise mouth no words would come. Until for once even his eyes would warm, their vast, unfathomable depths glow with thankfulness and wonder. He would hold her close and say, "Lady, weep not. For you have lost nothing and I have gained a friend. No man ever lived that was truer to his comrade. What did not happen here last night is a marvel to awe even us that fashioned men."

He would tell her the truth after all, and she would understand, being Goddess to his God, and together they would marvel at the

honor of Pwyll, Prince of Dyved, Pwyll who could have soiled the
bed of a God and had not. The bed of Death himself, whose other
face is Life.

From that time forth, says the *Mabinogi*, friendship grew strong
between Pwyll of Dyved and Arawn, Lord of the Abyss. And because
of where Pwyll had been and what he had done there even his own
people often called him Pwyll, Lord of Annwn; a title that surely
must have displeased Arawn had both been mortal. But no man can
either hurt or spare the unreachable dignity of an Immortal; even
that talk in the golden bed must have been all a dream in the tired,
wine-befuddled head of Pwyll.

But neither his new friendship nor his new title pleased his
druids, always jealous for their own power. So they, who had more
magic than wisdom, set about turning his good luck to bad. But for
three years their evil spells could accomplish nothing; for those three
years the whole Island of the Mighty prospered; Beli the Great was
healed of his sickness and his son Caswallon ceased to plot.

Book Two

RHIANNON
OF THE BIRDS

"... NOT BEING ... in such gross bodies as we, they are especially given to the more spiritual and haughty sins." A somewhat simplified quotation from the Rev. Robert Kirk's *The Secret Commonwealth,* perhaps the first great book on Celtic fairy lore. Kirk died young; his parish seems to have believed that the fairy people had "taken" him, presumably for betraying their secrets.

1

Trouble Comes upon Dyved

FOR THREE winters and three summers Dyved thrived. The snows bedded her gently and lovingly; beneath their whiteness the brown earth slept the warm, fertile sleep of a bride. When she brought forth her fields blazed with golden grain, her fruit trees sagged with their weight of fruit. Nuts and berries were as many as the stars in heaven. The cow who did not bear triplets bore twins, and it was the same with the ewes and the mares. The women did not do quite as well, but they did very well. No land could ever have had better proof that it had a good King, for according to ancient beliefs a strong King brings good crops and good seasons, but a weak King makes the land grow barren and the people suffer. Deeply did all Dyved love Pwyll, her Lord.

But the fourth winter came howling like a wolf. The icy wind of his breath tore down tall trees, it brought sickness on man and beast. Spring came late, and she was not bright and eager, like a bride, but wan and weak, like a sick woman. She cowered before untimely frosts; what fruit grew was small and scarce and worm eaten. No cow bore but one calf, no mare but one foal, and most of these died.

When the frosts ceased the rains came. What grain grew rotted in the fields. What calves and colts were left sickened and died, as did many of the children of women.

The druids came before Pwyll. White-robed and bearing their holy golden sickles they came, and the oldest spoke. "Lord, your people perish. Soon Dyved will be a waste, and what few of us are left will fall before the wrath of the Old Tribes, from whom our fathers took the land."

Pwyll answered as best he could. "Beli the High King will forgive

us the tribute this year. He is not the man to punish men who are
doing the best they can. And next year must be better."

"Will it? And how many of us will see it? Gwynedd lies at our borders, and no trouble is on her people, near us as they are. Mâth the
Ancient, her King, is still a mighty man of war. If he marches against
us, many folk of the old blood will hail him as a deliverer."

"Mâth is a mighty guardian to his own, but never does he set foot
beyond his own borders. You know that well, wise man; you knew it
before I was born."

"We who have lived long know that there is always a wolf to tear
the throat of the weak. Also folk must eat. When your father was
Lord over us the crops never failed."

Pwyll saw it then, the knife they held at his throat. To make way for
a new King was the God-forsaken one's ancient duty: the law that the
New Tribes had brought with them from the mainland. It had brought
bloody death to many kings, yet never, in the pride of his young
strength, had Pwyll dreamed that it could be invoked against him.

He laughed grimly. "So that is it, old man. You want a new Lord.
I am too old and feeble for your taste."

They were silent then. They had not meant to speak out quite so
plainly yet. But their faces were set as the unchanging faces of those
God-Shapes that hung motionless forever, carved into the trees of
their holy groves, their eyes like ice-encrusted pebbles, cold and
hard. Only in the face of his cousin Pendaran Dyved, the youngest
of them, could Pwyll see sympathy and human fear.

The High Druid spoke again, that oldest of them all. "Put no
words into our mouths, Lord. We ask only that you do your duty. The
land of Dyved is a mother, the ancient mother of all her folk. But
even a Goddess must have seed to make Her womb fertile. Every
King of Dyved has given Her his since Kings came among us. Save
only you."

For a breath's space there was silence again. Then Pwyll said quietly: "We have spoken of this before, Lord Druid. In due time I will
take a wife; meanwhile I do not hoard my seed. Has any bride that
slept with me ever complained that she went to her man a virgin? Or
been slow to bear her first child?"

But the old man's eyes pinned him. "You may have done your duty
by your men's wives, Lord, but those brides were not the Holy Bride.
The White Mare of Arberth must be brought forth; you must lie with
her and give her your seed, then slay her and drink of the broth made
of her blood. Then and then only the earth may bear her good fruits
again, and the curse be lifted from land and folk."

"Seven winters ago I refused to sleep with the White Mare, Lord. Yet six of those winters have been good."

"The Goddess has been patient; She has waited for you to outgrow the follies of youth. But now you must prove your manhood—if indeed it is still strong within you."

To some it seemed that Pwyll flinched as if a hot coal had touched him; but then his jaw set hard. "And I say that the Goddess is glad because I did not mock Her with a beast. Get your mare a stallion, old man—let her live and bear foals, and not have her blood drunk by any. So will she do her best for herself and Dyved, without my help or any man's."

Then indeed silence fell, like a blow. Men could hear their own breathing. Never before had any man, even a King, dared speak so to the High Druid. Those who loved Pwyll most wondered, shivering: *Has madness come on him? Is his wisdom gone?*

But the old druid drew himself up to his greatest height, and that was great indeed. In the firelight his golden sickle gleamed like another flame.

"None has ever mocked Her as you mock Her, Pwyll, called Prince of Dyved. You scorn the White Mare, you who have known the embrace of the Corpse-Devourer? You who have been Death's servant, fighting his battles and sleeping in his bed? With his own bedfellow, her that is yet more ancient and terrible than he—"

"She is beautiful above all women!" Pwyll cried in indignant amaze. "But though I lay beside her I never lay with her. Never gave her my seed."

"She wound her arms and legs about you; she laid her bonds upon you. And the seed you denied her has shriveled within you. Never again will you beget son or daughter, only boast of the fruit of other men's good seed. What child born here since you came back from Annwn has had a face like your face?"

"*Aa-aagh!*" Pwyll's voice rang through the hall, wordless as the cry of a tortured beast. Like lightning his sword flashed, but its gleaming arc that would have sliced off the old druid's head like a head of grain stopped in mid-air. Corpse-white the Lord of Dyved stood and fought himself; when at last he spoke his voice was low, as if forced through the stiff lips of the dead.

"We will not help our people, Lord, by railing at each other like dogs fighting over a bone. Let the Gods judge. Tonight I will go up upon the Gorsedd Arberth, and if good counsel comes to me in my dreams there I will come down and take a Queen to bear me sons. For from of old the feast at which a king takes his kingship has been called his wedding feast, so maybe I did wrong to take my father's place without taking a wife. That much right may be with you, old man."

"The King sleeps with his kingdom; those are the ancient words." The High Druid's face was as stony as ever. "The Queen who makes a man King must have the old Goddess of the land within her. Here no woman does. Only the White Mare. . . Would you lie with her if you came down from the Gorsedd? Few Kings ever have, and none of them was vowed to sacrilege like you."

He stopped, and all men shuddered, as if through the walls around them seeped the black, chilling shadow of that awful Mound called the Gorsedd Arberth—that dread Mound that had always towered above the folk-filled, life-filled palace, waiting. . .

"Better that than be burned in my own hall, or dragged to the vat or the tree! I know the ways Kings die." Pwyll laughed savagely. "I will go up to that high place, with my foster-brothers and chosen battle-comrades round me, the True Companions of the King. And if they beat me to death with their spears as old men whisper that my grandfather's True Companions beat him—I will not lift hand against them. But I will be surprised if they do it!"

"The choice is yours." The old druid's face was unmoved. "A King's choice."

"But one that I did not make alone . . . You have got what you played for." Pwyll laughed wryly, then his eyes left the High Druid's face, left all those carven faces and blanched faces and came to the one that was troubled. "If he wins and the Gods strike me down—for my True Companions will never do it—I lay it on you, Pendaran Dyved my kinsman, to be King here in my place. You are no man of war, but your heart is sound, and our people will need you."

"I had no hand in this, Pwyll." The other young man's voice was full of misery.

"You did not have a finger in it, lad. I know that. The Gods be with you! The druids will—that too I know."

Then the High Druid rose and went forth from that hall, and all the druids went with him. Even Pendaran Dyved, but Pwyll had known that that must be so. He wasted no time, but straightway gathered together his True Companions, and they made ready as if for war.

Back in his own place the High Druid sat alone. Pendaran Dyved came to him there. "Lord, let me go back to my cousin. Let us speak alone together, and maybe I can yet make him see what he should do. For he has both the heart and the head of a King."

"It is time for him to go back to the Abyss."

"Lord, he meant no insult to your high dignity. He is a bull of battle, and in his great hurt rage blinded him. Let me entreat him—if he lies with the White Mare, surely his seed will swell again within him. What one Goddess has taken, Another must be able to give back!"

The old man smiled thinly. "I do not serve Her, yet this I will say for Modron the Mother: She harms no man's seed. Life is Her business, Death only prunes Her garden."

"Then he is not—?" Joy flashed sunlike in Pendaran Dyved's face.

"He is. He has walked in the Land of No Return, in that Abyss from which no man should come back to earth save through the womb of woman. In a new body."

"You mean—he could not come back whole?" The joy died in Pendaran Dyved's face.

"Arawn and his shadows needed strength to fight the White Shadow. Strength lower, grosser than their own—the strength of a mortal man. Not from malice but from need, to save both their world and ours, they drained Pwyll's. Else men would have become as beasts again—and worse than beasts."

"But then—if Pwyll's sacrifice saved both Gods and men, surely She must forgive and help him, our Goddess who is Herself born of the Abyss!"

"Modron, whose care is the whole world, has many daughters, and all of them are Herself. She is one of them, She who watches over our fields and our forests, over our beasts and us."

"She who *is* Dyved. The White Mare!"

Again that thin smile. "Boy, under the Oldest Tribes Queens alone reigned in Dyved, and all of them were the Shadows She cast among men. When Kings came, they were Her sons at first, and later, when a new people came, Her husbands. Even among us of the New Tribes, no King may yet reign in his own right; he must always wed the old Goddess of the land."

"The land herself—I know. My forefather and Pwyll's seized the last Queen, but she bore him no girl-child. A pity. For Dyved's good Pwyll would have married any woman."

"It is no pity, but a blessing that that line of witches came to an end. To make men stronger and women weaker we druids devised the Bridal with the White Mare. In her name we wield the Queens' ancient power."

Pendaran Dyved's jaw dropped. "But the Goddess—"

"Boy, there is no more of Her in the White Mare than in any other she-beast. A little of Her dwells in every creature that holds a womb.

But sometimes it is needful for the wise to deceive common men."
His smile was dry now. "It is time for you to learn that, you who are
of our Order."

After what seemed to himself a long time Pendaran Dyved whispered, "Lord, how can wisdom lie?"

"It speaks in symbols. The Old Tribes have but one symbol for
creation: the womb. Here we have changed that, but children must
still have their toys. If the people lose the White Mare too soon, the
power of women may wax again."

Pendaran Dyved said slowly: "I have known women who were
wise and strong. Seed and womb—what is one without the other?"

"We serve the Man-Gods."

"But I thought we still revered the Mothers—as do the Old
Tribes, who were druids before us. They made us brothers in this
Order that is older than the world. Druids helped to shape that
world, and only when that work was done did they plan and put on
the flesh of men. Or is that too a lie?"

"The Old Tribes have grown too old. They cling to ways that are
past and done. The day of the Mother is done. She must sink back
into the Abyss, into that Night which was the Beginning and shall be
the End."

"But then—all must change. What is to come?" Pendaran Dyved
shrank from him, bewildered and afraid.

"A day when men will fly higher than birds, when they will fare
deeper undersea than the fish. When the lightning shall be shut in
little boxes, and serve them like a slave. And all these wonders will
be worked by the hands and wits of men. Woman—she who only
receives our seed and carries it while it shapes itself in her darkness—how can she claim then to be a creator? The fields we tread
shall be ours as are the shoes that also are beneath our feet—
no longer a holy trust, no longer *Her* holy flesh, the Breast of the
Mother whose milk is our bread."

Pendaran Dyved said yet more slowly: "Lord, I cannot understand. My mind is like a dish out of which all these wonders pour as
fast as I put them into it."

"Then go to your bed and meditate upon them."

But by the time Pendaran Dyved got to bed he had found a lid for
that dish. One that fitted snugly, and shut out all wonders.

"So we shall fly higher than birds and swim deeper than fish?
Even High Druids can reach their dotage, it seems. Old men dream,
and sometimes hate women, whom they can no longer enjoy . . . But
Pwyll's men still love him, so he will come down safe from the

Mound and marry, and most likely beget sons. The troubles that
plague the land will pass too—never could the Gods forsake a man
like Pwyll."

Such thoughts comforted him, and he slept. But the old High
Druid sat and smiled, he who could read, even from afar, the minds
of all who once had yielded their wills to his will.

"So I dream in my dotage? Yet by our arts we spent old men have
brought all these woes upon Dyved, to save her from a mad boy's
folly. You will make a good King, lad, well guided—as you shall be!
But the stuff of a High Druid is not in you. And tomorrow you shall
be disappointed, for the people do not love rulers who cannot ease
their sufferings. Not for long. . . Most of Pwyll's men still love him,
but not all. And I myself shall mount the Mound tonight, too see
that all goes well . . ."

A while he brooded there, his face yet more awful than the faces
of his carven Gods. Awful as the face of Fate's ageless, all-mastering
self.

"You would not be ruled, Pwyll. If one said, 'This is right,' and you
thought it wrong, you would not believe him, even if he were the
High Druid himself. And in this new world of which a God whispers
to me in the night, there will be room for those who think for themselves. Even our wonder workers must be children, save when han-
dling those materials we give them to work wonders with. To keep
order always has been hard, but it will be ten thousand times harder when men's hands are filled with marvels. They will be like children, playing with earth-rending toys. We rulers will talk much of
freedom, but in the name of freedom, we must destroy freedom.
Questions can be more dangerous than swords."

2

Pwyll Mounts the Dreadful Mound

IN THE fiery light of sunset Pwyll left his palace. Ninety-nine men followed him, his chosen war band, the King's True Companions, whom he trusted as a man trusts the fingers that grow on his own hands. Not one of them but was young and mighty, a bull of battle and a woe to Dyved's enemies, and not one of them but wished he was going somewhere else.

Black as night it loomed above them, that huge and awful Mound: the terror of their childhoods, the ancient, fabled home of fear. Monstrous it seemed, too vast to be the work of human hands, yet the long dead had piled it above the bones of Dyved's first King, of him whose name and race no man now knew; and the gates of whatever world had opened to receive him never had quite closed again. Tribe after tribe had held Dyved since, and all had learned to shun this place. Only when disaster tore the land might mortal feet be set upon its slopes; then a living King must make that dread climb, his men about him.

Will we bring Pwyll's corpse down tomorrow? That was the question that burned the heart in every man's breast, beat upon his brain like a hammer. Always the bloody carcass of each King who died upon the Mound had been borne down by his own True Companions, by them who should have died for him, yet had been alone with when he died. Comforting mothers told boy-children that when the King was death-doomed deep sleep fell upon him and all his comrades, who woke to find him butchered. But men knew better, and Pwyll's men were afraid, afraid. Could the Powers that haunted these heights make them go mad and slaughter him they loved above all men? Like the beaks of dark birds sick dread clutched each man's heart: *Will I be the one? Tomorrow and forever must that worst of all guilts and shames be on me? Woe to my hand that it has slain my Lord!*

Yet a few—a very few—thought: *Better perhaps for all of us—better for all Dyved—if he dies tonight.*

Only Pwyll was happy, because at last he was doing something, he who for long had not known what to do. True, he was doing what the old man wanted, what that sly druid had goaded him into doing, yet action is action, and only the Gods can tell how it will turn out.

There was nothing in it; there could not be. Yet whenever he passed a band of playing children old enough to have been born before he had gone down into Annwn at least one of them would smile up at him with his own eyes. Always young mothers had stopped him, proud and dimpling, to show him his own likeness in the faces of their first-born babes. But now few did, and their eyes looked greedy and sly, so that his lip curled even while he made them the coveted gift. Had that begun only during this last black year, or had he been too happy in his gay pride to notice it during those earlier, good seasons? Sometimes he thought one thing, sometimes the other; such thoughts could grind out a man's brains and twist off his screeching head to send it spinning on the awful cold of the upper winds forever.

Kings must be perfect; the King who lost arm or leg lost his kingship. But any man who lost that power! But *he* had not lost it; he could not have! He enjoyed women as much as ever, they enjoyed him as much as ever. Perhaps the old druid himself had sent him those black fancies; certainly he had read and played on them, as on a harp. *But I will show him! Be on my side, Powers that haunt this place. Help me!*

The path twisted; it wound round and round the Gorsedd Arberth, like a snake. There was a chill, an emptiness here, against which a hundred men could not warm each other. Or was it emptiness? Their feet, scuffing pebbles, seemed to scratch at a silence that nothing could break. Their voices tore at it vainly, and soon were silenced.

How had *he* died, that first King of Dyved? Somewhere beneath their feet his bones still lay. Long ago the passage that led to his last bedchamber had been filled up, sealed, lost forever. But Otherworld folk still used it; man-shaped or monstrous, they passed through solid walls to bring blessing or woe upon Dyved.

Their world was not Annwn; Pwyll knew that much; Arawn could not help him here. Upon this Mound the King of Dyved must face them alone, save for his own people, who in this place alone he could not trust. For the first time Pwyll thought, with sudden, deep loneliness: *Can one of these with me be a traitor? One of these friends of my boyhood? One, even, of my foster-brothers, of them I slept with and fought and played with, when we were little?*

He could not bear to think of that. He turned his thoughts to a lesser hurt: Arawn's silence through all this long, evil year. Well, doubtless the King of Annwn would have helped if he could. *I only hope,* Pwyll thought grimly, *that he is not preparing a place for me in his court.* It would be a good place, the honored place of a brother, but Pwyll's body was still young and strong and pleasant to live in; he wanted to stay in it a while longer. Also he did not want his enemies to triumph over him.

They came at last to the top of the Mound. Many stones crowned it, rough-hewn seats set about a huge central stone. The high back of this overshadowed its hard seat, made it black in that red light. On this grim throne Pwyll took his place, none too comfortably; on the lower stones his men sat, ringing him in. He looked up at the vast, crimson-splashed heavens, where Powers beyond man's imagining still seemed to be doing battle in the wounded, bleeding sky. He looked down upon the darkening earth below, upon those black shadows that now seemed to be creeping quietly uphill after him, and he smiled.

"All my life I have lived within the shadow of this Mound, yet never before have I mounted it. Well, the view is good."

One of his men grinned back at him. "When I was little I tried to climb it, Lord, but before I got more than two steps up it my old granddad caught me and gave me a good belting. For a whole week I wished, whenever I sat down, that I had been born into the Old Tribes, who never whack their young ones."

All laughed, and Pwyll grinned back. "I got off easier. It was my nurse who caught me, a woman of the Old Tribes, and she said, 'Nobody of your blood ever got down from there in the same body he went up in. Not unless he saw a Wonder.'"

Most looked puzzled, but one man chuckled. "That should have sent you right back up again as soon as her back was turned. You have ever been one for running after wonders, Lord."

"She knew that. She said also, 'Only the King may see that Wonder, and you are not yet King. So you would lose your body for nothing.' That made me a good boy."

Again all laughed, but their laughter died quickly. Uneasily they looked at the shadows already lying black around them, beneath the rugged rocks; at those others rising as blackly from below. A cold wind blew about them; they shivered. But Pwyll thought suddenly: *The Wonder—what is the Wonder? Will I see it, the glory that the lucky King sees?*

The Goddess Herself in all Her beauty? No—She was supposed to wait for the Kings below, in the White Mare. The White Mare—she was a good mare, he would have liked a good gallop on her, but never would he lie with her, give her his seed. His eyelids were heavy; his eyes were closing. He had not known that he was so tired.

The eyelids of the others were sinking too. Some thought surprised: *It must be the wine we drank before we left the palace.* The most honest thought: *The wine we drank to keep our courage up.*

But those very few thought: *Is this how it happens? While the others sleep we can do it, we can rise up and kill him.* But then their lids fell and they too slept. The King and all his Companions slept, the true and the untrue.

A sound roused Pwyll. A thin sweet sound clear as pure water, fresh and clean as the water of mountain springs. Yet it was golden too, golden with the tender gold of young mornings, far finer and more precious than the hard cold gold of earth.

Pwyll's eyes opened and he saw light. Not the last red of the setting sun—that was gone now, swallowed in a grave of gentle twilight. But a clean golden light, tender as the songs of birds.

There were birds—they were flying in and out of that light as it drifted below him, on that twisting path that he and his men had followed. Their wings sparkled in it, and they were singing—that thin sweet sound had been the far-off sweetness of their singing. They were nearer now. But they could not be there at all. This was a black cold autumn, and no birds were left to sing in rain-soaked, frost-bitten Dyved.

Pwyll rubbed his eyes, but the birds were still there. They and the light too. What was that light? A fallen star? No, for it moved, and with a slow, unhurried grace that a man could think proud.

It was a horse and rider! The horse's white, flying mane shone like moonbeams, and the rider's flying golden hair shone like the sun.

The rider was a woman.

Pwyll sprang up. He ran as he had never run before, his eyes straining as if they would fly like her birds, cross the space between them and behold the wonder of her face. The Wonder—*she* was the Wonder, and she had come.

The turn that led to the hilltop was just ahead. He must reach it before she did! He held his breath, ran as if he would burst his lungs.

He reached the turn first. Tall he stood there, his breast heaving, yet fine to look at, a true King. She was very near; through the dawn-gold, thin stuff of her dress and veil he could see her flesh glowing, warm and softly rosy. She must see him now—her eyes must find him and her face must change and light with that smile that would be for him only. Not with surrender, but with a self-giving gracious and lovely as the sun's own. For she was his; she had been sent to him!

She did not seem to see him. She rode on, round the Mound. Past the turn and past him, as though he was not there.

Wordless as a beast's, Pwyll's cry flew after her, in shock and agony that tore his throat. But her head did not turn. She rode on as if she had not heard.

Rage and disappointment burned Pwyll like fire. His jaw set. "So you want to play a little first, my pretty? Well, you shall have your fun—and then I will have mine!"

Still she did not seem to hear him. Unhurried, her horse ambled on.

Lightly, swiftly, Pwyll ran after her, smiling now. It would not take long. He could outrun any man in Dyved, he could outrun many horses, and though he doubted if he could outrun this one, she soon would have to make it show its speed, or there would be no game at all. For the first time it struck him as strange—that slow, even gait in a mare that shimmered like morning, and looked as fleet as the wind.

Soon something else struck his as even stranger: he was not gaining!

He could not believe it at first, but presently he had to. He set his teeth then. As a spear is thrown he threw himself—high as the birds that twittered round her head his great body flew through the air! That mighty lunge should have brought him abreast of her, or even ahead of her—to a place where he could easily have pulled her down from her horse.

He landed on his feet, but he only stood panting, reeling, shaking his head in wonder. She was as far ahead of him as ever. Her horse jogged along as slowly as ever. Her birds twittered undisturbed, flying in and out of the light that clothed her.

No man has ever run faster than Pwyll ran. Perhaps no man has ever run as fast. But he got no nearer to her. Her horse ambled on, unreachable as a star.

The High Druid came to the top of the Gorsedd Arberth. Slowly he came, leaning heavily upon the arms of two of his youngest, strongest druids. But he himself bore his golden sickle.

He looked down at Pwyll and his men as they lay sleeping, the King and his True Companions, the night around them gentle as the bond of their sleep. He frowned. "The God has sent the slumber He promised, but it should not have bound His chosen. . . You two must strike."

The young druids shrank back, their faces blanched. His eyes flashed and they cried, "We will, we will!" but through chattering teeth. His lip curled. "You fear to kill your King? Well, I am old, but the God will give my arm strength." With raised sickle he advanced upon the sleeping Pwyll.

Then through that windless night a great wind rushed. It struck him to his knees, the golden sickle fell. His eyes blazed with rage and fear, staring at the unseen.

"Who are You to stand between this man and Doom? *Who?*" The voice choked in his throat, and his men ran to help him. He gasped a while, then spoke again, but not to them. "You—still have power. More power than I—thought. You bind all these men with dreams, but *his* dream is a test, and if he fails You can shield him no longer. And he must fail. His work is done. He must go back to Annwn. And when he falls I will be here, waiting . . ."

He crouched there shaking, but with his jaw set. At his sign the youngest druid ran to fetch the fallen sickle and laid it across his knees.

Pwyll could run no more. His tongue was hanging out like a dog's; he was panting like a dog. He stopped because he had to stop. He thought sickly: *I can do no more.* And that was the first time that Pwyll, Prince of Dyved, ever had acknowledged defeat.

All the other women who had ever run away from him had wanted to be caught, but if this one did she was going the wrong way about it. Or was he? He sat down and let his tired body be still. He tried to think.

For indeed I have not been thinking. I have not been acting like a man. A man thinks. I have only been chasing her as a dog chases a deer, or any beast his food. I have been wrong; the Gods' gifts are not to be snatched. Neither will they drop like ripe fruit into a man's lap. They must be won. How can I win her? How?

He sat as a man sits at the bottom of a pit, and the moon shone high above him, so high that her rays could not reach down into his darkness. And then he heard the singing of her birds again, he saw the light through which they flew—he saw *her.* She rode by him, and as a tired, winded god rises and follows his master so he rose and plodded after her. She was no farther from him than before, but never could he get any nearer to her.

Only magic can win you, Lady, and I have none. Yet if I had my good Kein Galed here we would give you and that white witch-mare of yours a good run—a good run . . .

He stopped, still panting. He threw back his head and whistled, that special whistle that he had always kept for that one horse. He did not know why he did it; the great Kein Galed was sleeping peacefully, full of oats, in his stable below. Far below, in that nearby, yet far-off world of men. Yet like a wish made flesh the answer came: an eager whinnying, the ring of quick light hoofs upon the stones, and there was Kein Galed himself saddled and bridled, galloping uphill, his lovely, fiery dark eyes searching for his Lord.

Pwyll met him, hugged him, in incredulous joy and love. "Welcome to you, my beauty, my darling, my Kein Galed, swiftest of the steeds of men!"

Kein Galed whinnied again, proudly, and nuzzled him. Pwyll stroked his mane, that mane that he had always said was glossier, more shining than any woman's hair. It could not be more shining than hers; it would not be as soft . . . For a breath's space he felt dizzy, thinking what that hair must be like, that hair and all the rest of her. He could not rest, he could know no peace, sleeping or waking, until he had her.

"But we are together now, my Kein Galed." His heart sang with hope. "The Gods Themselves must have sent you to my help." Light-swift, all his weariness forgotten, he swung into the saddle.

And then it came—the steady, light clip-clop, clip-clop of the mare's hoofs returning! Pwyll waited, holding his breath. He must be careful now. Man's wits and beast's strength together . . .

They were coming! The mare's mane shone silver in the moonlight, the woman's golden, under her living crown of birds.

"Now!" Pwyll drove his knees into the stallion's sides. *"Now!"*

As a wolf springs, so they sprang, man and horse together. No deer could have escaped that spring, the wind itself could not have.

And yet it missed.

When Pwyll's dazed eyes found them, the white mare and her rider were some thirty paces ahead of them, ambling along as leisurely as ever!

Madness took Pwyll then. With a great shout of rage he drove his knees into the stallion's ribs again, urged him brutally, as he never before had urged him. He must have her—she was the answer the

Gods had sent him, the Queen who would bear him sons, the blessing bringer who would make fruitful again both Dyved's fields and
his own loins. Above and beyond all else, she was his darling and his
heart's desire.

Until the sun was high Kein Galed ran; until the shadows that
had shrunk with morning began to reach out long black arms again.
Fast as the wind he ran; faster than the hawk plummets when he
swoops down upon the dove. And still the white mare's lead neither
lengthened nor shortened. Always she and her rider were jogging
along just as far ahead of them as before.

On and on Kein Galed ran, though his breath came in great, sobbing gasps, though his eyes were glazed and bloodshot. Sweat stood
on his heaving sides, yet still he ran. Blacker and longer grew those
shadow arms that daily reach across the world.

Pity pierced Pwyll at last; broke into that sealed chamber of himself where for so long there had been room for but one sight, one
sound, one purpose. He stopped and dismounted.

"The horse can do no more," he said. He took the tired head
between his hand and fondled it. "There is Illusion in this indeed.
Never for any woman's sake would I have driven you to your death,
my Kein Galed, who was foaled in my lap."

Weakly the stallion whinnied and nuzzled again at the gentling
hands. Pwyll led him downhill then; back to his own stable in
Arberth of the Kings. With his own hands he rubbed down the worn-
out chestnut, and gave him water to drink, and food that he could
not eat.

Then Pwyll braced himself and went back alone into his palace,
that he had left so proudly with so many men around him, to challenge the Gods upon the Gorsedd Arberth. But when he went inside
all ninety-nine of his True Companions were already sitting there,
drinking around the hearth, and they and all men greeted him as if
nothing had happened. He ate and drank with them, but his heart
was heavy. Would the horse ever be as good again? Would he even
live? Whatever game she was playing, that wonder woman had cost
him too dear. She had made him ill-use a friend.

Yet when he went to bed he could only toss and turn, wondering
where he could find another steed half so swift to follow her on
tomorrow. All night long that question burned him.

Before dawn he was up, having all his other horses and all the
horses within reach of Arberth led before him. All were good, and
some were very good, but none was half the equal of Kein Galed. All
Pwyll could think of to do was to have the best of them stationed

along various points along that snakelike, twisting path. So he could keep changing mounts, always ride a fresh horse.

But at the last moment, just as he had mounted to ride out, there came a great wild neighing and stamping from within the stable, and Kein Galed himself broke from his grooms and ran forth. Straight to his Lord he ran; he laid his head upon Pwyll's knee and whinnied piteously. He could not have said more plainly: "Lord, you are mine, as I am yours, and I cannot bear to see you ride upon any other horse's back."

Pwyll looked at him and marveled, for he seemed sound and fresh again. He remembered how his own wounds had healed in Annwn, yet he said cautiously: "Well, then, for a little while, Kein Galed. Until we come to where the next mount waits. You I will not risk again."

Upon Kein Galed's back he rode forth, feeling humble as he never had before; he who had stood proudly before Arawn, King of the Underworld. Humbled by the love of this creature whom he had used only as a means to his end; whose misery he had forgotten in the flame of his desire.

Would she come again? *No matter; whatever happens, I have you, my great Kein Galed, fleetest of steeds and noblest.*

Then, upon the hillside, even before he saw the light about her, he heard the singing of her birds. Knew how great had been his fear that she might indeed have vanished with the night, that he might never see her again.

But she was there—there in her shining splendor, with her singing crown, and Pwyll's heart leapt within him, and beneath him Kein Galed's mighty muscles flexed. The great steed did not mean to let himself be outdone this time, and Pwyll did not try to check him. Round and round the Mound they raced, but all went as it had the day before. Never could they get any nearer to that strange, gleaming, unhurrying horse and rider.

Pwyll thought: *There has been enough of this. I must rein Kein Galed in.* And then: *Surely I can let him run a little longer. To where the first of my other mounts waits. Already we must have passed that place many times.*

But they ran on and on, and never saw hide nor hair of any of the other horses. Pwyll told himself: *We must be going so fast that we pass them before I can see them. I must be more careful. Soon—soon, surely—I will see one of them.*

But then he saw a place ahead where it seemed that they must be able to cut through the bushes and head off the woman. *Strange that*

*I never noticed this spot before, but no matter. Now we will catch her—
now!* His heart beat high, he urged Kein Galed on. Nobly the stallion charged through bushes whose thorns cut through his glossy
hide to tear the flesh beneath.

But when they came out onto the road again there she was,
ambling just as far ahead of them as always.

Pwyll's heart sank then, and rage burned him like flame. He drove
his spurs into Kein Galed's sides, that never before had felt them;
the spurs that he had put on that morning, expecting to ride other
horses.

But when the great horse flinched and cried out, when he looked
down and saw the blood on the heaving flanks, Pwyll's own heart and
mind came back to him. He groaned and dismounted; stroked the
stallion's quivering neck.

"Forgive me, Kein Galed! I did not mean it—I forgot that I was
riding you!"

"Would another horse have liked it better?" Coldly a soundless
voice asked him that. Pwyll started, then forgot all else in the knowledge that smote him like a blow. *You are through, Kein Galed. I must
turn back.*

Yet the other horses must be near! They could not be anywhere
else. Soon he must find one of them—soon, soon!

He mounted again. "Just a little farther, Kein Galed, my beauty—
then you can rest."

But that snake road seemed suddenly to have sprouted new coils,
new twists and turns; surely there had not been half this many of
them before! Surely all these bewildering, clawing bushes had not
been here before. He was like a fly tangled in a spider's web; a web
studded with stabbing spikes.

"Just a little longer, Kein Galed, my darling—just a little longer.
Watch out for that bush! We will find the other horses any minute
now . . ."

Then, with a sudden cold, terrible absoluteness, he knew that he
was not going to find them. Accepted that fact at last.

On his own legs he could feel Kein Galed's sweat. Feel through
them how hard the great heart beat; how hard the breath was
whistling through the great chest . . . And Pwyll fought himself as he
never had fought the Beast who bore the Severed Heads, or the Bird
who guarded the Gate, as he had not fought even the awful longing
to give Havgan the second blow—the blow of mercy. All the demons
of custom and upbringing came swarming, like winged wasps, to
reinforce the burning flame of his desire; in his ears they cried the

words that men would have used. *"Only a horse; only a horse! What is that against your kingship, your life, your woman?"*

Then again Pwyll saw her shiningness, that for a little while the bushes had hidden. Peace came to him, strangely and suddenly. He stopped; his hands loosened on the reins. As his body stiffened to dismount he took one last, longing look at her.

It came to him then—the thought that would have made any other man he knew laugh at him. Men of the New Tribes could be kind to women, but they asked no favors of them; the suppliant must always be the woman. And to abase himself before her who all this time had not given him one look . . .

He did it. He called clearly, loudly: "Lady, for the sake of him you love best, stop! Stop and wait for me!"

She did stop. Her mare stopped—that accursed ambling that had seemed as if it would never end ended. Across the space between them came her voice, clear and pure as the voices of her birds: "Gladly, Lord, since you have the courtesy to ask it of me."

3

What Come from the Mound

HOW HE reached her Pwyll never remembered. But when Kein Galed drew abreast of her mare and she saw him, her voice leapt at Pwyll like a flame. "Far better for your horse would it have been, man of Dyved, had you had the grace to ask me to stop sooner."

The new-born joy died in Pwyll's face.

"Lady. I did not spare my own strength either."

"That was yours to spend as you chose. You have also spent the strength of him who could not choose—who could but obey you. Well, I will do what I can."

Her birds flew from her, they left her crown of light, and circled, still singing, round Kein Galed's head. His breathing ceased to whistle, his sides grew smooth again, unmarked by sweat or blood. Pwyll watched in joyous amaze.

The birds flew back to her. One perched upon her head, the other two upon her shoulders. All four looked at Pwyll, and he had a sudden queer feeling that all four were one, and that he knew that One. That cold still voice that he had heard a while ago, had that been hers, even though now her speech crackled like fire? Then, remembering Kein Galed's bloodied flanks, he fought shame, as he had long ago when his mother or his nurse had caught him doing something that he knew was wrong. For even the greatest warriors are born of women, and women are the first judges and the first lawgivers that they know. Which may be why some men who respect nothing else respect women, and why others strive forever to make them small.

Through her veil that was like a mask of light she studied him. "I have lived so long in a world where no blow is ever struck that I have forgotten many of the ways of men . . . You have much to learn, but you are neither mannerless lout nor horse killer, so I need not leave you to your druids, as for a while I feared I must."

Pwyll understood few of her words, but "horse killer" stung him. He remembered that he was Lord in Dyved and she, whoever she might be, a stranger in his dominions, no judge set over him. To remind her (or perhaps himself) of that, he began to ask her such questions as the Lord of Dyved had the right to ask of such strangers.

"Lady, who are you, and where do you come from?" Her hooded eyes fixed his, deeper and more beautiful than the eyes of mortal women. "I am Rhiannon of the Birds, Rhiannon of the Steeds, and I have come from my world to yours."

"But—those are the names and titles of the Goddess, of Her who reigned in Dyved of old." Pwyll's voice shook; awe chilled him.

"Too much of Her is in me for me to be run down by brute strength, whether it runs on four legs or two. I can give, but I cannot be forced."

She could give—again Pwyll's heart leapt within him—and she had come here, and stopped at his call. Was she enough like the daughters of men to become the wife of a man? He said, feeling his way, "Lady, what business brings you here?"

"My own business, and I am glad of this meeting, Lord of Dyved."

A two-faced speech, Pwyll thought somewhat grimly. She put him in his place, yet at the same time showed her friendliness. He fell back on the simple dignity of a host.

"Welcome to you then, Lady. Whatever business brings you into Dyved is a good business."

She smiled then; she threw back her veil. For the first time he saw her face, and it was as if for the first time he saw dawn, and he wished that he need look upon nothing else forever.

"It is a wonder you are indeed, Lady. The wonder of this world and of all others. The face of every young girl and of every ripe woman I have ever seen has been pale and plain beside your face."

"Even the face of Arawn's Lady? She you lay with when you rode down into Annwn, the Abyss?" Her smile mocked him now.

"I lay beside that Queen; I never lay with her!" Pwyll spoke indignantly. "Lady, had she been you—"

"Then by now my beauty too would have been forgotten. There was Another whom you met in a garden. She was once the fairest of all. Until the next night, when you saw Arawn's Queen." Those deep, beautiful eyes still fixed his.

Inside Pwyll's head far-off bells rang faintly. Great weariness— apples and flowers and a quiet place. A woman crowned with light and

living birds—but no! That woman was here before him now, and he
wanted no other, forever. He tried to tell her so, but still she smiled.

"You showed great courtesy to Arawn. Courage you have, and
honor, as men know it. So much I knew of you. But your ways with
beasts and women—with beings you hold lesser than you are—these
I had to learn for myself."

Pwyll's heart stood still. "Why, Lady? Why?"

"Because you are the business that brings me to Dyved."

Pwyll cried joyfully: "Those are the happiest words that ever I
heard in this world! But are you truly the Goddess, Lady? Or only
one who has Her name and some of Her powers, and so can take a
mortal husband? I want you always—not only for one hour here on
the Mound."

"I am Rhiannon, daughter of Heveydd the Ancient. He is a king
in the Bright World now, but once he was King in Dyved, and this
Mound you call the Gorsedd Arberth was heaped over the bones he
used then. I am woman enough to wed."

"Then," Pwyll cried, joyful again, "surely he means to give you
with his good will to me who am King in Dyved now!"

"He will not. He seeks to give me to another man against my will."

Pwyll stared. "Is that how they do things in this high fine world of
yours, Lady? To me it has always seemed that the Old Tribes had one
good notion: that a man and a woman should not share a bed unless
they also share desire."

"The Old Tribes cling to the Ancient Harmonies. But with every
gain comes loss, and every gain is a test. My world, that thinks itself
as far above both earth and Annwn as you New Tribes think yourselves above the Old, is forgetting the ancient holy things of Earth
the Mother. Yet, since all force is against our law, force may not be
put upon me. If, within a year and a day, you come to the hall of
Heveydd the Ancient, our wedding feast will be ready, and Heveydd
must give me to you."

"Most joyfully will I keep that tryst!" Pwyll cried. "By the sun and
the moon, by the heavens above and the earth beneath us, if I had my
choice out of all the ladies of all the world it is you I would choose!"

"Then remember that, and keep tryst before I am given to another
man. Now I must go my way; I have no power to stay here longer."

And for all Pwyll's urgings she would not stay, even for the littlest
while, but left him there. Although the *Mabinogi* does not say so, she
must first have told him how to reach that other hall of Heveydd the
Ancient, beyond the grave; for surely no living man could have found
that way by himself.

Pwyll went back to his sleeping men and woke them, and in the golden sunrise all went down from the Mound together, back to Arberth of the Kings. And the druids dared say nothing, since Pwyll had come down alive.

That winter was not a bad winter, but as good as a winter can be. In the long hours beside the fire men wondered what Pwyll had seen upon the Mound—some Wonder they knew he must have seen since he had escaped death, but he would not answer their questions, or as little as he could. More men asked him why he did not wed, as he had promised to do when he came down from the Mound. Many had had hopes for their sisters or daughters. But always he answered: "My bride is chosen. I must wait a year and a day—the ancient customary time of betrothal—and then I will go to claim her." So men thought that their new Lady was unlikely to be a woman of Dyved, but that was all they knew.

Strangely, Pwyll himself never wondered why earth-time and this Otherworld's time should be the same, when that of Annwn had been so different. Or if he thought of it, he remembered what he had learned in Annwn: that the time of other worlds is not fixed and inflexible like the time in ours.

Spring came, sweet as a bride. The sun shone, the crops grew. Seas of fragrant blossom covered the fruit trees. In the fields the beasts frolicked, and inside the houses men and women loved. Never had there been so much conception in Dyved.

Harvest time came; the golden crops were gathered. Autumn came, with her fiery mantle; all the leaves of all the trees blazed like flames.

On a frosty bright morning Pwyll called his True Companions together. "Today we go to fetch my bride." And in marveling eagerness they set about making themselves and their steeds and their weapons fine. But Pwyll said: "On this journey we must go unarmed and on foot. Only wear the best you have, and bear lighted torches."

They marveled still more, but they did as he said. Back to the Gorsedd Arberth he led them, and the sun shone cold and clear upon its rocky sides, but as they drew near a black gap opened in that terrible, fabled hillside. It yawned before them like the gaping hungry jaws of night herself.

They shrank back, but Pwyll said, "We must go through darkness to reach light."

He held his torch high and entered those black jaws, and some of them followed him because they loved him, and others because they were ashamed to have men know that they had turned back.

Down a long dark passage they went. It seemed to grow ever narrower and lower, so that at last they went single file, with bent heads. One whispered to another, "Can this be that long-lost passage by which Dyved's first King was carried to his last bed?"

They came out at last into a great chamber, and in the center of it stood a man in golden armor, in a golden chariot. But the steeds that had drawn that chariot were long dead, their bones shone white in their harness, and their Lord too was dead. His head almost had been won by his enemies; they could see the cracked, hewed neck bones beneath his white skull. But his own folk had saved it and his beard had grown after death; like a great silver coverlet, spun from moonbeams, it reached to his feet.

Pwyll said, "Hail to you, Heveydd the Ancient, first of those who held my place before me."

But that dead shape was silent, and Pwyll's men, looking round, saw that in the stone walls of that chamber there was no door, no opening through which a mouse could have crawled, save only that one by which they had entered. And the air around them was scant; it was heavy and close; it made a man's head swim.

One cried: "Let us get out of here as fast as we can, Lord! While we still can! You will find no bride here but Death."

Another, one of Pwyll's own foster-brothers, said more calmly: "He is right, Lord. If we stay here long we will not have breath enough to get out again, and you will get as bony as he is."

And then they all screamed, for the skeleton was moving in its chariot! And of a sudden all their torches went out, as if blown out by a great wind.

In that black sightlessness they held their breaths and shivered, and listened to the rattling of those ancient bones. Then a fiery light filled the chamber, and they saw that the skeleton was about to step down from the chariot. It faced toward Pwyll, the eyeless sockets in its skull seemed to hold black flames that glared at him. And what had been its right hand was lifted, and in it gleamed a great sword from which the light came, a sword that blazed like lightning.

All the living men in that death chamber screamed, all but Pwyll. He felt the hair of his head rise, stiff as thorns, but he stood like stone. Slowly then, very slowly, he stretched out his hand; he knew that he must move before the skeleton stepped down from the chariot, or all would be lost.

His fingers closed round those bones that once had been housed by fingers. He spoke again, and keeping his voice steady was harder than walking along the edge of a precipice.

"You have gone to a world where none lifts hand against another, King Heveydd. You have no more need of this sword. Give it to me who am King in Dyved now, and will be your daughter's man."

Gently he took the sword from those skeleton fingers, and though it looked like flame it did not burn him. Gently he set the skeleton down again, in its ancient place. He smoothed out the great silver beard, so that those poor bones were covered again.

Then he straightened and held up the sword. And under its light the mighty stone wall that he faced quivered like a wave of the sea. All its massive hardness left it; grey stone became grey mist, a solid barrier no longer. Pwyll walked into it as before he had walked into the darkness. Once again all his men followed him.

On the Gorsedd Arberth, in the white moonlight, the High Druid's arm fell again. Once again the golden sickle fell; it passed within an inch of the sleeping Pwyll's head and dropped, still clean of blood, upon the earth.

The old man's body shook again; his face twisted with rage and hate; the young druids shrank before his awful glare.

"She has won again! This test too he has passed. But next time he shall fail—*he shall fail!*"

Wandering in the mist, his men like shadows about him, Pwyll felt the sword hilt crumble in his hand. And was glad, because this must mean that he had reached at least the threshold of the Bright World, where no weapon could enter.

But he missed the ancient weapon's glow which, though dimmed by the mist as it had not been by the darkness, yet had kept him from falling. He had to move very slowly now, to creep as he had seen snails creep on earth. Then he looked up and saw a great rainbow ahead. Almost he had missed its shining gorgeous splendor, so intent had be been upon his feet. He shouted, and his men saw what he saw, and shouted in answer. All together they ran forward, under that rainbow, and out onto a green sunny plain, under a sky of beauty like no other.

A road of pale shells stretched before them, almost white, yet glowing with the very souls or spirits of all colors ever seen beneath the sun. They followed it, knowing that it would lead them where they were meant to go.

4

In the Hall of Heveydd the Ancient

FAIR INDEED is the Bright World. None can say which is fairer: the blue of the sky that covers it, or the deep blue of the sea that rings it round. None can say which is more delicate and lovely: the white clouds with their great purity or the many-colored clouds, gold-shot glories that gleam with every hue from dawn pink to sunset red. Lovely too is the crystal foam that makes manes for the blue green sea horses, they that play upon the silvery sands forever, born of a stormless sea.

Sweeter than the song of earthly birds is the laughter of those playful waves of the Bright World. Sweeter than any sound man can imagine is the song of the birds in that World. Pwyll's men marveled, and Pwyll marveled too, though he had seen the glories of Annwn, and the soft loveliness of the Moonlit Land.

But this sunlight was as soft as moonlight, gentle as the fragrant, tender air through which it shone. On earth too much light can blind a man, but here, where the splendors of light are far greater, they might glow and gleam and sparkle, but never dazzle. Nothing here, Pwyll thought, could ever hurt.

Then, above a tree not far ahead, just over a bough on which a small golden bird sang, he saw the dark shadow of a hawk's wings.

Like polished bronze shone that huge fierce beak, purple and gold the pinions of that winged death glistened in the sun. Splendid and terrible it hovered there. Many times on earth Pwyll had laughed with joy to see the sheer splendor of a swooping hawk, but now his heart shrank within him.

With exquisite, heartbreaking purity the golden bird sang on, as though it neither saw that black shadow of death above it, nor heard the rustling of those awful wings. Joy, the glorious, undimmed joy of life still poured in a lovely flood from that little throat.

The hawk struck.

Deep within the flesh of its prey that fierce beak closed; deep within the rosy flesh of a fruit that hung just above the singer's tiny, golden head. Another fruit sprang forth, ripe and luscious, as soon as the first was eaten. Peacefully the hawk settled down, on one branch with the songbird. He ate on, and the smaller bird sang on.

Pwyll thought, humbly and in wonder: *Yet all this she will leave for me.*

Then his heart leapt with a delight that swept away all else. *Tonight she will sleep with me. Tonight!* With quickened step he hurried on along that road of pale shells, that road that must lead to the house of Heveydd the Ancient. Joyously he went, and joyously his men followed him, awed yet full of pride in him, their Lord. In him who was to get a woman to wife from this wondrous place.

And in the gentle splendor of sunset, like, yet gloriously unlike, the sunsets of the world we know, they came to a palace beautiful beyond mortal imagining.

Living birds roofed it, as they did Arawn's hall, but these walls were all of crystal. They mirrored the lovely light around them; they mirrored every nearby tree and every green leaf and every delicate, glowing Otherworldly flower. They mirrored the birds that flew among those trees, birds that shone with many colors. They made a marvelous, many-hued, ever-shifting tapestry, never to be matched on earth.

And there, before tall, wide-open doors of pale rose, doors that looked as if they might have been carved out of one giant seashell, Heveydd the Ancient stood waiting, alive.

His smile made them jump, recalling that grinning skull, but though his new bones were probably much the same as his old, now firm, warm flesh covered them. He looked just as any very fine man on earth might look, save for the unearthly, piercing brightness of his deep blue eyes. And around him played the same light that Pwyll had seen about Rhiannon, the light that clothed all in this many-colored land.

"Welcome to you, my son," he said to Pwyll, and embraced him. Side by side they went in through those lovely doors, and Pwyll caught his breath at sight of the gorgeous throng within.

Heveydd said, "All the noblest Lords and Ladies of this world are gathered here for my daughter's wedding feast. To honor her and me, and the man she has chosen."

At his wedding feast a bridegroom was expected to give many gifts. Pwyll said in sudden shame, "Lord, I have no baggage with me."

"No matter. Your world holds no treasures fit to be gifts at a feast like this. And here on his wedding night the bridegroom sits in the host's seat. Give of my treasures as if they were your own, and give unsparingly. Do not shame your bride and me by being hesitant or cautious."

I hope he will not mind if I take him up on that, thought Pwyll, and thanked him. Then he saw Rhiannon, and saw nothing else. Golden-fair she sat in the bride's seat, enthroned like a Goddess or a Queen, and her smile made all his blood beat hotly to one cry: "Soon! Soon!"

He looked too hard at her to see the splendors that struck his men dumb. But his nose caught the delectable smells of hot, steaming foods and the finer, more delicate fragrances that rose round him at every step, as his feet crushed into the piled blossoms that carpeted the hall. Blossoms that rose again in unhurt, smiling beauty as soon as his feet had passed. He reached her, he took his place beside her, and Heveydd sat down beside them. Pwyll's men sat down too, and whatever dish was set before each man, under his eyes it turned into whatever he liked best. They ate so happily that they forgot their awe, and wondered at nothing but the goodness of that food.

Pwyll ate as much as anybody, but what he ate he never knew. He thought only of his bride; his eyes never left her, but hers were troubled. Once he squeezed her hand: "Be glad, my joy."

"When we are safe in bed I will be. Not before."

"Why? If that other man who wants you tried to kill me I could not blame him. But here in this gentle world he can do nothing. Even if he is here. Is he?" With sudden interest Pwyll looked around.

And saw a wonder. For on the far side of Heveydd the Ancient, in the guest place of highest honor, sat a mighty Shape or perhaps Shadow. Storm clouds boiled round him, hid his face; only the great Noble lines of him showed mistily. Huge he was, beyond the sons of men, and red lightnings darted through the darkness that eddied round him.

"Is that the man?" Pwyll stared. "If so, he looks angry. Very angry. I hope he is too well bred to thunder."

"Hush! Do not mock him." Fear was in her voice. "He is not Gwawl the Bright, who wooed me, but he is Gwawl's dearest friend. He is also the Lord of us all—the Grey Man, the son of Him That Hides in the Wood."

"Death!" So this was the Grey Man of her world. Pwyll looked again at that clouded Shape, and said somewhat doubtfully: "Does he always look like this? Myself, I would far sooner see Arawn coming with all his hounds. Even if we never had sworn any oath together."

"No. His face is beautiful. But tonight he is angry for Gwawl's sake. Gwawl himself will not come to see me wed another, but the Grey Man must, being High King and my father's friend and overlord. Be careful! They are foes to fear."

She was like other women after all, Pwyll thought comfortably. Afraid of fancies, when all peril was past. For he had reached her, and here none could strike him down. He patted her hand. Yet it made him more comfortable to look away from that Shape among the boiling clouds, and when a servant passed with more wine he took some and drank it off quickly, more quickly than he had intended, so good was the flavor. It made him feel very warm and happy, and a little hazy. It must have been strong, much stronger than the wine they had served before. His eyes were closing—they had closed. He could not open them; he could not move at all.

"I cannot warn him; our pact binds me." That was Rhiannon's voice, clear as crystal, hard as crystal, but somehow very far away. "Yet all the laws of our world will be mocked if I am forced into Gwawl's arms. If you, Mighty One, doom my right man's neck to the blade of a butchering traitor."

"The Law will be kept." Beneath the vast cold might of that voice Pwyll shivered, even in that far place where somehow he was. "No hand will be laid on you, Lady. You will but keep the bargain you have made."

"I made it, not knowing what guile you planned."

"In this world no hand will be laid on Pwyll. The druid's deed will be his own."

Rhiannon laughed bitterly. "That fine lady who is too dainty to kill a fowl, yet has her servants wring its neck and roast it for her table? What worth has her blood-guiltlessness?"

"It is a little thing, daughter, the death of a mortal man." Heveydd's voice soothed her. "Arawn will care well for his friend. And in Gwawl's arms all this folly will soon be forgotten. Your joy will equal his."

"What I feel in Gwawl's arms will bring corruption here where corruption never has come before."

"Here it can never come. Peace, woman." In the deep voice of the Grey Man was such power—passionless, irresistible—as in the avalanche that hurtles down from snowy mountains to crush out all life on the green plain below.

For the space of a few breaths there was silence, such silence as follows the avalanche. Then Rhiannon said quietly: "Perhaps it has already come. Fair indeed is this world we have reached, this world where the sun never burns, where the bee never stings. But the wisdom that won us this lovely home fails us. We who know no pain have forgotten pity. We look with scorn upon those who still struggle in the blood and mud of earth, as we once did. We have grown proud, and pride breeds corruption."

The bleak fury of the Grey Man's answering voice made Pwyll remember how once, as a little boy, he had run out barefoot upon ice and screamed, thinking that he trod on burning coals.

"So? We are proud. And you are not—you who have set up your will against us all? If you go back to earth you will learn what corruption is, woman. You will learn what pain is. In that gross flesh in which you have trapped yourself a myriad pains' great and small, will torment you ceaselessly. You will spew up your food, you will walk clumsy and misshapen behind your own swollen belly—until the agonies of childbirth rend and tear you. Age will wither your youth and beauty, and at last death will take the tottering, toothless, shameful wreck of you. And all that before a year has passed over these laughing, glad-eyed girls who are your playmates here!"

"All those ills I know. I have borne them many times before. And I can bear them better than mortal women, I who know them for the passing things of a moment."

"Can you? Pain can seem long and hard to him—or her—who bears it, woman. It can blot out all else."

"That too I remember, Lord."

"Then remember this also—only bits and scraps of the knowledge you have here will be left to you there!"

"That I know. As now I know too, Lord, that those bits and scraps will be as small as you can make them."

"You deserve none, who would break the first law of the Great Going-Forward. Sink back to wallow in that slime from which once you rose!"

"Lord, is the Great Going-Forward a ladder up which we can climb straight to the top? Or is it a winding mountain path whose turns twist and sometimes confuse? Those who have climbed high may turn back to help those below. Gods themselves have done it, and will again: Showers-of-the-Way."

"And you think yourself strong enough to show that way, girl!" Heveydd's voice was rough with anger. "You knew better when you came here, raped by the forefather of that fool who lolls drunken beside you!"

"And coming last, became daughter to you who once called me mother. I erred, but not enough of the Goddess is in me to tell me

which time: when I did not come here first, to try to keep this lovely world sweet and clean, without pride, or when I fled from earth
that had grown vile. Mothers can sway their sons; I might have lightened the darkness sooner had I stayed."

"Dreams, girl—foolish dreams! You came here when you were fit
to come, and now you look back. The wise look forward. But you lust
after this mortal clod."

"By his own strength and in pain Pwyll has done great deeds,
Father; and if he was not always alone he thought he was. Men of
our world cannot know such pain and loneliness. In some ways they
are like children beside him, whatever he lacks."

"On earth a dog will fight and die for his master. Does that make
its brain equal his?" Pwyll could feel, though he could not see, the
curl of the Grey Man's lip.

"Dogs, like all else, will become our equals, Lord. They are only
younger than we. You know that as well as I."

"Would you live among dogs? Never hear human speech?"

"Maybe I can help dogs to learn to speak, Lord."

Heveydd snorted. "Folly, and more folly. Mortals are base, and
grow ever baser. We who had it in us to rise, have risen."

"That is true." The Grey Man's great deep voice was gentle now, as if
reasoning with a child. "The Old Tribes dimly remember wisdom, but
they cling to ways that must pass. Men's future lies with the New Tribes;
I have sought to lead them through the minds of the druids, but always
fools and men of blood twist my words. I shall speak to men no more."

"You teach without love, Lord. I would kneel down among the
weeds, as you will not, and try to pluck them up—give their goodness room to grow. For it is there."

Heveydd laughed harshly. "Many have tried to do that, girl. Once
I did."

"I remember. In those days we both loved Dyved, Father."

"And now I am awake, and you still dream like a child. What
could you do alone when we could do nothing together?"

"I can do something. I can keep Old Tribes and New from rending each other. Pwyll does have a foolish love of fighting—he might
back Caswallon against Bran when Beli dies. But with me beside
him his word will be for peace."

"You could not do worse." The Grey Man laughed now, and that
laughter was like thunder rolling in the hills. "Under Bran will come
such war as the Western World has never seen—and all that blood
and woe will be but the beginning. Through age after age men will
bleed and tear each other in the darkness."

"That World-night must come; all of us know that, Lord. If Bran's war hastens it a little yet it will not be fought on the isle that holds Dyved. There, in sea-ringed quiet, what is left of Old Tribes and New will grow into one people, without the bitterness that burns between conquerors and conquered. Something will be saved, and something may flower."

"A poor stunted flower." Heveydd snorted.

"Maybe. But I will sow seeds, and though many will be lost, some may grow. Some man or woman may be kinder because of a kindness I did him or her as a child—or did his father's father or her mother's mother. Poets will make songs of Pwyll and me, and of how we loved each other, and some of the men and women who hear those songs may seek finer things in each other. Many things—little things; it is from these that great things spring at last."

"Folly, girl; more dreams and folly!"

"My dreams and my folly, Father. I will follow them if I can."

"About that Gwawl will yet have a word to say." The Grey Man's voice, low yet vast, seemed to fill all space with immeasurable power, immeasurable cold . . .

"Drink!" Rhiannon was shaking Pwyll's arm and holding a drinking horn to his lips. Such urgency flowed from her that it beat against him like a wave. He opened his eyes and drank, then gasped and choked. This drink, though strong, was neither wine nor sweet. He did not want to finish it, but she made him.

"Drink! Your head must be clear."

"Why?" Pwyll grinned foolishly. "A man's head is not the most important part of him on his wedding night."

"You must get your head clear as fast as you can—and as soon as you can!"

"But why?" Pwyll asked again, and then his head reeled before the wild jumble of half-remembered memories that swarmed hornetlike upon him.

"Did they drug me?"

"No. We have no drugs, who know no pain, but they did give you a drink too strong for a man not of this world. It has dulled your wits."

"But why do that? To keep you virgin one night longer would help them little; and by the God my people swear by, nothing could make me too sleepy tonight to—"

"You have had enough to drink. I will give you no more, and you must take but a sip of what others bring you."

She sounded exactly like a wife, Pwyll thought somewhat hazily:

any ordinary mortal wife. Well, soon she really would be his wife. Visions of delight dizzied him, dimmed that queer, wild pack of memories. Nothing could go wrong now. She was here beside him, his lovely bride. And a man could not help but drink at his own wedding feast.

A bard rose and sang. Pwyll thought he never had heard any song so lovely, though what it was all about he had no idea. Another man refilled his drinking horn, and Rhiannon kicked his foot under the table, not at all gently. Pwyll jumped, then grinned at her. "Soon we will be where I can take revenge for that, Lady," and wondered why her face went white.

Then he saw a tall, auburn-haired youth coming toward them. A golden mantle was on the stranger, and a golden light was about him too. *I know him,* Pwyll thought, blinking, trying to remember.

"Hail to you, Lord Heveydd." The voice of the late-come guest was deep and sweet as a bell. As a golden bell. "Hail to you, Lady Rhiannon, fairest of brides, and hail to you, bridegroom who tonight will be happiest of all men."

Pwyll liked him and grinned again. "Welcome to you, friend. Sit down. There is still plenty to eat. And to drink," he added, with a yawn he could not suppress.

"Lord, I have not come as a guest, but as a suppliant. Let me do the business that brings me here."

"Do it then"—Pwyll yawned again—"and then sit down."

Eyes blue as cornflowers fixed his. "Lord, my business is with yourself. I have a boon to ask of you."

Those eyes were very blue; bluer than any flowers; bluer and deeper than the sea. The boy was young; very young. He was as beautiful as morning. He was like—but even if Havgan the Summer-White had been reborn into this world he would still be a little child. Yet such love welled up in Pwyll as he had never felt for any man before.

"Name your boon, lad. Whatever it is, you shall have it—if I can get it for you."

Rhiannon shrieked as if a knife had pierced her. "Woe to us! What made you give that answer?"

Triumph blazed in the stranger's face, the light about him flamed like the rising sun. "Yet he has given it, Lady, and all these Lords are witnesses."

Through stiff lips Pwyll spoke. "Friend, what is it that you ask of me?"

He knew. He knew who this man must be, and what he would ask for. And the answer he expected came.

"Lord, the lady I love best is to sleep with you tonight. I ask for her, and for this wedding feast."

Like a great tree struck by lightning, all its green leaves shriveled and blasted, life and growth gone from it forever, its dead mightiness stripped and bare, yet still abiding in its age-old place: even so Pwyll sat there, unmoving, unspeaking.

But Rhiannon's face and the light around her blazed like flames. "Sit there mute as long as you will," she cried. "Never has any man made worse use of his wits than you have done tonight."

Pwyll said heavily, "Lady, I did not know who he was. And you did not tell me."

"I could not; I was under bonds. But now you know! He is Gwawl, son of Cludd—Gwawl, to whom they would have given me against my will. And now you yourself must give me to him, or be a dishonored man forever!"

5

The Breaking of Many Things

PWYLL LOOKED at the ground at his feet: he wished that he need look at nothing else forever. He wished that he need never speak again forever, yet every eye there was like an auger boring into him, like a rope round his neck and pulling at him, tugging at him. Forcing his mouth open, his set teeth apart.

He spoke at last, and by some marvel the words were his own, not those that had been put into his mouth.

"Lady, never can I bring myself to give you up." He added stubbornly, fiercely: "And if I could, what shame could be greater than that? To give up my wife?"

"You must," said Rhiannon. Her face was still a flame, bright and terrible. "You must."

She rose. She looked straight into the gloating eyes of Gwawl. "Lord, I was Pwyll's to give, so now I am yours. But this feast was made for the man of Dyved, and it is not any one man's to give away. Go home now. Come back in a year and a day, and our bridal feast will be waiting for you, and our own bridal bed."

Gwawl's eyes ceased to gloat. Fire flared round him, an angry, green-shot scarlet. "What trick is this, Lady? Would you still put me off for the sake of this witless oaf, him who threw you away as a man throws a bone to a dog?"

"Would you feed your men dogs' leavings, Lord?" Rhiannon's eyes were steady. "This feast is already half eaten."

In shame and in sorrow Pwyll left that hall he had entered so gladly, in such pride and eager joy. He could not even resent those insults, he who could fight magic and knew that he had only one duty left: to get his men safely back to Dyved. He went, and they went with him, and all those beautiful, fine folk smiled to see them go. For now all was right with the Bright World again; he who belonged there had got back his own.

Through the softly shining twilight the men of Dyved plodded, for true night never came to that world; but the blackness that was not before their eyes was in their hearts. They came to that glorious rainbow bridge, but now its gay colors seemed to burn like hot coals, even as Pwyll's heart did. They stumbled through the grey mist, and Pwyll wished that he might be lost in it, mind and body together, and cease to be forever.

When they came at last to that black tomb chamber he hoped that this time the dread Shape in the chariot would rise and strike him down. But this time it was only a bag of bones, empty and frail beneath that silvery blanket of beard. The wall closed behind them, and Pwyll knew one last tearing pang. Now the way to the Bright World was sealed against him forever; yet what good would it have done him to go back? He had lost her forever; more, his folly had killed her love, and doubtless that was good, since now she must sleep with Gwawl the Bright.

Long and dark the passage seemed; the way his life would be without her. When they came out of it Pwyll stopped and said: "Go back, all of you, to Arberth of the Kings. I will go up the Mound again to that rocky seat upon its top, and await what the Gods send me there. For it is clear now that my luck is bad, and I will bring no more woes upon Dyved."

Many tried to dissuade him, but his mind could not be changed, and at last they obeyed him and left him. Only on their way to the palace a few slipped away in the shadows, unseen by their comrades, those few who had meant to kill him had the magic sleep not come upon them. They thought: *Now it will be a mercy to slay him, for the joy of life is gone from him. And we will make Dyved safe . . .*

The moon shone high and clear above the Gorsedd Arberth. Pwyll sat down again upon that rocky throne where he had sat when first he had seen her. She would never come again; he would never see her again. His lips were dumb, yet in its burning agony his heart cried out against his fate that seemed harder than the rocks. Until at last, unbelievably, the moon shimmering on those rocks soothed him and he slept . . .

She stood before him, shining in all her loveliness. He thought, *I am dreaming.* Then again, *But I could not dream beauty such as this. It is not in me, or in any man. Such beauty must come from without.*

He said, "Have you forgiven me, my Lady, and come to say good-bye as people who love each other should? Or has Death come in your shape? But I have always heard that upon this Mound Death comes in evil guise."

She smiled. "It is easy to be angry with you. But it is also easy to forgive you. And you are my man, my choice out of all the men of all the worlds I know."

"I have been a fool," said Pwyll humbly.

"You have. And we are in sore straits, for my own oath binds me as well as yours. I bargained with my father and with the Grey Man our Lord. We three sinned, making that bargain, but they sinned doubly, for from the beginning they plotted your death."

"Lady, I do not understand."

"Women out of what you call Faery often take mortal lovers, but seldom do they follow them home. To be free to go with you I bargained with what no woman has a right to bargain: the way between my legs that leads to the child-shaping, holy cup of life within my body. I said, 'If I cannot get Pwyll I will take Gwawl.'"

Pwyll groaned. "And it is as he said—I threw you to him as a man throws a bone to a dog."

"He shall never possess me. Listen well now." They talked long together, and in the end she sighed and said: "Great will be the sacrilege. Perhaps, if I were a whole Goddess, instead of a mere aspect of one, I could think of a better way. But I cannot, and I am not altogether sorry.

Pwyll chuckled. "Neither am I, Lady."

"Then remember well. Now I must be gone, for my flesh sleeps in Heveydd's hall, and there are those who will suspect me if I am too long out of it. They know me. . . But first I must show you a sight that you might not understand if you woke and found it for yourself."

"What is that, Lady?"

Then his sight seemed to widen and he saw as though they lay before him, six men who lay shriveled and blasted some paces behind his rocky throne. Only by their arms and their garments did he know them; fire had seared away their faces. And he cried out in sorrow: "My men—my men. What has befallen them?"

"Most truly these True Companions of yours crept up behind you to slay you in your sleep. But they—or rather, he who sent them— forgot that I still have some power in the world of men."

Pwyll looked at her face, so fair and sweet and unruffled. Then grief drowned wonder and he groaned again. "These men and I played together as children, Lady—we have ridden and hunted together and fought side by side all the days of our manhood—and yet they would have slain me!"

"The Gods play strange games with men. They are not always to blame, for priests like your druids invoke the might of their names to justify great crimes. But when the Grey Man said last night that he would speak to men no more, those words meant little. For he cannot keep away from his playthings long, men give him great sport That is a common weakness of the high: they depend on and need those they think of as the low."

"You mean—it was not of their own wills that these poor fellows tried to slay me?"

"Not wholly, I think. But I would not grieve for them too much. Now indeed I must be gone. Again I say: remember!"

In the gold of dawn Pwyll opened his eyes for the first time (they had been shut while they beheld her, his beloved), and stretched and rose and found a little bag at his feet. An ordinary leather bag, to look at, but he remembered his dream and seized it as if it held all the treasures of the East. Then, his lips tightening, he went behind his throne and found the dead men there.

With his own hands he bore those poor charred corpses down from the Mound, one by one. He gave them honorable burial, as if they had indeed been True Companions, and folk said, "He is generous." And also, "The Gods still love him. They smote down those who would have been his murderers."

In Dyved the seasons did indeed remain good. Next year's crops grew tall, and were safely harvested, and the young of women and beasts were plentiful.

Then, on another bright frosty morning, Pwyll called his True Companions together: the ninety-three who had ridden with him before, and the six stout new fellows he had chosen. He said: "Men, today we go back through the Gorsedd Arberth to that fair place that most of you have seen before. And we will see who sleeps with my bride tonight—I that am her right man, or he that stole her from me by trickery!"

The True Companions applauded dutifully, but not very enthusiastically. They had no taste for more adventures in strange places into which they must go unarmed.

As they walked toward the Mound one man grumbled to another: "I hoped he would marry a good, solid, buxom earth-girl this time— one who would be proud to get him and whose family would be proud to have him. Myself, I thought he was well out of that business last year."

"Why? You did not like the looks of the bride?" His comrade was one of the six newly chosen True Companions.

"Her looks could not have been better. She was the cream on the milk and the juice in the apple, but she had a tongue as sharp as a knife. Sharper even than my wife's, and that is saying something."

The other's lip curled. "A man must know how to handle women. If she was so pretty, what else mattered? Pwyll had only to knock out a tooth or two and then she would keep her mouth shut and look as beautiful as ever."

"She might have," said the first man dubiously, "but if he did she might have done something else. I have a feeling that it would be better to let that one talk."

"Would you have a man act like a mouse?" His comrade spoke scornfully.

The first man thought that over. "It is better," he said finally, "for a man to act like a mouse than for him really to be a mouse. You cannot tell, with these women of Faery."

It was the second man's turn to think things over, and when he had done so he said nothing at all.

They came to the hillside, and again that black mouth opened before them. Yawned as if to swallow all of them up. They went down that long passage that was as black as night, its blackness seeming to beat against their torches. They came to the chamber that was blacker than night, where the bones that once had held Heveydd the Ancient still sat in his golden chariot, under his silver beard.

Pwyll opened the mouth of the shabby little leather bag he carried (all men wondered where their King had got so poor a thing, and why he had brought it along). He took out a sliver of wood, and in a breath's space it grew to the size of a sturdy torch. Of itself it burst into flame, and Pwyll held it up so that its light fell upon the stone wall. Then all men saw a marvel: for the great grey stones of that wall shook and quivered, swayed and softened and became grey mist.

"The way is open," said Pwyll. "Let us go." And he marched into that mist, and all the ninety-nine followed him, twice ninety-nine eyes popping in their heads.

This time there was no danger of being lost in the mist, no trouble with their footing, Pwyll's magic torch was so good a light. Only when they came to the rainbow bridge, that glowed and glimmered again as gloriously as ever, did that torch itself quiver and wink out like a firefly. In Pwyll's hand it shrank again, almost as swiftly, to a mere sliver of wood.

"You have been a good torch," said Pwyll, "but your work is done." And he threw it away.

All men gasped then at the beauty of that shining world that lay before them, even though most of them had seen it before.

But all was not quite as it had been the year before. That pale road of heaped shells was covered with people and horses, all singing or neighing or laughing, all hurrying joyfully toward the hall of Heveydd the Ancient.

Pwyll's jaw set a little. "They are happier than they were over my wedding feast. Well, let us join them."

The eldest of his foster-brothers said in wonder: "But they will see us, Lord. I suppose that we meant to take those feasters by surprise."

"They will not see us yet a while, brother."

"But we have come out of the mist!" The objector's jaw dropped, so far that it seemed likely that he would have trouble getting it back into place again.

"It is still around us, but now it shines clear and bright, like the air of this world. People see only its shining; when they hear our voices they hear only their own gentle, fragrant winds."

One or two men wanted to ask him how he knew that, but they had not quite got their breaths back, so they followed him as humbly as the rest.

They came within sight of the hall of Heveydd, that hall that glowed like a jewel of shining light. But Pwyll led them away from it, across green lawns, down soft and fragrant, to a place from which they could look down upon that palace: a place that was the sweetest to smell of all.

It was an apple orchard. Apple blossoms still sat among the green leaves of many trees, their pink-and-white color lovely as the tenderest hues of dawn. But in others luscious apples glowed, some red as a woman's lips, others golden as morning.

"We must wait here quietly," said Pwyll, "but you may eat all the apples you want."

Joyfully they leapt to obey him, but he himself ate nothing. Somehow the place made him think of some other place; the dim memory hurt him. Presently he opened his bag again; he took out tattered, many-colored clothes and put them on.

One man saw him and cried out. All of them stopped chewing, even those whose mouths were still full, and all stared at him.

"Lord," said the second eldest of his foster-brothers, "what are you doing in those clothes? They are a beggar's clothes." His voice was as full of disapproval as his mouth had just been full of apple.

"They are indeed," said Pwyll. "In them I am going to the hall of Heveydd the Ancient, and all of you will wait for me here. Until you hear this horn." And suddenly a golden horn hung from his neck, dangling upon a golden chain, and as suddenly both were gone.

The third of his foster-brothers gasped. "Lord, they will know you! Even those clothes cannot change your face. They will know that you are no true beggar."

"In this world," said Pwyll, "there are no beggars. Also Heveydd and his folk have eyes from which no disguise, no shape changing even, could hide me. Yet these clothes will serve their purpose. But if by moonset you do not hear my horn, then get back to the rainbow bridge and into Dyved as fast as you can—if you can. For I shall be past help."

His men watched him go, and then fear came upon them. Such fear as they never would have known if they could have gone with him; such fear as they never would have known if he had left them anywhere in the world they knew. Presently the youngest of them said, his voice troubled: "What harm could come to our Lord here? I thought the people of this place were gentle and never killed anybody, even though they do not like strangers."

"They can turn him into a beetle or a gnat." The eldest of the foster-brothers spoke harshly.

None answered him. They sat down upon the mosses, among the fallen fruit and flowers; the fragrance rose around them like the breath of the Mother, sleeping quietly in that vast brown bed that is Herself. They sat there seeing beauty, breathing beauty, and never had they been so afraid.

Atop the Gorsedd Arberth the High Druid staggered, his white beard singed as if by flame, his hand shaking, though it still was locked tight about the sickle. The young druids tried to hold him back.

"Be still, Lord! The fire from heaven smote you as it did those others—they that woke from their sleep and drew their swords and would have crept upon the King. At first we thought you dead too. Be still, Lord."

"I will not! I will slay him! This last time he will fail. I will slay him."

6

Again in Heveydd's Hall

IN THROUGH those tall pale doors of rose Pwyll waked, those same doors out of which he had once gone in shame and sorrow. Again he saw that hall, full of light and fair folk and laughter. For a breath's space it was as if all that year of pain and longing had been but an evil dream; as if he had only gone outside a moment to relieve himself, as warriors often had to do at earthly feasts.

But then they saw him, and their laughter ceased. All sound ceased. A boy who was carrying a beaker of wine dropped it, and his jaw dropped also. Through that broken silence their laughter broke forth again. It burst from between the jaws of noble gentlemen, it rang from between the sweet red lips of fine ladies; it made all the many-colored lights about them quiver and shake, as if a fallen rainbow churned there.

All the way down the hall that laughter beat upon Pwyll like whips and cudgels; it crashed against him and about him, and no way he had ever walked had seemed so long. *Once I came here as a bridegroom. Now I come ugly and grotesque, a figure of fun. Well, so a proved fool should come.*

Rhiannon did not laugh, where she sat in her bridal finery, and her father's lip only curled. He who was bridegroom now grinned broadly, he who in scarlet and gold outshone the sun.

One place was empty; that place where last year storm clouds had boiled. Where Pwyll, going forth an outcast, had seen over his shoulder that huge and beautiful man whose smile had made him think of a cat that has licked cream. That mighty Presence was not there now, and Pwyll was glad. Least of all because of that remembered smile.

The laughter was dying down. One lady whispered uneasily to another who sat beside her: "He must be dead. Alive he never could have found his way back here. But why is he not feasting with his fathers, in Arawn's hall?"

"Because he cannot forget what happened here. Because he died in woe and longing these tattered rags are on his ghost. Yet dead or alive he should not have been able to find his way back. Among us he has no place." The second lady frowned.

"Could he and Arawn be plotting?" The light around the first lady quivered, almost went out in darkness.

"No, sister. On earth Arawn could help him. There his strength is greater than ours, being grosser, but here he has no power."

Pwyll came before the bride and bridegroom, and Gwawl grinned yet more broadly. "Well, scarecrow, this time you come fittingly attired. Have you come to beg pardon for your past presumption and to wish us joy?"

"That you have without me, Lord. I have come to beg a boon in my turn. Once I granted yours." Pwyll's eyes and voice were steady.

"So you did, fool." Laughing, Gwawl lolled in his seat. "Well, make your aims reasonable, and you shall have them. A man should be generous on his wedding night."

A great chuckle went up from many. Yet that chuckling died as the tall, gaunt figure in its tatters moved closer to the splendid bridegroom. One man whispered to another: "He was a great warrior. He must have taken many with him in his death."

Pwyll laid his shabby little bag at Gwawl's feet.

"Hungry and thirsty I left this hall, Lord. Hungry and thirsty I have been ever since. On earth I found no comfort; when foes took my head and ravens plucked my bones I thought: 'Now at last I shall have peace.' But even the mead of Annwn cannot slake my thirst, even the dainties of Arawn's table cannot fill me. Some scrap I must have from your plenty—one crust from this table where I won all and lost all. Some morsel to carry back to the Abyss. Without it I cannot rest." He leaned forward, and the light fell upon his strong brown neck, upon the line of darker brown that circled it, like dried blood. One woman shrieked.

"Enough food to fill this little bag, Lord. That is all I ask." Pwyll's voice came clear in the silence that followed that shriek. "Then I will go back whence I came and trouble you no more."

Gwawl said: "Men, fill that bag."

They ran to get food, such haste on them as if they felt the hot breath of foes on their necks. They brought enough food to fill a dozen bags, they put some of it in, then more of it in, and then all of it in. But the bag looked no fuller.

"Get more," said Gwawl.

They did. They brought all the food in the kitchens, all the food from the storehouses, they finally even stripped every bite from the guests' plates and put that in too. Yet still the bag looked no whit fuller than before.

There was deep silence then. Everybody looked uncomfortable. The guests looked down at their empty plates and looked especially uncomfortable. Gwawl still grinned, but his grin had grown still.

"Man," he said to Pwyll, "will that bag of yours ever be full?"

Pwyll said: "Not if you put all the food in the world into it, Lord. Every bite in your world, and every bite in mine. Not until the true Lord of wide lands and great possessions, of every kind of noble possession that there is"—here he looked very straight into Gwawl's eyes—"shall put both his feet upon what is inside it and say: 'Bag, enough has been put into you.'"

Then the silence became yet deeper; deep and cold as that at the bottom of some winter-bound, icy chasm. Everybody looked at everybody else, and saw only the mirror of his own bewilderment; his own nameless fear. But then at last Rhiannon did laugh. She looked at Gwawl, and for the first time she spoke.

"Rise up, noble Lord of mine. Easy should that deed be for you."

Heveydd her father said quickly: "Do not do it, son-in-law. There is art in this."

Gwawl sat and looked at Rhiannon, and his eyes narrowed. "That could be so, Lady. Was it truly by mischance—a most sad mischance indeed, wife—that when our Lord the Grey Man was bidden to this feast the wrong night was named? So that he guests elsewhere, and cannot be here before tomorrow night?"

"What could he do if he were here?" Rhiannon asked smoothly. "This man only asks you to keep the promise you have made. As he once kept the promise he had made you."

"There is some trick in this, woman." Gwawl's eyes grew yet more narrow.

"How can there be, husband? Unless indeed, you who are Lord of wide lands and great possessions are not true Lord of every noble possession that you hold?"

Fire flashed and leapt about Gwawl. "You are mine, woman! By my wits I won you from this oaf!"

"Some things must be given, not won, as at dice. If you are my true Lord, you have nothing to fear. Rise up quickly, dear husband,

and end this. We are all shamed. Never before have guests gone empty from my father's table."

Heveydd's face whitened, where he sat in his age-old majesty. He said: "Maybe we have all grown careless, forgetful of the laws of the Mother, here so far from the darkness of Her womb. Mine be the shame. I say again: son-in-law, do not put your feet in that bag!"

Gwawl looked at the guests, and across their empty plates they looked back at him, without fondness. The man who has let himself be made a fool of has few friends in any world. Also to refuse what was asked of him would be to admit before all (and most of all, to himself) that Rhiannon was not rightly his.

Gwawl sprang up. "Kneel and hold that cursed bag of yours open for me, mortal—as the base slave you are!" He leapt. He hoped to break by accident the laws of his world and to stamp upon Pwyll's hand; at least he would stamp on the food. To stamp on anything would be good.

His feet landed in the bag. Pwyll sprang up and back.

The bag grew. It shot upward, it spread sideways. Gwawl was like a man round whom a black pit is rising, a man whom a great snake is swallowing. He screamed, and so did all the women but Rhiannon. His men leapt to help him, but already the bag was above his middle. Even as they reached him its black mouth closed over his head and engulfed him.

They tore at the bag with their hands, they snatched knives from the table and slashed at it. But they might as well have tried to cut through solid rock with those knives, or through the untouchable, all-touching softness of air.

The golden horn appeared, dangling from Pwyll's neck. He seized it, raised it to his lips, but even before it reached them its wild sweet notes blew through the hall, rising above the screaming of women, the shouting of men.

Like ants pouring from a hive, Pwyll's men poured in though those doors of rose, crying, "Pwyll! Dyved!" They seized Gwawl's men, and bound them; they trussed them up like so many bundles. The folk of the Bright World were helpless, they did not know what to do, they who had never borne arms, never even clenched their fists. Only the women did anything, and they only screamed louder than ever.

When all was done Heveydd the Ancient rose up in his cold majesty, his face like carven stone. "You have won this time, man from earth. None here can open that bag, save only my daughter, who must have given it to you. And well I know that she will not. But soon he comes who can open all things, undo all things. Flee while you can—and flee swiftly. But first set an hour and a time for Rhiannon to follow you. She has made her choice."

Pwyll's jaw set. He looked straight into the eyes of that first Lord of Dyved. "By the God my people swear by—they that once were your people too—I will not go from here until my wife goes with me. No more tricks shall part us."

Tall Heveydd the Ancient had been. Taller yet he grew. His head brushed the rooftop; the light about him, that had been bleak as a winter day, flared into golden flame.

"You have no wife. You gave her to Gwawl, and he has not given her back to you. By magic you have entrapped him, violating all that we of this world hold holy—seizing him brutishly as beasts of your low world seize their prey! But not long can you keep him penned up in your little darkness—soon he will be free! And then he will have power to follow her from world to world and to seize her wherever he finds her. Yes, even in the very halls of Arawn, Lord of the Abyss! For her own oath binds her."

Men shrank and women's breath caught in their throats. But Pwyll said quietly: "Yet that little darkness of mine will hold him yet a while, Lord. Before your Grey Man comes he may grow generous and forego his claims on her who has always loved me, never him."

High above him Heveydd's lip curled. For a breath's space the flames about him burned smoky red. "You threaten him? In this world, boy, we die only when we choose and as we choose—when we have learned all that we can learn here, and seek fresh knowledge and fresh sights."

"Well," said Pwyll, "according to you I have come far and done much for nothing. Yet this one night at least I will sleep with Rhiannon."

From the bag came a howl like a wolf's. "Sleep with her, and for ten thousand lives you shall be blown through the air like flies, you and all who followed you here! Fire shall shrivel your wings, cold seas shall swallow you. And through ten thousand more lives you shall crawl upon the earth as worms, and heavy feet shall trample you into bloody pulp!"

Those fair folk grew pale; the lights about them wavered and dimmed; they were not used to hearing of such horrors. Pwyll's men paled also, they to whom such things might happen. But Pwyll laughed.

"Truly, you have a gentle heart, man of this gentle world. But your words make my task easier."

Heveydd had shrunk to his usual size; the light around him had paled too, and his face had changed. "Man, will you bring that doom upon your men?"

"What do you care for them or me?"

"This much. I too have fought and bled for Dyved—in my time I have died for her, something you have yet to do. Long-gone folly; yet a man may look back with tenderness upon the poor, clumsy toys of his childhood. I still see some beauty in the bond between a Lord and his men. Save yours—they have followed you loyally."

Pwyll answered quietly: "I would like to believe that those are true words, Lord, and not the last of your tricks. But you who led us long ago have forgotten many things, and one of them is this: the men of Dyved do not like a Lord who runs home with his tail between his legs, like a whipped dog."

Some of Pwyll's men looked as if they were not too sure of that, but the faces of most brightened and their shoulders straightened, drawing courage from his courage.

"Then what must be will be," said Heveydd heavily.

"It will be, father-in-law. But now I will go to wash off my travel sweat in the stream outside, and two by two my men will follow me to do the same. People with noses less dainty than those of you fine folk here would have the right to expect that of me at my wedding feast. And when I come back I will sit where Gwawl sat—in the place that is mine by right—and my men will sit where his sat."

"And the best of food will be before all of you," said Rhiannon. "I will see to that."

Heveydd said nothing. From the bag too came only silence; and no man or woman there broke that silence.

But when Pwyll came back, laughing in the clean pride of his sun-bronzed nakedness, he sat down beside Rhiannon and threw his arms about her. And as she threw hers about him joy made her shine like a rainbow.

"I did not want to wed you in those rags, Lady."

"I could have made you fine, Lord. But indeed you look best this way. I never have seen so much of you before, and all that I see is good."

They kissed and were happy, for all the cold eyes upon them.

The first two men who had followed Pwyll out came back then, and one carried in his hand a bough cut from one of the apple trees. To reach his seat he had to pass the bag. He stopped and looked at it in feigned wonder.

"What is in there?" said he.

"A badger, I think." The man with him laughed.

"A big badger, indeed." The first man laughed too, and as he passed he switched the bag once, hard, with his bough. The second man kicked it hard with his foot.

Two by two Pwyll's men came in, and every man who had a branch switched the bag in passing, and every man who had not gave it a good kick.

For what seemed a very long time there was no sound but the sound of those blows. Once a woman started to cry out, but the cry choked in her throat. In spellbound horror the people of the Bright World sat watching this deed the like of which never had been done in their world before. Listening to the thuds and thwacks of the kicks, to the savage swish of the switches, until it seemed to them that they never had heard anything else, and never would hear anything else forever. Rhiannon's face was as white as any there, and Pwyll and Heveydd sat like carven images.

Twenty men had come in, and thirty, and forty. They kept on coming. The fiftieth stopped between the doors.

"What game are you fellows playing in here?"

"'Badger-in-the-bag' it is called." The forty-ninth grinned.

The fiftieth grinned back. 'Well, that is a new game and there are plenty more of us stout fellows here to play it. Let us in."

He advanced upon the bag, his foot raised to kick it. He was the biggest man who had yet come in, and he had the biggest foot. When that kick landed all shuddered.

The bag broke its silence at last. It did not cry out, but the voice that came from it was hoarse and changed. Few would have known it for the voice of Gwawl, the bright son of Cludd. "Lord, hear me— let me not die in this bag!"

Pwyll looked at ancient Heveydd. Slowly, through stone-stiff lips, the words came. "Son-in-law, make an end of this. Truly I had forgotten the ways of men, and evil they are to remember. Take her; we cannot withstand you."

The fifty-first man, switch in hand, had almost reached the bag. At a sign from Pwyll he stopped. Pwyll's eyes swung back to that earlier Lord of Dyved. "Father-in-law, I will take your counsel and Rhiannon's. Tell me what I should do."

Rhiannon spoke quickly, before her father could. Her voice was clear and hard as crystal, and as cold. "This is my counsel, Lord. Make Gwawl swear never again to seek me, in love or in hate. To take no vengeance on us or ours."

"Gladly will I swear those oaths." The bag spoke in haste.

"And gladly will I accept them." Pwyll rose, but Rhiannon caught his arm. "This too he must swear, Lord—never to stir up his friends and kin against us."

"We will take that oath with him," Heveydd said heavily. "All of us here. Only set him free."

Pwyll looked at Rhiannon. For a breath's space she hesitated; then she said: "With those terms we must be content."

At Pwyll's touch the bag opened like a mouth. He put out his hand to help the man inside, then flinched as Gwawl's golden head rose out of that darkness. Once again he seemed to see the white face of Havgan, dying beside the ford. The love that twice already had nearly been Pwyll's bane welled up within him. But then Gwawl thrust his extended hand aside, and he met those blazing tormented eyes and knew them for the eyes of one who never could give love or friendship. For all their baffled rage they were cold with an inner cold wide as the heavens and deep as the sea: a loveless, self-filled vastness never to be warmed. To this man the thwarting of his own desires was the only sin, and that a sin unforgivable.

Clumsily, painfully, Gwawl freed himself. The leather sides of the bag had shielded him somewhat; no drop of blood stained his fine wedding clothes. But blood stood in a red, ugly line on his lips, where he had bitten them through, and he moved stiffly. He did not look at his men, whom Pwyll's were unbinding.

"Bring him wine," said Heveydd, his own lips tightening. They did, and he drank it; faint color began to creep back into his face. His eyes, now blank and hard as bright stones, turned to Pwyll.

"Lord, I am sorely bruised and hurt. Have I your leave to go?"

Courteously Pwyll made answer: "If that is your will, Lord."

"It is as much of my will as I am likely to get." Again those eyes chilled him.

From the wide doorway Pwyll watched them go, Gwawl and his men, riding off into that clean, sweet twilight, their own lights glowing dull crimson and smoky purple about them, soiling that shining cleanness as they went. And great unhappiness was on the Prince of Dyved, a woe beyond his understanding.

"You grieve, Lord?" Rhiannon stood beside him.

"Lady, I have longed for this vengeance; all this long year I have dreamed of it. Yet I have had no joy of it. A man should meet his foe face to face."

"Never would Gwawl fight fairly, Lord."

"I know that now. In whatever world one meets him he knows no pity, and that of other men is only his tool. Yet never have I honored pity overmuch. I am a warrior sprung from warriors, and I have always thought war the one right business for a man, and all the works of peace unmanly."

"But now, Lord?"

"Now I do grieve. Not for Gwawl, but for the foolish innocence of your people, who had forgotten what man can do to man. For your trees, that my men and I have maimed, lopping their branches, that should have borne flowers and fruit, yet now have died in order to deal pain.

"I too grieve, who devised the deed." Both her face and her voice were very quiet.

He spoke on, his thoughts jumbled, wild and bitter like the blows that had rained upon Gwawl. "That hawk, too—him I once saw sharing a bough with a singing bird. Will such a thing ever happen again, even here? Or will some invisible darkness stain this clear, light-filled air of yours, making the weak fear the strong, and the strong learn the terrible pleasure of hurting the weak?"

She laid her hand on his arm. "This is not the first world into which sin has come, Lord, nor will it be the last. Long since the seeds had been sown, or Gwawl never could have been born here."

"But all was beauty—all was peace . . ."

She said dryly: "Not so. Remember what Gwawl and the Grey Man planned for me. Truly only beauty can be born into this world, and Gwawl has achieved beauty. But he uses it to sway others to his will, not to draw their gaze upward. For he himself was the first to fall in love with his own beauty, and now he thinks all others made only to serve the wonder that is himself. In lower worlds he must add fighters' skills to that beauty, to dazzle your warrior-kind, but wherever pride is, he is."

"Lady, a man has a right to pride."

"Not to such pride as his. That tenderness and service are parts of love he has forgotten, and had he been able to hold either your mind or my body, in time all Dyved must have become as he is. Save for his lying, snaring beauty."

"Then we have done no harm?"

"I did not say that. I have brought violence here, where violence never was before, and for that I must pay. But the debt is not yours, who were only the stick in my hand."

"You are my wife!" He turned and caught her to him. "None shall hurt you, now or ever! Not while I live."

She smiled gently, as a mother smiles at the child who boasts of protecting her. "Tonight none shall harm either of us. This is our wedding night."

She took his hand and led him back to their places beside Heveydd the Ancient, her father. Pwyll's men were all there, each sitting just where he had sat the year before, and it was indeed as if nothing had ever happened, as if they were still making merry at that first wedding feast. They sat there, they ate and drank and laughed until it was time to go to sleep. Then, by the light of that silver gold moon that shone as bright as any earthly sun, Pwyll and Rhiannon left that lovely hall; they went together to her chamber. To her bed, that was made all of flowers, dove-soft, fragrant, and unwithering. There at last his arms clasped her, and gladly she gave him her maiden head.

Riding home, stiff and sore, through that cool, shimmering light, Gwawl thought of them in that bed and his heart writhed within him, even as his beaten body had writhed in the bag. Savagely he comforted himself. *No oaths bind the Grey Man. None of us had power to swear for him—as well she knows. He will avenge me.* But then he remembered Arawn, and how, in the thick air of earth, the might of the Lord of the Abyss could prevail over even the Son of the Hidden One, of him who lurks forever in the primal Wood of the Uncreated. And there in that world that knows no darkness, blackness came over the bright son of Cludd, and flames seared him; he ground his teeth. *Yet men live but a little while, and if Pwyll dies before you, beware, Rhiannon! For then again you will be ours, and Arawn will have no right to shield you.*

7

The Golden Sickle

ALL WHO could find chambers in that wondrous, many-chambered palace had found them; in the wide hall beds had been made for the rest. Only Heveydd the Ancient still sat in his high seat, alone in that silver quiet, as now he must always be alone. His brooding eyes stared afar off, into memories and mysteries beyond the ken of man.

One of Rhiannon's maids slept there with one of Pwyll's foster-brothers. At first they were happy, but when joy was spent and they lay still her heart grew sore for her lady, whom she must lose, and she mocked him.

"What a surprise you will get tomorrow morning, all you fine fellows from earth, when you wake up back on your own barren hillside. With cold, hard stones for beds!"

He grinned, half awake; his hands found her breasts again. "Indeed they were not like this bedding, girl. But it was last year we slept on those stones, the first time we mounted the Gorsedd. Yesterday we had no time even to sit down there."

She laughed in his face. "Man, if by the Gorsedd you mean that mound that was piled over those discarded old bones of our Lord's, you have mounted it but once. You never went down again."

"That cannot be!" He started; his jaw dropped.

"It is. Pwyll and all of you think he met our Lady two years ago, yet by your time it was only yesterday. And by ours not two hours, though here our great ones can make an hour long or short as they please. Time does not chain us."

Gaping, he stared at her. "Woman, it cannot be. We were back on earth a whole year. There Pwyll chose six new True Companions to replace the six traitors. They mounted the hill with us yesterday . . ."

"Dreaming he chose them, and in dream, empty eyed, they rose from their beds and mounted the hill. Now all ninety-nine of you sleep round your King, but those six lie nearest him. For not having been out of their bodies as long as the rest of you, they can move more swiftly if need be. To do her bidding."

"Her bidding!" He shook her, fear and fury in his face. "She is in it too then! She and all you cursed folk have tricked us! She whom Pwyll loves as he has loved no woman.

"Fear nothing." Her smile was bitter. "Many Illusions have been arranged between our Lady and her kin. But she loves him. She will wake tomorrow on your Gorsedd beside him."

"Then all is well." Heaving a deep sigh of relief he sank down again beside her.

"It will never be well! I do not see how she can bear it! When she wakes her flesh will be mortal, no more light will come from it, ever again. She will grow old, as your women grow old. And though the poor among you may love her, remembering the Goddess their own folk worshipped of old, your proud ladies of the New Tribes will hate her because he loves her. Because he chose her, not one of them. It is not good to be a woman alone among other women who hate you. And with the powers of your own kind gone from you."

He laughed. "Jealous hags can be dealt with. Our Lord will have his Lady."

She sighed. "Well, her birds will always be with her. They are part of her."

Of a sudden his eyes sparkled; he caught her to him again. "Girl, come with me—then she will not be alone. I can always spare my woman to tend Pwyll's Lady."

But she shrank back from him and shook her head, mute with horror.

In their moment of highest ecstasy, when that moonlit chamber seemed full of a glory greater than that of sun or moon, Pwyll started and cried out. "I know You now! I remember! You are She whom I met in Annwn, after I had slain the monster. The One who sat in the garden, making birds."

Gentle and amused, the voice of the Goddess answered him. "True. Birds are among the least of My creations, yet they fly the highest. Men will fly higher one day, but they must make their own wings. I cannot do it for them, else they would remain children forever."

"How could any man rise higher than to possess You?"

"That was all of Me, Pwyll, that Maker of Birds. More of Me than any flesh may house for long, even such flesh as this Bright World breeds. Yet I am woman enough to have wondered sometimes how long it would take you to remember."

"I should have known when first You lifted Your veil, and showed me Your face. When I thought I had lost You forever, and woke in the black night to find You shining before me. How could I ever have forgotten?"

"Because you are only a man. As I am only a woman. Your woman." Now again the voice was only the voice of Rhiannon, his wife. But she herself was enough— blessedly enough. . .

When he slept again she held him, the light that for this one more night was still hers playing round them both. "You learn slowly, beloved, but you learn. And it is what is learned slowly that sinks deep within. You men and your Gods! You mock at the Mother for snail slowness, for creating blindly in the dark. Yet when you create without Her, swiftly and in the light, you will create blindly indeed— shaping, maybe, a world's death! Well, poison sea and sky, the air you breathe, and even the sweet brown skin of Her breast, that always She has allowed you to tear to give you grain. Kill and kill until nothing is left but bare bones upon barren, polluted earth. The Mother is mighty; She has many bodies, and your world is but one of them. In Her mightiness She may yet heal Her wounds and make earth bloom again—yes, raise up you men along with it, even if She has to bear your whole race again. For a good mother is patient; she knows that a child must stumble many times before it learns to walk. . . Also you do have your good points. Who should know that better than I?" She laughed, and cradled Pwyll's head upon her breasts.

On the Gorsedd Arberth the High Druid lay dying, his own golden sickle protruding from his heart. Both young druids knelt beside him, one held his head. A little breath was left in him; he spoke to them, gasping: "She—has not—won altogether. Tell Pwyll—that— never will he beget a son!"

He died without seeing the silent, closed look on their faces. Never would they speak such unpalatable words in the ears of the great; in that new age that he had said was coming, Kings and warriors, men of earthly power, plainly were to be the ones the Gods loved. Had they not just seen the High Druid himself smitten down when he raised his hand against the King?

Unharmed, the King still slept with his ninety-nine True Companions around him. Six men had climbed that hill, empty eyed in the moonlight, to sit in the places of those six Untrue Companions who had fallen. "In his dream he has chosen them," the High Druid had said, laughing. "Little good they will do him!" But they had done him good; when the sickle had been poised above him those six it was who had sprung up and seized it in its fall and driven it back, deep into the heart of its wielder. Then, empty eyed as ever, they had gone back to their places. Now they slept peacefully, as did those others whose selves had been gone longer from their bodies.

As the young druids bore their Lord's body downhill one said to the other: "Maybe we should tell Pendaran Dyved the last words of him he will surely follow. Then a High Druid will have the knowledge, yet if he uses it the words will come from his mouth, not ours."

His comrade said doubtfully: "The high usually can find some way to blame the low, brother—and to let the low suffer alone. Yet Pendaran Dyved loves Pwyll; if he speaks it will be to warn the King, not to harm him. So we can be true to our order without offending him the Gods love more."

END OF THE FIRST BRANCH.

Sources—and Thank-Yous

DRUIDS WERE famed prophets. They foretold Rome's downfall and the domination of Europe by its northwestern people. Also, Giraldus Cambrensis' account of that strange Irish coronation rite— the king's bridal with a white mare, who was afterwards killed and her blood drunk in a holy broth—is now accepted by most Celtic scholars. Since the worship of the Horse-Goddess was popular throughout the Celtic world, the rite does not seem likely to have been confined to Ireland. The Welsh Rhiannon has been identified with the Horse-Goddess.

Parts of the First Branch of the *Mabinogi* have long puzzled Celtic scholars. Why should Pwyll's great adversary bear the name of a benevolent deity, Havgan, "Summer-White"? It has even been suggested that Pwyll himself may have been originally a Power of the Underworld; that is to say, we are really sympathizing with the wrong person. To me, the only clue seems to lie in Eastern influence; years ago Heinrich Zimmer pointed out that certain elements in the old Welsh story seemed unsuited to the British climate, and suggested that they had been brought in by the Phoenicians. The term "Phoenicians" is not as popular as it used to be, but we do know that the ancient Sumerians identified their blazing summer sun with Death himself, and worshipped him so at their temple in Cuthah.

The *Mabinogi* gives Arawn's entrance a weird majesty that is truly like a wind from another world; I felt presumptuous for retouching it. But when Arawn assures Pwyll that fighting Havgan will be perfectly safe—just one blow, and it will be all over—he does not exactly build up suspense and scare people. Doubtless medieval audiences and readers already knew what was coming, and cared only for the way in which the old tale was retold; about a hundred years ago Irish farm-folk still grew old listening raptly to the same tales of Dierdre and Finn that they had heard as children. But now we story tellers who crouch over typewriters instead of using harps and our own voices, have to try to keep our readers guessing. So I remodeled the combat scene to resemble the fierce duels of Irish epic heroes, and even gave Pwyll two new antagonists, creatures shown on two mysterious relics of the mainland Celts: the so-called "Monster of Moves," and that Bird who keeps age-long vigil above the skull-adorned pillars of the grim Temple at Bouches-du-Rhone.

The late Roger Loomis identified Arawn's never-named Queen with Modron the Mother. To an article by the distinguished Nora Chadwick I owe the suggestion that Pwyll's whole experience upon the Mound was a dream. (Dream in one world, reality in another— can we be quite sure what reality is?) And the late Robert Briffault's monumental work, *The Mothers,* gave me several intriguing ideas to play with. He believed, as I understand him, that civilization first evolved from the efforts of childbearing women to provide for their families, and that when men took over they invented nothing really new until our own machine age appeared, an almost exclusively masculine creation. Pollution has dimmed that last glory a little; I hope I will not be accused of sex bias for saying so; I like penicillin, electric toasters, jet travel, etc., as well as anybody. But when we were superstitious enough to hold the earth sacred and worship her, we did nothing to endanger our future upon her, as we do now. That seems a little ironic.

—EVANGELINE WALTON
Tucson, Arizona, 1974

The Children of Llyr

To that great Welsh-born man of letters,
the late John Cowper Powys, whom the author never met,
but without whose interest and encouragement this book
might never have been written.

The Beginning

LLYR LLEDIAITH was a Chief among the Old Tribes, and the woman he slept with was black-haired Penardim, Penardim who was beautiful. Her brother was Beli of the Deep, High-King over all the Island of the Mighty. Even the New Tribes paid him tribute, the fierce invaders from beyond the sea.

But Beli ruled by the law of the Old Tribes. When his time came he would choose his heir from among his sister's sons—his nephews, the sons of Penardim and Llyr.

Penardim did not call Llyr husband, nor did her children call him father. The Old Tribes had no such words. Easy to imagine a young man scratching his head and saying, "Yes, I know, Grandmother. But the New Tribes say that their girls do not have children till after . . ."

"The New Tribes! Impertinent good-for-nothings! It is not that easy to make a woman's belly swell. Children are the gifts made to women by the Mothers, by the ancient Powers that bring spring and summer. Their beginning is among the Mysteries."

"Yes, but . . ."

"And as for those girls of the New Tribes, I know them! And so do you! It is not because they do not have men that they do not have children before they have husbands."

And the young man would grin and remember (or pretend to if he did not), and say that that was so. Besides, a child certainly was not made every time a man lay with a woman. At that rate any brisk young fellow ought to get dozens every moon. Better to leave such matters to the Gods; a man should not presume too far.

So it was when Llyr Llediaith and Penardim the King's sister came together, and to them man and woman meant only Llyr and

Penardim. All others were but sexless, secondary shapes floating out-side the rich warm island of being that was these two. So it was among these two when Llyr made the circuit of the land to collect tribute for Beli; when he came to the house of Eurosswydd mab Maelgwn, a chief among the New Tribes, and stopped there.

Taxes are seldom paid gladly, and no tax collector could have been less welcome to Eurosswydd than Llyr. Between these two dislike was somehow as inevitable as between fire and water. Llediaith means "Half-Speech," for Llyr spoke the Island tongue brokenly; he had come from the mainland, where the New Tribes were tri-umphant, and his memories were bitter. Yet he had many friends among the New Tribes; only when he looked at Eurosswydd did he remember how this man's people had fallen upon his with fire and sword. And whenever Eurosswydd saw Llyr he thought, *None ever forget that my grandfather and his folk were not born here. Yet although this man himself was born elsewhere, he has got many more friends than I have, both among his people and mine. He has got the King's own ear. He has got the King's sister.*

Thinking thus, he felt himself unjustly made small, and the idea of paying taxes to Llyr made him feel smaller, and he was a man who liked to feel large. So he drank too much, and in the end he pound-ed on the table, and refused to pay.

"For my father Maelgwn pledged taxes to Beli, and to Beli I will pay them, but I am no man of yours, Llyr Llediaith, to pay you any-thing at all!"

"I am sent by Beli," said Llyr, "and all I get I must give account of to Beli. When he asks for what is lacking, shall I tell him that Eurosswydd, Maelgwn's son, withheld it?"

"Tell him why I withheld it," said Eurosswydd, "and that to him-self I will pay it."

"What if he comes after it?" said Llyr, and his voice was soft, as the fur of a pouncing cat is soft.

Beli might not have come in war. His dignity was too high to be above patience, and his lifework had been the welding of friendship between Old Tribes and New. Llyr did wrong to make threats so soon. But the hot fumes that he kept out of his face and voice seethed round his brain.

They flashed out of Eurosswydd like sparks out of a smitten anvil. His voice leapt at Llyr like a beast. "Then he may get it, and my head with it, but it is not you who will get steward's fees out of it, stum-bling-tongued outlander!"

Then his voice too grew soft, but as rotten fruit is soft, and he said, "Yet why let you go to babble lying tales to Beli?"

Llyr saw the spear at his throat then. In that banquet hall Eurosswydd had three men to each of his. But his face did not change and his voice was as cool as ever as he said, "Death is a fair woman, Eurosswydd; or so some say. But are you so much in love with her that you would throw yourself into her arms for the pleasure of pushing me into them first?"

"By my hand," swore Eurosswydd, "it is not into the arms of any woman I wanted that I ever would push you! I am a man—I keep my women to myself. Not like you honorless bastards, you half-men, that come when you are called and go when you are bidden, obedient as puppy dogs to your women's lusts! Women! I know a better name for them." He spat as he said it. "I would take a whip to all their backs—these strutting sluts of your Old Tribes—and teach them what a man is. They would soon forget you puppy dogs!"

All round the hall there was a bright flicker of swords—the snick of one being drawn wherever a man of the Old Tribes was. But Llyr raised his hand, empty, and all the swords fell.

"You have refused Beli's tribute to Beli's officer," he said quietly, and his eyes pinned Eurosswydd. "In the morning, when your mind speaks, and not the wine in your belly, you may think better of that. If you do not, I will go down to the ford and fight you there. So shall our men go unharmed, and the quarrel be between us, and nothing to Beli."

His eyes did not turn from Eurosswydd's nor relax their spearlike fixity until the red angry eyes of Maelgwn's son fell.

Eurosswydd said low and sullenly, "So be it. But you will not come back alive from the ford, Llyr."

"That is as may be," said Llyr. "Let us eat."

But upon that feast had fallen a gloomy silence. Like a black bird it perched upon each man's shoulder. All ate, but none tasted his food. The bards harped, but their harping brought no beauty to birth; it only made a noise that seemed afraid of silence.

Llyr thought, *I have come to a fertile field, and I have sown bad seed—the kind it was fittest to grow. Will I get my men and myself out of this alive? And if I do, how have I served Beli whom I talked so loudly of serving?*

His men and Eurosswydd's were thinking too, thoughts as like as twins: *Had we better sleep with our swords on? There may be treachery in these Other Tribe folk. There is bound to be—they have always stunk with it. But if we sleep armed, they may say we planned to rise and slay them in their sleep. Make that their excuse . . .*

Their thoughts turned red and they mused, *it would be good to rise up and slay these Other Tribe folk now and let their blood run out. Then we could sleep in peace.*

Eurosswydd sat still, and looked at the long red hairs that grew, grass-thick, upon his hands. He was unhappy. He was ashamed, because he glared at his own hands and feet, and not at Llyr. *Was it by magic that he made my eyes fall? The Old Tribes are strong in magic . . .*

In his mind he saw the ford, and the cold gray of dawn.

He said angrily in his heart, *Magic will not help him now. I will carve him as a side of beef is carved.* His mind drew joyous pictures of that carving and the accompanying bloodletting. He felt free and powerful and happy, certainly the better man. He saw himself a hero; to follow him the New Tribes would rise to a man. *I will set Llyr's head upon one of my doorposts, and Beli's on the other.* Until a voice whispered, a small cold voice in the back of his own head, *But what if his magic prevails over your strength? As it made your eyes fall . . .*

He tried to think that hand-to-hand, Llyr could not do magic. But he could not feel sure; one could not be sure, with a magician. He thought angrily, *It is not fair.* All along Llyr had outwitted him, goading him to fight, cleverly robbing him of the advantage of superior numbers. It had seemed fair and chieftain-like, that offer of single combat, so chieftain-like that he could not turn it down before his men. But if it was not—if it was not—if Llyr counted on magic to spit him like a sheep . . .

He thought, *Guile is fair against guile,* and again, *He sleeps in my house tonight.*

If Llyr had slept anywhere else, Eurosswydd could have waited honorably enough for morning. He would have thought his face lost forever if he had not gone down to the ford. But now every moment seemed like a spear that lay in his hand and that time twisted from him, saying as it passed, *"This is gone, and you have not used it. You fool, who sit here waiting for him who lolls in your own hall, full of your meat, to slay you by craft."*

Faster and faster time twisted them from him, those precious bright minutes. Like gold falling from a bag's mouth into the sea.

Gold that might well be his own lifeblood . . .

His mind began to work. It was the part of him least used to exercise, and it burrowed molelike, scurrying here and there in dark, crooked passages.

He called a bard to him, a man whose mother's kin were druids, but whom the Old Tribes had cast out for some crime. He whispered to that man, whose eyes grew narrow and bright.

"I can do it, Lord. But there will be none to help you when it is done, for the charm falls upon all alike. You yourself had best go quickly from the hall."

Eurosswydd said, "Make me a sign when the danger comes."

"I cannot, Lord. The charm will take all of me. But not long will you be safe, staying."

He went back to his harp and sang. That song was a marvel and a mystery. It was sweeter than honey, more monotonous than a day-long fall of rain. It was softer than those lowest notes of lullabies that are lost in the throats of mothers; sweet shadows of sound. It was the distilled essence of all sleep; it was the shadow of death.

Weariness came upon the feasters. Mist gathered before their eyes, their lids grew heavy as stones. They slid from their places limply, grotesquely, legs rising and arms falling, like dolls dropped by children. Only Eurosswydd, stumbling, lurched out of the hall while the others fell. Like brothers his men slept beside Llyr's; beside Llyr himself.

The torches guttered out, untended, and night, no longer held at bay, crept in softly through the doors and took back this one tiny nest of rebels. Wrapped them all in the vast, gentle cloak of her blackness . . .

The sun came and burned that dark coverlet away, and still the men lay there; only now Llyr's were weaponless, and heavy thongs bound their arms and legs. Like flies caught in the web of some coarse giant spider they lay there. The men of Eurosswydd still slept beside them. But the bard sat smiling broadly, a new gold chain about his neck. The slaves who had been called to bind the sleeping guests had all gone back to their huts.

Eurosswydd the son of Maelgwn sat and looked at his captives, and the mole in his head worked on.

To kill Llyr now would mean outlawry. His honor would go out with his foe's life, like a torch in a fetid pool. For Llyr had been a guest in his house, and never could he prove to any, not even quite to himself, that Llyr would have used magic at the ford.

Yet Llyr the Prisoner was also Llyr the Hostage—they would swear Eurosswydd peace, those chiefs of the Old Tribes, they would give him gold and lands to get Llyr out of his hands alive and whole. And Llyr himself would walk a shamed man forever after, memories burning him like whip weals. Oh, but he should have memories! Before he went free he would know who was master. Llyr the Very Proud, the father of the King that would be!

The King that would be! Penardim's boys were Beli's heirs. That pride never could be taken from Llyr. His seed would lord it over the New Tribes in days to come.

Over my own children, whatever vengeance I take.

Like lightning a thought struck Eurosswydd. Like a fresh log falling upon the fires within him. It flared up in a blaze that dazzled his mole brain . . .

He laughed and pounded his chair with his fists. His eyes shone as he called the smiling bard; their pupils were like little murky fires dancing evilly in the reddened whites.

"You are the only man of mine that is yet awake. You will bear my words to Penardim the sister of Beli. To Llyr's woman . . ."

He spoke these words, and the man heard them and trembled, but he had to repeat them after his Lord. His little time of power and praise was over.

Not happily the bard came before Penardim, in her house, where she waited the sister of Llyr.

She was tall, the sister of Beli. Her hair glistened like blackbirds' feathers; her high sweet breasts, still girlishly erect, the pure lines of her head and body made music. She was like a torch shining in a dark quiet place. She was straight as a torch, cleanly and beautifully made.

"You bring me tidings from Llyr Llediaith?"

"Not from, but of him, Lady. He stopped at the house of my master Eurosswydd, and he is a prisoner there."

She quivered once, as if beneath a sudden blow. Then her face became hard as stone; colder than stone.

"Llyr was not easily taken. By what treachery?"

"Lady," he stammered, licking pale lips, "Lady, there was a quarrel. The Lord Llyr made magic with his eyes, and struck my master dumb in his own hall. But in the household of Eurosswydd is a man who has this quality—he can sing a song that will put sleep upon the worst-wounded man, upon the most fevered and pain-torn. That man sang the Song of Sleep to Llyr and his comrades, and they were disarmed and bound."

He shrank. He hoped that she would think that man far away, yet feared that she would not. All his thoughts seemed like fish swimming in clear water, bared to her gaze.

She saw them but did not think of him. She faced the need to save; she would not yet face the need to avenge.

"Your master has Llyr," she said, "and presently Beli my brother will have him. Has he thought about that?"

"He has, Lady. Many days will pass before Beli who is in Arvon can gather the Cantrevs and march to my master's house. By then he can be safe in Gaul or Ireland with chiefs who will give great gifts to him who can show them where and how best to ravage Beli's coasts. He gives you this day and this night to decide in—whether you will pay him Llyr's ransom, or he shall send you Llyr's head."

"How much?" Her voice that was cold as snow bargained; she was a good housewife.

He looked at the ground. He looked at her shoes, and tried to count the stitches on them.

"Well?" she said.

He tried to answer; he opened his mouth, but it worked only soundlessly. Death was the least of his fears now. He was remembering much that in Eurosswydd's house he had half forgotten: the powers of her ancient royal line that was younger only than the Gods. The might that not only could sweep him from the earth, but bring him back to it as a mouse or a beetle or some yet more lowly thing.

Perhaps even unself him, make him nothing . . .

At last he got sound out; it was low and quavery, but it was sound. He had no power to keep back one word, to plead, or evade, or soften. "Lady, he asks this: that you come to his house and mate with him. In the morning both you and Llyr may go unharmed. By the sun and by the moon he swears it, and by the vigor of his body, that he would have you taste."

The druids came to her in her Sunny Chamber. Tall men with white robes and beards, and in their hands the wands that were said to have power to put upon a man the shape of bird or beast.

They said, "Lady, wait. A man in battle does not throw away his shield, and Llyr is Eurosswydd's shield."

She said, "You are wrong. He has boasted that he will take Llyr's head off and he will do it; he would be afraid not to. He is a small man trapped in his own big words, and there is nothing more dangerous than that."

"There is, Lady. There are dark beings that lurk between the worlds, seeking bodies and birth. Often such have been born into the Eastern World, tyrants and torturers. But here where we live under the Ancient Harmonies, simple folk still close to the Mothers, no woman's body has yet been a door to let them in."

"You speak of the Mysteries," said Penardim, "and I revere the

Mysteries. But it is my man I am thinking about now Not to escape one night's misery will I lie all the nights of my life without Llyr by my side. No—I have borne children, and though this is worse than childbirth, like that it will pass."

Her women were there, and one of them said, "Llyr himself may not like it, Lady."

"Where a woman of our people sleeps, and with whom, is for her to say. So it always has been, and so it always will be. I am not giving away lands or goods of my man's, that he might ask account of if he were fool enough to want to die for them. Nor would Llyr wish Beli my brother to lose men and slay men for his sake."

"If Llyr and his slayers and avengers do not die, many more men may," said the eldest druid. "Go, women." And they went swiftly, shivering.

But Penardim sat and faced him, and her eyes were steady. "You need not have sent my women away. They know as well as I do that I may bear a child to Eurosswydd. Have not you wise druids learned that most women know that much nowadays? Maybe all women that have loved a man much. Could I doubt it, who see what Llyr must have looked like, and he little, every time I see my Manawyddan's face?"

"Would you give him a monster for brother, woman?"

"Strong words, druid. I will count it bad enough if I bring forth another Eurosswydd, and he is no monster. He is too small for that. And indeed, I think that, whoever else dies, he will soon be smaller by a head."

"Lady, well you know that all lovers are strings of a mighty harp. All that live, man and woman, bird and beast, the fish undersea and the snake that crawls through the deep grasses, all make that music. No woman of the Old Tribes ever yet has sought a man and conceived his child save when it sang through her being. That music is life's source and love's delight. It is the one chance of man and woman to be as Gods and to fashion breathing life. You who would go to a man you hate, who seeks you only for spite—will you open the door of your body to what may come?"

She said, "I cannot let Llyr die. And as for my child, who knows in what image it may be fashioned? I will close my mind against the Red Man. I will see only Llyr—think only of Llyr."

"You are a strong woman," said the druid, "but you will not be able to do that. Not all through the night . . ."

She looked past him. She looked through the walls and the waning light; and with her heart's eyes she looked into the face of Llyr, that shone warm and clear. Her own face was as set as her will; again a face carved in stone.

She said, "I will not let Llyr die. The Island of the Mighty must take its chance with my child—the child that may never be born."

In the red of that sunset she began her journey. And the winds bared their knives and the leaves moaned and shuddered beneath their cold bite. The whole Island of the Mighty shivered in the grip of descending night.

The druid stood and watched distance take her.

He watched longer, while darkness piled up about him like smoke, and what he watched only himself knew, and perhaps not even the mind of him; there may be that in man which goes where mind cannot follow. He drew his cloak about him and shivered beneath those biting winds.

"So be it," he said, "since so it must be. Night falls now, a World Night, and a dark age draws on. The end of all we have known, the beginning of the new. Well, so long as all be part of the Great Going-Forward, so long as good comes again at last, rising out of evil."

So began the journey of Penardim the Dark Woman, the mother of the sons of Llyr.

She came to the House of Eurosswydd, and the housefolk welcomed her with so many torches that the path to his door seemed as though lined with fallen stars.

Eurosswydd met her there, before his door. He laughed his high neighing laugh and flung out his arms; he gave her the host's kiss of greeting, and she gave it back again.

She went into his hall and ate with him, and later she went to his bed. She stood beside it and unfastened the brooches that held her robe; and it seemed to her that no deed in the world ever had taken so long or been so slow. She felt like a bowman who had been standing rigid, cramped, for hours, every thought and nerve and muscle fixed on keeping his arrow aimed, his arm steady.

On not relaxing, not letting go . . .

Beside her Eurosswydd was stripping his broad, hairy body. The red bristles on it made her think of a pig's back she once had seen; hunters had carried it in from the forest, the carcass swinging on a pole. But the pig had been cold; Eurosswydd's body would be horribly warm . . . *Do not feel, do not think, except of Llyr!*

Only tonight, only this one night! Tomorrow night, and for all the nights to come, Llyr again, only Llyr! He will not be here long, this other, you will not have to grip yourself like this long, not to see him, to keep him out. Be strong. Oh, be far away, that which is I!

She felt his hands, hot upon her body, upon her breasts. She felt his kisses, hot and wet and sickening. He was laughing, pulling her down onto the bed—and suddenly something inside her shrank and scurried back, sick, into the innermost recesses of herself.

He cannot enter you. Your flesh is not you; it is a garment that you have not always had and that will be replaced. . . No! O Mothers, no!

Leave the body there upon the bed; let him have it. You are separate from that; you must be. You must stay away, hiding in some inner space, clinging to Llyr . . . See only Llyr, think only of Llyr. Oh, be very far away!

In the morning they both went to the place where Llyr lay bound. With eyes like colored stones he looked up at them, eyes emptied of all feeling, carefully, fiercely blank. He saw how white and drawn Penardim's face was, her eyes tired and sunken. He saw Eurosswydd's grin.

The Red Man strode to Llyr and stood over him. His grin widened until it seemed like the sky. Immense, inescapable; it covered the world.

"You are not the only man who has fathered a nephew of Beli's, Llyr. Not if I know my strength, and I never put in a night to better purpose—by the Gods, this will be a fine tale to tell! How Llyr Llediaith came to my house and slept so hard that he could not get out again until his woman came and slept with me—a livelier sleeping time that!" He threw back his head and shook with laughter. Like thunder it rolled, and the room shook with him.

Penardim knelt by Llyr. As she cut his hands free she said, "I have paid dear for your life, Llyr. Do not make that go for nothing."

Eurosswydd still laughed, but his face turned a slow, blotched crimson. Llyr's was as white as death.

"This is his time for talking, woman; let him do it. Now cut these ropes round my legs."

"Not so fast," said Eurosswydd. "First you must promise not to stir up Beli against me."

Llyr looked straight into his eyes and calmly. "I will pledge you Beli's peace, but not my own."

"Beli's is good enough for me," said Eurosswydd; and chuckled.

But there was little heart in that chuckle. His vanity was bleeding; he had hoped to make a good impression on the woman. Also those two still stood together and against him, as if in some druid circle that he could not enter. He kept reminding himself that that was not true; he had had the woman.

He got no happiness out of the memory of that morning save for that one sudden blanching of Llyr's face.

And on a day in autumn, when frost had turned the trees to marvels of gold and fire, his own face blanched. For Llyr rode with his own men out of his own land, and spears ringed round the house that had heard the Song of Sleep.

Llyr spoke to those within through a trumpet, and this is what he said. "Come out, Eurosswydd, and we two will go down to the ford at last. Come out, and I will let your folk go free."

Eurosswydd did not want to go. But there were too many eyes on him; there had been too much talk about the trickery he had used before. He was afraid his own men might think him a coward. He raked together the faggots of his pride and kindled them to a final blaze. In savage and nervous hope he went down to the ford.

He went farther than that.

He went out of his body and out of the Island of the Mighty, and that was the end of him, there and elsewhere. For wherever he is now he is not Eurosswydd, any more than an oak is the acorn from which it sprang. Arawn, Lord of the Underworld, judged him and no doubt melted up most of him, yet saved the little that was good enough to be used again.

He went and men forgot him, because he had not been memorable; also he had gone in fair fight, so that neither New Tribes nor Old need hold a grudge.

Except for two reasons, his very name long ago would have been forgotten, but because of those two it never can be so long as the Island of the Mighty remembers the tongue of its youth. A few moons after he died Penardim bore those two, and they were her sons and his. Nissyen and Evnissyen were their names.

Three winters passed, and spring came again, and when the land was fragrant with blossoms she bore another child—Branwen, daughter of Llyr.

1

The Coming of the Stranger

BRAN, FIRST son of Llyr and Penardim, was King over all the Island of the Mighty. In Llwndrys, later to be called London, his name had been cried, and there he had been crowned.

Pwyll of Dyved must have seen that crowning, he who reigned among the New Tribes with Rhiannon, the Queen who had come to him out of Faery, though well she knew that age and death must be the price of her love for him. Mâth, son of Mathonwy, must have seen it, that avatar who was called the Ancient. In many bodies he had ruled over the people of Gwynedd, the pure stock of the Old Tribes, and would rule them until the time came for both him and them to change. That time was drawing near. His successor was already born, his sister's son, Gwydion, son of Don.

If those two chiefs said yea to Bran's crowning, none could say nay, though Caswallon, son of Beli, may have watched with secret, dreaming eyes . . .

Bran the Blessed he was called, for he was kind and just, and in his time every cow that calved twinned, and every field and orchard bore double. But his woman died young, and he kept her only child, and called the boy Caradoc, son of Bran. People were not so surprised as they once would have been. Belief in fatherhood was growing; nobody could quite forget that there was some difference between the children of Penardim. Between the children of Llyr and the sons of red Eurosswydd.

On a day when young Caradoc mab Bran was in his teens the court was camped upon the Rock of Harlech. Bran sat there looking down upon the shores of Merioneth, and in the mists that rose up from the sea his great form looked like that great rock's topmost crag and pinnacle. He was mightily made, the biggest of the sons of men. The *Mabinogi* says that no house or ship could hold him, though if that tale has not grown in the telling, houses and ships must have been small then. One thing only seems certain: Bran was very big.

Two of his mother's sons, Manawyddan mab Llyr and Evnissyen mab Eurosswydd, were with him there, and so was Caradoc, his own son. Caradoc was playing with a golden ball, throwing it up into the air and catching it as it came down again. Evnissyen eyed that game with disfavor, as he soon did all sports in which nothing was killed or maimed.

"You will be a long time hitting the sky at that rate, boy. You have not come anywhere near the lowest cloud yet."

Caradoc missed the ball then; it fell, and Evnissyen chuckled. The boy turned, saying in a voice that was sharper than he meant it to be, "I am not trying to hit anything, uncle. And why should anybody be fool enough to try to hit the sky?"

Evnissyen grinned. "Myself, I would rather aim at something than at nothing, but maybe it is as well that you lack ambition, young one. In the south young Pryderi will be king in Dyved after his father Pwyll, but you, the High-King's own son, will be lucky to get one or two miserable Cantrevs. Branwen's sons will king it after Bran, not you."

Manawyddan said peaceably, "Dyved is a little kingdom, brother, such as could easily pass under the New Tribes, and so from father to son. But Caradoc here is what no man in the Island of the Mighty ever was before—the High-King's acknowledged son. Caswallon and his brothers always have had to be content with saying that Beli was the man their mother slept with."

Evnissyen promptly became very fond of Caradoc. Threefold opportunity dazzled him—to forgive and defend Caradoc, who had snapped at him, and yet at the same time thoroughly to annoy both his brother and his nephew. He pounced on it as a cat pounces on a mouse.

"Well, it is nice to be able to boast of one's high descent, but it would be nicer still to have what goes with it—the fruit as well as the rind. But then I too might praise Caradoc's lack of ambition, Manawyddan, if I were in your shoes. They are a good place to be, since Branwen is staying a virgin remarkably long."

He smiled as he spoke. He had as keen a nose for pain as a dog has for deer, and he knew that Manawyddan hated to be reminded that he was Bran's heir, should Branwen fail to have issue.

"I have always refused to hold either land or lordship,"

Manawyddan said quietly. "That you and all men know. Let the boy be."

"Now I call that unfair," said Evnissyen. "He answered me shortly just now, when I asked him a simple question, and yet I have been taking his part."

"In your own way," said Manawyddan, then bit his lip. To answer Evnissyen was always unwise; it gave him an excuse to speak again. Yet the place that is always being pricked grows sore.

Manawyddan knew the dangers of Evnissyen's endless pricking. Big, good-natured Bran would have wanted to pull down the moon if his baby had cried for it, and though Caradoc, left to himself, would no more have dreamed of crying for kingship than of crying for the moon, Evnissyen was forever reminding him of what otherwise the lad would have taken for granted. Making him feel deprived of something, and making sure that he could not forget that deprivation.

Evnissyen shrugged now and said, "Well, whatever I do is always wrong. I should be used to your thinking that, you sons of Llyr. You are both better than I; all my brothers are better than I. I have always had the pleasure of knowing that everybody thought that. And maybe it is true. For if ever I refused lands and lordship, it would be because those offered me were not big enough. Because I hoped to get more by waiting; by being good, so very good that presently people would thrust what I wanted upon me as a duty."

Manawyddan looked straight at him with the sea-gray, sea-deep eyes of Llyr. "It is to be hoped that such cunning would take more baseness than is on you, son of my mother, as it would take more than is on me."

Bran said disapprovingly, "That was a big long mouthful of nothing, brother Evnissyen."

He had turned from the cliff drop and the mist, and was watching them, but Manawyddan wished that he had not. Here was mist more blinding to a man.

Evnissyen flushed. "Then you love Caradoc less than you claim to, brother. Why should not the boy have all that kings' sons in the Eastern World already have?—what many think that some day all kings' sons will have! With Manawyddan's help, that surely such an unselfish man should hurry to give, you could change the laws. Make Caradoc king after you."

Manawyddan said, "You have heard my answer to that over and over—you and Bran both. For Bran to do that would be to declare himself no rightful king. Then Caswallon could say justly, 'Why should Caradoc follow Bran, when I could not follow Beli?' All the Island of the Mighty might become chaos, with sons and nephews fighting one another for inheritance."

Bran sighed. "That is true—and yet hard to take. For some day the change will come."

"Then why not now?" demanded Evnissyen. "In time for Caradoc. I know you love peace, but if trouble must come, why not get it over with?"

"Because in time to come that trouble may be less," said Manawyddan. "By then so many people may want the change or at least be ready to accept it that it may come without turmoil and strife."

Then he bit his lip again and thought, *I should have let Bran answer him.*

Evnissyen grinned again. "Well, you cannot be blamed for wanting things to stay as they are, Manawyddan. You are the man who would lose most by the change."

Bran opened his mouth to speak, then closed it. Silence fell; silence that seemed to stretch and knit and tighten, like cords around living flesh.

Evnissyen could have hugged himself. He lay down and threw one arm over his face to hide the joy in it. *Bran will not believe anything that I have said, but it will bother him. And it will bother Manawyddan, and seeing that will make Bran wonder. If he ever should believe it—!* He shivered with delight.

He did not know why he wanted to set his brothers at odds; he did not hate them much more than he did other men. But his belief that he had been wronged and insulted all his life was by now so deep-rooted that he never bothered to think who had wronged him or how, only revenged himself constantly upon all. This was the quality of Evnissyen; he held his own dignity and that of any other person with whom he might briefly identify himself (he never exactly liked anybody) to be as delicate as eggshell. lie could think of a thousand ways in which that precious fragility could be hurt; he hunted such hurts with an eye keener than a hawk's. He could convince a man whose elbow had been jostled in a crowd that that jostle had been long premeditated and deliberate, and he could make that man burn to avenge the malicious outrage. People said that he could make trouble between a man and a woman about to lie together, between the woman's own two breasts. Certainly trifle-twisting and troublemaking were his gifts. And he had made trouble now.

Manawyddan sat and thought, *My brother cannot think that I want his place. Yet he heard what Evnissyen said; he sat there and said nothing . . .*

Bran wondered uneasily whether he should have rebuked Evnissyen again. Yet to keep rebuking such twaddle was to seem to take it seriously. Manawyddan knew Evnissyen as well as he did. Why was he getting so sensitive about what the boy said? And why should he be so set against Caradoc's getting the kingship? Caradoc . . . Caradoc . . . The lad would make so fine a king.

What he thought was clouded by what he felt and wanted, and the poison of Evnissyen worked on.

Caradoc too was silent. Like nervous birds his eyes flew back and forth between his father and his uncle, wary yet yearning. If those two willed it, he could be a king . . .

Manawyddan caught those glances. The silence began to weave itself a tongue, and that tongue accused him. He rose.

"Have I your leave to go, Lord?"

Bran stiffened. "Why should you wish to go, brother?"

"It seems to me best, Lord."

Bran looked down; thought wearily, *Why should I always have to be telling him how honorable he is? I have said nothing against his honor.*

His hesitation lasted a little too long. It pierced Manawyddan like a spear. He said in a low voice, "I think it is the King's will that I should go."

Bran said with a rumble like a bear's growl deep in his great throat, "Why should I wish that, Manawyddan?"

Manawyddan said with a coldness that was like an icy crust over boiling heat, "That is for you to tell me, Lord. But I think that you will not—to my face. For you only play with it in the darkness inside your head. You know well that it is not worthy of the light."

Then Bran's voice leapt forth like the roar of a lion. "I dare say whatever I think, brother. Why do you think that I am thinking evil about you—unless you have first got that evil formed in your own heart?"

Manawyddan's face went death-white. "Name that evil, King."

Silence again; silence that tightened around necks like a noose. Bran looked at Manawyddan, and Manawyddan looked at Bran. Evnissyen leaned forward, his face eager as fire.

The silence dragged at Bran's mouth and tongue like wild horses. His mouth opened; he was afraid of what might come out of it. He wanted to shut it, but could not. The muscles of his throat moved. Sound whistled between his teeth and died there.

Somebody had laughed.

Laughter, cool and sweet as the bubbling of a spring, it shattered that grim silence as gently as though melting it. And the fierce suspicions of Evnissyen's breeding and begetting slunk away like dogs, their tails between their legs.

"What is all this about?" Nissyen, the son of Penardim, looked at his elder brothers. "Why are you two making the air red around you? Tell me."

But of a sudden they both knew that there was nothing to tell Nissyen. They felt him, as if he had been cool air in a heated place; a cool clean wind, blowing through their hearts as well as their lungs. Bran himself laughed, as if at some vast and incredible joke.

"Nothing at all, Nissyen, nothing at all. Manawyddan here is insulted because he thinks I have got it into my head that he wants to be king after me. A long reign he would be looking forward to, since I am only two winters older than he is, and very healthy."

He beamed down upon his younger brothers, tolerant, enlightening, jovial. "I would be the world's biggest fool to keep a notion like that in my head long," he said.

"As big a fool as I would be to think you could," said Manawyddan, and put out his hand. Bran took it, and they both laughed. Nissyen laughed with them.

"You would be a pair of fools," he said.

Evnissyen sprang to his feet, savage as a hungry dog whose bone has been snatched away. "It is I that had better go away," he said. "I am not wanted here. I never am."

Bran looked at him levelly. "It is not you that are not wanted, boy. It is the kind of thing you start."

But Evnissyen was already gone, his red cloak whirling round him like a flame hissing over dry leaves.

"He is hurt." Nissyen looked after his twin, and in his eyes was pity. "He thinks always that you two hold it against him because he is Eurosswydd's son. Always, since we were little, whenever anyone has been angry with him he has thought that that was the reason— not anything that he himself has done."

"Among the Old Tribes it never has mattered who a man's father was," said Bran. "And whoever his mother was it always has been held that he himself deserved good treatment because he was here at all. But if Evnissyen does not watch out, some day it may matter who he himself is."

"So far he has done nothing but what others let him do," said Nissyen. That was the quality of Nissyen; he always told the truth.

Bran did not answer that. He sighed again and sat down beside Manawyddan. Nissyen sat down near them. Caradoc went back to playing with his ball. There was quiet again upon the Rock of Harlech, and peace settled down like a nesting bird. That too was the quality of Nissyen; he made peace.

Bran looked out to sea again. The mists had lifted, and in that clearness and from that great height, he seemed to be looking out into unearthly space. Sea and sky were before him, and sky and sea, and far away the two seemed to meet, vast blueness clasping vast blueness, in an embrace that looked like the world's end. In earlier times, when boats were new, and a thought but recently shaped into wood by the hands of men, folk had believed that blue wail solid. The boldest had tried to sail out to it, to see what it looked like near at hand. But when always it had recoiled before them, a space farther off for every space that they advanced, they had concluded that it was magical, a druid work set up to veil Other World secrets from the eyes of men.

Bran watched the delicate shining mystery of that wall until the sun came down to cleave it, filling the sky with blood and spilling gold upon the darkening sea.

Then he saw speckles cross that flaming disc. Speckles that grew and swelled into strange shapes, like huge ants crawling across the face of the dying sun. Swiftly they grew—speeding forward, out of Illusion, into the world of men.

They became birds, great birds with white wings spread, darting toward the land, their prey.

Bran raised his hand. "Ships are coming—and coming fast."

There was a sudden stir around him. All men were on their feet, all eyes looking where he looked. Excitement the many-fingered, that has hands enough to grasp all near her, had them by the throats. One or two strange ships might be either pirate or peaceful traders, but never before had so many ships come toward the Island of the Mighty save as invaders.

Bran said, "Do you go down and lead men out to meet them, Manawyddan. But go as a herald; find out whether they come in peace."

Some men stared as if they thought him mad, but in the faces of others hope dawned. The King was not sure that the strangers came as foes.

Manawyddan signed to men who took spears and shields and followed him. Round all their hearts the subtle many-fingers tightened—so swift and sure and silent was that advance across the reddened sunset sea, with the wind behind it, the wind upon which ride Other World folk and the disembodied dead.

On the shore below, men were milling around, rushing to arm themselves. With shouts they greeted the son of Llyr, thinking he had come to lead them. Manawyddan smiled and raised his hand palm outward, commanding peace.

"Have your spears ready, men, but do not cast them until I give the word."

Then all were silent, looking out to sea.

Nearer the strange ships came, and nearer. Never had the men of the Island of the Mighty seen ships more splendid. The stranger-vessels glowed and bloomed with many-colored banners of rich stuffs, with men in many-colored clothes and shining arms. In the red light their bronze breastplates and spearheads shone like fire, brighter than gold.

One ship sailed ahead of the others, and as they looked, men lifted up a great shield above its side, pointing outward, in token of peace. Manawyddan's heart lightened when he saw that, for the sons of Llyr did not love war; but he did not sign to his men to lower their spears. There might be treachery.

Behind the shield a tall man appeared, scarlet-cloaked. The sharper-eyed saw that he wore no helm; the sun caught in his bright hair and in the brighter circlet that banded it. A king's crown.

When the ships came close beneath the Rock of Harlech, he raised his arms and from his throat and from the throats of all his men a mighty shout pealed across the waters.

"Greeting! Greeting to Bran the Blessed, Lord of the Island of the Mighty!"

From his place high above, Bran heard them. He leaned forward, and his own great voice boomed out across the waters. "The Gods give you good, strange men! A welcome is with you here. Whose ships are these, and who is your chief?"

His voice seemed to come from the sky above them, and the strangers started and stared. They had taken Manawyddan's tall, tree-straight figure waiting on the shore for the mightier son of Llyr. Then a herald rose and said, "Matholuch the High-King of Ireland is here. These are his ships, Lord, and we are his men."

"Why is he here?" said Bran. "Is he coming ashore?"

"He is not," said the herald, "unless he gets what he wants. He has come to ask a boon of you, Lord."

"Well," said Bran, "what is it?" He made no promises; granting an unnamed boon could be a riskier business than buying a pig in a poke, as Pwyll Prince of Dyved had learned at his wedding feast, when Gwawl tricked him, that dangerous supplicant out of Faery.

"It is Branwen of the White Breast, Branwen the daughter of Llyr. Let her go with him and be his wife, Lord, that you and he may be as brothers, and the two Islands of the Mighty be leagued, and both grow greater."

Then indeed silence fell. Men stood and stared, too thunder-struck to be angry. Never had a woman of the Old Tribes left her kin and her island save as the victim of fraud or force. Such a thing was unheard of, incredible; and the woman so asked for was Branwen, their noblest lady, the mother of the kings that were to come.

Bran broke that silence; he rubbed his chin. "Well," said he, "that is a boon. I am no king of the Eastern World to give my sister away like a cow. But let your king come ashore and feast with us; let the girl get a look at him, and we will talk about it."

On the shore below, men stared and stared again, as though they could not believe their ears. But the herald smiled, and the tall man with the crown whispered in his ear.

"Lord, King Matholuch thanks you. He will gladly come ashore."

Near Manawyddan one man plucked up heart enough to slap his thigh and mutter, "Well, when that outlander comes ashore he will get what he has asked for. And it will not be Branwen!"

Another laughed. "Bran is clever! He has to get the fellow ashore to be able to punish him."

A man of the New Tribes said thoughtfully, "At least he is com-ing ashore without knowing whether he will get her or not. Bran has made him back down."

Manawyddan said nothing; he stood like a tree, like a rock. He knew better than to hope that there was guile in Bran's offer; he knew his brother. For the first time in his life fear froze him; icy fear. *Will he send the girl away with strangers? So far away that we can know what happens to her only by hearsay? Rob her of her home, and her children of their heritage? Can he dote on Caradoc enough to do that?*

The Irishmen came ashore; proud, fine men clustering around their king. He was tall and comely, Matholuch; indeed, no man with any blemish might be High-King in Tara. His silky hair and beard were almost red, but in the dying sunlight they shone with a glitter that was golden. His keen eyes were almost blue, yet too pale for blueness; no young comely woman ever looked into them without dreaming of being the sunrise that would warm them.

On the shore he gave Manawyddan the kiss of peace and greeting, and on the Rock, Bran gave it to him. Then Branwen came, the daughter of Llyr. Bran had sent for her and her maidens.

She was beautiful, the sister of Bran the Blessed. Her hair was like the wings of blackbirds, and her breast was like the breast of a white dove, soft and warm and sweet, the loveliest of all flesh in the world. Matholuch's whole face shone when he saw her.

"By the sun and by the moon, and all the elements, Lady, you are worth a journey to the world's end! Sorrow is on me for all the nights I have slept without you!"

Her face crimsoned, even her white breast. She said, "Greeting, and joy be with you, Matholuch of the Irish."

He laughed a great laugh. "Indeed it will be, Lady, if you will it." He took the mead cup that she offered, his great hand brown on her white arm. And the shadows that were lengthening over Harlech grew blacker.

Like a great cloak darkness fell. Fires gleamed; beasts were slain and turned on spits above those fires. The men of the two islands sat and ate, and the women of the Island of the Mighty ate with them.

Branwen sat across from Matholuch, and her eyes were filled with the beauty end brawn of him. Her heart sang, *Here is my man, my first man and my last, the one for whom I have always waited.* Yet some space deep within her was cold with dread. To leave her home and her people forever—the girls she had played with and grown up with, her kin, her brothers, Bran and Manawyddan, Nissyen and Caradoc, even Evnissyen—how could she do it? Yet if she did not, if she watched this man sail away, would not all things that were left behind be cold and empty and hollow?

If she could have gone back to that morning, to the time when she had never seen him, how gladly, how happily, she would have fled there! But now, whatever she did, everything must be changed; pain and rending loss were inescapable.

And yet—and yet—did she truly wish that she had never seen him? Missed the sight and sound and warm nearness of him, the knowledge that such a man existed?

She could not go with him! she could not! Yet . . .

Her eyes begged him to make her go, yet not to make her. To do the impossible, and take the pain out of sorrow.

With green, hungry cat's eyes he watched her; the clean, swan lines of her head and throat that curved down into the warmer, richer beauty of her breast. He burned to lay his head and hands there, on that warm white sweetness that was a nest for love. Yet he never forgot what else that lovely body was: a strategic treasury, the shaping place, the gateway into this world of kings to come. Of the lords of this island that was greater than his own . . .

Not until near dawn were the sons of Llyr alone together. Then, when the fires had burned to embers and all other men had gone to rest, when the moon had set and the earth lay lightless and forsaken, they talked together.

"Well," said Bran, "it is plain that Branwen likes him. What have you to say, brother?"

"I do not like it," said Manawyddan. "No king in the Western World ever before has sent his sister away with an outlander."

"You give the best of all reasons for doing it," said Bran. "That word 'outlander.' The Old Tribes dwell in Ireland, as in our own isle. The New Tribes followed them there, as here. We are of one blood; or of the same bloods. Yet a little strip of sea has built such a wall between us that men of each island call those of the other 'outlanders,' and make of that name a suspicion and a stink."

"That would be as wrong if our bloods were different, brother."

"True. It is not honorable or a hero's deed to kill a man because he does not live where you live, or in some other way is different from you. But all our young men, Matholuch's and ours alike, think it is; by stealth these young hotheads raid each other's shores and slay and steal and burn. It is no use to talk about who did that first, or who does it oftenest. The thing to do is to stop it."

Manawyddan said, "I am not one to hold any man's race against him, Bran; you know that. But this man Matholuch is a stranger to us. And he springs from the New Tribes, whose ways are not our ways."

"He seems well-bred and well-favored. All that a man should be, brother."

"Maybe. But I wish I could see him with his beard off. Many a face that is good at the top is poor at the bottom. All we know about his jaw is that he can eat with it."

"A needful accomplishment." Bran grinned.

"A father of kings needs more. Also, hate of outlanders will not die overnight. If Branwen's boy is born in Ireland his seat will not be easy when he comes here to rule."

For a breath's space Bran was silent. Then he said, "A king's seat is never easy."

"And Branwen herself, brother? The storm in her blood may drive her to Ireland, but there she will be what the man is here—an outlander. If troubles rise between them—and what is so chancy as this

hot, all-creating, much-destroying love between man and woman?—
she will be alone. All there will be his friends, not hers. And in
Ireland the New Tribes have won the mastery; they who think that
man should be master over woman."

"Matholuch would never dare to offer her harm or insult," said
Bran. "Too many traders pass between the isles; it would soon reach
our ears. Also, why should any man wish to hurt such as she?
Branwen is lovable as well as lovely."

"Many women have been both, brother, yet woe has come to
them."

"To come home again will always be in her choice," said Bran.
"She is a woman of the Kings! No man dare lay bonds upon her. Beli
made peace in this island, brother. If I could make it between the
two islands . . ."

With the part of him that loved all men and all women Bran
looked upon that picture and saw that it was good. If, deep in the
darkest, unacknowledged places within him something whispered,
*Branwen's son will be born far away. He will be a stranger in the Island
of the Mighty, when Caradoc is known and loved,* he did not tell himself that he heard.

Manawyddan sighed. "I see how you will speak in council, brother,
before the chiefs. As you know well how I would like to speak. But
I will not go against you there. I never have."

He thought, *Friendship between peoples, the death of old hates—
with what fine clothes you have covered the nakedness of your desire.
You hide your true purpose from yourself, but it is there.*

2

The Insult

IN THE Council of the Chiefs that Marriage was agreed upon, the first marriage ever made for reasons of state-craft in the Island of the Mighty. Bran the Blessed and his sister wished it, and his brothers Manawyddan and Nissyen said nothing against it. His brother Evnissyen was not there to say anything. Since that day when he had failed to estrange his elder brothers upon the Rock of Harlech no man had seen his face.

The *Mabinogi* says that it was settled that Branwen should first admit Matholuch to her bed at Aberffraw. So Bran marched there with all his men, and Matholuch sailed there with all his ships. Too many were those wedding guests to have been got into any house. They ate and slept in tents and around campfires. At night the stars, watching those many bright fires upon the once dark earth, must have wondered and searched the sky for a gap in the constellations, shivering lest they too should fall.

Beside one fire sat the sons of Llyr, and across from them sat Branwen the daughter of Llyr beside Matholuch, and the hands of the two lovers were forever touching, and their eyes stealing long deep looks. Manawyddan watched them and thought, *It is like wine, this thing between them. I hope that it will last. But I do not like it, this plan for two people to sleep together for the good of two islands. Desire will not always come when it is called. A dreary road to set winding through the ages—the loveless beds of weariness, and the children begotten without joy. Well, maybe it is as well for the Great Going-Forward that Bran is king, not I. I am not one to open up new roads.*

He looked again at Branwen, at her sweet, flushed face and her eyes that saw only the Irishman, and he prayed to the World-

Fashioners by the name he knew Them by: *"O Mothers, who made the earth, make my sister's road as good as you can!"*

That night Matholuch slept in the arms of Branwen the white-breasted, the daughter of Llyr.

Day came again and night, and after them day and night again, the black and the gold shuttling back and forth as they will till the world ends. For the marriage between light and darkness seems likely to have been the first ever made, as it will certainly be the last, when that energy which has been perverted into darkness is at last purified and drawn back into that Breast of Divine Fire from which it came.

Branwen and Matholuch were happy. Day after day the Irish King hunted and feasted with the men of the Island of the Mighty, and night after night he lay down beside his wife, and for them there was no sunset and no darkness, only their own fire that rose up and walled them in and left them alone to love each other.

His men hunted and feasted too, and found the women of the Island of the Mighty most hospitable, and his horses grazed all the way from Aberffraw to the sea. The Irish men and the Irish horses lived on the fat of the British land, and one may wonder which frisked the more.

Evnissyen came upon the horses on his way home. What happened makes it certain that he did not come upon many Irishmen. Likely there was only one Irishman, with the horses, and he old.

Evnissyen had been in the hills, sleeping upon hard ground, and eating what game he could catch, hearing no human voices, only the cold winds that blew over him and paid no heed to him. Such impersonal foes, unlike an angry person to whom one hates to yield, do not challenge the proud *I* and are often very cooling. Evnissyen was ready now to forgive his brothers; indeed, he felt almost friendly toward them.

He wanted to get home, but when he saw the horses he stopped to look at them, and no wonder, for they were well worth looking at. From hock to forelock they were perfect, from mane to tail they were all swift, shining beauty. Their eyes and their sleek coats shone like stars. Ireland has bred many fine horses, but none anywhere have ever outshone these.

"Here are fine beasts," said Evnissyen. "Whose are they?"

"Who is your honor himself?" said the Irishman, grinning. He thought that this was Nissyen, being playful. The two sons of

Eurosswydd were as alike outside as they were unlike inside, dark slender youths with great beauty in their faces, like Penardim their mother.

Evnissyen did not grin back. He felt that he was being made fun of, and his ever tender dignity promptly puffed up again and became as prickly as a porcupine.

"I am brother to the High-King of the Island of the Mighty, fellow. To Bran the Blessed himself. I am Evnissyen, son of Penardim. So keep a civil tongue in your head, oaf."

That wiped out the Irishman's grin. "If you are a brother of King Bran," he said, "I take it that it is not because of you that he is called the Blessed. But if so, these horses are your kinsman's horses, for they belong to Matholuch, High-King of Ireland, and your sister Branwen's man."

Evnissyen went as red as fire and then white as death. "Is it so they have dared to deal with a girl like Branwen—giving her to a dog of an outlander? My own sister too, and my counsel unasked? My brothers could have put no greater shame on me than this."

It seemed to him that Bran and Manawyddan had arranged this marriage on purpose to punish him, to show him and all the Island of the Mighty of how little account he was in their counsels or in any great matter, the least of the sons of Penardim. They had not waited for him, they had jumped at the chance to settle this unheard of great business without him!

His hands shot out and grasped the old man's throat. "By the Gods your people swear by! Is this shame true?"

"It is true, and no shame," said the old man sturdily. Evnissyen's sword went through his belly before he could say more. He fell, and the son of Eurosswydd stood and watched him die, glad of every groan. Then he rushed upon the horses and cut their ears off. He cut off their lips, and left their bare teeth with the blood running down them, gumless. He cut off their silky tails. He hacked away their eyelids. He did them every hurt he could, short of killing them, and all the while their screams were music in his ears. In his own mind he was cutting this off Bran, and that off Manawyddan, and several things off the unknown Matholuch. For once in his nervous, self-harried life he was happy, for if his revenge was incomplete and in part dream, he yet was spoiling complete beauty, and there is a kind of miracle in being able to undo such a miracle as that.

When he had done all the things he could think of to the horses, he went away. On the road he met another Irishman and stopped him.

"Tell your outland High-King," he said, "that he had better go look at his horses, for they were never so well worth looking at before. Also it is a pity to leave such fine beasts unguarded, and the man who was minding them is in no shape to do it now.

"Tell him too that this message comes from Evnissyen, brother to Bran the High-King, him that rules over by far the greatest of the Isles of the Mighty."

Laughing, he went upon his way, that no longer led home.

But the Irishmen were not laughing when they came to their King. Their faces were as red as blood, and their hands were knotted fists.

"Lord," they said, "you have been disgraced and insulted as no king in Erin ever was before you."

Matholuch stared. "How?"

"Lord, the horses have been cut and hacked about, castrated and left to their blind screaming. The cruelty of it passes belief. And Evnissyen, your lady's own brother, himself boasted of it to us. This must be what these other-island men have been planning from the beginning, while they slobbered over you and made-believe to be your friends."

Matholuch sat as stiff as a dead man, staring from crimson face to crimson face. He felt hollow, as if his vitals had been knocked out of him. He wanted time, time to think, but there was no time. All those red, staring eyes beat him like whips.

He tried, once, to use reason. Himself, he would have liked to wait for explanations; he was a temperate man. He licked his lips and said weakly, "It is a wonder to me why, if they meant to insult me, they let me sleep with so noble a lady, the darling of all her kin."

The hard red stares did not soften. "Lord, it does not matter what kind of a wonder it is. It is so. And since there are not enough of us here to fight them, there is nothing for you to do but to go home."

He saw that if he did not go they would despise him. He said heavily, "Let us be going then."

A white-faced girl brought news of that going to Branwen the Queen. At first Branwen laughed. The tale seemed madness, one of those ugly frightening webs that imps weave, out of the sleep-relaxed and unguarded brains of men. But the day was plain and sane around her. The encircling soberness of reality pressed the tale upon her, something that must be disproved and thrust back into the land of dreams.

She went outside. She looked toward the road on the other side of her pavilion, the road that led down toward the sea and the Irish ships. She saw the Irish there, marching away, Matholuch at their head, tall and straight in his scarlet cloak. His face had the curious, carved look that all faces seen in profile have. Feelingless, masklike, image-like. He was going past her, they were all going past her, like stones set rolling by an avalanche. Men no longer, only moving images. It was a kind of death.

"Matholuch!" She tried to scream his name, but a sudden growth in her throat choked her. She tried to run after him, but her feet had grown roots that shot down into the earth and held her.

She wanted to throw her arms around him, and turn him back from image to man again. *Yet what if she should touch him, and he should not come alive?*

He was more a stranger now than on that first day. An image going away from her with the images of his men. No cry of hers could reach him, or that silent company, any more than if they had been dead men going down through the Pass of the Dog's Mouth, down into the misty fields of Arawn, Lord of the Underworld.

It was surely her death. For her man, her lover, wanted to go.

Bran and Manawyddan sat in council in the royal camp of Harlech. Evening had come, but not the peace of evening. The sky blazed with terrifying color, blood-red and fire-gold.

Their councilors sat with them, but they talked low. Branwen was in the pavilion behind them, and the sons of Llyr hoped that she was safe in the arms of sleep, that gentle sister of death. She had not wept, but her silence had been worse than weeping, heavy and dumb as the pain within her.

Bran had sent messengers after Matholuch. They had spoken with him aboard his ship, that his men were loading. They had said, "Lord, this business was not willed by our King or his councilors. The shame on Bran the Blessed is worse than it is on you. It is unblessed he has been this day."

That is what I think," said Matholuch. "His face is more blackened than mine. But he cannot take back the insult. He cannot undo the pain."

Bran's men made offers of atonement then, and Matholuch looked around at his men. But he saw only one face engraved on many faces, eyes bright and jaws set rigid with pride in their own anger. And he said, "Red was the wrong, and red must any atonement be. And that kind I do not think your King will want to pay us, since the man who did the wrong is who he is."

The messengers brought these words back to Bran, who sat long in silence. Every man heard that silence; felt it, like a knife at his throat. For but one true atonement could be made to Matholuch.

Manawyddan spoke at last, and his voice was like the unsheathing of a sword. "Two things we must settle. What we are going to do about the Irishmen, and what we are going to do with Evnissyen."

"We could exile Evnissyen," Bran said drearily. "The Mothers know he has deserved it, and without sinning against the Ancient Harmonies we can offer Matholuch no greater face-price. Never among the Old Tribes has brother slain brother. Even among the New it is still accounted an evil deed. We cannot do it."

"If we exile him," said Manawyddan, "he will turn pirate and treat the people of Ireland's coast—and maybe of ours—as he did the horses.

Bran groaned. "Why could not one of those horses have kicked him in the head?"

"It did not. We were not fated to get peace so easily, brother."

Bran groaned again. "This is an ugly business. His killing the Irishman I can understand. He has always liked despising things; naturally, he would despise an outlander and see no great harm in killing one. But this business with the horses—I have never heard the like. No man can have acted like that since the world began. Does he know no pity?"

His great face looked as heavy as if all the gloom of night had gathered there.

"We were fools not to foresee trouble," said Manawyddan. "He did have a right to sit in the council that decided to let our sister go with Matholuch. And his dignity has always been a tender part of him."

"I would like well to use my hand on another tender part of him," Bran growled.

"That too is against the custom of the Old Tribes," said Manawyddan, "To beat our young. We might have taught Evnissyen cunning, but we never could have taught him fear stronger than his hates."

Bran said grimly, "Many men might live if he died now. The druids were right, brother. You remember? When Nissyen was born they looked at him and shook their heads in wonder. They said, 'How could such a child have come of such a deed?' But when Evnissyen followed him they shook their heads again and said, 'Never let this one grow into a man upon the Island of the Mighty.'"

"I remember well," said Manawyddan. "I still can hear our mother's weeping. Llyr stood against the druids for her sake, and Beli would not judge between his people and his kin. He sent messengers to Mâth the Ancient, who replied that every child was a destiny, and that this one would not have come here if the island had not earned him. So Evnissyen was kept and named."

"Evnissyen—'unlike Nissyen,'" said Bran. "Which the Mothers know he is." He sighed. "I do not see what we island folk had done to earn him."

"Our mother Penardim did a deed," said Manawyddan. "Eurosswydd did a worse. Deeds have been in the air ever since the New Tribes came, because change has been in the air. Change that seldom bears a single child, but mostly twins—good and evil. But because Evnissyen is unlike Nissyen, are we to make ourselves unlike Bran, unlike Manawyddan? The Ancient Harmonies are in your hands to guard, brother. They and, I hope, the shape of the world that is to be."

Bran looked off into the night, that was moonless; at the stars that seemed to watch him like a myriad bright eyes. Such eyes as might shine from dark colossal faces watching, with quiet, age-old wonder, the turmoil of earth.

He said finally, "There is nothing we can do about Evnissyen. You could not let light into him, not if you made a hole in him. But the Irishman is another matter. Go after him, brother, with Heveydd the Tall and what other men you choose to take, and tell him that though I cannot give him the head of my mother's son—as indeed I would like well to do—I will give him such a face-price as never was paid to any king before." He named that price over.

"It is more than he is worth," said Manawyddan.

"It is his due. Nor do we want bitterness between the two islands, and all his young men raiding our coasts. I could not hold our folk then. Besides, this business is breaking Branwen's heart."

Manawyddan stiffened. "Let it break here, not in Ireland. Matholuch is not good timber to build a peace with, brother. He has not been staunch to Branwen."

"He has not. I know it. Yet he is not such a one as Evnissyen. So long as nothing stirs him up he will do well. I have the peace of two islands to guard. Help me, brother." Manawyddan was silent awhile; then he said heavily, "Sooner would I give him our brother's head than our sister to take home with him, out of our sight. Yet I see that you cannot withhold her if she is still willing to go. But do you hunt Evnissyen down and keep him under guard. Else there is likely to be something else to stir our precious new kinsman up."

"There will not be, Lords." Tall Heveydd had heard, and had come forward. "The Lord Nissyen has gone to look for his brother. Yesterday he bade me tell you so, but so much has happened that I forgot."

Bran and Manawyddan exchanged a long look. "

"Strange," Bran muttered, "how Nissyen always knows! A pity that he did not find Evnissyen before Evnissyen found the horses. But he will find him; that is sure."

Manawyddan nodded. "Yes. You and I would have had to set druids to looking into water and into crystal to find out where Evnissyen is, but Nissyen's feet will lead him to him of themselves. It is a queer bond between those two."

"It is indeed." Bran grinned. "When they were little and Evnissyen bit the nurses and kicked the dogs and tore up whatever he could lay hands on, so that Branwen herself had to be guarded from him in her cradle, he never once lifted hand to Nissyen. If his twin came up and looked at him he would stop whatever evil he was doing, and then shriek with rage and run. Does he love Nissyen, or does he hate him most of all of us, I wonder? Well, that is one problem settled. May you have as good luck with the other, brother."

"I will do my best," said Manawyddan.

In the last hour before dawn, when quiet and blackness lay heavily upon all things as though the world mourned for her own death, he came to the ships of the Irishmen. He hailed them; by the light of their guttering torches be saw how their eyes glittered, sheen without color, peering at him watchfully from under their helmets.

Their spokesman said, "Go back, British man. There is nothing to talk about. Our King sleeps."

"Wake him," said Manawyddan. "Tell him that Manawyddan, son of Llyr, is here. The brother of his own wife."

"I am here." Beyond the man who had spoken a tall figure loomed up, faceless. He stood out of reach of the torchlight, many others pressing about him.

Manawyddan peered toward him, strained his eyes, trying to make out that featureless patch of paler darkness that was his brother-in-law's face. Suddenly, startlingly, it came to him that he was seeing Matholuch as clearly as he ever had seen him. Was darkness much more veiling than shape and color, than the pride of him among his fighting men?

The son of Llyr gave his message. Matholuch said, "I will talk this over with my men."

Manawyddan and his men waited. The black of night gave way to a sickly colorlessness that made the earth look old and tired and misshapen. The east grew gray as an old woman's hair. A cold wind blew, and on it the shrill buzz of voices came to the envoys: "A great face-price . . . If we do not take it we must raid their coasts for vengeance . . . Then they may invade us . . . Likely that is what they are trying to get an excuse to do . . . If we refuse this we will get more trouble and maybe more shame, and never again such an honor-price."

The dawn reddened. Matholuch came to the ship's side and leaned over. He looked down at Manawyddan and smiled his old frank, friendly smile. In the red light his hair and beard shone almost red, with e glitter almost golden.

"Come up, brother," he said, "and clasp hands with me. Meat and drink shall be set before you and your men. Nobody in the world could refuse so fair a face-price. My men and I are agreed on that. And it is glad I will be to get back to Branwen, my wife."

3

The Peacemaking

AT SUNSET Nissyen the son of Eurosswydd had come to a hill not
far from Aberffraw. Trees and rocks were there, but no sign of man.
Like a gashed and burning greatness the sky brooded above it; blood-
red, as though from mighty wounds. The rocks and trees shone dully
in that red glow, that was like the shadow and the soul of blood.

Nissyen saw an oak, and something that crouched within the
shadow of that oak, so still that to any searcher less subtle it might
have seemed part of that shadow. But Nissyen felt the red darkness
that boiled round it, foul as fetid waters, fiercer than the burning sky.

"Evnissyen," he said. "Brother."

His twin jerked as if pierced by a dart; then averted his eyes as
though sight of that calm face were intolerable.

"It would be you." His teeth showed in a snarl like a beast's. "Why
can you never leave me alone?"

Nissyen said nothing. He sat down beside his brother; he did not
look at him or away from him. His undemanding, undisturbed friendliness was like the tranquil power of earth herself, that is too big for
any man to shatter, too strong and soft and fertile for any fire to burn.

It made Evnissyen feel empty and futile. He clutched, as with
both hands, at the fury that was slipping from him. He tore at the
earth and got fistfuls of grass, and so the satisfaction of hurting
something a little.

"He sent you!" he raged. "Bran."

And the bulk of Bran, that he had always feared a little, loomed
over his mind like a great cliff, like the huge ice masses of the far
north, immensities that, if one set in motion, might crush and chill
all things.

"Is he still so pleased with the trick he played upon me, our glorious brother? He that has not guts enough to do what he wants and make his own son king? He has not pith enough in his whole vast clumsy carcass to resent an insult or insult anybody—except me. Except me!" He howled as a wolf howls. "All my life he has despised me. All of them have, all of them have always hated me and tormented me and twisted everything I ever said or did. Because I am Eurosswydd's son, not Llyr's."

"I too am Eurosswydd's son," said Nissyen. "I have never felt that hate."

"No, you crawling bootlicker! You hound, always whining at the heels of the sons of Llyr! But *I* have had to bear it all my days, and I will have to bear it all my days." He snarled and writhed in his agony, and tore up more grass.

"Grass feels less than horses," said Nissyen.

Evnissyen sat up. He laughed and ground his teeth in that laughter. "This anyway I have done! I have frightened them—Llyr's fine sons! I so nearly had them at each other's throats—I would have but for you, you blighting pest—that I made them afraid. This time it was me they tried to get even with—me." His voice rose in triumph. "Not our father. *Me.* Evnissyen."

"They should not have done it," said Nissyen. "But they did not do it out of malice. They forgot you."

Silence then, crashing silence. The sons of Llyr never could have made Evnissyen believe that they had been forgetful, not spiteful, but Nissyen made him believe. That knowledge made him feel small, and there was nothing in the world that Evnissyen feared so much as smallness—the smallness of himself. He loved giving pain, and so making himself large in the consciousness of that which felt the pain. He could have borne pain with secret delight in the knowledge that his own doings had been important enough to produce this violence that he suffered under, this disturbance and exertion in another being. To the chilled and starving inward person punishment can give a bitter nourishment. And now Evnissyen's source of food had been snatched from him.

When he spoke again his voice was low. "I will teach them to forget me! I am not a safe person to forget. If our good brothers have not learned that by now, soon they will learn it. Eurosswydd made them remember. I am glad of that. Glad that our mother had to have him when she did not want him. He got as much done with her in one night as Llyr had in all the years before. Two of us, as there are two sons of Llyr. He was a man, our father! And Llyr had to remember every night thereafter, as long as he lived, that Eurosswydd had been everywhere he had been—" He laughed wolfishly. "Well, I will not be less than you, Father. I too will make them remember me. I have only begun."

Nissyen did not answer. Shadows were everywhere now, like dark, long-limbed invaders swinging down from the sky. Ever thicker, blacker, stronger—a host of them covering the earth.

Evnissyen said presently out of the darkness, "I could have been happy if they had not hated me." He moved restlessly, his hands still tugging at the grasses, but no longer uprooting them. He was tired; his fury was spent. For all his boastful words he had no idea what he could do next to make Bran and Manawyddan remember him. His beautiful upturned face was tragic, pure with the purity of pain, and so more than ever like its calm counterpart beside him.

"Do you suppose Bran will be able to make peace with that outland king, brother? I hope not—I hope not!"

If he cannot, I will still have done something. I will still have size.

"Bran will offer him a great face price," said Nissyen. "More than he could win in battle."

"He might get my head in battle. Maybe he hopes to get it anyway." Evnissyen laughed grimly, but uneasily too.

"You know Bran would never give him that, brother."

"Truly that is great goodness in him—the son of my own mother! I do not even know that it is so, but no doubt you do. You know many things, you creeping spy—too many! But you did not know enough to find me before I found the Irish. How you would have loved to save those horses from me!" He laughed spitefully.

"I should have indeed," said Nissyen. His voice was like the night-covered rocks around them; it had no color and no weakness and no passion.

"Dog!" Again Evnissyen's wolf howl rose. "Dog, unworthy of our begetter. If you had been my true brother, if you had stood beside me against the sons of Llyr . . ."

"I have always stood beside you. I stand against none."

This time Evnissyen made no answer. He hid his face and gave himself up to his sick hatred of all things. Nissyen lay beside him and thought, *I have given him a little light, and it is burning him worse than his own fire. Well, it is my business to bring light.*

Presently he rolled over and laid his hand on his twin's shoulder. "Get up, brother. Let us go up into the hills for awhile, both of us. Away from other men."

Obedient as a child Evnissyen rose, but he kept his eyes averted; they burned with unabated loathing.

Together they went up into the hills, and no man saw either of them again until the Irish had sailed for Ireland.

Bit by bit the sun let down her golden hair upon the earth. Through that brightening greenness Manawyddan and Matholuch marched back together. Tall Heveydd had gone ahead to warn Bran of their coming, and when they reached Aberffraw the feast spread there was as great as that which had been spread for the wedding. Bran sat waiting for them, and with him Branwen. Pale and still as a carved image she sat, deep circles round her great dark eyes. Ever since morning she had been thinking, *When he comes, will it be the same? Everything all right again, and I sure of him, my man? O Mothers, let it be the same!*

Yet could even They undo what once had been done?

Manawyddan and Matholuch came to Bran, and gave him the kiss of greeting. Then Matholuch came to Branwen. He took her in his arms and gave a great laugh—laughter, that needs no logic, is often more useful than words—and kissed her mouth, and rumpled her beautiful hair that had been smooth as black feathers.

"Well, girl," he said, "I missed you last night. Did you miss me?"

She laughed too and kissed him. But her eyes did not smile. They searched his as a tired swimmer's might search the horizon for land.

He sat down beside her, and ate. All ate, and soon talk buzzed as merrily as bees. Now that peace had been made and their mouths were full the Irishmen liked the British better, and because their mouths were full and the danger to their coasts was over, the British liked the Irish better. The two hosts liked each other.

Only where the Kings sat was there still a kind of silence, cold depths that the talk rippling over their surface could not warm. It may have had a quiet that came from Branwen; it certainly had an ugly red gloom that came from Matholuch.

For now that his men had forgotten the insult, he was remembering it. They, who had been honestly offended and outraged, could forgive. But they had dragged him after them. He, who should have been the head of the dog, had been its tail instead, and a well-wagged tail at that. He felt lessened. Both Branwen's silence and Bran's cheerful friendliness grated on him. Had his men been right at first? Was Bran laughing at him? At a little quarrel with a lesser king?

A lesser king . . . The darkness around him thickened.

Bran saw how white Branwen was, the depth of trouble in her still unsmiling eyes. He felt Manawyddan growing quieter and quieter beside him, saw the glitter of the sea growing in those sea-gray, sea-deep eyes. The eyes of Llyr their father.

Bran made a decision. He looked at Matholuch and said, "You are not as cheerful as you were, sister's man. If that is because you think the face-price less than you have a right to, you shall have any other goods of mine that you may ask for."

That was an offer as big as Bran, and for a breath's space it and his ox-big, guileless eyes washed Matholuch clean.

"Lord," the Irish King said, "that is a princely offer."

"It is meant to be, brother. I will add to the face-price; I will give you a rare gift. A cauldron that was not made upon this earth. This is its quality: if a man of yours were to be killed today," here he remembered sadly that Evnissyen had killed one of them yesterday, "you could throw him into it and he would jump out of it alive and whole, save that he would lack the power of speech. For it would not be himself that was in it, but some other thing in his body, something unable even to think in the tongues of earth. But he would fight like the demon he probably would be."

Red leapt into the face of Matholuch. His eyes shone.

"I give you thanks, Lord! That must be the greatest treasure in the Island of the Mighty. With it a man could conquer the world!"

"It is the best treasure a man could have," Bran said dryly, "to make invaders afraid to come against him. But a wise man would hate to use it. For those unearthly beings that can do nothing but fight might be worse to deal with, once his battles were won, than any earthly foe."

"I see." Matholuch's face fell. "Too great a risk would he take who tried to go forth and conquer with it. But it would make him safe from conquest. For at worst those Other World beings would walk the earth in flesh that once was of his own race. His people never would have the shame of bowing to outlanders."

Bran said still more dryly, "A hard choice. But you see what I meant you to see."

Night had come again; all the feasters went to their rest. Branwen and Matholuch went to their pavilion, his arm around her. So it had held her on other nights, cradling her, warming her like wine. But now, back again in that longed-for, magic-making circle, she still felt cold and lonely, like a lost woman wandering in the winter night.

They were in her pavilion now, and she heard him sending her women away. "Go and get some sleep now, girls. I will help your lady get her clothes off." Always before that laugh had thrilled her; it did not now.

She sat down on the bed; she felt tired, as a worn-out old woman is tired, for whom nothing has glow or sweetness any more. Her feelings had passed over her like years, slow and hard and aging years, and she had no longings left. Unless it was to be alone, not to go through a mockery of what had once been beautiful.

She felt his hands on her, undoing her dress, slipping down— somehow it offended her, as though he really were making love to an old woman, or to a corpse.

She said, "You did not want me so much last night."

He laughed again. "Did I not? Little you know about it, woman!" and pulled her close. He held her so tightly that she felt the reddish-gold hairs on his chest, the hard beating of his heart.

"Let us stop talking, sweet woman. Let us waste no more of the hours of this night!"

His arms held her fast; she could no more keep them out of her blood than she could have kept them off her body. Yet in them she could have wept because she was still shut out from him, still the wandering woman, peering through a lighted window at unreachable warmth and joy . . . Two Branwens; the body that was being comforted, and the woman who watched, alone with her inexorable knowledge, in the cold and the dark.

When he had possessed her and she still had not fully responded, he asked her what ailed her. "Nothing," she said, and her voice quavered on the word, and that shamed her; she was very young. Then, for the first time, she wept.

"Oh, how could you leave me without a word?"

He had no mind to quarrel with her; he wanted her and he wanted the Cauldron. The Island of the Mighty seemed a good place to him that night; pleasant and full of treasures. Besides, the cause of her distress flattered him. He held her tenderly and said the one thing that was left for him to say. "I was mad last night. I was shamed and grieved and enraged. I did not think."

That made him sound like a child carried away by his fury, and most women have tenderness for the hurts of a child. And though she did not want to she was still weeping, and he was fondling her to soothe her, though she still thought that she wanted him to go away.

"Branwen," he said, "Branwen." His voice was a lover's; the music that is at once delight and demand. His hands were stroking her breast, and they were warm. They brought a melting sweetness to every chilled hurt place within her.

"Matholuch!" she said. "Matholuch."

This time she was wholly his.

The Cauldron pleased the Irish. Before the feast was over, Bran's men had set it before the tents of the outlanders, huge and round and dully glinting, like a burnt-out, fallen star. It's new owners were full of wine and food and happiness, but they could not sleep for touching it and looking at it.

Yet all feared it a little. It seemed colder to the touch than it should be. Unearthliness was on it, the chill of black wastes beyond earth. Metal does not belong to our world alone; it may come to it from without, housed in meteors, those strange strays from the dark fields of space.

One man said, "I wonder if that British King was fooling us again." And he ran his hand along the side of the Cauldron gingerly, as if afraid it might resent his doubt and bite him. "Or if you really could kill a man and stew him in this, and him jump out as good as new except for not being able to talk."

"That last would be an improvement in some men I know," laughed a second. "Many a tongue has wagged off the head it was in."

"Indeed and indeed I would like well to see this Cauldron at work," said a third. He stared at it with wide, fascinated eyes.

"Until we do we cannot tell what it will do," said a fourth. "We have only this King Bran's word for it, and him an outlander, no Irishman. It would be a nice thing if, when we got it home and put a dead man in it, he only cooked."

"Before you can try it out you must have a dead man to put in it," said a fifth, "and nobody around here is dead."

They were silent awhile then. They were all eager to see the Cauldron work, but none of them wanted to be dead.

"We might draw lots," one hardy soul said at last.

But another promptly said no to that. "If the Cauldron did not work, then the King would be short a man."

They all discovered depth and greatness in their love for Matholuch. They said loyally, "That would never do. Here in the midst of his enemies. He needs every man he has."

"We might creep up on one of these outlanders and slit his throat and fetch him here," suggested one.

"That would not be honorable," said another.

"Nor safe," said yet another. "He would be missed in the morning, and we might be suspected. We might be caught killing him too, and then folk would say that we had broken the peace."

The first man sighed. "It is a pity not to be able to kill even one of them, after what they did to the horses. I helped rear those horses." He sighed harder. "Is there nobody we can kill at all?" he said.

"There is not," said the most cautious man, "but there is somebody we can dig up. Our comrade who was slain. Let us go and get him."

There was another brief silence. They all looked at one another doubtfully. "He has been dead a little while," said one. "He must be getting used to it."

"It happened only day before yesterday," said the man who wanted to dig him up. "He cannot have gone very far, and it is likely that he is still surprised and homesick."

They went and got him, and it took all of them to do it, though he had never been a big man. They shivered when they heard the wind moan as they carried him back through the quiet fields, for they thought his soul might be riding it, wondering angrily why old friends and kinsmen disturbed his rest. Death makes a stranger of a man; however easygoing he may have been in life, none can be sure how his temper will be when he is dead.

Gently and carefully they lowered him into the Cauldron. The moonlight shone down upon his still face, that was as blank as a doll's, yet full of awful mysterious wisdom, like the face of that Corpse-God who is said to have been the teacher of ancient poets. It looked familiar to none of them, though some there may have been his sons, or his sister's sons.

One said to him, "Brother, we are doing this for the honor and glory of Ireland. It is proud you should be to help us."

But then he sprang back sharply. That still face seemed so without interest, so unhearing.

They brought wood and set a fire and lit it. Little flames licked up toward the Cauldron. Men looked at one another, troubled.

"It must be hot in there," said one.

Another said, "He cannot feel it." Then, with a shudder, "At least not yet."

The flames rose higher. Quickly, as if some unseen thing reached down, eager to draw them upward. The Cauldron glowed red and baleful, like a fallen star that hated its prison, the earth. Smoke began to rise from it and, suddenly, a hissing sound like the voice of a mighty serpent.

The hair rose on the heads of the watchers. They all leapt backward. One man tried to giggle, "Have you never before heard a pot boil?" but in the midst of that giggle his teeth chattered. They were all shivering again, though the heat of the fire reached for them like hands.

The smoke rose higher, blotting out the moon.

Then, of a sudden, it quivered and vanished. The fire sputtered and went out, as if all power had been drawn out of it, into some Otherwhere. The moon shone again.

From within the Cauldron came a sound of movement, of something stirring there. A yell went up from the men closest to it, and they jumped back still farther.

The men behind them made room for them joyfully. All shrank, and most wanted to run, but could not. Their feet seemed glued there, and their eyes, that longed to look away, were glued to the Cauldron.

On the lip of the great vessel hands appeared. Fingers that looked unpleasantly long, unpleasantly eager. There was a scrabbling sound, and a body swung itself over the side, its long legs, its shaggy hair and beard half covering the setting moon.

Its eyes shone greenish, and the dead firelight seemed to glow on within them, evilly.

It came to the ground in one spring, and glanced about it, without recognition, into the faces of the Irish. Its nostrils worked, like a dog's, as if seeking a scent it could not find. Then, with an unhuman scream of rage, it leapt for the nearest Irishman.

Before he could move, its teeth had torn out his throat. Before the swords and the combined weight of all there brought it to earth, it had seized two more men and knocked their heads together, so that their skulls smashed like eggshells. Bran and Manawyddan came running from the British tents, and Matholuch came running out of Branwen's.

They heard what had happened. They looked down at what lay dead again, hacked by many blades, and Bran mopped his forehead.

"You see now, brother," he said to Matholuch, "what I warned you of."

"Truly," said Matholuch, his voice shaking, "I never would wish any man of mine a rebirth like that."

"Your man himself was never troubled," said Bran. "He was safe with Arawn in the Underworld. With him who has power to hold what he has taken."

Matholuch shuddered and said no more. He went back to Branwen, as if seeking shelter from the Unspeakable.

"I am glad he takes it like that," said Manawyddan, looking after him. "He will be careful with that Cauldron now. I remember my thankfulness when you got it from Llassar. And my heart sank like a stone today when you gave it away again. I never would have."

"I gave it to Branwen's man," Bran said simply. "To prove my friendship beyond all doubt, by giving him what could make his island safe from ours, the bigger one, forever. I did not think that too great a price to pay for our sister's happiness, and for the peace of two islands."

"Can any but they two buy their happiness," said Manawyddan, "she and Matholuch?" He looked off into the gray gloom of the fields and the heavens. "I think, too, that it takes more than gifts to buy peace, brother."

4

The Iron House

A SECOND night they feasted, the men of Ireland and the men of the Island of the Mighty. And Matholuch said to Bran the Blessed, "Brother, where did you get that Cauldron?"

"From a man who came from your country, brother."

Matholuch started. "From an Irishman?"

"Where he first came from I do not know, but Llassar—the Flame— is the name he uses upon earth; and he is flamelike enough. He came here with his woman, Kymideu Kymeinvoll after they had escaped from the Iron House that your people heated red-hot around them. It is a wonder to me if you know nothing of that business, brother."

Matholuch smiled; a frank, open and soldierly smile. "I do indeed, for as High-King I ordered it heated red-hot around them. There seemed to be no other way for men born of women to defend themselves against those two, and their brood. I should have known that Cauldron again; they were carrying it when I first set eyes on them."

"Tell us," said Bran.

"I will. One day I was hunting, and somehow I lost my way, and my comrades. I rode on and on, but whichever way I turned I seemed only to get deeper and deeper into the forest. Nothing but trees, trees everywhere; no beasts, no birds, not even a cricket singing. Only greenness and a great stillness, as if Earth Herself were holding Her breath down under the trees and grasses, waiting for Something that was to come. As if all life that had legs or wings had fled before that Something could come."

"Indeed," Branwen breathed, her lovely face flushed and her lovely eyes star-bright upon her husband, "you must have been riding into great danger."

Matholuch laughed and patted her hand. "No need to worry about that, girl, since I am here with you now. But then I did feel like a fish caught in a vast net, for the trees got so thick that I could not see the sky between their branches. Glad I was when toward evening, I saw the shimmer of water ahead, between the bushes. That meant a chance to drink, and an open place. But as I spurred toward the light a wind arose and screamed through the hidden sky. All the trees in the forest bent and shook and twisted. My horse and I rushed on, with branches snapping off and falling all around us. And then I heard a mighty, crashing splash, as of many trees falling into waters, and I knew that that shimmer must be a lake, and deep.

"We came out into the open, and I saw the surface of that lake churning as if there were a storm beneath it as well as above it. And in a breath's space I saw that that was so—that Something was heaving itself up from below."

He paused. Branwen caught her breath, and so did all the women there. The faces of most men were tense. Only the sons of Llyr sat calmly, their sea-gray eyes fast upon the face of Matholuch.

He went on. "I saw a huge man's head and shoulders rise out of the lake. If you could call him man—his yellow hair was dripping, and his face was vast. Whiskers grew out of each nostril, and fringed each great thick roll of lip; fire-bright whiskers that looked as if they could burn up anything that touched them, and it was a pity they had not burned up the face. So I first saw Llassar, the Flame, and the sight of him was even more dreadful than fire, for which he is named.

"He rose out of the waters and waded toward shore, and I saw that he was carrying a cauldron on his back—this same, I suppose, that you gave me yesterday, Bran. But then I paid no heed to it. The waters were still churning, worse even than before he had come forth; and in a little while a woman's head rose out of them—if you could call her woman—and it was twice as high as his head, and twice as good to look away from. She waded after him like a farmwife shooing a hen. They came toward shore, and I saw her belly, and I hope I never see anything like that again!" He sighed, spat, and took a drink.

"What then?" Young Caradoc's face was eager.

"They saw me on the bank and called to me, 'Good day to you, Lord, and good be with you!' And I went down to meet them though I felt good might be nearer me if they were farther away from me. 'Well,' I said to the man, 'this is Ireland, and I am High-King of it, and why are you in it?'

"He said, 'This is the cause of our coming, Lord. In a month and a fortnight this woman with me will bear a son, and we must have some world for him to be born in. We ask your hospitality, Lord, for we are two strangers alone in your land.'

"Whoever or wherever they were I could not but feel sympathy for whatever people evidently had wanted that son of his born somewhere else. But to refuse such a plea would have been unkingly, so I took them home with me—I had no trouble in finding my way out of the forest once I had found them—and gave them a good farm. And the woman's womb, now that it was out of its own element, shaped flesh after the pattern of our world, for she gave birth to a stalwart, shapely youth. A sword, a spear, and a shield came out of her along with him, and that did surprise me, but I was glad not to have another monster on my hands, I was only one stout warrior to the good, and that sooner than could possibly have been expected.

"But next month she had another son, and the month after that another, and the month after that yet another. And the night that their youngest brother was born all four went out and stopped a party of nobles on the road to Tara. They stripped the men and took all their valuables, and they lay with all the women. Some of the women liked that and some did not, but none of the men liked it. They complained to me, loudly.

"I sent a man to complain to Llassar, but he found only Kymideu Kymeinvoll and the children at home, and he did not stay to deliver all his message, but went away quickly when Kymideu Kymeinvoll rose up and asked him what he meant by scolding her little ones so harshly."

"I begin to see," said Manawyddan, smiling grimly, "that you may have felt that your hospitality was ill rewarded."

"It was, brother. And next month Kymideu Kymeinvoll had another son, and that night all five went out and committed another and bigger outrage. Their mother said they were only playful and that we Irish could not take a joke, but Llassar seemed more understanding; he said he thought his boys might settle down if they had women of their own. So I gave them women, but they promptly got them with child and went on molesting my people the same as before. And every month there was another of them to help do it. At the year's end the chief men of Ireland came to me. 'Lord,' they said, 'you must choose between your realm and these children of Llassar the Killer—between his folk and your folk. If you keep on holding your hand over them we will outlaw you along with them, for we cannot stand them any longer. They must die.'"

"'They may be hard to kill,' said I, 'for their father and mother may object.'

"'The Old Ones must die too,' said they, 'them above all; for how can we ever hope for peace in the land while those two keep at it? No decent woman's insides could shape swords and shields. It is too tough that woman's insides are,' said they.

"So I sent men to slay the strangers by night, but Kymideu Kymeinvoll woke and killed twice as many of them as her man and boys did. I saw that I might lose a whole army that way, so I called a council of all Ireland. But while we were debating she had twins, and when we heard that we did not feel any better.

"Then a druid said, 'The great stone that fell from the sky last year has become metal; the metal that the Eastern world calls Iron. Iron is harder than bronze itself, that we make our swords from; none can break through it. Hollow a hall out of that stone, and it will hold even the Children of Llassar. Great was the toil, but we did it; then we made peace with the Llassar folk and bade them to a feast there, and we made them drunk. Then we slipped out and piled up charcoal, and built a great ring of fires round the Iron House."

"I know that part of the tale," said Bran shortly.

"It was a sight to see, brother. Every smith in Ireland helped, and every man that owned hammer and tongs. Flames roared like beasts, they shot up as if to eat the stars out of the sky. Soon would the heat within have grown unbearable to common flesh, to the children of men. And at last we heard a scream, as though a man's hand or arm, or some other part of him, had touched a red-hot wall. Some of us laughed then, for they had done many wrongs, they who were roasting in that oven."

Branwen was telling herself, *He had to do it. There was no other way.* But she was unhappy; when Matholuch paused for effect she said, "Did none of them get out?"

"Not then, Lady. The smiths blew upon the fires with bellows to make them yet hotter, and the people fetched yet more fuel. They danced round that ring of flame shouting and jeering at those within. But never another sound came from the Iron House. Until in the last hour of the second night, when those walls that had been red-hot glowed white as death, there came a great crash as the iron-plated doors burst outward. There the roaring walls of fire were thickest, but Llassar the Flame charged through them, and after him tramped Kymideu Kymeinvoll, her huge shadow dwarfing even his. Their children followed, but they were not so tall, and the flames blinded them. We spitted them like chickens, we thrust them back into the fire, though their giant parents fought hard to save them. Those two brushed aside our spears like pins, they thrust their long arms full-length into the flames. But in the end they had to flee, with only their Cauldron, whose power we did not know—good luck it was for us that they did not manage to fish out any of their boys' corpses to put into it! Where they went we never knew, nor did we care, since they went out of Ireland. I suppose they waded across to you, Lord?" He looked questioningly at Bran. "Through the Sinking Lands?"

"They did," said Bran, "and people here were not glad to see them coming. Many chiefs were for killing or driving them out. But I knew that that would cost many lives, also that, since they were here on earth, they had a right to live somewhere. So I made a bargain with them. They gave me the Cauldron, whose power they fear, and agreed to distribute their sons, as fast as they were born, among different towns and parts of the Island of the Mighty."

"You mean they are still here? That you have found no way to kill them?" Matholuch's jaw dropped. "How could you dare to give away the Cauldron?"

Bran laughed his great, deep, jovial laugh. Never was any sound on earth at once as mighty and as mellow, as thunderous yet serene, as the laugh of Bran. "We do not need it. We have eaten up that people and digested it."

"We did not have to cook it in an Iron House either." Disgust showed plain on Caradoc's young face.

For once Bran frowned at Caradoc; he did not consider that speech tactful. "Be still, lad. That savage brood is vast, Matholuch, but there is not much of it m any one place, nor does it know itself and hold together. But its people always prosper, and every town they live in they strengthen with the best of men and arms."

"You trust them?"

"Yes. I am not saying I am glad they came. That warlike stock, working within us, may yet change our race. But already we have changed them; they are part of us, of a large and peaceful people. Had I driven them on, they might have come upon some lesser land, and eaten up its folk."

"They may yet eat you up. Kymideu Kymeinvoll bears sons fast, brother."

This time Manawyddan laughed. "Not so fast now. In a whole year she has not borne a single warrior, yet you say that when your people got afraid and plotted her death she bore twins. Like breeds like, be it thought or flesh, and fear is wine to fury."

Bran said, "She did bear one more pair of twins, the first night after she came ashore here—the only children I have let her keep so far. But soon I will not be afraid to leave her sons with her long enough to learn their parents' ways. These are changing. Nobody who is comfortable and unafraid ever wants the risks and pains of war."

"Keep a man's belly full and you will have no trouble with him? Is that your thought, Bran—that a rich man can always buy peace?" An edge had come onto Matholuch's voice.

"Men whose bellies are full seldom leave their homes to fight," said Bran comfortably. "Only great fear or great wrath can make them do that, and such madness is usually the work of cunning liars. It is our business, my brothers Matholuch and Manawyddan, to see that no lies come between our two islands ever again. Let us drink to that."

The sons of Llyr drank, and Matholuch drank, shining-eyed; thinking how one day his son would be king of the Island of the Mighty. Heir to all the wealth of Bran.

Many days the men of the two islands feasted together in peace and gladness, but at last the time came when the Irish made ready to sail.

The day before that sailing, Manawyddan went to see Branwen his sister. She and her women were packing. He said, "Send these girls away, Branwen."

She did, then looked up at him wonderingly. "What is on you, Manawyddan?"

He put his hands on her shoulders. He held those two slim shoulders as if they were very precious things.

"Yourself, girl. This is your time to feel, and I am going to try to make you think."

She smiled up at him. "About what, brother? I am doing what Bran and the Council want, and I am happy."

"Happy? Branwen, girl, are you sure of that?"

She said simply, "Not altogether. You know that I could not be, brother. It is hard to leave my kin and my home and my friends, but who can have all she wants? I love my man, as our mother loved our father."

"You will be going far. Out of sight and reach of us all, with a man whom three moons ago you had never seen. Penardim did too much for Llyr, but never that."

She winced, but her eyes were steady. "I know what is in your mind, brother. Because he went away and had to be brought back, you do not trust him. You are hurt and angry, for me, as he was hurt and angry for the sake of his horses—those beautiful horses! But I trust him; I know he loves me."

"No doubt he does. You are the fairest of women. And you, because he is a fine figure of a man, you think his heart must be as fine. But such loving passes; like fire, it burns high, then burns out. Desire will come and go as long as your two bodies are healthy, but friendship and respect must be there always if a man and woman are to live happily together through the long years. Think, girl, before you go with this man! Do you respect him now as you did before Bran had to buy him back for you?"

She shrank, she stared past him. Trying to see, not that night of cold and loneliness and hurt, but Matholuch, only Matholuch, still warm, still magnificent, still hers.

"What kind of friend is he, girl? You have heard, from his own mouth. Once, I think, he hoped to gain power and glory through the Children of Llassar, but he forsook them at his people's bidding, as once already he has forsaken you. Will you give him another chance to do that?"

But now the picture he was drawing seemed too callous, too unlike the man she knew. She raised her head.

"He is my man," she said. "You forgive a child for forgetting love when it is hurt and angry, and I have forgiven him."

"Your man—yet a child? He can hardly be both."

She laughed softly, assured again. "What man is not, sometimes? There are times when every man needs the mother in his woman, maybe when every woman needs the father in her man. The Gods did not give us Their own strength, brother."

"True enough, but those times had better not come too often. You cannot be Matholuch's mother."

Branwen suddenly dimpled. "I do not want to be. Can one ever gain much without risking much? If the first woman who burned her fingers had put fire out of her house forever, what would we be doing now? Eating our meat raw, like beasts."

"You blind yourself, girl."

Again her smile flashed into dimpled wickedness. "Did she leave so sour a taste in your mouth, brother— that beautiful Queen in the south, of whom I have heard tell?"

Manawyddan said shortly, "He—or more likely she—lies who says that Rhiannon of the Birds ever loved any man but Pwyll, Prince of Dyved."

"Then how did she get her son—she who was childless so long that Pwyll's folk turned against her and told him that if she did not bear a child within twelve more moons they would not let him keep her? And that same year you visited Dyved, my brother, and somehow Rhiannon got her boy. Nor have you ever looked long upon any woman since, although you say that such fires always burn out."

Manawyddan laughed impatiently. "Every man in Dyved will tell you that young Pryderi is the image of his father Pwyll."

"Will they? Those who wish to can see great family likenesses between any two faces that each hold one nose and two eyes and one mouth."

"You tease me to keep away thought, girl."

"You too do not think of everything, Manawyddan." She was serious again, a grave-eyed queen. "It is too late now to speak against Matholuch. Our parting would be a fresh insult to him, one that might breed war."

"It would be no insult, girl. Bran would have to give him some more gifts; that is all. You are not property to be given away like the Cauldron; none can blame you if at the last you feel you cannot bear to go so far from home. Here the Old Tribes still rule, and we are the mightiest of the Islands of the Mighty; no smaller isle will send an invading host against us."

Branwen said, "I cannot be happy without Matholuch."

Manawyddan's hands dropped. "Then may you be happy with him, little sister! None wishes that more than I."

With her Irishman Branwen sailed from Aber Menai. From the shore the sons of Llyr watched her go. The day was gray; the heavens brooded low, like vast, sad-colored wings, upon the earth. As long as she could see them Branwen looked back at her brothers; they looked at her until she shrank to the size of a child, dwindled to the size of a doll. At last only the ships were left, toy-sized, passing down into the gray maw of the mists. Distance, the witch that has power to make the greatest small, had swallowed them up.

The sons of Llyr went back to Harlech, and most of the way they were silent. Once Bran said heavily, "What will the girl look like, suckling her own baby? It seems only the day before yesterday that she herself was nursing at our mother's breast. I wish Ireland were nearer, or that we were not such busy men, and could go there oftener. Say what you are thinking, Manawyddan, I know well that you are thinking it: that I never should have let her go."

Manawyddan said, "I will not say it. She is gone now. But I too wish that Ireland were nearer. She said that the man was like a child. Well, every woman must keep in practice for motherhood, and she is wise as well as foolish. But it is a man's business to be a man."

5

The Blow

MATHOLUCH BROUGHT Branwen to Tara, and they were welcomed there with joy that blazed like fire, and was louder than song. The New Tribes were glad to see their King back in triumph, and the Old Tribes were glad because the new Queen was of their blood, and might make their lot easier. Branwen's beauty and treasures dazzled all; Bran had given her great wealth with which to win friends. The *Mabinogi* says that for a whole year not one chief or lady that visited her came away without a jewel of great price.

Then her son was born, Gwern the son of Matholuch. The King swelled with pride. His dreams were becoming flesh and blood. What an unheard of great kingdom might be built were both islands to become the boy's heritage!

Subtly and cautiously he began to work toward that end. He spoke to Amergin the High Druid, the oldest and wisest man in Ireland. But Amergin said, "No son has ever followed his father in Tara. Men of your tribe took it from the Priest-Kings of old, those God-chosen ones who were named when we druids sang a Spell of Truth over a sleeping man, and he in his dream beheld the King that was to be. But you New Tribes made Tara the prize of the strongest; he became king who killed the king. Until your uncle died in his bed, and you said that the Gods had taken him because it was time for you, his sister's son, to wear his crown. A good change, and one that fitted our ancient laws. It is soon to make another."

Matholuch smiled; he gave Amergin and all the druids great gifts. "Times change rapidly nowadays. Go read your stars; I think they will tell you that Gwern my son will be the best High King the Irish have ever had."

They went, but they came back grave-faced. Amergin said, "Evil will it be for Ireland, Lord, if your son is ever king. Evil that will be remembered to the end of life and time."

Matholuch paled. "Why? What will happen?"

For a breath's space Amergin hesitated, then he said, "Lord, why vex your heart with woes that need never come? No man is the better for black visions. Let your boy be reared here, learning to love Ireland and the Irish, then go home to be king in his uncle's land. So, and so only, will your marriage bear good fruit."

Wrath flamed in Matholuch's face. "Do the stars say that? Or is that your own word, old man?"

But the steady eyes of Amergin met his, and the King's eyes fell. Later he said to Branwen, "We must go slowly. In time these old men without vision will die off, and with them the grudges they nurse. Meantime I will be winning over the younger druids. You too must keep on giving gifts, Branwen."

"I will. But," her face was troubled, "what did the Lord Amergin read in the stars? He is old and wise."

He laughed shortly. "Druids' wisdom and your Ancient Harmonies! Both are old wives' tales, woman."

She winced and thought, His rearing speaks. The ways of the New Tribes. Not his own nature.

He went on. "In the end I will get my way. I have before. Unless," and he frowned "the people should get to know of the insult your brother Evnissyen put on me. That my war chiefs would never brook."

She winced again. "But they must know of that already. All your men knew, that sailed with you."

"The druids I had with me laid it upon them as *gessa* not to speak of it. Or of the Cauldron. Your brother made me a two-edged gift there, woman. What use is victory if one must be torn limb from limb by one's own victorious warriors when they can find no more foes to kill?"

"My brother paid you the best face-price he could, Lord. Not many kings would have given up that Cauldron."

"I know that, woman. I have never denied it."

But he did not laugh and kiss her as once he would have. He was used to her now, and no longer a great lover by day. But Gwern crowed and held up chubby hands to her, and Branwen cuddled him and was content. She knew that when night came his father would need and love her again.

He did. That night, and for many nights. She was watching herself for signs of another conception when Amergin died. Many wept, for Amergin had guided Erin long and well; he had been the last pillar of a golden age that was gone, the last shield of the Old Tribes. Mighty were his funeral games; mightier than would have been held for any other man save the King. And the night those games ended, one of the men who had sailed with Matholuch got drunk and talked. Maybe with the High Druid dead the ancient terrible bonds of *gessa* seemed less frightening, maybe too some of the lesser druids worked on him, fearing the King who had new ideas and wanted to open up new roads. Anyhow he did talk, and though the Gods may have attended to him thereafter, the men of Ireland attended to Matholuch.

All over the land a cry of rage went up. From every chief who had the blood of the New Tribes in his veins.

"Lord, you have reddened the face of all Ireland!"

"That outland King was spitting on you! You have let him send you home like a beaten pup, with a few pitiful bones in your mouth—you, the High King of Ireland! We are ashamed to hold our heads up."

"You should have got that Evnissyen's head, and you have not got even one ear off it!"

When the King went out in his chariot, refined people looked the other way, and the vulgar jeered and spat at him. The harassed man no longer had friends or kinsmen or subjects; he had only a swarm of maddened hornets. Or rather, they had him. They buzzed in his ears, and at last they buzzed inside his head. And always, underneath all, were the words that were never spoken, yet rang loudest in his ears: *Lord, you had not the courage to try to take the head of him that shamed you. Lord, you are a coward.*

Branwen was his only comfort. Her tender arms and white breast, her clear shining eyes and soft voice that still admired and praised him, a great man whose clear-headedness and farsightedness his people could not understand. When he came to her sore and humiliated he went away feeling noble; well puffed up again. He even tried using some of her arguments in the council chamber, but his councilors sneered at him.

"Lord, you have been lessoned by a woman. The Queen is bound to defend her own people, but honor leaves the man who is a woman's tool."

Matholuch began to wonder, *Is she speaking from her heart when she praises me? Which does she love more—me or the princes of the greater island of the Mighty?*

After that he sometimes spoke harshly to her, and seemed to blame her for his troubles. But at others his need made him cling to her. Branwen bore his tempers as she would have borne her child's had he been sick. She hoped that the storm would pass.

But it did not. It grew. In every breeze the people seemed to hear the laughter of the men of the greater island, mocking them whose King they had belittled. Any people can be worked up, or down, into a mob; and a mob must have something to tear. In the end they had an idea. It may have been hatched in the brain of some unworthy druid, cunning replacing the wisdom that had died with Amergin.

A deputation came to Matholuch; too many great men for the King's comfort. Some of them seemed to want to look the other way, but their spokesman faced him squarely.

"Lord, these are our terms. Take them or leave them."

Matholuch looked at them, and his face was stony and calm, as became a king. But his eyes were green and shifty, like the eyes of a cornered fox.

"What is it you ask?" he said.

"This, Lord. That you put away the woman you have with you, Branwen the daughter of Llyr, the sister of the King of the other Island of the Mighty."

There was a brief pause; the King moistened his lips. He said, "Very well. The woman is a good woman, yet her going is not too great a thing to grant to make my people happy. I love them more." He thought, *Branwen loves me. She will make a fuss about this, but what is one more fuss among so many? She will not make it to her brother; she will not want him coming after my head.*

Easy for her to say that she went home of her own accord, because she was homesick; to the Old Tribes that would seem natural enough.

The man answered, "Lord, we will not let her go. We have not got her brother, who reddened your face for you, and all Ireland's through you, but we have got her. This is what we will do." And they told him.

In her Sunny Chamber Branwen heard those terms before the King himself heard them. Her women watched her face hungrily while they told her, as a hawk watches chickens. With a consuming eagerness to pounce and pierce, and miss nothing that they could tell other people about afterward.

She laughed a little. She said, "You are dreaming."

They shook their heads, their eyes shining. "No. It is true. Lady, we grieve for you."

She knew that they did not. She knew well, now, how much friendship her gifts had bought her. For many long days these tale-bearers had been besieging her, telling her everything they heard and a good deal more, and trying to make her talk about it. That they had to make up nearly all the answers that they repeated to others as hers was perhaps a slight nuisance to them, and her one comfort. She was a queen bred in queenliness; she never had shown temper or fear.

But she was also young, and alone under many hostile eyes, and now at last she had to admit to herself that she was afraid. Not of these foolish threats, of course; Matholuch never would let anyone touch her. But what humiliation it must be for him to have to listen to such shameful proposals. That his men should dare! Never could such a thing have happened in her own Island of the Mighty.

This was her fear, one that made her heart beat so hard that she was afraid all these greedily watching women might hear it—what if Matholuch lost his temper with these traitors? What if they should hurt him?

She wondered; she became a flame and an intensity of wonder: how was he facing them? Easy, so easy, to picture how her brothers would have faced them: Bran with a great bellow that would have blown them all out of his presence, their hair standing on end; Manawyddan with a few cold words as quiet as steady, even rainfall, as crushing as hail. His voice would have been the coldest thing in the world, and it would have chilled them to the bone.

But how would Matholuch, her own man, face them? Carefully she locked and bolted the doors of her mind against any notion that he was less of a man than her brothers, but she was afraid. What if he should go mad and splutter? Then they would mock at him and humiliate him, and he had already been so much humiliated . . .

She rose. She could not keep still any longer. She said, "If the men have gone I will go to the King and ask him what they really did say. You have made me curious.

They smiled; they thought that she was afraid for herself. And so she left them, never dreaming that it was for the last time.

Silence greeted her in the corridors. As many silences as there were people, and as many qualities of silence, all weaving them-selves together into one great silence. Once someone tittered, but she turned and stared that mocker back into silence, her eyes the eyes of Llyr as long ago he had faced Eurosswydd in the Red Man's hall.

She came to the council chamber, she knocked on the door and waited for an answer. None came, and she opened it. Matholuch sat inside, very still. He did not move or look at her.

She stared at him and could not find him. His face was once again an obstacle, a painted, carved mask hung between him and her. So much familiar jut of nose, so much brightish beard below eyes that now were gray as faded, sunless water. Eyes that avoided hers, nose that jutted purposefully into nothingness, beard behind which his jaw had always lain hid.

She stared at him as though she would throw out all her soul through her eyes, to pierce the shield of that face and find the man hiding beneath it. And in that very hiding—not in any reaching of him that hid there—found at last her answer.

An answer that seemed to open the earth beneath her, to send her sliding down into a limitless gray abyss. So far down that her out-reaching hands never again could come at anything warm and human forever. And as she sank into that awful solitude memories mocked her, whirling shapes of what had been, voices crying for the last time as they vanished into nothingness, *"Branwen! Branwen, daughter of Llyr!"* Her girlhood in the Island of the Mighty, and all the tenderness and joy. All the pride in her, and all the hope that she, the strong and beautiful, might lie with heroes and bear the mighty ones of the earth.

This was the man she had loved, and allowed to father her child! This was her shame, and the shame of the Island of the Mighty! *But most of all your shame, your sorrow, Branwen, you who are alone.*

Matholuch stirred, and he looked uneasily at his feet and said, "Go away, Branwen. I will talk to you later."

He never meant to see her again. He did not want to face her. Clearly, in that last hour of their life together, she saw him and understood. It was not that he wished her ill. For a little while he would miss her—it would be hard to find as fair a woman for his bed. So little she mattered to him, or any other woman, save as they touched his comfort.

Her face turned red and then white again. She laughed, an awful laugh, like the sound of a heart breaking, and cried out at him.

"Oh, Matholuch of the Mouse's Heart, it is more shame to me to lie in a coward's bed than in his kitchen. That is my disgrace and my sorrow that there is no amending—that ever I should have lain with you!"

Matholuch sprang up and struck her in the face. Red came out on her cheek and delicate ear, but still she laughed.

That was the first blow that ever was struck Branwen, but it was very far from being the last.

They set her in the big, waist-high pit where the cooking was done. They set the huge cooking spit itself upon her shoulders, so that she had to bow beneath it, sweating in the heat of the flames. Every day for three years she, who had been Queen in Tara, toiled there in its kitchen, a drudge. And every day the butcher came and gave her a box on the ear; people came from far to see that, and to laugh.

"As her people have reddened the Goddess Ireland's face, so let her face be reddened!"

Quiet years those were outside the kitchen, quiet in both islands. The *Mabinogi* says that his men said to Matholuch, "Lord, forbid all ships to sail to the Island of the Mighty, and all folk that come from there, let them not go back again to make this thing known," and that the King obeyed them; once again the head of the dog had become its well-wagged tail. But it seems more likely that he sent false messages to her brothers in Branwen's name. So long a silence surely would have waked suspicion in the sons of Llyr.

6

Branwen and the Starling

IF BRANWEN had any consolations during those years we are not told of them. She had hard work to do, and that must have been the least of her torments, and her only salvation.

Eyes and hands and tongues jabbing at her like wasps; curiously, ceaselessly, greedily, with a vicious playfulness. There is always a bit of Evnissyen in every mob.

An outland woman alone among enraged and outraged this-landers; a Queen handed over to scullions crazed with excitement by the very height and depth of her fall, so that class took revenge upon class. The doom of the daughter of Llyr.

The women must have harassed her in many little ways. The men may have pawed and leered. She may have learned to sleep with the kitchen spit in her hand, perhaps with water boiling on the kitchen fire beside her; water that the women would spill on her if they could . . . Not good to look too long into abysses or to try to plumb their fetid depths.

Branwen set her teeth and bore all. Never should these outlanders see her weep. All that they could do she could endure and live through; never would she ask mercy. *They* would ask it—easy enough, when the time came, to shame them as they never had been able to shame her.

In all save one thing. One red scar, one fouling shame, of which she never could be free until she was rid of the soiled body that had betrayed her.

She had loved Matholuch; her flesh had responded to his flesh . . .

That was what sometimes, when her aching head rang with all the whirling, maddening noise of the great kitchen, almost broke her—hours once sweet that burned her memory now more than the butcher's hard palm could burn her skin. Times that made it seem not worthwhile to fight, to try to save anything so cheapened, so degraded as herself.

Do you want your kin and your friends and the whole Isle of the Mighty to know what you loved— how he loved you, the beautiful, the proud? It is not pleasant to be pitied when you have been proud. Here at least you are not pitied.

And she was not; that was very true.

Die and let the earth hide your shame. Help could not bring back happiness to you, only expose that shame.

She gritted her teeth and said to herself, I will not break. I am a princess of the Isle of the Mighty, and before I am that I am a person, and I will do the duty of both. There is my baby. I gave him the Mouse-heart for a father; I must not wrong him more. I must see to it that my blood rules in him, not theirs.

Time must have eased her lot a little. One grows used to anything, also her humiliation had gone on so long that it was no longer a show. People no longer came to the kitchen to watch and jeer, people who once would have been glad to boast of a word or a glance from her; and her fellow servants grew used to her being there. Since she did no spiteful acts herself, some even began to feel a secret, sneaking pity for her.

Once, as they worked together, a woman whispered, "Your boy is in fosterage among the best men of Ireland." She named the place. "They make much of him there. The King and his Council still hope to get good from your people through him."

That was the one bright day in all those long dark years. But Branwen could not even whisper back her thanks. She saw the head steward watching them, her implacable foe, and had to stare coldly and turn her back. The woman either did not understand or understood too well and was afraid; she offered no more kindnesses. She finally rejoined the ranks of Branwen's tormentors.

Days and weeks, and moons and years. Lying down each night exhausted and waking each morning to know that the butcher would come, and that somebody would laugh.

Once when all were sleeping she rose and went out into the night. The wind was cool on her bruised face. The moon was full, and she looked at it, wondering at the vast peace of the cloudy sky. She bathed her soul in the stillness, that after the daylong torture in the hot, noisy kitchen was sweeter to her than music.

In the eaves of the palace there was a starlings' nest; now a faint cry came from below it. A small cry, a bird's cry, but it shattered the stillness. Pain was back in the world again. Branwen moved toward it. She thought, *Maybe this once I can turn aside the whip.*

She found a fledgling fluttering and crying, and the cat watching it, green-eyed. Blood showed, where already the cat had pounced once.

Ordinarily the cat and Branwen were good friends; it was the one inmate of the kitchen that never had mocked or hurt her. Often she had fed and stroked it on the sly, afraid that if she were seen to fondle the beast it would be made to suffer. But she had no mind to let her friend have this living meal. She snatched up the fledgling and carried it back to the kitchen, where she got water to bathe the wound, that was not deep. The cat came after her and mewed plaintively, rubbing against her legs, unable to understand her unkindness, but she paid no heed. She put the bird in the hollow of her kneading trough, and tended it there, a dark little puff of down with red blood running down one half-feathered wing.

She said, when the wound was staunched, "I have done all I can. You must live or die now, as the Mothers will." And she carried it back, but the nest was too high for her to reach. Then, harder than the butcher's palm, a thought smote her, sharp and dazzling as lightning in the black night.

Lightning indeed, cleaving long night . . .

The starlings that Penardim our mother used to keep! How we used to love to teach them to talk, and we little! It is a sign. It is the road— my road! My chance, at last.

She carried the small starling back to the kneading trough, and she gave the cat cream, reckless for once as to whether it would be missed or not. "You have served me," she whispered into those furry ears, "served me well, whether you meant to or not, and it has been long since anyone did that."

In the morning the butcher was there to strike her again before the grinning servants, though fewer may have sniggered than at first. The sight was an old story now.

But now she had a refuge—something to do besides bracing herself against the trough and making a blank of her face.

She had hope. There in the trough she had wings, and they would grow and strengthen until they grew great enough to fly across the sea to the Island of the Mighty.

She had a tongue beside her tongue, and in the end it would pierce her enemies like a spear.

She was a smith, and that tongue was the sword she was forging. She was a poet, and it was her pupil.

She became as wily as a serpent, as persistent as death. She worked slowly, for sureness, for safety. They must never suspect, never guess what she was about, there in the kitchen of Matholuch.

At night she trained the bird, whispering softly into its feathers while others slept. Sometimes she took it out into the darkness, where she could speak louder and it, too, could learn how to pitch its voice and articulate clearly in the alien tongue of men.

She packed it with words, and she packed it with food, that turned into strength and size and muscle, into the strength for rising immense distances, for flight . . .

It thrived, there in the kneading trough. It forgot the nest and knew only her. Sometimes it would reach up and peck her fingers caressingly, then take a bite or two of dough before settling back again into the hollow.

We do not know how she kept it from speaking in the daytime, or how she taught it where it must go. In those days when the subtle senses were not yet lost, when the walls between the worlds were not yet so firm but that outlaws like Llassar and his wife could flee from one to the other, and thicken and harden into earth's denser mold, understanding may have been easier between men and birds.

Nor do we know the full powers of her royal druid line . . ."

The *Mabinogi* says she taught it what kind of man Bran her brother was, so she must have been able to make pictures pass from her mind to that small mind.

Summer came; sap flowed like holy blood, quickening the veins of earth. The trees were full of life, green life and singing life, the sky smiled, and the starling grew restless. Branwen saw that she was old enough to fly.

The discovery was delight, and it was terror. It was an end . . .

She had had hope, she had had suspense, she had had an end to work toward. Now she would still have hope and a far greater suspense, but again she would wait helpless, with bound hands.

How long—how long, O Mothers—before she can reach Bran? And then how long—how long—before Bran can come? Wait—and wait— and wait—and then perhaps he will never come. A hawk may take the starling, or storms drown her in the sea, or she may forget all and follow a lover, as once you followed one, Branwen, daughter of Llyr!

All one night she crouched under the stars, the starling against her breast. She talked to it, she muttered charms that later men would call mesmeric. She poured power out of herself, she could feel mind and will flowing out of her like blood, into that little feathered shape.

Dawn came. Age seized upon the night, all her years came at once upon that proud sweet darkness, and upon the world. Her black hair turned gray, trailed its dead wan ghastliness upon the earth. The east whitened, then began to bleed, like a woman's smitten face.

Branwen rose. One last time she repeated her speech to the bird. One last time it repeated her words to her.

She held up her hands to the east, the bird in them, she kissed its head, and threw it into the air. It sped away like an arrow, straight toward the Island of the Mighty.

Branwen looked after it, then suddenly burst into tears. "O my bird, it is long and hard, the journey that is before you! I never should have let you go!"

She had sent away the one friend of her loneliness; she had won its love, then used it as a tool.

And that was the first time in more than three years that Branwen, daughter of Llyr, had wept.

Long and lonely was the bird's flight. She was young, and she never had flown far before. She saw strange fields green beneath her, and she saw the different, grayer green of the Irish Sea, stirring constantly and softly, like a great snake. She feared that bleak vastness, she who never had seen more water than that in the horse trough, or in a puddle at the kitchen door.

She flew on.

She flew until she was so tired that it seemed she must drop into the sea, until her wings were heavy as stones and her eyes began to make their own night.

Then a wind blew in her face, a warm wind, sweet with the scent of green, succulent growing things. The good smell of earth again, and trees, trees on which a tired bird could perch. She was hungry and worn out, and she smelled food and rest.

But the wind beat her back, it blew her this way and that. She had to fight against it, beating her tired wings against the shining air.

Cliffs rose out of the sea, gray and stark, and again her heart rose. Solidness to perch on. Blessed rest, blessed freedom from upholding the weary weight of oneself . . .

Then she saw great birds, far bigger than herself, wheeling and circling round those cliffs. Their screams smote her ears like the very voice of death.

One had seen her and was speeding toward her, his long neck outstretched, his black eyes glinting, his beak shining, greedy, cruel as death. With a scream of her own she turned and fled seaward again, back toward the death of weariness, the drop into the cold gaping waters that at least would have no beak to tear one with, no fierce greedy eyes to gloat while that beak tore one's flesh.

But she was tired, too tired. And the gull was swift. It headed her off; she saw another coming, hovering there above the sea.

She turned back and dived lower, in one last frantic burst of speed, looking madly for some crevice in the cliffs to hide in, some little place where no bird of prey might follow.

She found none.

But she saw something else—a boat below her, piled with fish, such as sometimes they brought into the kitchen at home for Branwen to cook. Two men were on it. She dropped, plummet-like, on the far side of that pile of fish, away from the men.

The gull swooped after her. But the men thought it was after the fish and shouted, and one waved a coat at it while the other snatched up a piece of wood to throw.

The gull rose and flew away.

They did not see her, hiding among the fish. She crouched there and shivered, exhausted; her heart beat like a hammer, as if it were trying to smash through her breast.

The boat came to shore. In a quiet, green place in the cliff walls, where there were no gulls. Her heart had steadied somewhat; she set herself, rose and was off through the air in a magnificent, painful burst of speed. She heard a voice call out behind her, but no stone whizzed through the air.

She reached the shore. She flew on, straight as a cast spear, a miserable and frightened and gallant little spear, looking for trees. She found them finally; what bliss it was to feel their green, blessed shade close her! Her feet closed upon a branch, and so upon heaven; her tired wings rested, furled at last . . .

She woke; she ate and attended to her feathers. Sleep came once more, like a great, dark, soft wing . . .

She woke again, and remembered Branwen.

She flew on, over this strange island in which she had not been hatched, looking for the man who was not to be feared because he was kind to all things, the man whose image Branwen had made her see.

The *Mabinogi* says that Bran was at Caer Seiont, in Arvon, and by that it probably means Caer Seon, later to be the lordship of Gwydion the Golden-Tongued, Gwydion the son of Don. Then it must have belonged to Mâth the Ancient, that great king who was so mighty a man of illusion and fantasy that only two men born ever can have equalled him: Gwydion, his own nephew and pupil, and that

far-famed Merlin who in a later age was to make Arthur king of
Britain. Most likely it was in counsel, not in goods, that Mâth paid
tribute to Bran the High King.

Bran must have been sitting in front of Caer Seon, for he could
not have got inside it, and there must have been other men with him.

The starling saw him, and she saw them.

She wanted to go to him at once, but she was afraid; one of those
other men might be a stone-thrower. She had learned fear too well,
in this vast, windy world outside the kitchen, to take many chances.

She perched upon the nearest tree: she found a bug and ate it.
She waited, brown eyes fixed on Bran.

If only those other men would go away . . . !

They did not, and the day wore. The blue faded from the sky; the
sun slanted downward, fire-red, in the bloody west.

*Night is coming, and I will get sleepy. I must get to him, and make
the noises she taught me. Before I am too sleepy to remember.*

With a wild cry of fear at her own daring, she sailed through the
air; made her landing in the only place where it seemed likely that
she could keep her footing if he tried to shake her off. Among the
stuff that was like thick, queer-colored grass on top of his great head.

A man or two cried out, but Mâth the Ancient lifted his hand; the
hand that had such mysterious might.

"There is meaning in this," he said.

"There is something in it," said Bran. "I am taller than other men,
but it is not usual for birds to come and sit on me."

He reached up gently, and the bird recognized that gentleness.
She let his great hand close upon her and lift her down. He held her
so that their eyes met.

"Little one," he said, "I am not a tree. It may be that you thought
so and have made a mistake. Or again it may be that you have a good
reason for coming to perch on me?"

He may have thought her no true bird, but a man or woman
bewitched.

What Mâth the Ancient thought no man knew. He stared into the
bloodstained golden west, and in his face was the sadness of a god;
of one who beholds an oncoming darkness vaster than night, far
more terrible than night . . .

Bran looked at the bird, and the bird looked at Bran. Her beak
opened; from it came a squeaky echo of Branwen's voice of beauty.
"Bran—Bran son of Llyr—greetings from Branwen, daughter of Llyr..

That night found Bran already on his way back to Harlech, and
signal fires blazing from the hills, like fallen stars.

7

The Hosting of the Island of the Mighty

BEFORE THE folk of fourscore and seven counties Bran told what Branwen suffered; and from side to side of the great rock his voice rolled as though the thunder had forsaken the clouds of heaven to find an earthly home and issuing place in his breast.

The people heard; their whole beings quivered like the strings of smitten harps. A red cloud, too fine for any but druid sight, covered Harlech; the airy beings, the Elementals that feed on blood, hovered in it, sniffing hopefully at those fumes of dark promise.

Ireland! Ireland! That was the name gabbled on all tongues, cried in all hearts. As a pack of starving dogs hungers for meat, they hungered to get there. *Ireland! . . . Ireland . . . Branwen! Branwen, daughter of Llyr!*

As wind fans flames, so Bran and Manawyddan fanned that blaze. They themselves were burning; for them there could be no rest until their bodies should be in Ireland with Branwen, where their minds already hovered, impotent, fleshless shades.

So ended the Golden Age of the Island of the Mighty, the peace of Bran the Blessed.

That night in council it was decided how many men should go with the High-King into Ireland, and how many should stay at home. No doubt the strongest and bravest went with Bran, those with the finest bodies and often the finest minds. In war the first-goers are always the fittest fathers of the future, perhaps not only of men, but also of poetry and thought. Our world might have been darker had Homer not been blind.

Another decision was made in that council, and in the morning it was proclaimed before the people.

Seven chiefs were named to hold the Island of the Mighty in the absence of her King. And the seventh and chief over the other six, for all his youth, was Caradoc, son of Bran.

The naming of that name made silence; silence deep as that at the bottom of a well.

A light kindled on many faces among the New Tribes. *Bran never would do this if he did not want Caradoc to be King after him. The Isle is turning from its old ways. To ours!*

The Old Tribes stood mute, dazed as men might be who, while sitting quietly at home, suddenly see and hear a great wind wrench away a wall or a ceiling.

Eyes moved with an incredible, covert activity. Eyes that were questions, eyes that were hopes and fears and suspicions. Eyes that held merely blank bewilderment.

A man with a rich uncle thought, *If Caradoc can be King after Bran, will I get my uncle's fields when he dies? Or will Kilydd and Kai get them, Kilydd and Kai that are probably his sons?*

A man with a rich father thought, *Will I be able to get Glelwyd's lands after him—and laugh at those sniggering sons of his sister, that think they will be so much richer than I?*

Doors opening everywhere, upon unheard of vistas, doors slamming shut upon the old and the safe and the known . . .

Many tried to think that surely Bran did not mean to make so great a change, that things would settle back into their old shape and be the same when he came home from Ireland. But the heart of every man who wished to inherit from his uncle grew cold within him, and the blood of every son who would have liked to inherit from his father quickened and grew hot in his veins.

But the sons of Beli stood like an island within an island, no light on their faces, their eyes dull as storm clouds. Only the eyes of Caswallon, eldest and ablest of them, began to smolder . . .

Young Pryderi of Dyved laughed and clapped Caradoc on the shoulder. "A good choice, son of Bran the Blessed, and may his blessedness be with you!"

He was the first to break that silence, and his word was the word of a chief.

All applauded then; Bran the King had spoken, and his will would be done. The Old Tribes, who alone might have wished to oppose him, had no other leader. Besides, they were divided against themselves, nephews and sons.

Only Manawyddan, son of Llyr, kept silence, and Mâth the Much-Born, the son of Mathonwy.

That decision truly had been reached earlier, while the King was waiting for his people to come in. Only the four sons of dark Penardim had been there, and Mâth the Ancient.

Bran had unfolded his plan, and Evnissyen had leaned forward, his face twisted with savage glee.

"That is good to hear. Never then will the Island of the Mighty come under the foul spawn of that outland dog!"

"Be still," said Manawyddan, "you who dug the pit they have put our sister into. And do not misname her son."

"He is the seed of Matholuch. A shame to her, and a danger to us! And did I make Matholuch a coward and a traitor? Is his baseness my doing?"

"We have no right to speak before our elders, brother," said Nissyen. "We who are the youngest here."

Manawyddan looked at him. "And what would you say, brother Nissyen?"

Nissyen said softly, "Sorrow and sorrow and sorrow. For Evnissyen's insult that brought her to this, and for hers that takes us to her in Ireland."

"You mean that now we are insulted as the men of Ireland were insulted, so that to go in wrath is only to keep the Wheel turning? I know that. I know that soon even our own men will be thinking less of her than of Irish heads on a pole. But Branwen is there: what else can we do?"

"Nothing," said Nissyen. "Nothing now."

Evnissyen showed his teeth at him in an evil snarling smile. "This is once when you will not be able to make peace—milk-drinker! And do not tell me again to be silent! Your time for speech is past, and you never did deeds. You are only a cloak over nothing. A wind would blow you away."

"It is I who bade you be silent," said Manawyddan, and though his voice was not loud, Evnissyen suddenly became still. Manawyddan looked at Bran. "I will not say again what I have said before, brother. How will Beli's sons take this? And Branwen herself, when we set her free? She has borne enough sorrow without your disinheriting her son. She bears it still."

He ceased, and in the silence all her brothers could hear the slap of the butcher's hand against Branwen's cheek. Remembered that it was not long until morning . . .

Bran said heavily, "You are always telling me to remember the good of the people, Manawyddan. And I have remembered. Branwen's son is the son of Matholuch, and can I trust the Island of the Mighty to the seed of a traitor? Of the man who has dealt with her as he has dealt with her?" His great hands clenched on the rock beneath him, so that a little of it crumbled in his fingers.

"The Mothers bear me witness, brother, that I wish the little boy all good—he is her son, and I am ready to love him for her sake-but to give him the Island of the Mighty is daring much. You may say, 'Wait and try him,' but how can we ever be sure? His father is fair and false. And I shall have Ireland to leave him—the land he was born in."

For what seemed a long time Manawyddan sat silent. Far below the gulls cried, and somewhere among the tents a sleeping man cried out, in the grip of evil dreams.

"There is some right with you, my brother," he said at last, "and that makes you more wrong. Your wrath against Matholuch is strong, and weds a new excuse to your old desire. Would that the veil of the Mothers still held, and that we men had never learned that we could father sons! I see that Mâth here is right in trying to keep that knowledge out of Gwynedd as long as he can. Without it you would see only Branwen in her baby, and we should still have peace to come home to."

"Matholuch would still be in him," said Bran.

"That is true, too," said Manawyddan, and sighed. "But there is good and evil in every man. All men must clean the evil out of themselves, no matter how many lives it takes. So the druids teach, and so we believe. And I think, brother, that we could teach any son of Branwen's, conceived while she loved the father, to manifest the good in himself oftener than the bad."

"The Island of the Mighty is a great trust," said Bran.

"Is that why you will bring a new kind of war upon it? One that will only be beginning when we come home? Those of us who do come home . . ."

Bran looked toward Mâth. "What is your word, son of great Mathonwy? Are you with my brother, Manawyddan, son of Llyr, or with me? You have lived longer than either of us; long before we were born men called you wise.

Mâth raised his eyes then, those gray eyes that seemed infinite as the stream of time itself, upon which floats all that has been and all that is. So vast his vision seemed, and so different were his eyes from the eyes of common men. Their greatness was equalled only by their sadness, the sadness of the farseeing.

"Does it matter," he said at last, "what my counsel is? For the old calm world of which we are the pillars is breaking, and a new world shaping. Old days and old ways are passing. Here is an end. For awhile longer I shall keep the peace in Gwynedd, but he that comes after me shall break it. For even Gwynedd that I have tried to keep remote from the turmoil of men is bread baking in the oven of the fates—already the stuff strains against me and tries to rise and escape from the shape into which I would knead it.

"And that is part of the Great Going-Forward. There can be no stopping; the world grows as a child grows, and no man is ever full-grown. He dies when the time comes for him to grow somewhere else.

"We have been guardians of earth's babyhood, kings who were fathers of the people, and the world would be happier if we could remain the only fathers. But now mankind must grow up, and each man find and train the King within himself. That is as it should be. To depend upon a leader is to fail to develop one's own strength or to strive for clear vision. He that fights must lead or obey a leader; only he that is strong enough to stand alone can stay at peace."

Bran leaned forward eagerly. "Then change is good in the end? If it brings evil for a time, that is only like a woman's birth pangs?"

"If it comes too fast it can bring long evil," said Math, "evil that will outlast all the birth pangs ever borne."

"You think that I bring it too fast?"

"If I said so, would you turn from the path on which your heart drives you? The path that maybe is destiny? Already, too, it may be too late to turn back. You have sent your sister away, you have lit the signal fires upon the hills."

Bran's great hands clenched again. "The Mothers know that if I could undo what I have done I never would let Branwen go from us! But the signal fires upon the hills," and his voice was as the deep growl of a lion sunk in this throat, "them I would light again! Men, they hold her there, bearing such shame and misery as among the Old Tribes never was inflicted upon any woman, queen or serf . . . Branwen! Our Branwen!" And he turned away his face.

Maybe Mâth thought of dark-eyed Don, his own sister, back at Caer Seon. He said gently, "True. The evil stinks to heaven. Yet Manawyddan and Nissyen and I could have gone into Ireland secretly and freed her. Against my Illusion no Irishman but Amergin could have fought, and had he lived this black folly never would have been. Your sister would still lie in Matholuch's bed."

Evnissyen gasped with fury that broke all bonds. "You would take no revenge? *Bear* the insult?"

Manawyddan and Bran stared at him in wonder. Only in Nissyen's eyes was there understanding; he smiled faintly, with quiet sadness.

"Many women of the Island of the Mighty must weep now, for sons and brothers and lovers. Is Branwen's reddened face worth that?" Mâth's voice was as calm as ever.

"All the peoples of the mainland would laugh at us, hearing that I let my sister be used like a dog."

"Can strength never afford to be laughed at? You fight the New Tribes with their own weapons. Already you have forgotten ours."

"War is evil," said Manawyddan, "but this one has been forced upon us. You yourself have fought, Math, when Gwynedd was invaded."

"And will again. Yet war itself, not any race or tribe, is the enemy that shall pull down all that we of the Old Tribes have built. Among us neither man nor woman was ever master; all walked free. Women created property; they brought houses and tilled fields into being, because they needed shelter in which to rear their children, and food that would not fail when the day's hunting or fishing failed. They could leave little to chance, unlike man the free, the roaming hunter. So ownership, one of her children, has always descended through the line of the woman. And for long she ruled the folk she gathered together."

Bran and Manawyddan looked at each other, and nodded. In Ireland itself, the triumphant New Tribes never had been able to blot out the memory that Tara and all the other great Irish strongholds had been founded by women.

Mâth went on. "But war came—for new peoples came, and it will always be the instinct of the hungry to take from those who have food. And men made better war chiefs, better defenders. A war leader with a heavy child in her belly is not much good.

"Yet woman, though she ceased to be a king* and man protected her, was still reverenced as the source of life. Only now when man is learning that she cannot give life without him does he begin to scorn her whom he protects. So she that created property will become property.

"So it is already in the Eastern World, so it will be here. And out of that constant injustice will rise continually more evils to breed wars and fresh injustice until men forget that there was ever a world at peace. When humankind lets one half of humankind be enslaved it will be long and long, even when that slavery wanes, before free-

---

*See Rhys, *Celtic Folklore*, p. 661, for probability that the Celtic title generally rendered "king" was once applicable to either sex. Also Macalister's *Tara* for Irish foundation legends.

dom is respected and nation ceases to tear nation; before the world unlearns the habit of force."

He ceased, and great Bran drew a deep breath.

"If I can prevent that, nothing else matters. Tell me what to do, wise son of Mathonwy, and I will do it."

"I can make no promises," said Math. "Already the evil is conceived, and the world labors toward the misbegotten birth."

Bran looked at him and past him, and into the gray mists that overhung the sea. Dawn was coming, the pale sickly dawn of a day that would bring no happiness. In that paling darkness that was not light they all looked into each other's faces and found no help; only wan, featureless masks.

Bran sighed. "It is not good that you see before the world, son of Mathonwy. It is a bitter thing to know that all this will come upon the folk, and that they must go backward instead of forward. Or at least go forward by a very roundabout way.

"Yet you that see so much—dare I ask you what you see for Branwen my sister? And for Caradoc my son?"

Again Mâth looked at him with those gray eyes that now seemed to unite in one the whole trinity of time—past, present and to be.

"I cannot see so clearly as that, son of Llyr. I can hear the cries of many that will be slain, and smell the blood that is not yet shed, but that is the fate of the many. For the few, those that I myself know, my heart blinds my druid sight."

Evnissyen laughed. "Well, that is one thing to be thankful for, Lord of Gwynedd. It is the first cheerful thing you have said."

Mâth turned his eyes upon him. "Even energy that has been turned to pure evil has its part in the pattern," he said. "But I think that only gods could bear to look at that pattern. It is well that men cannot."

That was the morning when young Pryderi of the South came in with the men of Dyved. Joyfully he came, his white teeth shining in a fighting grin beneath his jewel-blue eyes and golden hair, his nose sniffing the air like a young, high-hearted hound's, eager for the chase.

"Greetings, Lords!" He came bounding up to the sons of Llyr. "Good be with you! And with the Lady, your sister. We will take off an Irish head for every blow that they have dealt her, and then we will open up that King Mouse-heart to see what queer kinds of insides he has got. Though by the Gods of both islands, I think somebody must have been beforehand with us and taken out his guts."

Then he saw by their faces how deep this went, beyond all grimness and all mockery, and his own face sobered, like a merry child's that suddenly feels pity.

"Indeed, and there would be no laughter with me either if the woman were Kigva, Gloyu Broad Realm's grandchild. Not until I had washed my hands in blood. I am sorry."

Bran smiled. "That lady has come to your house to sleep with you, has she not?"

"Three moons ago," said Pryderi proudly. "My mourning time for my father is over and I am king now, so I thought it was time I got my woman. And indeed, since I got Kigva," here his eyes danced, and a dimple in the left side of his grin danced with them, "I have wished for nothing except that I had got her sooner. It is a pity to have wasted so much time."

Bran chuckled. "Well, I see now that we owe you even more thanks than I thought for having come so soon."

Pryderi tossed his yellow head. "I am not wont to be slow on my way to battle, and if I had been this time it is not in the arms of that redhead that I would be lying. More likely the toe of her boot would be helping me forward."

"The women of her kin are warriors, are they not?" said Manawyddan. "Witch-priestesses of the tribes who dwell beside the Severn?" He thought, *I hope that Kigva has not got their temper; it would make her an ill housemate for Rhiannon of the Birds.*

"That is true, king's brother. I do not think any man ever lost his head over any of Kigva's aunts except when she took it off his shoulders." He grinned. "Nine of them, all old witches, and not a one but has a face that would scare a man away, even in the middle of the night. It is from the other side of the family that Kigva gets her looks. If her aunts could do her kind of witching, maybe they would not have taken up head-slicing."

Their ugliness may have been one reason why the Nine had become warriors, yet there must have been another. To keep the lands and the freedom that had been their foremothers' and that peaceful priestesses could hold no longer, they had taken war, their enemy, for their servant; and he had become their master. Was transforming, through them, even the face that their Goddess showed upon earth; so many are the traps set by change, the inexorable.

But what made them as they were Pryderi never stopped to think. Indeed, he seldom seems to have stopped to think, which is a little surprising, considering the blood that was probably in him. Perhaps he was too m love with life, too busy enjoying every breath of it, to stop for anything but sleep.

So at least, in the days that followed, Manawyddan read him. He loved to watch that zest, that young eager strength. Yet sometimes thought, never far from him, would come and lay a cold hand on his shoulder.

Risks enough at best, even for the young and swift and bold. But if Matholuch should use the Cauldron . . .

That would mean war such as the world had never seen. Extermination for the men of both islands, and the earth covered with savage speechless demons.

No man would risk that. Yet when panic drives a coward . . .

Manawyddan may have been glad that he had little time to think.

Like ants driven from their hills, men milled in that camp below Harlech. Ships were being built, weapons smithied. All eyes turned toward the sea, toward that gray road of waters that led to their goal.

Soon we shall be there! Soon we shall teach them! It is their whole heads we will have for a face-price, those dogs.

Many were grimly happy. Evnissyen was happiest of all. He thought proudly, *This is all my doing. Except for me there would still be peace. Bran would still be fooled.*

He could have hugged himself for joy in his own cleverness, pride in his own farsightedness. He never had been fooled by the out-landers' smooth, lying tongues.

Some men shared his own view of his shrewdness; for the first time he had a following. Foremost among his new admirers were Keli and Kueli, those sons whom Kymideu Kymeinvoll had borne within her womb when she broke out of the Iron House. Save for the ugly fire-red mark that twisted one side of his face no man could have told Keli from Kueli, and in their hatred of the Irish both burned with one flame.

"Our parents and our brothers trusted in their promises; in peace and in friendship they went into the Iron House. We know them, those outlanders who burned our brothers." Keli's eyes burned hot-ter than the brand upon his face.

"You can trust no promise they give, no oath they take. Every man, woman and child of that blood should die. Else all will be to do over again." That was Kueli, his eyes as fierce.

"So long as one of them walks the earth treachery will be breed-ing. No man of another race can walk without fear of a knife in his back, no child rest safe in its mother's arms or womb." Keli's blazing eyes had widened; his voice had risen to a grim chant.

They praised Evnissyen's discernment until he purred like a cat. He drank in every word; both their praise and their savagery went to his head like wine.

8

The Sinking Lands

THE REASON why so many ships had to be built was that they were not ships at all, but rafts and canoes, such as could sail in shallow water. Sails they had, but little else of true ships. The fleet could not take its natural road through the deep, because Bran was too big to get aboard a ship.

He might not have been able to get to Ireland at all had it not been for the Sinking Lands.

Many of them were gone already, those "lost lands" of Wales. The sea covered the tall forest that once had made the shores of Carnarvon one with those of Anglesey,* that sunken forest in which, in later ages, have been found not only the bones of the great bear and the red deer, but also those of oxen, the ancient servants of men.

The lands between Anglesey and the shores to the south were sinking, but not yet sunken. Trees still rose here and there through their muddy waters, giants defying the flood that had doomed them; fish swam through their lower branches and seaweed grew thick and rank where once fields had waved their plumes of golden gram. No beasts were there, and no birds but the white screaming gulls. All that water was salt, and no land thing could live in those lands, but left them to their lonely death. Like the Corpse God's own dominion they stretched there, a waste of sullen dirty waters.

Bran would have to walk through them, and his men dreaded that. But he laughed at their fears.

"Most of the time my chin will be above water, and when it is not I can swim."

*Sir William Boyd Dawkins.

"It is an unpleasant walk you will have," said Pryderi. "I would hate to wade through all that mud." He looked at it and shuddered; for once his gaiety was quenched.

"Maybe," said Bran, "but Branwen is having to bear far worse things than getting her feet wet."

"That is true," said Manawyddan, and pain crossed his face like a black wing.

"But do you be careful," he added. "You cannot see your footing through the darkness of these waters, and the ground is treacherous. If you sink, we in the ships will come close and try to pull you out, but I cannot say what will happen."

"I can." Bran smiled his big, good-natured smile that was the widest in the world. "The ships will overturn, and you will all get a mud bath."

"So long as that is the worst of it," said Manawyddan.

Frowning, he looked out across that hostile waste, that wilderness where the peace of death had not yet come, but only the ugliness and pain of a huge, once fruitful body in its death throes, hating to give up the warmth and goodness of the past. And he thought, *With how many of us will that be so before we come this way again? . . . Well, death too is a part of the Great Going-Forward.*

Naked, Bran waded down into the Sinking Lands, save for the ropes that Manawyddan insisted should be put upon him. They bound him to the ships that kept as near him as they could, and he walked as close as he could to the boundary of the Sinking Lands, to the edge of the true sea. But in that too was danger. It brought him nearer to treacherous drops, to the edges of unseen cliffs.

Sometimes there was firm ground beneath his feet, and sometimes the squashy softness of wet sand, and over that he went as quickly and lightly as he could. Bran could run lightly, for all his bulk.

Again he felt hard rock under his feet, and there he went slow and carefully, guarding against a fall from unseen heights. And then again the thick mud squashed and belched under him, like some monster of the Underworld spitting under his heel; and he put on fresh speed because that mud sucked at him like lips, it pulled at the sinews of his mighty legs with might that made even him atom-small, with the strength of forces that dwell forever in darkness and have no gift or power but destruction.

Then he fell and, like arms, that sucking death closed round and over him, like jaws whose teeth were the more terrible for their softness, annihilation blacker than night.

But out of those clinging depths great Bran surged up, fighting, writhing, every muscle pulling, with heart-tearing effort, against that black, enveloping embrace, every toe groping, like a separate being, for foothold, solidity, safety. Yet remembering, even in his agony, as the harpooned mother whale remembers not to let her threshing flukes strike her young in her death throes, so Bran remembered not to pull upon those ropes that bound him to the frail barques that bore his men.

Then the groping toes of one threshing foot found and lost what they sought; brushed, for a breath's space, solidity. Fiercely he scrabbled back—thought it lost—found it again. His toes closed; through the clutching mud the other foot fought its way forward. With set teeth, his mouth and nose filled with muddy death, he braced himself for one last tremendous effort; the force of it seemed to snap his straining muscles, to split his whole being.

His head broke water. Above him he heard the shouts of frightened men. His mud-plastered eyes would not open, yet freed from that depth and extremity of darkness, their own smeared, blackened lids seemed like very light, clear and bright as the sky that once more looked down upon him.

He staggered on, and Nissyen, the lightest of his brothers, swam out to him and bathed his face, and brought him wine to drink.

He laughed then, looking up at the sun that he never had thought to see again; and from the ships his men applauded, and Manawyddan, still white and unsmiling, drew a deep breath of relief.

Beside him, Pryderi laughed. "It would take more than mud to kill Bran the Blessed!"

But for once Manawyddan spoke sternly to the young King of Dyved. "Be still, boy! You have seen a victory greater than any that ever will be won in Ireland, and one that was dearly bought."

Yet in truth no man had seen it, that battle fought in the darkness underwater, in the deeper darkness of that corrupted and envenomed earth, against that death like a mountain-huge, devouring tongue. Alone and unseen Bran had fought it and won it, and that no other man ever born could have done.

He plodded on, and the day wore. Sunset came. The pale shores of the Island of the Mighty had sunk into the gray arms of distance, and the white cliffs had darkened. The sky flamed like a mighty funeral pyre.

From the shores they had left, those ships looked small now, such toys as a child may launch on still pools or small streams while nurse or mother keeps guard. Bran's great figure, plodding through that treacherous waste, had shrunk to the size of a common man; had

looked little and lost and wholly human, there in the vast graying
loneliness.

It had dwindled to doll's size; then vanished altogether.

From the heights of those forsaken cliffs four men had watched
it as long as they could: the sons of Beli.

When they could no longer see anything but the sails of the ships,
Caswallon stirred. "I wonder what happened that time he fell. He
was so slow in getting up that for a breath's space I wondered—but
the blessing is still with him."

Lludd his brother sighed. "He will get to Ireland. Some of us
should have gone with him. In my heart I knew that always. I hope
he gets Branwen back safely. They say those Irish prize no trophy so
much as a woman's head upon a pole."

"Because of the trouble the women of the Old Tribes gave them;
they fought hard for the old ways." Caswallon shrugged. "Also it was
Bran who sent her to Ireland, not we. And he cheated when he did,
for he knew well that the Irish wanted her so that presently an Irish-
born man might sit upon the throne of Beli. And all the time he
meant that seat for Caradoc."

"Then his was the first wrong!" young Eveyd cried eagerly; he was
the fourth brother. But Lludd and Llevelys, his elders, were silent,
and presently Caswallon turned and looked at Lludd.

"You are the first-born," he said. "If you wish to claim your right I
will support you."

Lludd looked back at him. "What right, Caswallon? The word has
two meanings. Bran has been a good lord to the Island of the Mighty,
and it is not I that will tear it, like a dog fighting over a bone, if
Caradoc should reign after him. He would be a murderer that broke
the peace and shed blood so, all for his own profit. While the land is
happy, under Bran or Caradoc or another, disturb it not!"

"Why should that whelp of Bran's sit in the high seat after him, if
we could not sit there after Beli?" Caswallon's laugh was like the
tearing of silk. "It is we that have first right, and it is not I that will
give that up! And since it is my right to be king, all people who do
right must back me, and I will kill only those who do not, and so do
wrong. The killing of wrongdoers is lawful."

"I have loved and dreamed of that kingship too long to defile it
so," said Lludd. "A king is the servant of the people; it would be queer
to kill some of them in order to get to serve all of them, and not so
do I understand kingship."

"Then you will stand aside," said Caswallon.

"And what if Bran comes back?" said Llevelys. "He probably will;

that Irishman is no match for him. Do you think the people will stand with you against him? I do not."

"There are many chances in war," said Caswallon. "It is in my heart that it is my destiny to be king."

"And would you kill Caradoc?" said Llevelys coldly. "You would have to, to sit safely on the throne, and that would be such a deed as is seldom heard of. Such as only the outcasts and outlaws have committed, they who walk accursed forever, to whom none may give food or drink or shelter."

"He is Bran's son, not Branwen's. No kin of ours . . ."

"He is our kin if we are Beli's kin. He is our cousin's son, our own blood."

Caswallon was silent awhile, then he said, "I have thought of that. Many people may think as you do, though indeed now the degrees and bonds of kinship will have to be reckoned in new ways; there will be much for a new king to do. And I will be that king. Bran has held our rights long enough; him I never could dethrone, but Caradoc I can. Him I will not stomach. But I will try to leave him alive."

Manawyddan looked back toward the island they had left behind. Back at the cliffs that now were a blur and a gloom, as though oncoming night already rested there. A black shrouding shape, she seemed to have settled upon the Island of the Mighty, like some huge bird upon her nest.

What eggs are hatching there? he wondered. But only the silence of the night answered him, the little whisper of the waters, the dull unhuman crying of the wind. And Bran trudged on through the Sinking Lands, steady, inexorable, as a mountain in motion, as one of the hills moving from their age-old places. So he went forward, blind as rock and earth, through the world that his movement already had shaken from its age-old foundations.

Herdsmen saw strange sights on the sea, and the word was borne to Matholuch.

"Lord, Lord, there is a forest rising out of the Sinking Lands—there where since our fathers' fathers' fathers' time nothing has grown at all—and it is moving! It is coming toward us!"

Matholuch called for his druids. "Use your sight," he bade them, "and tell me what it truly is that these fellows think they have seen."

They said, "Lord, such journeys of the mind take time and preparation." But he would give them no time.

He would give them no time, so they closed their eyes and their lips moved soundlessly. Then for a few breath's space they were silent. Then all their mouths opened at once and they said, "Wood—wood—yes, they are wood. Many, many of them and tall—a multitude of them, and all moving . . ."

"But is it a wood?" demanded Matholuch.

"Something walks beside them, Lord. One, beside the many—something taller than a man, not so tall as a forest tree . . .

"What is it?" Matholuch leant forward in his carved, gold-ornamented chair, his hands grasping the arms so that his knuckles showed white.

"Lord, it is moving . . . Twin brightnesses gleam near its top. Like water they gleam, but red . . . It is moving, Lord! Everything is moving! Toward the land. Toward all of us!"

They opened their eyes and shivered.

Matholuch sat like stone. His hands still clenched the arms of his chair, and his face was as white as his knuckles. He must have known: forests do not rise out of the sea, and only one reason could take ships into or so near the Sinking Lands.

Only one man could wade those shallows . . .

All there must have known, but with all their might they pushed the knowledge back, slammed and bolted the doors of their minds against it. *Let us not face it—let it go away—let it not be . . .*

But it was there. With every breath they drew it was drawing nearer. They all knew that; the King knew it. He licked his lips, and spoke at last.

"Well," he said, "well." And stopped. Then, "Nobody can know what this means unless Branwen knows. Ask her."

He did not offer to go to her himself.

They went, the nobles and the druids. They lifted the heavy spit off her and her out of the pit. They told her the tale, and it lost nothing in the telling.

". . . And beside the forest is a great mountain, and it moving. And near the top of the mountain are two bright shining lakes . . . Lady, what do you think this is?"

Indeed, they saw less Bran's body than his mind, and the wrath that overhung all of them like an avalanche.

Branwen's eyes shone; a faint, hard smile played round her mouth. "I am no Lady, but I can tell you what this is. The men of the Island of the Mighty are coming here, for they have heard how I am punished and dishonored."

Not a man there but had laughed to see her lowered into the pit.

Not one of them all but now suddenly fell in love with his own feet; stared down at his shoes, as if trying to see through them, down into the wriggle-some and delectable and fascinating mysteries of his toes.

But they still hoped against hope. Naturally she would want to think that her people were coming, but it might be something else— it might be . . .

"Then, Lady," they asked politely, "what is that wood?"

"The masts of the ships," she answered. "As thick as a forest, the ships that bring the host from the Island of the Mighty."

They shuddered, and looked up toward heaven, but the ceiling was in the way, and it may have seemed to them that Bran was almost as depressingly near.

"Lady," they asked still more politely, "what is that mountain?"

She bloomed like a rose. Her face, that for so long had been wan and white save when the cooking fire or the butcher's palm reddened it, shone like the dawn.

"That is my brother, Bran the Blessed, wading through the shallows."

Bran, whom no ship could carry! They shuddered, but they tried once more. "Lady, what are those two lakes?"

"His two eyes, looking toward this island. The King is wroth, thinking how I have been treated here."

They left her then; they went back to Matholuch. They were eager now to let him have that leadership of which they had once deprived him, eager to let him be the head of the dog, not its tail. Like frightened children, they hoped that he could think of something to do.

But he railed at them. "This is all your doing! I never wanted to drive my wife from my bed, and insult her mighty kin. You are my councilors, and a fine job you have made of it! Now think of some way to undo what you have done, or I will take all your heads off. Surely they will be as much use off as they ever have been on."

They said nothing. Their silent faces were the mirror of his own despair. He raged at it and them.

"Speak! You did enough talking once. What emptinesses you have got on top of your shoulders! Lugaid, my love . . ."

He turned to his champion, that armed, bold hero whose like always stood near an Irish High King. Most likely Matholuch kept a regiment of them; he would not have wanted any ambitious man to get near enough to him to take his life and so his crown, as was the bloody way of the New Tribes.

But his chief druid got a little courage at last. No doubt he remembered Amergin.

"Lord, maybe it would have been better for all of us if you had given that order three years ago. But now it is too late. The deed is done, and you need all the men you have."

Matholuch remembered that forest of masts. The rage went out of him, and he sank back into his chair.

"Have we no hope at all?" he said weakly.

"We have Branwen," said the druid.

"Fool! All of you said that, three years ago."

"And the use we made of it was folly. But it is still true."

"Fool! Would you provoke him further? He must have a hundred men for every one that I can get together here before he strikes, and if I could win time it would help him, not me. In the north there are still many men of the Old Tribes, and they would rise to him, both to save their own skins and to take vengeance upon us."

"That too is true, Lord. We cannot keep Bran from avenging her. But the men of the Old Tribes hold their women dear. He may want her back safe and sound even more than he wants a face-price."

"I do not like your plan," said Matholuch, "but I will hear it."

"First, take her back to the House of Women," said the druid. "To her own Sunny Chamber. Send ladies to wait upon her there. Then let us prepare messages to send to him."

The men of the Island of the Mighty came ashore. They beached their ships near the mouth of the River Boyne, that sweet stream that is named for an ancient Goddess, the mother of Angus of the Birds. Not many miles from Tara of the Kings it flows, and past the Brug na Boinne, that splendid stone tomb that may be older than the oldest of Egypt's pyramids; it cannot be much younger. One thing is certain: not for Matholuch or the likes of Matholuch was it built.

Bran bathed there, in the Boyne. He washed off the mud of the Sinking Lands, and he got a hot meal at last, and a good sleep. His men feasted and rested too, but not all of them slept at once. The host kept a close watch.

The messengers came while Bran still slept. Manawyddan gave them food and drink. "When the King wakes you shall speak with him."

"Why waste good food and wine on the dogs, brother?" demanded Evnissyen. He took good care that they should hear him.

"Because, although they do not know the treatment that is due to women, we know the treatment that is due to heralds," said Manawyddan. "We are men. If a dog bites us, we do not bite him back. We have our swords."

"Although it is not on heralds that we use them," he added, seeing that Matholuch's men still looked unhappy.

Evnissyen flounced off, and Pryderi looked after him thoughtfully. "There are dogs and dogs," he said. "And a mad dog must bite somewhere."

The he bit his lip and looked at Manawyddan. "I forgot that he was your kin. Indeed, Lord, it is hard to remember."

Manawyddan smiled. "Only those who have madness in them need go mad because of any bite," he said.

Matholuch's messengers ate in peace, or in such peace as their own hearts would give them. They had hardly finished before they were brought to Bran. Even in his sleep he may have felt their coming; he whose heart was set now unalterably, sleeping or waking, upon one thing: one person's freedom and peace.

They looked at him, those messengers, and thought with relief, He is human, after all. A man like others.

Then they looked again, and thought, less comfortably, But he is very big. And something in his face awed them more than his bigness.

"Hail to you, Lord," they said, "and good be with you. We bring greetings from Matholuch the High King your kinsman. And from his noble lady Queen Branwen, your sister."

Bran thanked them, then said, "Have you word or token from Branwen the Queen?"

The messengers hesitated; they looked at the ground. But then they remembered their training; they stiffened themselves and faced him, like men going into battle.

"Lord, the Queen is safe in her Sunny Chamber, and there is nobody in Ireland who is not sorry that she was ever out of it. Nobody who would wish harm to a hair of her head, but . . ."

They stopped. Under Bran's eyes the words died. Their own eyes darted about like frightened flies, from sky to earth and side to side, and back again. They lit everywhere but on his face. They did everything but buzz.

"Would you threaten her?" said Bran; and his great voice was like a bear's growl deep in his throat. It was like a wind from angry heaven, a wind with power to sweep all things before it, and it blew Matholuch's messages away.

9

The One Vice of Bran

THE MESSENGERS knelt before Matholuch; they told their story, and their voices ceased and died away.

Silence came then; silence that seemed to seep out of the council chamber through every nook and corner of Tara. The silence of the grave, or of a room in which a man lies murdered, of a place where life has made a sudden and more than usually unwilling end. Men heard their own breathing, and it was a mere thread plucked loose from the great cloak of that silence.

Matholuch lay back in his splendid chair and thought of what was to come.

He did not feel ready to face it. He felt queer and cold and sick inside. He felt empty; hollow where he should have been solid. His whole self was only a crust over hollowness.

He looked around at his men, but they too looked hollow; masks that his clutching fingers might twitch off to find empty air behind them. Nowhere the warm solidity of loyal hearts, loyal brains, loyal arms, to scheme and fight for him.

They were committing treason—they were not seeing him. They were seeing only themselves, their own fears, their own danger.

He was alone.

He tried to cry across the barriers, more terrible than any walls or any space, that separated him from them.

"You have undone me. You have betrayed me again. You have thrown away whatever chance I had."

But what chance had he had?

He moistened his lips and moistened them again before he could speak.

"Men, what is your counsel?"

"Lord," the eldest druid said, "there is only one counsel: you must give up the kingship to Gwern, your son. That may be a face-price that will satisfy even Bran, for it will break the laws of Ireland and make his heir our king. And it will save Ireland, for then we will not have a foreign prince over us."

And Matholuch bowed his head.

Messengers came again to the banks of the Boyne. Excuses buzzed around them like a swarm of bees.

"For nothing that was done with his good will has your kinsman Matholuch ever deserved anything but good of you, Lord. Indeed and indeed, that is so."

"Indeed, it is not much good that his good will is then," said Bran.

Pryderi put his hands on his hips and laughed. His white teeth shone scornfully.

"Indeed, if ever men of mine tried to deal so with my woman, it is fewer of them and none of myself there would be before they got it done."

The messengers were careful not to hear this. They said politely to Bran's feet, and not to his eyes, "All that he can do he is doing, Lord. For the shame that was put upon you and upon the Queen, by his own people but not by his own will, he is ready to step down from the high seat and give up all that he has. To Gwern your sister's son he yields it. So shall the heir of the Isle of the Mighty be High King in Ireland, and Matholuch the Throneless shall be maintained here or in the Island of the Mighty, or wherever you please."

Many stared in wonder. Light leapt into Manawyddan's face and into Nissyen's. But black fury twisted Evnissyen's, and his hand flew to his sword hilt. The men around him looked downcast and disappointed.

Their thought beat through the silence. *Have we come all this way to be bought off with lands and goods, when blood alone—seas of blood—can wash out the insult?*

And not even lands and good for ourselves, but for the outlander's own whelp!

Before they set forth on that hosting, not a man of the Old Tribes would have given such a name to Branwen's son. But Evnissyen had sown seeds; war and wrath had watered them.

Yet not even Evnissyen dared speak before the envoys were answered. Bran must answer them.

And Bran said nothing.

Like some great monstrous stone he sat there, like the great Sun Stone itself where it still rears up, rugged and gigantic, amid the stone circles of Britain's oldest temple; it upon whose head each summer solstice still brings the sun's self to rest, like a terrible blazing crown.

He sat and said nothing, and Manawyddan's hand tightened on the arm of the young King of Dyved beside him, until Pryderi gasped.

In Nissyen's face the light faded; as it faded in the sky above. The day wore toward evening.

Still Bran brooded. He thought unhappily, *A good offer—a good offer—I wish it were not so good. It would save the Irish pride, and every man needs pride. It would give Branwen's boy what I want him to have. But I could not keep the little King of Ireland always with his mother and me in the island of the Mighty; the Irish would have to have him part of the year—keeping him Irish, yet filling him always with this notion that he is heir to the Isle of the Mighty. While if he grows up in my court as a young landless prince, expecting to get Ireland at my death as Caradoc will get the Island of the Mighty . . .*

He opened his mouth, and then shrank from the thing that came out of it. So shatteringly loud it sounded in that stillness, and so much was shattered by it.

"Am I not to have the kingship myself then? When you offer me that, I may think about giving you peace. But from this time until that you will get none from me."

The men of the Island of the Mighty laughed loudly, for joy. The stricken faces of the Irish did not look too surprised; whatever they had hoped, those envoys of chiefs who had given little mercy can have expected little, knowing little of it. With folded arms and sad eyes Nissyen stared into the sunset, that now was making the sky bright again, making the west blaze like a burning world. Manawyddan's hand fell from Pryderi's arm, and his face was gray as death.

But Evnissyen laughed loudest of all, and the fires of the sunset glowed red in his dancing eyes.

"Now nothing shall stay our vengeance!"

They bore that word back to Tara. It brought night with it, black and complete. For here ended the hope of the Irish to keep their pride as a free nation. Here too were opened the red gates of butchery and slavery and rape.

That was a court of white faces and scared eyes and taut mouths. Every man went mantled in gloom, and every woman had in her eyes the dread of the sons of Llassar, whose brothers had shrieked and died in the Iron House.

Many of them must have marched with the sons of Llyr; be sitting by those distant campfires now. Eating Irish sheep and Irish cattle, as soon they would eat up all Ireland, crunching the green pleasant land in their mighty jaws.

They would be the most merciless of all, they whose stock had been merciless before they had anything to avenge.

The women who had been set to serve Branwen circled round her as though she had been a wolf. They told her nothing, and she asked them nothing. Speech had been scarce in the Sunny Chamber, since the first hour of the Queen's return; they had fawned on her then, but their ingratiating cluckings had died before the cold calm of her eyes. She thanked them for service done, as a Queen should, but unsmilingly. Now she saw that they suddenly seemed more afraid, and her heart leapt.

Can that mean that my brothers are drawing near? My brothers . . . !

Matholuch, the one man who had dreaded the making of peace, was the most frightened of all now that it had not been made. From the shadows his own face grinned at him, on its way back to the Island of the Mighty, on top of a pole.

He wondered if it would do any good to cut off the heads of his councilors—the heads that had spawned the cruelty and the insult—and send them in a kind of bouquet to Bran. In a last brief rush of rage he thought, *It is they that ought to die! They that have done it all!*

But he was not sure that any command of his would be obeyed now. They might well be plotting, those traitors, to send his own head to Bran . . .

He said at last, "Bring Branwen."

As a queen comes, she came to him. Like dawn rising after long dark night she came, beautiful as morning. Painted roses bloomed on her white cheeks, red satin hung about her, draped as though in flaming triumph those bones that would always be a poem, however age or drudgery might wither the flesh upon them. The noble thighs, the curved hips narrowing into invitation at the waist, the firm, sweet breasts like rare white apples; almost it seemed the same, that body that had been shaped to bear kings and be the lodestar of desire.

Matholuch put out his hands to her. It is likely that he never had loved her as he loved her then. "Branwen!" he cried. "Branwen!"

For to him the sight of her was morning. She was his one hope and his last chance. This was no ragged, accusing drudge from the kitchen, no stranger—she was his own, his Branwen. His wife, who had loved him. Surely she must still be enough herself to save him, to beg his life from her brothers.

But she looked at him, and his hands fell.

"Lord," she said, "what do you want of me?"

"Branwen." He could only stammer her name again. "Branwen."

"Speak," she said. "I still have one ear to hear you with." And she touched the still delicate-looking shell that could not. "For one thing I must give you thanks: that all these years your butcher has always struck the same side of my head."

"Branwen," he said, and his hands shook, "it was not my fault. I never meant it to come to this. I sat there wondering what to do, and then you came and had no faith in me. You were angry, and I grew angry too . . ."

Again she looked at him, and he was silent.

She went on looking at him, and her face was like a carved face, that can neither be warmed by triumph, nor softened by pity.

She remembered many things, and she understood him now. Never would he have fought for her. That first time he had turned from her, in her own island, he had hated to leave her; as a hungry dog hates to leave a bone. He had had no thought at all, let alone pity, for her grief at losing him. After she had hurt his vanity, here in this same room, three years ago, he had tried only to forget her, not out of guilt or hurt love, but only out of hurt pride. Now he yearned for her again, as a scared child yearns for the warmth of its mother.

He drew courage from her silence. In her place he would have railed at his betrayer. If only he could get her into his arms, wake her passion again . . .

"Branwen—!" His voice was thick with a desire that she remembered well; one that brought back many other nights.

A stride had brought him to her, his hands were outstretched to grasp her, but she crossed hers upon her lovely breasts. They showed callused and chapped and ugly, rough against the shining silk.

One of them was blistered, and the nails of her long, tapering fingers were broken. Above their ruin her eyes shone cold as the ice of high mountaintops, ice that shall never melt till the world's end.

The King's hands fell again.

She said, "Call your councilors, Matholuch. We have nothing to say that should be said alone."

He sent for them, then waited, fidgeting, trying to avert his eyes

from her face that yet drew them like a terrible magnet. So in its
seeming blankness a stone face, or the dead moon's face, may seem
secret with an awesome secrecy. Far more chilling is such a mask
when it comes upon human flesh . . .

They came, those men by whose counsel she had suffered. They
greeted her warily, and she looked at them with those cold, calm
eyes.

"Tell me how matters stand between you and my brother, Lords."

The eldest druid cleared his throat. He cleared it twice.

"Lady, we have offered your brother this face-price—" and he told
her what had happened.

"Lady, surely it would be pleasing to you to see your son High
King, and you cannot wish to see his realm laid waste. Nor can you
wish to see the blood of the men of Ireland spilled for your sake,
when the blood of men of the Island of the Mighty must flow with
it and, living, they that have insulted you must bow down to you and
be the servants of your son. They, and their children after them."

Branwen stood thinking, and that carved face did not change, any
more than the bleak peaks of mountains change. The men who
watched it shivered and held their breaths.

She said at last, "You give better counsel, Lords, than you did
once. The King my brother should have been the first to see its goodness—he must be angry indeed. Are you sure that you have told me
all that was said to him?"

"We swear it, Lady, by our hands and by the Gods we swear by."

"Then what has happened that you have not told me? Is one of
my other brothers dead?" Her unwavering eyes fixed them, many-
layered darknesses.

"No, Lady. There has been no fighting yet. We have told you all
that has happened, as it happened. By the sun and by the moon, by
fire and water, earth and air, we swear it."

She said, puzzled, "It is not like Bran to want blood."

Matholuch said eagerly, "We could send him the butcher's
head—or the whole butcher to kill in any way he likes."

Then the darkness of Branwen's eyes flashed lightnings. "It would
be beneath my brother's dignity to kill a servant for obeying his master's orders. He will not take the butcher's head unless I ask him for
it, and I will not!" Her eyes said plainly, *"Ask yourself whose head he
is likeliest to want, Matholuch, you who could not be more dead to me
with it off your shoulders than with it on!"* and Matholuch shrank.

Aloud she ended, "Yet must we think what to say to my brother. I
would not have men of my own people shed their blood for me."

"Lady," said the eldest druid, "you know him. Unless you can give us counsel we have none."

She thought, she searched her memories as a woman searches in a bag of old garments, rummaging among all that is cheap and all that is dear; among high cherished moments and the small commonplaces that time and death may yet turn to treasures fabulously dear. Great happenings and little happenings, and here and there an incident all shining like a jewel in the glow of some ancient tenderness. Memories that she had treasured and polished like jewels many a time during the long nights of those years when memory had been her only comfort.

Like the sudden opening of a door into a lighted room it came at last, the one she sought and needed, and she smiled, thinking how childlike all men were, both her great angry brother, and these who cowered guiltily, like scared children, before the whip of his coming.

"He hated it," she said, and a little tender smile brought back the dimples to her mouth, "he hated it when he grew too big to get inside a house. He never complained—he is no complainer. He joked about it, but he hated it. I was very little then, but I remember; it is one of the first things I do remember. Build him a house."

The hope that had lit their faces died. "Lady, how could we build him a house if he himself cannot?"

"He is not so big as all that," said Branwen. "He could build himself a house if he were willing, as he puts it, to squander so much of the wealth of the men of the Island of the Mighty. Wealth that is needed for things the people need. But I need not tell you the drains that there always are upon even the wealthiest king's purse. Or that there is nothing your own people now need so much as his good will."

They knew that, though they may have been thinking more of themselves than of their people. But their faces remained grave.

"Lady, the building would take time. And will he give us time?"

"Try him," said Branwen. "Say also that you will put the kingship in his hands to deal with as he sees fit. Once he yields a little, he will yield all. He is like that, big in all things."

They bore that word to Bran, where he sat in the camp of the men of the Island of the Mighty.

He sat with a naked sword across his knees, a sword the length of a lad near manhood. The heralds saw it and shivered, thinking how far it would reach and how its great sweep would slice a man like cheese.

"We hope this face-price will please you, Lord."

Bran said, "This is a lie to get time with."

"If you will give us time, the house will stand, Lord. Already the trees are being cut to build it. And this is done by the counsel of the Lady Branwen your sister, who hopes that you will not lay waste this island with war. This island that, if you will it, will be her son's kingdom."

"Branwen—" said Bran softly. And the thought smote him, *She may want that. To see her son a king.*

But he thrust that thought from him. He told himself again how unwise it would be to make Gwern king. And these men were wily; he glared at them.

"How do I know what she said or did not say?" he thundered. "What words you are putting into her mouth?"

But it was Manawyddan who answered, and his eyes were as deep as the sea they were the color of, and as steady as the changeless stars.

"These words are Branwen's own, brother. The Irish never would have thought of building you a house—that is her thought. Remember when she was a little girl and cried at bedtime, because you must stay outside in the dark?"

Bran looked past him; his great face worked. Then, "She shall weep no more because of me," he said heavily. "I will take the face-price."

The faces of the Irish shone like sunlight. Many of the men of the Island of the Mighty looked like dogs from whom a bone has been snatched, but as many more looked glad.

Bran's own huge shoulders were slumped as if in defeat, but the faces of Manawyddan and Nissyen were all light. Manawyddan thought within himself, *You have won a greater victory now, brother, than when you strove against those sucking depths in the Sinking Lands. The greatest you will ever win.*

Then of a sudden he heard a strange and very evil sound: the grinding of Evnissyen's teeth.

10

The Price of a Crown

TREES CRASHED and fell, giants that it had taken ages of sun and rain to rear fell prostrate on that brown earth from which they had sprung. Across the green plain of Tara men and horses dragged them, and down the dark shining rivers they floated, bound together into rafts.

Night and day smiths toiled at their anvils; hammers crashed and fires burned. Metals glowed and melted, became screens and panels of gold, or of bronze chased with gold. Night and day wood-carvers toiled, straining their eyes to make in haste the intricate lovely patterns that would make plain brown wood as fine as shining metal. Nobles' houses yielded up vessels of gold and silver, and jeweled cups of ivory; coverlets and cushions of silk and fur and embroidered linen. Tara itself was looted. Nothing was spared that could make splendid the House of Bran.

Where it rose we do not know, there is no record left; but somewhere between Tara and the sea seems likeliest; where great Bran himself could watch its building, Branwen beside him. She was with her brothers now, she had her own pavilion in their camp, as once before she had had it in Aberffraw, for her wedding.

Great joy had there been at her coming. For the first time in three years—save for that one night she had sped the starling on its way—Branwen had wept, seeing her brothers, and no shame had been on her that the Irish who had brought her saw her do it, they before whom she had been proud and tearless so long.

"Bran!" she said, "Bran." Then, "Manawyddan!" And Bran passed her like a doll from his great arms to their brother's, his own eyes wet, and when Manawyddan took her his gray eyes too had the wetness of the sea for once, as well as its color.

Nissyen came then. His eyes were dry, but full of a great soft light.

"Good be with you, sister," he said, as his arms circled her. "Now and always."

She laughed and clung to him. "Good always will be with me, Nissyen, brother, while you three are."

Then she bit her lip, for she saw Evnissyen behind him. She changed her words quickly. "While you four are, sons of my mother."

He embraced her; he never would have foregone anything that was his due, but his eyes were hurt and angry.

"I came as far and as fast as the others, sister, and I am the only one that never would have given you to that Irish hound to chew. But because I always knew him for a foe and treated him as one, you hold it against me. That is like a woman."

She answered, "Evnissyen, it was only that I did not see you, and my heart was so full of the three I did see that I could remember nothing else. You are my youngest brother, the last to come from our mother's womb before me. How could I not be glad of you?"

But he thought only how ungrateful she was to him, the only one who would have saved her. How, as always, he had been slighted and rebuffed.

He glowered and gloomed, but he always had, so Branwen was not troubled. Even Evnissyen's jealousy and evil temper seemed good, they had such a flavor of home.

Her heart sang so loudly in its joy that the whole world seemed good.

Sometimes, alone in the dark watches of the night, she may have remembered that other pavilion at Aberffraw, where her lover had lain beside her. But all that seemed long ago, farther off than her childhood, that her brothers' coming had brought warm and close. Almost she could have smiled, as a woman smiles when in her housecleaning she finds some old toy that as a child she had lost and wept for, and now sees as something worthless and tawdry, all its magic gone.

All that is gone, it is over. It does not matter any more. Not unless Gwern should be like him, and I will not let him be. He has my blood too.

Gwern! Her heart cried that name as a lost child cries for home, as a man lost in a desert place cries for water. He was her one lack, her longing for him was unassuageable.

But I must not be greedy, I who have so much now! I who for so long had nothing. it is only for a little while. As soon as the house is built they will bring him, their king, for the feast and the peacemaking. A king belongs first of all to his people; we must not tread their pride underfoot too much. I must remember that, I, his mother, must learn to love them for his sake.

Soon now, soon! His uncles will see him, and I will hold him in my arms again—Gwern, Gwern, my baby! My son, who will be king of two islands some day.

But she cared nothing for that kingship, save because he would be proud of it. All she wanted was himself; bigger now, of course, but still warm and round and laughing. Still small enough to be carried in her arms.

The sons of Llyr saw her longing. Bran said, "Should we not send for the little fellow at once, brother?"

Manawyddan said heavily, "You know why not. It is not good for a people to feel conquered; they need what signs and symbols of freedom they can keep. We are bearing hard upon them, as it is. Most of these Irish chiefs will be plucked to the bone."

Bran said, "I must gift my men to repay them for this hosting; they are getting neither plunder nor battle glory from it. And as for these Irish chiefs, never was plucking more richly earned. When I think what they did—these woman-beating dogs—I still could take all their heads off!"

But his anger stemmed from more than one cause now. Those lords who must give him "gifts" undoubtedly were wringing as many of those gifts as they could out of the little people, the tillers of the soil. The many were paying for the brutish folly of the few.

Later it will be different, he told himself. *When all is in my hands. Justice will be done between all men then, as it is done now in the Island of the Mighty. I will bring back the ways of the Old Tribes.*

He chafed because he must tolerate and profit by injustice, because he must humor these men he despised. Not for the first time a thought crept through his mind like an ugly, sluggish worm. *They are taking much for granted. I have not yet said that the boy is to be king.*

If Gwern were not a king, Caradoc's crown would be safer. If he were not—if he were not . . .

Manawyddan felt his brother's unease. He said, "If we had taken the heads off these dogs, we should also have had to bury some of our own men, brother. Where no road is good one can still be better than another, and you chose the better."

Bran fidgeted. "I still have many choices to make, brother. Nothing is settled yet."

Manawyddan glanced at him keenly. "Surely the greatest matters are. Though it will be a delicate matter arranging Gwern's household: one man of ours for every Irishman, and each of them a sober man that will not step on Irish toes—"

Bran laughed shortly. "A household of cats and dogs that would be, surely! Better to take the boy home with us. Then he can be with Branwen always, and no trouble about it."

Manawyddan opened his mouth and then closed it again. He said at last, slowly. "Then he will return as a stranger, an outlander. He will be hated and plotted against always. While if he stays here he will be Ireland's own; most folk will cleave to him, even though for years our task will be no easy one."

"It will not. That we can depend on." Bran laughed again, yet more shortly.

"Yet in his manhood Gwern can bring about such peace between New Tribes and Old as our own isle knows. Do we not owe the people of this island that much, Bran? The Old Tribes, our own kin? The many little folk upon whom we have brought fear and hardship because of the deeds of one pack of high-placed hounds?"

But Bran stood like a mountain wrapped in storm clouds, in gray sullen darkness charged with thunder and lightning. He was divided in his own mind; he no longer knew whether he was going to do what was best, or what he wanted to do. He only knew, with the terrible stabbing suddenness of a spear thrust, that the two might not be the same.

Through all the years of his kingship he had striven to labor only for the good of his people. But was that true now? And when had it ceased being true? He looked into Manawyddan's eyes, and then swiftly looked away again, for those steady gray eyes gave him answer. *When first you set love for Caradoc above love for our people.*

He could not bear that knowledge, and so he could not bear the sight of his brother. He turned on his heel and left him.

It is easier to shut light out than to let it in; easier to block up a hole in a wall, after some fashion at least, than to knock that hole in it. Carefully, painstakingly, Bran filled up the hole that had let in the light he did not want to see.

As a dog guards a bone, as a miser guards his treasure, so Bran brooded over and cherished his doubt.

What kind of man would Gwern be?

Surely it was only prudent to wait and see. A boy cannot hide his nature as a man can. In six or eight years, maybe in only four or five, it might be possible to tell whether Gwern was Branwen's true son.

And the joy of having him with her would solace any hurt to her pride in his future.

But the Irish will never believe that you are waiting. There will be unrest here and plotting, and finally bloodshed.

Bran brooded, and Evnissyen and his friends took heart again. They swaggered and preened themselves, and behind his brothers' backs they bullied the Irish in little ways.

Yet fear is hope's twin, and they were like dogs under whose nose a bone is held, a bone that at any second may be snatched away. Evnissyen thought with sick fury, *Why did the Irish have to surrender? Why did Branwen have to make Bran sentimental, just when he seemed to be getting sense at last? And all for the sake of that outlander's whelp! Of that wolf cub who will grow into a wolf* . . .

And beside him were those other twins, the sons of Llassar.

Kueli said, "Will the King your brother let them build him another Iron House? Can you not stop him? You did before."

Kueli's teeth shone like a hungry wolf's. "Let them try it! Some parents here may see their children burn."

Evnissyen started; his nostrils quivered, his eyes grew wide. *Yes, I could stop Bran again!* He knew how now; and that knowledge was both terror and dizzying delight. It was a dream—something he never really would do, yet something he could do. A deed no man would dare; yet from that hour it tugged at him, lured and tormented him; he was afraid, and to ease his own torment he taunted Nissyen.

"You were getting your hopes up again, brother, but you have failed. Never will Bran hand over this island to the traitor's whelp."

Nissyen said, "What will be will be. It shapes in the wombs of the Mothers."

Evnissyen thought, *But I can shape it! Wipe the smiles off all your faces. Show all of you, who have always thought that I did not matter, that I am stronger than all of you put together. Able to destroy whatever you can build.*

He felt Nissyen's keen eyes. To blind them he laughed. "An easy way out. Will I never be rid of your whining, fool?"

Nissyen smiled. "You can never escape me, any more than I can escape you. For we were one being once, and shall be again."

Evnissyen stared. "Now that is madness, even for you! Two people more unlike than you and me cannot walk the earth."

He flung away, and Nissyen looked after him, still smiling. "In every man is something incorruptible, however low he sinks, however invisible his true self may become, to himself and others. But you do not understand that, brother. Time was when you still could hear my voice across the gulf, but now . . . Well, every man must undergo many lives and many births before he can cleanse himself of the darkness and return to that Light whence all light comes. What does time matter, time that also must end?"

Had Branwen been less busy she must have seen that trouble was on her brothers. But Bran's house was nearly built. She was there from morning to night now, planning, overseeing.

Once fear did strike her. She laid her hand on Manawyddan's arm. "Brother, are you keeping something from me? Have you and Bran heard some rumor? About Gwern . . .?

He smiled. "None, little sister. Your son will soon be here."

That eased her; they walked on to the house together. She was eager for his opinion of this and that.

"I want it to be just what Bran will like. This is his house, the first he has ever had..

"It seems to me that you also want it to be what Branwen will like." He smiled again.

She dimpled. "You always see everything, Manawyddan. But when you and Bran go back to the Island of the Mighty, Gwern and I will live in this house. When he is a man Tara must be his home, I know; but never again can it be mine."

He looked down into her face that had sobered, suddenly aged; the face of the woman he was beginning to know. The young, laughing sister he had known from her birth was gone again.

"Girl, it is not Matholuch . . .?

"Not he. Not one thing, but all . . . In this house they have dug no pit for a woman to cook in, brother; I have seen to that. Queens know too little about what goes on in their palace kitchens; maybe it is a good thing that I had to learn that. When I die no woman in Ireland will be toiling in a hot pit with the cooking spit on her shoulders.* I will lay it on my son to see to that, if I cannot manage it before he is a man."

"We will make it part of the peace terms, if need be. Bran will not like your staying here, but I thought you would not he parted from the boy again." There was a grim note in his voice, yet pride also. "Few women would wish to stay here after what has happened, but you have a brave heart, girl."

---

*In the seventh century St. Adamnan's mother actually did enjoin upon her son to bring this relief to Irish cooks, as well as to secure other rights to women.

"And kin who are good friends to me. I had one other friend." She looked up at him. "Where is my bird, Manawyddan? Bran told me that he had given her into your keeping, so I knew that she was safe. Yet I am ashamed not to have asked before."

"I gave her to one who keeps many birds, sister, but cages none."

She laughed. "So Rhiannon has her! Well, may my son grow as tall and fine as hers! You have a right to be proud of him, brother. I had hoped to see my starling again, but if she mates and nests in Dyved I will leave her in peace."

Then her mind swung back to the house; to all the preparations that must be made for the night when Bran first entered into it.

"It will be the greatest feast that either island ever has seen, brother. All our men, and all the chief men of Ireland; all the kings that pay homage to the High King at Tara. And this time they will pay it to my son. Could any woman be prouder than I shall be? Or ask a better revenge?" Suddenly she laughed. "What does all that matter? Gwern will be there. My Gwern!"

Her whole being was centered upon him now, with the terrible single-heartedness of the woman who has turned her back upon love, and knows that her firstborn will be her last. Deep within Manawyddan something shivered, as if in great cold; he thought he knew why. He prayed within himself, *May no fresh sorrow come on you through him, sister! From us, your brothers.*

On a day the house was finished. On its right stood the men of the Island of the Mighty, on its left all the great men of Ireland, their folk about them. Matholuch the King stood there in his red cloak and golden crown, and in his heart was a bitterness that almost outweighed fear.

Evening was near. The sun streamed red-gold across the plain, soft as a woman's hair; but under the trees the shadows lengthened. Black and monstrous, they stretched out many arms, and dreadfully, from the bowels of approaching night, their mother. Toward the House of Bran they reached. Hill-high it stood there, proudly disdaining their dark tentacles, seeming to create about it its own small night.

Into either side of it were set double doors of bronze, inlaid with gold. The widest doors ever seen.

Beside Pryderi another high-born young man of Dyved eyed them uneasily. "I wish we had not had to give up our arms, Lord."

"The Irish have given up theirs too," said Pryderi. "Under Queen

Branwen's own eye the servants and ladies of Ireland are hanging up each man's arms above what will be his place at table. That takes time; it is why we must wait out here."

But he too felt uneasy. That vast pile, deep in its own black shadow, looked more like one of the mammoth tombs of the *Brug na Boinne* than the palace of a living king.

Then at last, and in the same breath's space, all four of those gigantic doors swung open.

Pryderi gasped; so did many men of both isles.

Huge indeed was that hall of Bran. Fire gleamed within its shadowy vastness, rose like red flowers from each of three great hearths set in the center of that great hall. A hundred pillars upbore the roof; a hundred tall trees that had been, stripped now of their green branches, encased in glowing gold.

All stood and stared; as if that hall that seemed too big for man were in truth the grand and aweful abiding place of a God; perilous for the feet of men.

Then Bran laughed his great laugh. "Come on, men."

Like the waves of the sea they surged in after him, and like another surging sea, through the doors upon the opposite side, swarmed the Irish, behind their gold-decked, bright-bearded shadow of a king.

So the men of two nations went into that hall that will be famed forever.

He did not go unhappily at the last, great Bran. While that house was being built he had thought of it with more annoyance than interest; it had seemed like a bribe and a trap. Long since he had ceased to miss the pleasant small shelter of houses; no roof can keep out the storms that beat upon a king. But now that it was here, that he was actually entering it, he felt boyish wonder and pleasure. He thought, *This is mine.*

The good smells of roasting meat and new-baked bread rose around him, brought a feeling of home.

On each side of each of the three hearths was a bed-place. Carved screens, glittering with gold, divided it from its fellows. There were set the couches where the children of Penardim and the King of the Irish would eat and sleep.

There Bran the Blessed met Matholuch; there warmth died, and cold courtesy took its place. Matholuch, drawing back to the other side of the great fires, the chiefs who had repudiated him around him, knew that there was no hope for him.

He will trust no pledge that I can give. He will neither let me stay here where I was born, nor go into exile in Gaul, where Gaulish chieftains might take up my cause. I must end my days a prisoner upon the Island of the Mighty.

And he thought of how he had first gone there in his pride, an army round him, to win the woman who now despised him. How different would this sailing be! Shame would pass; soon his main concern would be what comforts they would still allow him, what crumbs of splendor. Like a caged animal, in time he might learn to live only for the filling of his belly. But tonight his pride, or that vanity he called pride, writhed in white-hot anguish. All this pomp that surrounded him for the last time roused him to savage hunger, mocked him.

When he saw Branwen coming, beautiful as a bride, shining in all the splendor that became a queen, he turned away his head. Not in shame, but because she was one more thing of which he had been robbed. He did not look once at the small form that trotted beside her, the firelight catching in its red-gold curls—his pride once, now, perhaps, his supplanter . . .

She did not see him; she saw only her brothers. She led her son by the hand; before the sons of Llyr she halted, the noblest ladies of Ireland clustering behind her.

"This is Gwern," she said. Her eyes said, pitifully and proudly, *If I have shared a base man's bed, if I have been shamed and betrayed as no woman of the Island of the Mighty ever was before me, yet out of it all I have brought one good thing.*

The child was as fair as Matholuch, but his square little jaw, his nose, and the shape of his face, were Branwen's. And his eyes, blue beyond all doubting, not the almost-blue of Matholuch's, looked straight up into the eyes of his uncles. With an interested if somewhat awed curiosity.

The *Mabinogi* says that nobody looked at that child without loving him.

Manawyddan looked at him once, and then at Bran. He thought, while he prayed for it to be otherwise, *Now will we see how small the biggest man can be?*

Bran looked at the child and then at the mother, and deep within him something turned over. Something melted, and left him immeasurably relieved and immeasurably happy and immeasurably free. He caught up the boy in his mighty arms and tossed him toward the ceiling. His great voice boomed out so that the rafters shook.

"Hail to the King of the Irish! Hail to Gwern the High King! Let there be peace and brotherhood forever between my people and his!"

Then the Irish shouts too shook the rafters, and then Bran shouted again, and the men of both islands shouted with him.

In that whole vast hall all faces were stars of light save four: the grim faces of the twin sons of Llassar, the white face of Matholuch, the King that had been, and the death-white face of Evnissyen. The son of Eurosswydd stood there and ground his teeth. The cries of the outlanders' joy slashed him like whips, ran like poison through his veins.

But Bran beamed. He beamed sunnily, benificiently, unbelievably; he looked upon everybody with eyes of love. He thought, *It is better this way. Better not to hold a nation prisoner until I die. Now Branwen will be happy. Both islands will have princes of their own blood and be happy, and build a sure road to peace. And Manawyddan will not be able to say anything.*

That last thought gave him great satisfaction too. He beamed a little more . . .

Branwen signed to the cupbearers and they brought drinking horns filled with rare wines. Bran sat down and called Branwen's son to him again. The boy came gladly. Children are not as fond of laps as most child lovers like to think, but here was one uncle who had a lap big enough to be comfortable. Gwern sat on it and approved of it.

From Bran he went to Manawyddan, whose lap was smaller, but not bad. Those sea-gray eyes were very friendly and warm and kind.

Then Nissyen the son of Eurosswydd called him.

This uncle was different. He was beautiful, as beautiful as Gwern's new-found mother, and as kind. His beauty seemed to flow out of him and make everything else beautiful, to find itself in all things and to fit all things into their places, and to show that those places were good. His very quietness made music.

Gwern could not have said any of those things, but he felt them. His eyes, that had been growing big and dark with excitement, grew soft. His head fell against Nissyen's shoulder; he slept.

Branwen found a moment to sit down beside Manawyddan. Her eyes too were soft.

"He was getting tired. I thought I should have to get him away from all of you, but Nissyen knew. What is there that Nissyen does not know?"

Manawyddan smiled. "Another woman would have said, 'He should have children of his own.' You are wiser. Nissyen loves all living things; I think he sees into each so deeply, with such knowledge of its inmost self, that he loves it as no other can. But for him there is no love that binds him to one more than another; no love that shuts others out."

"You are wrong, brother. His love may know no bonds, but he is bound. To Evnissyen, as to none of us."

As if her words had been a wand to put his shape upon one of the shadows behind him, he was there. His eyes gleamed, restless as the leaping flames.

"Good be with you, my brother, my sister, noble children of Llyr. Surely it is, tonight. You have both got the stake you have played for." He moved forward, out into firelight.

The strange voice roused Gwern. He raised his head; the eyes that were as brilliantly blue as jay's feathers stared in wonder at the face that was like a mirrored image of the one above him. So like, yet so unlike . . .

Evnissyen smiled his wry smile. "First Bran, then Manawyddan, then you, Nissyen. All of you but me. Why does not my nephew, the only son of my sister, come to me? I would be glad to hold the boy, even if he were not King of the Irish."

Branwen sighed. "Gwern must go to him now, or he will be insulted again, and all of us will have put the child up to it."

Bran said, "Let the lad go to him, and welcome."

Gwern was used to being shown off. He rose and trotted obediently toward this new uncle.

Evnissyen sat down and dropped his hands between his knees, that none might see their frantic working. With the madness of twisting, spitting snakes his fingers writhed.

Two breaths, three breaths, four—then I will have him!

The little feet reached him; stopped.

With a howl of triumph Evnissyen sprang. In one lightning-swift movement he seized Branwen's son and hurled the child headlong into the fire.

11

War

THE LITTLE body hurtled through the flames and crashed through the burning logs like a club; his skull smashed like an eggshell.

One shriek the child had given, as Evnissyen seized him, a cry that changed horribly as the flames swallowed him. Branwen too had shrieked, and to Manawyddan, at her side, it seemed that that scream would ring in his ears forever.

Arrow-straight she leapt for the fire, but he sprang after her and flung her to one side. With his cloak thrown over his face to save his own eyes he bent and lifted that seared eyeless thing out of the fire. Branwen screamed again when she saw it, but its agony was over. Then Bran's great arm grasped her, and his shield covered her. From all sides the Irish, yelling with rage and horror, were leaping for their weapons. Their King had been killed before their eyes, and the war that Evnissyen had willed had come.

The men of the Island of the Mighty sprang for their own weapons. Smitten shields roared like thunder; swords and spears flashed. Men screamed as their flesh was pierced. From place to place Evnissyen leapt and slew, his face still aflame with unholy glee, and beside him leapt and slew the sons of Llassar, Keli and Kueli, their white teeth shining, their eyes red as the flames. Nissyen kept his shield over Manawyddan, while the son of Llyr fought the pain in his burned hands and arms. Like a lion Bran raged before them, his huge sword, longer than any other man's, clearing a circle wide enough to keep all harm from Branwen, crushed between his shoulder and his shield. Hampered as he was, that whirling blade often helped or avenged his men. That hall was like the home and birthplace of all thunders, the crashing, shrieking core of all storms that ever have battered the earth. The *Mabinogi* says that no such uproar was ever heard beneath any other roof, and in their far places the Gods Themselves may have heard it, and shuddered at the power They had given men.

Many were falling. Blood made the ground slippery, and men tripped over bodies that lay forever feelingless or that twisted and screamed again beneath that new hurt. Friend trod on friend; the dead and the dying were trampled beneath those milling feet.

Bran saw what was happening. His voice rang through that tumult like the battle horns that shall blow on the day of earth's ending. "Out! Out, men of Bran the Blessed!"

He ploughed forward, through the press, his giant sword whirling like a scythe before him, and all men shrank from it. And all that were his own followed him, hewing down those that barred their way.

Outside in the moonlit twilight he stopped and got his breath, and the men of the Island of the Mighty gathered round him. Manawyddan, his hands bandaged in strips torn from his cloak, found that he still could handle sword and spear.

A breath's space, and the Irish were around them again, like dancing flames, and Matholuch came too, the center of an eager, swirling circle; he had seized his chance; however little they honored him, the Irish were used to following him, and they had nobody else.

He fought well; many a man of the Island of the Mighty fell before him that night, but he never pressed too close to that place where his mighty brother-in-law towered.

But for awhile that rush needed no stronger leader; frenzy begot it and frenzy fed it. And when vengeance was forgotten another madness took its place. They were no longer men who fought there; they were deaths, lowering dreadfully at one another. To himself each man was still flesh, but those who came at him were grinning at him through skulls, and clawing at him with the bony hand of extinction; and as he saw his fellows so they saw him. Each man rammed sword and spear into as many of those living threats as he could reach.

Dawn found them there, gray men fighting amid gray shadows; as perhaps every man who fights in war fights a shadow, the death that he sees as death because it sees him as death; so that out of their common passion for life all are turned into its foes and kill.

Dawn fell on their worn faces, and their fever left them. They shivered there in the harsh gray light.

The Irish retreated toward Tara, and Bran and his men went back

into the house that had been built for him; the house that was to
have sealed the peace.

Within that vast hall all was ruin; the fires out, the furniture
smashed, the floor covered with blood and dead men, and with the
moaning wounded.

They laid what had been Branwen's son upon the couch prepared
for the King of the Irish; Branwen slept like one dead upon her own
couch, and Nissyen sat beside her, those strangely magical hands of
his near her head, where at need they could fetter her faster in sleep.
Sometime during the slaughter she had fainted behind Bran's shield;
and oblivion was the one good left for her. She slept . . .

Bran and Manawyddan did not sleep; they saw to the treating of
the wounded, the carrying out of the dead. Food and wine were
found; the preparing of a meal begun.

Before the relit fires Evnissyen and Keli tended each other's cuts;
Kueli, who had taken a real wound, sat down. Evnissyen's eyes still
danced; he had not yet noticed that all men but those two had drawn
away from him.

He said, laughing, "Long will the Irish remember this night!"

Then he felt the eyes of his brothers upon him, the eyes of the
sons of Llyr, and a great coldness came over him. The laughter faded
from his face. But he gathered himself together again, and burst into
quick, savage speech.

"Well, brothers, what have I done but the sensible thing? He was
the traitor's whelp, and the bigger you let him grow the harder he
would have bitten. Our sister made his flesh—fair flesh—but the
seed it was shaped round would have rotted the heart out of it.
You love peace, Bran—what peace could you have had while he
lived? Would you have wanted his knife in Caradoc's back? Or, more
likely, his poison in Caradoc's belly?"

Bran said slowly and grimly, "Speak not to me of Caradoc, Evnissyen,
lest I remember what will be in my sister's heart when she awakes.
What would be in mine if it had been Caradoc."

Manawyddan said as grimly, "Many men of the Island of the
Mighty died last night for this sensible deed of yours, Evnissyen; this
kin-murder. And many more will die."

Evnissyen cried out wildly, "It was not kin-murder—you cannot say
that! I was careful not to shed his blood, I only put him in the fire . . ."

He stopped before Bran's face, that was bleak as wintry dawn on
cliffs that frown, eternally relentless, above northern seas.

"Do not remind us that that is not shedding kindred blood," he
said. "Do not speak of fire. It is not safe for you."

Evnissyen shuddered and for once was still. For awhile all men there were still.

Then Pryderi looked up from the sword he had been cleaning, and his eyes were as bright as the blade.

"Indeed," he said, "I am no kin at all to this son of Eurosswydd. If you would like him to die, Lords, I will be glad to go outside with him and persuade him to do it."

Evnissyen's teeth flashed like a wolf's; he was himself again. "When we get back to the Island of the Mighty and have no born foes to fight, I will make you answer for that, Pryderi, whom Pwyll was fool enough to call son!"

"You will get that answer," said Pryderi. "But why try to sneak out of asking for it now? It is ready I am to give it."

Bran said, "Let no man here shed blood of the Island of the Mighty. The Irish will do enough of that."

He turned his great back upon them, and again there was silence.

In that silence Evnissyen found that men looked away when he looked at them, and drew away when he neared them. He came at last to the doorway by which the twin sons of Llassar were sitting, fierce Keli and Kueli. He began to tell them how wise and farseeing he had been.

"That cub might have ground the whole Island of the Mighty under Ireland's heel. I stopped that; yet what thanks do I get?"

But then he stopped speaking, for he saw that nobody was listening to him. Kueli's wound was worse than he had thought, and Keli was busy with it, trouble on the side of his face that looked like other men's.

Evnissyen sat still and looked at no one, and knew that once more he was alone.

Only Nissyen, who sat by Branwen, looked at him, and his face was saddest of all.

The day wore. Bran had his dead burned and a great pit dug to bury their ashes in, and the old women of the Irish came and dragged away their dead.

Some of Bran's men grumbled, and said that they wished that the men of Ireland had come instead. A few laughed and said that the Irish cowards had got a bellyful soon. But most said nothing at all. They were beginning to wonder, *When will they come?* The man who can rejoice most savagely when he meets his foe face to face, still likes to know where that enemy is, and what he is doing.

They could see the hill of Tara; the ramparts that surrounded the place called the Seat, where kings had dwelt from of old. Since the morning of the Western World, when all kings reigned in accordance with the Ancient Harmonies.

Nothing moved on those heights; there was only sunlit silence.

The shadows grew blacker; the arms they stretched out over the plain grew longer and longer. Nothing happened.

The sun set, red and wrathful, in the west.

The men of the Island of the Mighty watched her go, and felt themselves grow colder. That was not strange, for autumn was upon them, and already the nights were chilly. They went inside, and ate and drank; they would have drunk too much, had the sons of Llyr let them. They sat round the fires, and piled the firewood high. Like angry snakes the red flames hissed. Branwen heard them where she lay and shuddered, covering her face; she could no longer bear the sight of fire. Nissyen stroked her hair gently, with his long, fine fingers.

There was a sudden stir at the door that faced Tara. One of the guards set there hurried to Bran.

"Lord—" he stammered, "Lord, there is something wrong with the moon. It—it is where it ought not to be."

"Where is it?" Bran's huge frame stiffened.

"Lord, it is too low." The man's lips worked. "Too low. It is not in the sky at all."

Bran rose and made for the doors. Pryderi would have followed him, but Manawyddan laid a hand on his arm.

"Best if we stay quietly where we are, lad. Where the men can see us. We want no panic."

Pryderi sat down again, though not happily. Bran reached the doorway alone.

Round and red it glowed there, upon the ramparts of Tara. A gleaming balefulness. A squat, strange witness to the mystery of shape, that can be shared by a child's ball and by the sun; by the tiny and by the infinite. The circle made solid; without end and without beginning, the very shape of eternity itself. Unalive, yet full of life; smoke rose from it like grim breath.

Bran looked, and his big face grew pale, and then paler, like a mountain whitening under winter snows.

"The Cauldron—the Cauldron . . .

The cry was Kueli's. He was running, staggering as he ran, he who since noon had not been able to rise, and his face was blanched with horror.

"Come back! You must be still—" Keli his brother caught him. Other men swarmed after them.

"No, brother, no! We must flee. They will send the dead against us!"

Kueli fought to free himself, to reach the doors, and suddenly a red flood came pouring from his mouth. He gasped; his head fell forward, and he fell forward, against his brother's breast. His breath rattled, and he died.

Keli laid him down. He turned to face Bran, and the red mark on his face worked like a living thing.

"My brother spoke truth, Lord. Yonder is the Cauldron that my father and my mother stole from the Underworld—the Pair Dadeni, the Cauldron of Rebirth."

All gasped; all stared. Not a man there but knew of that Cauldron, in which memory must be drowned before each soul could rise from it to return to earth and find a new body in the warm womb of a new mother.

"Yes, they stole it," Keli's laugh was wild, "they, the only two since time began to break out of that world by force! *They* did not choose to lose their hard-won battle skills in its depths—they thought to set mankind free from the Gods forever, free to shape his own destiny."

"But how—?" Pryderi stared; he had come up with Manawyddan.

"How have the Gods managed without it, you mean?" Keli's laugh was still wilder. "Somehow They have, for there is still birth in the world. My mother herself was afraid for awhile; she told me once that she feared she might not be able to get souls for her own sons. Well, we soon shall know. They will slay us all, those demons that come out of the Cauldron now!"

"Be silent," said Bran harshly.

Keli swung back to him. "Woe on the day when my father Llassar gave It to you, against my mother's counsel, Bran no-more-the-Blessed! You that gave It to that Mouse-heart, to him who forsook your sister as he had forsaken us! Once traitor, always traitor, till the Cauldron has washed the soul times without number. Did the Mothers turn their backs on you, or the Gods make you mad, that you rushed like this upon your end?"

Bran said, "I am not yet ended. No man ever has been, and no man ever will be."

Yet again Keli laughed, and the scar that was no scar twisted like a crimson snake.

"Maybe, maybe not. No men before us ever have met their deaths by such hands as we shall die by. You that we called our friend, that should at least have been your own, you should have known better than to give the Cauldron into the hands of those that burned the

children before the mother's eyes. I could have told you what these
Irish were—I on whose face they set their mark while it was still
within my mother's womb! Well, Kueli is dead now—the one of us
two that women liked—and I thank the Gods, those foes of all my
kin, that he died as other men die! A clean death, not such a one as
you and I will know."

Laughing like a madman, he turned and fled into the night.
Pryderi would have sprung after him, but this time it was Bran who
laid a hand upon his arm.

"Let him go, boy." He turned to the men that crowded around
them, clustering white faces already ghostlike, stiff with a fear that
ghosts cannot know. "Let us get to bed now, men. Tomorrow we will
need our strength."

In his vast quiet there was something quieting. It soothed them all.
One man even laughed, though that laugh was not steady on its legs.

"Here is one that they cannot raise again!" He held up a head that
he had taken the night before. "Or if they can, it will be hard for him
to see where to smite."

His comrades laughed uproariously, though there was a queer
twitch in their laughter. But Manawyddan looked at the head and
said thoughtfully, "Were I you, I would guard that well."

The man's face whitened a little. "I will," said he, and tied it
firmly to his spear by the hair.

They lay down with their shields and swords beside them. They
slept, and their souls went out of them, held to their bodies by those
slender silver cords that but one knife can sever, that which is held
in the hands of death, sleep's sister. They slept soundly; to know the
worst is to find a kind of peace.

But in the last watches of the night, in that deep darkness that
goes before the dawn, a great cry rose up and the sleepers woke.
They snatched up sword and spear and looked about them for the
foe, but whichever way they looked the darkness covered their eyes,
the vast bodiless enemy that hemmed them in.

Until torches were lit, and they saw a man cowering and gibber-
ing on the ground, past screaming now, but still pointing with his
hand . . .

At a spear that was bounding over that ground before them, and
as they looked, astounded, they saw what made the spear move. A
head whose hair was tied to it was hopping swiftly, grotesquely,
toward the doors. Its glazed eyes shone red and its bared teeth shone
white.

All men gave a yell and sprang backward. Only Bran and

Manawyddan sprang before the doorway, where the entranced guards stood staring at that head as birds stare at a snake.

Pryderi leapt forward and grasped the spear by the haft, as far as might be from the head. But it spun round and sprang at him, somehow aiming the spear at his throat. That deadly lunge seemed sure to spit him; again all men cried out.

Light-swift, Pryderi twisted to escape the thrust, then yelled as the head itself jumped sidewise and fastened its teeth in his throat.

He tore it away and hurled it to the ground. For a breath's space it lay stunned, then sprang at him again. But this time he side-stepped, and drove at it with his own spear. Again and again it dodged and leapt, trying to reach him again, while he as vainly tried to spear it.

Bran and Manawyddan made the doors fast, and Bran set his great bulk against the nearest. Manawyddan turned to help Pryderi.

But in that instant Pryderi kicked at the head with his left foot, while it was watching the spear that drove at it from the right. That kick caught it and sent it bouncing into the embers of the fire, where it screamed like a man in agony. Pryderi leapt after it and stamped upon it; time after time he drove his spear into it, but still it sprang at him, howling with rage and pain.

Then Manawyddan brought him an axe, and with that he smashed its skull, though he had to smash it into little bits before the pieces stopped leaping at him.

When all was over the men rejoiced. They shook their spears and laughed. "So must we all do tomorrow! Cut off their heads and smash them! Then they will not rise again."

Pryderi sat down and rubbed grease on his scorched feet, and Manawyddan bathed his wounded neck. The son of Llyr used druid power on that wound, as Bran had on his burns, for there was no telling what poison might have lurked in those demon teeth.

But Branwen wept for what those screams had made her remember, and could not escape again into sleep.

Morning came, and with it the host of the Irish, and some had the faces of men, but most had foaming mouths that snarled and slavered and gnashed bared teeth, yet made no sound. Long and hard was that battle; many men died. Matholuch kept those demon-housing bodies always in front, so saving the living and wielding his deadliest metal, the Undead.

One by one those dead men fell, cut into too many pieces to rise again. Living Irishmen took their places, white-faced men who shrank from the devils they fought beside.

Bitter and long was that battle; it ended only with the day. Then the Irish went back to Tara, and the tired shrunken forces of the Island of the Mighty turned back to the House of Bran.

A man named Rhun turned aside to drink at a nearby stream; he was the man who had cut off the head that had fought with Pryderi. Night was falling, and he thought he heard a rustling behind him, but when he turned to see if one of his comrades was there, he caught only a glimpse of someone scuttling clumsily through the bushes; someone too short to be a man.

Is it an Irish child? he thought, He called after it, but only once, for he was very tired. He went on, down to the stream. He stooped to drink, and in that instant something pounced on his back, and long arms grasped his neck . . .

His comrades heard his scream, and came running. They found him lying there, his head twisted from his shoulders. A thing the like of which they never had seen before was dancing upon his body and brandishing his head. Its own body was a man's, but from its shoulders rose no head, only the red stem of a severed neck.

Screaming, they ran back to the House of Bran.

"Well," said Pryderi when he heard, "it has got Rhun's head in place of its own. It is me it will be wanting next. I will not keep it waiting."

He rose and rearmed himself and went down to the stream. His blue eyes and his sweet, gay young mouth were set and stern; for once all his smile was gone.

The thing could not have seen or heard him coming; it had neither eyes nor ears. Yet as he came within sight of the water it sprang.

He was ready. He sidestepped its spring and with a great slash of his sword cut it in two. Its legs fell one way and its arms the other. Yet in a flash those arms were reaching for his neck, and the legs were twining round his. He seemed to be fighting four foes at once, all of them quick and fierce as lightning. He had a hard fight before he got them all chopped into little bits.

But next day only dead men came against the men of the Island of the Mighty. With horror Bran's men recognized the faces of men they had killed not once, but twice; the cauldron had power to weld the smallest bits of flesh together again, into a whole man. And that night scouts brought word that more Irish were pouring in along the roads that led to Tara. The men of the Island of the Mighty were in hard case; they could hope for no reinforcements, and their dead did not rise.

"Once the Old Tribes might have helped us," said Manawyddan, "but not now. Not since they have heard how uncle burned nephew."

He looked at Bran. "Shall we try to reach the ships, brother?" The night was well worn, and the chiefs sat alone in council.

Nissyen raised dark eyes. "What of our wounded? Many of them could not walk so far."

With stern sorrow Manawyddan met those eyes. "Better to lose some lives than all, boy. And our sister is with us."

Bran said heavily, "We could never get there. What whole men we have left could not fight their way so far, with those demons free to come at them from every side. Here we at least have walls at our backs."

"Let us make a surprise attack," said Pryderi. "If we could capture the Cauldron—" His eyes sparkled.

"The ramparts of Tara were well planned," said Bran. "And the spot where the Cauldron sets is well chosen. Two of those devils could hold it against an army."

For a space there was silence. Then Manawyddan said at last, "There is only one thing left to try. Tomorrow we must hold the Irishwomen, so that they cannot bear warning to Tara, and burn their dead along with ours. I doubt if even the Cauldron can raise men from ashes."

But next day at sunset when, after great carnage, the dead were burned, only one armload of Irish fragments was thrown onto the fire. Somehow its fellows knew and fled. Like an enormous pack of rats they scampered off toward Tara. Over the green turf they rolled and hopped and bounded, a grisly squirming mass. Weary and bleeding the men of the Island of the Mighty pursued them, but in vain. He who caught up with them was tripped and thrown, and in a breath's space the flesh was stripped from his bones, so fierce were the nails and teeth of those bodiless hands and feet and heads.

That night, for the first time, the doors of Bran's House were closed. Men huddled round the fires and tried not to think of the Cauldron glowing balefully, like a star of hell, upon the Ridge of Tara; of those shadows that even now must be squirming over its sides: the dead swinging back, with lithe and dreadful suppleness, into the world of men. Within that house was darkness far deeper than that of the night outside; long indeed it seemed to those within since they had set forth in their pride and strength to punish the outlanders, they who now waited like trapped beasts for the butcher.

Sleep came at last to seal their eyelids, to bear them to worlds that the waking brain is too coarse to remember.

When the darkness was deepest Nissyen woke. He heard stealthy movement near the doors, and softly he rose and crept toward it. His hand found another hand and touched it.

"Evnissyen," he said.

"You again!" The whisper was an angry hiss. "Would that I had slain you in our mother's womb! There at least there would have been no fools to cry 'Kin-murder!'"

Nissyen said, "What do you seek to do, brother?"

Evnissyen said, "I have not made up my mind yet. But something must be done."

They went out together, and closed the doors behind them. They walked over ground that would have been white with frost had there been light enough in the world for anything to be white. The moon had set and clouds veiled the stars, but upon the hill of Tara the Cauldron still glowed dully. No shadows moved round it now; for that night its work was done.

"He had a good notion, that loudmouthed pup of Manawyddan's," said Evnissyen, "As far as it went. To destroy the Cauldron would be easier than to capture it. If we could throw it down from the walls . . ."

"First we must reach it," said Nissyen. He thought, *You play with straws because you cannot keep still. Because you know in your heart that you have brought death upon all our folk.*

"There must be a way."

For awhile they walked in silence toward Tara, then Evnissyen laughed harshly.

"They say that this island breeds no snakes, yet it has bred Matholuch. See what his snake's cunning has brought us all to."

Nissyen was silent.

"Even you must have wit enough to see what game he plays, brother. He looks to his living dead to kill us all and to us to kill enough of them before we die that the men of Ireland can handle them afterward. Then he can sit in peace at Tara and smirk. Oh, he is clever in his slimy way, the outland snake! If only Bran had not been fool enough to give him the Cauldron . . ."

He screamed then, as a spear shot through the darkness and struck him in the leg.

They fled, but all around them the shadows were coming alive. Flowering terribly and blackly into the arms and shouting voices, into the running feet of men. Arrows and more spears whizzed after them. Nissyen half carried his brother, but even so Evnissyen stumbled and staggered. And behind them a torch blazed into red light.

"Quick, brother!" Nissyen's grasp tightened. "If these are living men, they will know you for their king's murderer . . ."

"Fool!" Evnissyen tore himself free. "You use that word—of the scotching of a young snake . . ."

Then such pain took him that he fell, writhing.

There was a thicket beside them. Light-swift, Nissyen tore off his own green cloak and the flame-red one that Evnissyen always wore. He pushed his brother under the bushes and covered him with the green cloak.

"Lie still, brother. Even if they catch me. You can do nothing, and I do not want to die for nothing."

He ran, the red cloak whirling round him, and the torchlight found it and made it glow like new-shed blood. Shone as mercilessly upon the face that might have been Evnissyen's own . . .

The shout went up, fierce as a hungry beast's: *"Gwern's slayer!"*

More spears hissed; he fell. They closed around him and laughed with savage glee. They would have liked more time; they would have liked to carry him back to Tara, where Matholuch could have shared the vengeance. But the House of Bran was nearer, and from it already voices were coming, and the clank of arms.

They did not have time enough to deal with Nissyen as they would have liked, but they had time enough. They hurt him as much as they could.

12

The Slayer of Two Kings

MORNING CAME, and with it the host of the Irish, and this time they carried Nissyen's head upon a pole. Cries of rage and grief went up from Bran's men when they saw it; like one man they hurled themselves upon the foe. The living Irish had to come to help the dead.

All day long that battle raged; sometimes it broke against the ramparts of Tara; sometimes it rolled back and broke like a wave upon the walls and doors of the House of Bran. Terribly it raged, like a fire that in time of drought seizes upon a forest and all the host of forest dwellers, and devours all, big and little, both the green trees and the winged and furred things that try to flee and cannot, so that at last only stumps are left, and bits of charred wood and bone.

The men of the Island of the Mighty took back Nissyen's head, but the life that had been in it they could not put back, and they paid for it with many of their own.

All through that battle Evnissyen lay beneath the bushes; sometimes he heard it and sometimes he did not, for his mind flickered in and out of him as a dying candle flickers.

I could call them now, they would hear me and come . . .

But he knew that he would not; that he never wanted to hear the sound of any human voice again.

Why should I wish to rise again, when I could not rise while you were still alive, Nissyen? When they were tormenting you . . .

Again his mind left him. When he woke again night was near. He moved a little, beneath that green cloak that was the color of all growing things. He saw the sky above Tara, the white vastness of it turning slowly to darkness, and he saw the Cauldron beginning to glow dully; they had lit the fire beneath it. Soon they would begin to revive their dead.

And he thought, *Not even that Cauldron could bring back Nissyen's own sparkle to his eyes, or his laugh to his lips, or the softness of his voice. How little power there is in miracles, that this one could make Nissyen walk and fight again, if he were put in it, and yet never could bring him back.*

He had never wept except for rage; his eyes did not know how. He could only lie there and feel the pain seethe within him, burning like fire, tearing him like claws.

He is dead, and he died for me. Not because he thought it his duty, but because he cared what happened to me.

The only eyes that had ever met his warmly, unshrinking, unrepelled. The only one who had never had to try to be kind.

I am all alone now, forever . . .

The others had always tried to be kind. He had always known that, and hated them the more for it. Because they had had to try. Why had everything always gone wrong? What had been the meaning of it all? He was too tired to think; also the eyes of the mind that belonged to his present body were not capable of seeing why.

He looked up and saw the Cauldron, red now as the sun that had set; red as a fallen star gleaming through the dusk of hell. Black smoke streamed from it, darkening the darkening sky.

Each day we kill them, but each day they rise again and kill more of us, and our dead do not rise. So it must go on until they kill us all, until they mow us down to the last man, as the reaper mows the grain. The host of the Island of the Mighty will be no more, and the outland cowards will take all our heads and laugh.

He told himself for the thousandth time, *It is Bran's fault, not mine. Bran gave away the Cauldron.*

But he was too weak to kindle the old fires, he who had always had so many fires of wrath to warm himself with. He was alone in the cold and the dark forever, and over the frozen wastes a voice howled, a voice that he could no longer shut out: *"It is your deeds that have brought the men of the Island of the Mighty to this. You hate the outlanders, and your hatred has given them this good gift: the conquest and destruction of your people."*

And within himself he reeled and gave the cry that erring humanity has given throughout the ages: *"I did not mean it! I did not know that it would be like this."* And the inexorable answered him, *"Yet so it is, and by your doing."*

He accepted that; and that was the first time in his life that Evnissyen ever had accepted responsibility for anything that went amiss.

He said, "O Gods, woe is me that I am the cause of this slaughter of the men of the Island of the Mighty, and shame be upon me if I do not seek their deliverance."

He lay very still, and out of his pain an idea was born, the far white shimmer of mountaintops upon it, as out of pain a child is born.

He threw aside the cloak, he pulled the spear from his leg. With blood and mud he smeared his face so that none could have known it. He rolled out from under the bushes; he kept rolling, painfully, until he came to a heap of the Irish dead.

They were two Irishmen without trousers, the *Mabinogi* says, who found him. They hoisted him onto their backs, grunting and groaning, "Here is a big one!" They were all mighty men, those sons of Penardim, men of beauty and power.

He did not have to pretend to be stiff. Upon that battlefield were many soulless, who still were soft and warm.

They carried him back to Tara, and up upon the ramparts. He felt a hot wind blowing upon him; it grew stronger.

The Cauldron . . .

They were lifting him higher; he knew why. The heat of its steam smote him. Fear took him, sudden fear of the boiling depths that were about to receive him.

Can I do what I meant to do? Can I do anything, in that agony? I must do it.

Doll-limp—be doll-limp. You must not stiffen now; they must not guess that you breathe. Doll-limp; like Branwen's dolls that you used to break, you who now have broken her last and most precious doll of all . . .

Their hands were loosing him, falling away. He was falling—down, down. He could do nothing but close his eyes.

O Gods, O Mothers. Agony indeed—hot, searing agony! Is this what Gwern felt?

Then, suddenly as it had come, it was gone. He still felt and smelled the heat and the fumes, the boiling bath of regeneration laved his whole body, but mysteriously it no longer burned. He had a feeling of vast spaces around him, of being outside the world, and yet deep within the world.

In the very womb of the universe . . .

He did not wait to see what it would have done to him. He stretched out his arms and legs as far as they would go. He stretched with all the might that was in him, and with all the violence and rage and fury with which he was gifted above all the sons of women.

He felt his sinews cracking, and then his bones. His lungs labored in fiery torment. He gasped for air, and let in burning heat;

the pain came back. He lived through eons of struggle and torture, he stretched and pushed and strained when it seemed that he could not, by any power human or unhuman, stretch and strain and push the least whit more. His heart was like a great puffed ball, pushing with unimaginable agony against his ribs, that pushed it back and cut into it like knives, inflicting yet more agonies.

Yet all that lasted through the space of only seven breaths.

Then the Cauldron burst, and the heart of Evnissyen burst with it.

The men of the Island of the Mighty, in that hill-high House of Bran, heard a crash as of the moon breaking and falling in fragments upon the earth. They rushed out in time to see a great mass of fire rising from the hill of their foes; then it flew apart and fell back, like a rain of flames, upon Tara.

The Cauldron of the Gods had gone back to the land of the Gods.

Bran said, "He did one good deed at the last. I am glad of that; for his sake as well as ours, for he was our young brother, and fair to look upon. He gave his life for the lives of all of us, and no man can do more than that."

"He did according to his nature to the last," said Manawyddan. "He saved us by destruction, that is his one gift."

All night long the druids labored upon the scorched, seared ramparts of Tara, every art they knew exerted to turn aside the fumes that had been freed by the bursting of the Cauldron. Like a tawny cloud these hovered over the land of Ireland; thick rolling mists shot with a strange fiery green, with purple, and with orange; and whatever color glowed flamelike or wriggled snakelike through those grisly vapors was, when seen there, hideous, a horror to the eyes of men.

Death was in them, those fumes of the Underworld. Birds fell from heaven, cattle died in the fields and foxes in their dens. So did the people, the nobles in their fine wooden houses and the poor folk in their clumsy huts of stone. By dawn no life was left in all that wide plain that stretches westward from Tara of the Kings; no man or woman or beast survived, save in Tara's ancient holy self, and in the House of Bran.

Such was the fruit of the sacrifice of Evnissyen, that strangest of the saviors of men.

He had come and gone, that dark diseased soul whom the druids had foretold. He had shattered a world as he had shattered the Cauldron whose shape symbolized the world, and his own darkness, dissolving into the elements more quickly than his broken body, may have helped to poison those fumes. Though with what unknowable powers his essence blended none can ever guess, what forces lurked in that Cauldron alien to earth: the giver of Life that, carried away by sacrilege, had passed through the Pass of the Dog's Mouth and become a poisoned, perverted shadow of itself.

He was gone, and with him had passed the world he had known. But his brothers did not yet know that, they who labored through the night as the Irish druids labored. They did know what gift he had died to give them, they to whose druid sight his last thoughts must have been visible, agonized images fading into the mists that had engulfed him.

All through the night the sons of Llyr labored, and in the morning they saw that they had saved all of their men who still could stand; but the more sorely wounded had died where they lay. Ever since her son's death, Branwen had lived for the need of those hurt men; it had given her refuge from her own pain, strength to hold shut the doors of past and future. Now she sat desolate, her red, ruined hands empty in her lap, her eyes emptier. In that gray dawn her brothers saw fully, for the first time, what those years in the pit had done to her.

Bran turned away his face, and in his eyes was sorrow beyond all telling. Then he looked at the brother and at the men who were left to him.

"Let us send a herald to Matholuch," he said. "Tell him that we take our sister and leave this land. His people cannot wish for more battle now, any more than ours do."

And in the worn faces all around him hope dawned, feeble maybe as the light that shone upon the corpse-strewn land outside, but still hope. *Home,* they thought. *Home.* Before their eyes rose visions of green fields they knew, of the faces of friends and kin. *It will be the same.*

They thought they could do what no man or woman has yet done, and go back into the past.

The herald went, and the others, tired as they were, almost feverishly set about gathering together and pack-big their possessions. Only Branwen still sat like a carved figure, with her quiet, empty hands.

Manawyddan went to her at last and said, "will you pack for us, sister? Bran and I have much else to do." She rose at once, smiled at him with her mouth and set to work, but though her hands were busy her eyes were still empty.

But Bran's eyes grew easier as he watched her. He said to Manawyddan, "It will heal her, our own land. The smell of the white hawthorne and the purple heather, and the sight of the sunlight on the cliffs of Harlech. She is too young not to go on. Not to want a man again, and feel how like a harp the body is when love moves it to music. Not to bear more children. However her heart is scarred, can any dead child's scream in the fire ring as loud in a mother's ears as the living child's cry for her teat? Home and time are all Branwen needs; life itself will do the rest."

"I hope so," said Manawyddan. He thought, *But home itself will be different, brother. Grief will come on many faces when they look at the few who still follow us and see that their own men are not there. Not until we are old can we hope to see again such a glorious crowd of young men as shouted once beneath the heights of Harlech.*

For many years now much of the Island of the Mighty would be a land of women. Those who had been girls with Branwen would be weeping for their brothers, and for the fathers of their children. She would know herself for the cause of that weeping; certainly that would not help to heal her wounds.

If they could still be healed . . .

The herald came back from Tara. The Irish had not been friendly, but they had been glad to know that soon the strangers would be gone from their island.

One more night what had been the host of Bran slept in the House of Bran. In the morning they would set out.

The moon shone down; coldly, upon a mined land. In the hall of Tara what nobles the men of Ireland had left came to Matholuch.

"Lord," they said, "you are King over a land of the dead. Maybe in the far north, in Ulster the stronghold of the Old Tribes, some folk are left alive. Maybe on the western shores, where the storms beat forever, there are yet others. We do not know; but there cannot be many anywhere. Neither do we know whether our poisoned fields will bear grass or crops again, or whether the few women we have left can still bear us babes. Children we have none—all were blasted."

"That is so," said Matholuch. He thought, *You have not come here only to tell me that which I already knew.* And stiffened with an old dread.

They looked at him with savage eyes, those few who were left him, those always savage captains of the New Tribes. The hard eyes of men who think they have nothing left to lose.

"Shall we let them go, Lord? To laugh at us?"

Matholuch said heavily, "It will be long before they laugh. Of those who crossed the sea not more than one out of ten can still be living. We have made them pay dear for their coming."

"Yet in the Island of the Mighty they may grow great again, may come back with a fresh host—many men must have been left behind to see to their farms and towns—to take this land that they have made a waste. Make it theirs forever."

Matholuch licked his lips. He said wearily, "What would you have me do?" This was an old story

"Let us follow them, Lord. Ambush them on their way to their ships. Two of the royal brothers are already dead. If we could get the heads of the other two—! Or even your woman's own, she that sat and watched her son burn . . ."

Matholuch remembered Branwen's face as it had looked when she saw that burning; heard the screams again, hers and the boy's. For a breath's space something seemed to swing back and forth inside him; almost it got free.

He said harshly, "Speak no more of that. He that burned was my son." Almost he had said, "Speak no more of her," and if he had got that one word out maybe he would have been a man, he who had given up his manhood that he might stay a king.

He remained a king; the king he had always been. He said, "But we will follow them. Yes, we will follow them."

In the morning the men of Bran set forth. It was a chilly, misty morning. Gray heavy rain clouds had followed those poisonous fiery vapors, as though earth tried to heal herself; but as yet no rain had fallen.

Bran looked back once at his house and laughed. "I will never go inside a house again," he said. Had Branwen not been within hearing he would have added, "Would that I never had seen this one." He did say, "All I will ever ask for again is the sky that arches over the Island of the Mighty. That is cover enough for my head."

All were tired and hurt, but all applauded. *Home!*

He marched off, his men around him.

Halfway to the sea it happened. There was a wood, and its leaves were withered; what greenness the coming winter had left, the Cauldron's fumes had charred and blackened. From beneath those ruined trees came death: a shower of spears like low-flying, bronze-beaked birds, and after them, with earsplitting howls, the Irish.

In that last battle the men of the Island of the Mighty fought as a great stag fights, surrounded by dogs, and the others fought like what they were—men whose wives and children, kin and homes and goods, all had perished by that smoky death. Men whose world had ended and who were willing to end with it if they could end the destroyers, the bringers of the doom.

Bran drove the Irish back into the wood. Like the giant he was he pushed forward, his sword whirling like grim light around him, until the black tree shadows engulfed him, reaching for him like the long black arms of giants mightier even than he. A great spear came from behind and pierced his thigh, but he fought on, the halt protruding from his flesh. Twenty more men fell by him before the poison on its point reached his great heart and he fell.

Over the body of their King his men made their last stand. All but seven of them died there, the *Mabinogi* says; and the names of those seven will never be forgotten so long as the Island of the Mighty remembers the glory of her youth: Manawyddan the King's brother, Ynawc, Grudyen, Gluneu, Taliesin, later to be famed for his many births, Pryderi Prince of Dyved, and Heilyn son of Gwynn the Ancient.

The Irish died to the last man.

They were faint and heartsick, those seven who were left. Through the gray rain that had at last begun to fall they stumbled and struggled, striving to build a fire and keep it alight, striving to build some kind of shelter, with broken branches and dead men's cloaks, above Bran where he lay. Branwen helped them, she whom Manawyddan and Pryderi had covered with their shields to the last.

Bran was alive, though he could not move. Like a net of fire the poison filled his veins, and like ice it froze bone and muscle. He suffered much, and all knew that there was no hope.

Stone-still and stone-white, Branwen tended him. Only her eyes were still alive, and all the life in them was misery.

"Sorrow on the day that I sent the starling, brother," she said, and her voice was flat and dull as the blade of a tarnished knife. "I never thought to remember those days in the pit as happy, but how glad I would be to toil in its heat now and think that my baby lived, and that you lived."

He could not touch her. He looked at her with eyes that were as tender as any touch.

"Do not blame yourself, Branwen, girl. On me alone the blame is. I never should have sent you into Ireland; I failed in wisdom, and what is worse, I failed in love—both to you and to, our people— and may my blood alone, and not my son's blood, be required in payment! But I do not know—I do not know . . .

"You do not understand, you cannot. Be it so. Only do not weep, small Branwen, for your tears are the one thing that are as bitter as the poison. Both together are more than I can bear."

She winked the tears off her lashes. She set her teeth and schooled herself again to stone.

"Evil indeed would it be of me not to do that much for you, Bran, brother—I that have cost you your life."

"You have not," said Bran. He looked at Manawyddan, grinned a little, with his pain-wrung mouth. "Tell her, brother, you who know it all and fought it all. But do not tell her until I am dead, for it is uncomfortable enough I am already, without seeing her eyes when she knows."

He said later, "I tore my own pattern—I pulled down, whose work it was to build . . ."

Then his eyes closed and for awhile he seemed to dream, and they sat around him quiet as the falling shadows, thanking the Gods and the Mothers that so, however briefly, he could rest.

Manawyddan kept his arm around Branwen, and her body yielded to the comfort of that hold, but her face still stared unseeingly into misery, with eyes that would never see the good common outer world again.

The night wore. Dawn came, gray and sorrowful. Then suddenly the far east glowed golden, like a door opening into the Shining World.

Bran opened his eyes. He looked, with patient, harried eyes, toward that gold. He said, "I should like to see the sun again; take me outside. It is bad luck houses have always been to me, from the day that I could not get into them until I got into this one-no blame to you, sister, for having it built."

They saw that he thought that he was still inside that house the Irish had built. They lifted him and carried him into the open, clear of the shadow of the trees.

He looked around him happily. "Thank you, men. I will die out here where I can feel the life of earth around me, where everything is always dying, changing, taking new shapes to live again. Walls stay dead forever. What man makes and not the Mothers, that alone can change only to decay; Their handiwork is ever-living."

Then the pain came back and he writhed.

"It is not to be easy then . . . Branwen? Where is the girl?"

Branwen had stayed behind in the dark. Bran looked back and saw her in that miserable shelter that now seemed like a door into darkness, and the saddest of all his looks was on his face.

"Girl, come here. No—" as Manawyddan, gray-lipped now with understanding, would have stopped him. "No. Why should I escape and leave you that burden too? The telling as well as the doing."

She came and he spoke to her. "Branwen, it is brave you must be. I am in too much pain to bear it any longer, and if I could there may still be some Irish left somewhere, and you that can live should be getting back to the ships."

She could not go whiter. She said nothing, only looked at him with dark eyes as piteous as though he had been about to pronounce her own doom.

He smiled into them. "You would not wish to keep me suffering when I could be well, Branwen?"

She bowed her head. He looked into the whitening faces of the men around him and they shrank back.

"Cut off my head," he said. "Whichever of you loves me best, though I think that one of you should be willing to spare my brother, who does."

They shrank farther back.

"Lord," said Ynawc, moistening his trembling lips, "we are not traitors. How could we do this thing to you?"

"You are my men," said Bran. "You cannot be traitors so long as you do my bidding."

"Then we are very loving traitors, Lord," said Pryderi. "We cannot do your bidding. I do not see how it could be done. Be a good lord to us," he urged, with his winning smile, "as you always have been, and do not ask it of us."

Bran ignored that smile, though it had got round most people all Pryderi's life long.

"I have asked it," said Bran. "Is it love to leave me in this pain?"

Manawyddan set his jaw and came forward. "I will do it," he said.

"That is what I expected," Bran said. "Good, wise Manawyddan; always dreading and foreseeing the hard thing that would not happen if you were listened to and always setting your shoulder to it when it has come. That is some men's luck in life."

Pryderi flushed scarlet and his hands clenched. He stepped forward. "Is there none of you that will spare his brother the deed, when that is the last thing the King asked of us?" He looked hopefully round the circle, but met only silence. "If there is not," he said and squared his shoulders, and his mouth tightened and grew white, "I will do it myself."

But Manawyddan had always a tenderness for that gay young king of Dyved. He smiled at him now.

"Your youth is the one brightness left on our earth, Pryderi; I would not have a cloud put on it before one must come. Take Branwen away, lad; that you can do. Go all of you, and leave us sons of Llyr alone."

They went, Branwen walking rigidly; the marks her nails made in her palms then were to be there till her death day. All her thought was, *I must not make it harder for either of them.* She was a will, no longer a woman.

When Manawyddan raised the sword, Bran smiled up into his eyes. "Long ago, Manawyddan, you told me that I who was so fond of building new roads might build a road that would break my neck. It breaks now. Who knows? When we get another birth I may heed you more, my best friend and my brother, son of Llyr."

Five men went on, with Branwen and the head, toward the ships. Manawyddan and Pryderi stayed behind to heap the cairn high over the body that had been Bran the Blessed's. It was wet, dreary work; the gray rain had begun again.

When it was done, Manawyddan looked toward the wood. "There is one more task to be done, boy."

Pryderi found his smile that for hours had been lost. His white teeth flashed in it, pearl-bright.

"Indeed I have been thinking of that, Lord," he said. "And hoping that you would let me have a hand in it."

They went together into the wood. They threaded their way among dead men, and among blasted trees and bushes. Until Pryderi gave a cry and stopped.

"I thought the spear must have been thrown from about here." There was no need to say which spear. "And it was! See . . ."

He held out a bit of red cloth that had been caught upon a branch; red cloth from a man's cloak; a cloak they knew.

"Branwen wove this and embroidered it." Manawyddan's face did not change as he took the rag. "Strange that he still wore it."

"You knew that it was he—?" Pryderi stared.

"He was not among the dead. Also last night I felt him fleeing; felt his triumph and his fear."

For a breath's space Pryderi was silent, awed. The New Tribes saw only with the eyes in their faces; they had not that other sight that the Old Tribes had— that sight that came and went, and often was not there, but could be such a thing of dread.

Then he laughed shortly. "Well, it is still true that the Irish died to the last man. He is good at dodging men, that King who is not quite a man. Will he find a way not quite to die?"

"Not with us behind him." Manawyddan's voice was as unchanging as his face.

They went on through the wood; they came out on the other side of it. The rain stopped and the moon shone. Pale as a ghost of the sun it shone down upon a desolate land, a land that lay as devoid of life as all lands may have lain before life was created. The birds lay dead beneath the trees, and the beasts in the fields. A woman lay dead beside a well, a fallen bucket beside her; also a fallen child. Not even an ant was there to feed on their discarded flesh.

But somewhere in all that stillness still lurked one living thing . . .

The rain had washed away all tracks, yet somehow Manawyddan knew which way to go. Perhaps the feverish heat of his quarry's own fear guided him, as the hare's smell guides the hounds. In the dawn at last they found him, asleep under some bushes. These might have hidden him, had he not still been wrapped in his torn red cloak, that made him look as though mantled in blood.

They stood and looked down upon him, and knew that the chase was over.

Manawyddan's face was set, as it had been set ever since that moment in which he drew his sword and advanced upon Bran. Set as a face carved in stone. He drew his sword again, but there was no joy in his eyes.

"The druids would say that I still had much to learn," he said. "They would be right. This will not bring Bran back. But it must be done. This that lies here has done more and brought about more than I can bear."

"Lord," said Pryderi very hopefully, "I remember that you never liked killing, and it is glad indeed I would be to step on this louse for you. So if you do not want to bother . . ."

"There is still a king to be killed," said Manawyddan, "and I will do it who for this hour and never again am a king, Beli's heir."

He put the point of his sword against Matholuch's throat and stirred him, not roughly, with his foot.

Matholuch started wide-awake. As though even in his sleep he had expected this, feared it and waited. His terrified eyes darted from side to side, from one man to the other, like trapped beasts.

"Manawyddan!" he said. "Brother! It was not I that killed Bran. It was not by my order that the man hid and did it. It never has been by my will that harm has been done to any of you, to my lady or to her brothers, my kin. Manawyddan, remember that we are one kin . . ."

"Rise up," said Manawyddan, "you who struck the weak in the face and the strong in the back."

But Matholuch the Mouse-Hearted had no mind to get up, even when the sword pricked a little deeper. Pryderi began to draw his.

"Indeed, Lord, now that we have caught our mouse, is there any need for us to play cats with him, because he will not act like a man? Let us kill him at once, like men."

Matholuch shrieked at that, he flung up begging, clawing hands. He had none of the props of pride left, and therefore no pride; he had no vanity; he had only flesh that wanted to go on breathing.

"Manawyddan, Manawyddan—" The words were a prayer.

Then he met those gray eyes that were as deep as the sea and as cold, and his tongue froze in his mouth. For a long moment there was silence, there in the dawn; the sun was rising bloodily in the east.

"O man of almosts," said Manawyddan, "this is the end of you. Rise up now and do one deed wholly; you have never done that, for even when you were born there did not quite enough of you come to make a man. Die like one now, give my sister, who has lain with you, one decency to remember; do not put more shame than you must on the memory of my nephew, whom you fathered. Die decently, for there is no way out of dying; I will not let you live."

Matholuch rose up then. He swallowed hard, three times; his tongue came alive and he licked his lips with it, though it was only a poor frightened thing, shivering there in the dry red cave of his mouth.

Pryderi stood watchful, his sword ready in case of tricks. But there were no more tricks in Matholuch; he had no cunning left. An end of all things had come to him, and here was the end of himself.

He fought, and he did not do badly in that last battle. The sun was high in the east when Manawyddan killed him. It beat upon his face as he fell, and turned his almost red hair and beard to gold. It gleamed in his glazed eyes, that looked straight up, at last without fear.

Manawyddan wiped his sword, and sheathed it.

"Are you not going to take his head, Lord?" Pryderi looked in surprise from those dead eyes to Manawyddan's, that were unreadable, gray and cold.

"No," said Manawyddan. "Branwen shall not look upon his face again. Besides, we have heads enough to carry. One head—I would not pair that with this."

13

The Wind of Death

THROUGH THAT night the five men from the Island of the Mighty had slept, exhausted, upon the cold seashore.

They had come to that shore, and they had found all changed. Their ships were wrecked or gone. The Sinking Lands no longer stretched like a marshy bridge from Ireland to the Island of the Mighty. They had sunk in that mighty catastrophe when the Cauldron had burst and its venomed fumes had spread over earth and sea.

Dead among the wreckage of the ships lay those few men who had been left to guard them. While war raged the outnumbered Irish had spared them; the older and cooler heads among them cannot have wished to cut off the enemy's retreat. But that cloud of death had spared nothing.

Weary and wounded as they were, the five men built a funeral pyre for the comrades they had hoped would welcome them. Then they made camp, as best they could. With the hulls of two broken boats they made a shelter for Branwen, and in it with her they set the Head of Bran, in the golden dish in which they had carried it, that dish which had been brought from Harlech to hold his food.

They slept then, but Branwen did not sleep. She knew what errand must be keeping the one brother she had left, and in the dark she lay and prayed to the Mothers.

"Let him be safe—let nothing happen to Manawyddan, my brother . . . Let the man who once was my man die better than he has lived . . ."

Would Manawyddan bring that head back upon a pole, dead eyes glazed above the gray lips that once had been warm on hers? And if he did, what would she do? Smite that cold cheek as once he had smitten hers, the outland coward, her brother's slayer? Or go mad and take it down off the spike and cradle it where it had wished to lie—for its own safety's sake, not for any love of her—that head of the father of her son? No, never that; he had killed Bran.

Bran! Bran, my brother! Gwern, my baby! You two I loved, and him I learned to hate, yet now that I too am guilty and broken I can see the terribleness of having to hate him of all men—Matholuch! I would have pitied Gwern if he had been afraid, yet his father I could not pity. A man should be a man. Not a walking, twisting fear.

Oh, Bran, my brother! Gwern, my son!

She prayed again. "Mothers, keep Manawyddan safe." But she could not feel the Mothers. She could feel only the great dark about her, the darkness that seemed as vast as the world. Both Those she prayed to and those she prayed for seemed as far away as the stars, and she was all alone, shipwrecked and solitary forever.

Then out of the darkness the Head of Bran spoke. "You are not alone, small Branwen. I am here."

She raised herself on one arm. She stared, no more breath in her than in the Head.

Its eyes had opened, and they were Bran's eyes. Its lips opened, it spoke again, and the voice was the old deep voice that had been Bran's when it was upon his shoulders.

"Child, not yet can I go to my rest, who have brought all of you to this."

She cried out at that. "No! I brought *you* here. To your death."

But the Head only smiled. "Girl, Matholuch and his butcher left you one ear; use it. He took you to get a son who would be King of the Island of the Mighty, and I cheated him, who hoped that if your boy was born afar Caradoc might be King after me. You were the pawn in the game we played. You have little to thank us for, husband or brother."

For a breath's space her eyes widened, but then memory overwhelmed her again.

"I had Gwern. Another man might have given me another son, but not him, and I cannot wish him unborn. Weakling though his father was, only we two together could have made *him.*"

"You two made his body, girl; not all of him."

"The body that Evnissyen burned!" That memory tore a scream from her; she rocked back and forth, moaning. "Go to your rest, Bran; take me with you! Then I may find him again. He may be remembering—he was so little, he cannot understand what happened that night. Even in the arms of the Mothers he cannot understand. What if he thinks, like the Irish, that all of us betrayed him, even I . . ."

"Peace, sister! He needs no comfort. That burning was only an evil dream. Evnissyen made all of us dream it, but Gwern was the first to wake."

"But he is gone. I cannot see him, I cannot hold him. I can see only his death—hear only his cry; day and night, sleeping and waking, I am burning with that sight and with that sound! I am dying, yet I cannot die. Give me rest, Bran; let us both rest!" She still rocked to and fro.

"Girl, these are only evil dreams; you torture yourself for nothing. In the pit you had courage to work and wait and be patient. Have that courage again."

"To what end, Brother? Oh, I know—I do not doubt what the druids say. Sometime I shall find my son again—but when, and what forms will we wear? I want my baby—not a strange man, or some shining spirit—and him I will never have again. Three years I waited—three hard bitter years, praying the Mothers not to let him change too much—and now I must wait again! For a stranger."

"You want the image that you cherished in the pit, Branwen; his chubbiness and roundness, the curls that you combed, and the arms that he put round your neck. But those things you may have again in another child; they are things that always pass. Not the true Gwern."

"I want the Gwern I knew!"

She wept until at last the Head wept with her; then she roused herself, and pitied its sorrow as she would have pitied the living Bran's. She wiped its eyes, where the tears trickled down the great face to the chin, and she tried to wipe away the blood that ringed its neck, but she could not, for that blood always stayed fresh. As she worked the Head watched her, and that look was not quite like the living Bran's.

"Sleep, Branwen," it said gently. "It is true that you need rest, little sister. Lie down and sleep."

Hope kindled in her white face. "You mean . . ."

"No. Your body is still too strong for that. But sleep, and if your sorrow does not bind your mind too fast to your body, you will find Gwern again, even though when you wake you may not remember the meeting."

"I must wake?" Her mouth trembled, her eyes were sick with pain.

But the Head looked at her, and under that strange compelling gaze, weights seemed to come upon her eyelids; she fell down where his feet should have been and slept. And the Head still looked down upon her, and its eyes were sad for her, and for all things.

"Evnissyen, can you bear to look on this, from where you are, you that burned her child's body in the fire and burn her spirit in it yet? Oh, the deed is hers also, that yields herself to the fires you kindled, but she is not the first of our blood to love a son too much. All these deeds sprang from my deed, and for me the time of payment draws near . . .

"Some day folk will believe in a God Who burns men forever and ever, and they will call Him a God of Love—and then as now, themselves Will still burn themselves. When will there be an end of burning, O Mothers? An end of the pain we children of women deal each other?"

And the Head looked toward the east, where the Island of the Mighty was. Out across the foam-tipped, troubled billows of the dark sea it looked, and through the moonlit darkness above. How far those strange eyes saw no man may tell, but agony rose through their calm, and for a space they were but the eyes of Bran looking upon his own misery.

"*Caradoc,*" the Head said softly. "*Caradoc.*"

In the Town of the Seven Chiefs, Caradoc sat with the Six. They were happy, because the storms and the undersea crashings that had come with the final subsidence of the Sinking Lands were over. Land and sea were at peace again.

The *Mabinogi* says that Pendaran Dyved was there, as a young page. But that seems strange, for Pendaran Dyved must have been an old man then. He cannot have been young twenty years before, when, as Pwyll's chief druid, he named Pryderi from that first cry Rhiannon gave when she knew that her longed-for little son was safe. "Now I am relieved of my anxiety (*pryde ri*) ." Most likely his druid sight had warned him of danger (between Dyved's princes and the Children of Llyr the bonds were always close), and he had left his own body behind in Dyved and come to borrow the page's for awhile. The lad's own spirit must have gone where sleeping folk go.

The Seven feasted, and the druid watched, wise eyes of age shining with the brightness of those borrowed young ones, and the night wore. The moon came down from her throne, and the heavens darkened; the earth shivered as if before the coming of vast cold. Inside Caradoc's hall was still light and warmth, but outside, in that last starless hush before the dawn, blackness lay like a great beast crouching at the doors.

"Lord, the wind is rising." The youth who had Pendaran Dyved inside him spoke to Caradoc. "Shall I shut the doors?"

Caradoc laughed and shook his head. "I feel no draught, boy. I never have known a stiller night."

"It is too still, Lord. The wind will be a great one when it comes."

Unic Glew laughed drunkenly. "Run along, youngster—have a drink and warm yourself. We have had enough winds lately; we do not want you scaring up more out of your head."

The page made no answer. He stood and eyed those doors that were all darknesses: watching eyes of night.

Heveydd the Tall and Gwlch drowsed; they were the oldest of the seven chiefs. But Iddic, sitting near them, stirred restlessly of a sudden. He ran his hand over the back of his neck.

"Hoo! That was a wind! Cold as a knife. Maybe those doors need shutting, after all."

Fodor the son of Ervyll was sitting next to Iddic. He started, looked behind him, then shook his yellow hair out of his eyes and laughed.

"You are right, Iddic. That was a wind! There must be many dead riding on it, to make it so cold. I hope our ships are safe, there in Ireland. It is a good thing that your father's new palace is too far inland, Caradoc, to have been flooded."

Llassar the son of Llassar frowned. He was the greatest warrior there, and he sat next to Caradoc.

"We may have missed a messenger from Ireland. Not one from your father, Caradoc—this fellow asked for me. But he must have known something about the host."

"Who? When? How?" There was an instant pricking of ears, a raising of heads. Caradoc's eager voice cut across them all. "Who was the man, Llassar? And how did you miss his message?"

"Because he died, Lord. Died saying, 'Llassar. Tell Llassar—' But what he would have told me only Arawn, King of the Underworld, knows."

"How did it happen?"

"My men found him on the seashore, beside the wreckage of a fishing boat."

"You think he had been caught in the sinking—?" Caradoc drew a deep breath. Awesome indeed was the thought of that convulsed sea, of the depths opening and swallowing up their long-awaited prey.

Llassar said simply, "No man could have lived through that, Lord."

"You have no idea who he was?"

"He could have been anybody but a small man, Lord, or one as big as your father. He had been a warrior, no fisherman; he had worn gold and scarlet, and he was covered with wounds, old and new. He was built like my brothers, Kueli and half-faced Keli, but whether he was one or either of them not even my mother, Kymideu Kymeinvoll, could have told. He had no face left at all."

"You think the sea had done that?"

Llassar said slowly, "No. Men must have fallen upon him just after he landed. Maybe he mistook them for friends. It was still dark when my men found him, yesterday morning, and they swear that they heard fleeing footsteps."

Caradoc frowned. "Robbers? I thought we had cleaned all of them out of these parts. But his news cannot have been important; no messenger from the King my father would have come alone and in a fishing boat."

Yet he still frowned, uneasy. No man could have wished to make that voyage. Even when no terrors rose out of the deep, that wild, already wintry sea was cruel to travelers. Bran and his men, with their fleet, would be mad to try to come home before spring warmed the winds and the waters. Yet one man alone had dared that journey—and when the sea could not yet fully have subsided after making its terrible and titanic meal. What fear, what need, could have driven him?

Can harm have come to the host? To my father—? Firmly Caradoc told himself that that thought was folly.

He shrugged. "Well, it is a strange business. But we must catch those robbers; I will not have more men killed."

Iddic looked up from his wine again. His eyes had a strange glitter, a glaze, like the beginning of emptiness. "It must have been he that I felt riding upon the wind. Your brother, Llassar. Why should he run his cold hand along the back of my neck? Keli never liked me—why should he come to me first? But your turn will come."

Llassar said sharply, "There is no proof that that dead man was Keli my brother."

Caradoc said, "We will send for a druid. One powerful enough to call him back and find out who he was. We will send into Dyved for Pendaran Dyved himself, if need be."

"I wish he could hold the fellow long enough to find out what his message was," Fodor muttered.

A mighty wind suddenly blew through the hall. The candle flames twisted, sank, and for a breath's space the long room seemed to tip over into darkness. Even the fire upon the hearth shrank down, as if in fear of hands that might seize it. Then the flames rose again; all was as before.

Caradoc said abruptly to the disguised druid, "That was a better idea of yours than we thought, boy. I would not have that draught come again. Shut the doors."

The druid did not move. He was staring hard into the shadows, as though trying to find in that dark, clustering troop one that might have life in it, a thicker, stronger shade.

"Too late, Lord," he whispered. "Too late. It is inside now. We do not want to shut ourselves in with It."

"With what?" Unic Glew laughed loudly. "You heard the King's son, boy. Go and get those doors shut." And he made a pass at the seeming boy's head.

The druid did not even bother to dodge, as any real boy would have done. He still stared into the shadows.

"Listen."

Outside a great storm broke suddenly. The black waiting stillness turned into raging sound. Wind shrieked round the house. Hail battered it, beating upon the roof like a myriad tiny, frantic hands.

Fodor whispered, "So it storms when the mighty die. When a man's Other World foes and friends fight around his house."

Caradoc went white to the lips. "If this means that harm has come to my father—or to my uncles . . ."

Iddic had still been staring with dulled eyes into his wine. Now suddenly he raised his head.

"So it is you, Keli? I thought so. No—you are trying to warn me? It is . . ."

As he spoke there was a flash of light and his head fell, and blood rose in a spurting jet from his neck.

His head fell upon the table before him and rolled along it, the eyes glazing now into complete emptiness.

For a space all men saw the sword that had flashed through the air to smite him; then, lightning-like as it had come, it flashed back into nothingness.

They had seen no hand. . . .

Fodor mab Ervyll screamed. He sprang up, away from the headless sitting body of Iddic. But even as he did so, even as that body crumpled, the sword flashed once more. It went through his back and out again through his breast; and mighty must have been the tug that drew it out again.

It dripped in the air and vanished, as if dissolving. Fodor fell and lay still; and the relaxing body of Iddic fell and sprawled across him, limply as a dropped doll falls from a child's hand.

Llassar sprang forward, across them both, and struck madly with his own sword into the air from which that shining death had come. But his blade found nothing. So for a little while he dueled with air; and the others ran hither and thither, striking about them with their swords. But they saw nothing, heard nothing; they smote only air, pierced only air.

Caradoc moved toward Llassar. "Back to back! If we stand so we cannot be reached from all sides at once. Back to back, men!"

He shouted, but they did not hear him. They leaped and ducked and sidestepped, they fled from corners and they dived into corners, crouching there and swinging their swords in fierce circles before them, to keep off that unseen foe.

Caradoc reached Llassar. And in that very moment the sword came out of the air again. Behind Llassar the son of Llassar, not before him. Blood from the blade spattered Caradoc's cheek as it clove downward, through Llassar's shoulder, to his heart.

He fell, and his weight bore Caradoc to the ground with him. The druid flinched, expecting to see the blade pierce that prostrate body, but once more it vanished. Caradoc stumbled to his feet, untouched.

"To the doors, men! Let us get out!"

They heard him this time, in the brief, dreadful silence that followed Llassar's fall. They rushed for the doors and he rushed with them, but between them and that sheltering darkness the sword flashed again, dripping now with the blood of three men.

Caradoc sprang at it; his own blade struck against it. "Smite, men! It cannot hold the door against all of us. There is a body somewhere behind it . . ."

But as he spoke the sword vanished, and then came again; and there came a terrible groaning scream from Gwlch. He crumpled to his knees; the sword flashed and dripped as it left his breast.

All courage seemed to leave them then, those last two chieftains, those warriors who had been brave in battle, Unic Glew and Heveydd, called the Tall. Like mice played with by an invisible cat they fled through the hall, their swords whirling round them. Caradoc followed them, but they paid him no heed; more than once their swords almost spitted him.

Backed against the wall, the page who was Pendaran Dyved stood silently watching, his old eyes showing through his young face, like a reflection under water . . .

That came which must come. The sword appeared in the air again, this time above Caradoc's head. Even as the druid shouted warning, even as his last two men jumped back, screaming, it crashed down through flesh and bone.

It pierced the thigh of Heveydd the Tall, and as he stumbled, dropping down awkwardly to the height of other men, it flashed again, smote again. The once high head of Heveydd bounced from his shoulders, and past the cheek of Caradoc.

Of the six chieftains five had fallen.

Only Unic Glew was left, and unfortunately his courage came back to him. He lurched about uncertainly in his drunkenness, trying to balance himself on legs that did not seem very well acquainted. Again and again he stabbed the air.

"Unic! Unic Glew!" Caradoc called him, but he only shook his head dizzily and went on stabbing shadows.

"Let me alone, son of Bran. The sword lets you alone—time after time that has been shown. You need no help and you can give no help. Let us fighters be."

He stabbed another shadow. "I have never run from a man with a sword," he mumbled with dignity, "and I am through running from a sword with no man onto it."

He walked out into the middle of the hall.

Caradoc knew what would happen then. What five times already that night he had seen happen, and he could not bear it. Within him something snapped, as an overtaut cord snaps. He sprang after Unic Glew and hurled him against the wall, covering him with his own body. With straining eyes he stared into and begged that deadly Nothingness:

"If you will not fight me like a man, at least let me die with my men. Do not put this shame on me, to see all of them die before my eyes while I strike no blow."

But nothing answered him. No sound, no movement, no flash of sword. The candles burned lower. The hail still beat upon the roof, frantic as helpers, defenders, that could not get in.

From his place against the wall the druid watched as quietly as God . . .

Caradoc threw back his head, so that his throat and breast made a target, defenseless and bared.

"Are you a coward to ignore a challenge? It is in my keeping this island was left; it is under me those six were. Take my life, and let this last man go."

He saw the sword coming. Like a ray of light it advanced, here glittering bronze, there the fresh scarlet of dripping blood.

He stood steady to meet it, eyes alert, sword ready. And then Unic struggled and twisted away from the wall.

"Here it comes! Let me at it, boy."

Caradoc tried to push him back, and in the struggle Unic's back was turned, and the sword flashed down into it. In horror Caradoc's hands fell, and Unic broke free and staggered back to one of the long tables. He clutched it, staring with astounded eyes at Caradoc.

"You held me—for it to stab me."

Those were his last words. He fell then and died.

The stiffening corpse lay there, and Caradoc lay beside it. The rain blew in gusts through the hall, and beat upon the breast that he had bared to the sword in yam.

Sometimes he talked to himself, and his voice and the shrieking wind were the only sounds that broke that silence.

"It is in my keeping that my father left the Island of the Mighty, and this is how I have kept it. What man would follow me now? I am all alone . . .

"Six times my heart has been pierced this night, and yet I live. All of them, all of them!" He named their names, and ground his teeth, and wept. "Yes, I live—my life he counts too poor a thing to take! And he has made it so . . . If I could get at him, if I could see him, for but one breath's space! There is no distance I could not spring across to seize him, no sword and no strength that could help him, once my hands were on him! But I cannot see him, I cannot reach him! He will only kill and kill, and let me live and watch . . . May the Hounds of Arawn tear him, may his soul hang red and ragged from their jaws!

"I can do nothing, I cannot find him, I cannot ask more men to follow me to a death that I cannot share. It is poor stuff for a king I am. Caradoc the cursed, son of Bran the Blessed."

The silent walls seemed to echo that in many voices, the rain that had followed the hail seemed to beat it out with tiny feet upon the hard-trod floor, thousands of sounds forged in the flaming anvil of his tortured brain into one sound:

"Caradoc the Cursed . . . Caradoc the Cursed!"

He lay there and his mind burned and his body burned.

He lay there and he died there, before dawn.

Morning came, and out of its gray shadows the earth reshaped herself, black formlessness and misshapenness taking on form and warmth and color. Out of those gray shadows where the dead men lay and the druid crouched, the form of the magician took on shape and humanity and color. He stood there a living man, clean and comely, save for his bloodstained sword.

He was Caswallon, the son of Beli.

He walked over to the dead son of Bran. He knelt and felt over him with his hands, then looked up at the still silent druid.

"This is not my doing; my hands are free of kindred blood. It would have hurt my heart to slay him, because he was my nephew, my cousin's son, and indeed there is no mark on him. You will bear witness to that, druid."

"You did not shed his blood. To that I will bear witness."

"I did not plan this; I did not foresee it. How could I have foreseen it? I never would have died only because other men died; it seems to me that the boy was a great fool."

"He will be called one of the Three Chief Guardians who died of vexation and grief. The *Triads* will give him that name and honor him long after both of us are dust."

"Who will the other two Guardians be?" A shadow crossed Caswallon's face.

"They will not be of your blood. No son of yours will reign after you. The Island of the Mighty will have many kings now, but none will reign in peace, and none will found a dynasty. And in the end fair-haired invaders will sweep over all and subject us all—New Tribes and Old alike. Bran might have prevented that had he not given away his sister and the Cauldron, that symbol of the cup within her body—the power of birth and rebirth, the power of woman. Now for ages women will be as beasts of the field and we men will rule, and practice war, our art. By it we will live—or by it, rather, we will struggle and die."

"For awhile at least I will rule, druid. Who are you? Mâth the Ancient?"

"I am Pendaran Dyved. Mâth's spells would have been strong enough to tear the Veil of Illusion from you. It was your good fortune—or your bad—that he never crosses the borders of Gwynedd, his trust from the Mothers."

"It was my good fortune—if he would have been strong enough. I am not bloodthirsty; I will be a good friend to all who pay me due homage as High King. I will not even harm those who do not, so long as they do not lift hand against me. I think they will be few."

"Did Keli lift his hand against you? He that came to warn his brothers of the demons that might follow him out of Ireland?"

"I did not want him to spread panic among the people. The sea rolls between us and Ireland; we have time, at least, to prepare for those demons. But when I heard what Bran's folly had led to I knew that it was time indeed for this island to have another King—one of the true line of Beli."

"You have wanted his crown these many winters, Caswallon; ever since he went into Ireland you have plotted to take it. But you need fear neither Bran nor the demons his folly loosed. The Cauldron has been destroyed, and so has our true King, and most of his people with him."

Light blazed in Caswallon's face; was swiftly veiled. "Hard tidings, druid. Yet if so, kin will not strive with kin. War and bloodshed will be banished from this sea-girt isle for ages to come. Your prophecies are as poor as your spells were when you strove against me, old man."

"Are they so? Before you die you will see invaders, Caswallon; bit by bit you and the kings that come after you will have to yield the land. We have been stripped of our young men as a tree is stripped of fruit, and soon the birds of doom will gather; they will never let us grow such another crop. They will attack and attack, and what strength they do not drain our own strife among ourselves will eat up. For you will be but the first of many, bloody, self-seeking plotters. Yet for awhile, if you keep some of your promises, you can give us peace. Reign then, son of Beli; your hour has come. I strive against you no longer."

Caswallon smiled and thanked him, but in the midst of his thanks the other looked around, staring as if he saw the dead bodies for the first time. With a scream of fear and horror he fled, and did not stop until the green wood of Edeyrnion closed round him. For a moment that flight startled Caswallon, then he smiled.

"It is only the boy. My kinsman's page."

So it was. For the druid had gone out of that borrowed body; Pendaran Dyved was back in Dyved.

Caswallon's thoughts turned then to the great funeral and the great mourning that he would make for Caradoc. He was very glad that he had not had to kill his young kinsman; one cannot doubt, either, that he was more than a little glad to have him dead. The druid's prophecies he thrust out of mind; ill-wishers are often wishful thinkers, and this was indeed Caswallon's hour. No ghosts should stand between him and its joy.

And in Ireland, in the gold of the morning, Bran's huge Head bowed itself where no breast was, over the golden dish that held his blood, and great tears dripped down onto Branwen's white sleeping face.

"It is finished," the Head said. "And it is begun."

14

The Birds of Rhiannon

THEY TOILED, those seven men of the Island of the Mighty who were left in Ireland; toiled to build a ship that would carry them home. They soon found that the charred wood of their wrecked ships was treacherous and rotten; nothing that the fumes of the Cauldron had touched could be made serviceable again. They had to go inland, to the forests, to cut trees and these they had to choose with care; there too the Cauldron's searing breath had been. Then they had to drag the logs to the shore; the work was not easy.

They saw no Irishmen; save for themselves that stricken land was deserted, and when their sweat was not running and their backs aching, they too felt like ghosts. So many had fallen; they were so few who were left.

They had no fresh meat; no game was left to be hunted, but some of the ships' stores were still edible. When Manawyddan first sat down to plan the work, Branwen claimed the task of cooking for them. Silence fell then, a heavy, shocked silence. Out of it Manawyddan said, "Are you sure, sister? Some of us can cook."

Never since her son's burning had Branwen looked upon a fire. Whenever she had had to be near one she had kept her back to it, ox at least turned away her face. But now she said, "I cannot fell trees, brother, nor shape wood into ships' parts, but here in Ireland I have learned well how to cook. I will do what I can."

So she did. While the men built the ship she worked as quietly as once she had in the kitchen of Tara, and what she saw in the flames only she knew.

Manawyddan thought, *Maybe it is the beginning. The first step. Maybe now she will come back out of the past, into the world of living folk.*

Branwen thought, *This much I can do. For this little while longer I am needed.*

One other thing she did. Near the place where she cooked, and where all of them ate, she built up a mound of earth and stones. Upon that mound she set the dish that held Bran's Head, and round it she wrapped his cloak, so that he himself seemed to be standing there, watching over them.

At first that act of hers troubled Manawyddan, but he did not like to oppose her, and he told himself, *Maybe this too is a step. She makes a baby of our brother's head, thinking she does it only for love of him, but in her heart she longs for a new child.*

And he was glad that the Head showed no signs of decay; its color stayed fresh and bright as in life, and the closed eyes looked as if they only dozed. Every day Branwen washed it and combed its hair, and every night she took it with her into her shelter.

The day came when the ship was ready; it was a day when the sun shone weakly, and no wind blew. Manawyddan said, "Shall we wait here for spring, we who are too few to defend ourselves if foes come? They may yet, for I think that the winds did not carry that death smoke over all Ireland. Or shall we take the gifts the Mothers have given and set sail, trusting Them to bring us home?"

As with one voice all said, "Let us go home!" But they did not fear the Irish, or trust the sea; the truth was that none of them could bear to stay in that silent land any longer, that land of death.

The seven set sail, and Branwen was the eighth of that company. With Bran's Head in her lap she sat and looked back toward Ireland until the mists came and hid it. Then she bowed her own head and hid her face in the hair of Bran.

Pryderi said uneasily to Manawyddan, "Is she weeping? You would think she would be glad to see the last of that land, where they treated her so cruelly."

Manawyddan said, "Her son was born there, and is buried there; Irish blood flowed in his veins. We are lucky whose love and hate can flow in single channels; not be mixed together."

But his hopes waned as he looked at her. *What has she to go home to? What all of us want is to go back to a place that is nowhere now. To home as we knew it, to an Island of the Mighty that has sat still, unchanged.*

But it would be changed, and forever. The feasts they went to would be filled with new faces or empty places, and Caradoc would sit as lord of them, never Bran. All their comrades had fallen, all their friends and all their foes, and now they were sailing back alone out of that dead ghost world, with her they had fought for, but the heart in her breast was broken. She was only the seared burning husk of that laughing girl who years ago had sailed for Ireland with her lover.

That prize, their only victory, was lost as well as won. Manawyddan accepted that fact at last, and bowed his own head.

Night found them fog-bound, unable to see their way through the mists, and the hopefulness, the laughter, that had attended their setting out, all gone. Their troubles had come back like homing birds, and all knew at last that they never would get home. Even if their bodies should still reach there, all would be different. There had been so much death that it seemed that all the world should be dead, and their own voices, muffled there in the fog, were like unnatural and irreverent sounds disturbing the quiet of the world's tomb.

Branwen lay with her cheek against Bran's. Once she whispered, "Brother, is this the end?"

For myself I would be glad to rest. But I do not want Manawyddan to die, or his friends. Least of all that boy who is our nephew, and who still has within him so much power to be happy.

In her mind she added those words, though she did not speak them aloud. She had come to think that there was no need to speak aloud to the Head of Bran. And it seemed to her that the Head answered, though she could not tell—since that first night she never had been able to tell—whether its voice came from anywhere but inside her own head.

"I will bring all of you home, small Branwen."

Morning came, and light. Out of the gray waste of waters rose the gray cliffs of Anglesey, the harsh and everlasting rock. But to all of them it looked as warm and inviting as the lighted door of home does to lost children. How they had got there they could not imagine, but they laughed and rejoiced because they were there.

The *Mabinogi* says that they came ashore at Aber Alaw in Talebolyon, that is on the holy Isle of Anglesey. Good indeed it must have been to feel solid land under their feet again, earth that was so nearly earth of the Island of the Mighty.

There was a wood near their landing place. As they stretched their limbs, Pryderi looked toward it and his eyes danced.

"We can go hunting now," he said. "It is glad I would be of some dinner, and it fresh." He tossed his bright head as if defying that dinner not to be caught and eaten, and he smiled.

Manawyddan smiled to see him smile and Branwen smiled at

both of them. But her smile was only a way her mouth moved; it had no light.

"Go hunting," she said, "all of you. I will gather driftwood here on the beach to make a fire with. It will be waiting to cook your meat."

But as she said it blackness came over her and for a breath's space the earth seemed to tip beneath her feet. *Fire—fire—will I never have done with fire?*

Pryderi had not seen; he was laughing. "There will be plenty of meat. And it is almost done with cooking you are, Lady."

She was not sure what Manawyddan's gray eyes had seen . . .

He was the first of the hunters to come back, though he did not bring much game. Together they cut it up and made it ready for cooking. They worked together, and the warmth and closeness of that brought back many things. Almost it built a warm and lighted house around her, walls that her mind could cower behind, like a deer hiding from the hounds.

They were many and strong, those hounds. They were within her, not without. Inescapable—bound to pull her down and devour her.

In time the others came back with their game, and she cooked it. She ate with them and sat by the fire. The sun set. Like the face of a dying woman the sky whitened, though here and there red light still stained it, as with the scarlet of fresh blood.

She thought, *Before night comes I must look at the Island of the Mighty, that I have yearned for so long. From this same shore one can see Ireland . . .*

She rose, she looked. To the west lay Ireland, a flame-tipped, darkening mass. To the east, so close that they seemed almost within her touch, lay the pale shores of the Island of the Mighty. Home . . .

She looked, and all her memories came upon her like hail; such fiery hail as volcanic mountains belch forth to blast the fields of men. She was burned from head to foot with memories; they seared her like coals. They were too many and too terrible for one mind to hold, yet like peaks turned to flames by the sunset the worst rose clear.

Gwern, if I had not sent for help, you would still be alive! What matter what happened to my body, that had brought forth its treasure? I had my island, my refuge then, and I did not know it.

Because of her Ireland lay waste, the green isle of her baby's birth. For her the bravest sons of her own island had died; soon women would be wailing there. Were all those dead any less dead, was her misery any less because she had not been to blame? Only what was mattered; what was, and could never be escaped . . .

She cried aloud to the white evening, "Sorrow that is my sorrow! Woe that ever I was born! For the good of two islands has been destroyed through me."

She moaned once, and her heart broke, and she fell . . .

Manawyddan kissed her cheek and closed her eyes. "Sleep may be best for you, beloved, for the world that we grew up in is gone, and you were too tired to help build a new. Sleep and find Gwern again, and our brothers. And maybe even Matholuch can find some new tale to tell, there before Arawn's face. Maybe it can be your comfort at last, not only your shame, that he was a coward. But it is sad my world will be after you, and the light of you gone out of it."

They buried her in a four-sided grave on the banks of the Alaw. Later the waters must have managed to encircle that last bed of her loveliness, for ages after an islet there was still called *Ynys Bronwen,* "Branwen's Isle."

They left what was left of her, as she had left them, and went on . . .

They crossed the Straits of the Menai, and came to the Island of the Mighty. They who had left it in a host thousands strong came back but seven, with no loot and no prize of victory.

On the way to Harlech a huge crowd met them, a crowd of men and women garlanded, yet sad-eyed. Manawyddan felt his heart turn over in his side when he saw them. He had thought that nothing in the world could touch him any more, but it may be that that is true of a man only when he dies. As Branwen had died, and Caradoc.

He asked the nearest man, "What tidings do these garlands mean?" and he had to moisten his lips before he could speak.

The fellow did not know him; he answered as he would have answered any other man. "Caswallon, son of Beli, has been crowned King in Llwndrys."

"But Caradoc—" Pryderi's voice shook; he had liked his cousin, "what of Caradoc, and the chiefs who were left with him?"

Then the seven who had come home heard what had happened to the seven who had stayed behind.

They went on to Harlech, and there was none to forbid them possession of it. It must already have been stripped of its treasures, if any had been left there, and Caswallon was too small a man to need the windy, roofless courts of Bran. They camped there, in that desolation that once had been thronged with folk and splendor. They sat there, and the Head of Bran sat with them, in its dish.

For long Manawyddan sat brooding, and the others waited. It was for him to speak; he was their King now, rightful King over all the Island of the Mighty, as indeed he had been, by all the ancient laws, ever since Bran died. Their waiting was like a sword that they were pressing into his hand. Their obedience commanded him; their silence made him speak.

He said at last, "Caswallon did not break the bonds of kinship. He did not shed Caradoc's blood; he only broke Caradoc's heart. And not even druid sight can foresee the age when men will call that murder."

"What does it matter what we call it?" Pryderi's hand clenched on his sword hilt. "Let us avenge it. We are only seven, but we are seven who came back from such a war as the world has never seen. And I am still a king; the men of Dyved will follow me."

"To what?" said Manawyddan. "We might win. We might take Caswallon by surprise, and I think there are still many who do not love him. But to win we must bathe the Island of the Mighty in blood. I will never do that. All the less, because the Island should be mine, will I do it—a true king never robs his people of peace."

Silence then; silence deep as that bedded in a grave or at the bottom of the sea. Manawyddan broke it; he laughed, a bitter grating laughter that rang through those barren rocky heights of Harlech, and found its only answer in the gray wash of the sea far below.

"I wondered why, when I cut Bran's head off, he bade me bring it to Harlech. Why he did not say to Edeyrnion. I wonder—that would have been a sad vision to come to a man in his last hour; and a man that so loved his son—" His voice broke.

Silence again, and then out of the depths of that silence came song. The song of birds, sweeter than any sound of earth; finer and more delicate than any music that ever came out of a human throat. That song had all beauty; its gentleness, its peace, were lovelier than the dream of love; than the cold white Heaven dreamed of by later men. It had the magic of Gods that never condemned, never bade or forbade, but lapped all in the music of their measureless charity; Gods who left man to burn himself until his eyes were clear enough to behold the wonder and peace of their gardens; to do what only oneself can do, and break his own bonds.

Three birds were singing, and they were still far away across the sea, yet by some strange sudden lengthening of their vision, the men on Harlech saw them coming; saw them plain and clear. A gold bird, a white bird, and a green bird, circling, with shining feathers, in the sun.

Pryderi caught his breath sharply. "The Three Birds of Rhiannon, my mother! All she brought with her out of her own world. They are hardly ever seen. I saw them once, and I little; I saw her kissing them, in the dawn."

And the Head of Bran opened its eyes and said quietly, where it sat in its dish, "You have decided as a King should decide, Manawyddan my brother; and as perhaps only you would have decided. Now for seven days we will feast here in Harlech, as we used to do, and my Head will be as pleasant company to all of you as it ever was when it was on my body."

For seven days the Birds sang, and for seven days the tired men feasted, and it seemed to them that all Harlech's old splendor was upon it, and they were happy there with Bran their Lord. All the evil that had happened was like a dream that they had wakened from, and troubled them no longer. Their plates and their drinking horns seemed always to be full, though how they were filled none knew. That feast was called by later poets the Entertaining by the Noble Head, and to none of the guests who enjoyed his plenty did it seem strange or sad that Bran's body was not there. He himself was, and that was enough.

Six of those seven did not think at all; but Manawyddan thought. Sometimes in the night, while the others slept, the sons of Llyr talked long.

Once Manawyddan said, "Why could you not help Branwen, brother?" And the Head replied, "I tried. But I could not break through the hot cocoon of pain that wrapped her; she was past shock or comforting. Nobody can love too much, but it is in our blood to love one person too much. So our mother dark Penardim loved Llyr our father, so I loved Caradoc, so Branwen loved her baby. And for her there was most excuse of all, our little sister whom I sent from us to spend those dark years in the pit."

"Could not even the Birds have helped her? They for whose loan you must have asked Rhiannon in her dreams?"

"No. They are fledglings of that race whose song takes away the pain of death, so that the dead go down happily to Arawn. They hold none back from rest."

"And she needed rest." Manawyddan sighed.

"As do all of you, whose minds are worse wounded than your bodies; who have seen and borne things that no men have undergone before you. Even on Pryderi there might have been shadows. But you seven I can heal here on earth; when you wake again to your memories you will have strength to bear them."

"You sound as if we were dreaming now."

"Who can be sure when he dreams and when he wakes? What you know now is good; be content."

Another time Manawyddan said, "There is one thing I should like to know, brother, though I suppose it does not matter. You should know, you who have one foot in this one world, and one in the next."

"I have no feet at all, I no longer need them. But I will answer your question if I can."

"It is this. How have the Gods got along without the Cauldron?"

"They never lost it," said Bran's Head.

Manawyddan stared hard at the Head, then scratched his own. "How can that be? I never could see how Llassar and his woman could have had power to steal that Cauldron, yet it is certain that they got Something that had power."

"It was the Cauldron," said the Head, "and it was not. Perhaps I cannot make you understand, you who still have your whole body, but nothing is ever so solid as it seems. Everything that is is many-layered, and each eye that sees a thing sees only part of it—and that a part that no other eye can see. Kymideu Kymeinvoll and Llassar stole the Cauldron *they* saw—not the one the Gods see. The true Cauldron is too fine for earth; it sits unharmed where it has always sat, throughout the ages. What Evnissyen broke was only a blasphemy and a mistake."

"You are right, brother. I do not understand you."

"It is simple," said the Head. "We are never destroyed, though we have all had many bodies that were. And it is the same way with the Cauldron, that never should have had an earth-self in the first place. Sleep now, brother."

A thought struck Manawyddan. "Can you sleep?"

"I need no sleep, who am beyond weariness, and all the bonds of time and space. When you sleep I go to our parents and our brothers and to Branwen. I am with my son also, my son whom I helped to bring to death, as I led so many of our people to death, because I wanted him to wear my crown. It alone is lost, my brother, and it, in the sense in which I wanted it for Caradoc, was only a trinket after all."

"I could have told you that while you were alive." Manawyddan only thought that, but the Head could hear thoughts. "But then you would never listen. Now that there is less of you, you seem to have more sense."

"Indeed I had to listen," said the Head, "for many a time you would not let me get out of it. But that too is over; it is not about crowns, or any other trinkets that we will bicker again, Manawyddan my brother."

On the seventh day the Head said, "It is time for us to go."

They stared at it in fear. "You will not leave us, Lord?"

"Not yet. We will go to Gwales in Penvro, and there we will feast for eighty days."

They did not question him further. They did not mind leaving Harlech, so long as he was with them; it seemed to them that they had been there seven years, though every hour of that seven had been happy. They set forth, carrying his Head in its dish; and the Birds of Rhiannon flew before them, singing.

They came to Gwales, perhaps now called Gresholm, the Pembrokeshire isle that lies farthest out in the gray murmuring sea. Upon Gwales they found a fair and kingly hall awaiting them; no man or woman was in it. Three doors it had, and two stood open; one faced toward green Penvro, and the second upon the gray-green sea.

"Do not open the door that is shut," said the Head of Bran. "Not now. The time must come when one of you will, but then my Head will begin to decay and the memory of all your woes and losses will come upon you, and you will be back in the world of men."

"Indeed, Lord," begged Pryderi, "please tell us which of us is going to open that door and kill you all over again, and we will kill that idiot first."

"Then you might stay here dreaming all your lives," said the Head, "and I will neither have that nor bring death upon any more of my men." And the Head looked very straight at Pryderi, and Pryderi looked the other way.

Days came and went, blue and golden, and after each day night came, like a tame dark bird alighting gently upon the hand. And still those Seven feasted and were happy, more at peace than the wholly waking ever are.

And his spies bore word to Caswallon, who had grown uneasy when he heard that Manawyddan and his men were at Harlech, that royal seat that many still held in loving awe.

"They sit in a fisherman's hut, Lord, a place that they found all tumbling down and deserted. They drink spring water and gather seaweed to eat, and they laugh and babble like children. They are all mad, Lord."

Caswallon smiled. "There is nothing to fear from them, then."

So in death Bran the Blessed guarded his men better than he had in life.

At night he and Manawyddan still talked. In afteryears, Manawyddan tried to remember those talks, that then seemed lost in a moon-silvered fog.

Once, he knew, he had said, "Nissyen and Evnissyen. Why were they so different, those two sons of the curse?"

Bran's Head had answered, mellow thunder out of that glowing fog, "Both of them were parts of an Immortal, and Nissyen is not such a part of it as ordinarily is born again into a body of our world. But he chose birth, he came back into this schoolroom that he had outgrown, to keep Evnissyen from doing too much harm."

"Indeed," said Manawyddan, "I cannot see what harm he ever managed to keep Evnissyen from doing."

"He did much," said the Head. "He kept you and me from going to war with each other instead of with Ireland. And he made Evnissyen, whose only power was hate, love him, so that in the end the boy broke the bonds that he had been forging upon himself throughout the ages, and sacrificed himself to save us."

Manawyddan sighed. "Seven of us he saved—only seven . . . Our mother should have let our father die."

"Do not blame her," said the Head. "He had to come. Such as he are part of the world's growing pains."

"You make him sound like something a baby must have cut its teeth on," said Manawyddan. "But he has broken most of our teeth, and to me it always seemed that he was doing the chewing, not we."

"Change will always bring forth twins," said the Head. "Good and Evil. We were born in times of great change, that for my own ends I tried to hurry. And change that comes too fast brings about a triple birth: Hatred and Fear and Strife. Now even I cannot tell in what age peace will come again or tumult end."

"You are not encouraging, brother."

"I am not encouraged. In the darkness that comes man will twist and disfigure both himself and those bastard Gods born of his reaching toward the Unknowable."

Another time the Head said, "Indeed it is not much use to try to make the world clean, as Beli tried and for awhile I tried, unless each person will try to make himself or herself clean. Change that is effectual must come from within the hearts of men; force is an ill broom to sweep anything clean with."

"So we were always taught, brother."

"Maybe we were not taught it well enough. Yet in teachers lies the world's only hope. Force should be used only to keep one man from hurting another; to give teachers peace in which to teach. Both governments and Gods will forget that, though the Gods, being shrewder even in their corruption, as the less material always must be, will always know that the One is all that matters. The individual, whoever or whatever he is. For is not each of us one? Alone, trapped in his separateness?"

"Nothing could be truer than that." Manawyddan sighed. Loneliness—sometimes he woke enough to fear it.

The Head went on. "But governments will think that only masses of men matter, that one individual exists only to make his image like to another, and it is then, when man, maker of governments and of man, sick of his corrupted Gods' cruelty, sets governments above them, that his hour of greatest peril will come. For then his own skills and knowledge, grown Godlike, will turn against him."

"May the Mothers be with him," said Manawyddan. Later he wondered what they had been talking about. Often in those night watches the Head used words strange to him; at the time he understood them, but in the morning their meaning would be gone.

That feast at Gwales was a beginning and an end. The end of the reign of the Children of Llyr, of that fabulous early world that for a generation longer Mâth the Ancient kept alive in Gwynedd. What it began is not yet finished; yet many mysteries lie between that time and ours.

Once again in the night Manawyddan woke, or thought he woke; perhaps he only dreamed. And in the silver twilight he saw the Head of Bran his brother staring into space, and heard the great voice say, deep and sonorous as the voice of earth:

"Again I shall be the Keeper of the Cauldron. Yes, my Head shall sit in a castle beyond the rainbow river that girdles earth and there order life and birth, and the age-old struggle between Life and Death his brother. For those two brothers of mine and of all men's were born in one hour, though Life is the elder, and both the predestined victor and the predestined prey."

Manawyddan started to ask what the Head meant, but as his lips were opening, a feather of sleep, the dark bird, brushed his face . . .

Indeed, that meaning was always hidden, and now seems lost. But one tale whose teller seems not yet to have heard of the Grail tells how a young hero who should have asked a question and did not came to a Castle of Wonders, and saw there a Bleeding Head upon a tray and a Bleeding Spear.

The Spear of Christ's wounding—or of Bran's?

There are many worlds, and maybe when the reign of the Ancient Harmonies ended upon earth, those Keepers of the Mysteries who had guarded them in the next world above ours passed on, and made Bran the Blessed their heir. For all Bran's mistakes had sprung from love, and at last he had understood himself, and therefore had won as much wisdom as man can, and was ready to become a God.

That would explain much; even why that demon brother of the Lords of Life is said to have crept about invisible, slaying men under the very noses of Arthur's knights. For death is necessary to make room for life. He sounds more like Caswallon than Evnissyen, but Caswallon may have taken Evnissyen's place as the Destroyer. For one was an individual and the other the beginner of a type and of an age. The son of Beli has slithered snakelike through the centuries, growing ever blacker. Greed is his God, so he is cheaper in his guilt than Evnissyen, who never seems to have cared for gain.

But these things can only be guessed at; never known.

In Caswallon's earthly realm time passed. Above Gwales the second golden moon grew round and passed into darkness. The third rose, slim and horned and shining, began to grow round. The eightieth day came and the eightieth night, and Heilyn, son of Gwyn, woke while his comrades slept. He saw the darkness fade, he saw the two doorways rise out of it, long and pale. He saw the third door, the closed door, appear between the walls, heavy and brown and richly carved, blocking out the dawn.

He was a man of inquiring mind, the son of Gwyn. Whenever there was anything he did not know about, he wanted to find out about it at once. That quality, like fire, can do good work or bad work. Without it man would have got nowhere; with it, many a man has got himself into places he would have given a great deal to get out of.

Heilyn looked at the door, and it seemed to look back at him. To say, *"You cannot see through me. You cannot be sure what is on the other side of me. I am like blindness; I shut you in . . ."*

Heilyn stared at it. He thought, *I could open you. I will not, because it would not be wise. But I could . . .*

The door seemed to jeer at him, as one boy thumbs his nose at another. *"You would never dare. You are afraid of what the Head said would happen. Are you sure it said that? How could a Head talk? Are you sure of anything?"*

He looked toward the Head, but it did not look back at him. The dawn shimmered faintly in its eyes, that might have been looking wisely into the mysteries of space, or might have been only glazed.

He felt suddenly dizzy, uncertain of himself and all things. He sprang up, as if by action to drive uncertainty away. He faced that taunting door; it at least was solid, real.

"By my beard," he said, "I will open this door and see if what is told about it is the truth."

He strode forward; his feet moved and then his hand moved; found that hard solid wood . . .

And then bells seemed to be pealing all around him; wild sweet elvish bells. His comrades started up; he saw their white staring faces, heard their shocked voices. And under his hand was nothing but air. He saw a rude wall with a gaping hole in it, and recoiled.

They all saw; saw what that wall had hidden. The dawn-lit sea and the shores of Cornwall; the mouth of the Henvelen, where it poured into that sea. And sea and sky and river looked as gray as death.

The peal of bells ceased, and they heard the last faint echo of a song. They looked up and saw the Birds of Rhiannon flying away from them, white and green and gold in the drab heavens.

They looked around, and saw no splendid hall, but a fisherman's bare hut. One cried, "Where are we?"

Of all the riches and beauty that had seemed to surround them, only one golden dish was left: the dish that held the Head of Bran. That Head turned its eyes a little now, toward Manawyddan, and smiled with graying lips. For a breath's space the face was still Bran's face, Bran himself was in the eyes and the smile. And then the eyes closed, and the Head slid slowly sidewise, like a ball dropped from a child's hand. It lay on its side in the golden dish, in the midst of the clotting blood, one gray livid cheek bedabbled and upturned . . .

A thin wind blew through the hut, a wind sharp as a sword, and as cold as death.

"It is finished," said Manawyddan. "We are back in our own world. And it is a world without you, Bran my brother, and without almost all that we have ever loved."

In sorrow they left Gwales, that gray place that had been rainbow-bright, and in sorrow they set their faces toward Llwndrys and the White Mount.

Their hearts were dead in their breasts, as dead as the Head they carried, forever silent now in its golden dish. Spring was coming, but they were desolate as naked men wandering in the cold of winter. In that black awakening it seemed to them as though all the dead had died but yesterday, and they grieved for them, and most of all for Bran their Lord.

They came to the White Mount, where now the Tower of London stands, and they buried the Head there, with its face toward Gaul, and the Triads call that the Third Good Concealment. For so long as the dead face of Bran looked toward the continent no invader might set foot upon the Island of the Mighty. So much power to bless had he, even in death, Bran the Blessed, son of Llyr whom dark Penardim had loved. The digging up of that Head is called the Third Evil Uncovering; Arthur dug it up in his young pride, ambitious to hold the Island of the Mighty by his own strength alone, without the help of the ancient mighty dead.

Caswallon must be given credit for doing nothing to hinder that burial, for he must have known of it. But then Caswallon was never the man to throw away an advantage.

When it was done, Manawyddan said, "We must go on now. If we could reach a good place and stop there forever, that would be good indeed. But that never can be. Nothing can stand still for long; what does not go forward must decay."

His face was sad as he said that, he who was no longer young, and who must go forward alone. But the others suddenly remembered people who might still be alive; people who might be glad to see them. Light came into their faces; the faint stirring, as of plants that sought to put forth new roots. Pryderi sniffed the air like a young hound; eager-eyed he faced westward, toward Dyved.

"I will go home," he said. "To my mother and my people, and to golden Kigva, my woman." He strutted a little. "Maybe I will beget a son. Men just back from war often do. It is a good time for it."

Some of them laughed. Even Heilyn grinned, he who since he opened the forbidden door had been almost as silent as the dead.

Manawyddan said, "Any time is a good time for that." He thought, *it is hard to be left behind, a man, when your kin have joined the Gods. To have none to work with or for.*

He who always had worked with Bran henceforth was to work alone. In little daily tasks he might have plenty of help; in great struggles none. That much was true; but how much work awaited him in that new world into which he was going, how little of it would be for himself alone, he could not yet dream. Now he thought that his loneliness would last as long as his body. But that tale is told in the Third Branch of the *Mabinogi*. The Second Branch ends with the burying of the Noble Head.

SO FAR, THE TALE OF BRANWEN AND OF THE CAULDRON; OF THE GREAT WAR AND OF HOW THE SEVEN CAME BACK FROM IRELAND.

The Song of the Rhiannon

To My Mother,
Who had a bright and gallant spirit.

1

The Last of the Children of Llyr

THEY TURNED their faces westward, toward the ancient path of the dead, those seven who were seeking a new life. Those seven who alone had come back from Ireland and from that great war that had stripped two islands of warriors; that war in which not only their comrades but the life and the ways of life they knew had died.

It was too late that day for them to get far on their way to Dyved, so they made camp outside Llwndrys, within sight of the White Mount, where they had buried the Head of Bran their King, he who once had been called the Blessed. They saw the moon rise, tipping with silver the trees and thatched roofs of that city of kings. And then sleep came to weight down their eyelids, and six of the seven slept. Only Manawyddan son of Llyr still sat wakeful, and thought of all that had been, and no longer was.

He looked toward the thatched roof of the King's Hall, and remembered how his parents had taken him and Bran there as little children, to visit great Beli, their uncle: and how long Bran had dreamed that Caradoc his son might sit there, Lord of that hall where no king's son ever before had been enthroned. For the Old Tribes counted descent through the mother, and a king's sister's son always had followed him as Bran had followed Beli.

But now Caradoc was under the earth with Bran, and Caswallon, son of Beli sat in that hall, safe in the place that he had won by magic and by murder. Bran's dream had been fulfilled, though not in the way that he had dreamed it. A king's son now sat in the seat of his father, and the days and the ways of the Old Tribes were done.

Manawyddan sat there and saw nothingness. He heard it and felt it, he tasted it and breathed it.

Had he been younger, he might have sought vengeance; have kindled and fed its fires, and found in them a refuge. An aim for the
aimless, warmth in that great cold.

*I could do it, I am still a strong man. But if I did it, more men would
die; surely some of these six faithful comrades beside me. Young Pryderi
himself might die, he for whom life can still hold much. I could do the
deed alone, but how? Creep upon my foe from behind, like a wolf? As
he crept upon the chiefs that Bran left to guard Caradoc? Make myself
over to fit his pattern? No. Better to die cleanly, in a ditch, like any
other wandering beggar.*

*For what are you but a beggar, Manawyddan, son of Llyr, who have
nowhere to go? For whom all roads lead nowhere.*

That was true. He had nothing left to do, no place to go, now that
Bran's last order had been fulfilled, and the Head laid in Its chosen
resting-place.

*If only you were alive, Branwen little sister! If only your child had
lived, or Caradoc. But Bran's dream was the torch; it lit the fire that
brought red ruin upon all of us . . .*

All the years of his manhood he had served Bran and the Island
of the Mighty: and though he had done his own thinking and sometimes Bran's, he never had done anything for himself, for his own
gain. He felt afraid now, stripped and helpless and afraid, as he never
could have felt had there been anyone left for him to work and fight
for. Nobody is so dependent upon others as the unselfish man; their
need is his fuel and his balance, so that he needs them and that need
is itself perhaps a queer kind of selfishness. When Manawyddan had
had dependents, he had had infinite resource. But now he had neither, and nothing.

He sat through that night and saw dawn come, like a faded, gray-
haired woman painting her withered cheeks. He saw the sun raise
her bright head in the east, begin her steady and inexorable march,
that march which called all other men to work and life.

He rose; he cried out as a man upon the dizzy edge of a precipice
might cry, "O Almighty Mothers! Oh, my sorrow! There is none but
me that does not know where he shall lay his head this night!"

"Lord—" The voice was Pryderi's. That youngest and dearest of
the seven had awakened. He stumbled to his feet, still awkward with
sleep, and came forward. And Manawyddan was silent, ashamed.

"Lord—" The young King of Dyved's hand was on his arm.

"It is not a bed or a roof I mean, lad. Those are little things no
beggar that wanders the Island of the Mighty but can have them, for
knocking upon any decent farmer's door. It is a place I mean, some-

thing that belongs to me and I to it. Wherever I go, I will be a stranger. It is an exile I am now, upon all the earth, with Bran and Branwen under sod, and all my kindred dead."

Pryderi was silent, trying to think. In that weakness of the strong man, of the oak without ivy, was something that it seemed indecent to look upon, such horror as later men might feel in seeing a tortured man's body naked in its helplessness.

"Lord, your cousin is king over the Island of the Mighty. You and he are of one blood, and in your youth you were friends. He sits in your place—I know that—but you never have laid claim to land or possessions. Always you have been known as the Third Landless Prince. And Caswallon needs peace as this land needs it—he would be glad to have you beside him to help him make it. As you helped Bran."

"He might indeed." Manawyddan laughed shortly. "The last of the sons of my mother his house dog, and all tongues silenced! But though this man is my cousin, I could not bear to see him in the seat of my brother, the Blessed. Never could I know happiness in one house with Caswallon!"

What more he might have said he did not say; the boy's intended kindness bound him. So this was what all men would think, even his faithful six. That because he, now the rightful High King, did not seek his heritage, he was willing to be Caswallon's tamed hound. A new height of loneliness opened before him, a new depth of pain.

Pryderi was silent again, biting his lip and thinking. Then of a sudden his eyes brightened. He straightened his shoulders like one casting off a load. His white teeth gleamed in an eager, beguiling smile. "Lord, would you be willing to listen to any more advice?"

"I stand in need of advice," Manawyddan answered wearily. He felt no interest, he spoke from courtesy only; but Pryderi seized upon that permission as joyously as a dog seizes upon a bone.

"Lord, seven cantrevs came to me from Pwyll my father; in them Rhiannon my mother dwells. With my wife Kigva I live in the Seven Cantrevs of Seissyllwch, and if you were my mother's man you two could enjoy my father's lands together. None are fairer or richer—it would make my heart glad for you to have them."

For a breath's space Manawyddan was silent; then he said, "I thank you for great friendship, Prince. Your mother might not; she is well able to choose her own man if she wanted one."

"I would show you the best friendship in the world if you would let me," Pryderi coaxed. "The Lady my mother would say what I say—ever since I was little I have heard her praise you as the noblest of men. Never has she forgotten that one visit of yours to Dyved, long ago. And she is lonely now, with my father dead and me a married man."

Manawyddan opened his mouth to say no, but as he did so, a golden bird flew overhead. A golden feather fell at his feet. He stooped to pick it up; in his hand the thing shone like light, and as he looked at it, he heard his own voice say, to his own wonder, "I will go with you, lad. To Rhiannon."

2

They Come to the Shepherd's Hut

SO THEY set out for Dyved by the western sea, and one by one their comrades left them; went back to their own homes to tell there such tales as old soldiers have always told. Surely no old soldiers ever can have told bigger ones, though that is saying much. For no other men on earth yet have fought against foes who held the Cauldron of Rebirth, that even when outraged and held captive in this gross world of ours, still had power to raise the dead. To send their unsouled bodies back, possessed by demons of the Underworld, to fight against living men.

Gluneu was the first to go. He left them that second night; and when the six lay down to sleep, Manawyddan groped for that shining feather and could not find it. He smiled wryly, without surprise. *Well, so I only dreamed. The Birds of Rhiannon are with her in Arberth, they that alone came with her from her own world. And I am not the man for whom she left it.*

For Pwyll she had given up everlasting youth; for him she, the daughter of a King in Faery, had put on mortal flesh and its pain. To get Pwyll and to keep him, she had borne many trials; and at last the uttermost had been required of her: to sit alone, through the withering years.

I will visit her, then go. So far my promise binds me. Yet deep within the son of Llyr something still stirred, as nothing had stirred since Bran had got his poisoned wound and had said, "Cut off my head." Memory that, for a space, could drive back even that black memory. *You cannot have forgotten, Queen, any more than I have forgotten. I did you a great service, yet because of that very service you may never wish to look upon my face again.*

She would not show that; she was a true Queen. They would meet and part graciously; one more parting should not matter much, in this time of many partings.

On the third day Ynawc left them. Grudyen went next, and then Heilyn. Taliesin was the last to go, he the sweet singer, the wonder of western bards until the world's end. Pryderi tried hard to get him to go on to Dyved.

"You can get the best hospitality in the world there," he urged. "You can sing with my mother's Birds, that some say can sing even sweeter than you, and you can talk wisdom with my kinsman, the old druid Pendaran Dyved."

But Taliesin shook his head.

"I have been with you long enough," he said, "and the deeds we shall do together are done. I would they were not, for you are both good company. But I must go where new deeds are shaping, for that is ever the law of Taliesin. You ride south into Dyved that men unborn shall call the Land of Illusion and Glamour, and I ride north, into the fierce sunlight of the future."

Manawyddan looked at him straightly. "You mean that we are the past? Well, so it may be."

Pryderi put his hands to his hips and hitched his sword around a little.

"I do not feel past at all," said he. "I am still doing things, and I intend to do more."

But Taliesin and Manawyddan did not heed him; they were looking deep into each other's eyes. The twilight was soft around them; under the trees dusk was settling, shadows that soon would ripen into darkness were already stretching forth long black arms. Only pink clouds still bloomed like flowers in the western sky. And for a breath's space the gay young King of Dyved felt as though he were touched by the fingertip of a great silence, of a finality that was also peace. Then the poet turned to him.

"I go now, to Gwynedd," said Taliesin. "I was there at the court of Don, before the birth of Gwydion. And now I would watch him grow."

"Gwydion?" said Pryderi, pleased to understand something at last. "Is he not the little boy who will be Mâth's heir?"

In the dim light Taliesin looked at him long and sadly. "He is a little boy, but that is not all he is. Or all he has been. He has borne many names. But now he is called the son of Don, the sister of Mâth the Ancient, and in time to come you will think that you know that name too well. And later all the world will know him, for there is a universal forge, and our world is metal upon it, and he is the smith who will hammer our part of the world into a new shape. What bloody fools like Caswallon do may be undone, but not the work of wise men who work through the mind."

"He has a great destiny on him," said Pryderi, impressed. "Maybe one that the rest of us could do without. Why should I think that I know him too well?"

Taliesin did not answer and Manawyddan rubbed his chin. "I remember now; a thing that Mâth once said. He knows already that this child has come to undo his work and do his own."

"He knows and accepts," said Taliesin. "What can be hidden from Mâth the Ancient? In the Eastern World there is a God, men say, who loathed change and its evils as Mâth does, and wished to keep His people at peace and in the Golden Age. So He forbade them to eat of the fruit of the Tree of Knowledge, and was disobeyed. But Mâth is a wiser God than that; He will not forbid his people to do what, soon or late, they are bound to do, and so lay upon them the sin of disobedience."

"That is because Mâth still wears a human body," said Manawyddan, "and can speak for Himself, instead of through the mouths of priests who cannot fully understand His Word."

Pryderi stared. "Mâth is a man. A man of Illusion and Glamour, but human. He eats and sleeps and does all the things the rest of us do. When his time comes he will die."

"All Gods die," said Taliesin. "By dying as a man a God can sometimes show most clearly that He is a God. But now the time comes for Mâth to withdraw from earth and cease to be worshipped for awhile, for now men want fiercer Gods."

"As it may be that that Eastern God is," said Manawyddan, "for He is a Father, while we bow to the Mothers. But I do not believe those who call Him jealous. The jealousy must be on His priests. No God would ever be such a fool as to wish to keep His people forever in ignorance, for the ignorant can never choose between good and evil and so master neither."

"All this goes over my head," said Pryderi, and scratched it. "But anyhow it will take this Gwydion of yours, who sounds like an upsetting sort of person, some time to grow up and begin making trouble."

So Taliesin the Much-Remembering left them, he who has had many births and will have many more. Who may be somewhere among us even now, though nobody knows where. At least nobody who will tell . . .

Pryderi made one more attempt to keep him.

"Indeed," he urged with his loveliest grin, "if you want to be around when somebody is rearing a son, it is with us you should stay. Kigva and I would have had a boy before now, if I had not had to go to war, and it is no time we will be losing now. Indeed, it may be that we already have one," he mused hopefully. "That was a good night, our last before I left Dyved. Triplets might have come of it."

But again Taliesin only shook his head and smiled . . .

So the Seven became Two and went on alone toward Dyved. And the Preseli Mountains guided them westward, those rugged, sky-piercing walls whose tops they had been able to see from Ireland in the bad days. To Pryderi then their sunlit craggy heights had seemed like the sight of a face from home, the home that he was not quite sure that he would ever see again.

Now no sea held him from them, only wild stretches of wood and moor that grew ever narrower beneath his eager feet. And Manawyddan, who would have been glad of a slower pace, knew what was in his heart, panted and kept pace with him.

Night found them in a fold of those windy hills, and there they came upon a shepherd's hut. He made them welcome, but he was old and his eyes were dim, so he did not recognize Pryderi. And Manawyddan said, "Let him think you a stranger; so he may speak more freely than before his Lord. You have been long away from Dyved; much may have happened."

The truth was that ever since he entered those wild lands his druid sight had told him that eyes watched them; hungry, brooding eyes. Maybe the eyes of Caswallon's druids far away, maybe those of druids serving some nearby foe who sought to ambush Pryderi on his way home.

To the shepherd he said, "I am a harper back from the war, and this is Guri, my son."

The shepherd's wife gave them supper, and watched them eat. Then the old woman said, "What war is this you speak of? I did not know that this Island had men enough left, or that those few who still live had heart enough in them to be fighting again. But that is the way of you men. Never resting, always after each other's blood."

"We fought in Ireland," said Manawyddan, "Ireland, where the young men of the Island of the Mighty died. And we do not want to see more death."

She stared. "No man came alive out of that great fighting, surely. Not one has come back to our hills; or to the plains below."

"There are always a few left to come back," said Manawyddan. "Even though they come slowly. We are only the first you have heard of."

The old shepherd leaned forward eagerly. "If you were there—there where the battle roared and later the wolves and the eagles fed on the flesh of our sons—you may know what befell our young Lord. He died there: Pryderi, the son of Pwyll."

"Maybe not," said Pryderi. "Maybe he will come back."

The old man shook his head. "He would have come back before now had he lived. To his people and his mother and his young wife."

"I have come back," said Pryderi. "Do you think my strength and my luck were greater than his?"

"The Mothers alone know what luck is." The old woman peered harder at him through the smoke. "You are like him. He was called Guri too; Guri of the Golden Hair was the name that was on him as a babe, and he grew up to be tall and golden—like you. But he did not come back."

"Is there trouble on Dyved?" asked Manawyddan. "Lordless folk often fare ill."

The shepherd shook his head again. "Not yet. But it is coming. The two Queens still reign in peace, with old Pendaran Dyved to counsel them, Pwyll's wise High Druid. But Caswallon sends gifts to our chief men, and the young men grow restless and mutter, 'We should have a King again.'"

"Then neither Queen has taken a new husband?" Manawyddan asked.

"No. But as soon as Pendaran Dyved is mounded, both will be bedded. Maybe by several husbands apiece before one man proves himself master and can settle down to grind underfoot and plunder those of us who are left."

"And Caswallon would let such things be?" Pryderi's hands clenched. "Never could they have happened under Bran!"

The old man laughed bitterly. "But the Blessing went from Bran the Blessed. He went away and left his son to rule us, contrary to the ancient Law. And now he and all his house are dead, and Caswallon says that he was always the rightful King. And maybe he is right, for clearly the Gods are with him. The Mothers grow weak, the Father grows strong."

Manawyddan was silent. He thought, *This is what all folk must be saying Victory proves a man the Gods' chosen, even if he be a murderer. And once all men loved and praised you, Bran my brother!*

Yet at the last Bran had broken the peace he had upheld; had undone his own work, and brought misery and death upon his people. That was true, and that truth was the hardest of all things to bear.

Pryderi said stubbornly, "It is the business of a High King to maintain order and justice. Not to let Under Kings butcher each other and their folk."

Now the old woman laughed, a harsh, shrill cackle. "He needs friends—Caswallon, the Father's choice. The seven chiefs he slew so as to oust Caradoc the son of Bran have left kinsmen and friends. Their hands reach out fast enough to take Caswallon's gifts, but their hearts do not love him. And if his luck goes bad, if crops fail or invaders come, many will cry, 'It is the curse of blood—the blood he shed!' So long as Under Kings call him High King, Caswallon will let them do as they please."

"Or play one of them against another to gain time," said Manawyddan. "Also to see their strength weaken while his grows."

"And Dyved is still a rich and prosperous land!" Pryderi's laugh was like the sound of ripping silk. "He would like well to see it weak and torn—as we left Ireland weak and torn!"

"Maybe so." The old man sighed. "Some say he backs one of our Lords, some that he backs another. But all these greedy lordlings are only waiting for the breath to be out of Pendaran Dyved's body. Fear of the old druid's curse still holds all men back, but he is failing. His end nears."

"I should think that Rhiannon herself could do a bit of cursing," said Pryderi. "She is no mortal-born Queen."

"Oh, she has her magics!" The old woman cackled again. "I would like well to have a tiny part of that magic! But it never was of a kind to keep men off her, and even in her youth she had no power to curse those lying women who swore that she had killed her own babe. None need fear her!"

"To have sent sickness or death on those women could not have cleared her," said Manawyddan. "Only have made folk fear and hate her more. I have heard that tale."

"You have? It is told in many ways. But I know the rights of it." And she launched into the telling, eager as a starving man sitting down to meat: all the troubles that were and would be forgotten in the wonders and now unterrifying terrors of the past.

Manawyddan thought wearily, *Here in this lonely place a chance to talk means much to her. And perhaps she is wiser than she seems. To forget what one cannot strive against—to enjoy what one still has—there are worse ways to dream away one's day. The question is: if one searched hard enough, might one still find a way to do, instead of to dream?*

He knew the tale she was telling better than she did. He let flow from his mind into hers such hidden parts of it as he thought it safe for her to know.

"Here on Preseli it all began." Her voice had risen to a chant. "Here the chief men of Dyved gathered to meet Pwyll their Lord. In the Holy Place they awaited him, within that double ring of blue-stones where folk have met in council since first men walked in Dyved. Old, old are those rings, and in the dark night their tall Stones rise and dance together. For they are the Eldest Folk, the firstborn of Earth the Mother. Each has a name that may not be spoken, and each has power to heal or blast. And no man dare go back upon the word he has spoken before them; else he would wither and die."

"I know of that place," said Manawyddan. "Great is the power of the outer ring, but that of the inner is yet greater. For its twelve Stones are said to be the first Twelve Gods born of Earth, archetype of all the mighty mysterious Twelves that are to come. In their sides is not only the color of the sea that once covered all things, but the ashes of those fires from which Earth the Mother shaped Herself, that mighty travail from which the mountains and the valleys sprang.*

The old woman stared at him, her jaw dropping. "You know too much. You can be no man of the New Tribes!"

"Good men spring from all tribes, woman. Were not your Pwyll and his Pryderi born of the New?"

The shepherd said sadly, "Yes. They have been gentle conquerors, the House of Pwyll. But those who come after them will be hard on the little man; on us shepherds and tillers of the soil. They will make all who spring from the Old Tribes little."

"Not forever," said Manawyddan. "In the end Old Tribes and New will become one folk."

"Maybe. But it will take yet longer—long and long—for the rich to become brothers to the poor."

"The House of Pwyll may not be ended," Pryderi cut in, his jaw set.

"Those men who met Pwyll in the Holy Place wanted to keep it from ending." The old woman went on with her tale again, firmly. "Pwyll came, and he said, 'Men, why have you sent for me?' And they said, 'Lord, we are sorrowful to see a man we love so much, our chief and our foster-brother, without an heir. You are not so young as some of us, and your wife is childless. Take another, and get sons. You can not stay with us always, and though you may wish to keep the

---

*Only from Preseli could the "bluestone circles" of Stonehenge have been brought, though their moving would have been a herculean, almost incredible task for any ancient people.

woman you have, we will not suffer it.' They did not say, 'That woman out of Faery is mortal now, and can be killed. Her own people will not avenge her, they whose wrath must have put barrenness on her. And if you do, we will bear it for love of you.'

"They did not say that, because it would not have been good manners, but Pwyll knew what they meant. He knew, too, his duty to his people. He said, 'The woman and I have slept together only three winters, and there is still time for her belly to swell. Give me a year and a day, and if it has not, I will do according to your will.' And they agreed.

"On May Day that pact was made, and on the next May Eve—in the very nick of time, just one night before her time was up—Queen Rhiannon bore a son. By what arts she got him the Mothers alone know, but get him she did. And she and her Lord were triumphant as warriors who ride home from battle, laden with spoil. Pwyll and his men made merry in the great hall, and in her great bed the Queen slept, and her babe slept beside her. Six of the noblest ladies of Dyved watched over them, so all seemed safe. Even though May Eve is one of the Holy Nights when the doors between the worlds open—when those who have put off our flesh or never worn it can come from their terrible unearthly places against us mortals.

"They cannot have been happy, those six fine ladies—each of them had a daughter or a sister that she said would have brought Pwyll four fine boys in those four winters instead of only one. A bitter pill it must have been, too, to know that now, because of her one son, this stranger woman would queen it over them forever. But they dared not say so; they had to pretend to be proud and happy. For no higher trust could have been given to any women in Dyved. They knew that they must guard that mother and son as each would her own two eyes. Yet by midnight every last one of them was fast asleep."

Here her husband managed to put a word in. "You can't blame them for that, old woman. That sleep must have been sent upon them, by Those the wise do not name."

She went on as if he had not spoken. "And toward daybreak, when they woke, all six of them, with a great start—the boy was gone. He was not there; he was not anywhere; it was as if there never had been a boy at all. Then great fear took them, who had slept when they should have kept watch, who, as many would bear witness, had whispered against their Queen, the stranger . . . "

Behind his hand Pryderi yawned and whispered to Manawyddan, "I never thought that I should ever have to listen to this yarn again."

Then his mouth grew grim. "If I had been my father, I would have drowned all those miserable hags like rats."

"And they the wives and sisters of his chief men? You know better than that, boy."

"So my mother says. That if he had, there would not yet have been peace in Dyved. But I still say . . . "

"Hush, lad! Our hostess will hear you!"

Indeed, the woman had stopped talking and was looking at them indignantly, but such a great silence promptly settled upon them that they looked as if it had been there forever, and she went on.

"The Queen still slept, so they killed a staghound bitch's newborn pup and smeared her face and hands with the blood, then laid the bones beside her. Then they rose up and scratched their own faces and blacked each other's eyes and screamed aloud, so that the whole court came running in. And they pointed to the bloodied face of the sleeping Queen and cried out upon her. 'Would to the Mothers that you had come when we called in the night! For this madwoman rose up and such demon's strength was on her that all of us together could not hold her. Before our eyes she tore her own son limb from limb and ate him raw!'

"So was joy turned to sorrow, and triumph to woe. Like fire the tale spread through the land, and his nobles came again to Pwyll. 'Put away this evil woman, Lord, this murderess who has devoured her own flesh and yours.' But Pwyll answered, 'You have no right to ask that. I agreed to put her away if she was barren, but now she has given birth. Keep your bargain, as I have kept mine.' But still they raged, and at last, lest she be butchered or burned alive behind his back, he had to say, 'Let the druids judge her.'

"And Rhiannon begged those women, 'By the sun and by the moon, who see all, by the Mothers in Whose shape we are all fashioned, charge me not falsely! If you lie because fear is on you, I will defend you.'

"But they answered, 'Truly, Lady, not for anyone in the wide world would we risk bringing evil upon ourselves.'

"'Is not my woe great enough?' said Rhiannon. 'The sorrow of a mother that has lost her child? What evil will come upon you for telling the truth?'

"But whatever she said, she got only one answer from those women.

"So in the end the druids came and heard all, and this is the doom they spoke: 'Lady, for seven years you shall sit every day upon the horse block before your Lord's house here in Arberth. And to every one that comes to his door you shall tell the tale of your bloody deed, and then bow down upon all fours—even as a beast would go, she that knows no better than to eat her own young—and bear that guest on your back into the hall.'

"Such was the judgment of the druids, and as they ordered, so it was done. But few would ride upon her back, for we folk of Dyved have hearts in our breasts."

3

The Man Who Fought the Monster

THEN, BECAUSE her own throat was parched, the old woman rose and fetched mead for them all. When Manawyddan praised its rare goodness, she smiled and said, "I have a little friend that helps me."

"A bogey, I suppose. More magic," said Pryderi. "Surely my father and all his men must have been magicked, not to know a pup's bones from mine. Those misbegotten hags would have done better to say that the bitch swallowed me whole, and that my mother had made a breakfast of raw pup to get even."

"Lad, do you want her to hear you?"

But because Pryderi's young jaw was set and his eyes smoldered the old woman poured him the fullest cup of the sweet yellow mead. Flattered because her tale had so moved him, she sat down by the fire and began again.

"Teyrnon of the Thunder-Flood was Lord of Gwent then, and there was no better man in the world. And he had a mare, and in all the land no horse or mare was more beautiful. But though every May Eve, in the dark of night, she foaled, in the morning there never was any foal beside her. What became of her colts no man ever knew. And one night Teyrnon talked with his wife. 'Woman,' he said, 'it is great fools we are, to let our mare foal every year and never get a single one of her colts.'

"'What can we do about it,' said she.

"'Tomorrow night is May Eve,' he said. 'And may I never look upon sun or moon again if I do not find what the Thing is that comes and carries away the colts!'

"She was frightened and tried to stop him, but he would not listen. He had the mare led into an empty hut, the last and least of the small houses grouped round his great house. On one side of it was the open moor, and on the other a door, the only opening. He had his men build up a bright fire, then bade them leave and shut the door behind them, for a bitter wind was blowing in from the moor. He sat himself down, fully armed, against the wall farthest from that door. There he could watch unseen, for thick shadows covered him. He waited there until the gray twilight ceased to try to force its fingers through the cracks round the door, and there was no light left at all but the red glow of the fire. The wind howled and the mare stood by the fire and shivered. Now and then she lifted her head and neighed pitifully, and it seemed to Teyrnon that her dark eyes looked in fear at the door. But he kept still and did not go to her, though he was a man whose nature it was to go to the help of all beasts in pain.

"Night had scarce fallen when she foaled—a big, beautiful hecolt. It stood up on wobbling legs, weak and wet and dazed, and the mother washed it. The feel of her tongue comforted it and it pressed closer and found her teats and sucked; it was happy again then, as it had been inside the warm dark nest of her body. So they comforted each other after the squeezing, rending pangs of birth; and so the foal, like all young, discovered this huge world and himself, and her who was the first sharer of its great and terrible loneliness.

"Teyrnon could not stand it any longer. He went to them and praised the mare and felt over the foal with his hands, proud of its size and of the strength with which it sucked.

"But even as he knelt beside them, a great crash came and the door fell in. Through the black opening a huge arm darted, thick as a tree and blacker than the night, and at the end of it a great, gleaming claw that grasped the colt's mane. Teyrnon sprang up and hacked at it with his sword, and when the mare saw that this time she had help, she too sprang upon the Arm, biting and kicking. Teyrnon needed her; he had been Pwyll, Prince of Dyved's man, and had fought beside him in many battles, yet never had he met a foe like this. His sword seemed to be hewing wood, and all three of them— man, mare, and colt—were being steadily, if slowly dragged through the doorway. Power to hinder that unearthly Power they had, but stop it they could not. And then all at once Teyrnon's blade worked through mighty muscle and sinew to the bone itself. Harder than rock that bone seemed, and at first Teyrnon thought that all was over, but he shut his eyes and held his breath and smote with all his strength. And then there rose up a shriek like no other shriek ever heard in this world; it seemed to fill all the space beneath the sky and to shake Earth herself. Teyrnon reeled back, his eardrums all but splitting, and when his head cleared he saw that the Arm, all its terrible black length, up to where the elbow should have been, lay there severed. Around it boiled a great pool of blood, from which rose a stench that all but choked him.

"On one side of the door the wall had been ripped like cloth and the roof sagged. He set his shoulder against that wreckage and broke through it, for that stinking, boiling blood blocked the doorway. He led out the mare and her foal, though she screamed as only a horse can scream and rolled her eyes, for the night was still filled with unearthly wailing. They stood there, all three of them, and gulped in deep breaths of the clean night air, and gradually the wailing dimmed, as that monstrous, wounded Thing, fleeing, sank back into the depths of the Underworld, into that unspeakable, unthinkable darkness from which it had come. And then through that wailing they heard another wail; a small sharp cry out there in the dark night.

"'What is that?' cried Teyrnon, and he ran forward.

"Near the doorway he found it, where it had fallen, just clear of the blood that still boiled from that monstrous, bleeding Arm. A baby, wrapped in a mantle of shining stuff, and yelling as if it would split its small fat throat.

"Teyrnon picked it up and unwrapped it and looked it over as he had the colt, and then he looked toward the colt itself and grinned.

"'You are a pair, the two of you,' he said. 'Both newborn and both stallions.'

"He saw that the foal had found its mother's teat again, need rising above the memory of terror, and how the mother was quieting, standing still to assuage that need, though her whole body still trembled. His face sobered and he looked down again at the screeching baby.

"'Well, that one of you who is four-legged seems to be the luckier now. We will take you inside, Master Two-legs, and see what we can do about that. I cannot see why people have not come running out to see what is the matter.'

"He went back into his great hall and found all there, men, women, and children, fast asleep. As fast asleep as the six ladies who, that same night, were watching beside Rhiannon's bed. But of them, of course, he knew nothing. He went on and came to his own sleeping chamber, and there he found his wife, as sound asleep as any of the others. He shook her and when her eyes opened and she stared at him, he grinned again.

"'Is this the woman that was not going to close either eye all night for fear of what might be happening to me?'

"She might have looked sheepish then, but at that instant the baby, who had stopped for lack of wind, got its breath back and began to cry again. That was a sound she must often have longed for, she who was a childless wife, even as Rhiannon had been. But now it made her give a great start.

"'Lord, what is that?'

"Teyrnon, still grinning, held the baby out to her.

"'Woman, here is a boy for you, if you will have him you never gave birth to.'

"'Who did give birth to him?' she said. And she sat up very straight, and looked at Teyrnon very hard.

"'This is what happened,' and Teyrnon told her all. She marveled much at that hearing, and she gave many little squeaks, both for terror at his danger, and of praise for his valor, but never did her eyes leave the child. And when she had warmed milk for it and changed its swaddling clothes, that by then were very wet indeed, and it slept at last, satisfied, she held up the shining mantle and looked at it with a careful, appraising eye.

"'This is good stuff; rare stuff. She that owned this mantle was rich enough to deck herself and her son in all the treasures of the Eastern world.' And she looked at Teyrnon and thought with relief that he did not know any such woman, and that if he ever had, it had been too long ago for her to have borne him this son tonight.

"'The boy is of gentle blood,' she said.

"'He is a fine boy anyhow,' said Teyrnon. 'Strong for his age.'

"'His age!' She snorted. 'He has no age—he who was born this very night.' Her eyes widened suddenly. 'Lord, let us have a game; a merry game with my women. We will call them in and say that I have been pregnant these many moons, but dared say nothing lest it come to nothing, I to whom the Mothers have not been kind.'

"So it was done, though I who am a woman do not think that the women of Teyrnon's household can have been fooled. Likely Teyrnon's wife wanted to see all of them as soon as she could to make sure that none of them showed signs of child-birth, shining cloak or no shining cloak—and likely they thought it wise not to contradict their mistress. Anyhow, most of Gwent—certainly all the men in it—believed the child to be Teyrnon's own son by his lady. They named the boy Guri, and because what hair was on his head was pure gold, they called him Guri of the Golden Hair. And by the next May Eve he was walking briskly and was as big as the biggest child three years old."

"This woman thinks well of me," whispered Pryderi to Manawyddan. "When I heard that tale at home I was only as big and fine as the biggest, finest boy of one year could be."

"That seems more likely," Manawyddan whispered back, "but be still."

"And by the second year," the old woman went on, "he was as big and fine as the biggest, finest child six years old."

Here Pryderi's lips pursed for a whistle, but Manawyddan trod on his foot in time, and he was silent.

"And by then," her voice sobered, "many were talking of the great woe at Arberth, and of Rhiannon's punishment. Word of it had reached Gwent that first winter, and Teyrnon and his lady had looked at each other once, and then looked away again. But the second year, when those tales kept coming, they took care not to look at each other. Indeed, they took great pains not to look at each other, and each would have liked very much not to be able to see his or her own thoughts.

"Teyrnon's wife said in her heart, He is the apple of my eye, but he is her flesh. Can I do this to another woman, I who have shared the burden of barrenness with her? But how do I know that he is her flesh—I did not see her give him birth! How can I be sure? And he is the apple of Teyrnon's eye too—Teyrnon who has no son! And Teyrnon fought the Great Arm and saved him; he gave him life at more risk than any blood parents could. Who has a better right to him than Teyrnon?'

"And Teyrnon thought, He is the apple of my wife's eye. How can I ask her who has waited so long to give him up now that she has got him at last? Yet I was Pwyll's man once, and we were friends—the Lordship of Gwent was his gift. But how can I be sure that the boy is his?

"And they both thought, *Rhiannon has conceived once; and whatever her woes are by day, every night she still sits Pwyll in his hall, his honored queen, and when the moon is high they go to bed together. Why should she not bear another child?*

Let her conceive—let her conceive . . .

"But the third winter came, and now Guri was running about and even being lifted onto the back of the young stallion who was, in a way, his twin brother. And still no word came that Queen Rhiannon bore any burden save the weight of any guest boor enough to ride upon her back. Every third or fourth moon that happened, though when such foolish fellows left his court, Pwyll had them followed and set upon and taught more gentlemanly manners. That much he could do for her, he who could not refill her womb.

"And May Eve came again, and Guri's fourth summer. A stranger came then to Teyrnon's house. Tall he was, and his hair was black as night, and his eyes were now gray, now green; they changed like the sea. His clothes were old and worn, but he carried a silver harp with golden strings. And nobody had ever heard a harp played as he played that one, or a tale told as he told it.

"Three nights he played for Teyrnon's household, and on the third night he played a song so sweet that it would have made women in childbed close their eyes in sleep, and wounded men in the sharpest pain forget their pangs and find rest. Every living thing in that house fell asleep; men, women, and children slept; the cats and dogs slept, and even the mice in the walls.

"Only Teyrnon was awake. He sat in his seat, the Lord's seat, with the child Guri asleep beside him, his head on his father's knees. And Teyrnon looked at the bard, and the bard looked at Teyrnon.

"'Once before, Lord of Gwent,' said the harper, 'you woke while others slept.'

"'How do you know that?' demanded Teyrnon.

"'I know many things,' the stranger said, 'and I have not stayed here these three days without feeling your thoughts burn in the night. Yours, and your lady's.'

"'A man's dreams are his own,' said Teyrnon, 'and no stranger has a right to come creeping into them to watch them, and learn secrets that are not meant for him!' His hand went to his sword.

"'My rights do not matter,' said the stranger. 'But others have rights that do. Look at that child there.' He pointed to the sleeping Guri. 'Have you ever seen such a likeness between father and son as between that boy there and Pwyll, Prince of Dyved?'

"Teyrnon looked down at the child, and his eyes saw what for two winters he had been shutting them against. Saw it too plainly ever to forget again . . .

"'Look at those eyes,' said the stranger; and as he spoke, Guri's eyes opened. They looked up, in sleepy wonder and trust, at the man he called father. And Teyrnon bowed his head.

"'They are the eyes of Pwyll,' he said heavily. 'The eyes of Pwyll, my Lord and my friend.'

"Then he looked at the bard again and his face changed; fury twisted it. He sprang up, thrusting Guri behind him. He crouched like a beast about to spring, and his drawn sword flashed in the firelight.

"'Who are you?' The gleam of his blade was not more deadly than the gleam of his eyes. 'Who are you, and what brought you here? Are you another Thing of the night?'

"But there was no answer; there was nobody there to answer him. He stood alone among the sprawled bodies of his sleep-emptied folk. Even the child Guri was asleep again, tranquil as though he had never waked. Teyrnon gathered him up and went from the hall, and his shoulders were bowed like an old man's.

"In the dark of that same night the Lord of Gwent woke his wife and talked with her. He told what he could no longer tell himself that he did not know. He said, 'It is not right for me to keep a boy that I know to be the son of another man. And it is not right for you either, to keep him, and so let so noble a lady bear such punishment.'

"The woman did not weep or cry. She said only, 'You are right, Lord. Long have I known that we should send the boy home.'

"Then for awhile they both sat silent, and in the dark his hand found hers, and she turned and wept upon his breast. But not stormily; she loved him too well to make his load heavier, and soon her mind turned, like a good housewife's, to what might yet be salvaged from the wreck.

"'In three ways we shall get good from this business, Lord. Thanks and gifts from the Queen for freeing her from punishment, and thanks from Pwyll for nursing his son and restoring him to him. And if the boy's heart is good—and well you know it is!—he will be our foster-son, and he will do us all the good in his power.'

"*Foster-sons come back to visit their foster-parents. He will come back to see us. We will see him sometimes—sometimes—*That thought was the only light in her darkness.

"In the morning she packed Guri's things and dressed him in his best and combed his golden curls. Then Teyrnon sat him beside him in his chariot, and together they rode away. Two of Teyrnon's best men rode behind them as escort.

"Evening was near when they came to Arberth. They saw Pwyll's palace, round as the setting sun that turned its thatched roof to gold. Behind it rose the blue rugged heights of our Preseli cloud-drowned, so that none might tell where mountain ended and sky began. And nearer, lower, yet terrible in its strength, loomed that huge and awful Mound that is called the Gorsedd Arberth, The Home of Mysteries, the tomb of Dyved's earliest King, though no man now remembers his tribe or name. Like the home of all shadows it looked, a blackness in which, even by day, night's own blackness might well take shelter and await its hour . . .

"Before the palace doors, that were wide enough to admit twelve men at once, was set a horse block. Beside that block sat a woman, and the sinking sun made her hair shine like a golden flame.

"She rose as she saw them come. Her face was set like a mask, like something carved by godlike craftsmen beyond the Eastern sea. When she first sat beside that block, she must have had to fight for that carved look, fight as hard as ever warrior fought in battle. But day had followed day, week had followed week, and the moons had grown into years; now it was part of her. She flinched only once; when Teyrnon lifted the child down, and he trotted forward by his father's side.

"'Lord,' her voice was clear and steady, 'come no farther. I will carry every one of you into the palace on my back.'

"Teyrnon's two burly men stopped in their tracks, then looked down with great interest at their feet. Anywhere but at the lady. But Teyrnon faced her, and she him.

"'This is my penance, Lord,' her eyes were as steady as her voice, 'for slaying and eating my own son.'

"She had no doubt that Teyrnon believed her guilty; never once in all those years of her sorrow had he, Pwyll's old comrade, come to see them. That did not matter. She had faced too many men to care what one more thought, but the child—his horror still had power to hurt her. She could not bear to see those young eyes widen; she kept her own fixed, unwaveringly, upon the father's face.

"'Lady,' Teyrnon's deep voice shook, 'never think me such a one. Never will I be carried upon your back.'

"He turned upon his men then, and so fierce was his look that they cowered, although such a ride was the last thing they wanted.

"The child Guri piped up, 'Neither will I be, Lady!' His troubled, friendly eyes regarded her.

"And suddenly Rhiannon laughed. The lost smile of her youth came back, and made that carved face alive and sweet.

"'You are one that I would like to carry!' she said, and swept him up in her arms. All of them went into the palace together.

"Great gladness was with Arberth that night. In that royal hall a royal feast was always spread, but when folk knew that Teyrnon, Lord of Gwent, had come, more oxen died, more fowl were roasted. The best mead and wine, the best silver and gold cups were hunted out, the best cheeses fetched and sliced. In the midst of all Pwyll came home from hunting; when first he heard who had come his face filled with joy, then clouded.

"'Did he—?' That question may have been looked, rather than asked.

"But when his smiling people shook their heads, he came forward with outstretched hands and face beaming like the sun. He greeted

Teyrnon and seated him between himself and Rhiannon, and the boy sat between Teyrnon's two men. Often the Queen's eyes sought him there.

"They ate and talked and drank, they drank and talked and ate. Pwyll was eager to hear everything that had happened to his friend, and at last he said, 'That fine mare of yours—that was a queer business. Have you ever been able to keep any of her colts?'

"'I have that,' said Teyrnon. 'Four of them now, all as fine horse-flesh as ever you saw. But it was a great baffle I had to fight to keep the first of those four.'

"And he told the tale of that night, and of the Arm that had come in the night, and women shuddered and men held their breaths. Guri's eyes grew round; he never had heard the tale before.

"Teyrnon told of his victory, and of how his foe had fled wailing to the Underworld. Then he told of that other cry. Of what he had found beside the door.

"Deep was the silence then; deep as a well. Men stared at each other and dared not speak. Each thought, *It cannot be—it could be—* And Pwyll looked at his lady, and waited for the light that did not come into her face. She thought, *I am dreaming again. I have dreamed so many times. Teyrnon does not mean what we think he means. Soon I will wake again.*

"Teyrnon rose and walked through that dead silence. Up to the child he had called his child. From under his cloak he drew the shining stuff that had wrapped the babe; he put it around Guri and lifted him again, as he had lifted him on that other night. He carried him to Rhiannon and set him in her lap.

"'Lady, here is your son. Whoever told that tale of your slaying him told a wicked lie. I think that there is none out of all this host here who does not see that this boy is the son of Pwyll. Look at him,' he pointed to his lord, 'and then look at the child.'

"From all there a shout went up, 'It is so!' There was power in Teyrnon in that hour; all saw that likeness, even as he himself had seen it, that night when the stranger bard had faced him in his own hall.

"Only Rhiannon sat in mute wonder, her eyes wide and blank as those of the staring child on her lap. Her arms had closed around him, as any woman's arms will close around a child, but she did not look at him. It was as if she did not dare to look . . .

"But then Pwyll rose and threw his arms around them both, and his eyes were wet. She began to shiver then, to shake all over, as a tree might shake in a great wind. She looked down swiftly into Guri's face and then buried her own in his golden hair.

"'Oh, my darling, if this is true, then I am delivered from the long fear for you, the long grief!'

"And the wise druid, Pendaran Dyved, came and said to her, 'Well have you named your son, Lady. Pryderi, son of Pwyll, he shall be called forever.'"*

*In old Welsh, "pryderi" seems to have meant something like "Anxiety" or "Grief."

4

The Son of Llyr Remembers

"SHE DID not tell the tale badly." Pryderi stretched himself luxuriously upon the blanket-covered straw that was their bed. "I think she got most of it right. All but one thing."

"What thing was that?" asked Manawyddan politely. He pulled back the covers that Pryderi's stretching had pulled off them. He hoped that Pryderi would soon be ready to sleep.

"It was what that stranger-bard did. He did not vanish into the air."

"What did he do?" Manawyddan's voice was without interest.

Pryderi frowned. "It is strange. I can still see that sword gleaming in the firelight, as Teyrnon's eyes blazed above it. Ready to flash up and down and then up again, dripping red with the stranger's blood. Almost I could see it happening. And my heart was in my throat, for I loved that bard."

"And did it happen?"

"No. He turned his back on that blade and on those eyes. Without hurry he picked up his harp, and without hurry he walked to the door. He went out through it, and we never saw him again."

"His work was done. He had nothing to stay for."

"But who was he? Where did he go? And where did he come from?"

"Surely it is enough that he was your friend, and your parents' friend."

"Yes, but who was he? Sometimes it has seemed to me that you have a look of him, Lord."

The son of Llyr laughed softly. "I am no helper out of Faery, lad."

"Nor was he! My mother's kin never sent her help, only harm."

"Do not put shame on your own blood." Manawyddan spoke sternly. "Folk of whom your mother could have been born never could have sent a monster to steal a newborn child. Remember Gwawl the Bright, Gwawl mad Cludd, to whom her kin would have wedded her. She escaped from Gwawl untouched, yet at a price. His hate will never die."

"I know that story. On the wedding night Gwawl came and tricked my father into giving my mother up to him unknowingly. To get away from him, Mother had to trick him into a bag, and then Father and his men each gave that bag a good hard whack with a good stout stick. Until Gwawl promised to release Mother and to take no revenge. By the awful, unnameable oath he swore—it that can blast even a God if he breaks it. Gwawl sent no monsters."

"Yet Gwawl had friends whom no oath bound. Had it not been for Arawn, King of Annwn, your father's own friend in Faery, all Dyved would have been blasted long ago. Surely you know that, lad."

"But if those powers dared not touch Pwyll, how could they have dared to touch me, his son? Unless they were of my kin on the mother's side, and so had a claim on me that even mighty Arawn must respect?"

Manawyddan said, "We cannot fathom the ways of the Otherworld, lad, we who are mortal men. Let us sleep."

But when they had settled themselves for that sleep, he thought, *Almost you tore the veil from more than secret tonight, Pryderi. But this you never have suspected, and never shall suspect: that no drop of Pwyll's blood flows in, your veins.*

That night had been as dark as this. Softly and quietly the moon had risen through cloudy darknesses, higher and yet higher, moving ever westward across the unthinkable vastness of heaven. In her pale light Pwyll, Prince of Dyved, had sat drinking with his guest, and both men had watched her gleaming roundness, so much gentler than the sun's.

"Nine more moons we have—Rhiannon and I. Nine only." Pwyll's voice was rough with pain.

"That could be time enough. Do not waste it."

"We have done all we can. We have lain together beneath each Stone of the Holy Stones, and done every rite the druids advised. We have done every foolish thing the old wives tell of. And nothing has happened. As I knew that nothing would happen."

He laughed harshly, bitterly, his face twisting. In puzzled pity the other man sat and watched him.

Pwyll recovered himself, turned to him and smiled, "But now I do waste time. There is one way left. The Gods must have sent you here, son of Llyr, brother of Bran my Overlord."

Manawyddan said slowly, "You mean the visiting overlord's right to sleep with his host's wife? That is not the way of the Old Tribes. Bran never would claim it. Nor will I."

Pwyll still smiled. "If Rhiannon were a mother, I would be glad indeed of your forbearance; I own that. But she is not, and the custom is old among the New Tribes, and it has good in it. The King is always supposed to be the best man in the Tribe, the strongest and the most skillful. And the more women he sleeps with the more sons he begets, so the stronger the Tribe is."

Manawyddan said grimly, "If I loved a woman and she me, any other man that went to bed with her would indeed have to be stronger than I." His face was hard; he was thinking of his own mother, dark Penardim, and of how to ransom his father Llyr, captured by treachery, she had had to submit her body to the captor and to bear the twins Nissyen and Evnissyen, those two who were unlike any other men ever born on the Island of the Mighty.

Pwyll said, "Shame is in what a man thinks it is in." His face was cold now; like a carven image.

"That is often the truth. But seldom is any saying true always." Manawyddan brooded. When first he had seen Rhiannon he had thought her the fairest of women; when they had talked together, he had known that their minds flowed in the same channels, that the same things would move them to laughter or pity. But also he had known that she loved his friend. Not until now, when the cup of cups was offered him, with no wine in it to slake his thirst, had he known the fierceness of that thirst. Yet the heat of his blood whispered in spite of him, *Yet you would have her. Touch her—hold her...*

He said violently, "Among the Old Tribes no woman sleeps with a man unless she wants him. Otherwise her child would be born outside the Ancient Harmonies, against the will of the Mothers. I will not beget such a child—nor would you want me to if you knew my brother Evnissyen. Get your own children, man!"

Pwyll's eyes met his steadily. "I cannot."

For a breath's space cold silence fell; then Manawyddan thrust back understanding "If your Queen's own people have made her barren, my seed will not take root in her either. Why do this ill deed for nothing?"

Pwyll said, "You have heard that in my youth I went into Faery to fight for Arawn, King of Annwn. To kill for him that terrible foe who would have wrested Annwn from him, and so have changed the course of our own world also."

"You did a great deed."

"And great has been its price. Those Shadow-folk needed earth-strength to fight the White Shadow—him who had brought bloody death even into their world. And only from an earth-man could they get it, violence being the element we are born to. But the man who has so used his strength cannot bring it all back to earth. He who has touched so much death must die a little. Leave something of himself behind, among the Shadows . . . "

"You brought back strength enough. I know that, who have seen you on the battlefield—" Manawyddan stopped and bit his lip. Too late he understood. Meeting those still steady eyes, the depth of pain and shame in them, he felt such horror as only a strong man can feel at sight of another strong man maimed. *He minds this more than I would mind the loss of my right hand, or one of the legs I stand on. He is ashamed, too; as only cowardice should shame a man . . .*

The son of Llyr had this virtue: he could pity with all his heart what seemed to him folly. No man should feel lessened by what he could not help; by a lack or a difference from other men. But if he did . . .

Pwyll said quietly, "Rhiannon knows. I could not let her blame herself. Being a woman, she is still noble enough or foolish enough to love me. Now we three know. And I know your honor too well, son of Llyr, to say to you, let there never be a fourth."

Manawyddan thought swiftly, *But you have let your people blame her—Rhiannon.* And then as swiftly, *But you are not like Bran and me. You have no brother, no near kinsman they have only you to turn to. And if they knew this—they who know your courage and your nobleness best of all—they would lose faith in you. Mill about like leaderless beasts afraid of wolves. That is what your knowledge has done for you, you men of the New Tribes, who are so proud of being fathers. We of the Old Tribes judge a man by his own worth, not by what his seed can do inside a woman's womb.*

Aloud he said, "I will do my best for you, Lord of Dyved. I will use the druid power that my House has, but seldom uses—I will put on your shape, so that Rhiannon will think that it is still yourself she lies with."

Pwyll smiled. "Yet I doubt if you could fool her all night long . . ."

"I know. And I will not ask what love words you two use together—those no third person ever should know. Go to her and tell her—I suppose she does know of this pretty plan of yours, does she not?"

"She does. She is a great lady. She said, 'When I came to you I accepted the way of your people. Tell the son of Llyr that I will welcome him as the mother of his son should.'"

"Yet I would not have her nobly endure me. Tell her that from tonight until I leave, you and she must not speak together in the night. So she will not know when I come to her."

Pwyll said with grave dignity, "Lord, I thank you."

When he went to Rhiannon his wife, he told her what their friend and guest had said. She laughed—a laugh that was half a sob—flung her arms around him and held him close.

"That is like his nobleness! I was afraid—I can tell you that now, Lord. I was afraid. To lie with any man but you—" She kissed him long and hard.

When he turned from her to take off his clothes, the shadows were thick about him. Had her mind been calmer she, the woman out of Faery, would have known that one of those shadows was a man.

His bare feet made no sound on the rushes as he left that quiet, moonlit room; left her. She was not listening; she was only waiting. Seeing, with what relief and happiness, the dear, familiar head turn back to her, the dear, familiar body advance upon her. "Whatever happens tomorrow night, tonight, Lord, we are still together!"

To Manawyddan her white face and out-stretched arms, the sweet loveliness of her two white breasts, still looked like things of Faery . . .

Now, lying awake beside his son and hers, he thought, *It was well done. She never dreamed that we would change places in the very hour that Pwyll spoke with her. The boy was begotten as the Ancient Harmonies would have all children begotten: in shared love and desire.*

Yet soon fresh trouble had come. The dread Otherworldly foes had proved their reality, snatching away the newborn life. He remembered the long misery, knowing what *her* fear and misery and shame must be. Remembered the long peering into that shining dish of clear water; water in which the druid-trained could see what was far away. Striving to keep his mind away from her face, from that accursed horse block—to find that other face, that unknown baby face that might be nowhere on earth. Again and again he had seen Teyrnon's house in the water; at last he had found it upon earth. It, and the sturdy little son he had never seen. The joy of that hour had been his own, if nothing else ever could be. A pity that it had had to end the joy of others . . .

You owe much to Teyrnon, lad; as much as any boy could ever owe his own father, maybe more. He fought a great fight for you on your birth night, but maybe the fight he fought with himself, later, was harder. He would have won that one too, by himself, if I had not hurried him. But whatever I did was good if it saved her one day by that horse block.

He had sent her boy home to her. He had helped Teyrnon to conquer himself; ironically in the event, he had even conquered Another, that unseen, unknown Might of whose terribleness that monster had been only the servant . . .

Or had he? Suddenly in that darkness Eyes met his, those same Eyes that he had felt watching them the day before. Eyes sea-gray as his own, but colder, deeper than the sea. Cold with the cold of vast and unfathomable space. *Look. Look and know your littleness. None can conquer Me. I am beyond age and death. To Me one of your life-times is less than half the passing of a moon. Though I wait a few breaths' space of My time to strike, still the blow will fall. And beneath it all you miserable mites will shriek and flee and be crushed into nothingness.*

That Voice that made no sound chilled Manawyddan's heart. He sank into a darkness that seemed to be that threatened nothingness.

5

Homecoming

IN THE dewy sweetness of the dawn they set out again. The way was hard and rough, straight up through those dark mountains that cradled the Holy Stones. But Pryderi sang as he went. His eyes shone like the sun that soon beat down hot upon them.

"Before nightfall we shall be home, Lord. *Home!*"

Your home, Manawyddan thought. *Will any place on earth ever again be home to me?* Well, nothing must dampen the boy's happiness; nothing must spoil this day for him. He trudged along unhappily. A black mood was on him; he could not understand how he could have been such a fool as to let himself be trapped into seeing Rhiannon again. To come as a beggar before her who was still a queen—what part was that for a proud man? For any man? Better far to have let her remember him as she always had; as one who had helped her in need, then had too much delicacy ever again to inflict his presence upon her. He had been the High King's brother when last they met, he who was now a landless wanderer, kinless and friendless forever.

No—not quite friendless. He could not escape the boy's hospitality now, whatever craziness had been on him when he accepted it.

He had been needed in Dyved once. Now he was not needed anywhere . . .

I dreamed something last night. What was it? Like a black wing, memory brushed him, and was gone.

Sunset was past when they saw the Gorsedd Arberth, that mighty Mound that all men feared. Flowers grew there, but no child ever plucked them. Gold might well be buried there, with that once great, now nameless King, but no robber was fool enough to seek it. Many generations of lords and warriors had avoided that Mound, as men avoid a bed of hot coals. Only in evil times, when trouble threatened the whole Tribe, had a few Princes of Dyved gone up there, daring death. The King who mounted that Mound was beaten to death, or else he saw a wonder. . .

Pwyll had seen a wonder. He had sat upon that Mound and seen its side open to let Rhiannon ride out, upon a white horse and clad in a golden gown. The Holy Bride meant for him. . .

But now that fabled Mound was quiet, purple in the gray evening, and as they drew nearer they saw smoke curling against its grim heights, and then the palace huddled below it, the palace where Pryderi had been born.

Pryderi gave a great shout of joy. "We are here! Here!" And sped forward, too lost in his gladness to notice Manawyddan's silence.

The great doors yawned before them, as once long ago they had yawned before Teyrnon and the little Guri. The doorkeeper saw them, saw Pryderi, and stared; stared again, then rushed inside. Men and women came swarming out, like bees out of a hive, all shouting together, "Lord! Lord Pryderi!"

Like bees they swarmed upon him, all trying to kiss his hands, his clothes, any part of him they could reach.

Then two more women came, and before them all fell back; opened a lane that led straight to him.

One hesitated, till she saw his face, then cried out and came running. She was young and tall and deep-bosomed, apple-sound and honey-sweet: Kigva, the daughter of Gwynn Gloyu. She flung herself upon Pryderi, and they hugged and kissed each other as though trying to squeeze themselves into one body, to do away with all separateness and all chance of any more separation forever.

The other woman came more slowly. But her eyes drank in Pryderi with a joy as warm, as enfolding, as touch. Time had clawed with graying fingers at the gold of her hair, had tramped across her face and left tiny footprints around eyes and mouth, but her beauty shone on through the aging flesh, as the light shines through an alabaster lamp.

She saw Manawyddan, and her eyes lit for him. For himself, not merely for her guest. She came to him.

"A welcome is with you here, son of Llyr! Long has it been since you came to this house, though there is no man we could be as glad to see, save my son himself!"

He took her outstretched hands, and by some magic he was no longer embarrassed or ashamed.

They went inside, and the feast was spread before them, the feast

that perhaps Rhiannon's Birds had told her to have ready. Rigva sat next
to Pryderi, but Rhiannon put Manawyddan between her son and herself. And the son of Llyr could no more look away from her than
Pryderi could look away from Kigva. The turn of her head, the lifting
of her hand, the shape of her mouth as she spoke each new thought,
all these were music. Each brought her some new form of loveliness
that he thought could not be bettered, and then she would move
again, and the new sight ravish him anew with fresh beauty.

He thought, *She is as beautiful as she ever was. She is more beauti-*
ful than she ever was. She has a grace that makes youth seem boisterous
and crude.

But Pryderi and Kigva were well satisfied with their youth. To
each it seemed that nothing could possibly be so fine and wonderful
as the other. They laughed and talked and ate together—Pryderi ate
a great deal—yet their eyes never left each other. And as the night
wore, they talked less, and Kigva ceased to eat and drink at all.

At last the time came they longed for. The feast was over, and the
young King and Queen went to bed together. Rhiannon went to her own
sleeping-place, and Manawyddan lay down in the one given him. Yet
his closed eyes still saw Rhiannon.

So it was for the next night, and the next. The nobles of Dyved kept
pouring in to welcome Pryderi home, and since those who had hoped
to get his throne had to take care to shout their gladness as loudly as
those who really felt it (often they shouted louder), there was never a
moment's quiet. During those three days any man in that palace at
Arberth would have been hard put to it to hear himself think.

Yet Manawyddan and Rhiannon talked together, and heard only
each other. Their minds and their voices flowed together, as the voice
and the harp of the bard flow together. And the longer Manawyddan
looked at her and talked with her, the more it seemed to him that that
far-sung beauty of the Queen of Dyved was sweeter and more comfortable now in her fading than it had been in her bright youth. She
too had lost, and had wept for her dead. In her too, as in him, were
barren places that never would blossom again, and where she too
must always be alone.

Yet she lived, as he lived, and she was lonely, as he was lonely . . .

And on the last night of the feast, when the moon was well on her
westward road, he said to the young Lord of Dyved, "Pryderi, I would
be glad indeed for it to be as you said."

'What was it he said?" asked Rhiannon, and though her voice was
curious, her mouth was not. It had all knowledge, that mouth; it was
sweet, and a little wicked too.

Pryderi looked at her and cleared his throat, then cleared it again. He had been too busy with his own affairs to see how things were shaping between his mother and his friend, and here, under her eye, his offer did not sound quite as it had when he had made it to Manawyddan. He had been sure then that she would gladly do that or anything else to please him—she always had, whenever she had felt that the thing in question would not be bad for him (a point on which, in his early youth, they had sometimes differed). But now he was suddenly aware that he had taken a good deal upon himself.

"Lady," he said, and cleared his throat yet again. "Lady, I offered you as a bride to the son of Llyr. Indeed," he rushed on before she could speak, "there is no finer man alive than he is, and when I said it I thought I would be doing good to both of you. Indeed and in very deed"—here he grinned at her as radiantly as he had when he was small and she had caught him doing something that he was fairly sure she would not want him to do—"I still think I am. If you will let me, Mother."

Then Rhiannon's smile opened fully, like a scarlet flower in the sun. "You have said it, and glad will I be to abide by your saying, Son."

In the morning Manawyddan awoke beside Rhiannon. He lay there beside her and looked at her, and it seemed to him that he felt life itself lapping about him in that chamber, lapping him like a warm sea. Life as surely as if it had been youth renewed, the rapture of the sun rising in the scarlet east, not the earth-fed strength of storm-blasted trees healing and thrusting forth new branches.

Not reborn, scarred but still growing, up and on—on . . .

Then he saw that she was watching him through her lashes, a quiet twinkle in her eyes, and he smiled.

"Good morning to you, Lady."

She smiled back and stretched herself as a cat stretches. "It is a good morning. The best morning that either of us has known for a long time. Did you truly think, Lord, that you and that overgrown child of mine could keep any secrets from me? That I had not thought of this and willed it, long before my boy thought of it and willed it?"

"Never, Lady. I feared that you had loved Pwyll too much ever to be willing to take another man."

She sobered. "I loved Pwyll, and I love him. But he is gone, so here on earth there is nothing I can do with that love. When my own son offered me to you, when my Bird flew over you, and the golden feather dropped at your feet, did you not hear my call?"

"I thought I dreamed, Lady. Out of my own longing, childishly."

She laughed softly; a tender, mocking laugh, and rubbed her face against his. "True it is, as they say: You are no claimant of lands or possessions, Manawyddan."

"I find myself enough to master, Lady. Without struggling greedily for mastery over things that perhaps should not belong to me."

"None will call you greedy, Lord. You will always let Caswallon wear your crown—and well I know why, who would hate as much as you to see this island bathed in blood! You will never even claim the son you yourself begot. And with all my heart I thank you for that, who know how much it meant to Pwyll to have Pryderi think him his father."

"He is ill-bred who takes back the gift he has given. I have wondered, Lady: did you ever guess on which night the boy was begotten?"

She laughed again and drew his head to her breast. "I knew. Not for awhile, but before the night was over. I knew that the man I lay with loved me—that I was not being taken like some rare dish a host sets before his guest—but there was a difference. So when you slept, I put your own shape back upon you for a moment to make sure— some little tricks I still know, who had to leave most of my powers behind me in the Bright World."

"I am sorry. I thought I had put no grief or shame on you."

"You did not. At the time I would have been better pleased if I could have felt a little grief or shame. Shame—" she sobered again. "You did the deed generously and with great delicacy, Lord; a deed that another might have made horrible. When it would have been betrayal to love and blasphemy not to love, you did your best to spare me both evils. For that, as well as for my son himself, I long have wanted to thank you."

"You owe me no thanks." His eyes twinkled. "That was the best night of my youth, Lady. It could have been better only had it been myself you loved and chose."

"I love you now." She put her arms round his neck.

Two more such nights they had. The third night was that of full moon, and toward morning laughter wakened them. Laughter coming from the other side of the wall, where Kigva and Pryderi had their bed. That new-fangled luxury, a window, had been cut in the outer wall there, and evidently the two young people were looking out of it.

Kigva said, "Look at the moon, Lord! Was it ever so round and fair before? Even now, when it is setting."

Pryderi answered, "It is two moons I see, on a white sky—rare the sight! Let me see if I am seeing double, Lady, or if they are really there."

Then silence, and then Kigva laughing, "It is to feel you meant, not to see—" and sounds that might have been whispers, but most likely were kissing, there in the morning dusk.

Rhiannon smiled. "We must have a window cut in here too, Lord. For years after I lost Pwyll I wanted to shut myself into the dark. It used to make me sad to hear those two children being happy, even while I was glad for them. When I lay here alone."

Manawyddan gathered her into his arms. "Lady, long will it be before you lie alone again!"

Yet that time was to come sooner than either of them dreamed.

That morning restlessness was on Pryderi. For one flashing second, when he saw his mother coming to the breakfast table, Manwyddan's arm around her, it lit up with the old loving mischief. But before and after that it was as heavy as the body of a pregnant woman near her time.

He fidgeted. His hands seemed to want to do something, yet to be dissatisfied with anything they undertook. His feet seemed to want to go somewhere, yet to be unwilling to lift him from his seat.

He did not eat. He only nibbled at his food and then threw it away, and nothing could have been more unlike Pryderi than that.

Kigva and Manawyddan sat and watched him, in worried wonder. Rhiannon sat and watched him awhile, then spoke.

"Son, it is a new face you have on, and I liked the old one better."

Pryderi threw back his head and looked at her defiantly. "I do not like it either, and soon I am going to have to do something that we will both like less. For that Caswallon Mab Beli who calls himself High King now, will soon hear that I am at home, if he has not heard it already, and if I do not go to him and pay him homage, he will get suspicious of me and maybe come after it."

He stopped and glared at his mother, as if that were her fault, and when she looked back at him unmoved, he glared at the ceiling.

"I do not know what to do except to go and give it to him, and if one must drink sour milk there is no use in putting it off."

He stopped again and looked very hard at the floors and the walls and the ceiling. He carefully looked anywhere and everywhere except at those three he loved best.

He was afraid, desperately afraid of what they might be thinking of him. Manawyddan, his rightful King, to whom this paying of homage to the usurper might well seem both cowardice and treachery. His mother, now rightful Queen over all the Island of the Migty, who might well see things in the same light. And Kigva—Kigva, who had always thought him the bravest and strongest of men. Able to tread all foes beneath his feet.

He waited for them to speak out, in a chorus of amazed horror and wrath. He waited for them to be silent, and their silence was what he thought most likely, and feared the most.

What did happen startled him as nothing else on earth could have done. Rhiannon took up a bit of meat and remarked calmly and casually, yet with admiration in her tone, "Son, you are growing up."

Manawyddan said, "It is the only thing you can do. Dyved cannot stand alone against all the rest of the Island of the Mighty, and by bringing me here you must already have roused Caswallon's suspicions. You are right—the sooner you go to him the better."

"There is no such hurry on him as that." Rhiannon swallowed her meat hastily, then turned to her son. "Indeed, Lord and dear, Caswallon is in Kent, as either of you two men would have known if you had bothered to ask questions. Wait until he is nearer: do not seem too eager. And there is this good in sour milk: it always keeps."

"It does," said Pryderi, greatly impressed. He sighed with relief and leaned back in his chair; then saw his breakfast, and went to work on it with great vigor.

He was brave. For himself, he would gladly have fought that usurping magician-king, for all his power to slay invisibly. He did not admire common sense, any more than any young man admires an ugly woman, but now he could not sacrifice himself without sacrificing other people, indeed all Dyved. So, since protecting them meant ceasing to admire himself, his plan, unheroic as he thought it, was probably the most heroic deed of his life.

But Rhiannon was troubled. That night she talked with Manawyddan. "We must not let him go to Caswallon too soon, Lord. Not until you have had time to school him. For Pryderi cannot think any way but straight, and Caswallon, who cannot think straight, will not understand him. All could so easily go wrong!"

Manawyddan put his arm about her. "Be at ease, Lady. Caswallon will not slay a guest. That would be worse than his old blood-guiltiness that folk are just beginning to forget."

"But accidents can be arranged! Poison . . ."

"Who would give Caswallon the benefit of the doubt? A name once smeared is never really clean again. And I think that

Caswallon will be truly glad to see the boy. Peace is what he wants and needs now, most of all."

Yet on him too there was fear. Discretion was a new growth in the young Lord of Dyved; that morning it had shown itself, but it still could be but a young and tender plant. Caswallon's own discretion should be dependable, yet constant strain and watchfulness tell upon a man. Blood-guilt, even smothered, unacknowledged pangs of conscience, may well drive him to shed more blood. And there was one danger that Rhiannon must never guess. If Caswallon suspected the secret of Pryderi's birth, saw in him a rival—there had been talk, if only guesswork and whispers. He remembered Branwen's gentle mocking, long ago.

He said, slowly, "Perhaps I should go with Pryderi. I offer my own homage."

"And thrust your own head into the wolf's mouth too? No. With you here, Caswallon will know that if he harms Pryderi, Dyved will not be left headless. Men from all of the parts of the Island of the Mighty would flock to you then. Not all men, but many."

Manawyddan chuckled. "So then it is safe for Pryderi to go. You yourself disprove all your fears."

"It is not as simple as that, and you know it! You are afraid too. Let us think . . ."

They talked much, and thought long.

Old Pendaran Dyved's dying won them some delay. He had lived only for Pryderi's homecoming, he who long had guarded queens and realm as best he could. But it was Manawyddan, not Pryderi, he asked to talk with at the last.

"I am glad to shift my load to your shoulders, son of Llyr. You may think you have borne loads enough, but the truth is that you are a man born to carry loads. Free, your eyes lose their sparkle and your shoulders slump."

"You are wise, old man. Wiser than I thought."

The old druid smiled. "You never thought me wise. And I know why: I knew why of old, when I was a guest at Harlech. As I fear another knew too."

"I was always courteous to you . . ."

"And no more. There is no time left for anything but truth between us, brother of Bran the Blessed."

Old wrath and old pain boiled up in Manawyddan. For what his sister had suffered in Ireland, for what Rhiannon had suffered here.

"Never would druids of the Old Tribes have let their Queen or any other woman be used like a she-ass—made to carry men on her back! Worse—to be made to keep telling and retelling those other women's hideous lies, accusing herself of such foulness! Their eyes would have pierced the lies—have made the liars blubber and wail for mercy. Pwyll was no Matholuch; only a decent man, striving to do his best for both his wife and his people. But you druids—I know your wisdom and your goodness, Pendaran Dyved, many times since then they have been proved, but never will I understand what was on you then!"

The old face grew grave. "I had no wisdom to strive against what menaced Dyved then, Lord. We druids here were all helpless: we looked into the water and the crystal, and we could see nothing but clouds. Only the Grayness—the Grayness. It had Eyes. Only I ever saw those Eyes." His face twisted; he gasped. "They came to me in the night. Their evil entered into me; made me mock her and give the most brutal sentence that we dared give, Lord. For the fear of Pwyll was on us too. But those Eyes . . ."

He struggled for breath. Manawyddan said gently, "Peace be with you, Pendaran Dyved. If you failed Rhiannon once, since then you have guarded her long and well. I grieve that I reminded you of what is over and done."

"It is not over! He—waits. Watch well, son of Llyr!"

The dying man cried aloud those words, his last. He spoke no more, though through two more nights he breathed.

Then he died and was mounded, and many mourned for him, Rhiannon the Queen not least. And a week later Pryderi set out for the Court of Caswallon. Nobly he went, dressed in his best, with the finest young men he had left around him. Golden ornaments glittered on his crimson cloak, and even on the trappings of his white horse, the finest of stallions, that was a grandson to the foal that Teyrnon had saved along with him, on that dread night long ago.

But Manawyddan watched him go, his heart cold with dread. For he was remembering those words of Pendaran Dyved's: ". . . *at Harlech. As I fear another knew too.*" What meaning could they have had except that Caswallon had scented out the secret of Pryderi's birth?

6

Before Caswallon

THE YOUNG lord of Dyved and his train were but a half day's journey from the house where Caswallon was, when a strange man met them on the road.

He was tall and old, and his ragged clothes were of as many colors as the rainbow. Over one shoulder he bore a dilapidated bag of hide, with most of the hair worn off it. But over the other hung a golden harp with silver strings.

He said, "Lord, may I travel with you?"

Some of Pryderi's young men looked insulted, and all looked surprised, but Pryderi stared hard at the stranger.

"Man," he said, "have I not seen you before?"

"Lord, I have sung in the halls of many chiefs. Maybe I sang in your father's, and you small."

"My father was Pwyll, Prince of Dyved."

"A noble man, and a far-famed. I sang in his palace at Arberth once, before he had a son."

Pryderi hesitated, trying not to be seen looking at the stranger's clothes. "I would like well to hear any bard that sang for my father, but now I am on my way to see the High King. If you will turn back to Arberth, my mother and my wife will give you good welcome there. I will soon be home again."

He thought that shabby man would shrink from facing all the fine bards of Caswallon's Court, but to his surprise the stranger said, "I would rather go with you now, Lord. If I may."

"Come then," said Pryderi. He turned to the man who had charge of his baggage. "Get him a cloak."

But the stranger shook his head. "You are generous, Lord, as is to be expected of your father's son. But these clothes and I are old comrades; we will not part now."

"Let it be as you please," said Pryderi.

So the stranger fared with them, and they all fared on, and before sunset they came to the place where the King was. It was a place of druidcraft, of wise men and teachers; later, men were to call it Oxford. Caswallon, once the pupil only of magicians, lately had turned to the study of the higher wisdom. He wanted to wipe out memory of his kingship's bloody beginnings, to be remembered as Beli his father still was, for nobleness as well as power.

He gave Pryderi a great welcome, and he and all his men made much of him. "I call this finely done of you, young Lord," he said, "you who were such great friends with my cousins, to come in so soon and wish me joy of my kingship."

"You are the King," said Pryderi, "and this island needs peace. May it be as blessed under you, as once it was under Bran."

That was all he could bring himself to say, and he nearly choked on it, but Caswallon shook his hand and laughed.

Deep into the night they made merry. Then Caswallon said, "I have one thing to ask of you, young Lord. Give it me and I will ask no tribute of Dyved again so long as you live."

Pryderi sat up sharply, the wine fumes clearing from his head. He thought in horror, *What if he means to ask me for Manawyddan's head?* He said aloud, his eyes fixing Caswallon's, "Ask what you will, Lord. So long as it is honorable for me to give, I will give it."

Again Caswallon laughed. "I see that you have not forgotten that other feast, your parents' wedding feast, when Gwawl the Bright came in disguise and asked a boon. When your father granted the gift but forgot to set limits to it, and Gwawl asked for the bride herself."

"But Gwawl got nothing by that Slip of my father's. Nothing but shame and stripes." Pryderi's eyes still pinned Caswallon's. In the shadows behind them one or two men gasped.

But Caswallon still smiled. "Your chiefs hold meetings and your druids rites in an ancient Ring of Holy Stones. To you New Tribes, it is spoil of war; your grandfathers' grandfathers never set eyes on it. But to the Old Tribes it is holy indeed; nothing that men can see or touch could be holier."

"To my people too it is holy." Pryderi was breathing more easily now, but his eyes looked puzzled. "Four generations of us have worshipped and held our councils there. We do no mockery or sacrilege against it."

"None says you do. But the wise men with me here—some of them druids who have served Beli my father as well as Bran my cousin—say that they know a place in which those God-Stones could sit and bring man such wisdom as he never yet has had. Where they could watch and time the ceaseless marching of the great Stars that walk through the sky like men—yes, and even foretell the coming of that great Darkness that sometimes swallows up sun and moon."

Pryderi said slowly, "My people would not like to give up the Holy Ring. Nor do I see how it could be moved."

"I say that it could be moved."

Pryderi was silent awhile; then he said, "This is a great matter. I must speak of it with my chieftains and my druids in the Ring itself. Those God-Stones are holy to all the men of Dyved. They are not the King's nor any man's to give away."

"A King speaks for his people," said Caswallon.

"A war-king does, in time of war. Not so the Lord of peaceful folk, in time of peace."

"To have their taxes eased soothes all men." Caswallon grinned.

But Pryderi stuck to what he had said, though the King pressed him. At last, maybe partly to ease that pressure, he asked questions about where the Stones were to go, and when he heard he laughed.

"For a bird in flight that would be a long journey. And stones are not birds—they do not fly. Come and get them if you can."

"Is that a bargain?" Caswallon's eyes were keen.

Pryderi laughed again. "It is, Lord. And if the Stones make themselves light as feathers and fly away with you, then indeed my people and I will know that it is the Gods' will that they go. For you could never carry them half that far."

"The Gods will help us," said Caswallon, "for it is Their will. And Their blessing will be upon you."

He held out his hand and Pryderi took it and grinned. "Yet meaning no disrespect to Them or you, Lord, I fear that Dyved will be paying you tribute this year and next, and for many a year to come."

Caswallon grinned back. "We shall see." But within himself he had ceased to laugh. He thought, *This young man is stiff-necked, if a little simple. It is well for a stiff neck to have no head on top of it.*

Next morning the feasters slept late; all but the stranger who had come with Pryderi. He rose early and went down to a stream near the house; he washed his face and hands there, and the wind blew cool and sweet in his face.

He looked about him, and saw that the land was green and gentle, and what else he saw in it only druid-bred eyes could know. He said to himself, *This is a place for birth. Not for the births of the body, but one where knowledge will be worshiped, and great thoughts born. By listening to its druids, Caswallon may achieve memorable deeds, but he will not do them for the people's sake, or for their own goodness. He will do them for his own pride and power. He has not changed.*

He lay down on those green grasses in whose place so many walls and roofs were to rise, roofs beneath which so much thinking was to be done, and he thought.

At first Caswallon was glad to see the boy. His mind was not made up. Not until he saw that the lad had manhood in him. That could be dangerous in any man who still loved the House of Bran. But most dangerous of all in the son of Manawyddan son of Llyr.

But if Caswallon had any inkling of that secret, as yet he had given no sign of it. Eyes that last night had watched the mind behind his face—the trained mind that could be almost, but not quite, as well guarded as that face—had found nothing

The day wore. By twos and threes the feasters woke and straggled out into the sun. Some of them had headaches, and some of them had bellyaches, and some of them had both, but when the women brought out breakfast many of the young men still had good appetites after all. Pryderi had, and Caswallon sat beside him and made as much of him as he had the night before. Drink never turned Caswallon's head.

The King had almost finished his breakfast when his eye lit upon the tall shabby man who stood among Pryderi's men. His eyes met the stranger's eyes, and their gray directness puzzled him. For a breath's space memory flickered through his mind then away again, as a moth or a gnat flicks past a man's face.

He said, "Pryderi, who is that tall fellow with the harp? He is not dressed like your other men."

Pryderi laughed. "That is a tactful way of putting it, Lord. He joined me yesterday. I offered him a new cloak, but he would not take it."

The King frowned. "That is a queer way for a beggar to act. Usually they grab at whatever they can get."

Pryderi said, a trifle stiffly, "He is no beggar, Lord. See, his harp is fine."

"Can he use it, I wonder? Here, fellow, come and give us a tune."

The stranger came up to their table then, and played for them, and no man or woman there ever had heard music that was sweeter.

When he had finished, Caswallon drew a deep breath. "Man, you are the king of harpers!"

The stranger said, "Some men are kings of one thing, Lord, some of another."

Caswallon's face changed; for a breath's space his eyes grew hard. Then he took the fine gold chain from about his own neck and threw it to the harper. The bard had to stoop to pick it up, and Pryderi, without knowing how he knew it, suddenly understood that this was what the High King had wanted—to make that straight back stoop and that high head bow to pick up his gift from the dust. To show all men what kind of kingship mattered, how little an artist's gifts and skills counted beside place and power.

But why? Pryderi thought, his mouth stiff with distaste. *Why should he care?*

But the stranger straightened, his brow unruffled, even a faint amusement in his eyes. He walked toward Caswallon, chain in hand.

"Such a gift is too great a treasure, Lord King, for a poor wandering man of the roads. Never could I close my eyes without fear that in my sleep some other man would cut my throat to get it. And some night some man would." He held out the chain to Caswallon.

The King said, "Your wanderings are over." He paused, and that pause seemed, strangely, to darken the morning sun. Then he added, his voice silken soft, "You shall stay with me always, and play that sweet music of yours for me every night."

"Lord, I could not hope to please so great a King for long. Some days my music is sweet, others it is sour."

"It is not every man that is offered the place of bard to the High King. Suppose I do not let you go, fool?" Caswallon's voice was low, but his eyes burned like hot coals.

The stranger said easily, "You will do according to your kind of kingcraft, Lord, as I will do according to mine. Would you like me to do tricks for you? I am a cunning man, as well as a musician."

Some stiffness, some dread that had been in the air, went out of it. People relaxed; some smiled. The harping-man had sense; he was going to give in, after all. But Caswallon's eyes did not soften, though their light grew cold.

"Well, fellow, show us what you can do."

The chain still swung from the stranger's hand. He laid it down on the table beside Caswallon, took down his own worn bag from his shoulder, and held that high.

"This little bag cannot hold much. Bear witness to that, all men."

He set it down and untied its mouth. He took out a ball of silver thread that glistened, moon-bright, in the sun. One of Pryderi's men whispered to him, "Small as that bag is, it could hold a hundred balls like that. I am afraid this is not going to be much good."

"Wait and see what he does with it," Pryderi whispered back.

Shielding his eyes with his hand, the stranger looked up at the sky. It was blue, bluer than the deepest sea, yet here and there white clouds floated upon it, delicate huge masses that looked heavenly soft, yet solid as the thatched roof below. Whitenesses with curly edges that grew ever thinner and finer until they melted into that depth of blueness and were lost.

The stranger spun the ball round in his hand. He spun it round and round. It shone brighter than silver ever could. It grew bigger and brighter. It shone brighter than the moon. It shone like the sun's very self.

All eyes were fixed upon the spinning brightness. Not one could have looked away even though a spear or an arrow had flashed towards that person from beneath that glowing, spinning ball.

A length of thread came loose from that ball. It did not fall earthward, or float upon the wind, as even the finest thread should have done. It darted straight up, like a bird.

Up and up and up it went, higher than any bird ever flew. They should no longer have been able to see its upper part, but still they saw its whole length, stretching from earth to heaven.

It came to a cloud, it wrapped itself around and around that cloud; became a shining bridge, fine as a hair.

"So far, so good," said the stranger.

He stooped to his bag again, put the ball back inside, and took out a white hare much too big to have been in there.

"Up, hare!" he said, and set it down facing the thread. And though any of its paws was many times wider than that narrowest of bridges, it sped upward without any trouble at all. Up and up, through the sky, until it reached the cloud, and was lost in that whiteness so like its whiteness.

All gasped but the bard. He stooped and took a small snow-white hound out of the bag. He set it on its feet and said, "Dog, go after that hare."

And the dog ran up the thread as the hare had done.

It too vanished, and soon the wild sweet music of its belling came drifting down from heaven. They knew that it must be chasing the hare through the clouds.

Again the bard stooped to his bag. This time he seemed to have trouble in getting out what was inside. A head came finally, the curly yellow head of a boy in his teens, and a woman screamed. But a chest followed the head, and then long legs that carried the rest. The whole boy stood there, handsome and grinning.

The harper said, "Boy, go after that dog."

The boy leapt for that thread. He shinned up it as fast as any other boy ever shinned up a ladder. He too vanished.

Again the bard turned to his bag This time too he had trouble, but before long a young woman stood there, so beautiful that every man caught his breath and forgot all about the wonders in the clouds.

"Girl, go after the others," the stranger told her, "and see to it that the hound does not tear the hare. That boy may be careless."

She went, and a groaning "Ah-h" rose from the throats of all the young men. They would have liked her to stay where they could get at her.

But she too vanished, and soon, mixed with the sound of the hound's belling that still came down to them from the sky, sweet and wild and strange, came the two young people's voices calling to him. All of Caswallon's people, and all of Pryderi's, stood there in awe, listening to that hunt in the sky, until at last all the lovely, strange sound of it died away. Then silence fell; an awed, stunned silence.

Until the bard shook his head and frowned. "I am afraid," said he, looking up into the clouds, "that there are goings-on up there."

"What kind of goings-on?" asked Caswallon.

"I am afraid that the hound is eating up the hare, while the boy makes love to the girl."

All the young fellows there stiffened or snorted. One said angrily, "A bad servant that fellow is, letting his master down like that. I would have the hide off him for that!"

But really each was angry only because it was not himself who was doing that lovemaking. Each thought enviously what a soft bed that white cloud must make, only Pryderi remembered red-haired Kigva waiting for him at home, and grinned in sympathy.

Caswallon's stern mouth twitched. "That is likely enough," he said.

"Well, I will put a stop to it," said the stranger. And he took out the ball again and began to reel the thread in. Once more all eyes were glued to that gleaming roundness . . .

Then all of a sudden both girl and boy were sprawling on the ground together, and nobody at all could have had any doubt as to what they had been doing. Next instant the dog plopped down beside them, one of the hare's legs still sticking out of his mouth.

Everybody there roared with laughter, even Caswallon. Everybody but the bard. His jaw set and he drew his sword and advanced upon

The Song of the Rhiannon

the lovers. In one flash the boy's head was off his shoulders and spinning along the ground. The body twitched like a beheaded chicken's.

Men gasped. Women screamed. Caswallon sombered and his eyes pinned the stranger's. "I do not like a thing of that sort to be done before me," he said with dignity.

A man near the house wall muttered, "Unless he does it himself." And then wished he had been silent, for in that sudden deep silence even whispers were loud.

The stranger shrugged. "Well, Lord King, if you are not pleased, what has been done can be undone."

Pryderi sank back into his chair and drew a long breath of relief. Until then he had not known how shocked and somehow disappointed he was. Inexplicably, since this manslayer was only a chance-met stranger.

"Undo it then," said Caswallon harshly.

The harper walked over to the head and picked it up. He threw it toward the still twitching body and it lit on the neck and promptly grew fast there. The boy sprang up, looking startled. But soon he looked more startled, for his face was looking out over his back, not over his chest. His head had been put on the wrong way round.

"Better for him to die than to live like that!" said Caswallon violently.

"I am glad you think so," said the stranger. He went up to the boy then and put a hand on either side of his face. Without effort he twisted the head around until it faced the right way again.

"Get back into the bag now," he said. "The lot of you."

They shrank and dwindled; the lovers became the size of children, the dog became the size of a pup, and the meat jumped out of its mouth and became a whole hare again, though a tiny one. They all ran for the bag and by the time they reached it they were the size of dolls. They scrambled into it and were gone.

The stranger picked up his bag and his harp and started for the gate. But Caswallon's voice leapt after him like a spear. "Stop that man!"

Men raced forward, massed themselves before the gates, the sunlight gleaming on their spear-points.

The bard stopped. Unhurried, the King walked up to him. "So it is war, Manawyddan my cousin?"

No muscle of the other's face changed. "It is peace if you will have it, Caswallon."

The High King laughed. "That is not for you to offer. Not with my men between you and the gate. I do not think that you can climb over them on that thread of yours."

He saw the memory that Manawyddan did not try to hide, and laughed. "It takes time to weave invisibility for oneself. Time such as I had when I prepared my attack upon the Seven who guarded Caradoc. I will not give it to you."

The son of Llyr said, unmoved, "Trick for trick, magic for magic, I can match you, Caswallon. And master you. Did you forget, because Bran and I seldom chose to play such children's games, that we were of the Old Blood, and knew more of Illusion and Fantasy than you could ever hope to learn?"

"I do not deny it. But men bar the gates against you now, cousin. Sharp spears end all Illusions."

Pryderi came up to them then, his eyes dangerous, his young mouth set. "This man came here in my following, Lord; so he is under my protection. What has he done that you should slay him?"

Manawyddan spoke before Caswallon could. "None seeks to slay me, young Lord. The High King and I have matters of which we must talk alone."

And Pryderi, to his own surprise, turned and went back to his seat.

Manawyddan said quietly to Caswallon, "He does not know who I am. Such glamor is on his eyes as still rests upon all here save yours. For awhile I blinded those too."

"Not for long. You came here to guard your whelp—though you hoped to find a chance to take my life at the same time."

"I did come to guard the boy; that much truth even you can still see, cousin. But whether he dies now or in old age he never will doubt that he is the son of Pwyll, Prince of Dyved. Crowns and thrones are toys I never would shed blood for—least of all would I ever risk his blood for them."

"You say that, but how can I trust you? You have caught me in a trap, Manawyddan, but it is you and your son who will die in it. Black as my name will be, I will still be King. A man can bear the burdens he must."

Manawyddan laughed. "My Illusion is upon your men's eyes; you know that. If I turn now and cry, 'Here I come!' each will see my face upon the head of the man next to him. While they are killing each other, Pryderi and I and all who follow him can go out by other doors."

Caswallon said grimly, "If that is so, why do you not make them see your face on my face, and make an end?"

"Because then I must sit where now you sit, and as uncomfortably. For we both have friends. I myself cannot see why it matters whether a man's own son succeeds him or his sister's son, so long as the new king serves the people well."

Caswallon's lip curled. "You give yourself one more reason to seek my place, father of Pryderi."

"It is your place, so long as you use it well. I do not say that I will make no move if you oppress the people, but I am still the fool you have always thought me. I would hate to make that move. For then I too would have blood on my hands, I too would always be looking back over my shoulder. I do not want that burden, nor will I put it upon Pryderi, whose nature is not fitted to bear it."

Caswallon said slowly, "The burden is heavy. But I do not hate it enough to lay it down. You must know that you can never trust me, cousin. Are you fool enough to let me live, knowing that?"

"I can trust you, cousin. Because I have too much knowledge for you ever to be able to creep upon me unsuspected, under any Veil of Illusion. And you know now that I can always creep upon you unseen. I will go now, and you will keep faith with Pryderi, knowing that I have power to avenge him. Also, when your men come to take the Holy Stones, your High Druid will come with them, to tell all men that Pryderi bowed to the Gods' own will.

"Fare as well as you can, cousin. As boys we two played better games than today's together, but I hope that in these bodies we now wear we will never meet again."

Caswallon bit his lip, then signed to his guards. As mist melts before the summer sun, so they melted away from the gate. Without a backward look the stranger who was Manawyddan son of Llyr turned his back upon them and strode out.

"He might have said goodbye at least," one of Pryderi's men grumbled.

But Pryderi was staring after him in wonder. He said slowly, "I know him now. I should have known him when first I saw him. He is the harper who came to Teyrnon's house in Gwent long ago, when I was little."

7

The Taking of the Holy Stones

AGAIN PRYDERI, the son of Pwyll, came home to Arberth, and again his people welcomed him. Torches burned like stars, and roasting beasts and birds smoked over gleaming fires, and harpers played and told their tales. But Pryderi bore with all that only to keep from hurting his people's feelings.

"I have had too much feasting and too much drinking and too much merrymaking," he told his family, when he was alone with them. "I need some fresh air. The Gods know how I need it after sitting all those nights with Caswallon's smile on me."

"You said the King received you well, Son." Rhiannon smiled her own gentle yet somehow mocking smile.

"He did so, but I do not like that smile of his. It is full of teeth and full of smugness and full of whiskers. It makes you feel as if he were a cat that had just swallowed a mouse, and you are not sure that you are not the mouse. Indeed—" and he sobered, "it was wiped off his face once, though. And that was a strange happening."

He told them then of the mysterious harper, and of how at last he had known him for the same man who had played before Teyrnon in Gwent, long ago.

"He did you great good then, Mother. Can it be that not all your kinsmen in the Bright World are so set against you after all?"

"None of them are set against me, Son. It is I that cut myself off from them, leaving the world of my birth to follow your father."

"So you always say. But then who put those years of barrenness on you? And who had me carried off on my birth night, when I finally got myself born at last?"

Rhiannon's smile deepened. "You take too much credit to your-self, Son. Your father and I were the ones who got you born."

"That is not the point. You know what I mean . . ."

But Kigva was bubbling over with wonder. "By the Mothers! How I wish I could see that strange man and thank him! Except for him you might never have come home to us. For why did he appear again unless Caswallon was plotting something against you?"

"That is true." Pryderi sobered again. "I have been wondering about that myself."

Manawyddan said, "Arawn, King of Annwn, owes your father much, lad. His whole Other-worldly kingdom. Maybe he wished Caswallon to know that you had strong friends."

Rhiannon said gravely, "There are many worlds, most of them bet-ter than this, a few worse. We who live in this one cannot know any ways but its ways. Even I cannot, many of whose memories went from me when my flesh coarsened into earthly flesh. Let us waste no time in vain wonderings. You are home again, Son; that is enough."

"It is indeed!" Kigva caught his hand and squeezed it. "But—" her eyes widened, "what if that Caswallon visits us here sometime? I do not want to sleep with him!"

Rhiannon laughed softly. "You will not have to, child. That night I will put your shape on a cow or a mare. Or a she-rat if I can catch one. She should make Caswallon a proper bedmate; true flesh of his flesh."

Pryderi and Kigva laughed heartily, but both looked relieved. Pryderi said, "But what about my fresh air? It seems to me that everybody in Dyved wants to sit here and eat until next year."

"Tell them you, who have been away so long, wish to make the circuit of your dominions," said Rhiannon. "Indeed, it is high time you did just that. Then every chief and rich farmer will go home and make his house and folk fine for you."

"And a good thing that will be too," she told Manawyddan later, when they were in bed. "For though our many guests have brought many gifts, the palace stores are getting low. When we ourselves are the guests and our hosts have to furnish all the food the feasts will not last so long."

Manawyddan laughed and hugged her. "You are a good housewife, Lady. You have learned the ways of our world well. Yet sometimes I wonder—can it be that you never regret your own?"

"Lord, I rode after Pwyll into the teeth of time, that I knew must tear us and gut us and fling us away like gnawed bones at last. I will not say I came without dread, but I came by my own choice."

"It was a great and unheard-of choice."

"It was. Yet all seems like a dream now, that Land of the Ever-Young, where people never die until they grow too wise for our world, and so ready for the next—one that we know as little of as you do of ours."

"So I have heard. And that death among you is different from our death."

"It is only deep sleep, without illness. Well I remember my fear when I first saw the ugliness of earthly death, and knew that it must come to me, and might come first to him—to Pwyll. But not even then did I regret.

"I have sorrowed, but I have not been sorry for my choice. And here tonight I am not sorry, Manawyddan, son of Llyr." Once more she put her arms about his neck . . .

So began for Manawyddan the happiness in Dyved, those long good days in that land that poets later were to call the Land of Magic and Illusion. He and Rhiannon rode with Pryderi and Kigva through those green fields, and thought that they never had seen crops richer than those crops, tasted honey sweeter than that honey. To Pryderi it was home, the home that he had long been away from. And to Kigva any land through which she rode with him would have seemed as sweet as Rhiannon's lovely Land of the Ever-Young. The glamour that was upon their young eyes gilded the eyes of the older couple also; they thought that they never before had realized the goodness and the magical simplicity of earth.

The *Mabinogi* says that those four were happy together; that they became such friends that they could not bear to be parted by day or by night. That sounds unlikely; each couple must have wanted some privacy; but surely they were happy.

They lacked nothing but the son Pryderi had wanted. He would have been very welcome, but he was not really needed. For they had enough, and rarely indeed can human beings claim that most perfect of conditions, they who live oftenest in hope of the future, and then, when that piece of it that they have planned and labored for comes, must live on and work on in the hope of a new piece.

Having enough—that hardest of all sums to obtain and the most impossible to keep—those four were very delicately poised upon a wonderful and slippery height. Their perfect balance, their deep content, could not last long; for it is the nature of time both to add and to take away.

Manawyddan and Rhiannon must have known that, and have talked of it.

She said, "For long I feared time, Lord, I who knew that it must take away my lover's strength and my beauty. But after Pwyll died I learned to bless it because now it had done its worst and could only bring me nearer to him."

"I understand," said Manawyddan. And sighed, thinking of Bran and Branwen.

"But when I had blessed it my vision changed, I saw that it was a teacher as well as a destroyer. I saw that, great as was my love and Pwyll's, I must not make a prison of its memory, a walled place, shutting others out. For every walled place is truly a small place, cramping the body and the spirit. And every man and woman is worthy of love, and each calls forth a love that can be given only to himself or herself, never to another. And I remembered you, and knew that I loved you, and that by that loving I need not cease to love Pwyll. It is hard to make clear, that lesson. Do you understand, Lord?"

Manawyddan said, "I do."

She shivered slightly. "Change will come again, I know—change the child of time. And I fear Caswallon your cousin. Do you really think that he can take away the Holy Stones?"

"I think so. He is sure of it, and in matters that deal with matter my cousin is no fool."

"Would to the Mothers that you could have kept him from tricking that promise out of Pryderi! Nothing could put such fear on the folk of Dyved as the going of the Stones. And it will be a weapon in the hands of the chiefs of the Seven Cantrevs of Seissyllwch too. They do not love Pryderi."

Manawyddan frowned. "I know. Those Seven Cantrevs were part of Dyved until the New Tribes came, and then, in Bran's last year, because the chiefs who held them were misusing the Old Tribesmen still there—as Pwyll never used those under him—my brother gave Pryderi leave to break the peace and to take back those Seven Cantrevs. And the poor folk in them have cause to bless your son, but those chiefs will always curse him."

"Yes." She shivered again. "I am not likely to forget that war, Lord. It was Pryderi's first, and he rode to it laughing. But I wondered if I ever would laugh again in this body. If he had died like his father . . . !"

His hand covered hers. "In the end you would have blessed time again, Lady, but it would have been hard."

"Too hard!" She clutched at him and her body shook. "That would have been the one thing I could not have borne. No man ever can quite understand the bond between a woman and the child that is born of her body—not even you, Manawyddan, wisest of men!"

"Something of that too I know, my Rhiannon." His voice was deep, heavy with unsayable things. He held her, he spoke her name, but he saw, not her face but Branwen's face, as it had looked on that black night outside Tara, when she had seen her little son thrown into the fire by Evnissyen, their hate-crazed brother; Evnissyen, who should never have been born.

Rhiannon heard and saw, she thought that his pain was for what might have befallen Pryderi. She said quickly, "Well I know that you love him too, Lord! You have guarded him and watched over him as well as any father could. But it is not the same."

He could not tell even her of Branwen, of that old pain. He thought, *This is excess, and therefore dangerous. Any lover has a right to die to save the beloved. As I would have died for Branwen, or Bran, or Nissyen. Or for Branwen's baby. But to lay all life waste because of what cannot be saved—that is to yield yourself up to the Destroyer you hate. To set your will against the will of the Mothers. But who am I to tell a woman how to serve the Mothers?*

Least of all this woman who had reawakened in him the joy of life . . .

He said aloud, "Lady, many of the druids Caswallon has talked with are wise men, though he is not. And my heart tells me that it is right for the Stones to go; that in their new home they will be a wonder and a mystery to men through the ages. As for Pryderi, we have given him life; from now on all we can do for him is to give him what love and counsel he is willing to accept from us."

His lady smiled tolerantly and tenderly upon him. She thought, *So the wisest of men is as foolish as the rest, after all.*

They went on being happy. Earth was their mother and their friend; for life itself is magical and the Great Energy that shapes all things a magician mightier than any Man of Illusion and Fantasy that the Welsh ever knew. The miracles we see daily seem commonplace and what the Head of Bran did at Gwales wonderful, only because the one event is seldom heard of, and the others happen all the time. Yet a Head that talks after being cut from its shoulders is not, if we stop to think, nearly so vast or all-moving a Mystery as the wonders of growth, or of sunrise and sunset.

We have made of "natural" and "everyday" poor words, ordinary and trite, when they should be *the* Word, full of awesome magic and might; of cosmic power.

On Gwales, Manawyddan had been less awake than he was in

Dyved. Or perhaps more awake, because there he had lived in eternity, and outside time. He had forgotten that Bran was dead, because Bran was there. Now he was caught again in the ancient inexorable pattern of time and loss, but again his feet were set upon a road, and the new pattern was weaving round him, rich in color and music. Rhiannon wove it, Rhiannon with her deep eyes and her warm mouth and her understanding that usually was as full and sweet and quiet as her breast. She was like cool water on sun-baked earth; like a warm fire in the chill of an autumn night.

"Best to love in the afternoon," he told her once. "After the storm, when the heart has learned wisdom and the body is not yet too old. When love is no longer strain and fear and wine that goes to a man's head, but the fire on his hearth and the food on his table."

She smiled her twisted smile, half elf's, half mother's. "Pryderi and Kigva would think that spent old man's talk. They are eating each other like honey. Am I no more to you now than a well-burning faggot or a well-done joint of beef? Time was when I could make a man drunk."

His eyes danced. "Let us see what you can do now. It is not spent I feel yet, Lady."

And presently she said that he was not, indeed . . .

Winter laid whiteness upon the hillsides. The winds shrieked and howled; they raged through that ancient Ring of the Holy Stones, as if striving to overturn what had stood before any green thing grew on earth; before life first took on a shape that breathed and moved. Cold as ice those winds blew; like knives they pierced all living flesh. But in the great hall at Arberth there was fire and warmth and laughter; summer still bloomed.

Spring came, and with it the men of Caswallon. Unarmed they came, save for sledges of heavy wood and ropes of twisted hides. They broke up the Ring, they moved the Holy Stones, those firstborn of Earth the Mother. In Her flesh they left torn holes, where of old Her children had stood.

The people of Dyved cried out in horror. They left their ploughs in the field, their food half-eaten on the table. They rushed to arms, but Pryderi had to stop them; to say, "I have promised . . ."

The High Druid spoke; he whom Caswallon had sent, as Manawyddan had bidden him. He said that this was the Will of the Gods, revealed to him himself, as he slept before the altar, upon a bull's hide. How the Holy Stones, the Unmoving First Folk, were going now to a place where they would be seen and honored by more folk than ever before. By the whole Island of the Mighty.

In silence the people of Dyved listened. Their faces did not lighten; they only lost what light the fire of battle had given them. In bewilderment and woe they watched that unarmed host drag the Stones away.

Some muttered, "They cannot get far. Their backs will break from weariness. They will slink away, back to this thieving High King, like hounds whipped away from the kill. And we will go to the Folk That Do Not Move, and bring them home again."

But others said despairingly, "The High Druid dreamed it. Upon the bull's hide he dreamed."

A few said, "Never would Pwyll have let the Stones go. If he had been alive . . ."

Yet fewer said, "If only he had married a woman of his own people, begotten a son who cared for his own folk . . ."

Bent beneath that load that seemed more than men could bear, Caswallon's men toiled toward the sea. Long and hard was that toil; their arms were almost torn from their sockets, their backs seemed bowed forever, but at last they came to the gray billowing water, to the waiting rafts. By sea the Stones fared then until they reached the mouth of a river deep enough to float them. From stream to stream they passed; long and winding as a snake was that road. But at last they came to their appointed place; in the midst of greenness, within a ring of giant sarsen stones, their own Ring was set up again. The Holy Place stood, and stands yet, and still men marvel.

Later men were to say that only magic could have moved those Stones; that wise Merlin, Arthur's guardian, brought them from Ireland. And indeed it may be that the New Tribes, or some part of them, had come into Dyved from Ireland.

But the only magic that moved those Stones was Caswallon's shrewd and ruthless will. He planned well.

In Dyved people still muttered, "Evil will come. Our luck has gone with the First Folk."

Summer wore. Their crops grew tall and golden, but still they stared at the sky, in dread of storm. All who could shunned the hills, but those who could not walked warily, each looking upward or westward or downward; anywhere but toward the spot that each man still saw stark and clear before him. That empty place upon the windy heights where from times unremembered the Stones had stood, guarding Dyved. Where they stood no longer, those Holy Ones, the first born of the Mother.

8

Storm over the
Gorsedd Arberth

THE RAINS ceased; the heat grew; the sun burned down upon the broad brown breast of the Mother, as if hating Her and all the life that sprang from Her. The fear in the folk's eyes changed. Some said, "We did wrong to fear the storm." And others added, "It is this way that the doom is to come."

Rhiannon said, "There may be something that I can do about this." And she called her women together, and all the other women that would follow her, and led them to a place deep in the woods. There they waited until the moon rose and what rites they performed then no man ever knew. Only shepherds and goatherds heard their singing, faint and far off, and loved the sound, yet shivered at it.

Dawn came, but quietly, without her wonted blaze of gold. Clouds veiled the sun's fierce face; the darkness gave way only to grayness, not to true light. And soon rain began to fall; like a myriad soft tiny paws it pattered upon the parched earth, upon the dying things that had been green.

It saved the crops. And then it stopped.

The sun shone upon the reapers. Men and women sang as they gathered in the harvest. Most said, "The old Queen is wise and mighty. She has appeased the wrath of the Gods." But some still said, "Wait."

In the great hall at Arberth a feast was spread. Men drank in celebration, drank to their own strength, and to Earth the fruitful Mother, to her who, with the help of that strength, had brought forth. For now they were sure of another winter's food, and food is life. All eyes turned with love to Pryderi; the harvest is good only when the King is good. He had not failed them; his power and luck were still with him, even though he had let himself—and them—be tricked out of the Holy Stones.

Pryderi knew what was in their hearts. For moons that knowledge had burned him, and the saving rain had not altogether eased that burning. For he knew that he had had no hand in bringing it.

He was too honest to forget that, and he was too young not to need to prove himself to himself. *Since I have not done this, this thing for which I am praised, I must do something as good. As worthy of praise.*

He rose, cup in hand. He said, "Drink this drink with me, men and women of Dyved. For by sun and moon, by earth and air, I swear that I will not eat or drink again until I have watched the sun rise from the Gorsedd Arberth."

There was silence then. Eye sought eye, and each was a terror and a question. Even by day, when the sun was high, men shunned the mighty Mound called the Gorsedd Arberth. By night even they who lived in the palace below it walked as far from it as they could, and shuddered when they heard a night bird call from its lonely heights. It was a place of power; of too much power for man.

Manawyddan looked at Rhiannon, and saw her face calm and still, masklike as the moon's. But her hands were tightly clenched; so tightly that the piece of bread in one of them was crumbling. And Kigva's round young face was white with fear.

Again Pryderi spoke, his voice loud and clear, so that all might hear. "Few Princes of Dyved have done this deed, but each Prince has known that he must stand ready to do it. Pwyll my father did it after he came back from Annwn; he who had walked in the Land of the Dead knew that he must cleanse himself of the death that still clung to him and win new power and life from the Mighty Ones of the Mound—including a Queen to bear his sons—or else go down again into the Underworld forever. And the Mound-Dwellers honored him above all men by sending him one of their own—the Lady, my mother." He paused and smiled at her, then faced the folk again.

"Now I, who have been farther away from my people than any Prince but Pwyll ever was, will dare the same adventure. I will prove once and for all that no ill luck is on me—that no doom has followed me home from that terrible great war beyond the sea I will take what the Gods send me!"

He drained the cup, laughed, and flung it from him, the smile on his young face bright as flame. As one man, his people rose, shouted and cheered him. All the young men shouted, "We will go with you!"

He smiled. "It is your right. My father went with his foster-brothers round him, and all his true companions."

Kigva rose, the daughter of Gwynn Gloyu, and the girlishness was gone from her young face; it was a woman's. "It is my right also, Pryderi. Of old, Queens mounted the Mount to die with their Kings."

"Or to be wedded to them anew." Manawyddan rose. "There is no need for dying now. But when you went into battle overseas, stepson, we two always went side by side."

Pryderi said in dismay, "I thought to leave the Queens in your care, second-father. Kigva has nothing to prove; let her wait here in our chamber, to hold the Holy Marriage with me when I return."

Rhiannon rose and threw her bread to a hound. "Kigva has already claimed her right, Son. And I stood upon the Gorsedd before you were born. I do not fear to stand there tonight."

In the end they all went, even the ladies who waited on Rhiannon and Kigva.

They bore no torches. The moon was full, and the top of the Gorsedd would be light as day. But though the way was short, part of it lay through the deep shadow of the Mound, and in that blackness none could see another's face. They could hear only footsteps, small scrunching sounds that seemed to disturb both the pebbled earth and her silence. Each heard his or her own breathing, too, and that seemed loud, another affront to that deep shroud of silence. Many thought wistfully of the torch lit hall where, but a little while before, they had been so merry. Where now the servants were eating the broken food left by the great ones could it really be only a few paces away?

Will we ever get back there? Ever laugh and drink again? That mute cry rose from a hundred hearts.

In the darkness Rhiannon's hand slipped into Manawyddan's.

He said, "Fear nothing, my Queen. Had the harvest not been good these 'true companions' might have seen signs bidding them slay him, but not now. He has won back their love."

She laughed shortly. "The last Prince who mounted the Gorsedd before Pwyll died—beaten to death with his own men's spears, I think. But that is not what I fear. Here on this Mound there is indeed a door into another world—that I know well, who once came through it."

Manawyddan was silent, thinking of what else might have come through it. Of that huge grisly Arm that had taken her newborn son from her side.

Rhiannon said, "There was no need for this. Before the rain came I feared that he might have to do it. But now, when all was well! What got into him? If it is some spell that is on him, drawing him to doom—" She shuddered.

Manawyddan said, "It is only himself. His pride has been hurt. Also I think he truly fears that the ill luck that came on us in Ireland clouded his judgment and so made him lose the Stones."

"And that too was only himself! His prudence has always been the least part of him. It is a pity that children's heads do not grow up as fast as the rest of them. Now I must watch him running into danger that once I could have pulled him back from—by the ear, if need be!"

"Lady, that last is the fate of all parents who see a child live to grow up."

"I know, but that does not make it less hard! If only I could have taught him more! But when I came through those doors that now I can re-enter only by dying your earth-death, I forgot much—and on much that I do remember my lips are sealed."

They went on in silence.

They came out of that depth of shadow, and found themselves at the foot of the Mound, their people about them. Ahead of them Pryderi and Kigva were already climbing, hand in hand, the girl bright-faced again because of that clasp. The elder couple followed, and the moon looked down on them with her pale, battered stare, like a golden face mauled by fiends from outer space.

They came to the top of the Mound. They sat down together, the four of them, upon the stones that had been set there, how long ago no man remembered, to serve as seats at such times as these. They sat there, with their train of folk around them.

They sat and waited . . .

They saw light below them, streaming out of the open doors of the palace they had left. Faintly voices seemed to be borne to them.

Kigva said, low, "I thought our housefolk liked us. How can they be so glad?"

Rhiannon said, "They do, but now the wine is in them, and drowns all else. And maybe not only wine. Do not begrudge them their moment of being masters and mistresses of all they work for every day, but never own."

And indeed, all of them there on that dreaded height felt like the dead looking back into the world of the living. Into a space and a life already far away, incredibly remote. Silence seemed to be wrapping around them, fold after fold of it, an ever-thickening cloak. It got into their mouths and into their minds; it stole over them like deep.

Then from far off, faintly, sweetly, came the sound of music. Music more beautiful than the song of birds, gentler than the lowest note of the lullaby in the throat of a mother who lulls her child to sleep.

Manawyddan felt peace coming over him and his lids closing, and then suddenly he felt something else—a sharp, jabbing pain. He started awake, reaching for his sword. But he saw no monster, but only his lady's white fingers leaving his arm, and then a yelp told him that she had also pinched her son.

"Ouch!" Pryderi rubbed himself. "It is my opinion, Mother, that there has been nothing dangerous here on the Gorsedd since you came out of it!"

But Rhiannon did not seem to hear him. She was looking into the vast dark sky, as if it were a face, and hers was whiter than the moon could ever make it. She was muttering, charms and words of power, but the deep strong sound of them, in some tongue that was soft as the rustling of leaves; a tongue not of earth. Both men knew that much; their hair rose on their heads as if given legs by the strangeness of the sound, and Kigva clung to a hand of each.

She too was awake, but no other man or woman on that hill was. All their heads were bowed, all their bodies slumped or sprawled, in deepest sleep. Like tall plants mown down by a scythe they lay there, or drooped in their places, emptied and soulless as dead folk yet unburied.

Rhiannon's muttering ceased. She turned and faced the three, and sweat stood like dew upon her brow.

"You fools! Would you sleep upon the Mound of Arberth? Better to sleep in the middle of the sea with no boat beneath you, or in the fireplace with the fire lit!"

They tried to answer her, they opened their mouths, but nothing came out. Their jaws only widened in great yawns. The night was still again; clouds gathered round the moon like sheep huddling round their shepherd.

Or like wolves closing in upon a sheep . . .

Manawyddan thought in angry surprise, *My mind is awake, but my body is not.* He braced himself and began to fight.

His lids felt heavy; very heavy; never in his life had he tried to hold up anything so heavy. He saw that Pryderi's eyes had already closed again, and that Kigva's were closing.

Rhiannon swayed, looking from one dulled face to another. Both her lips and her fingers worked, as if she did not know which to use first.

Then Manawyddan's eyes flashed open. He shook Pryderi awake, and Rhiannon did the same for Kigva. He drew his own sword and then Pryderi's, and thrust the blade into the younger man's slack hand.

"We must walk. Round and round, sunwise. And if one tries to fall out of the circle, the one behind must prick or pinch him!"

They did so. They stumbled, their eyes kept closing; it was as if stones were tied to their legs, dragging them down. But they kept moving; their circle was not broken.

Rhiannon's tired eyes began to shine. She whispered to Manawyddan, "If we can only hold out till sunrise . . ."

Silence fell again. They stumbled on, their eyes clinging desperately, hopefully, to the still blackened east.

The moon was gone; the clouds had swallowed her. There was no light anywhere; only darkness and that deep silence.

Suddenly Kigva looked around her and behind her, like a child that is afraid. She said, "It is too still. It is as if the earth too were frightened and waiting for something to happen. I would like to hear a noise; any noise in the world."

Like an answer, thunder crashed around them; like a hammer big as the biggest mountain it smote the earth. All caught at their ears with the pain of it; they felt as if their eardrums had been smashed and had fallen back bleeding into their skulls.

Like a sea, mist fell from heaven. They saw it boiling white above their heads, between them and the black sky; thick as sea water, furious as foam, falling, falling.

Then it was upon them, around them, and they were each alone in a terrible roaring world that had neither color nor form left in it, not even the negative color of darkness.

They could not see each other. They could not see anything. They knew that the earth was yet beneath their feet but only because they felt it there.

Manawyddan felt as if he were fighting to keep his head from being blown away, from rocking, away like a bobbing ball upon that immense stream of sound, that incredible and unheard-of din; the roar of that storm that was like no storm of earth.

He groped, like a blind man, with his hands. "Rhiannon! Pryderi! Kigva! Give me your hands! We must keep our circle. We must not let one another go!"

Several times he had to shout that, each time louder, before he could hear his own voice. Then at last he felt Pryderi's strong palm slip into his, and on the other side of him Rhiannon's smooth one, and he heard her voice, that carried through the wind and the thunder like the thin clear ring of a silver bell. "I have one of Kigva's hands. Have either of you men got the other?"

Pryderi tried to say yes, but the rushing sound carried away his voice.

They stood with clasped hands, those four; the thunder cudgeled their ears; the wind lashed them like an icy flail acres long, acres wide. Kigva was knocked to her knees. Manawyddan said, "Better if we all lie down. But we must not let go each other's hands."

They lay there, hands still tightly clasped. The wind could no longer beat them, but they shivered in its icy, unnatural cold. It roared through the vault of night like the waves of a roaring sea, an ocean risen out of its immemorial gulf to drown all life. Again and again the thunder crashed; it seemed that the Mound itself must be leveled, and earth herself break apart and fall into the vast abyss of outer space.

Yet even through that din they began to distinguish other sounds; tiny, far off, they rose from below. Thin and feeble as the piping of insects, they yet pierced that mightiness of sound, and with a terrible finality. Shrieks, the death cries of men and beasts.

The four shuddered; they clasped one another's hands yet more tightly, hearing their world die.

But all things end except ourselves, and even those, as we know them, have an end . . .

They did not know when the roar slackened. They were too deafened to think; the noise had got into their heads and rolled on there, dazing and ceaseless.

But they saw the mist begin to thin. When they began to see one another as dim blobs thicker than the surrounding dimness, their stunned minds woke. Anxiously they watched those blobs take on shape, line; saw those blurred forms sprout faces, become individuals again.

There is something left. We are here; we have each other. The world goes on.

Morning was coming; the mist was almost shining now. Through it Pryderi's hair gleamed golden. Kigva's red hair lit itself again like a torch. Manwyddan's eyes found Rhiannon's, and they smiled at each other.

The sun came up red, proudly, reclaiming her own. The whole sky glowed with a light that was pure and pale as pearl. Defeated, the mist shrank down through that new gentle silence, to the earth below.

The four looked around them, and saw that on that bare hilltop they were alone.

Not one of all those who had followed them up that hill was there. They had vanished, as if dissolved in the mist.

Kigva caught Pryderi's hand. "Did the wind blow them away?"

He said, through stiff lips, "I do not know."

All four looked down; intently, desperately, as if their eyes were spears or arrows that could pierce that white blanket of mist that still lay below.

It, too, was thinning. Soon the thatched roofs of the palace began to rise through it, the roofs of home, and for a breath's space the sight was sweeter than honey, like a mother's face to a lost child. Then, "There should be smoke coming up," cried Manawyddan. "There is none."

"Maybe the wind blew all the fires out," said Pryderi. "Let us go down and see."

He started down, but Rhiannon caught his arm. "Wait, Son. Let us see a little more."

They waited, they watched. Soon they could see the good everyday green and brown of earth. But something was wrong, something was different. They strained their eyes, peering down into countryside that should have been filled with peaceful farms; with the fields and herds and the small snug dwellings of folks.

It was not. Only the fields were left, the quiet, empty fields. The trees and the green meadows.

There was no house, no beast, no man. Not even any charred ruin where lightning-blasted houses might have stood.

Terror clutched their hearts like iron fingers. They ran stumbling down the hillside. They came to the palace. Its doors were not barred and bolted against the storm. They stood wide open, black mouths of desolation.

They went inside, and no man greeted them. The great hall stood empty, except for overthrown chairs and tables, and dishes and spilled food littering the floor.

They searched the whole palace, the sleeping-places, the storehouses and the kitchens, and still found nothing but food and furniture and garments, all tossed and broken and torn by that mighty wind. No living thing was left, not even a dog.

They cried into that silence, that was no longer menacing, but only empty. That gave them back nothing but the echo of their own voices.

Pryderi stopped at last and scratched his head. "Everybody in Dyved must have been blown away," he said.

Kigva clung to him, her teeth chattering. "What does it mean? What does it all mean?"

Sudden hope lit his eyes. "Maybe we are dreaming," he said. And he pinched her arm experimentally.

"Ouch!" said Kigva. "You need not do that to see if I am real. I will see if you are." And she pinched him.

"Indeed," said Pryderi, "there are pleasanter ways of proving it."

He gave her a kiss on the mouth then, and she gave that back to him also. They kissed each other several times, and began to look as if they felt better. Rhiannon looked at them soberly.

"You should not have challenged my people, Son. When a man stands upon the Gorsedd Arberth, he takes his mind along with him, and they can seize that mind, and use it. When I was of that world and longed for your father Pwyll, I could not come to him until he sat upon that Mound and so placed himself and his own world within my reach."

Manawyddan said, "We had better eat and sleep now. Then we can go forth and see if the whole land is like this."

For a day and a night they rested, and then they set out. They searched from end to end of Dyved, but they found neither man, woman, nor child. Neither cattle nor sheep, nor even a lost dog. Man, and every living thing that belonged to man, had been swept away.

Nearer the sea they did find empty how. White butterflies flew strangely thick around these, and sometimes one would fly into a vacant house and touch some object—bowl or bed or garment—tenderly and lingeringly with their delicate minute feelers, as if it were something that they loved.

Manawyddan and Rhiannon looked sadly at each other when they saw those little winged visitors.

"It is such shapes that the lesser druids claim to see come forth from the mouths of the dying," he said. "Are all our people dead then? We have found no bodies or bones."

Rhiannon shook her head. "Hard it is to tell what has happened. We do not know what glamour may yet be over our own eyes. But I am sure that our people have died no ordinary death. Maybe they were too afraid, and all of them that was gross matter shook to pieces under the force of His will that sent this Illusion forth. For it is an Illusion that has come on Dyved—a spell from my own world, and so is Gwawl avenged at last."

"You think that the Avenger was one, not many?"

Her eyes half closed. "I do not know. I cannot say. It took great power."

"Well, what matters is this—will what has been done content the doer? Or the doers?"

She shivered as if a cold wind had touched her. As if the inner light of her flickered in some unearthly chill.

"Again I do not know. I cannot be sure—they tried hard to take us that night. I used all the power I had left, and when that was gone you saved us. They may be satisfied, seeing us brought down from kings and queens to wanderers in a waste."

"It is not a bad life this is," said Manawyddan. "We have our health and ourselves, and the sky is blue above us, and the sun shines on us. If now we have to hunt and fish to feed ourselves, yet the lands we live and work in are our own, and the food when we get it the sweeter-flavored for being a greater prize."

"That is so," said Rhiannon. "And a good reason why they may not be willing to leave us in peace."

9

The Change

AUTUMN CAME like a torch, and set the trees on fire. The birds
flew away to warmer lands, but still Manawyddan and Pryderi hunted and fished, and Rhiannon and Kigva cooked what they brought
home. Winter came, and white snow, and again winds howled over
Dyved, though not such winds as had howled on that terrible night.
The men sat at home oftener, and Rhiannon and Kigva made bread
from the crops that had been harvested before the Terror came.

Spring came again, and greenness, and birds. And again they left
the palace, those four, and went wandering through the land, living on
game and wild honey. Until autumn came again, and another winter.

No man came near them. No travelers or messengers entered
Dyved, and at first that seemed strange. But Manawyddan said, "The
druids must have seen in their crystals something of what befell on
that night of doom. They think us gone with the others, and
strangers fear to enter and take possession lest the curse still cling to
the land and rise and smite them." He did not add, No doubt they
think that no curse would have come had the Holy Stones stayed at
home in their ancient places.

Pryderi snorted. "Caswallon must be pleased He thinks he is rid
of you for good."

"So he is," said Manawyddan. "Certainly we four never will go up
against him in battle. Doubtless he would make us welcome if we
came to his court seeking his bounty—then he could show all men
our poverty and his kindliness. But that too I think we would not
wish to do."

Pryderi snorted again. "It is the last thing we would do! And I
think it would be the last, for I would hate to trust my head long to

that kindliness of his. The very thought makes it feel loose on my shoulders."

"You wrong him there," said Manawyddan. "None could be more tender of our lives. He would, as I have said, make a great show of us."

"We could go to Mâth, the Ancient in Gwynedd," said Kigva. "He might be able to help us. No man on earth is said to be mightier in Illusion and Fantasy than He."

"No power on earth could match the Power that has struck down Dyved," said Manawyddan. "Caswallon knows that, or he would have sent men here before now. But I have no doubt that Mâth would hold out the hand of friendship to us if we went to Gwynedd. A true friend's hand, not that of one who sought to glorify himself by parading our need."

Pryderi said harshly, "I never will go as a beggar to him whose fellow king I once was," and turned his back upon them all. Later he grew friendly again and merry, indeed so very merry that that night everybody was glad to get to bed and so end the strain.

Later, where they lay side by side in the dark, Rhiannon spoke to her husband. "The boy grows weary of this life here."

For a little Manawyddan was silent. To hear what one already knows can be hard. Then he said, "I have wondered that trouble did not come upon him before. They are his people who are gone, the sheep to whom he was shepherd."

"And he loved them. He was so proud, too, of having made Dyved a kingdom again—it that the New Tribes had split into petty princedoms. You did not see him when he came home with his head high, after taking the Seven Cantrevs of Seissyllwch."

"And now all that is undone."

"Yes, but for awhile he did not realize that. He is so young; all this new life was like a game to him, a boy's lark."

"But now his mind, that for awhile was stunned, is rested. This has been like that other time, that rest beyond time when the Head of Bran my brother talked with us and healed us of our hurts. Your Birds sang to us then. Your Birds, Rhiannon. Could you not have them sing to Pryderi again and bring him peace?"

She said sadly, "My Birds sing no more. Sometimes I go to meet them in the wood, and they perch on my hands or rub their beaks against my face in love. But they make no sound; that dread night took their voices."

He sighed. "Then there is no help for it. We must go forth into the world of men again. And we have been happy here. I would not want to go, even if I trusted Caswallon as far as I tried to make Pryderi think I do."

"I did not think you trusted him. For himself Caswallon would still fear your powers, even though he knows that you could not save Dyved. No man could have."

Manawyddan laughed shortly. "He might not fear me—seeing me so utterly overthrown. But I cannot be sure of that. And whatever happens the boy must not get any ideas into his head about fighting Caswallon. Once many men might have risen to follow us, but not now. For when ill luck has come on a man, who can tell when or if it will leave him? And surely Pryderi and I have shown that the ill luck that was on us in Ireland still clings to us."

"That is not so. You came back to a curse that had waited for me and mine since the night I first slept with Pwyll. The night that he and his men beat Gwawl who had tried to take me from him. I should have known that that doom would fall at last."

"When the sun shines, Lady, it is hard to believe that misfortune will come. But what is done is done; what matters now is what is to come. Since Pryderi will not be content to stay here much longer, and since he and I cannot make any fight for place and power, we would do well to take new names and live quietly among humble men."

"Lord, that will not please Pryderi."

"Yet it must be tried. Let us talk of ways and means."

So, once again, the son of Llyr braced himself for change.

Spring drew near. Every day Pryderi grew more restless. He prowled up and down the lonely hall of Arberth, and looked at the benches where once had sat a host of men. And he seemed to look at their silence and to listen to their emptiness, as if both had been a cry.

The day came at last when he said, with energy, "I cannot stand this. It is like being buried alive. Let us go some place where there are people—people who stay where they belong, and do not get blown away."

Rhiannon, who had been sewing, laid down her work, and Manawyddan, who had been polishing a spear, set it down. Both thought how glad the people of Dyved would have been to stay where they belonged, but neither of them said anything. They knew the soreness that must be in Pryderi's heart; the sick cry that must rise there: *If only I had never mounted the Mound of Arberth* . . .

He spoke again. He said, "Let us go where we can hear a child squalling, or an old woman talking about how to cook beans, or a man boasting about all the other men he has killed in battles he never fought in. Once I thought those three sounds the dullest that ever mauled a man's ears, but now I could love anything that made a noise!"

"It is true that it is very still here," said Kigva. Her bright eyes looked wistful, as if recalling all the live, delightful noisiness that that hall had once held.

She touched her ears, that perched delicately as butterflies under her shining hair. "Indeed, ears, you used to love singing and harping and tale-telling, and the sound of women telling what other women were doing or wearing, but it is little of that you get now."

"If mine do not get something to do soon they will dry up and fall off," grumbled Pryderi.

He walked down the hall again, very fast, and then back up it. Rhiannon looked at Manawyddan, and Manawyddan looked at Rhiannon.

"Indeed," the son of Llyr sighed, "we must not go on like this. The life here is pleasant—or it was—but it is no real trouble, and I am afraid," and he sighed again, "that it is the business of men to have trouble."

"Let us go out and have some," said Pryderi. He threw back his yellow head and hearkened, like a young hound sniffing at the breezes. Longing to hear the fleet hooves of the quarry ahead of him, and the belling of the other hounds beside him.

"We will have it," said Manawyddan. "Men always must." A third time he sighed.

So they left Dyved and went into Logres, that green pleasant land that later was to be taken by the Angles and called England. They came to the town later called Hereford, and there they had a strange mishap. For when they opened the bag of gold that they had brought with them there was nothing in it but dry leaves. Pryderi would have thrown these out in wrath, but his mother stopped him.

"It is still really gold, Son, only the appearance of leaves has been put upon it. This is more of the work of my people."

"Indeed, Mother," said Pryderi disgustedly, "I am very fond of you, but it is not fond at all I am of any of my other relatives on your side of the house."

Rhiannon gave Manawyddan a wry smile. It said, *How little he dreams that I am the only one of my House who has had anything to do with this.* Husband and wife had planned this small magical trick between them; Caswallon was more likely to hear of rich people than of poor ones.

Aloud she said, "The innkeeper may trust us for a little while, but not long enough for us to go back to Dyved and get more gold."

"And what good would that do? It would turn into more leaves on the way!" Pryderi laughed angrily, but looked a little troubled. Never before had the Lord of Dyved had any reason to worry about debt.

"We could go to Caer Loyu," said Kigva. "Nobody would dare to stop us if we said we were going there."

Pryderi turned upon her sternly. "You are forgetting that your father Gwynn Gloyu is dead, and that your aunts the Nine Witches now rule in Caer Loyu."

"That makes no difference," said Kigva. "When he was alive they ruled there all the same. I know that you do not like my aunts and that they do not like you, but indeed," she added reflectively, "they never like anybody. Even me, of whom they are very fond."

"I will go anywhere and do anything except live with your aunts!" said Pryderi violently.

"There are worse people than my aunts," said Kigva "They will be glad to see us. They are always glad to have company because it annoys them, and it is so much fun to think of ways to annoy people who annoy them. They are very good hostesses, once you get used to them."

"I will not get used to them!" said Pryderi. "I will not try to!"

"We shall have to learn a trade then," said Manawyddan, "and learn it quickly."

Pryderi stared. "Work?" he said. "For our livings? As if we were not gentlemen born?" Already the New Tribes were learning that kind of pride.

"You wanted trouble," said Manawyddan.

Pryderi digested that, then laughed, "Well," he said, "I have cast the dice and I will play the game out."

They became saddlemakers; it seems unlikely that they knew how to make saddles, but equally unlikely that they knew how to do anything else that ordinary breadwinning men must do.

They only knew how to eat and they had to find a way to keep on doing that.

At first it did not occur to Pryderi that they could not do anything they had a mind to do. He had seen saddles, so it seemed to him that he ought to be able to make saddles, though naturally his first few attempts might be clumsy. But soon the image of a fine saddle made by himself, that image which had seemed as comfortably near as the house across the lane, flew away like a bird and lit upon a treetop where it sat and cawed at him.

"Indeed," he said, scratching his handsome head, "there seems to be a trick in this. I never thought that there was such power in sad-dlemakers; it seems strange that they should be able to do anything that I cannot. Perhaps," he added hopefully, "it is like fish swimming or birds flying. There is a knack to it, and if you were born of sad-dlemakers you have it, but if you were born of queens, like us, you have not got it.

"We were not meant to have it," he ended with conviction.

"We have stomachs," said Manawyddan.

"That is true," sighed Pryderi. And went back to work.

But soon Manawyddan said, "It will be long before our skill equals that of men who have worked at this all their lives. We need some new thing; something to draw folks' eyes to our saddles."

"We can gild them," said Pryderi.

"We can do more than that. There is a stuff called Calch Llassar. I learned the art of its making from Llassar himself, the fiery Giant from the Lake."

All one night Manawyddan stayed up brewing the Calch Llassar. Kigva said, "I have not seen such cauldron-work since I left my aunts the Nine Witches." But neither she nor Pryderi liked the smell, and they soon went to bed.

Rhiannon stayed by the fire, sewing, and Manawyddan said to her, "He was a great craftsman, Llassar. I have seen him make this stuff, and marveled at how he could catch the very blue of the sky in it. I asked him to show me how it was done, and he said, 'Send me a man you trust, and I will teach him. It does not become yourself to get your hands dirtied and your fine clothes spoiled, king's brother.' But I have always found it best to keep knowledge in my own head, so I did my own learning. Though until now the only use I ever made of it was to paint a wooden doll's robe blue for Branwen; she was little then. I can still see her eyes when she first saw that doll."

He paused, and said in wonder, "Yes, I see it. I, who thought I never should be able to see Branwen's face again, save as it looked when Bran dragged her back from that fireplace in Ireland, where her boy died. As it looked at Aber Alaw, where she died. Two sights that burned my heart like fire."

"But now those are only two faces out of all her faces," said Rhiannon. "Out of all the many you remember."

"It is so. I have lived on and been busy with other things; I have not known that I was forgetting her. Yet by that forgetting I have regained her. It is a Mystery."

"Her sorrow was on her, it was not herself. You had to forget it to remember her. She was dearest to you of all, I think; your young sister."

Manawyddan hesitated. "Bran and I were always together; each of us would have felt one-armed without the other. But I never felt such tenderness for Bran as for her. She was loveliness. She was our mother, for there is a mother in all women from the time the girl-baby reaches out her arms for her first doll. And she was our child; we had taught her to walk." And too much came back all at once, and he groaned, "O Bran, brother, why did you have to destroy even her for Caradoc?"

"Because Caradoc was part of him," said Rhiannon. "I know. I never yet have felt as if Pryderi were quite all out of me, though only for nine moons did I carry him safe in my body, and for many years now he has been running about, getting himself into all the kinds of unsafety that he can find. Yet whatever touches him still touches me." And she laid her hand on her breast.

"That is the way of women," said Manawyddan.

The day came when the saddles were ready. Manawyddan and Pryderi showed them in the marketplace. Many came to look, and all who could buy bought, whether they needed saddles or not. For never had there been any saddles like those saddles; the gilt upon them shone golden in the sun, and the blue enamel called Calch Llassar glowed as blue as the sky above it.

By evening there were no golden saddles left.

Manawyddan and Pryderi paid their bills, which must have been many unless, as seems likely, Rhiannon had quietly turned a few dead leaves back into gold pieces. Then they set about making more saddles.

These too were sold as soon as they were made. And so it went with the next batch, and the next and the next. People came from far away to buy those saddles. Everybody was in love with them, and anybody who was not would have been thought blind in at least one eye.

But the other saddlemakers in Hereford did not sell anything at all. They did not like that, and they held a meeting about it.

"We might ask the older man to tell us how to make the Calch Llassar," said one, but not very hopefully.

"He would not tell us," said another flatly.

"We could try to make him tell," suggested a third. "We could do things to him until he did," he added.

"That would hurt him, and be unlawful," said yet another. "It would likewise be wrong. We are honest men, and honest tradesmen. We cannot do anything that is not law-abiding, and proper."

"No," they all said sadly; and though they had been gloomy before, deeper gloom came and wrapped itself about them like a cloak.

"A man's knowledge is his own," the thoughtful one continued, "and nobody has a right to deprive him of it. But our trade was ours,

and he has deprived us of that. It always has been lawful for decent
men to poke a spear into a wolf, and this man who makes the Calch
Llassar is more dangerous to us than any wolf. It would be decent
and law-abiding of us to kill him."

These words seemed to light a torch in each man. Their slumped
bodies straightened, their eyes gleamed, and their ears listened.

"Would it?" they said happily.

Only one man objected. "We will have to kill the young man too.
And what about the women? It seems a pity to kill them, for they are
good-looking."

"It would not be sensible to do anything else," said the plan-
maker, "for they may know something about the Calch Llassar.
Besides, they probably would bear us ill will for killing their men,
and a woman's ill will is unlucky."

"Then we will kill them all," said the others. "Though indeed we
would not do it if it were not right, for we are decent, law-abiding
men."

By then it was nearly dawn, so they decided that it would be better to wait until the next night to do anything. They all went home
to bed, and their thoughts that had been heavy as stones were light
as feathers, and their sleep that had been uneasy and haunted was
sound and sweet.

Only one man could not go to sleep, the man who had objected.

He thought, *When we go to kill them, we must all go, so I must go
too. We will certainly kill them, but since they are all four healthy able-
bodied people they may kill some of us first.*

They might even kill me.

*We are many; there are many others they could kill besides me. I
have no way of knowing that it would be me.*

I have no way of knowing that it would not.

I may get hurt, even if I do not get killed.

Indeed, he groaned, *why could not all this have been settled peaceably, without such a fuss. If they only knew that we were going to kill
them they would run away. Anybody would run away . . .*

Like lightning blazing across a dark sky, the thought smote him:
they could know, for he could tell them.

The thought burned him like fever, it froze him like ice, but he
could not get away from it. In the end he rose and went out into the
morning twilight. He went stealthily, by back ways and strange ways.
He had borrowed his woman's hooded cloak, so that nobody would
know him if he were seen: and indeed he devoutly hoped that
nobody was the only person who would see him.

He came to the door of Manawyddan's house and knocked.

Kigva and Rhiannon were already getting breakfast, and it was Kigva who answered that knock. When she saw him her mouth and eyes became three round moons, and while she stood and stared he tried to back away, but Rhiannon called from within, "What is it, girl?"

"It is a woman with whiskers!" said Kigva. And she became a leap and a pounce and a spring, and what she pounced on was those whiskers. The man yelped.

Rhiannon came to them, and her eyes were hard.

"Explain yourself," she said. "You who would sneak into decent women's kitchens pretending to be another woman."

He explained.

Rhiannon called Manawyddan, and he came and listened, and asked a few questions, which the man answered.

"You will run away?" the man asked eagerly. "You will run away?"

"I do not know yet," said Manawyddan. "I must take counsel with my son. But if we stay, and if we kill anybody, it will not be you."

"It will be anybody Pryderi can lay hands on," Kigva said, her eyes flashing, "once he has heard this."

The man fled.

But when Pryderi heard, he did not seem angry. He merely cocked his head on one side and smiled. His eyes shone and his teeth shone.

"Let us kill these people," he said joyously, "instead of letting them kill us."

"It would not be wise," said Manawyddan.

"It would be great fun," said Pryderi. "I have been getting very bored with all this work. Let us do it," he urged.

"We will not," said Manawyddan. "We will take what baggage we can carry, and leave this town today."

Pryderi's mouth fell open. "You mean that we will let them make us run away?"

"We will make ourselves run away," said Manawyddan. "It is only just. We have hurt their trade, and they must live."

"We must live too," said Pryderi. "You have said so often enough."

"We can live somewhere else," said Manawyddan. "In some place where we have not made enemies."

10

The Gold Shoemakers

THEY CAME to another town, a town that the *Mabinogi* leaves unnamed. It says only that they came there.

"What craft shall we take here?" asked Pryderi. "Let it not be saddlemaking," he begged. "I am sick of saddles. Who needs saddles? A man should sit on what the Gods gave him to sit on. That is well padded enough."

"Let us make shields," said Manawyddan.

"Can we?" Pryderi stroked his chin, for he suddenly remembered that it took time to learn how to do things. "Do we know anything about how to make shields?"

"We will try," said Manawyddan.

They tried, and presently they succeeded. Pryderi never found it very interesting work, but he said that at least it was better than making saddles.

"Though it is a man's work to carry a shield, not to make one," he grumbled.

But it is true that to learn to do a thing well takes time, and the townspeople kept on buying from the local shieldmakers. From the men who knew their trade, the men they were used to. The newcomers could not make a living; they tried to undersell their competitors, but found that if they did so they would not have enough profit left to live.

There came a week when they ate lightly, and the next week they ate more lightly still.

"Maybe there is some good in saddles after all," said Pryderi. "Leather is a little like meat." He rubbed his flattened belly and said, "It is hollow I am. Hollow as the big tree that the birds used to nest in at home."

Manawyddan said, "We need some new thing. Something to draw the customers' eyes."

That night he stayed up to make some more of the Calch Llassar. He painted all his shields blue, and then showed them, glowing like great jewels, in the marketplace.

After that it seemed to rain blue shields and to hail them and snow them. If a man did not have a blue shield, he himself was blue, and he made haste to get one, and so get back his own right color. And if by any chance he did still like his old shield and did not want to part with it, his woman was blue, and could not be comforted until he got himself a fine new blue shield, and looked as smart as the men of other women.

But the local shieldmakers were bluer than anybody else, for nobody bought anything of them any more.

Rhiannon said to Manawyddan, "Lord, what if that happens which happened before?"

"Let it," said Pryderi comfortably. There was a large haunch of beef before him, and as he spoke he cut a large slice off it. "If the other shieldmakers want to kill us we can always kill them."

"If we do, Caswallon and his men will hear of it," Manawyddan looked troubled. "You are right to have fears, Lady; but it seemed that I had no choice."

"Well, perhaps nothing will happen for awhile," said Kigva. And she looked around the house at the new pots and cups that she and Rhiannon had just bought, and at everything else that they had bought and done to make the place comfortable and handsome.

"It is pleasant here," she said. "I should like to stay."

"You shall," said Pryderi. "Who would dare to drive us out?"

"They did at the last place . . ."

But Pryderi stuffed a big juicy bite of the beef into her mouth and silenced her.

Time passed. Manawyddan and Pryderi made shields as fast as they could, and sold them even faster. They had far more orders than they could meet.

One day a young servingman came to the house. It chanced that he found Rhiannon alone, for Kigva was helping the men to paint the shields.

"Woman of the house," he said, "let you tell your man to make haste with my master's shield. He wants it by tomorrow noon."

"Who is your master?" said Rhiannon.

"Huw the son of Cradoc."

Rhiannon thought a moment. "There are several ahead of him. We cannot have his shield ready before the third noon from now. But I will speak to my man. We will do what we can."

The young man looked offended. Huw the son of Cradoc was a chieftain, and one of the richest men in the cantrev; few said no to him.

"You must do better than that, woman. My master must have his shield by tomorrow noon."

"Even if men who ordered their shields before him wait for theirs? That is not the way we treat our customers, young man." But then suddenly Rhiannon checked herself; her eyes narrowed. "Why does your master want the shield so soon, boy. What has put such haste on him?"

Her eyes were eyes no longer. They were spears, they were arrows, plunging into his. They were inside him, in the depths of him, and against his will his mouth opened. His tongue did her bidding, not his own.

"Because after that he cannot get it, Lady. Because tomorrow night the other shieldmakers and all their kin and friends will come here. They will burn this house over your heads, and if any of you stick those heads out they will cut them off."

"Well," said Rhiannon, "I cannot altogether blame them. Go now and give your master the message I gave you. You will tell him nothing else."

And indeed, the moment her eyes left his, that young man clean forgot that he had told her anything at all except what his master had bidden him tell her. He felt only annoyance because these unreasonable people were going to get killed before they had done what Huw the son of Cradoc wanted. And a little uneasiness for fear Huw might blame him.

But whatever the son of Cradoc may have done, Pryderi the son of Pwyll was soon raging.

"This is not to be endured from these boors! Let us go out now— tonight—and hunt them out like the treacherous rats they are! Let us butcher them!"

"Then we will be the lawbreakers," said Manawyddan. "It will be Caswallon's chance to put us out of the way quickly and quietly, pretending that he does not recognize us."

For a little Pryderi was silent, breathing hard. "What shall we do then? Run away again? *Again?*"

"We will go to another town," said Manawyddan. And so they did.

* * *

Again we are not told where that town was. Likely it was farther
from the heartland of the Island of the Mighty than the one they had
just left, for there Manawyddan seems to have feared the nearness
of Caswallon. Perhaps it lay somewhat nearer the blue hills of Wales
and the wilderness that once had been Dyved.

Wherever it was, they came there; and Manawyddan said to Pryderi,
"What craft shall we take? It is your turn to choose."

"Anything you like so long as we know it," said Pryderi. "I am not
in favor of learning how to do anything new; we have to learn too
often."

"Not so," said Manawyddan. "Let us make shoes. For I notice that
the shoemakers here are peaceable-looking folk, and that there are
not many of them. I do not believe that they will have any stomach
for killing. I am a little tired," he said, "of people that are trying to
kill me."

"I am not," said Pryderi. "What I am tired of—very tired of—is
not trying to kill them."

"Son," said Rhiannon, "your father is right. Here we must try to
keep out of trouble."

"I need exercise," said Pryderi. "I cannot get it sitting in a shop. I
need a fight. And I do not know the singlest, smallest thing about
shoemaking."

"I do," said Manawyddan, "and I will teach you to stitch. We will
not try to dress the leather, we will buy it already dressed, and then
cut the shoes out of it."

"Indeed," said Pryderi, "I would rather be cutting the heads off
those people that keep running us out of town." But he subsided
then; that was his last protest.

The *Mabinogi* says that Manawyddan bought the best leather that
was to be had in town, and that he found the best goldsmith in town,
and had him make gilded clasps for the shoes. He watched that making until he knew the method of it. Then he gilded, not only the
clasps, but the shoes themselves. They shone like gold; no shoes so
beautiful were ever seen in the Island of the Mighty save those that
Gwydion made, the golden-tongued son of Don, when he too played
shoemaker in order to trick sun-bright Arianrhod and so get a name
for that little son of theirs whom she hated and he loved. But all that
befell in later times.

Kigva and Rhiannon marveled at that first pair of golden shoes.
They held them up this way and that way and several other ways,
and were delighted and dazzled by them.

Pryderi whistled. "I would hate to be in the shoes of the other shoemakers once we have a good stock of these. They are a better reason for killing us than anybody has had yet."

"They are beautiful," said Kigva. Her eyes could not leave them. "Too beautiful to make anybody angry," She tried them on.

"I hope so," said Rhiannon. But though her voice was doubtful, her eyes could not leave the shoes either.

If that town stayed the same at the top, it became brilliant at the bottom. It flashed as though all the stars in heaven had fallen and were going about its streets in pairs, with a person sprouting from each pair.

Feet glowed and gleamed, they flashed and sparkled. They twinkled like fireflies, they moved sedately like the moon, they strode ponderously and stately like the sun marching triumphantly toward noon.

They were golden, and so was the waterfall that poured into the purses of Manawyddan and Pryderi.

None of the other shoemakers sold anything, and none of them liked that.

But for four moons the Gold Shoemakers made their golden shoes in peace. Then a woman came to the shop after nightfall, and found Manawyddan alone. She said to him, "If you will make me a pair of golden shoes for nothing, I will tell you something."

Manawyddan stroked his chin.

"Something more precious than gold? That would be something indeed," said he. "What is it?"

"When I have the shoes I will tell you."

Manawyddan stroked his chin some more.

"You will get the shoes when I get the knowledge," he said. "But I will measure your feet now. Once the shoes are made we will both lose if you do not get them, for it is unlikely that they will fit anybody else."

"Well, do not be too long about it," said she, and he did not like the look in her eye when she said that.

He told the others of the bargain he had made, and Rhiannon rose at once.

"I will begin packing," she said with resignation. "Kigva, do you see to our clothes and the linens. I will take the kitchen shelves."

"Indeed and indeed," lamented Kigva, "I am tired of getting used to new houses. We have no sooner thought out the best way to place the pots and pans, and I have no sooner learned to remember where they all are, than we are running away again."

"I am tired of traveling! I am tired of being run out of town! I am tired of towns!" And she sat down and wept.

"That looks pleasant," said Rhiannon, "and I would like to do it too. But this is not the time for it; we must pack."

But Pryderi put his arms around Kigva and comforted her.

"You shall have a head off one of these boors to put in every pot," he said tenderly. "And another to put in every pan. You shall not have to run away anymore."

"Only once more," said Manawyddan. "Towns are no place for us; that is clear. We could buy a farm, but we would be almost as lonely there as we were in Dyved, and the land never would be really our land. Let us go back to Dyved and farm there," said he.

For a breath's space Pryderi and Kigva looked at him blankly; then a light dawned in their faces, like dawn coming up over the midsummer marshes, faint and cool and sweet, the promise of a fresher, clearer day.

"Dyved—!" said Pryderi. And a hundred memories rang in his voice, of big things and little things, of trees climbed and fish caught, of glad homecomings and eager goings forth. All the memories of a lifetime, of a life that had been good.

"Indeed," he breathed softly, "there is not a better place in all the world to go back to. Dyved . . ."

"Indeed," said Kigva, smiling through her tears, "it is a nice place, Dyved. Nobody ever ran us out of it, and nobody ever will, for there is nobody left there to do it."

But Rhiannon was not smiling, and her face looked white and still as some beautiful, snow-covered country caught fast in the chill grip of winter. Her eyes seemed to see far spaces, and her voice had the sound of wind; of a cold and far-off wind.

"You have got what you have played for, Husband," she said, "and what I have wanted too, but it may be that it is not wise. We will go back to Dyved, for that is the fate that is on us, but Something may be waiting for us there."

11

The Trap

IN THE springtime they came back to Dyved, and the land lay fair and still before them, and the Three Birds of Rhiannon flew before them, their wings shining in the sun.

Once Rhiannon went apart and held up her hands and called them. They came and lit upon her fingers, and she spoke to them, in some strange sweet chirping tongue. And with chirps as sweet they answered; for the first time since that dreadful night they made sounds, although they did not sing.

But when Rhiannon came back to the others, her face was white and grave, and when they asked her if she had learned anything, she shook her head.

"Nothing that I can tell in the tongue of men. They do not know all, and I cannot recognize, in their tongue, the name they speak. It is a great name, it casts a great shadow—a twilight in the heart, and a stillness all around, as though Earth Herself, our Mother, hearing it, held Her breath and was afraid."

"But this I know: The Birds said clearly, '*Be watchful. Be watchful. Watchful . . .*'"

The Birds left them when they came to Arberth, to that quiet palace waiting with the golden sun upon it, and its lonely chambers all dark and still within.

They built a cooking fire, and pastured the cow that they had brought with them. They tried to talk, but the silence seemed to drown their voices. Those desolate chambers seemed to have a dead feeling that they had never had before, as if the voices of all those people who had been violently swept away from their life here cried mutely from the walls. Cried for warmth and breath, and all that they had been deprived of.

Toward evening that silence was broken, shattered by a great belling of hounds.

Pryderi ran out through the palace doors and was all but knocked down by a rush of upward-leaping paws, and upward-leaping bodies, and frantically licking tongues.

"It is my dogs!" he cried. "My dogs!"

He patted this one's head, and scratched that one under the chin, and another behind the left ear, and yet another behind the right ear. He patted and scratched and tickled, and they leapt and licked and wagged their tails as if they would wag them off.

"I have come back to you, my darlings!" he exulted. "I have come back." And his eye beamed with tenderness and pity for them, who had thought that they had lost him.

Then suddenly he sobered; looked down upon them with an eye grown stern. "Indeed, it was not I that ran off and left you. I had not seen you for years before I went. You must have run away."

The dogs whined. They looked back uneasily toward the dark forest from which they had come. Their hackles rose and they whined again and shivered, and crouched down as close to Pryderi as they could get, looking up at him with great troubled eyes, as if trying to tell him something.

Rhiannon said quietly, "The dogs did not run away, Son. They were taken . . ."

She and the others had followed him out, and Pryderi swung round to her, silent for a breath's space. Then he said, quickly and sharply, "But they have come back!"

His words were a statement, but his eyes were questions, bright and eager, and Kigva slipped her hand into his. She breathed softly, round-eyed, "Do you suppose that some day the people could come back too?"

Rhiannon shook her head. "Anything could happen. But I do not think that that will. Build no hopes upon it, children."

"But the dogs were not killed! They have come back. They are here!"

Both young people had spoken together, and Pryderi added, looking down at the dogs and scratching his head, "But where have they been all this time? And how did they get back from there?"

"Ask those questions of Whatever took them, Son. But no —I pray to the Mothers that you may never get the chance."

Something in Rhiannon's voice brought back the silence. As if a great cold finger had been laid suddenly upon each of their hearts . . .

Then one of the dogs whined again, and Pryderi stooped to pat him and said magnificently, "Be still. I will not let anything get you again."

All the dogs believed him; he even believed himself. They looked up at him thankfully, and their tails wagged again, and their panting tongues lolled so red and happily and gratefully that they-too seemed to be wagging.

In their bed that night Manawyddan said to his lady, "I hope that the dogs will stay. Or be allowed to stay. That will mean much to the boy."

She said, "I do not know what I hope. They may have been sent back for a purpose."

"Well, we must be careful," said Manawyddan.

The dogs stayed, and Pryderi went hunting with them, and brought home many a dinner. They were the same as always; wherever they had been, that place of Mystery had not changed them. It takes a great deal to change the loving simplicity of dogs.

The leaves reddened and fell. Winter came howling down from the blue mountains; whitened all the land. Spring came, and the woods foamed white again, this time with hawthorne bloom; and still nothing happened. By then everybody was less careful. People who walk warily at first, half-expecting a monster to pop out from behind every bush, and a happening to be hiding grimly in every corner, could not help but be very surprised if, a year later, there should be anything but emptiness or another bush behind a bush. Or anything but shadows, and maybe a cobweb or two, in a corner.

So summer found them: happy and unsuspicious.

Then the rains began. They lashed those wind-swept heights where once the Holy Stones had stood; they drenched the deep green woods and made mud of the brown breast of Earth the Mother. Pryderi let the dogs into the great hall, and there he and they padded restlessly, tired of having nothing to do. He and Kigva quarreled, though they soon made it up again.

"But it will not stay made up long," said Kigva to Rhiannon, "unless this rain stops and he can get out of the house."

"Maybe this is my business," said Rhiannon. "He is acting like a little boy again. Shall I tell him so?"

Kigva considered. "No. It is our quarrel. Do you and Father look the other way, and let us fight it out in peace."

But in the morning the rain had stopped. Pryderi and Manawyddan rose early and went out to hunt, the dogs leaping happily around them.

For awhile they got nothing but muddy feet. Mist steamed around them, they could seldom see their way, but they were free of the house, and that freedom seemed good.

The morning wore; the mists vanished, but the sun did not come out. The sky was gray and shining. Not a breath of wind stirred, not a leaf moved.

"It is very still," said Pryderi. "I wish the dogs would find something."

Manawyddan too had been thinking that it was very still. He said, "Give the dogs time."

But they tramped on and on and nothing happened.

The sun, the golden lady of day, fought to pierce that silver veil. As a man may see his own face dimly mirrored in deep water, so moon-pale images of her glimmered here and there among the trees. One seemed to be sinking straight ahead of them, shining in the green dusk.

Manawyddan said in wonder, "I have seen such sights beside the Usk, but never this far west."

But at that very moment the dogs set up a great barking. Like a flight of thrown spears they shot forward, and with a gleeful shout Pryderi plunged after them. Manawyddan followed, running as fast as he could.

The race ended as suddenly as it had begun. The dogs stopped, growling, before a thick green bush. For a last dizzy moment, as he ran, Manawyddan thought he saw that mock moon sinking, in a flash of white light, behind that same bush. Then he stood beside Pryderi, panting and rubbing his eyes.

The dogs turned and ran back to the men. Their hair bristled; it stood straight up on their backs. They were afraid, desperately afraid; they who never before had shown fear of any quarry.

Pryderi laughed. "Let us go up to that bush, and see what is hiding in it." His eyes shone. Excitement was on him, like a kind of drunkenness.

He sprang toward the bush.

Like lightning a huge gleaming body leapt from its green shelter; leapt and was gone.

But not far. It turned and stood, its small evil eyes flaming, its terrible curved tusks ready. It was a wild boar, a pure white boar, and there was something awful in that whiteness, A chill as of a color (or a colorlessness) too white to have any place in all nature. To the son of Llyr it seemed the chilling, repulsive whiteness of death.

Pryderi did not feel it. His face flamed with delight. "At him, Gwythur! After him, Kaw! Get him, Fflam! Take him, my darlings!"

Always before they had leapt at that command, joyous and arrow-swift. But now they shrank and cowered; they looked up at him piteously, as if to say, "We would love to kill him. We would love to please you. But we dare not—we dare not . . ."

He was inexorable. "At him! Are you dogs, or are you mice?"

They could not bear that; they charged.

The boar stood and fought them, savagely. He ripped up one on his tusks, and the others wavered, then charged him again.

Pryderi, seeing his dog killed, charged too, yelling with fury. Again Manawyddan ran as fast as he could, fear tearing his heart, striving to reach his son before Pryderi and the boar met.

The dogs were still snarling and leaping, but the white boar seemed to be playing with them. To be waiting for their master.

Not ten feet from him, Manawyddan caught up with Pryderi. Side by side, they rushed on. Then and not until then, the boar turned and fled. Was off, incredibly swift, incredibly, deathly white, into the forest.

Pryderi sped after him, shouting to the dogs. Manawyddan was left behind again. He could not keep up with them; his legs had not the springy swiftness of youth. But he was tough; they could not shake him off.

The hounds ran, the men ran, and always before them, like a flash of pale, cold light, was the white boar.

Often, even in the heat of the chase, something like a door had flashed open inside the son of Llyr, and he had felt a queer kind of oneness with the quarry. A pity for the thing that must die to feed him. But now he felt only loathing. That white beast was hideous to him, he would have gagged over its flesh, yet he would have rejoiced to see it die. It was a thing that should not be.

He was running too fast to think. His body ached, his ears were filled with the singing of the blood in his bursting head. From very far away, almost as if from another world, he heard the quavering, frightened, yet still fierce baying of the hounds: heard Pryderi urging them on. His swimming eyes saw the coldly gleaming boar flashing in and out of a green mist. Trees . . .

The trees must be running too, their very roots sliding frantically beneath the earth, striving to get away from the chill of that beast that was too white to be a natural thing . . .

He could not see where he was going; he could not see anything clearly. Every breath tore his chest. But he must keep on; he must not lose Pryderi.

The boar had stopped. He was getting bigger. His whiteness was glistening, shimmering, expanding into a sparkling ball . . . It was not the boar. It was that fallen moon, and it had grown as big as a hill.

He was climbing it. He could still hear Pryderi and the dogs ahead of him, and he called out to stop them.

"Pryderi! Pryderi!"

Then he saw it. The opening in that white, shining hill. Like a black mouth it yawned beneath the massive, intricately carved stone lintel. Snow-white the boar flashed across that black mouth and dived into it; dwindled and grew small in its darkness, a racing point of white light.

Baying loudly, the hounds plunged in after it. Like a mouth indeed, the darkness seemed to swallow them up. Pryderi would have leapt in after them, but Manawyddan caught his arm.

They stood there, like men waking from a dream; realizing suddenly that they never had seen this place before.

Pryderi whispered shakily, "It was never here before."

They looked up at the gray shining sky; it was the same. They looked down, and saw that beneath their feet was neither grass nor earth, but pebbles of white quartz. A solid mass of them, that covered the whole hillside.

What hillside? And whence had these white stones come?

They looked back toward the dark mouth of the passage.

No bark came from it, no sound at all. The dogs must be lost in those depths, beyond light, beyond sight, beyond sound.

Silence seemed to creep out of that black mouth, like exhaled breath. To creep up around them and cover them, like a rising mist.

They turned and ran uphill.

At the top they stopped, panting, and gasped, but not for lack of breath.

They stood upon the top of the Gorsedd Arberth, of that gateway between the worlds.

"We have been led here," Manawyddan said slowly. "Blinded and led."

Pryderi did not seem to hear. He looked back the way they had come, and his eyes were both fierce and troubled.

"The dogs," he muttered. "The dogs."

"Let us wait here a little," said Manawyddan. "This is a high place. There could be no better spot for spying them if they come out again."

So they looked and listened, with the greenwaste that had been Dyved outspread below them, but they saw nothing and heard nothing. No bird flew across the sky; no wind stirred a leaf.

Restlessness came on Pryderi; settled on him and grew.

"Lord," he said at last. "I am going to go into the hill and find the dogs. Or at least find out what has happened to them."

"Are you mad?" said Manawyddan. "Whoever it is that cast a spell over this land has opened up the hillside and entrapped the dogs."

"I know that, but this is the Mound of the Testing. This may be my test."

"It is a trap. You said that this passage was never here before, but it has been. Through it the first King of Dyved was taken to his burial chamber, and then his Mound was built over him and covered with white quartz to make it shine like the moon, like the tombs of Irish Kings. Then for ages it was sealed, and strangers drove out his people, and the white stones were carried off or covered with grass. That lost entrance may well be what common men mean when they speak of this place as a gateway between the worlds."

"It is not lost now, but found." Pryderi pulled impatiently at the hand that again had grasped his arm.

"It is found. Death has opened his jaws. Would you walk into them?"

Pryderi tried to speak patiently. "You do not understand, second-father. You were not born here, you do not come of the blood of the Lords of Dyved. I do, and I accept the destiny that is laid on me."

"I understand that you would throw your life away. Think of Kigva and your mother."

"I do. These last years have not been easy for them. Maybe if I go into the hill the spell will be broken everything put back as it was before. Our people freed."

"If they live. Boy, that is a fair dream, but it is a dream."

Pryderi pulled his arm free. "In any case I cannot give up my dogs like this."

Manawyddan's hand dropped; he understood. This boy who had brought disaster upon a whole people could never knowingly forsake even a dog. The guilt that for years had crouched deep down under all his gaiety had not kept him from driving these poor beasts, too, to their doom. But that driving had added the last straw to the old load. Not again could Pryderi bear to walk unscathed while those who had trusted him perished.

Sadly the son of Llyr watched that straight young figure stride down the hill. "Loyalty is strong in you," he said softly. "You are a true son of kings, even if not of those you think sired you."

He thought of Bran, and of Beli their mother's brother, Beli who had been called the Mighty. *They would have been proud of you, boy, though they would have thought you a fool.* But then black realization smote him, burning through the last threads of that web of glamour that had numbed him too. Loss drowned pride. He writhed in such agony of soul as he had not known since Bran fell. But his training held; his mind was still his master. No use to try to follow the boy now; no earthly power could save Pryderi. If help ever were to reach him, it must come from the free. Not from one who shared his doom.

He knew that waiting was useless, but he waited. The day wore. The sun set, in a sky that seemed to hurt the watching man's eyes; flaming and blood-splashed, as though from a whole world's death.

He sat quietly under its rage, still as the stones around him.

Night came; the moon rose. And still Manawyddan waited . . .

He said to himself at last, *This is foolishness. You know that there is no more hope.*

Down below, the women must be waiting in fear; knowing that if something had not happened their men would have come home by now. Unkind to keep them waiting; unkind, too, to tell them what he must tell them . . .

He went down from the Gorsedd. He drew his cloak around him, for a wind had risen. It whined about him as he went; cold, colder than any summer wind he had ever felt. Like an ice-cold breath it smote him as he passed that black mouth that had opened in the hillside; that doorway that loomed dark even through the darkness of night.

Manawyddan glanced once at that opening. He thought dully, *Why has it not closed? Its work is done. Can He that waits inside be fool enough to think that I will still give up the game and come in to Him?*

Then bitter laughter seemed to ring inside his head: his own. *What game have I to give up? What good have I done Dyved, in all the years since He laid it waste? What good can I do my son? My son! My son!*

He went on. That is all a man can do: go on.

He saw the lights of Arberth. They streamed out to meet him, for the great doors stood open.He went into the hall. Rhiannon sat there, sewing, Kigva sleeping at her knee. He had only a breath's space in which to think that that sleep must have been mercifully induced, either by magic or by herbs, for then Rhiannon saw him. Gladness sprang into her eyes, opened there like a flower. She jumped up, her lips parting to speak his name, her arms going out to him.

And then she saw that he was alone, and all her gladness withered.

Her arms dropped, her face froze. Her eyes became spears piercing him, though her voice was only a whisper. *"Where is he that left here with you?"*

Manawyddan braced himself. He had expected pain enough from the sight of her pain. He saw now that he was to have an even more bitter cup to drink.

"Lady," he said, "this is what happened."

She listened, her face whitening until it grew as white as death. All the life that drained out of it seemed to burn in her eyes. They flamed; they blazed. They were not Rhiannon's eyes, but only the eyes of Pryderi's mother, and behind her of all that vast long line of mothers, scaly and furred, hairy and hairless, that have been robbed of their young since time began. Manawyddan wished with all his heart that she were still Rhiannon, his Rhiannon, for he had his own grief, and he was very tired. Stupid with fatigue, he groped for words to reach her, to bring her back; at least to comfort her a little.

He ended, "Lady, do not give up hope. For you know, better than we who are earth-born, that it is unlikely that he has died an ordinary death."

Quick as lightning, and as terrible, her wrath lashed at him. "Man without honor, without courage! A bad comrade you have been, and a good comrade you have lost!"

As flame darts over dry leaves she darted past him, and was gone. He followed her out into the night; he cried her name. "Rhiannon, Rhiannon!" But he caught only a glimpse of her, a tall slender shape vanishing into the rising mists.

He still followed, still calling desperately, "Rhiannon! Rhiannon!" But he was spent and dizzy and his whole body ached; and she was fresh, and of a less weighty make than the women born into our world. He lost her in those ever-thickening mists. Bushes caught at him spitefully, trees thrust themselves in his way. A huge trunk struck him; knocked all the breath out of his body. He fell; rose only to run round and round helplessly, blindly, like a man in a maze. For how long he never knew . . .

With an earsplitting, earth rending crash, thunder blasted the night. The black sky shuddered away from the sizzling, titanic blade of fiery light that seared it.

When Manawyddan's head cleared, the mists had lifted. The moon shone down with a ghostly gentleness. From far to the west came a sad, sweet crying. Three birds were flying seaward, the moon silvering their feathers, the white, the green, and the gold.

The Birds of Rhiannon, singing their farewell to the world of men!

He understood. The Enemy had foreseen that Rhiannon would seek Pryderi. He had sent the mists and the maze-Illusion that Manawyddan might not stop her. The dark opening in the hillside was closed now. That black mouth had swallowed her, the mouthful for which it had waited.

Rhiannon. Rhiannon, my beloved!

With bowed head and stooped shoulders the son of Llyr walked back to Arberth, where this time she would not be waiting. He walked like a very old man, and he felt as if all the weight of all the mountains of the world lay upon his heart.

The Son of Llyr Goes On

HE CAME back into the Hall of Arberth, and again he came alone.

The fog had come before him. Only the red embers of the dying fire glowed sickly, faintly, through the mists that stalked the hall like gliding shadow-shapes.

Kigva still slept. Her emptied body, lying there, was no more than another shadow.

He sat down heavily, crouching over those red embers. He felt like a man who sits amid the wastes of winter in the farthest north, in that dread place where sea ends and ice begins. Alone forever in sunless darkness and everlasting cold.

The Mothers alone knew which he grieved for most: for the man whom he had loved as much as Bran had loved Caradoc, or for the woman who had been friend and lover.

Rhiannon and Pryderi. Pryderi and Rhiannon.

O Bran and Branwen! Was it not enough that I had to lose you? I should not have had to lose these two as well. O Mothers, no man should have to bear this twice!

He had known spring and summer, and mighty winds had come and felled the great trees, and lashed all the flowers to death. He had known the chill of loneliness that is greater than the chill of death, since death at least must wipe out loneliness. For the dead are many, and at worst there is no loneliness in sleep.

He had known late summer, with its golden warmth, its tender delight in watching youth when one is no longer torn by the fierce confusing energies of youth. But now once again the trees were stripped and down, and all was over. He was back again in the great cold.

Yet the Enemy who had taken these loved ones, being beyond death, might not deal in the death we know. He had said that to Rhiannon, and it was true.

Yet how can that help you, son of Llyr? How can you, a man, fight with a God? With a God you cannot see?

There was no way; none. Hope was only a mockery.

O Pryderi, should I have gone with you after all? Then at least we would all have been together . . .

But he knew in his heart that that, not this, would have been surrender, flight. He would have given his life to save Pryderi, but he could not throw it away. It was not in the son of Llyr to waste anything

Pryderi had comforted himself with dreams of a capricious, ruthlessly testing Power that in the end might reward courage. Manawyddan had no such belief. An unearthly Power might be good or evil, but it would be no child-brain, wasting stupendous force in cruel tricks.

Yet in evil there is always weakness. Wisdom is above malice, above vengeance. Even on earth the highest druids taught that. Even beyond earth a Power that cherished such passions could not be invulnerable, might overreach Itself . . .

But how could such as He overreach Himself so far as to come within a mortal's reach? A baby cannot knock down a man.

Well, hope might be a mockery, but a man cannot live without hope, even if it be only the paltry hope of getting his dinner in the evening. *And in evil there is weakness.*

Kigva stirred and moaned. Her hand groped beside her, and Manawyddan's eyes closed in sudden sick pain. She thought herself in bed, with Pryderi beside her.

Her eyes opened, stared blankly around the great hall, then wildly. She saw him, and her whole face glowed.

"You have come back, Lord! But Pryderi—where is Pryderi?" Her voice quivered and broke, like that of a child staring into a great darkness. She had seen that he was alone.

Manawyddan braced himself again. She too must be told . . .

"Where is Pryderi? Where is Rhiannon?" Kigva's voice rose sharply, as if any sound, even the sound of her own speech that told her nothing, were better than waiting. This waiting that strained toward knowledge as toward a monstrous, unimaginable birth.

"Where is he? Where were you? You did not come, and you did not come—and the night grew darker and darker, and I grew more and more afraid. Until she made me lie down and stroked my head with her hands. But she has made me sleep too long . . . where is she? Where is *he?*"

Manawyddan thought of Rhiannon's hands; those white hands that were full of little magics, small sweet magics of her woman-hood, and of others, little wonders left over from that Bright World where she had been born. Was she back in that world now? Or in some other?

Rhiannon, Rhiannon, where are you?

Kigva said again, "Where are they? Where is Pryderi?"

"Child, I do not know."

He told her all he did know, and now and then she broke into his tale with questions, the questions of the suddenly grief-stricken, that try to find a way for truth not to be true. And then she wept.

She wept, the daughter of Gwynn Gloyu, as if she could wash away all that had happened, and float Pryderi back to her on that flood of tears. As only the young can weep, remembering, if uncon-sciously, how enough tears once brought gifts or mercy.

She wept as if she did not care whether she lived or died.

Manawyddan made breakfast at last, and brought her some, but though by then she had wept until she could weep no more, she would not eat. She only sat silent, staring into nothingness, and sometimes, as the day wore, she looked at him when she thought he did not know it, and then she shuddered.

I am alone with this man, who has lost his woman as I have lost my man. We are far away from any other men or women. Anyone would say that we ought to comfort each other . . . I cannot. I will not! O Mothers! O Pryderi! Pryderi!

She saw, not Manawyddan himself, but only a man.

He saw her sight of him. He thought wearily, *This is what comes of the ways of the New Tribes. In the old times, in Harlech, no girl would have thought that a man could enjoy her unless she shared that joy. Had we not grief enough without this?*

It hurt him that this woman who for years had been as his own child could fear him.

He stopped in front of her, too far away to touch her. He looked at her until her eyes rose to meet his. Afraid or not, she had plenty of fighting blood in her.

"Lady," he said, "you do wrong if you fear me. I declare to you that if I were in the dawn of youth I would keep faith with Pryderi who was as a son to me. You shall have all the friendship that is in my power to give, and nothing else from me, so long as this sorrow is on us."

So quaintly and formally the *Mabinogi* says he spoke to her, and perhaps in no other way could he have reached her. She looked at him, a long, still look. Then she smiled at him, suddenly and brightly and fondly, as a relieved and repentant child might smile at the person who has promised not to hurt it.

"Indeed, Lord, that is what I would have thought you would do, if I had been thinking of you yourself at all. I am sorry!"

"Child, it is forgotten. But we cannot stay here. Alone and without dogs, I am not hunter enough to feed us. Would you like to go to the Witches at Caer Loyu?"

"No," said Kigva, and her lip quivered. "They would tell me that I am well rid of Pryderi, and I could not bear that. Not now! Lord, let me stay with you."

"That is what I hoped you would say," said Manawyddan. And she sprang up and kissed him, and they were as good friends again as ever they had been.

So they left that haunted land where every place spoke of Pryderi and Rhiannon. Where the silence was so loud that it rang in the ears like a cry. They went back into Logres, and at sight of new things and new places, Kigva's eyes brightened, as Manawyddan had hoped they would. She was too young to be always sad.

They found a town they liked, and they stopped there.

"Lord," said Kigva, "what craft will you take? Let it be one that is seemly, for I am still tired of being run out of town."

But for once Manawyddan was contrary; his own load of bitterness was too new and too heavy.

"I will take no craft but the one I had before. I will make shoes."

Kigva looked very straight at him then. As perhaps she had seen the witches look at Gwynn Gloyu.

"Lord, you know well that competing with boors always gets you into trouble. And shoemaking is no business for a man so nobly born as you."

"Well would it be," said Manawyddan, "if no highborn man ever did anything worse. I make shoes, and another man pays me for them, and if they are good shoes and fit him, where is the harm? Did Caswallon earn his throne as honorably——that throne that people are beginning to forget that Bran my brother ever held?"

Kigva said sternly, "We are not talking about Caswallon, who is a bad smell. We are talking about you."

"I will make shoes," said Manawyddan.

He made golden shoes as before, and once the work was begun, Kigva took Pryderi's place and helped him cheerfully enough.

"Though I know how it will turn out," said she.

The moons passed; they prospered. But before the year was quite up, Kigva began to notice that some of the townswomen were not as friendly to her as they had been. She spoke about it to Manawyddan.

"They are all shoemakers' wives or kin, Lord. It seems to me that it would be better if you did not make quite such good shoes."

He sighed. "That is a weakness that is on me, girl. What I do I must do as well as I can."

Kigva sighed too. "Well, enough wisdom is with you to call it a weakness. It is going to get us into trouble again."

That night Manawyddan awoke. The room was dark and still, the moonlight did not reach his bed. But he could see, quite plainly, a little brown bird sitting on his breast. He said, without surprise, "You are Branwen's bird. The starling she reared in the meal trough and sent to tell us how she, who had gone into Ireland a Queen, was now but a beaten slave."

The bird said, "That is so. And before you went to Ireland to deliver my Lady, you gave me into the keeping of another Queen. Of Rhiannon Oset of Faery."

Memory came to Manawyddan. "She told me that you had found a mate and flown away."

"Yes. She set me free to love my love and build my nest and rear my broods as a bird should. Until that dread night—the night of the storm that came upon Dyved from beyond the world. I died then, of the great sound; I who was no longer young."

"Then why did you not go back to Branwen?" Manawyddan asked, still without surprise.

"I did, and glad was our meeting. But for this one night she sends me back. For your sake, as once she sent me upon a long journey for her own. And this time I know the meaning of the words I speak. She says, 'Brother, beware.'"

"Of what? Or of whom?"

"Of men who are losing their living because you outdo them at their own craft. Who will kill you if you are still here when the moon rises again."

"Well, that is not to be wondered at. Is that all her word?"

"No. She says that when you go back to Dyved—as well she knows that you will go back—you must still beware of—of—oh, I cannot speak the name! It clutches my throat like a hand, it weighs down my tongue like lead!" He felt how her tiny body trembled, even though no weight or substance of earth was in it any longer.

"Rest, little one," he said. "Be still. Perhaps I can help."

He spoke words of power then; words such as the wisest of High Druids seldom spoke but twice in a lifetime, and then only when they taught or were taught them, mystic mighty sounds to serve against that terrible uttermost need that most likely would never come. But his own tongue seemed to swell and harden until it was like a stone in his mouth. The sounds would not come dearly. Sweat stood on his forehead.

The night outside was quiet, but within that room a thin wind rose. It ruffled the starling's unearthly feathers; blew ice cold through Manawyddan's hair.

"I must go," the bird whispered. "Back—to—her. There—even He cannot reach me."

"He?"

She set her beak against his ear. Soft as the sound of grass growing was her whisper now. "The Gray Man—the son of Him that Hides in the Wood—*Oh-h Oh-h! Beware—beware!*"

As a feather is swept away by a wind, so she was whirled away. But just before she vanished, Manawyddan saw a ray of moonlight strike her, enfold her like a shining mantle. Glad at heart, he thought, *Branwen has power to guard her messenger.* Then darkness took him, and he sank again into that mysterious healing gulf that men call sleep.

When he woke, the sun was high, and the good smell of food came to him; Kigva was cooking breakfast. For a breath's space he lay still, then remembered all and leapt up.

"Girl, we must be out of here before nightfall!"

Kigva dropped the spoon with which she was stirring their porridge, and it fell into the hot porridge, and splashed her, and made her jump. Then she said with some asperity, "Well, Lord, I told you so. But who else has told you?"

"A little bird."

Kigva looked at him sharply. "One with feathers?"

"It had feathers once."

Her face grew grave. "Not—one of the Birds of Rhiannon?"

"No. If they have found her, they stay with her. Make haste and pack now girl. There are things I must do."

"There certainly are things you ought to do, Lord—there are indeed. Why should we bear this from these boors?"

"Boors or not, they have a right to live. It is time for us to go home, girl. Back to Dyved."

"Home," said Kigva; and her face changed and softened. "Home!"

But that night, when they were tramping through the lonely

392   EVANGELINE WALTON

woods, three laden donkeys with them (buying and loading those
beasts had been Manawyddan's task), she grew curious again.

"What did give you warning this time, Lord? Have the winds
begun to carry men's words to you, as they do to Mâth the Ancient?"

"Mâth hears men's thoughts, not their words, girl; and in this age
that gift is his alone."

"Then have you taken to sleeping upon a bull's hide? I have never
seen it when I made your bed."

"Child, no druid of the Old Tribes ever slept upon a bull's hide.
Only they of the New Tribes, that learned druidry from us, but still
refuse to live by the Ancient Harmonies, ever needed such devices
to focus the Eye within."

Kigva thought that over. "I have heard Pendaran Dyved say
such things, Lord, and he talking with Rhiannon. But if things
that cannot move of themselves truly have no power over men,
why did all our ill luck come on us after Caswallon took away the
Holy Stones?"

Manawyddan said slowly, "To us four the taking of the Stones
made no difference. But to the people of Dyved—who knows?
Generations of faith and worship may pour power into a thing even
as sailors putting out to sea pour water—that may well mean life to
them—into jug or cask. And when the Stones went, they of Dyved
who so long had put their faith in them may not have had power
enough left to withstand the fear that shook them out of life and
time."

Kigva thought again, then shook her head. "Lord, I would like to
say I see. But the truth is that I do not see at all."

They went on awhile, then she spoke again. "Lord, next year will
be the seventh year since the Great Storm. Folk say that in the seventh year, and in it only, can Otherworldly spells be broken and all
that has been taken away be brought back. Could all Dyved come
back? Could—even *they* come back?"

Manawyddan knew who she meant by "they." He said gently,
"Pray to the Mothers that it may be so, child. But do not set your
hopes upon it."

She spoke no more that night.

Cold and lonely was that journey. Winter's teeth already were biting, frost-white, through the autumn winds. The trees that at first
flamed like torches soon were stripped and bare, their naked boughs
shivering in the gusts, the fallen leaves beneath them brown as
themselves. All their brief glory of red and gold was gone, withered
as their summer greenness. Soon man and girl wore their heavy

cloaks even at midday, and when night came they tethered the donkeys where the trees grew lowest, and there was most shelter.

"This is not nice," Kigva said once, shivering as the wind's teeth sought to pierce her cloak. She drew the good wool closer around her.

"It will be worse," said Manawyddan, looking worriedly at the vast, darkening cloud masses above them, "if rain comes."

Before long rain did come. Cold and gray it beat upon them, soaked them through. It turned their sodden clothes from friends to foes; foes that clung clammily, implacably, to their chilled wet bodies. Mists hid all. Long before night came they were stumbling, squishing blindly through unseen, clawing entanglements of branch and briar. When night came the blackness was utter; they could not light a fire. If Manawyddan's long, patient labor did raise a spark from the damp faggots they gathered, the black, savage downpour beat it out.

They went on unrested, unwarmed by food or drink. The next day was the same, and the next night.

On the third day the ground became more stony, ceased to suck at their wet feet.

"This is better," said Kigva hopefully. "We can move more quickly now. Get somewhere sooner."

By "somewhere," she meant a house with a roof over it and a fire inside it. Manawyddan, who knew that in that drenched, darkened world they might already have passed near many such pleasant places, had the heart to answer only, "Maybe."

The ground grew stonier; sloped steadily upward. Soon they knew that they must be on a hillside. The wind slashed at them more fiercely, the climbing put fresh strain upon their tired legs. But Manawyddan's eyes lit up, and he peered forward, through that blinding, beating sheet of rain.

"These must be the hills of the Preseli" he said. "I thought that we should be getting near them. Near home."

The Preseli, thought Kigva, where the Stones were. And she remembered how different everything had been when the Stones were in their ancient places; all the light and laughter and warmth at Arberth, and Pryderi joking and scuffling with her in the daytime, and lying lovingly beside her at night.

She plodded on quietly, but now the wetness of her face was no longer cold; it was hot and salty. It rolled slowly down her cheeks, beneath the rain that still beat upon them.

Night was falling when at last they saw the walls of a house. They ran toward it, their hearts leaping with gladness, yet full of fear too. What if this longed-for refuge should turn out to be only a wish-shape, something that would vanish in the mist?

It did not. It was solid. Its doorway loomed dark and still as night, yet to them seemed warm and welcoming as a fire lit hearth. They rushed in, and Kigva dropped down, spent and gasping, giving up at last. Manawyddan groped until he found the fireplace; there was wood in it. Soon the fire blazed up and he saw the bare walls around them; saw the pots and pans and scanty furniture, the long-unused bed-place. Saw and caught his breath.

This was the shepherd's hut where he and Pryderi had guested on that long-gone night before they came to Arberth. Everything was just as it had been then. Only the old shepherd and his wife were gone.

In a chest were blankets, dry and clean. On a hook hung the old woman's cloak, as free of dust as if she had just washed and dried it. Manawyddan brought it and one of the blankets to Kigva.

"Get out of those wet things as fast as you can, child: you are soaked. I will take another blanket."

Kigva reeled to her feet. "I will start supper first, Lord. Do you change now; you have done enough, starting the fire by yourself."

"It was no trouble; these logs are dry."

"It will take only a minute to start supper." Kigva's jaw was set, though her teeth chattered a little.

"It will take longer than that. First we must bring out food and unpack it . . ."

"Because it is on the donkeys. Help me bring them in."

And Manawyddan helped her, because he did not want to lay hands on her, and there was no other way of stopping her. While she cooked and the donkeys huddled as close to the fire as she would let them, their shaggy hides dripping, he went to the bed-place and at last began to take his wet clothes off. The blessed warmth of a dry blanket was just closing around his tired, soaked body when he heard a thin, nastily delighted cackle of laughter behind him.

"It is not much fear you are able to put on your woman, Man of the Big People."

Manawyddan spun around. Deep in the deepest shadows he saw something.

Brown knees were there, and a small brown face gnarled as old wood, and the biggest mouth he had ever seen on anything, with the laughter still coming out of it, between whiskers that were as gray as cobwebs and as dirty.

There was great originality in those whiskers, for they grew upward instead of downward, and out of their owner's ears and eyebrows as well as his cheeks and chin.

"Indeed," said Manawyddan, "you must be a bogey."

"Indeed I am," said the bogey, "and it is glad I am to see anybody, even you and that pert chit of a girl, to whom something will soon happen if those miserable donkeys she would drag in dirty up my nice clean house. It has been a long time since I have had anybody to plague. A very long time." And he sighed.

"I am sorry for that," said Manawyddan courteously, "though if you try to plague either of us you will soon be sorrier. But I should have known you were here. This house does not look like a house that has been deserted for years."

"It does not indeed," said the bogey with pride. "You would think the shepherd's wife had just stepped out. She used to say that she did not see how she could ever have got along without me, and since she always put out a bowl of fresh milk and the best of everything for me, I never let her find out. Indeed, since she has been gone I have found out that she could manage to do a few things by herself."

"I do not doubt that," said Manawyddan.

"It is true, though I would never admit it if I got her back. Women should never be allowed to get above themselves. Like that one of yours, who would bring in those donkeys."

"She did well," said Manawyddan. "They are cold and wet."

"If they do what I am afraid they will do I will rub her face in it. We bogeys have our rights. We can make the work of a house go as smooth and easy as pouring cream out of a jug, or as full of accidents and mishaps as a fishnet is of holes. There is nobody like us."

"There will soon be nobody like you here if you try to play tricks on Kigva." Manawyddan said quietly.

"None of you clumsy Big People could ever get a hand on me," said the bogey comfortably. "I will be here long after both of you are gone."

"Maybe. But I or any other druid-bred man could put an awl through your nose and raise a wind that would blow you away to be spun through the upper air above the eastern seas for the length of twice seven generations."*

For the first time the bogey met his eyes squarely; those sea-gray eyes of the son of Llyr. He squirmed.

---

*For the disciplining of an objectionable household bogey see John Rhys's *Celtic Folklore*, vol II.

"Do not do that," he begged. "It was done to a cousin of mine, and he is not back yet. His mother is afraid that when he does get back he will have rheumatism forever. Those upper winds are cold—nobody knows quite how cold." He shivered. "I did not dream you were a man of knowledge, Lord; seeing how foolishly easy you are on the girl."

"You know it now, Remember it."

"I wish I did not have to. But truly it is good to have people here again. I am so glad to see you that there will not be a single lump in the girl's porridge tonight; though that will not be easy to manage, for it is plain that the little fool never has been taught how to make porridge. Or anything else."

To that Manawyddan had no answer. Little things can be vexing as well as great ones, and often, since he lost Rhiannon, he had been ashamed to think how glad he would have been if the Nine Witches had taught Kigva to cook. Rhiannon evidently had found it easier and more tactful to use her own magic on the food than to teach a grown daughter-in-law.

Kigva called, "Supper will soon be ready, Lord. If you will come and watch it, I can change now."

"She cannot hear my voice," the bogey said composedly. "Not unless I want her to. And I do not want her to. She is not a person with whom one could carry on an intelligent conversation."

"Any conversation between you and her would soon become a quarrel," said Manawyddan, "so none had better start." To Kigva he called, "I am coming girl. You should have changed long ago."

13

The Warning, and the Sowing

TOWARD MORNING Manawyddan woke, or seemed to wake. He saw the little house about him, gray and still. Then of a sudden that grayness grew, widened and expanded, into infinite space; into depths terrible and unknowable, through which Eyes watched him. He heard a Voice that made no sound say clearly: *"Here we first met, mortal, your eyes and Mine. Turn back now lest we meet once again, and for the last time. For no man may dwell in Dyved, that by My will must be a wilderness forever."*

Manawyddan started up. But now, in the fading darkness that was still more black than gray, the house was small and snug around him. He heard Kigva's quiet breathing, and remembered how, on that other night, when it was Pryderi who lay near him in the dark, he had faced in dream or vision that danger that then as now he could not remember, yet knew to be terribly real. *"Why do You veil Yourself from my waking mind, Enemy? Would You turn me back or drive me on?"*

Beside him came again the bogey's cackling laughter. "So there is Something that has power to put fear on you too, O Man of Illusion and Fantasy."

Manawyddan said, "What did you see, imp?"

"Only you. You and that girl, who at least does not snore. But I saw you jump, Lord."

Manawyddan said more slowly, "What did you see on the night of the Great Storm? When Dyved was laid waste?"

The bogey shivered. "Not much, Lord. Yet too much. The shepherd and his wife were already sound asleep. They might not have been, at that time of night, had they been younger. I can remember lively times in this sleeping-place." He chuckled. "Age draws the heat out of men and women, Lord. Mere tiredness took it out of you and the girl last night."

"My stepson is her man, not I."

The bogey cackled once more. "Your stepson! You never had one. Only Big People would have been big enough fools to swallow that tale, Lord. I know who you are now; we bogeys too have our ways of coming at knowledge, and last night I used them." He sobered, looking puzzled. "But Pryderi has been gone a long time. Why isn't his woman your woman now?"

"Because she still loves him. And I am neither young enough nor old enough to want to sleep with young girls."

"Well," said the bogey, "these giggling, ticklish girls can be a nuisance in a sensible man's bed. They have not even got sense enough to stop talking and let a man sleep when he has had enough and wants to rest. They are forever wagging their heads off, and it is not that end of them that is interesting at all."

"They are not the only tongue-waggers. I asked you what happened on the night of the Great Storm."

The bogey shivered again. "I would rather wag my tongue about anything else. I never think about that night. I have forgotten as much about it as I could."

"Yet this once remember all you can. Tell me all you can. I will not ask it of you again."

"Well, as I said, Lord, the old couple slept. And my work was done, so I listened to them snore, as I had many another night. They did not do it in tune, and sometimes one of them did it louder than the other, and all those snorts and wheezes and rumbles were very interesting to listen to. More entertaining than the noises the old folk made when they were awake."

"You still play with words. Get to the point."

"I am doing what you asked, Lord; telling you everything I can remember. That was a night like many other nights. And then the thunder came." He paused, and this time Manawyddan waited, and did not hurry him.

"The thunder came, and then the rain, and the great winds." The bogey shuddered. "There are always riders on the winds, but that night there were many, many. Not your ordinary human dead, that look down with regret and longing or else with forgiving friendliness—maybe even a little wink—upon this earth that once they walked.

There was no regret in these, and no friendliness. Only power;

power, and the will to destroy. I was afraid." Again he stopped, his teeth chattering.

"What did they look like, those riders?" urged Manawyddan. "Tell me."

"I cannot. They can be seen only as graynesses and whirlings; they whirl and whirl, and have no shape. In their own world they must wear forms, but in ours they have none. But they were terrible, and they came.

"The whole house rocked and shook, as if they were trying to tear it off the earth, and hurl it out into the night beyond the world. I crouched in my corner and shook; I shook like a leaf in that mighty wind; and the shepherd and his wife woke and shook also. Once she screamed, but in that din the sound was little, no more than the rustling of a leaf. After that she and the old man only clung together, burrowing into each other's warmth. But still they shook.

"We all three shook, so that it was a pain, a wrenching, jerking pain tearing at the very us inside us. An agony that could end only with our ending, with the very shaking of ourselves into bits. Not while one toe or finger held together, not while one hair grew beside another, could we know peace.

"We shook, the shepherd and his old woman and I, we shook . . .

"Had I been as solid as they were I would have come apart as they did. I saw their bodies wink and waver like torch flames, and finally go out. I saw where they had been, for they were not . . .

"And after that I did not know much, I did not feel or think much, for a long time.

"In the morning, when everything was quiet and golden again, and I was still sitting here, stunned and dizzy, two dragonflies flew into the house. They looked all around, they settled here and there, and then flew away again. But I knew them.

"Sometimes they used to come back, often at first. I could tell which was the woman by the way she hovered over her possessions, and sometimes lit on them and felt them with her feelers, as if loving them and remembering. But that was all she could do, and in time I grew tired of it, and of their queer fluttery ways, and began chasing them out whenever they flew in."

"That was very cruel of you," said Manawyddan.

"It was very bogeyish," said the bogey.

Toward sunset Manawyddan and Kigva and the donkeys came to Arberth. And never had Manawyddan been better pleased than when he saw his home again, and the green lands where he had walked with Rhiannon and Pryderi. Never before had he realized how fully it had become home, this house where his son had been born, though he had not.

Even to see Harlech again would not be like this. Harlech was my home because it was Bran's home; there I laughed and worked with my brother and helped him—or thought I helped him—to build peace and happiness for the world we knew. To weld Old Tribes and New into one people. But here I lived with Rhiannon; here in our youth and her ignorance we joyously begot our son; here in our ripeness and in our knowledge we loved. We too laughed and built and worked together; for ourselves and for those who would come after us; some of them of our own blood. Now has all that too come to nothing?

His mind said yes; all the quiet ruin around him said it. Yet in his heart the foolish-seeming gladness would not die.

Kigva, watching his face, braced herself and thought sturdily, *He is getting old. I have acted like a little girl, making him bear my tears and my fears and my loss, that is no greater than his. From now on I must be strong. Let him sit and dream; his time for that is coming, and he has earned it.*

And she thought with wonder that she loved him better than she ever had her own father Gwynn Gloyu, that great, swaggering warrior who had tried so hard to be a man in spite of the Nine Witches, and never had quite brought it off . . .

Somehow the great lonely halls of Arberth seemed to have a quiet friendliness about them that night; not the chill and crying emptiness the homecomers had feared. And when she and Manawyddan had unloaded the donkeys and made them comfortable, Kigva set herself to cook the best supper that she ever had cooked. She succeeded: both to her surprise and Manawyddan's it was as good as any that Rhiannon had ever set before them. Not until later, when she had gone to bed, did the son of Llyr find out why.

He was sitting alone beside the fire when in the shadows something moved. He started, then relaxed. *Good would be any ghost that came here. Perhaps it is my wife; or my boy.*

It came nearer, out of the shadows, into the light. Something more solid than memory; something small and brown and gnarled.

"I am here," said the bogey.

"So I see," said Manawyddan. "But I thought you bogeyfolk never left a house unless ill-treatment was put upon you there. And in the shepherd's hut none was. Before we left, Kigva and I cleaned up the mess that I will admit the donkeys made."

The bogey looked embarrassed. "It is our custom, Lord, as you say, never to leave the house we have chosen until some fool offends us. But this I will say: I was old before the oldest oak in Dyved was an acorn, yet all those years before did not seem so long as the few I have spent in that hut since the shepherd and his wife blew away. Clumsy and stupid and ill-tempered as you Big People are, one gets bored without you. I would like to come and haunt your house."

Manawyddan stroked his chin. "That could have both advantages and disadvantages," he said.

"What disadvantages? Did that fool of a girl ever cook you such a supper before? Nothing you eat will ever be underdone or overdone or anything but good—very good-so long as I am with you."

Manawyddan stroked his chin again. "And Kigva? How will it be for her?"

The bogey looked at him imploringly. "I will not play many tricks on her, Lord. Just enough to keep my hand in. If she treats me with proper respect, nobody could be nicer to her than I will be. Most of the time, anyway."

"All of the time," said Manawyddan, "if you stay here."

The bogey drew himself up with great dignity; he looked all of three feet tall, "Lord, it is custom too for a bowl of milk and bread to be set out every night for a bogey. If she is careless—if the milk has begun to sour, or the bread is just a wee bit stale—then she must pay. That too is a bogey's right; worth even freezing in the upper air for."

"I think you had better go home," said Manawyddan.

"Lord, I would not scald her in any place where it would show! I might trip her up now and then, but I would not break an arm or leg on her—that I swear. By the sun and the moon, and by the oath that bogies swear by."

"Bogey, I thank you for a good dinner, but my daughter and I can manage by ourselves. Good-bye."

"Are you sure, Lord? That girl is so clumsy that she could have worse accidents by herself than I would ever arrange for her. She likes and understands nothing about a kitchen, and nothing in a kitchen likes or understands her."

"Are you threatening us?" Manawyddan's voice was suddenly silken-soft. All the bogey's whiskers stood up in alarm.

"No, Lord. Into many houses I could enter unseen and make mischief, but here I dare not risk it. A man of knowledge like you would find me out. But consider—think of the meals you had yesterday and today, and of all the ones you had before. And a young woman gets above herself when all goes well and she thinks that she is doing it all herself—she needs a lesson. And both in the kitchen and out of it she is the better for having learned one. Think of your comfort and of the girl's own good, Lord. I will do her no real harm."

Manawyddan said, "I myself will prepare and set out your bowl each evening, and if you have any objections to what is in it, we will fight them out together. But raise one burn or one bruise on Kigva, and I will blow you away into the upper air for three times seven generations. That I swear by the sun and the moon, and by the oath my people swear by."

The bogey brightened. "Lord, I will watch over her as if she were the tenderest of lamb roasts."

And so he did. From that day on, no man and woman could have fared better than Manawyddan and Kigva did. When he hunted and brought home game, the meat never burned, and if Kigva gathered herbs that were too green, they somehow ripened in the pot. And when she did her washing, the dirt came out as easily as if it had only been perching like a bird on the top of the cloth, and never had got down into it at all.

Kigva always had been one for losing things too, but now she could find whatever she wanted at once, even when she could have sworn that she never had put it in the place where it suddenly appeared under her nose.

All this good luck and easy living began to get on her nerves. She tried to think that Rhiannon was watching over her and helping her, but the Presence that she sometimes felt near her did not seem at all like Rhiannon's.

Then one night on her way to bed she remembered she had forgotten something and turned back to the kitchen to see to it. She saw Manawyddan setting out the bowl of milk and bread, and understood.

"Lord, there is a bogey in this house!"

"Let there be no fright on you for that, girl," said Manawyddan placidly. "He does no harm. He only helps."

"There is no fright on me," said Kigva. "Is the niece of Nine Witches to be frightened of a little mite of a bogey? But indeed—" and as she thought things over her face lengthened until it became very long indeed, "this does explain things. Too many things."

After that she was more nervous than ever, and the bogey complained to Manawyddan. "It is even harder than it was to keep her from having accidents, Lord. I never saw such a girl for doing things wrong."

Kigva complained too. "It is hard on me always to be wondering where he is. Whether he is in front of me or behind me, or on which side of me he is. To know that he is watching me, and that whatever I do I cannot get away from him. And I always feel that he is laughing at me, Lord."

"I am not," said the bogey, who was still there. "She makes me too much work for that."

"Can you not feel grateful for his help?" said Manawyddan.

"He is very useful," said Kigva, "and indeed I wish he were a bother. I wish now that I had let my aunts teach me magic, as they wished to do. But witches always use black magic; they sing a great many incantations over a great many bubbling cauldrons full of queer things. I never felt that I could bear to memorize all those rigmaroles and then sing them in the middle of such a bad smell. But if I had . . ."

"He does not stay with you except when you are at work," said Manawyddan comfortingly. "He and I understand each other. There is no need for you to worry your head about him."

"What head she has," said the bogey, grinning.

The bogey was a great help to Kigva, but he was also an insult. She could no longer take pride in her own handiwork, knowing how much of it was likely to be his, and to have too little pride is as unhealthy for either man or woman as it is to have too much. Manawyddan saw her trouble and pitied it but he did not know what to do. His bargain with the bogey was made, and he pitied the gnome's loneliness too.

Winter howled over the land. Ice covered the rivers, snow whitened the brown earth and made shining lacy beauty of the leafless trees. Winds beat against the palace walls; sharp as knives, stronger than the arms of men, they tore at the thatched roof. Manawyddan had to climb up to mend it, and the bogey went along to help him. Kigva burned a batch of bread in the kitchen, and clapped her hands for joy.

Now if I work fast I can make and bake the next batch by myself. O Mothers, let it be good!

It was. That night, when at last the tired Manawyddan was safe back in the warm hall, she served it proudly and he complimented her upon it. Her face shone like the long-gone summer sun.

"Indeed, Lord, now you see that it was a good thing to have that bogey up there with you, keeping you from breaking a leg on that slippery roof, and not bothering me in my nice kitchen!"

The bogey snorted, and Manawyddan said "Shh!" But the light in her face did not die.

In his weariness, Manawyddan even let her fill the bogey's bowl that night, though he cautioned her sternly to taste everything herself and be sure that it was of the best. She did so, but when she set out the bowl and a generous helping of her new-made bread with it, she said proudly, "Sure I am that you never have tasted better, bogey. Remember well now that you had no hand in the making of it. It is not I who ever needed you or asked you here, but the Lord Manawyddan. Though of course you are welcome, being his guest."

"It was fairly decent bread," the bogey told Manawyddan later. "Which was as well for her, in spite of you, Lord."

"Remember our bargain," said Manawyddan drowsily.

"I do. Otherwise I would have tweaked that turned-up nose of hers for her, Lord. I nearly did anyhow."

"I am glad you did not. The upper winds would be especially cold now, little friend."

The bogey said, "I know it. Still, that girl of yours had better watch her tongue, or tomorrow or the day after she may take a bite of something while it is still too hot."

But Manawyddan looked at him then, and for the rest of that evening the bogey was only two feet tall. His height varied according to his mood; sometimes he was three feet tall and sometimes less, for bogeys do not belong to so solid a crust of the universe as the world we know.

Spring came at last. Ice and snow melted; under the brown bark of the trees and under the brown breast of the Mother a multitude of tiny lives stirred; they that rise up to make all greenness, leaves and grass and moss.

Manawyddan took the last load of grain, the one he had saved for seed. He chose three fields, he ploughed and he planted. The bogey went with him and helped him, so once more Kigva had peace in her kitchen. Sometimes things went wrong, but often they went right. She was learning; given time, her hurt pride, her desire to show that she could do things well by herself, would make an excellent cook of her.

Summer came, with her arms full of flowers; that most ancient bride who is ever honey-sweet, ever-young; she that rises in ever-renewed maidenhood to be clasped in the arms of the Young God, Her deliverer. He whose warm winds stir Her to inexhaustible and joyous motherhood.

She came, and the wheat in the three fields sprang up. The *Mabinogi* says that no wheat in the world ever sprang up better.

The bogey looked at it and not only grew three feet tall, but stayed that way. He said to himself, *This is the fruit of my help.*

Manawyddan and Kigva looked, and were happy. She said, "Next winter we will have plenty of meal, Lord."

There had been a little time, when the meal had grown low and what grain was left had to be saved for seed, when the ice still covered the fish, and it was not safe to track game far in the snowy woods, when they had been hungry. Not hungry enough to make them afraid, but hungrier than people like to be.

Manawyddan smiled and said, "No. Next winter there will be no need to tighten our belts."

No doubt he did not fear the ordinary hazards of weather as an ordinary farmer must; his druid power could keep them off. Yet he does seem to have been overconfident; the glamour was falling over his eyes again, that same glamour that for seven years now had fallen so easily upon any eyes in Dyved, that Land of Illusion. He of all men should have remembered that the Enemy might still be watching, playing with them as a cat plays with mice.

The summer wore; harvest time drew near. Manawyddan went to look at the field he had first planted, and saw it was ripe. "Tomorrow I will reap it," he said.

"Why not now?" said the bogey beside him.

"Because the sun is already high. Before I had finished I would be as wet as the sealfolk that dwell in the sea."

"Not with me to help you, Lord."

"Maybe not, and my thanks be with you, but the crop will only be the better for one more day's ripening."

Manawyddan, too, like Kigva, did not feel that it would be wise to become too dependent on the bogey.

He went home and told Kigva, and she rejoiced and cooked a fine supper. Once, when a pitcher of milk upset and then seemed suddenly to steady itself in midair, and then sailed quietly back through that air to land quietly on the table, she even smiled and said, "Thank you, bogey."

They ate and slept, but the blackness of night had hardly begun to pale before the oncoming tread of morning's bright feet when Manawyddan rose. He breakfasted, and set out.

He saw the stars twinkle and go out, vanishing into the grayness like golden jewels snatched away by unseen-mighty hands. He felt the dew upon his face, like heavy tears except that it was cold.

He walked under a gray heaven, through a gray land, for as yet the dawn was not strong enough for color, that eldest child of light, to be reborn. He thought suddenly, coldly, *Grayness, grayness*—Like a bird, the half memory hovered above his head in that pale darkness, then flew away and was gone.

He came to the field; and he stopped stock-still. For nothing but ruin was there. All was trampled and crushed as if by a herd of great beasts. He went through the field from end to end, and saw that not only was every stalk trampled flat, but that every ear of wheat had been cut from each stalk, as cleanly as with a knife, and that each ear was gone.

Nothing but straw was left.

He went to look at the second field, and every stalk in it stood upright, straight as a young warrior or a young tree. Tall and golden, and heavy with ears of the finest wheat. He stood and looked at it long, his gray eyes narrowed. Then, I will reap this one tomorrow, he told himself.

"Why tomorrow? We will reap it today!" Kigva raged, when he came home and told her what had happened. "I will go with you and help! So will the bogey: we will get this crop in before anything can happen to it."

"Tomorrow we will reap it," said Manawyddan.

Kigva looked at him with wonder. "Lord, what is on you? It is not yourself that is acting like this."

"Tomorrow we will reap the field," said Manawyddan.

That night supper was not so good. When Kigva upset something, the bogey forgot to catch it. It went all over her feet, and she did not like that, because it was hot. She was very angry, and used language that she had learned from the Nine Witches.

For the first time the bogey appeared before her.

"Lady," he said, "I did not do that on purpose. It was only your own clumsiness. If you will promise not to tell the Lord Manawyddan what has happened, I will do a little charm that will unburn your feet at once."

"Do it then," said Kigva, "and I will not."

He did it, and she felt of her feet wonderingly, finding the skin as white and smooth as ever. Then she said curiously to the bogey, "Why are you afraid of the Lord Manawyddan? He is the kindest of men."

"He could blow me away onto the upper winds, Lady."

"He has not got sense enough left to do any such thing," said Kigva "But if you let me spill anything more, I will tell him and see what he can do. For we cannot afford to waste any more food. It is in my mind that we are going to be starved out of Dyved this time. And if we try to live anywhere else we never last long." And she sighed.

"You may not last long if you stay here," said the bogey. "For something is happening again, and every time something has happened before, somebody has vanished. And this time there is nobody left to vanish but you and the Lord Manawyddan. I shall be sorry to see him go, even if he is unreasonable at times." And he sighed too.

"Vanish yourself," said Kigva, and threw a pot at him. He did, into thin air, and she went to bed, but not to sleep. For long she tossed, restless and miserable and afraid, and then suddenly the sun was shining in her eyes. It was bright day, but when she rose she found that she was alone in the palace. Manawyddan was gone. So was the bogey, for the kitchen had the feeling of a dead place that can have no life in it, seen or unseen.

She sat down then and wept. And sobbing, thought, *I would not mind vanishing if I would be with you again, Pryderi. Whatever kind of place we were in, I could be happy there with you. At least a little happy. But what if we were not together? What if vanishing means being alone in the cold and the dark? Or even*—her teeth chattered—*being nowhere?*

In the gray of dawn Manawyddan had come to the second field. Had looked at it and seen that it was ruined as the other. Nothing but trampled straw and trampled stalks were left. Not one ear of corn remained; only the useless, earless straw.

He looked and he raised his arms above his head and shook his clenched fists at the heavens. "Woe!" he cried. "O gracious Mothers, who is my destroyer? But I know well who He is: He that sought my ruin from the beginning is completing it, and He has destroyed the whole country along with me!"

Then he strode away as fast as his legs would carry him. He came to the third field, the last that was left, and now the young sun was coming up, and under her tender rays it shone like a whole field of gold, as beautiful as any wheat that ever grew. He looked at it, and his jaw set.

"Shame upon me," he said, "if I do not watch here tonight! Whatever robbed the other fields will come back to rob this field, and I shall see what it is."

But when he went home and told Kigva his plan, she raged again. "Lord, has all the wisdom gone out of you? You that were once so wise?"

But her words did not trouble him, any more than if she had been a sea gull beating her wings against a cliff.

"I will watch the field tonight," he said. And he got out his spear, and all his other arms, and set to work polishing them. "I will be ready for whoever comes."

"Pryderi was armed," said Kigva, near to tears. "Armed he went into that place he never came out of. Rhiannon had her magic, yet she too never came back. Whatever will come tonight is strong—too strong for any power known to men."

"I ploughed those fields and sowed them, girl; I put my strength and my sweat into them. I will not be robbed without a fight." Manawyddan's jaw was still set; the look in his gray eyes was not his own.

Kigva wept aloud. "Will you leave me here all alone, Lord? The only human being left in this whole land? What shall I do? How shall I live?"

"I will watch the field tonight."

Kigva's sobs ceased. She said quietly, "Lord, I see that your own good mind has left you, and that whatever Spider caught the others has you in His web. Well, I will go get you a good supper; it will be your last."

She went to the kitchen, and called softly into the air, "Bogey, give me something to put in his food—to make him sleep here through that third field's ruin. This blow at least I will try to stop."

Above her the bogey laughed. "Girl, you are wiser than I thought!" For the second and last time she saw him, swinging comfortably among the rafters.

But that night it was she who slept soundly; so soundly that she never heard Manawyddan rise and leave the house.

14

The Gray Man Comes

BEFORE MOONRISE Manawyddan came to the field. He sat down under a tree close beside it, and waited. He saw the sky darken and the stars come out, that myriad shining host that each night keeps watch over the earth and perhaps prevents even darker deeds than do happen in the darkness. He saw the moon come up, queenly and proud among them, her cheeks flushed with the red-gold of harvest time.

He heard the sleepy twittering of the birds, and the silence that followed it. He heard an owl hoot somewhere in the woods. He saw the dark shadow of the Mound of Arberth loom black through the blackness, with a darkness so deep that it seemed no light ever could reach or pierce it forever. That Mound whose black side had closed upon the two he had loved best on earth . . .

He sat there and waited. The night wore.

"It is getting late," said the bogey.

Manawyddan looked around and saw him crouching among the gnarled roots of the tree. He was small; he was very small; smaller than the son of Llyr had ever seen him.

"You here! Where is Kigva?"

"Safe at home," said the bogey. "She cannot follow us or worry. I drugged her as you bade me, though I still think hers was the better plan. I do not know what made me foolish enough to come with you myself."

"You were indeed a fool. Your being is too light and small to face What will come here tonight. Go—go before you get yourself blown away, not for twice seven aeons, but forever."

"I would," said the bogey, "if I dared." He shivered. "Whatever is coming is already on Its way. I can feel that, though I cannot tell from which direction It is coming. Maybe It is vast enough to come from all ways at once."

"Then lie still; maybe you can escape Its notice. Do nothing, for you cannot help me."

"You cannot help yourself either," said the bogey.

"I can try. That is what men are sent to earth for: to learn and to try."

The bogey made no answer. They listened hard, but they heard nothing but the silence; silence that is always a web of a myriad of tiny, interlacing sounds. Their own breathing became strands in that web; part of its dreadful, waiting quiet.

But nothing happened. Not one footfall out of all those pattering clawed softnesses came near them. Not one sound took on size or purpose; any purpose that had to do with them . . .

The moon rose higher. The night wore. Midnight came.

It happened then. That terrible, blazing spear of light shot out, stretching from end to end of heaven, slashing across the moon's bright face. All the stars of heaven seemed to be falling, and as they fell, the sky roared with thunder. Earth herself seemed to shake beneath the force of that blast that was the loudest ever heard.

When Manawyddan and the bogey took their hands from their ears, when their stunned eyes saw again, the stars were landing. Each of that bright swarm, as it struck the earth, lost its radiance and became a mouse. And each of that numberless host of mice sprang light-swift for a stalk of wheat and ran up it. So many were they that the tall stalks bent beneath their weight as if before a great wind and crashed to earth. Then, still light-swift, each mouse fled away, a golden ear between his white, shining teeth.

With a cry of rage Manawyddan leapt among them. He beat at them with his spear, he stamped with his feet, but they ran across his feet and leapt over his spear. He could not touch them, he could not reach them, any more than if they had been birds flying through the sky. He tried to fix his eyes upon one single one of them, hoping that so he might make his aim true, but he could not, any more than if they had been a swarm of flying gnats. But he kept on trying; not again, as in that first mad rush, would he let panic overwhelm him.

Was one going a little slower than the others? The least, least bit slower? No faster than the fastest horse might race? He prayed that it was; prayed that hope might not blind his eyes as the glamour did.

It was going slower—if the swiftness of the fleetest hound or horse could be called slow. Its dark round sides were plump; almost

misshapen. Being fatter than the others, it found the great golden
ear of wheat harder to carry.

Like a hound himself, Manawyddan raced after it. Again and
again he thought he had it. Twice he fell, when it was just a bare
inch beyond his outspread fingers. Always it managed to keep just
out of his reach.

They were nearing the field's edge. Soon the bushes and tall
grasses would hide it.

He was gaining. It was a mere yard ahead of him. A foot ahead. An
inch. He put forth all his speed. His heart seemed to be battering against
the walls of his chest, as in the besiegers' hands a log batters the gates
of a fortress. His strained muscles seemed to be tearing with each leap,
each bound.

Not an inch ahead now. Not half an inch. Though the bushes,
too, were not the length of his foot away.

With a gasping cry of triumph he pounced. And fell, his thwarted
hands clutching the grasses: empty of all else.

But in his despair he heard another cry of triumph; shrill and
small, but no mouse squeak. A voice he knew. It changed, even as
he heard it, to a sharp cry of pain.

Manawyddan wrenched apart the grasses before him, He saw the
bogey grasping the mouse, whose sharp white teeth, already sunk in
his shoulder, were ready, as soon as its squirming body could wriggle
a little higher, to close in his throat.

Manawyddan's iron fingers tore it away: gasped with pain himself
as those sharp teeth met in the flesh of his palm. The bogey sprang
forward. "Quick! Put her in this!"

The son of Llyr stared. He saw a glove of his own, and a piece of
string with it. But in the same breath's space he was struggling to
thrust his prey into the dark opening of the glove. He and the bogey
between them could hardly get their tiny, squirming captive inside,
hardly make the cord fast in time to keep it from wriggling out again.

When the deed was done they looked around, panting, more than
half expecting to go down beneath a million sharp, fierce mice teeth.

But all was quiet in the moonlight. No living thing was left among
the bare straw that littered that lovely field. Every mouse, like every
ear of wheat was gone. For awhile they stared in wonder. Then
Manawyddan said quietly, "Force is not their weapon."

"They have got enough of it for me." The bogey rubbed his shoulder. "Both of us together could not have held her if I had not brought
that glove."

"How did you happen to bring it?"

"I had just followed you out of the house, Lord, when I turned back to fetch it. A little bird flew low over my head and told me to."

For a breath's space Manawyddan was silent. "So? Well, I thank you, little friend; for that, and for brave and loyal friendship." Under his breath he said softly, "You too I thank, Branwen."

For another breath's space he seemed to meet her eyes, dark and shining, glad as they had been in childhood when she thought that she had helped her brother to win some game. And he had always let her think so, whether it was true or not.

And this time it was true, beloved, whether it is yourself or my memories that I see.

The bogey said, "I would not have come at all if I had known what I was getting into."

"But you did come," said Manawyddan.

Silently they went back to the palace together. In the hall they found Kigva, asleep before the fire. She sprang up, her eyes still dazed from the drug, but when they saw Manawyddan they became two lights.

"You are back, Lord! Safe!"

"I am, girl." Manawyddan went over to a peg on the wall, and hung the glove upon it. "We have lost our last field of wheat, but I have caught one of the robbers. Tomorrow I will hang her, and by the sun and the moon, if I had them, I would hang them all!"

Kigva stared. "Lord, what kind of robber could you get inside a glove?"

He told her then of the plague of mice and of the capture, and her face grew troubled.

"I would not want you to let it loose inside here, Lord—there is no love lost between the race of women and the race of mice—but why not let it loose outside? It is beneath a big man like you to hang a miserable little mouse."

"Girl, I would hang them all if I could catch them, and this mouse I will hang."

Kigva shrugged. She was feeling ashamed of her earlier fears; mice seemed unlikely allies for the Power who had laid all Dyved waste. The loss of the crops was a bitter blow, and the old man was taking it hard. Better to humor him.

"Well, Lord," she said, "do as you please."

They went to bed then. When Manawyddan rose the dawn was not gray, but flame-red and flame-gold.

He took down the glove, and felt one quick spasmodic jerk inside it. After that his prisoner lay still.

From the firewood he took sticks with which to build a doll-sized scaffold. He put them and the glove into a bag and with it over his shoulder he left the palace and the sleeping Kigva, and started for the Mound of Arberth.

Dark it loomed before him there in the rising sun, a grim stronghold of old night that the powers of day could never truly vanquish, and even the rays of light that touched its summit looked like a crown of all-devouring fire.

Manawyddan set foot upon its slope, and the bogey appeared beside him.

"Do you think this is wise, Lord?"

"Maybe so, maybe not. We will see."

"I do not want to see Why challenge the Enemy here, on His own ground?"

"Little one, if force were His weapon He would have struck us all down long ago. It took Him years to entrap Rhiannon and Pryderi. It is by terror and by magic that He kills."

"And this is the best place for Him to do it, this Mound that is the entrance to the Underworld. Turn back, Lord, while you can! Let Him come after His mouse if He wants her."

"Another day in our world might be her death; I do not know the laws of her being. And only here, I am sure, can He show Himself by day."

"Well, good luck be with you!" said the bogey. "I am not brave enough to go with you this time." And he turned and trotted back down the mountainside.

Manawyddan went on. He knew that now indeed he was utterly alone; beyond all help from creatures of earth or even the loving dead. He had only himself to rely on now, and he knew that beside the powers of the Adversary any arts he knew were like a child's toys against the weapons of a man.

He came to the top of the Gorsedd; he came to its highest part. And there, with the red light beating down upon him, he set up two sticks. Only the crossbeam was needed to make a gallows. As he reached for the third stick he stopped stock-still, and his hand dropped at his side.

A bard was coming toward him; not a true bard but a singer of the lower rank, an old man in old, threadbare clothes. The man smiled at him and tried to meet his eyes, and Manawyddan suddenly knew that it would not be good to look long into those eyes. They were deep and strange, and as gray as his own.

"Lord," said the stranger, "Good day to you."

"The same to you, and my greeting, singer. But where have you come from?"

The stranger went on smiling; his eyes were still trying to catch Manawyddan's. "I have been singing these many moons in Lloegyr, Lord. Why do you ask?"

"Because for seven years I have seen no human beings in this land but four of my own family, and now yourself. And it is quickly and strangely you have come. I did not see you walking up this hillside, that most men fear to tread upon."

Still the stranger smiled. "I go through this land to my own. Perhaps you did not see me coming, Lord, because you were so busy with your work. What are you doing?"

"I am hanging a thief that I caught robbing me." For one second Manawyddan's sea-gray eyes met his and flashed like sunlit ice.

"Then where is the thief, Lord? I see only ourselves, and something moving in that love you have laid out there: something that can be no bigger than a mouse. It ill becomes a man of such birth and breeding as yours to handle vermin like that, Lord. Let it go free."

His tone cajoled, but his eyes clung to Manawyddan's, that he thought he had caught at last. They pulled and drew, as softly and inexorably as the tide pulls the swimmer caught in its silken-soft, irresistible might.

With a tearing effort Manawyddan pulled his eyes away. "I will not, by the Mothers! Stealing from me I found it, and it shall die."

The stranger took a little bag out from under his cloak. From that he took silver, which he tossed up and down so that it sparkled in the sun. It sparkled too much. Manawyddan strove to look away from it and could not; knew that he had been trapped.

"Lord, this is all the little store I got in Lloegyr, by singing and by begging. I will give it all to you if you will let that vermin go."

Again, with an effort that it seemed might tear his eyes from their sockets, Manawyddan pulled his eyes away. "By the Mothers! I will neither free it nor sell it."

"As you will." The singer put his silver away, shrugged, and walked off down the other side of the Mound.

Manawyddan bent to place the cross-stick on the two forks of the gallows, but his hands were shaking so that for a little while he could not do it. He was getting it fixed in place at last when he stopped, his hands frozen in midair.

A druid was coming now, by his white dress and gold ornaments one high among the followers of Keridwen, the Dark Queen of the Lake, the Goddess that is older than any God. As indeed is only fitting, since She-That-Brings-Forth is the first symbol of creation known to man.

"Good day to you, Lord." His deep voice had the tone of a harp.

Manawyddan showed him proper respect. This time he asked no questions, but it was not long before he found himself answering them. With surprise he heard himself saying more than he meant to say, though his eyes were safely fixed on the ground. "The creature is in the shape of a mouse, Lord, but I caught it robbing me."

Again the shocked protest, again the offer to buy. This time gold was offered, and Manawyddan had to raise his eyes, he could find no excuse to keep them lowered. The druid held the gold pieces in his right hand, above his cupped left. Up and down he tossed them, up and down. They shone like falling stars. They were growing bigger. They were too bright for moons. They glowed like blazing, falling suns . . .

He heard his own voice saying harshly, "I will neither sell it nor set it free." The voice seemed to come from another man's throat, from a self deeper than the self he knew. "As it ought, so shall it die."

"Well, do as you please, Lord." The druid, too, shrugged and went away.

Manawyddan sank to his knees beside the tiny gallows. His whole body trembling, he covered his face with his hands. Would he have strength for another battle?

When he thought that his hand was steady enough, he made a tiny noose, then quickly opened the glove. His fingers shot in and grasped his prey.

She screamed once, a pitiful little scream such as a mouse might give in the teeth of a cat, then thrashed from side to side, kicking, biting so fiercely that he could hardly hold her. Somehow he got the noose about her neck.

She went limp then, like a woman fainting, and for the first time he saw her body clearly. Saw and understood why she had been less quick and light in her flight than the others. He flinched and turned away his head, for the son of Llyr was a kindly man. Nevertheless he swung her tiny, furry body toward the gallows.

Then stopped, as he had stopped before, his victim almost falling from his nerveless hand.

Up the side of the Mound a High Druid was coming, riding in a golden chariot, and in his hand a sickle shining golden in the sun. Tall he was, and white-robed, and brighter than the gold glowed the crystal ring on the hand that held the sickle. That ring was of the holy mystic stone called *Glain Neidr;* that stone is made by serpents, and both its making and its using are among the Mysteries.

Behind him his following stretched down to the plain; splendidly dressed men in splendid chariots of bronze, drawn by the finest horses that the son of Llyr had ever seen. How far that line stretched he could not tell, yet he knew that it was better to look at it than into the face of the High Druid, and one quick flashing glance at those oncoming men told him much.

Their eyes were too bright, as their Lord's own were too bright, yet each man's eyes were subtly, strangely vacant. Not of sight, but of self. Each was like a single facet of a jewel, mirroring but a single beam of the light that blazed through those tremendous, sunlike, Otherworldly eyes that shone through the whole company as through a mask.

Eyes that must blaze directly from the High Druid's own proud, serene face.

Manawyddan clutched the mouse closer. With his free hand he set the point of his knife at its throat.

"Your blessing, Lord Druid." Reverently he spoke, looking carefully past that noble, high-held head.

"You have it, my son." The deep voice seemed to enfold him like water, with the depth and softness and strength of sun-warmed water. To lap at the edges of his mind steadily, gently, inexorably, as waves lap at the rocks that in the end they will wear away.

"Is not that a mouse in your hand, my son?" Still that soft, enfolding pressure, tightening a little, like a snake's coils . . .

Courage came to Manawyddan. He raised his eyes and met those eyes that were beaming mildly, benevolently, too dazzlingly, upon him. Eyes that he knew, yet now was seeing more fully than he ever had seen them before, their unearthliness burning through the veils.

"It is a mouse," he said, "and she has robbed me."

Still those dazzling eyes beamed mildly, benevolently upon him. "Well, since I have come in the hour of this vermin's doom, I will ransom it from you. We who are Lords of Life like not to see the taking of life. Especially when the creature is with young, and so sacred to the Mothers."

"By the Mothers themselves, I will not free it!"

"Look first at the ransom I offer."

But this time Manawyddan turned his eyes away from the shower of gold, and would not look. Not though its luster seemed to fill the air around the High Druid as though with fire. Not though it glowed so fiercely that the sun-brightness of it burned through his closed eyelids.

"I will give you all this gold and more than the gold." Again the deep voice enfolded him. "I will give you all these horses you see here and upon the plain, and I will give you the chariots they draw, and all the treasures they carry."

"I will not set the beast free." Somehow Manawyddan got the words out. It was hard, hard as pushing heavy stones uphill, yet he knew that he was winning. The unearthly force that was in him, as in all men, was standing firm. Eyes and voice were losing their power over him slowly, bit by bit.

But now the resonant deep voice changed; grew stern. "You who come of the Kings of the Old Tribes will violate the Ancient Harmonies? Slay the mother who is heavy with young?"

The hand that held the sickle was lifted, as if to curse. But it was no fear of curse or sickle that made Manawyddan shrink back, made his tortured hands close tighter on knife and mouse. The light of the ring, of the *Glain Neidr,* was burning through his closed lids. Burning with terrible, unguessable splendor, burning him with all the cold fire in all the eyes of all the snakes that ever lived . . .

He could see it. He could see that shining death as clearly as if his eyes were open and he held it in his own hand.

Desperately, agonizingly, he raised up other images to set between himself and it. The face of Rhiannon, young and tender, as a ray of moonlight fell upon it that night when he begot Pryderi. That same face, aged but more deeply beautiful, that second night when she lay beside him at Arberth, knowing him now, truly his. Pryderi himself, laughing and playing with his dogs; the dogs that the Mound had swallowed.

He opened his eyes; he looked straight into the eyes of his tormentor. Not striving to match sparkling fire with fire, but with that sea-cold, sea-gray look that had been Llyr's. That kept always its own chill, quiet depths.

"I will take no price that you have offered, O Gray Man, Son of Him that Hides in the Wood. That, I think, is near enough to one of your names, and another, I am sure, is Death."

That sparkling, beaming radiance ceased to beam and sparkle. Clouds boiled up suddenly, blotting out the sun. All that long train of chariots, men, and beasts shook, wavered, and winked out. Only the bare gray hillside was left. Gray too was that Lord who sat there in his golden chariot, alone but not diminished, baleful yet defeated, for all his measureless might.

"Name your own price, man of earth. I will pay it."

"Set Rhiannon and Pryderi free."

For a breath's space the iron jaw tightened, the deep eyes that until that day Manawyddan had met only in dreams shone with all the serpent fires that had blazed in the ring.

"You shall have them. Set the mouse free."

"I will have more. Take the enchantment and glamour off Dyved. Put back the people and beasts and houses as they were before."

"That will take longer. To gather together souls that have been born and reborn into butterfly after butterfly, dragonfly after dragon-fly—that is not the work of a moment."

"Yet you will do it."

"I will."

Mists covered the earth below. The Mound became an island in a gray sea of fog. Presently the Gray Man said; "The charm is work-ing. Set her free."

"Not yet," said Manawyddan.

In his hand the mouse struggled and cried pitifully; she had wak-ened from her swoon. Her small bright eyes strained longingly toward the Gray Man. So a woman in mortal fear cries out to the man she loves.

"I will not let her go until I know what all this is about," said Manawyddan.

"Hear then. I am a King in my own world, as once I was a King here on earth. And Gwawl the Bright is my friend—the man whom her father chose for Rhiannon. He still lies in his bed, sick with the bruises of Pwyll's beating. For in our world that wrong was done less than three nights ago, though in yours, where time rushes by like a frightened horse, trampling all, Pwyll has grown old and died."

"Pwyll sought only to get back what was his own. The woman had a right to choose her man."

"And she chose like a fool. She who might still be Gwawl's new-married bride, young and lovely—what is she now? You know best, who have kissed her wrinkles and tasted her temper. All the worlds I know of—and I know of many—are but training grounds, school-rooms for those to follow. But how a woman so mulishly self-willed as Rhiannon ever reached the Bright World I do not know. She belonged on earth, and she returned to earth."

"Then you should have left her there." Manawyddan's own jaw tightened. "You yourself—have you grown so far above us? You, who to avenge a few weals on the back of a man who tried to take a woman against her will, had a babe torn from its mother's arms to be the prey of a monster of the Underworld."

The Gray Man smiled faintly, wearily. "When I did that I had

just seen Gwawl's back, and those few weals you speak of were
fresh and not so few. Never will I forget that outrage; it is beyond
your understanding, man of a low, gross world. In Annwn, the first
world above yours, there is still violence; Pwyll won Arawn's
friendship by killing for him.* But in the Bright World we have
outgrown violence. We still war, but with magic and trickery, we
who have far more brain than you to trick with—and other powers you cannot dream of. We hate the sight and smell of blood,
and any sight or sound of the pain of the body. Those gross evils
we have banished."

"I am glad to hear it," said Manawyddan dryly, "considering how
long you have held Rhiannon and Pryderi prisoners."

"I have not hurt them," said the Gray Man. "Though I have taken
pains to inconvenience them, and wish now that I had taken more."
He sighed. "Rhiannon did evil—such evil as the Bright World had
never seen—when she plotted that violence against Gwawl. For that
blasphemous invasion I blasted all Dyved; I meant to keep it a desert
forever."

"So you might have had you let well enough alone. Had you been
satisfied with the capture of Rhiannon and Pryderi I never could
have reached you."

The Gray Man said grimly; "You sowed grain where I would have
no grain grow. You made fruitful a tiny patch of My wilderness."

"A small patch, surely. Kigva and I were not young lovers who
might have repeopled the land."

"You did enough. You set yourself against My will. Twice the men
of my household and my foster-brothers came to punish you; as bulls
and as stags they trampled your fields. But on the third night my wife
and the ladies of my court wanted a share of the sport, so I turned
them into mice. You think you have outwitted me, mortal fool, but
had she not been with child, you never could have overtaken her.
Now let her go."

"Not yet," said Manawyddan. "Swear me an oath that never again
shall any enchantment be put on Dyved."

"I swear it. Let her go."

In the gray twilight that he had made, the Gray Man was changing. Strange lights and colors were playing over his face and body,
that seemed to shift and un-shape and reshape beneath them, not
being fast in one form like the bodies that we know. Again
Manawyddan felt danger.

*See the First Branch of the *Mabinogi*.

"You will take one more oath," he said. "To take no more vengeance on Pryderi or Rhiannon, and none on me, forever."

For a breath's space the Gray Man's shifting shape became black as night. It shot up and towered above Manawyddan, reaching almost to the clouds. From his eyes flashed such lightnings that it seemed the old terrible thunder must break again over the Mound. Then he shrank back again to the size of a tall man. He beamed again, mildly, amused, with genuine respect.

"I swear that. And by the Mothers. It was good thinking in you to ask it. Otherwise the whole trouble would have come upon you."

"For fear of that I chose my words with care," said Manawyddan.

"Now give me my wife," said the Gray Man.

"Not until I see mine free before me. And our son with her."

"Look! There they are coming," said the Gray Man.

From the east came a sudden barking of dogs, the sudden sound of laughter. Manawyddan started and whirled around, for he knew that laughter. Pryderi was running toward him, his hair streaming red-gold on the wind, his dogs leaping joyously about him, while he laughed as joyously.

Neither man knew what made him turn his head . . .

From the west Rhiannon was coming, and in her face was a deep gladness, a new wisdom. The gladness outshone the gold of her robe, that was such a dress of shimmering light as she had worn when first she appeared to Pwyll upon that same Mound, long ago; only shot with silver now, as her hair was shot with silver. But never had she looked more beautiful to any man than she looked to Manawyddan now.

He set the mouse down, gently. He ran to meet those two, and they ran to meet him. The *Mabinogi* does not tell us whose arms first closed upon whom, but for a little while all three must have clung together, close as one body. What they said is not told either, and perhaps it is right that it is not, for those words and that hour belonged to them only, and perhaps the words would not have made sense to anybody else, anyway.

When at last they turned, the Gray Man had become a shape of gray cloud. Only his eyes were still human, if indeed they had ever been human. Beside him in the chariot sat a young woman lovely as morning. Even her shape was wonder and invitation and delight; it may be that in the higher worlds, approaching motherhood is not disfiguring as it is here.

Manawyddan walked across to them. He faced that grayness that was still a Mystery and a mighty Power.

"Do not think that I am gloating over my own cleverness, Lord. Well I know that of us two you are by far the mightier. But throughout our struggle I loved and you hated; ask yourself what difference that made. Ask yourself too—you who think I cannot understand what you felt when you saw your friend's back—what you would have felt had you seen your brother writhing in the agony of a poisoned wound. Had you had to cut his head off with your own hand to end his pain."

The Grayness darkened a little, as sometimes a storm cloud darkens. The eyes did not change.

"Indeed, I did underestimate you, mortal. You played your game well. Lamenting in the fields and grumbling in the house, and letting the anger over your loss flow free over the surface of your mind, while you kept the depths clean and cool—all so that I would think you a common man, a mere murderous earth-fool who might slay my Queen."

"So you could see into my mind," said Manawyddan. "I was not sure."

For a moment the Grayness turned back into a man again. It smiled. "We can always see into your minds, earth-fool. We can see your thoughts and if we please we can play with them, as a cat with mice. Use you as the tiny beings of the air use you, they that you cannot see, yet that bring sickness and death on you. Wise men of the future will learn that much—soon, as I count time—but in their puffed-up pride it will never occur to them that they are being used by their betters as well as by their inferiors."

"If you mean that we are only your puppets," said Manawyddan, "I do not believe you. We can think of enough ways to hurt ourselves."

"I do not deny it. And of yourselves, as you have said, you can love. Most of the time we leave you to your own folly—but sometimes we have a purpose that you can serve."

"Not often, I hope," said Manawyddan.

"No. And when we do, we usually help you, as the higher should help the lower. I think that no Lord of the Bright World will invade earth openly again. Mind is growing stronger, even among mortal men, and the walls between the worlds are growing firmer. We may play with your thoughts again, but only with your thoughts."

"Remember your oath, and do not play with mine, Lord. I have had enough of playing cat to your mouse."

Those last words reminded Manawyddan of something. He turned to that young Queen of the Bright World. "I am sorry to have put fear and trouble on you, Lady, but I was sorely pressed."

She smiled. "Truly you put fear on me, Lord. Had you hanged me, my child would have had to find another body, and my Lord might have had to search long for my soul. It might have fallen into Arawn's hands, and have been kept from Him long and long."

"Speaking of souls," said the Gray Man, "my task is done. Look down upon your land."

As he spoke, the clouds rolled away from the sun, and the mists vanished from the land below.

And Manawyddan looked, and saw the fields of Dyved all golden with grain. He saw herds and houses, as of old. He saw the smoke rising from the housewives' cooking fires, and he heard faintly the songs of the reapers.

"It is good," Rhiannon breathed beside him. "It is good." Her hand slipped into his.

On his other side Pryderi squeezed his arm and pranced. "It is glad Kigva will be to see us, especially me!"

They three were alone upon the Mound. Chariot and Grayness and that Queen from the Bright World—none of them were anywhere. Like dreams from which a sleeper wakens, they had gone.

15

The Seven Years End

AT TWILIGHT the son of Llyr sat outside the Palace of Arberth. Its
seven years' silence was over; it hummed like a beehive, and through
those many noises, all of which sounded good now, he could hear the
three he most wanted to hear: Rhiannon's, light and brisk, talking
with her maids as they cooked supper; Pryderi's and Kigva's, laughing and teasing each other. He thought of what Rhiannon had told
him, her mouth curving in that tender, half-wicked smile whose wisdom was not quite of earth.

"Tonight I think they will get that son they have longed for."

And her hand had touched his, and her eyes had made promises;
they too would have joy that night, though their child-getting days
were over.

He thought it would be pleasant to see his grandchild grow and
play about Arberth, as he had not been there to see Pryderi play; a
smallness and a round pink chubbiness, some tears and many yells,
and a great deal of laughter . . .

The bogey came out of the bushes and looked at him. "Good
evening to you, Lord," he said, "and goodbye."

"Why go? You have been a good friend."

"I know I have," said the bogey. "I am not embarrassed because I
did not go up onto the

Mound with you; I could have done nothing there. I did catch the
mouse."

"You did indeed."

"And for that you never could thank me enough. But I can do no
more for you. Rhiannon does not need me, and besides, she can see
me, and that would make it risky to play tricks on her. I did manage to

play a few on Kigva, in spite of you."

"Are you sure of that?"

"Yes." The bogey grinned. "I can afford to own up now. I am going back to the shepherd's hut. They need me there. I can do things for them and to them, and make them marvel at my cleverness."

"Do not do too many things to them . . . And good luck be with you."

"And with you, Lord." The bogey vanished.

Manawyddan sat alone again, and wondered if he had ever really played any tricks on Kigva, or had only boasted of what he would have liked to do.

He rose and walked a little way from the palace and listened to the hum of the evening. To the gentle music of the open fields, it that at nightfall is more soothing than any other sound of earth. He saw those fields, their gold dulled by the twilight, and above them the white width of the sky, vast beyond belief; darkening now, yet pure still with the purity of its unearthliness that mirrored the infinite. He heard the low chirping of birds, settling themselves for sleep, and he smiled. Good to be alive—alive, and with work to do, and those you loved around you. What better lot could there be in any world?

But in the Bright World, on his fabulous throne made of the stuff of sunsets, shining red-gold with their heavenly fires, the Gray Man may have sat and smiled. You *have worked hard and fought hard, son of Llyr, and for a few days of My time you have won. But your son has not faced his last foe.*

And in Gwynedd, in the Court of Don, the child called Gwydion, heir of Gwynedd, he whose greatness Taliesin had foretold, sat and played with his toys. As one day he, a man, would sit alone in the strange, rich chambers of his own brain and devise ways to play with other playthings. With men themselves, like fate . . .

THE FATE OF THE CHILDREN OF LLYR, AND THE END OF THE THIRD BRANCH.

For Pedants and Some Others

MY ORIGINAL rule was never to alter anything I found in The Four Branches of the Mabinogi, whatever I might add or subtract. But if I have not broken this rule in my treatment of the Third Branch, I have at least bent it considerably.

I have changed the disappearing magic "castle" into a disappearing magic opening in the side of the Mound of Arberth; But since castles came into Britain with the Norman Conquest, I assume that this one was a monkish addition. Chambered tombs, buried inside great mounds, are a definite part of the Celtic picture, though probably they were built by pre-Celtic peoples.

Since the location of Arberth seems to be debatable—the late Professor W.J. Grufydd said that the traditional site would not be appropriate for the capital of Dyved—I have taken the liberty of placing it near the Preseli Mountains, where we are definitely told that his nobles conferred with Pwyll—or, rather, gave him orders.

Geologists agree that the Preseli Mountains must have been the original home of Stonehenge's famous "bluestones," so that gave me another batch of ideas. It also provided motivation for Pryderi's somewhat mysterious mounting of the Mound. The *Mabinogion* does not consider it necessary to say why he suddenly took it into his head to do such a risky thing, but we modern authors have to give our characters reasons for their most unreasonable actions. We lack the glorious freedom of the old bards, and perhaps that is just as well.

I take it that the original Mound, wherever it stood (or did not stand), had attached to it some grim pagan ritual which the monkish transcribers of the *Mabinogion* either did not understand or wished to suppress.

They also probably did not think that magic powers should be attributed to so good a man as Manawyddan, but he belonged to the mightiest kingly house in the Four Branches, and of these royal houses Sir John Rhys said: ". . . the kings are mostly the greatest magicians of their time . . . the ruling class in these stories . . . had their magic handed down from generation to generation." So I have felt free to de-whitewash Manawyddan and have him perform several of the magic tricks attributed to his Irish counterpart, Manannan mac Lir. The resemblance of one of these to the famous Hindu "rope trick" seems to me very interesting.

If Gawain's renowned "Green Knight" really should be called the Gray Knight, as many think, (Irish *glas* meaning either gray or green), a connection with our Gray Man seems clear. And in his fascinating *The Corpse and the King,* the distinguished scholar Heinrich Zimmer identified this mysterious Knight with Death Himself.

The Island of the Mighty

*Dedicated to My Mother and to Her Mother,
the two who first had faith in Gurydion and in me,
and to all who, known or unknown to themselves
have helped.
May that help return to them!*

Foreword

THIS IS the Tale of Mâth, Son of Mathonwy King and perhaps originally High-God of Gwynedd in the druidic days of Britain, not quite as it is told in the ancient *Red Book of Hergest.* I have altered little, but added much.

I owe many thanks to Professor Robinson, of Harvard University, who made me a special translation of some obscure passages dealing with Gwydion's metamorphoses; also to Miss Elizabeth Albee Adams of Quincy, Massachusetts, for the use of her article, "The Bards of Britain" and to my cousin, Clifton Joseph Furness, author of *The Genteel Female,* who procured me the help of both. I should also thank the late Sir John Rhys. Doubtless no man today could gather again the harvest he reaped among the Welsh country people. Old beliefs and traditions are fading everywhere. Without those he saved and his clear, careful analysis of ancient British customs to build on, this book could not have been written. He might be annoyed with some sections of the house I have built over those foundation-stones. Nobody can prove that the two social systems implied in *The Mabinogion* ever met while both were still in full force—just as nobody can really prove that they didn't. But when peoples like the Picts first began to suspect what mid-Victorians would have called the "facts of life" they must have gossiped and speculated very much as the people in this book do. Even nowadays there is nothing so laughable as a new idea.

Neither has anyone but myself ever suggested that the tribes of Gwynedd and Dyved were of different races. But Pryderi, succeeding his father Pwyll upon the throne of Dyved, shows us that fatherhood must have been an acknowledged and accepted fact there, while in Gwynedd the Pictish custom of the mother-right still prevailed. So it seems valid to picture the strife between the two kingdoms as part of the great prehistoric struggle in the Isle of Britain, the Celtic later invaders being fiercely resented by the Picts or Prydyn, the earlier lords of the island.

—EVANGELINE WALTON

BOOK ONE

THE PIGS OF PRYDERI

Which was first, is it darkness, is it light?
Or Adam, when he existed, on what day was he created?
Or under the earth's surface, what the foundation?
Whence come night and day?
The ebullition of the sea,
How is it not seen?
There are three fountains
In the mountain' of roses,
There is a Caer of defence
Under the ocean's wave.
Illusive greeter,
What is the porter's name? . . .
Who will measure Uffern *? . . .
What the size of its stones?
Or the tops of its whirling trees?
Who bends them so crooked?
Or what fumes may be
About their stems?
Is it Lleu and Gwydyon
That perform their arts?
Or do they know books
When they do?
Whence come night and flood? . . .
Whither flies night from day;
And how is it not seen?

> *(From the First Book of Taliessin, as translated in*
> *Skene's Four Ancient Books of Wales.)*

*The Underworld.

1

The Love-Sickness
of Gilvaethwy

GILVAETHWY the son of Dôn was in a bad way. His face, that had once been round and merry as the moon, was grown long and lean as a hungry wolf-hound's, and his sun-browned skin had bleached to a green and sickly pallor rather like that of an anemic cabbage.

He had forgotten how to laugh and how to joke, though jokes and laughter had once made up the greater part of his conversation. He who had been wont to be in the joyous thick of every game and every fray now barricaded himself behind that new long face as behind a wall, and he sat in corners and moped. His temper had soured on him and his appetite had left him.

His trouble was not of a new or a strange kind. It wore skirts, and was footholder to his uncle, Mâth the Ancient, King of Gwynedd, who held court at Caer Dathyl.* Goewyn was her name, daughter of Pebin of Dol Pebin in Arvon, and she was the loveliest girl of her land and time, save perhaps for Gilvaethwy's own sister, sun-bright Arianrhod, who lived in her own castle in the sea.

What was new was for love to be a trouble to this youth. Girls usually came and went easily with Gilvaethwy. Either they made eyes at him and he followed them acceptingly, or they pretended to flee from him and he caught them; and afterwards he forgot them again with the same satisfied ease with which they forgot him.

But Goewyn was another matter. She would have been nowise willing to give up her honored post at court (which required ritual virginity and included not only the holding of the king's feet, and

*Pen y Gair in Carnarvonshire in modern Wales. Gwynedd, *Gwyneth:* Welsh *dd* has the sound of th in they.

even the scratching of the royal skin whenever it committed the treason of itching, but also the valued perquisites of tax-exemption and
a share in the gift money of the king's guests), to become either
Gilvaethwy's wife or sweetheart.

And to live with an unattainable desire always under one's nose
but just out of reach is the most aggravating of conditions and the
greatest increaser of desire. It was not good for Gilvaethwy.

Lacking Goewyn he lacked everything; the air itself was sour to
his breathing, and food to his taste. He made himself a cocoon of
gloom in which he lived hazily and miserably, without hope of hatching. Yet he had no wish to advertise his condition. He may have
feared consequences, for love-sickness, though then recognized as a
disease in the Three Isles of Prydain,* was not one towards which
elder male relatives were invariably sympathetic. That his uncle's
curative methods, however drastic, might have taken his mind off
Goewyn and thus automatically have restored his sense of propor-
tion, never occurred to him, or if it did it failed to interest him. He
did not wish to be cured.

So he was alarmed one day when he became aware that his
brother Gwydion's eyes were dwelling on his face, for that which
Gwydion's eyes missed had to be something even smaller than nothing. They were now boring into and searching and mapping his
young brother's long face as though they would dig up the lengthening thoughts behind it.

"Boy," he said, "what is the matter with you?"

Gilvaethwy tried to think of an ailment offhand, but could not.
His mind scuttered around hunting for a lie, but was picked as bare
of lies by that gaze as a skeleton is of lice.

"Why," he said feebly, "what do you see the matter with me?"

"I see that you are getting bony and big-eyed, and will do nothing
but sit around on your haunches and mope like a sick cow. Your
appetite is not with you either; and when you do not eat there is
something the matter with you. There always was. I see enough,"
said his brother, "and will you tell me why that is?"

Gilvaethwy fidgeted and looked with great interest at his knees,
and then at his feet. But his brother's look, that unknown to him had
for days enfolded him as lightly and completely as air, now drilled
him like an auger; and he could not squirm free of it. He said at last,
sullenly:

"Brother, it would not be good for me if I told anyone what the

* The British Isles.

matter is." And he added after a space, as Gwydion still looked down upon him: "You whom he has trained to succeed him doubtless know far more of Mâth ap Mathonwy's powers than I do, brother. But he has one power that nobody in Gwynedd ever forgets, and that is that the wind is his servant and carries to him every sound that is ever made, howsoever far away. I am not going to make any sounds!" he said with energy.

"Much good that will do you!" said Gwydion. "You misunderstand even what you do know. It is thoughts he hears, not sounds. If he were thinking of you"— smiling at his brother's sudden look of horrified dismay—"he would know what ailed you at once. Just as, if he were watching you, he would know what you are forever looking at the way a hungry dog does at a bone. I do," he said quietly "it is Goewyn."

Silence then. Silence deep as mighty waters, in which it seemed that the movement of the clouds in the heavens was audible, and the growth of the grain in the fields. And across that pregnant stillness the two faced each other, the boy's white, aghast look intent now as his brother's; the man's face enigmatic still, with its sword-straight eyes and whimsical, twisted smile.

At last, with a great, groaning sigh Gilvaethwy heaved himself up out of the deep pool of that silence. He could find no words, could only sit staring in dumb guilt at that face where no intention could be read and no thought deciphered.

Gwydion was the eldest son of Dôn, the King's sister, as it seems likely that Gilvaethwy was the youngest. The name of their father (or fathers) is unknown. Marriage was still but a recent innovation in Gwynedd, fatherhood a theory eagerly discussed by the young, and smiled over dubiously by the old. Women had had children for ages; it might be that the mystery of life's reproduction was an art that did not lie in their power alone, but all this was still unproven fancy. A man could be sure of kinship only with those born of his mother, or of his mother's daughter.

So Gwydion ap Dôn was Mâth's rightful heir and his pupil in magic and the Mysteries, nearer to him than any other man: Official Controller of the Royal Household, one who should above all others have warned the King of his younger nephew's designs upon the royal footholder, or else have dealt with them himself.

Yet inconvenient pity hampered him. To Gwydion the world was a many-storied edifice where to Gilvaethwy it was a level plain that had suddenly disclosed a precipice. Mâth's heir, instructed in secret things, had walked on planes of wonder and power and beauty far above the hot, earthy sweetness of the meadows where Gilvaethwy had always romped merrily all unaware that their horizon was not an end but an entrance and a veil. Yet at times, deliberately seeking novelty in baser pastimes, Gwydion, still turned back to those fleshlier fields. He was young enough to understand the cruel intensity of his brother's desire and its seeming eternity; young enough to side with youth against the sober rulings of age in that war which is as old as life, and shall end only with the world.

"But you need not worry," Gwydion presently answered that confessing sigh. "Since Mâth has not thought about you already, it is likely that he may not until we have had time to get this business safely settled one way or another. He is busy with the thoughts of too many people to take time to wonder what yours are, especially since you generally never have any. And do not sigh, little brother. That is never the way to get what you want."

"You mean that you will help me? That you will not tell?" Gilvaethwy's mouth came open and stayed so, and his eyes brightened in unbelieving radiance.

"I will manage it," said his brother, and sighed in his turn, "even if I have to raise Gwynedd, and Powys, and Deheubarth. For nowadays Mâth never leaves the court except in time of war, and assuredly you cannot get near her while she is holding his feet.

"There is a way too," he added, "in which war might be good for Gwynedd. Only do you cheer up so that if Mâth notices you he will not see anything amiss and search your mind for your ailment. For what I have been days in doing, he could do in a minute, and you might not like his medicine."

They went to their uncle, Mâth the son of Mathonwy, where he lay, huge and still as some great ancient mountain, upon his royal couch. His long beard covered him like a glittering snow field.

He was old, so old that the deeds of his youth are not now remembered, even in legend, and yet they muse have been high deeds and many. For he had seen the earlier ages and the world moving upward out of the mists of the Great Beginning. He knew the laws of the cycles, the courses of the earth, and the movements of the stars. Even the stranger yet more mysterious movements in the minds of men. He had been the avatar who saw it as the duty of his kingship to guide his people upward upon the foredestined path of evolution. And he knew how life had been in the beginning, and it may be that he knew dimly how it will be in the end.

Goewyn was sitting at his feet, which she held in her lap. But she did not look at Gilvaethwy. Nor he at her; he was careful of that. Both young men ignored her and greeted Mâth the King. They had an air at once businesslike and ceremonial.

"Lord," said Gwydion, "I have heard news. Some strange beasts have been brought to the South, and they are of a breed that was never before seen in the Island of the Mighty."

Mâth scratched his chin.

"What is their name?" said he.

"They are called pigs, Lord. Their flesh is said to have better flavor than that of cattle, though they are small beasts."

"So they are small?" Mâth said, and rubbed his chin again. Or rather, that place where it must have been, under the pale cataract of his beard.

"Yes," said Gwydion, hurrying over this detail, "and their names change also. They are now called hogs or swine.

"Who owns them?"

"Arawn, the King of Annwn in Faery, sent them to Pryderi the son of Pwyll. They are one of those gifts that have been passing between Dyved and that portion of Faery which lies in the Underworld, ever since Pwyll changed shapes with Arawn and slew Havgan in Arawn's stead. And this time Pryderi has surely got the better of the bargain, since he has added to the food and the wealth of the world."

"Indeed," said Mâth, and he looked at his nephew with those sea-grey, sea-deep eyes that none might ever read. They were piercing, and yet not piercing, for they seemed to look not at a man but through him and beyond him, into the far mists of the horizon and beyond the veil of place and time. "I remember well enough that that friendship between Dyved and the Dead did not end when Pwyll died and went to dwell with Arawn in Annwn, but was kept up with Pryderi. . . . And how do you propose to get some of the swine from him? For I can see that that is what you are leading up to."

Gwydion made an eager gesture: "Lord, I will go with eleven others disguised as bards, and we shall seek Pryderi's court and see what we shall see."

Mâth rubbed the fleecy whiskers at his chin.

"It is possible that Pryderi will not give any of the new beasts to you," he said dryly.

His nephew's quick smile flashed at him. "I am not bad at a bargain, my uncle. I shall not come back without them."

"Go then," said Mâth, "and good fortune with you."

But he looked at the doorway for a long time after his nephew had gone out through it.

"He has an intention," said he, "and he has energy. How will he use the one and carry out the other?"

Goewyn lifted her beautiful face from the contemplation of his feet. She had not looked up while the Princes were there. Of late it had seemed to her at times that Gilvaethwy's eye tried to catch hers; and she, who had heard much of the rovings of Gilvaethwy's eye, had no mind to encourage it in that pastime.

"If you fear for your sister's son on this journey, Lord, why did you let him go?"

"Because, soon or late, he who is to rule after me must act by himself, and it is good to know how he will act, child. Do we let the blade rust for fear that it may be flawed, when we know that one day it must be wielded? Besides, this is a good venture. A new race of beasts might prove precious to Gwynedd."

"A new race of beasts," the girl mused, and sighed with a child's wonder. "What will they be like, will they be as good to eat as Gwydion has heard?"

"That too is to be seen. Be it enough that they will come. Gwydion will bring many new things to Gwynedd."

She looked at him awhile from under the fine silk of her long lashes. She was not afraid to speak to him. There was friendliness between them. She was too young for long silence, and Mâth the King liked nothing about him to be twisted or strained out of its natural shape. But for a little while she was quiet, thinking out her thought.

"Do you then find new things good, Lord? My grandmother does not. She says that many new things have come into the world since she was a girl, and that it is the worse for all of them. She holds that the marriage-bond is a craziness, and that all this talk of the making of children is impertinent and blasphemous. Women and the gods have always managed that well enough, she says, why should young men go meddling and getting conceited notions into their heads?

"But my mother feels otherwise. The year before I was born she had a lover whom she would have liked to keep, but he went away and lives now with Creurdilad the Fair-Tressed, in Arvon. And that he could not have done, mother says, had she made a marriage with him. But grandmother says that it would take more than a few new-fangled vows to bind a man; that men have roving feet, and so women should have a roving eye. Is grandmother wrong?"

The King stroked his beard again. "It might seem that marriage has come too soon," said he. "For marriage is a noble and beautiful idea that the most of humankind are as yet unfit to put into practice, and in grasping at what lies too high for their reach they fall lower than ever they did before.

"In my youth men and women desired each other and were joined, and parted when desire was over-past. Nor was there argument or curiosity or lewd speculation concerning the origin of children, for these were the gift with which the high gods blessed woman: her share in the work of creation. We had no disrespect for women in those days. They were our loves and our creators, our source and our solace: free to give and to withhold. We warred and wandered and built kingdoms. We left to them the care of houses and the giving of life and the drawing of food from the earth.

"But when the kingdoms were built, when the red-hot metal was shapen and ready for the burnish, we too began to think of houses and fields and the training of those who were to come after us. And when our work merged with women's as never before, arose new ideas and new struggles and new curiosities—the shaping of unknown laws.

"So now when a man and a woman desire each other they begin to marry and pretend that their desire will never pass, and that the eyes of neither will ever stray to another. And an unmarried woman must pretend to look with cold eyes upon all men. Yet, people go on behaving much as they have always done. And there is no virtue in a lie," he said, "there never has been, and there never will be.

"So ancient respect for womanhood waxes dim, and young men develop a desire to lay violent hands upon this new thing called chastity to see if it is really as cold as it pretends to be. They convict all women upon the evidence of the one whose window they still find open.

"Yet change is inevitable and good and must ever bring fresh evils for its birth-pangs, because the energy in a new idea always stimulates the lower as well as the higher, though in the end only the higher shall endure though ages pass ere it mold the world to its desire.

There is great energy in an idea. But these things are not for me. While my day is I shall rule according to the Ancient Harmonies, and with these new laws which shall be his laws Gwydion must deal when his turn comes."

"You have made it all clear, Lord," said Goewyn, "but still I do not understand."

But the King did not seem to hear her. His hand was still at his beard. He muttered as if to himself: "He should be ready. I have given him knowledge, but I could not give him wisdom. That a man must get for himself."

When they had left Mâth's chamber and come forth into the sunlight, Gilvaethwy stared round-eyed at his brother.

"How did you dare to tell him such a tale?" he cried, aghast. "He will find out that there is no such thing as a new race of beasts in Dyved or anywhere else. And what will happen then?"

"He will not find it out," said Gwydion very reasonably, "because there is such a race of beasts, idiot. And you would have known it if you had not been in such a state these three weeks past that you could hear nothing but the rustle of Goewyn's skirt. I never tell a lie to Mâth; he would see it in my mind and that would be unfortunate. If I am not telling him all the truth I think only of that part of it that I am speaking of while I am with him."

"Then there really is a new kind of animal called by that outlandish collection of names you mentioned— pogs, or higs, or was it swine, or all three?"

"Of course. And one pig, roasted, would be worth more than tumbling about with all the girls in Gwynedd, which is a thing you have done so often that it ought to be stale by now, anyhow. But roast pig is a new thing under this sun. There is only this one drove of pigs outside Faery, and plenty of girls everywhere, from the farthest shores of Pryderi's kingdom in the South to where the coasts of Alban meet the northern sea—and plenty more beyond that, in Gaul. Though virgins are less common, I admit.

"The pigs are there, right enough, and one day or another I would have gone after them. It might have been better to wait, but since you must either have this girl or fuss yourself into your grave, there is no time for that."

"There is not, truly," said Gilvaethwy.

Gwydion gave him a swift and raking look. "I wonder if you know how much we are risking," he said, "and how we may both live to sorrow for my soft-heartedness of now. Well, enough of that. What I have promised I will do, and I would not have promised it if I had not thought that I could manage it. Now let us plan our journey to Dyved. You shall come with me, for you need exercise if you are not to appear before Goewyn when the time comes as a whey-faced, shaky-jointed lover that any decent woman would spit at. Moreover, it is not right that you should escape all the work."

And for the rest of that day they were busy, for there were ten others to be chosen, and sometimes re-chosen when a few of their original choices found they had other matters on hand and could not go to Dyved. Also there were bards' dresses to be bought or borrowed or procured in various other ways. Harps likewise. All gentlemen had harps; these were the essential badge of gentility, their lack ranking a man as a serf. But those of Gwydion's choosing may have had a look all too suspiciously shining and unused. It was hard to find twelve bards in Gwynedd who could do without clothes for even so long a space as was like to be required for that journey to the South. But the genius of Gwydion proved equal to this, though it may be that some luckless poets woke in the morning to miss their harps and perhaps other more intimate and necessary pieces of their attire quite unexpectedly.

But by that time the twelve adventurers were well on their way to Dyved, singing as they went.

They were young men all that Gwydion had chosen, fond of a lark and a song and not afraid of a fight. There was not one of them whose mouth was not watering for a bite of the new beasts, after the hearing of Gwydion's tales—save indeed Gilvaethwy, who walked wrapped in his own dream. Pork had been hitherto unknown in Britain, save through the savage boar of the forest, the hunter's fiercest foe. And to imagine his grim wildness pent in a sty, waiting tamely for the butcher, was a novelty beyond the strangeness of dreams; as though the wolf should turn sheep-dog, or the eagle sing the thrush's song.

They hoped to accomplish their mission thoroughly, if not exactly peaceably. They thought it might be better if they could get their way without trouble, but they were ready to meet trouble more than half way. Gwydion knew their temper, but no doubt of his power to control it. Not one of them had one-tenth of his intelligence, and none could have been more fully aware of that than he.

It might have suited them better to swoop down and raid Pryderi's sty under cover of darkness than to try barter and diplomacy in the guise of bards, but Gwydion ever loved a trick, and he may have feared his uncle's opinion of open banditry.

Besides, the sty might be well guarded. . . .

So he enflamed his men with talk of the joke that it would be on Pryderi to welcome thus the heir and nobles of a neighboring land, come to seek his precious things, without suspecting that they were other than a band of wandering poets on the hunt for nothing grander than beds and a meal. He played upon the joys to be had in the acting of a role until he roused successfully that love of the drama which has been inherent in the heart of man since the first savage danced in the moonbeams, and perhaps before.

And as their steps drew farther southward, he told them tales of
Dyved and its greatness, and the greatness of its past, for there is no
glory in pitting oneself against any but a worthy foe.

Nor were these tales untrue, for though Dyved was held by folk
of the New Tribes that had come into Britain ages later than their
own ancient, magic-wielding race of the Prydyn, whose birth may
have been in lands now lost beneath the western sea, while the New
Tribes came from the far eastern valleys of the Altai, still had the
South had full measure of perils and marvels. True, there was no
magician there of Mâth's might. No tale tells that Pryderi ever practiced magic arts at all. But his mother had been a princess out of
Faery, Rhiannon of the Wondrous Birds, they whose sweet singing
could hold back time and so enchant a man that he did not note the
passing of eighty years; and Pwyll her husband had been a friend of
Arawn, King of Faery, with whom he had changed shapes for a year,
deceiving even the latter's wife and Havgan his mortal foe.

And the South was still called Gwlad yr Hud, "The Land of
Enchantment," in memory of these things. True, it had once been
devastated by magic in the days of Llwyd ap Kilcoed, the great wizard, and Rhiannon and her son had borne bitter captivity. But in the
end Llwyd had been driven off in ignominy and since then no enemy
had dared to menace Dyved or its lord.

"It would be a great thing then if we could do a deed against him,
we twelve alone," one of the ten said. He stood very straight, gave his
sword a flourish, and fingered it lovingly.

"And so we will, if that King does not see reason and give us some
pigs," said another.

"There are many kinds of reason," said Gwydion, "and some of
them are unreason. And it may be in those that our best hope lies.
But be quiet. I think he will give us the pigs."

"So do I," said the first, and there was a significance in the way
he said it.

"There should be no danger now that old Manawyddan ap Llyr is
dead, he who outwitted Llwyd ap Kilcoed, the great magician out of
Faery," put in a more cautious spirit. "He was of our own old stock
of kings—a brother to Bran who once ruled all the Isle of the
Mighty; not, like Pryderi, one of these upstarts of the New Folk who
have set the fashion of marriage and think they can tell what man's
a woman's son is.

"Who could be sure of that," said he, "even if one were positive
that there was such a thing as fathering at all?"

"It should be easy to fool such trusting people," another laughed.

"I do not see how they can reckon genealogies at all," said Owein ap Gwennan, who meant to be a herald some day when he was older and felt more inclined to settle down. "To make a lifelong habit of lying with one particular woman—a monotonous business at best—and then to say whenever she had a child that it was yours, that would be a great chance to take, and flimsy evidence to base the succession to a throne on. And generation after generation—what would be the use in keeping a record of such guesswork?

"Now all in Gwynedd know that Mâth and Dôn were born of the same mother, and the women still live who saw Dôn give birth to Gwydion. Our royal house is above a doubt, and our kings know that their own blood will reign after them. That is the way to have things. What you have seen with your own eyes you know."

"Sometimes you know things that you have not seen with your own eyes," said Gwydion. "There are many unfound knowledges in the world. And I talked once with a trader from the East, who said that his kings, that he called pharaohs, used to have the habit of marrying their sisters so that they might hold the throne the better and know their sons for their own kin, or some such reason. A better one than marriages are generally made for."

"That would be an idea," said one young man, scratching his head, "though it would shock the New Tribes that think it such a sin to lie with a woman of your near kin.* But I would not bet much on Pwyll's chances of having been Pryderi's father."

"Some say that Manawyddan ap Llyr was," said Gwydion. "He married Rhiannon after Pwyll died, and it is certain that he was keen enough to rescue Pryderi as well as his wife from Llwyd. But we are not interested in Pryderi's parents, but in his pigs."

"—Which you can tell more about," said Owein. "After all, if a woman's sleeping with a man makes a child, why does she not have more of them at a time? How can we be sure how many gettings into bed, or how many men, it takes to make one child? It might have several fathers; you cannot tell what goes on inside of women. . . . I myself have slept with some who have never had any children at all, and I am a proper man. You cannot be sure that that is what does it. It may be irreverent to the gods to say so."

* See Caesar's comments on the prevalence of incest—possibly only among the inland tribes—in Britain. He does not state that it was done for dynastic reasons, as in Egypt. These would have been political, the last survivals of a once universal custom.—Egyptian beads have been found in a grave near Stonehenge.

That night they ate beef at a farmer's house and dreamed of pork. But in the dark watches of the night Gwydion, lying beside Gilvaethwy on a heap of straw (the house was too poor and small to provide them with better), heard him moan and mutter in his sleep; the moan sounded like Goewyn's name. And with his lips curling in scorn that was not void of a weary tenderness, Gwydion put his arm about him and so quieted his sleep.

"It is a pity," he thought, "and it would be too harsh to put him to such misery any longer. Nature overdoes her work. For this is frenzy, not loving, and the only salve for it is the girl, who likely will cure him quickly enough. No woman is worth making such a fuss over, not even Arianrhod; and she is worth ten of that cold-eyed minx who cuddles Mâth's feet.

"Arianrhod I love, and could not be myself if I did not love. But if I never saw her again, or if she hated me, her beauty would be before me yet, and the days when we played together at Dôn's knee. I should have enough of her left to be a happy man and my need of other women would be small. That is good. It is more than these passing fevers that sometimes leave a man or a woman burnt to a crisp behind them.

"No human being, if irreplaceable, can ever be wholly lost, for the desire to touch and handle seeks the flesh and not the individual. And a thing truly precious must be drawn into the lover's heart and spirit to abide there an image forever."

2

The Magic of Gwydion

THEY CAME at sunset of another evening to Rhuddlan Teivi, where
Pryderi's palace was. They saw the round houses of the royal stronghold rising dark against the burning gold of the round, sinking sun.
So the buildings of the Southern court seemed as though mounted
awesomely upon a plaque of flame, and the adventurers caught their
breaths, remembering golden-maned Pryderi and his battles that had
never known defeat. But then they recollected deep-moated Caer
Dathyl and their own King, over whom even time had won but a
doubtful victory, and the might of his ancient wisdom, and his mysteries that were as old as dawn.

Only Gwydion smiled ever, without awe. . . .

But qualms lasted but a little time with them. They were tired
and hungry and soon grumbling again as they raced with dusk to
reach the palace. Their stomachs spoke, and their feet.

"I hope that King will kill a pig for us," growled one. "But no doubt
he is too mean-minded and stingy a skinflint to offer guests his best.
And if he is, I say let us kill him in his bed and help ourselves to all
the pigs in his sty."

"And help ourselves also to the spear-points of his guards in the
places where we would least like to get them!" said Gwydion. "You
yap like a pack of curs. Be content; it is possible that he may give us
swine for supper and it is possible that he may not. I am as hungry
as any of you, and you do not hear me bawling like a cow that has
lost her calf."

So he quieted them, but in truth he did not care whether there
was pig for supper or not, for his hunger was of the mind. His desire
was for a stream of pigs, pigs breeding and growing and guzzling and

being guzzled in Gwynedd forever, adding to the wealth of the land and its pleasure so long as the custom of eating should endure; and the fleeting immediate satisfactions of a supper weighed as nothing.

And the keeper of Pryderi's door admitted them, twelve bards, of whom some carried their harps as if they were more used to shields or spears.

They came before Pryderi, where he sat on his royal couch spread with stuffs of crimson and with golden embroideries from the East— a great lion of a man, though his golden mane was greying now and no longer shone sun-like as it had when he was Guri of the Golden Hair, before he got his second name of Pryderi (Care) because of the woe that was brought upon his mother Rhiannon when demons stole him from the guard of the Seven Sleeping Women, including the Queen's self, upon his birth night.

Now Pryderi the son of Pwyll was his name, which means Care the son of Thought, and today none knows what was the truth of these tales: why Thought went to Faeryland and slew a foe of the gods there; or why a Faery princess appeared to him upon a hill of perils and wonders; and why Care was stolen on his birth night and rescued by Teirnyon, who cut off the Demon's claw. Or if some know, they do not tell. . . .

Yet even these things are lesser mysteries than how Pryderi could have feasted for eighty years with the Talking Head of Bran, that was cut from the King's shoulders after Morddwydtyllyon, and yet have returned still young to Dyved, to a wife and a mother unchanged by time.

Either the scribes must have made error, or these lands they tell of were not the earthly Dyved and Gwynedd, but their counterparts in Faery, that first layer of it that lies in the Overworld, above our earth and Annwn; and their heroes were not men, but those who had already worked to freedom from the bonds of earth-flesh, the lesser gods whose deeds symbolize and inspire the deeds of men. For world may well fit within world, and each be but the shell of the next. . . .

But if so, these gods were very human, not over-upright elder brothers to men. Even if they were gods it is not strange that they are now dead. For death is the means of transportation from world to world, and a time comes to gods, as to men, when their work in one is done. All that is must pass through every world until it reaches the Last of All. . . .

We are not told whether Queene Kicva was present in the banquet hall that night that Gwydion came to Dyved, she who lived under Manawyddan's protection while Pryderi was in the power of Llwyd. But it is likely that Gwrgi Gwastra was, he who was of so much importance in the realm that it seems probable that he was Pryderi's son and hers, and of whom we shall hear again.

But we know that Pryderi welcomed the travellers well, whether he gave them pork to eat or no. For the law enjoined the giving of hospitality to bards, that never needed to lack food or shelter from land's end to land's end, if a house were within their sight. And a great and gracious king would have been generous, for his own honor's sake, in the fulfilling of the law.

But bards too must give. . . .

The son of Pwyll set Gwydion beside him at meat, and when all had eaten and drunk their fill, he turned to his guest and said:

"Indeed, and I would be glad to hear a song from some of your men here."

Gwydion looked around upon the eleven that were better at wooing women and encouraging a dog-fight, than at song.

"Lord," he said, "on the first night that we come into a great man's hail it is our custom to let none but the chief of bards try his skill. As you wish, I will be glad to tell a tale."

His own men grinned then, for they knew Gwydion's songs of old in Gwynedd, and had felt the power of his tales of late. So Gilvaethwy took the harp and Gwydion sang, and the hall rang with golden sound. Tones of silver he had also, touched with other colors that were tender as hues of the rainbow after the summer storm. And every word made the receiving ears raven for more, and the more they got the less they felt that they could ever get enough in this world. And when one tale was ended, Pryderi and his people would have another, and another, and others after that. But what tales they were that Gwydion told in song none now knows. All that has come down to us is that Gwydion was the best taleteller in the world. . . .

When the night had come to its darkest hours and the silence of the Underworld itself seemed to be pouring over the fields of men, they were still about the board, and all eyes were bright and keen, undimmed by the veils of sleep. Then Pryderi questioned Gwydion concerning hidden meanings in some of the tales that he had told; small, secret, hinted things. And Gwydion answered, though his answers that seemed to illumine like torches only swelled the mystery in the end; and it may be that none of them were true.

But at last he fell silent, and only sat staring at the King, his eyes bright as silver and deep as the sea.

Pryderi grew restless under that gaze. It grasped his mind too closely, enfolded it, like a closing hand. . . .

"Was there something you wished to ask me?" said he.

"Yes," answered Gwydion, and looked at the King a while longer. "I wonder," said he, "if there is any whom you would rather have do my business with you than myself?"

Those words were a warning. Had the King of Dyved thought, in those dark night hours, of tales of demons that must be invited before they can cross the thresholds of men, he had given a different answer.

"Indeed," said Pryderi, "that is not likely. For if you have not words enough, no man under the sun has."

Then Gwydion's gaze ceased to baffle and charm and grew straight as a sword.

"Lord, hear then my mission. I have come to ask you to give me some of the beasts that were sent you from Annwn."

"Indeed," said Pryderi, "that would be the easiest thing in the world to do, if I could do it." And he moved uneasily in the royal seat; for he had a sudden great desire, why or whence sprung he could not have told, to give Gwydion the swine.

"There is a bond between me and my folk concerning those beasts," said he; and suddenly found it hard to remember it. So like for a moment were those eyes to lakes in which he was foundering, a poor swimmer, who, if he were not careful, might drown . . . . "And the bond is that not one of these beasts shall leave Dyved until it has bred double its number in the land."

Gwydion smiled upon him. "Lord, let not that trouble you. I can free you from that bond. Do not promise me the swine tonight, nor not promise them; and in the morning I will show you that which might be traded for them."

"Be it so then. I hope that you can make good your words," said Pryderi. And wondered, the next moment, if he did. . . .

When Gwydion and his eleven went to the chamber where they were to lodge, the men of Gwynedd all acted stupid and sleepy, as indeed they should have been after all the wine that they had drunk, until they were sure that the palace folk were out of earshot. Then they all together pounced upon the son of Dôn like one noisy and enormous and clamorous question.

"What luck did you have? Did you get the swine? Have you asked for them already?"

He raised his arm and they were silent. His face had, in that mood and in that moment, all the command of Mâth's.

"Men," said he, "we shall not get the swine by asking."

"He has refused them to you? The skinflint! the miser! The miserable, unkingly, sticky-fingered, greedy old guzzler of meat and of songs of other men's deeds!"

"He would not give away a dry bone and it seven years old!"

"He has tricked all those tales out of you, and now he will give you nothing!"

"A decent king would have given you land enough for a whole Cantrev for half such a night's entertainment!"

"He will give us all land enough for our graves if you keep on howling out your opinions like this," said Gwydion, "and relieve us of all necessity of eating pig or anything else again into the bargain. The law that makes sacred the lives of bards is a very convenient one for us—as I thought when I chose that disguise—but it will not shield us too far.

"How do you think I am to achieve anything with such a pack of curs yelping at my heels? It is good that you were too drunk to listen while I was talking with him, or you would have spoiled all. I thought to charm him tonight. I have lost the throw, but there are other tricks to try."

"There are!" they shouted. "Let us go stick our swords in him and his chief men while they are asleep and not expecting it, and then open the sty and drive all the pigs back to Gwynedd!"

"And lose all the pigs in the dark," said Gwydion.

"We could fire the palace to make a light," suggested Gilvaethwy, whose spirits were rising under the excitement of his fellows and of the quest.

"And have the whole Cantrev down upon us before we had time to make a start for Gwynedd," said Gwydion, but he smiled.

The ten looked unhappy. They were like bladders from which all the inflating air had escaped.

"Well, how will we get the swine then?" they said.

"What business has this old miser to go setting on all the pigs in the world, like a hen on eggs?" they grumbled.

"It is only right that Gwynedd should have her share!"

"And he nothing but an upstart king of the New People, while we are of the ancient race that ruled all the Isle of the Mighty long before his grandmothers ever had the impudence to sail here!"

"And what did they bring but a pack of foolish notions about men and women and childbirth that set people to asking a lot of questions that can never be answered, and will still be making trouble for our grandnephews? Nothing else that was ever any good," cried one, "and even that is not good."

"Except the pigs," said another.

"And how are we to get those?" sighed a third, and scratched his head in several places.

"I will get them," said Gwydion. "Go to bed."

And with the words peace fell upon them, and assurance, and they went to bed.

But Gwydion did not follow them there. Long after the last of them was snoring he still stood erect and alone in the darkened chamber, and with a slim wand traced designs at his feet by the moon's white glow; circles he traced, and triangles, and other shapes and symbols whose power we do not know. . . .

Gilvaethwy woke once in that eerie, silvered darkness and watched him. He knew better than to become a disturbance by asking questions. But Gwydion turned presently and answered him as though he had spoken. They had strange powers of hearing, those who had studied the arts of Mâth.

"I am making a charm," he said, "and if you wish, you can go and fetch me some fungus, and then watch."

And that last was permission that ordinarily would have been eagerly besought and snatched at like the greatest of prizes when offered. Gwydion was not always willing to show the making of his magic. But Gilvaethwy suddenly remembered his unhappiness, and that it did not become him to be interested in anything in the world. He had come too near to forgetting that earlier in the night. So now he wrapped himself in tragic dignity and turned his face to the wall. He was a man in great sorrow and great longing; no child to be amused with toys.

"My sorrow, brother, but there is nothing anywhere in the world that it would interest me to see, except one thing, and that is not here," he said, and sighed—a deep, manly sigh.

"Is that so?" said Gwydion. "Still, you can go fetch me the fungus. I saw it growing near the palace gate. The exercise of that should help you to sleep and perhaps dream that you see what you want to see."

"If you had waited another breath I should have told you that I would be glad enough to oblige you, however heavy my heart was," said Gilvaethwy reproachfully, and sighed again, and departed. It may be that he did not altogether like that mention of dreams, for the instructed of the House of Mâth may have had power over dreams, and Gilvaethwy did not wish to ride a nightmare, or be ridden by one.

He had some trouble in finding the fungus, for there was little light. The moon was already bleached to a sickly and wan-checked misery; and it seemed to him that the wind that blew over the fields from the borders of Gwynedd was colder than its wont, and that there was something mocking in its whistle, a cunning not of earth. . . .

Dawn had begun to fade the night by the time that he had filled his arms with fungus and turned back to the palace. And in that grey, spidery twilight wherein all things are blurred and seem half of this world and half of another, dim shapes and ghosts of inanimate things settling now into stillness again after the darker, more active life of night, he entered and laid his burden before Gwydion.

Then, shivering too much to heed his brother's thanks, he tumbled into bed again and into sleep too deep for dreams.

Gwydion smiled on that sleep and worked on. . . .

He had much to do and to think of before the sun should be too high for the binding of spells. He loved his work. He may not have been so entirely certain of the failure of his comrades' plan for stealing the swine as he had pretended, but its carrying out would have required the taking of tremendous risks. And though he had daring, and had not yet outgrown flashes of the primitive battle joy that was his friends ecstasy, he seldom took risks unnecessarily, at least for slight aims.

For to him a well-turned trick was always better than the most glorious battle, as indeed the pleasures of his body were all but always underlings to those of his mind. Marvelous the coordination of warlike hand and leg and eye might be, but far greater adventures were to be won through the brain that, after all, must ever direct hand and leg and eye.

Mâth's mysterious sap of divinity was not in him, but he was the forerunner of the intellect: the first man of a world that was yet to be. He was an artist, one of the earliest that we have note of in our Western world, for those of Greece and Rome had felt the guiding hands of Egypt and the East. And he loved to use his wits to shape and polish a plan as his brother Govannon, the first of smiths, loved to use his tools to shape and polish a sword.

Perhaps it was his artistry that made him less scornful than his comrades of the New Folk and their ways. For he could not bear to leave a door unopened, or to reject new notions untried.

Moreover, he knew that there was something in them. The Triads name him one of the Three Famous Tribe-Herdsmen of the Island, and say that he cared for the cattle of Gwynedd Uch Conwy; and that probably means not only that he practiced mystic arts for their welfare, but that he studied them and their ways and the conditions of their being also. In those days the duties of kings and princes were often simpler than now. He may have held the sick calf's head on his own knee, and his own hands may have tended the horned mother in her birthing hour of pain.

And it is easy to imagine what experiments that brilliant, inquiring and unreverent mind would have led its owner into, how much he may have proved, through these mute creatures, of the reasons for birth and barrenness, and of the laws of life.

He was thinking of these two things when the charm was done at last and he lay down to rest while the sun rose and crept through every crevice and cranny in jets of airy flame.

"For I have noted that if I have a cow put in a field alone, she is barren, and if I place other cows with her she is barren, but if I let a bull into the field, even once, she becomes with calf. And after the calf is weaned, she becomes barren once more, and remains so, unless I let the bull into the field again. And if it is so with beasts, why not with men and women?

"Folk cry out that beasts cannot be thus compared with humankind, that such questions blaspheme the gods—women in especial cry it, grudging new power to men—but this is arrogance and fools' vanity, and has no part in the wisdom of my uncle Mâth. We are not so different; we were planned by the one Planner, and the calf is suckled on its mother's milk as I was on Dôn's. . . . They are co-heirs with us of destiny. All that is, is eternal and nothing passes but to return again, unless, at the end of the ages, it be time and change. . . .

"No, the New Folk are right this once. And it would be sweet to know a child one's own, part of the essence of one's own body. I have always envied women that miracle. . . ."

And he toyed awhile with that thought and caressed it, dreaming. The idea enchanted him. In its realization might have flowered in fragrant bloom the tenderness whose bud he felt for Gilvaethwy, and which had brought him on this errand, as he well knew, at an unpropitious time. But now the bridge was crossed and there could be no turning back.

"For I will not go back to Gwynedd shamed and pigless. Mâth would say nothing, but I would read it in the calm behind his eyes that I was young and unripe, and over-sure of my own powers. And Gilvaethwy would not be helped. . . ."

He brooded awhile and then his thoughts turned back to sweeter paths. "A child? Yes, I could get a child—but how be sure that the one that came was mine? Marriage is an awkward and uncertain shift, at best. The New Folk might have thought up a better while they were about it; yet how could they when even I cannot? It would be unfair to ask faithfulness of women when we should find it so dull ourselves. Yet faithfulness would be essential. . . . But I will sleep now. Soon I must go to Pryderi."

And within his own being he gave whatever orders were necessary and slept. . . .

The day was fresh and golden as a young maid's hair when Gwydion came again to Pryderi where he sat in his seat of state.

"Lord," he said, "good day to you."

"May the gods prosper you," said Pryderi. "I hope that you and your comrades found all to your liking in the lodging I gave you. But you must have, for your look is fresh and bright-eyed as though you had slept like a child; though that is the nature of youth." And he sighed for his own youth, that had gone in the long years of entertaining the Head of Bran after the slaughter of Morddwydtyllyon, and in the years that seemed longer when he wandered through Britain with Manawyddan son of Llyr, homeless fugitives both, while Dyved lay under the charms of Llwyd.

But Gwydion smiled and said: "We have naught to complain of, Lord. Your hospitality is great as your name, and it would be a man's own fault if he went sleepless here. But I have come to keep my word. I have the wherewithal to trade for the swine. Come to the door of the palace and you shall see."

So Pryderi went to the door of the palace and outside he saw Gwydion's eleven men standing watch over twelve horses with bridles and saddles of gold, champing on bits of gold; twelve white-breasted greyhounds with collars and leashes of gold; and twelve round gold-covered shields that sparkled like a heap of small suns upon the stones. Or like late-lingering stars that had been surprised by day and had fallen, in the haste of their flight, from heaven.

Pryderi looked and he thought that each of the twenty-four animals in turn seemed the finest that its kind had ever produced; yet when he looked back from the last beast that had seemed supreme among supremacies to the first, that one was still as fair as ever, and as uniquely superb. And the gleam of the gold dazzled him until it seemed to enlarge and fill earth and sky with its shining, and he would have been glad to look away but could not. Yet when at last he did, Gwydion was still smiling upon him with his quiet, subtle smile. But Gwydion said nothing at all.

"It is these you would give for the swine?" the King stammered. And suddenly wished, he knew not why, that he had not been first to speak.

"It is these," said Gwydion, and his eyes never left him. "Are they not double the number of twelve pigs, Lord? And the shields thrown in also, for not one tiniest piglet more. Will not your people say that you have driven a good bargain and won a treasure far more precious than a few of the new beasts?"

"That is right," said Pryderi, "and yet there is something wrong with it." Then he looked away from Gwydion and the gold, for both worked on his head in some strange way like that of wine, and he felt better when he was not looking at them. "I will take counsel with my people," said he. "I have made a bond with them, and I will not do anything that could be said to break that bond. They shall agree to our bargain before it is sealed."

"So be it," said Gwydion, and smiled.

But at the door of the palace the King stopped and looked back a moment at his young guest. "There is one thing I would like well to know," he said. "How did you get all these creatures here by morning? You did not bring them with you, or my men would have spoken of them last night. They are not things to be overlooked."

"I sent a messenger for them in the night," said Gwydion, and said no more.

By noon Pryderi's chief men and nobles were assembled and they talked of Gwydion's offer in sight of the glittering things that he had brought. Nor was there one that did not marvel over these treasures, the splendid beasts and the gleaming gold; nor loathe in his heart the thought that such riches might leave Dyved, and be seen there no more. Yet the new beasts too were a unique and priceless possession, a race of beings that had come from out the glamorous, mystical regions of Faery, and were held by Dyved alone, of all the lands of earth, her singular and choice crown.

"And what are dogs and horses against that?" said one. "We have had dogs and horses for ages; and nobody else in the world has pigs at all."

But another looked at Gwydion's horses and hounds, at the light that gleamed from collars and saddles and shields. "We have not had many dogs and horses like those, nor trapped like those," said he. "And even if we give up twelve the new race of beasts will continue to breed in Dyved. Nor is it wise perhaps to keep this gift of the gods altogether to ourselves, for that would breed envy and greed in other lands and cause our borders to be harried again as they were in the old days before Pryderi stood strong and safe as Lord of all the South."

"Let them attack us if they dare!" cried one who was younger, laughing boldly. "That will be good sport too—good as eating pig. I have a little one here who is thirsty for a drink from the veins of such visitors!" And he patted the sword at his side.

"That is right!" exclaimed another of his own years. "We can hold what is our own! And anybody who thinks he has a right to share in it had better think otherwise. Such caution is old man's talk and folly!" But for all that bravery of words his eyes dwelt longingly on the beasts and the gold.

"Be silent, puppies!" said Pryderi, "and keep your tongues off your betters until you too have fought a war or two. I am glad to know that my young men's sword-arms are ready, but there is no glory in being ungenerous, nor in stirring up hatreds through niggardliness. And there is here no talk of invasions or battles; we are being offered a fair exchange for the pigs."

"That is true too!" said they and looked long on the splendors that were Gwydion's proffered price.

"What I would like to know," said a captain of war, rubbing his whiskers, "is where a wandering chief of bards got all these treasures from. He is other than he seems."

"Doubtless some king who dwells afar gave him them for his songs, as he might well do," said Pryderi. "Or else the young man is in the service of some other king in the Isle of the Mighty, and offers this price on his behalf. I would he were in mine," he sighed, "for I have not been so well entertained in years as I was last night."

"We should find out from whom he comes then!" said the young men zealously. "He should be inquired into!"

Then an aged man who had been steward to Pwyll, Pryderi's father, and likewise to Manawyddan ap Llyr, the brother of Bran the Blessed and husband to Queen Rhiannon in her later days, looked up and spoke from out of his pale, thin beard:

"Lord, the stranger has a golden tongue. His voice last night was the sweetest sound that I have heard in the hall since your mother, Queen Rhiannon, passed and her birds flew back to Faeryland. But there was magic in his song as in theirs, spells that come from greater realms than mortals know. And if there was magic in his coming, may there not have been guile also? Remember Llwyd, and the days when you bore the knockers of his palace about your neck."

"No visitant from Faery would come seeking pigs," Pryderi said. "They have enough of them there, and to spare."

"Yet there are tribes in the Isle of the Mighty who deal in magic arts also," said the old man, shaking his head. "They who were here before us and are wiser than we in old wisdoms that men wrung from the gods in earlier days before the wall was firm between the worlds. Among them there are masters of glamour and dealers in illusion who could steal a man's own senses and make his very thought obey their will. They have no cause to love us who invaded their island, and they do not forget. They are very wily Lord," said he.

"Those simple-minded folk who do not even know why women have children!" one young noble said and laughed scornfully; and all the young men laughed with him. "I would like well to see them try to play a trick on us! They mutter of magic because they were not strong enough to drive us out with spears, and now they would hide their weakness with silly mummings. Nitwits who do not even know that a woman cannot get with child by herself!"

"But maybe they are not such fools at that," he laughed, "to count kinship only by birth, for their women are so untrustworthy that there would be no telling any other way. I have been among those tribes!" And he preened himself and licked his lips as if over pleasant memories.

"Are they worse than men? Are they worse than our own women would be if they were not afraid to break faith?" the old man demanded. "You are young and you do not know how strangely ignorance and wisdom may be blended. To each race its own secret gifts. The Old Tribes are as I have said." He turned again to Pryderi. "The Lord Manawyddan, your second father, knew something of that power, Lord. He weighed it well when he freed you and your mother before he would trust word or bond of Llwyd."

Pryderi turned and grimly stared into silence that youth who had mocked at the ancient servitor of his house. Then he said gently to the old man: "I know it well. But Llwyd was of Faery, and that power is going from the Old Tribes. There is no such lord of illusion left, unless it be Mâth, the old wizard King of Gwynedd; and he has never meddled with us, nor we with him."

"Mâth ap Mathonwy is an honorable man," said one of the captains, "but Gwydion his heir is said to be wily, and his uncle's pupil in his secret arts."

"Mâth has always been content to hold what he has," added the old steward, "but Gwydion is young and will want new things."

"Gwydion, Prince of Gwynedd?" said Pryderi, and it seemed to him for a second as though a voice of warning rang in his brain, or those words evoked a face that floated fleetingly before his vision, but that second passed, and the shields glowed round and golden and unwinking, and the bodies of the horses shone as sleek as polished bronze.

"We have no reason to fear magic!" cried the young nobles. "What matter if this bard who came from the direction of Gwynedd tried to use it? Our King has been too much for him! He would not give the swine for a story and a song. The poet has had to dig out his treasures and offer us a fair price!" And they laughed in triumph and looked with hot eyes at the gold.

"Yet he should be inquired into!" said others. "We should know all his purpose, and his prince's name."

Pryderi raised his arm.

"That would be an unkingly business," he said. "It has never been the custom of a host or a prince in Dyved to meddle with a guest's private business. He has done us no harm. He has made a frank request and offered us a fair trade. That alone concerns us. Do we accept or reject?"

"There is certainly no magic in that!" cried one. "The gifts are good. We have seen them, and what we have seen with our own eyes we can believe in."

"They can make cow-dung to appear like gold," the greybeard mumbled, but nobody heeded him, and he stared into the fire with his old fading eyes as though he saw there shapes and splendors from the fabled, faded years that could never come again, and perhaps also the disenchanted greyness of the years whose coming could never be stayed.

So they wrangled, but all the while the circular shields shone more and more like small golden suns, until their glow riveted all eyes as steel is riveted by a magnet, and that strange luminescence that played not only on greed but drugged like the light that is sometimes found in deep waters, or in the depths of an enchanter's crystal, sank into their souls. And Gwydion's will was done.

3

Flight

AND WHEN the sun was still an hour's journey from his flaming
bed in the west, Gwydion and his men set forth from the palace at
Rhuddlan Teivi, the twelve swine with them. They did not go in
haste, but they did not go slowly either; and they were glad that there
were not many to watch their going.

And the reason for that lack of watchers was that the men of
Dyved were drinking mead to celebrate the bargain they had made,
and all were merry and glad except only Pryderi, whose trouble was
a thought that he knew he ought to remember, but could not. It was
not far away. Again and again it crossed his mind, as swallows fly,
high and far and fleeting, but he could never catch it, any more than
he could have caught a swallow in its flight.

His will should have been bow and arrows to bring it down, but
it was as if another will than his lay on him, numbing and blanket-
ing it, bidding him forget. And that lost thought was: "We talked
until near morning. How then could that stranger bard have sent a
messenger anywhither to bring him back these beasts and shields
and golden trappings before mid-morn?"

But his men were merry, and Gwydion's men likewise were merry
as they took the Gwynedd road. When they looked back towards
Rhuddlan Teivi it was with mocking shouts and jeering laughter,
until Gwydion silenced them with a movement of his hand. In that
there was command that all obeyed, even those who were farthest
from him and had not seen, catching the vibrating silence from their
fellows and knowing what their Lord had willed.

"Men," said Gwydion, "do not waste your breath, for you will
need it. We must travel fast tonight. The glamour will last but a day,

and by tomorrow's dawn the illusions I have traded to Pryderi for his swine will again seem only the common fungus that they are. Else we would have stayed in the palace in comfort tonight, and not have risked suspicion by this sudden going."

They all stared at him then, for that was the first he had told them of the origin of the things he had traded to Pryderi. And though they had been sure that he had used magic, their inborn love of turbulence and commotion had made them a little afraid that the swine had been honestly paid for.

"So that was what you wanted that fungus for!" said Gilvaethwy, and forgot not to laugh.

"I would like to see Pryderi's face in the morning when he goes to look at his fine new horses and hounds!" chuckled another. "That will be a sight!"

And the exquisite humor of that idea set them all guffawing so that they could hardly stop.

"To think that we thought you might actually have paid the old fool a fair price!" they gurgled, "that you might really have given him all those good things; for we did not know but that they might last after you had once made them. But you were too clever for that!"

But a shadow crossed Gwydion's face. "If I were able to make real things so easily, it might have been cleverer to have given them to him," he said quietly. And for a moment it seemed to him that he was looking into the grey crystalline depths of the eyes of Mâth; and a thought pierced his heart like a wound: "Soon some of these gay comrades that are now exulting in my trickery may be dead because of it."

But he turned his mind swiftly from that profitless thought and let the mood of his men flow into and over him. He could delight in his triumph more than they, for his was the joy not of mere satisfied tribal spite, but of the artist and craftsman in work well done. And soon the battle and warfare that must inevitably come began to seem good to him also, and light harm beside the prize that he had won for Gwynedd. Must not all men take their chance at death?

But the others had no qualms at all.

"How that King will blink and stare and gape!" they giggled. "How he will rub his eyes and look again, and still not find his dogs and horses, and think that he has been robbed! That will teach these New Tribes a thing or two! They will learn to be respectful to their betters, and to the things their betters know that they do not."

"How soon will they come after us?" said Gilvaethwy.

"Long before we get to Gwynedd, baby," said his brother.

"I meant when would they march into Gwynedd," said Gilvaethwy with dignity, "not the little chase they will make after us. You could not think I would be afraid of that, brother. It is the war I am looking forward to."

"That is not far off," said Gwydion. "It will not take Pryderi many days to call his host together from the one-and-twenty Cantrevs of the South. But first you will have a nice long walk, little brother, to cool off your battle ardor."

He knew that what brightened Gilvaethwy's eyes was the thought of Goewyn and the palace at Caer Dathyl left unguarded by his uncle. But the other ten clapped their swords caressingly and preened themselves.

"Let him come as soon as he likes! There will be a welcome for him! We will give him spears instead of swine!"

And they strutted as they walked.

Their laughter made their feet lighter, and that was well. For now night was unfurling her black banners and drawing down upon them, and each shadow was a forewarning shade of a soldier that Pryderi would send at dawn. If they were not quick they would be taken, and they knew that if any of their company survived that taking it would be only the pigs. Moreover, they faced a night that would be sleepless and supperless. But they were not doleful, for there was a thrill in the thought of that race against pursuit, as there always is when the odds are even enough for the health of hope. And they had supped and slept many times before, and would again if they were not caught and slain; But death, the death of oneself, is something that youth can never really believe in, though it can with an entire ease, pleasant or painful as the case may be, envision the death of everyone else.

Our own hour must come, since all others' does, yet it cannot. And it may be that this is not mere sanguine strength of young limbs, and body, but some sure instinct of the heart that realizes what folly is even the dream of extinction, until age and pain cloud that first clear unconscious memory of eternity which we brought with us into the world, and we lose all awareness of our immortality.

Be that as it may, these twelve were not afraid, at least not with more than the little pleasant shiver of fear that adds zest to the game and fresh vigor to wits and limbs. For without darkness one cannot value light, nor without the dread of sorrow, joy.

They were all young enough too, to like prankish play and to chuckle constantly over the trick that their leader had played on Pryderi; and they had their hands too full for abstract apprehensions.

For the gifts of the Lord of the mystic Underworld proved obstreperous, also too short-legged for speed. Now one would grunt and squeal and dodge across the moonlit road, trying to escape into the fields, or another would stop and lie down and have to be poked and prodded into going on or else carried awhile in strong young arms.

Then, tiring presently of that strange undreamed of confinement against a stranger's breast, it would grunt disapprovingly and wriggle free and move off in the wrong direction. Only Gwydion would they always obey, for there was magic for all beasts in his hands and voice.

But morning found them already in a part of Keredigion at a spot which for ages after was to be called Mochdrev, or "Swine's Town," because they stopped and rested there. Yet they dared not tarry long but had to march on again through the green lands of Melenydd; and before they set off again Gwydion cast a charmed slumber upon the swine and bade the young men carry them. They protested somewhat at this, but he was firm.

"The pigs are tired," he said, "and we might lose some of them if we made them walk today. And it is certain that we could not go with much more speed than snails if they did."

"We are tired too," said the others, "and we are all nobles born, not burden-bearers. This is not a fit work for us," they ended with conviction.

"You will not die of it," said Gwydion. "And it was not to take your ease that you went with me to the South. You thought you were strong enough to fight. Are you so weak that you cannot carry home the prizes we have won, but must leave them straggling along the road for Pryderi? It is the first time that warriors of Gwynedd were ever as flabby-muscled as that. Take up the pigs," said he.

And they took them up. But they were twelve tired men who stopped the night between Keri and Arwystli at the town that was later known as the second Mochdrev. Each of them was nothing but an ache and a groan and a great longing to stretch out and sleep, save only Gwydion and even he did not stay awake long enough to practice his divinations and learn how close behind them the men of Pryderi might be. He fell asleep and dreamed of a Gwynedd full of squealing, succulent pigs, and of a Gilvaethwy hale and brighteyed again, eased of his lovesickness. But for that one night Gilvaethwy had forgotten even Goewyn and snored beneath the stars as peacefully and emptily as his comrades. Only Gwydion was never empty of thought, awake or asleep.

By morning men and pigs were both rested and they marched on together into Powys. And the place where they stopped that night has been since called Mochnant, "Burn of Swine." Gilvaethwy had remembered his woes and put on his air of tense brooding again, but the spirits of the other ten had risen, and they were garrulous and jubilant. Gwydion watched them closely for he knew that such a stage of success is like a drunkenness, and that they might become too enterprising. Presently they did.

There was a fight between two pigs, young boars that had perhaps caught the spirit of the hour from their herdsmen, and Gwydion stopped this, though his fellows would have liked well to see what the New Beasts could do to one another. But after that they looked long and meditatively at the swine.

Presently one said: "Why not have roast pig tonight?" And quick as light the others took up his cry: "Let us roast a pig tonight! Let us have something at last for all the work and trouble we have had!"

"Those pigs owe me a debt for porter's work," said one. And he unsheathed his sword, that shone like a frozen moonbeam in the firelight, and looked harder than ever at the pigs while he ran his finger along the sharp edge. "Let one of them pay it now," said he.

"They owe us all such a debt!" shouted his comrades. "And what better way could there be for them to pay it?"

The ten grew a stare and a greed that were focused upon the pigs, and it was evident that in a moment they would sprout a movement also. But Gwydion rose from his place in the shadows.

"There could be no better way at all," he said, "if I should allow it, which I will not."

But a clamor of expostulation went up from them at that.

"Lord, do not be mean-minded! Do not be like Pryderi. We of the North are generous and openhanded. We share and share alike in all good things! And it is just one pig we are asking for—one little lone pig—that big fellow over there who would be enough to make a good taste apiece for all of us. Eleven swine will breed as twelve when you get them home. And besides, that one is a he; he would not have little pigs."

"They would breed as fast as eleven," said Gwydion.

"Then you will not?" said the young man, and became very martyred. They looked at him like ten two-legged and angry incarnate reproaches, but all the while their hot eyes were still looking past and through him to the swine.

"Put up your sword," said Gwydion to the young man who had drawn it, and he gave that one a stare that was as deep as the sea, and as cold. But the youth did not catch it, for he was staring as hard at the boar that had been mentioned as if he already saw the fat haunches that were now whisking about on the little hoofs growing brown and greasy and fragrant over the fire. He still fingered the sword on his knees, and when the men saw that their clamor grew louder and angrier.

"Lord, we have carried these pigs all the way from Dyved for you, and now you will not give us even one. You have put upon us hard work that was not fit for gentlemen, and now you will not give us even laborers' hire. Is that a way for a lord of Gwynedd to act? You should have brought twelve asses with you from the North; it is beasts of burden you want, not good comrades."

"I did bring eleven asses," said Gwydion, "though they are shorter-eared than most."

But they were insulted by that.

"Is that all you care for us then? Well, we are men, and we will be treated like men. You and your brother are two, and we are ten. Suppose we were to eat a pig in spite of you?"

"Then you would be treated like men indeed," said Gwydion. And he stared very fixedly upon the young man with the sword. "Like men who have used a new kind of speech to a lord of Gwynedd, and a kind that is not healthy. You fools," said he, and his voice was like the sudden rising of a wind, "do you suppose I have tricked and robbed a king and brought war upon Gwynedd for the sake of filling your bellies on the way home? It is more important to get these twelve pigs safely home than to get you there, for there are dozens of dozens of men more in Gwynedd, but only these twelve pigs in all the world outside of Dyved and Faery. And if I had to blot you all out of life and sight to do it, the price would not be too high. But I will not do that; I am a merciful man," he said.

"So you will not do it?" they said hopefully. And they all moved forward towards the pigs again, though they had shrunk back a step while he spoke.

"No," said Gwydion, "I will not. I will only put a spell upon you so that if you eat pig tonight whatever other flesh you may eat again in all the days of your lives will give you such vomitings and pains and belly-wrenchings that you will curse your mothers for the day of your birth."

They stopped at that and looked at him and at one another with scared aghast eyes, and their faces shone white under the moon.

"Lord," said one, "could you truly do that?"

Then, of a sudden, the young man who was fingering his sword let out a screech and dropped it. And they saw that the sword was not lying flat and straight on the grass, but wriggling and gleaming

there under the moon. It was a shining silver snake, coiling itself to
strike. They all looked, and they all produced a simultaneous howl
and jump, and a leap that carried them so far backwards that they
almost fell in the fire. Indeed, one of them got a spark in his cloak
and had to be put out by his fellows. Only Gwydion stood unafraid
and alone in that suddenly emptied space and looked down with narrowed eyes at the snake.

"If you will pick up things and play with them, you should be
more careful," said he, looking at the quaking young man who had
drawn the sword. "That thing might have bitten you."

And the hissing snake still coiled itself and reared its dreadful silver head in menace, but it made no move to strike, even when his
cloak brushed it as he went back to the fire.

"Why must you tell them that you had brought eleven asses from
the North?" asked Gilvaethwy aggrievedly, after they had lain down
for the night. "I was not making you any trouble, brother."

"Which it is well for you that you were not," his brother said. "For
you have made enough already, and will make enough more. I know
what kind of flesh you are hankering after," he said, "and it is not
swine's flesh. And my mind would be lighter if it were only to steal
pigs that I had cheated Pryderi and had had to bring war upon the
lands and threaten my comrades."

But Gilvaethwy had closed his eyes, and appeared to have gone
to sleep.

4

The Hosting of Mâth

IN THE MORNING the young man who had lost his sword found it beside the fire where the snake had been; and they all went on as before.

Yet with a difference. For after a thing has happened nothing can ever go on quite as it did before. We may say that it shall, and that it does. We may even believe this. But a happening can never be un-happened and, faint or strong, its color will creep into the shade of all things and modify it with its own infinitesimal but all-pervading bit of change.

Itself becomes a thread in the vast web, one that cannot be torn out until time himself destroys the whole fabric, if even time can do that, for there will be happenings as long as there is life, which is eternal. And since that is so, memory must likewise be eternal in one form or another, and while there is memory the web of happenings must go on weaving, at least until there come the ultimate Inconceivable Change which is greater than death. So it is a serious thing for something to happen; or would be if anything that could happen could be serious in the end.

Something had happened to ten of these twelve adventurers. They had learned that there were forces too great for them to pit will and strength against; and they looked smaller that morning because they felt smaller.

But by evening they looked as large as ever, their self-esteem hav-ing swelled out once more until memory was merely a tiny but inescapable pin-point that might some day prick it into deflation again: one of the depressing beginnings of wisdom.

Gwydion had helped them to enlarge again by himself simply and

promptly forgetting everything that had happened the night before—
the course he deemed wisest. He had good control of his thoughts
and he could forget anything by the simple process of sending these
out in directions that he thought more practical. He sent them out
now in every direction of power save in that of the man who had
taught him so to control them—the man whom he was not quite so
anxious to meet as he might have been—Mâth his uncle.

He knew that he could count upon the attitude of the people of
Gwynedd. They would be delighted with the victory that his craft had
won over Pryderi and as puffed up as if it had been their own
performance. They would think the prizes that he had won well worth
a war with the ever dutifully hated New Tribes. All the young men of
Gwynedd wanted for such a war was an excuse. They would have
seen no glory in waiting for a day when the swine could be safely and
honestly purchased.

And Gwydion set all his resolution to willing himself into that
same mental attitude also. It would be the safest one with which to
face Mâth, who would not share it but always made allowances for
honest conviction. Gwydion, a pupil, could teach lessons to the
untaught, but it was conceivable that from his own master he might
still have to learn a few that he would rather have avoided.

But he was too confident of his own powers to expect this worst
to happen, and he did not let his thoughts, that might have been
read from afar, dwell upon it. He turned them to more immediate
dangers and wondered what Pryderi was doing. Himself and the
stolen pigs were now well within the borders of Gwynedd, but these
would prove no very effectual barrier against a pursuing and angry
king. Mâth could have learned all the enemy's movements in a
minute, but Gwydion was not so adept. He could not send his questions through the clear spaces of ether to pierce the brains of others
while he was both driving pigs and marching.

But that night they stopped in the Cantrev of Rhos, at the place
that thus became the third Mochdrev. They stayed in a house of
their own people that night, the greatest need for haste and the
avoidance of endangering others seeming past, and Gwydion let his
men be feasted and tell tales of their true exploits, and of several that
were not true, to thrilled ears and admiring eyes.

Only Gwydion himself rose and went from the feast and from the
house into the darkness, and came to a pool in the fields outside
where the mirrored stars were like candles under-water, and the
moon spread her light in a blanket of silver upon the glossy face of
the waters, yet would not yield it the wonder of her own ancient,

fabled face of mystery. The moon which is dead, yet rules the tides and alone lights the earth for love. For it is one of the Mysteries that lovers, who are earth's creators of life, never love under the sun, but always in the quiet dark under the cold radiance of a star that died ages before man was born.

But it was not for thoughts of love that Gwydion stared into the light upon the pool, and gazed and gazed until he saw all that was to be seen there, and all that was hinted but not seen, until that lustrous stillness became a whirl of shining mysterious movement, and then at last a curtain rolled away leaving him free to see in clear depths deeper than waters of earth, things that moon and stars had never mirrored there.

Arms he saw, and marching men, the land they marched through, and the fury in their hearts. He had drowned his consciousness in that moonlit pool as other men might have drowned their bodies there and it had yielded him the secrets of all moonlight, and all that he cared to know of what it saw upon the earth. Yet all this, that sounds like the work of hours, had not taken many minutes, for it had happened in realms wherein the initiated can escape time; and before he had been long missed he strode back into the feasting hall and faced his men.

"Comrades," he said, "we must be ready to push on with all speed at dawn, for already the hosts of Pryderi are on our track."

At that those who had been chewing stopped chewing and those who had been drinking set down their drinking-cups with a clang. Their eyes shone and their hands went to their swords.

"Is there a chance that he will be upon us tonight, Lord?" asked one.

"No," said Gwydion, "we can still reach the fastnesses of Gwynedd. It takes time to move one-and-twenty Cantrevs, but he already has the men of three on our heels, so there are no hours left for us to lose."

"War!" cried Gilvaethwy; and he leaned forward with flushed cheeks and shining eyes and tensed hands that closed upon nothing as though upon a thing that the others could not see.

The householders did not look very happy at these tidings, but the ten let out an exultant yelp.

"Why should we run away?" they cried. "This is our land, we are among our own people. If that old fool of a Pryderi wants his pigs back let him see what will happen when he tries to take them! If he cannot keep them when he has got them what business has he invading our lands? So long as we run he will follow; would you have us let him chase us into the sea? Let us stay here and welcome him!"

"No," said Gwydion, "I would have you take the pigs into safety in the fastnesses of Gwynedd, and then we can turn back in time to join my uncle's host and get our share of the battle. If we were to stay here now, before the men of Gwynedd are assembled, Pryderi would get his pigs back and the heads off our shoulders along with them."

They all preferred to keep their heads where they were, so there were no more protests, but a few grumbles.

"I hope that that battle will not be too soon," sighed one. "It would be a nice thing if it were to be fought and finished before we got there and others were to get all the glory while we were kept busy dry-nursing pigs. I still think," he growled very low, "that it would have been more hospitable to wait and give that King the greeting that is coming to him."

But low though the growl was, Gwydion had heard it.

"Do not worry," he answered, "there will be fighting enough to go around."

The householders looked unhappier still at that. Gilvaethwy had already become a grey and hollow-cheeked depression again. "Are you sure of that, brother?" he asked wistfully. "Sure that it would not be wiser to go back to Caer Dathyl at once?"

"I am sure of that, little one," said Gwydion. "And that there will be time enough also for you to kiss all your sweethearts good-by before you go into battle. Which is needful," he added, "because after all you might get killed."

"What do I care for that!" said Gilvaethwy, and became a beaming radiance once more.

So in the dim dusk between night and morn they ate the food the scared house-people brought, those peaceful folk who saw as yet no visions of a sty full of grunting, squealing, delicious food in the years to come, but only of the fire and sword that were like to ravage their farm and home upon the morrow. Yet they served faithfully their Lord's heir and his friends. And as for these, they left house and folk behind blithely enough and marched on with the pigs to Arllechwedd, where was the mightiest fortress of their time, placed in the highest of that district's towns, and so deep within Gwynedd that only conquerors who had overrun the whole land might hope to storm it. There a sty was built for the swine, and because Gwydion and his comrades, beast and human, stopped there, that town has ever since been called Creuwyrion, or Corwrion, though nobody knows exactly why.*

---

*Creu-Wyrion would seem to mean Wyrion's Sty, not Gwydion's, or the Sty of the Descendants.

But the morning after that the strange band parted company, for Gwydion and his men turned back to Caer Dathyl, while the pigs stayed behind in Arllechwedd with, one may be sure, all the injunctions that Gwydion could leave as to their care, about which he had doubtless inquired while in Dyved. But his men were glad of the parting, for they thought better of the adventure ahead of them than of one that had turned out to be all flight and pig-nursing.

And all the way to Caer Dathyl they found fields empty of people and roads full of armed men hastening towards the royal fortress. There were women weeping in doorways as they watched their men departing, and women laughing encouragement as they buckled their men's arms upon them; and children standing about, round-eyed half with dread and half with a queer scarce-understood elation, as they watched their uncles and brothers go.

Excitement hung over all like a subtle cloud that it was wine to breathe; and the veins of Gwydion and his men began to tingle. For they were young and strong and carried swords. None among them was a woman or a child.

So they came at last to the round, moated houses of Caer Dathyl, and into the presence of Mâth the Ancient, where he lay upon his couch no longer, but stood erect and armed for war. The sword-dancers chanted their war songs outside his chamber, and their circling blades made a spiky ring of blue and deathly light beneath the sun. All his chief men were with him, the nobles and lords of his Cantrevs, and the other sons of Dôn, among them Govannon, Eveyd and Amaethon.

Gwydion touched Govannon the Smith, the second son of Dôn, upon the arm. "What are the tidings, brother?" he asked. "What does all this mean?"

His brother looked at him in wonder, and then grinned. "You should be the last to ask," said he. "Pryderi is gathering all the Cantrevs of the South to give chase to you. It is a wonder that you have been so long in returning. We were worried for fear he might have caught you."

"He did not," said Gwydion.

"Nor will he," said Govannon, and chuckled. "I have swords and battle-axes ready, brother, that will chop the men of Dyved the way one chops a cornstalk. The night that Mâth first told us you were pursued I had an idea for a new axe, a beautiful axe that will slice into a person's brains as softly and easily as a knife into cheese."

"Is that all that you can think of to do with brains?" said Gwydion. "Your talk is always as edgy as your knives or as heavy as your axes,

Govannon! You cannot think of anything less solid than a lump of iron. You have not even asked whether I brought the pigs from the South."

"I have no doubt at all that you did," Govannon chuckled. "I know you too well for that. And it will take my knives and axes to get us out of what your pigs have got us into."

That was so true that even Gwydion could not find an answer to it, and the first craftsman of Gwynedd rubbed his hands and went on chuckling. But the elder brother thought with a moment's chill of his adventure and of the strange, far-reaching power of his uncle's mind—that mysterious, all-knowing vigilance which might have companioned him unseen through all the night watches and the days since he had left Gwynedd. "He knew that I was pursued. How much else does he know?"

Then outside the ritual clashing of the blades waxed louder, and the chanting voices of the dancers:

> Fire and water, blood and earth!
> Fire! Fire! sword and fire!
> Fire and water, earth and blood!

And all doubts left the heir of Gwynedd. He let the wild winelike music flow into him and over him, bringing him the turmoil of the blood that to the brain gives peace. He had acted for the good and the glory of Gwynedd, and his fear of Mâth's judgment, that had been in part fear of his own, was vanquished. Craft and wit had played their part and the hour of the sword was come. And who should regret it that was not too weak to have a warrior's heart?

Mâth had seen the newcomers, and he looked at his nephews from under his frosty brows. "So you are come at last," said he. "Where are the beasts you went to seek?"

"In a sty that I have had built for them in the Cantrev below, Lord," said Gwydion.

He went forward then and greeted his uncle, Gilvaethwy behind him, pressing close as his cloak. The boy was awed and astounded, for never before had he seen his uncle stand upright. Always since he had been old enough to come to court Mâth had lain encouched at Caer Dathyl, listening to the myriad vibrating sounds of the universe.

Upon his couch he had planned and upon his couch he had given judgment; and his nephews had been his hands for the doing of deeds as the winds had been his spies. Gilvaethwy had feared his uncle's magic and the power of his kingship, but he had thought that the strength of a man and the power of deeds were gone from him, lost in the unmeasured depths of years.

And now it was as if one of the immemorial cliffs had moved from its place and was walking forward over the fields of men.

"That was well done," said Mâth, "the building of this sty. And of the rest you have done it is now too late to speak. The host of Pryderi is within the borders of Gwynedd and we must fight for our own."

But the second sentence he did not speak aloud, and only Gwydion heard it in his own soul.

But the men of Gwynedd all echoed the King's words in a great cry: *"We must fight for our own!"* and their swords waved above their heads like a field of some strange and shining grain that would be baked into no bread but death. And outside the trumpets called and the clang of the sword-dance swelled.

"Have my men come from Caer Seon?" asked Gwydion. "Or is there still time for me to gather them?"

"Your brothers have gathered your men with their own," said Mâth, "and now they are waiting for you. Go you and take your place among them, for we march within the hour."

And that night they got as far as Penardd in Arvon, where they made camp. And in the distance they could see the campfires of the host of Pryderi gleaming like fallen stars; or like the red, baleful orbs of some fabulous, many-eyed beast outspread there in the blackness to threaten the homes and the lands of Gwynedd.

In the camp of the men of the North balled fists and sharp spears were shaken threateningly at those watchful little eyes of flame. And there was harping, and chanting to battle-songs. And warriors ate and drank against the morrow when many of them would eat and drink no more. When the evening meal was over Gwydion and Gilvaethwy left their comrades, and came to a clear space under the stars, away from the fires and the noise around the fires.

Gilvaethwy moistened his lips. "They will think we have gone off to sleep with women," he whispered. "They will only laugh. Many will be creeping off to do the same tonight."

Gwydion watched him and waited, a faint, scornful smile upon his mouth.

"But those women will be waiting for them," the boy whispered again. Once more he had to moisten his dry lips. "They will not be footholders to a king. What if she should tell?"

"Are you afraid?" said Gwydion, and there was the curl of a whip in his voice. "If, after we have come so far and done all this, you should lack courage to snatch what I have put within your grasp and go back to moping and puling again, I will give you something besides love to be sick for. She will not tell. There is no woman in the world but would have enough sense for that; her place depends on it. I have dared the anger of Mâth. Are you so much a coward?"

"No!" Gilvaethwy flamed. "I am not a child for you to threaten, and I have been undergoing torments that you could never dream of, fish-cold as you are! Nothing in all the world could keep me from her now! But may a man not look into the gulf he must leap?"

"Not too long, if he is to leap without falling," said his brother. "And if you keep on quaking and hesitating like this, Mâth may smell your fear on the winds, and then you will get at least a change of torment. Whom did you borrow all that fine phrasing from, by the way: Mâth or me?"

"I have not been hesitating!" said Gilvaethwy. "I have not hesitated at all. It is you who have been glooming and glumping and fretting about, and poking your nose into every corner to hunt for catastrophes. Let us go back now to Caer Dathyl and I promise you there will be no more glooms and frettings and mopings in me after tonight!" said he.

And he turned, quick and vibrant as a stag, and stared with star-bright, intent eyes through the night towards where Caer Dathyl lay under the virgin blanket of the dark.

"I cannot see what you find in it," said Gwydion. "but I have schemed and plotted to get you your way. So be it. For this time I have outwitted Mâth. He would never pardon this, if he knew. But he will never know."

Caer Dathyl lay still and lovely under the silvering moon when they came back to it. Only old men and women and children were left there, for the armies of Mâth were between it and the advance of Pryderi, and how could the palace have to fear any foes within the land? There was great hubbub at first sight of the Princes. All wanted to know if a battle had already been fought, since they had returned, and if they were fleeing, or if they were heralds of the victory of Mâth. But Gwydion made short work of their questions, one and all.

"No, there has been no battle fought, but there will be one tomorrow. My brother and I came back to the palace for a thing we had forgotten. We will sleep here tonight, for we are tired of tramping over the countryside and sprawling on the ground where we stop. I will go to my usual quarters—do some of you see to it that they are ready for me—and my brother will seek my uncle's chamber and look around and collect the thing that he has left there."

So Gilvaethwy went to Mâth's chamber where Goewyn and the maidens who were with her were sitting round-eyed and blinking, startled from their sleep. They had been all ears, trying to catch what the commotion was about, but when the youth entered they became a forest of white young breasts and big eyes, frightened or flashing, and of nervous giggles. Only Goewyn sat straight and rigid as a statue in her white beauty and her eyes shone like levelled spear-points. The glances of the others were all sidelong, but Gilvaethwy jerked the nearest to her feet with his right hand, and spun the next nearest to her with his left, and sent them both spinning towards the doorway.

"Get out," he told the rest, "or I will throw you after them. There is no need of you here."

When they had gone, with much flurry and a little screaming, he stood staring at Goewyn, who alone had not moved. She stared back at him with rising anger.

"This is your uncle's chamber," she said, and she did not call him "Lord" as she would have Mâth or Gwydion or Govannon. "When he returns what will he say to you for this discourtesy to us maids?"

But Gilvaethwy still stood looking at her, and it seemed to him that he could never look long enough. For all of her seemed to flow together like the lines of a poem. She was clean and fine as a sword-blade, she was lovelier and warmer than the light of the sun. How red and sweet her mouth was, even in its pursed anger; how beautifully her hair fell, soft and bright as a shining mist, over the white slope of her shoulders, about the delicious, beckoning curves of her slender rounded body; how velvety the narrow milky path between her breasts! . . . She was rising now. She was white as the moonlight. And he saw that there was a glint of red in her hair; he had remembered it as pure gold.

"Since your manners seem to have got lost altogether, king's nephew, I will go."

But he barred her way.

"Will you let me pass?" she said, and her voice was hard as a frozen stream in winter.

Gilvaethwy grinned ingratiatingly. "But I don't want you to go," he said. "I want you to sleep with me."

She turned red, then white; she stamped her foot.

"I will not sleep with you!" she cried.

She tried to run under his arm, but he caught her, and she scratched and kicked him with all the fingers and feet available, and bit his shoulder.

"You can sleep or not as you like," said Gilvaethwy, "but you will stay." And he lifted her in his arms, and carried her back, screaming and fighting and biting, to Mâth's couch. . . .

When the first red of the dawn was beginning to creep like blood into the east, Gwydion strode into Mâth's chamber and, laying his hand on his brother's shoulder, shook him into wakefulness.

"Get up," he said, "we must be back in time for the battle. We cannot afford to be missed."

"I have been in a battle already," growled Gilvaethwy, and he yawned and rubbed his eyes, one of which was black.

But he clambered out of bed at the urging of his brother's hand and voice, and dressed himself, glancing from time to time at the girl upon the couch. But she lay as if she were sleeping: still and with closed eyes. Even when he came back to the bed and bent over her and kissed her white shoulder she did not stir.

"Good-by, sweetheart," he said; and could not tell what lay hid behind the moveless, bronze-gold curtain of her lashes: sleep, or what deeps of grieving rage.

"Do not waste time," said Gwydion sharply. "We must be gone." He spoke with impatience. He had not glanced at Goewyn, yet he had been well aware of her there beside his brother; he was well aware of her now. How still she was after all of last night's clamor! Still as death, though her breathing was not that of a person asleep, and with a stillness that made this matter seem grave beyond his reckoning. "But women do not die of it," he told himself, "or they would be dying often—those of them who are not foot-holders. How can it make so great a difference whether she wanted Gilvaethwy or not? He is a handsome youth."

Gilvaethwy was arming himself, fussing with his weapons. "I cannot find my sword," he grumbled. "I threw it off last night. I was in a hurry; *she* was trying to get it." And he glanced again towards the bed.

"Here it is," said Gwydion, "in this corner. You threw it far enough. Hurry now."

"Shall we not stop for breakfast?" asked Gilvaethwy.

"No, idiot," said Gwydion. "Do you want to?"

They looked into each other's eyes, and in the ears of both rang the many sounds of the night before.

"Well, perhaps I do not," said Gilvaethwy, and his face turned slowly red. . . .

The palace was silent as a tomb as they left it. Their footfalls and the clank of their arms rang through it as through immemorially deserted spaces, heavy with a silence that was more still than sleep. They went in haste, yet not with too much haste, for though they were eager to trade that tomb-like stillness for the stir of the bright, awakening fields, yet they somehow feared to rouse its quiet into wakefulness and sound. They knew that their uncle was far away, the dreadful omniscient spies of his thoughts safely busied with the battle and the host. Yet between these walls of his desecrated majesty some shadow of his power seemed to linger like a dark, accusing ghost.

"Walls are not winds," Gilvaethwy whispered, "they will not carry him messages."

Not unless he asks them to," said Gwydion. And that was all he said.

But no voices but their own broke the quiet, and if any saw them go they never knew it. The old men slept who had failed to guard the palace of their King; the children slept in their sleeping mothers' arms. Only the girl upon Mâth's couch did not sleep. Not until the last sound of the young men's going had died away did she move. Then she opened her eyes under the red radiance that streamed upon her where she lay alone, and looked long, with dark, wide gaze, into the bloody east. And out of those wide eyes tears began to fall, heavy and slow, bright as rosy crystals in the morning light, coursing down her white face. But she made no sound at all. . . .

"Well, are you satisfied?" said Gwydion to his brother. They were riding through the fields in the golden vigor of morning, and the wind blew strong and sweet m their faces, fragrant with the scent of warm and fertile earth.

"I am satisfied!" said Gilvaethwy violently. "I am sore all over from kicks and she has scratched half the skin off my neck and chest."

"That is no matter. Your neck will not be seen if you wrap a scarf round it, and your clothes already cover the rest. But your face is something else again." Gwydion turned and looked at it wryly. "Your beloved must kiss like a bumblebee," he said.

Gilvaethwy grinned ruefully and ran a hand over his inflamed and swollen lips.

"She bit me every time," he said.

"She has good teeth; that is plain to be seen."

"She did not like me," said Gilvaethwy, and his tone was childishly aggrieved. "All the others always have— if they scratched a little and made a fuss at first, they were as eager for me before the end as I for them—and they were always careful not to get away. I thought it would be the same way this time. But she did not seem to be pretending."

"Well, you would have your fun," said his brother. "And do not let me hear any more complaints out of you," he growled, "for I shall have enough to do to cover this up without the bother of sympathizing with you. Especially since I cannot do that last sincerely. She made noise enough for a dozen. I would not have dreamed that so big a sound could come out of one woman's mouth. If there is one person in the whole palace who is ignorant or careless or malicious enough to remember what he or she heard last night when Mâth comes home—!"

"What would happen?" said Gilvaethwy, and looked alarmed for a moment.

"We should not feel any easier if we knew," said his brother. And they rode on.

Gilvaethwy whistled as merrily as a cricket, for his qualms had passed with the sight of the frowning walls of Caer Dathyl, and his spirits rose in answer to the vital beauty of the morning, blithe with the blitheness of one that is eased of a heavy burden after long strain. He went gaily towards the battle now, thinking with pleasure of the onset, the thrusting of spears and the smashing of shields. His brothers and comrades might rally him somewhat upon his damaged eye, but their inquiries would not be too close, and his dread all-knowing uncle would never notice so small and material a detail. Or if he did, he would not know that it had not been there yesterday, when a certain shyness had moved Gilvaethwy always to keen Gwydion or some other person between him and his uncle's line of vision.

But Gwydion's mood was more silent. His nerves were still shaken by the din of the night, and no less by the stillness of the morning. Things that were past were always less dim for him than for Gilvaethwy. He thought of the cattle he had studied, and of Goewyn. "Will she have a child? Footholders never do; that has been noticed even by the most pious and conservative; and if she did there would be no deceiving my uncle with talk of the gods. He knows too much for that.

"Women, too—the younger ones, at least—would make a mock and a stink of her name. For it is one of the treacheries that these customs of the New Tribes breed in women: they turn their tongues against one another and lose all loyalty to their own sisterhood. Even the old-fashioned ones, who themselves have had a score of men apiece, would think an unfaithful footholder a sacrilege against the gods."

And he felt ashamed of the violence of his hope that Goewyn would not have a child. It seemed somehow wrong that so great and lovely a miracle as birth could ever be dreaded or regretted. "But then this would be no way to get a child," he thought. "in such a noise and a racket as that, with half the court peeping in, scandalized, through the cracks in the door. . . . No, it should be done quietly, in some solitary hour of beauty with the woman you hold dearest. . . .

"This was ill done. It violated what Mâth would call the Ancient Harmonies. Yet was it needful for Gilvaethwy's sake. Now in my place Govannon would have thrashed him when he first found out what his ailment was. But for me such simplicity of action is always too crude. It is awkward to be able to see both sides of a question, to know what you would feel if you were in the other's place."

But he could not put himself in Goewyn's place. He could not conceive of chastity except as a market value and a pose—something contrary to natural laws. Arianrhod, his favorite sister, was the only other girl in Gwynedd who made such vehement assertions of it as the footholder; and it seems probable that Gwydion, whose lands lay nearer hers than did any of their brothers', already had the best of reasons for knowing what value to put upon those assertions. . . .

What harm was done so long as Goewyn kept her post? Mâth would be as well off as ever, for he would not know what kind of a lap his feet were now resting in.

"Yet it is a great risk to have taken, and if I were bringing up a boy I should give him plenty of other things to think of besides his body, that he might be able to amuse himself without so many of these awkward fevers."

And his mind turned with that to more pleasant paths, to his own desire for a child and thoughts of ways and means. "But even if I had a child I could not bring him up to be my heir. The people of Gwynedd would never feel sure that he was mine. My nephew must succeed me, and I have not got him either. I could love a child of Arianrhod's, but she is too taken with this silly fashion set by the women of Dyved to give me one. It is awkward that virgins never have children. . . ."

5

The Battle

SO THEY came again to Penardd, and went into the hall where Mâth ap Mathonwy took counsel with his chiefs. Grey and old he seemed as he sat there: ancient and strong as the mountains, and as shrouded in unalterable majesty. And he looked at his late-come nephews with those grey piercing eyes that could see so far and so deep.

"You are late again. It would seem that you are getting a habit of lateness," said he.

Gilvaethwy, having made formal obeisance, stepped back quickly towards where Eveyd stood with Govannon and Amaethon. But Gwydion bowed before his uncle with a mind that was carefully blank, emptied of all revelations.

"We had business to attend to, Lord."

"So it would seem," said the King. And glanced, after all, at Gilvaethwy's black eye.

"My sorrow if I have delayed the council," said Gwydion. "I thought not that there would be much to take counsel over; that we would either wait for Pryden here, or retreat into the fastnesses where it will be more dangerous for him to follow."

"It is that that we are debating," said his uncle, "whether we shall meet him here or in the strongholds of Arvon."

"Why should we wait here?" asked Gwydion. "Last night the sight of our campfires held Pryderi from harrying Gwynedd. He knows now that we are ready and in arms against him. He will come after us, and not scatter his men to ravage the dwellings of the folk. And why should it not be in a fortified place that he comes up with us, where it will be the harder for him to attack us, or to retreat through the steadings of our people?"

"That is well spoken," said Mâth, "and spoken as I would have expected you to speak it. Men, my word is with my nephew's sword on this matter. What have you to say?"

But some of the young nobles cried out: "And shall we let him think that he has us on the run? He will say that we were scared away by a sight of his fires in the night, that we dare not hold our own borders! Can we not fight without a fort at our backs?"

And Gilvaethwy had the imprudence to yell with them, until he was stilled by a look from Gwydion and a vigorous nudge from Govannon that almost made him lose his balance.

"It is plain to be seen that you are spenders, not savers of life," said the King, and he looked upon them all with his deep ancient eyes that overawed them by the very mystery of that ineffable calm that seemed passionless, yet stored with the strength that is at the source of all passions—vital and not bloodless, placid yet inexorable. "And that you think that a war should be fought to spill the blood of all, including your own, and not to save in so far as may be the lives and lands and homes of Gwynedd. Yet it is that is my charge, and shall be my care. We go into Arvon, men of Gwynedd, if you follow me to war."

And the older men cried out that he was right, the captains that were skilled in war. And the younger ones were silent, though they cast longing glances back toward the distant camp of Pryderi as they made ready for the journey to the strongholds.

And only Gwydion wondered if that council and that weighing of the courses had not been arranged as a test for his own judgment, and if there had ever been uncertainty at all in the mind of Mâth. . . .

The men of Gwynedd did not have to go far. They stopped between the Maenors of Penardd and Coed Alun, that is now called Coed Helen, and there they made their stand.

Nor had they long to wait, for the hosts of the South were soon drawn up before them, and they could see where Pryderi paced before his men, heartening and haranguing them, a great figure in his gleaming war-harness, with his gold beard glowing flame-bright beneath the sun. Like a trumpet his angry voice rang out across the space between the armies, and one heard as well as the other what it was that he cried:

"Men of Dyved, shall we chase these thieving foxes farther? These curs, with the hearts of curs, that had not the courage to rob, but must sneak into our land with tricks and lies, hiding behind magic to cozen us out of our goods and win what they were not men enough to take? Let them find shields that will not melt in a day to hold between our spears and them! Let them learn that there are swords and stout arms in Dyved that can make an end of magic!

"Men of the South, we are the sons of conquerors. Are we to stomach such craven, thieving neighbors, or leave any part of the Isle of the Mighty in their grip? We will eat them up with fire and sword! We will conquer them as our forebears have always conquered theirs! We will waste their land with fire, and their folk shall be the slaves whose hearts they have!"

The sons of Dôn heard him where they stood by their chariots, ready for the onset, and Eveyd and Gilvaethwy, the two youngest, ground their teeth at that insult to the men of Gwynedd: the putting of such shame upon their name for courage. And Govannon stroked his axe as tenderly as if it were a woman's hair. But Gwydion's face wore no look at all. . . .

Then the men of Dyved met the men of Gwynedd in the field and shields crashed against shields with a roar like that of earth breaking at the Crack of Doom. And swords and war-shouts rang louder than any tempest under which ever writhed the sea. There were spears that missed their mark and rang harmless on plates of bronze, and spears that split soft flesh and sank deep within. There were blood and severed limbs and fallen men, yet living, into whose torn bodies the heels of the fighters ground.

Ever the men of Gwynedd made a wall of shields around their King, though his sword bit as many as did theirs. And ever he stood in and over the battle like some old, mighty tower, impregnable and unbreakable.

But again and again Pryderi left his own men and raged lion-like through the ranks of Gwynedd, his bright eyes and his red sword ever whirling, questing, yet ever unsatisfied, as though there were one certain, unfound face he sought. . . . His chariot turned in all directions, in that Briton battle-mode that confused the legions of Caesar, so that the men broke and fled all around him, not knowing which he would come at, and he mowed them down like grain.

Five times he pierced to the very heart of the Northern host, and each time he left a trail of fallen men behind him, and among these a man of the ten that had fared with Gwydion and Gilvaethwy to Dyved. Yet it seemed that no weapon could reach or touch him, that his arm was always quickest and his thrust was always strongest.

Then when the press grew too close for driving he sent his chariot back and continued his attacks afoot, but still he took no scathe and scattered men as a hawk does chickens, swooping and striking. So there were many who began to lose heart to fight against this man who leaped among them untouchable as death himself, this man who had been one of the seven that alone came back alive from the slaughter of Morddwydtyllyon in Erinn, years before. And none stood firm except the group where Mâth was.

"This will never do," said Gwydion to Govannon the Smith. "He will break the ranks entirely if we do not drive him back."

"Or end him, brother," said Govannon, and drove the axe that had been a new idea but was now a red reality, messy with bits of scalp and brain and hair, through the skull of a man of Dyved who had come too close.

"He may insist on that," said Gwydion, "or else on making an end of us. But there is no choice but to make trial of that."

So he went forward, and his own men from his lands around Caer Seon saw him do it and raised a cry of *"Gwydion! Gwydion heir of Gwynedd! Lord of Caer Seon!"* Pryderi heard and met him as he came. There had been a man of Gwynedd in the Lord of Dyved's way, between him and the sons of Dôn, and he aimed a blow at Pryderi, who parried it by striking the arm that smote. His sword grated in its bones and pierced them all, so that the arm fell to the earth at Gwydion's very feet, and blood spurted like a red spring from the shoulder that had held it.

Gwydion glanced once at that arm that his countryman had raised to defend him, quivering there upon the earth as if to clutch at it, with fingers that would clutch no more. . . . Then he had no time for look or thought, for Pryderi was face to face with him. For a moment in the din of battle there was an inner hush as those two looked into each other's eyes. . . .

"So it is you!" said Pryderi. "Coward and liar," he cried, "your hour has come, and now will I pay your right wage for that song you sang to me that night in Rhuddlan Teivi!"

Then Gwydion raised his sword, but it was for that Pryderi had waited, and his own crashed down with a force that struck sword and shield from the arms that held them, and would have gone through shoulder and breast likewise had Gwydion been one second less swift in his recoil. But as he stood shaken and swaying Pryderi's sword rose again, and it was the axe of Govannon that stayed and shattered it in its fall.

Then a wail of horror went up from the men of the South as they saw their Lord stand thus, disarmed, and a roar of joy from the men of Gwynedd. But Pryderi snatched up the nearest of these, a little man that had fought beside Govannon, and bore him before him like a shield, and that one's blood reddened the swords of a dozen of his own countrymen that had tried to reach Pryderi, before the King of Dyved won back to his own men.

Yet that chance turned the tide of battle against the men of the South, for both the hosts had seen the retreat of Pryderi. The men

of Gwynedd pressed forward with a great shout, and the men of
Dyved began to flee. And presently the folk of the land were left
alone upon the field save for the dying and the dead.

But they made no stop there, but hastened after the fleeing host
until they caught up with it again, at the brook which is called Nant
Call, and there they hewed men down by hundreds, weary as those
were and disheartened by the blow of that first defeat. And on this
field the men of Gwynedd took small scathe.

What was left of the host of the South fled on again, toward Dol
Pen Maen. There the captains of Pryderi came before him, dust-
stained and smeared with blood. "Lord," they said, "the men can go
no farther; the heart is gone out of them and they are done."

They watched him closely as they said it. Some of them may have
quaked to say it. But he heard them out in silence. His face was still
as a stone, grey and storm-scarred as a stone. But once he turned his
head and looked away towards the south, towards where lay the fair
and rolling lands of Dyved and the folk that had cheered him, trusting and glorying in his might, as he rode forth in his pride and battle
splendor to redress their wrong and his. But between him and Dyved
loomed the grey wall of twilight, darkening with the falling night. . . .

"Let us make camp then," he said. "Better to die like men than
like scared rabbits scuttering back to our burrows. It is done."

The men of Gwynedd saw the fires of that encampment in the distance, red embers under the grey pall of dusk. The warriors were worn
with the days of marching and slaughtering. Many of them had bitter
wounds. Yet being still hot with their battle triumphs they would have
liked to go forward and make an end. Word of this was brought to
Mâth, where he sat upon his warhorse, mountainous and still.

"Lord," the chiefs said, "shall we suffer them to escape back into the
South and gather new hosts there? Were it not well to make an end?"

"Who is there left for them to gather?" said Mâth. "The men of one-
and-twenty Cantrevs followed Pryderi in this hosting. He has no more."

"Men who flee south today may ride back another day," said
Govannon, and he played with his unwashed axe.

The King rubbed his chin.

"They know that they cannot well escape out of our land now
without our leave," said he. "They wait for death, or for such peace
as we, the victors, give. There is no shame in peace."

"They would have it all the same if they were dead," said Eveyd
the son of Dôn. "Shall we not set watchmen to see that they do not
steal away in the night?" he begged.

"There is no need for spies," said Mâth. "It is done."

6

Peace

GWYDION THE SON of Dôn came presently back to his uncle when all the rest had gone about their businesses. Evening had fallen. The meal was cooking over the campfires and the wounded were tended. All others were gathered round the red dancing light. Long the old King had sat there, aloof and passionless as a god in his solitude, gazing down upon the host. And the calm in his eyes no man might read, whether it was sad or glad or eternal, or brooded upon the emptiness of all things.

"Lord, will you not come and eat with the men?" said Gwydion. "This is victory, and well have we won it. There were few men of ours lost at Nant Call, no more than you might count upon the fingers of your two hands," said he.

The King turned his head and looked at him. They saw each other's faces in misty wise in the moon-shot darkness, spectral and wan.

"That is well," said Mâth, "yet it might have been better. Many men died in that field between the Maenors. So many men have not died in Gwynedd in all the days since you were born."

Gwydion looked down at the moonbeams where they fell to earth from between the leaves of the trees, stabbing the warm darkness with their lances of cold light that gleamed like spectral swords.

"Yet is it victory, Lord," he said.

"True," said Mâth, and rubbed his chin again. "And what else besides?"

Gwydion answered in a voice that was quick and hot with passion, strangely young. "Did they not invade our land, Lord, as aforetime they invaded this isle in the days when our folk had the lordship of all the Isle of the Mighty?"

"They are invaders and have always been invaders," said Mâth, "yet for many years we had dwelt with them in peace. And I say to you there will be a day when the New Tribes and the Tribes of the Prydyn shall be one people, a single race again between the mountains and the sea. For it is so the cycles move, and the new can never be driven out or absorbed, but must merge with and leaven the old. Nor is it good to retard the course of the cycles and to pour fresh hate into the cauldron of destiny. Peace cannot be won through blood, but through union. Have these doings hastened that day, my nephew?"

"Would the folk of Gwynedd wish to hasten it?" asked Gwydion.

"No," said Mâth, "but would not you?"

And to that his nephew could answer never a word. . . .

On the morrow, in the golden hours of morning, Pryderi sent messengers to Mâth the King, asking his terms of peace. So Mâth took counsel with his chiefs as to what those terms should be. This was no light matter, for if the host of the South was broken and had lost half its number, still the host of Gwynedd that had been the smaller in the beginning was lesser by a third than when it had first gone forth. And some of the chiefs still thought it would be safer to fall upon and destroy the host of Dyved now while it could not risk another battle.

But Mâth said no to that. "We too cannot risk another battle," he told them. "Small good it would do to fling away our own men that we might annihilate Pryderi's, and leave the one land as crippled as the other. We can spare no more men," said he.

"Since we dare not leave these Southerners alone in the land, let us march with them to our borders, so that we can be sure that they do not turn back or harry the folk on their way," said Gwydion.

"But what if they should attack us by night, or turn upon us during the march with some sudden treachery?" demanded the chiefs.

"They are not clever enough to be traitors," said Gwydion, "but by night—?" and his fine brows wrinkled.

Mâth stroked his beard.

"Indeed," said he, "it is ill to leave the fangs of a foe undrawn while he has hate the whetstone to sharpen them again."

And in the end it was arranged that Pryderi should leave his son and the sons of three-and-twenty of his nobles with the men of Gwynedd as hostages while he fared back to the South. So Gwrgi Gwastra and his three-and-twenty comrades went from the camp of the men of Dyved to that of Mâth. And Pryderi sat with his back turned that he might not see their going; sat alone, with a face so grim and stone-like that his men, even those of them that were his oldest and dearest comrades, dared not speak to him. . . .

Then the two hosts marched together to the Traeth Mawr and crossed it. And there was no harm to the land, nor to the people of the land. But as they journeyed side by side into Melenryd trouble began. For the foot-soldiers of the two armies were marching only a few yards apart and the men of Gwynedd, still drunk with victory, could not help but laugh and shrug their shoulders at their neighbors, making easily overheard witticisms about the grand intentions of the Lord of Dyved, and how he had carried them out.

At first the men of Dyved had borne all that in black dejection and helpless rage, but by the time they had crossed the Traeth Mawr their courage and their spleen had begun to come back. The sparks that the men of Gwynedd were blithely sowing sank into dry kindling. Those jests chafed more every hour. They seemed to grow and swell and bloat, to sprout new annoyances in as many places as a potato has eyes. To men whose pride is already sore and smarting a pinprick can be a spear-thrust; and the more the men of Gwynedd saw their shots hit the mark the more pleasure it became to shoot.

But no less figurative kind of shooting began until at last a man of Dyved lost his temper and answered a gibe.

"You brag a great deal about a victory you would never have won, if our Lord had not lost his sword, and that probably by magic," said he to an offensive man of Gwynedd. "But we of Dyved have never had to play nurse-girl to foreign soldiers marching out of our dominions. We never let them get there," said he.

The man of Gwynedd looked surprised and then suddenly turned purple.

"What is that you are calling me?" said he, thrusting his chin so far out that it was a wonder it did not come loose from the rest of his face.

"What you are," said the man of Dyved. "You are afraid to take your eyes off us for a single minute." And he laughed in his enemy's face.

But before he had done laughing an arrow had whistled between his open grinning jaws, and stuck out through the back of his neck. He fell and the man next to him gave a cry of rage and shot down the man that had killed him.

After that the two armies could not be kept from shooting at each other whenever their officers' eyes were elsewhere, and word of this was brought to Mâth.

"Well," said he, rubbing his chin, "what is to be done?"

"Gwydion might cast a few illnesses about as I have noticed that he sometimes does when he is annoyed," said Govannon, "but that would

take time and might be too subtle for the understanding of any but the
men of Caer Seon, who are trained to it. I could take a few heads off,
which is a simple thing that everybody could understand, but whenever I was not looking the tongues would be wagging as much as ever
in those that were still on; and so the arrows would still fly."

"Is death so simple?" said Mâth. And he pondered awhile as if
staring into those deeps of destiny and time that were veiled from all
eyes save his alone.

"Let none be slain," he said, finally, "for we cannot stay them.
When hate is once raised it cannot be laid until its fires have burned
themselves out. But ill have we kept our bargain with Pryderi." And
his eyes dwelt long on Gwydion who paced beside them, splendid
and restless as a flame in his crimson cloak. And those old royal eyes
had love and pride in them, but likewise a deeper shadow.

"He dare not protest," said Gwydion. "His son and the sons of his
chiefs are in our hands."

"Then the ill is all the greater," said Mâth. And in his nephews
there was something that saw his meaning, as men still in a valley
see the shape of a mountaintop afar off, and tied their tongues.

Pryderi and his captains were giving thought to these same matters also: to the hostages and the broken peace. The chiefs were
grouped around Pryderi, where he sat on his horse.

"Lord, we are losing men every hour," they said, "many men. It
cannot go on. Before we leave Gwynedd there will be battle joined
again."

"And if there is?" said Pryderi. A sword lay across his knees, and
his hands stroked it all the while, but there was no joy in his looks;
rather a pitiful uncertainty, such as had come to haunt his eyes since
Gwydion had charmed him at Rhuddlan Teivi and strength had
failed to win back what the mysteriously conquered mind had lost.

They hesitated. They looked at him and at one another, and in
their eyes was the woeful longing of a dog that gazes, slavering, at
savory meat, yet holds back for fear of the whip.

"We could risk it, Lord," they said. "The host has got its heart
back. And if we have lost many men, the strength of the Old Tribes
was not in the beginning so great as ours. Yet is there one thing."

"My son and your sons," said Pryderi. "Well I know it." And he
gazed gloomily upon the hands that stroked the sword.

There fell upon them all a silence that was like the weight of
mountains, thick and dense and dark.

"Yet if battle comes how will it fare with them at the hands of the men of Gwynedd in any case?" A red-bearded chief spoke. "These folk are poor trothkeepers. The heir of their land bargains with false goods, and they break the peace they have sworn. Must we wait like cows for the butcher? All goes ill; if we struck swiftly might it not go better? There is such a thing as rescue."

"Yet if we rescued the dead?" said another.

Nobody found any answer to that. For they were weighing chances beyond their reckoning, gambling with destiny for stakes too high, yet which fate itself had trapped them into pitting. There was danger in advance and in retreat. And fear that was not for themselves chilled them. Fear that was not for their own bodies, yet was for their own flesh. A bond that Gwydion alone of all the men of Gwynedd truly dreamed of. And upon them all still weighed the disheartening memory of that new thing—defeat.

So they brooded in the chill heaviness of their hearts. And Pryderi brooded likewise, his hands upon the sword, his look dull and lowering as a thundercloud, conscious in every thought and nerve of all their perplexed misery around him, and feeling the rasp of it through all his being.

For he was the King. Upon him were the woes of all, their cause and their solving. And yet he was only a man whose griefs were one with theirs.

He thought of Gwrgi Gwastra, and of the sons of his chiefs, and of all the woes and shames of that sad homeward road. And a gloomy rage burned in him, a ventless agony, poisonous with impotence, that seared him like a flame and might be eased by only one thing in the world: the feel of one throat between his hands.

Gwydion! Gwydion, heir of Gwynedd! Day and night the name roared in his ears unceasing, maddening him with a hate that it seemed must burst him yet only burned on and on in torment. The man that had gulled and cheated him; the cry that had turned the battle-fates against him on the field between the Maenors.

Gwydion! From first to last it was he that had undone them. He that was the curse and the bane of the men of Dyved. To choke into silence forever the golden voice that had beguiled him; to put out the light in those eyes, whose charmed stare still haunted some chilled, secret chamber of his brain, and see them glaze in death: that might ease him, might free and give back to him his manhood. Never again could he be himself, never again could Dyved know strength and honor while this man lived.

Flesh to flesh a magician would surely be as other men. His

bones would break as easily; his blood would flow. . . . Pryderi's hands clenched and unclenched. Action was his sphere, the only one he knew; yet he was denied action.

Or was he. . .? Clear as lightning, and as sudden, a thought flashed across the heavy storm clouds of his mind. He raised his head and faced his chieftains.

"Send a message to Mâth," he said. . . .

They bore that message to Mâth the son of Mathonwy where he sat in his camp among his captains of war. The sons of Dôn were with him, the chiefs of the clans and the lords of the Cantrevs. And the ancient King sat there in his age that looked to be the age of earth itself, hoary with the frost of all the winters of time, and listened with grey, sea-deep eyes to what the messengers spoke.

"This is the word of Pryderi," said they. "He prays you, Lord of Gwynedd, to stay your folk as he will stay his, and to leave the battle and the combat between him and Gwydion the son of Dôn, who has caused all this."

Mâth stroked the long, frosty vastness of his beard. For a time it seemed as though he brooded, pondering within himself the demands of destiny and all that might chance or could chance, locked into those deep and lonely spaces where his spirit must forever range alone, or uncompanioned by shapes of earth. But at last he turned his eyes to them and spoke.

"Verily," he said, "I call the gods to witness that if Gwydion the son of Dôn is willing, I will be glad to leave the battle and the combat between him and your King. Never will I send any into battle unless I and mine do our uttermost."

Then all eyes turned in question towards Gwydion, save the King's that dwelt on his nephew indeed, but with a look that none might read. And the folk of Gwynedd thought that their Prince looked handsome and warlike and a very flame of life, but sullen and lowering as though something preyed upon him.

Ever since the making of the peace great restlessness had been upon the heir of Gwynedd. He had seen earth and sky through a sultry cloud whose red murk vibrated with death-screams and the groans of wounded men. In him those subtle senses of sigh and hearing, that are above the grosser senses of the body, were too well trained not to discern the hideous welter of pain and rage and of the ugly elementals that feed on blood, the psychic debris that haunts the scene of violent death. Yet he had not Mâth's ineffable serenity to raise him into spheres above that vision; and those deaths had been died, and that blood shed, for him.

Of Goewyn he thought not at all. He dared not, for fear of the strange powers of Mâth. What he had done to Pryderi troubled him little; Pryderi was not of his tribe or kindred. The equality of outlanders with ourselves is still owned oftener in theory than in belief. It has no true place in the dealings of nation with nation; and in Gwydion's age it was unconceived of, even as a senseless dream.

He did not know whether it was Mâth or his own soul that sent the thoughts that haunted him now, the thoughts he was forever arguing away: *If many are slain, are the pigs not won?* Could I build a house without cutting down trees? *Is any good thing won without strife and warfare, whether of the body or the mind?*

Yet a flame of trouble consumed him, a vast unease. A voice cold as a blast from the Underworld rang through his soul: *That which I could have got peacefully for a little waiting, that which I bought so cheaply and cleverly for illusions, in the end has it not been dearly paid for with the blood of the men of Gwynedd? Mâth will not speak. He leaves me to the judgment of my own mind that he has trained. He knows that battle triumphs cannot drug it long, nor fear of him deter me in the days of my own kingship when he is gone. . . .*

. . . Is this the way a king learns? Then must his folk pay dear for his lessoning.

So his thoughts had moved for days in a burning, wearying round. And now came this challenge, half welcome escape, half menace; for Pryderi was still the champion whom no foe had met hand to hand and overcome. His mind flew to his uncle's, seeking with all of his master's art that he knew to ferret out the wish and purpose there. Was this punishment or but the risk whose taking Mâth deemed the duty of kingliness?

But the King's eyes and mind were blank to him. They waited in silence, unhelping and unhindering, for his free choosing . . . if himself could yet concede himself the right to choose.

"In truth," said the messengers, "Pryderi says that it would be fairer for the man who has worked him this ill to meet him face to face, and let their tribes go unharmed."

Then Gwydion leaped up and sprang forward to face the messengers, his crimson cloak whirling about him.

"The gods bear me witness," he cried, "I will not have the men of Gwynedd do battle for my sake. Since I have leave to meet Pryderi myself, glad will I be to set my body against his!"

7

Gwydion and Pryderi
Speak with Swords

THEY BORE THAT word to Pryderi where he waited in the camp of the host of Dyved. He smiled to hear it; and in that smile there was something of the fierce joy of storm, of the ecstasy that lashes the roaring sea.

"Indeed," he said, "I shall need none but myself to claim my rights."

That night the men of Dyved were merry and sang in their camp, while those that attended on Pryderi made sharp the weapons of their Lord and washed them of the last trace of the blood of common men, that they might be pure for the red draught that should heal all the woe and shame of Dyved.

They burnished the armor that had been given him by Bran the Blessed, he that had been King of all the Isle of Britain, and whose head was as sweet-tongued and good a comrade for eighty years after it was cut from his body as it had ever been when upon his shoulders. It was he that was in one sense the greatest of all Britain's kings, for he was so vast in size that no house ever built could hold him, save that one in Erinn where he got his death. And no British monarch has ever since achieved a size like that. Perhaps the attendants thought that in that gift that proved their Lord's alliance with the fabulous and mighty dead there might be a charm to withstand the wizardries of Gwynedd. For Bran too had been of the Tribes of the Prydyn—a Prince of the race of Bell of the Deep, whose name may be a reminiscence of that Mighty Being for whose sake the Celts, through immemorial springtimes, lit the fires of Beltane.

Bright as torches burned the hopes of the men of Dyved that night. But the mirth in the camp of the people of Gwynedd was less loud; or, if it made as much noise, the sound sometimes rang hollow. For some remembered with dread Pryderi's battle-might and glories, and the wars he had fought in of old, wars that were already fabulous and would be sung in saga forever: all the tales of a strength that had never been put down.

Nor was it great comfort to reflect that he was growing old, for all had seen with their own eyes how Mâth could rise from his couch of seeming feebleness to stride forth, a lord of war.

Some wondered how the wily son of Dôn looked forward to the morrow, he who must now meet sword and spear with their mates, not with magic and songs. Seemingly the combat had been left to his own free choice, yet after his uncle's words and the heralds', he could not have accepted the shame of refusal and have hoped to lead again in war.

But in the place where Gwydion's quarters were Govannon was giving his brother asked help with his weapons and a good deal of advice that had not been asked for. Gilvaethwy and Eveyd and Amaethon were there too, full of questions and suggestions, until Govannon chased them out.

"Our brother must sleep," he growled. "How do you think that he can fight in the morning if he listens to you young magpies chattering all night? Your jaw wags bravely enough now, Gilvaethwy, but I noticed before the battle that there was never a cheep out of you, and that you hid behind everyone you could get on the backside of."

"I did not hide behind you at any rate!" said Gilvaethwy.

"No," retorted his brother, "you knew better."

"Are you going to quarrel with them all night, Govannon?" asked Gwydion. "For their chatter would be as easy to sleep through as that."

"No. But there would be less quarrelling if you encouraged less chattering. You have almost ruined Gilvaethwy," grumbled their brother, as the youths fled at last before his shooing hand. "First, he must be pining like a bitch that is full enough of pups to split her belly, and now he is running about everywhere squealing as gleefully as a woman that has found out a secret that her best friend did not want her or anyone to know."

"He did well enough in the battle," said Gwydion. "Is not that all that concerns us, brother? Such matters burn out quickest when let alone. You understand metals but not moods, Govannon."

"Metal sometimes has moods, but I hammer them out," said

Govannon. "I would like well to know what Gilvaethwy's moods have been about, but maybe we will be luckier if we do not find out."

He did not see his brother's face as he ended, for as he spoke Gwydion had moved away from the fire so that a shadow covered him. He wished that it might have covered his memory, also, from the mind of Mâth that might even now be watching them.

"But speaking of battles, now that you are going to have one all to yourself," observed the smith, "I have brought you my axe. It has done you good service against Pryderi once already. It may be that it will get you out yet," he said.

Gwydion thanked him and took the axe, but he smiled, half strangely. "Do you think it will take no more than a new shape of axe to overcome Pryderi, my brother?"

"I think it will do more than anything else. There is no other like it. I hope you will not get killed," Govannon grumbled, "for I should not want Pryderi to get this axe and the men of Dyved to make others like it. It is the first steel-bladed axe that has ever been seen in the Islands of the Mighty. I am not sure that I could make it again myself without this one before me."

"You should learn to keep track of your ideas better than that," said Gwydion, "for they are more a part of you than are your axes."

"If it were not for your ideas I could be more sure of keeping track of my axes," said Govannon. "It may be an axe that gets us out of this, but it was not an axe that got us into it."

And then they embraced and parted for the night.

When the earth gleamed again with the gold of morning Gwydion ate and armed himself and went forth. He took leave of his brothers, they shouting for his victory. And he took leave of Mâth the son of Mathonwy, where he sat in his immemorial calm, under which he may have hoped and feared as ordinary men hope and fear when their dearest go forth to danger. But he sat in silence, inner and outer, and would not, with his will or his prayers, swerve destiny.

And Gwydion went down to the Velenryd, that is a ford of the river Cynvael, and the meeting place appointed between him and Pryderi. He had feared that he might be early and that the men of Dyved would mock him, saying that fear had made him loath to wait—young magicians are not above the folly of such fancies—but Pryderi was there before him, eager as a hound that has sniffed blood.

They looked at each other, and the ring of earth narrowed to the little space of the ford, and they two alone in it. For only one of them could it ever widen again. The watching hosts were drawn up farther back on either side of the river, out of ear or bowshot. All save themselves was gone. . . . Long they looked and the eyes of neither fell, but Pryderi's grew strained and he whipped up his rage as an angry man whips on his dogs to the hunt.

"Coward and thief!" he cried. "Liar, your magic will not aid you now. Pray to your gods of the Prydyn, for today you die. You shall go to be judged before Arawn in the Underworld and there you will find pigs enough!"

A new gust of fury blazed up, crimsoning his face. As though upon the topmost peak of his malice a spirit brooded, like a wind from some malevolent Outerworld, putting words into his mouth.

"You have wanted the flesh of pigs to eat," he shouted. "May pigs eat your flesh, and vermin crawl in it! May your own magic turn against you and all the victories it wins you destroy the prize that you have played for! My curse upon you, heir of Gwynedd! my curse upon you, till you are bitter and emptied as I am now!"

So it was uttered, the curse that was to be so strangely fulfilled and yet never fulfilled, in the years to be.

"Have you prayed to your own gods, Pryderi?" asked Gwydion. "I took the pigs from you, and those from whom you are sprung took the land of Dyved from the people of the Prydyn; and I have held the swine by force of arms as you have held our land. Is there so great a difference between us?"

Pryderi found that unanswerable, yet altogether wrong and entirely enraging, so he set it down to magic, as men do whatever they cannot understand. The dark spirit had passed from him. He was ruled again by his human vengeance and human purpose.

"I want no more of your words," he shouted, "who have had enough of them to last me to the end of time. Traitor and cheat, leave off your lies and fight! You are not slinking into decent houses now to steal the goods of honest men. If you can fight as well as talk, come and get your death!"

As he spoke he flung his spear, a great cast that would have pierced both shield and man, but Gwydion leaped aside and his shield turned the spear, though by but a hair's breadth. He flung his own then, but already Pryderi was plunging toward him, closer than the length of its cast. So Gwydion drew his sword and went to meet him, and they fought there in the ford in silence till the end. . . .

All day they fought, and the air rang with the clash of weapons, and the waters of the ford were stained with red. The shadows shortened and the sun moved forward in his triumphal march above the world.

Noon came and went. The shadows lengthened and the sun moved downward toward the west. And the two distant camps were shrouded in a stillness in which the beating of the heart could be heard, and that made thunderous the rustling of the leaves in the wind.

And Mâth the King sat with unmoving eyes upon the unmoving sky. What question he asked or did not ask of it only the powers that shaped the world may tell. He had set a strong guard around Gwrgi Gwastra and the other hostages lest the men of Gwynedd do them harm if Gwydion fell. And since then none had dared come near him with movement or speech; and at last they had forgotten him, as men forget cliffs or the nearness of the infinite sea.

Yet those two in the ford fought on as though they could never end, as though evenly matched as night and day. Now Gwydion was beaten back and reeled before the storm of Pryderi's mighty blows, now Pryderi was forced to make retreat before the whirl of Gwydion's attack that was all about him, swift and searing as lightning, and as little to be grasped at, until his battle fury renewed itself and he swept back his foe with the very force of his bull's onslaught.

Long ago he had forgotten what it was they fought for, what was the cause of his hate. He had become that hate and it nerved his arm and drugged his soul, though his muscles began to stiffen and grow sore as the hours wore toward evening.

They were not men, those two; they were arms tearing at each other, and legs advancing and leaping, swerving and retreating. They were hate and anger, and the lust to kill. They were that deepest of primal instincts, which is to survive.

And only by flashes did Gwydion remember Gwydion the magician, the man of art and science, the heir of Mâth. But one of those flashes came toward evening, as he fell back before the charge of Pryderi, and for a second that outer solitude in which they two had been so long alone faded into the distance, and he was alone with himself the watcher, that Dreamer who had ever shaped all his deeds. . . .

A second only; it was his trained body that escaped and drove back Pryderi. But of that second something had been born, a seed germinated. . . . And Pryderi, being beaten back, suddenly saw his foe's eyes, bright and keen as steel, deep and mysterious as the sea, the eyes of that strange bard in Dyved. He knew memory and hate and the old strange chill. . . .

He rallied and beat his foe back, but his breath was getting shorter now. Even when his enemy retreated he was still looking into those eyes, hateful and brilliant) and making his very soul swoon with hate. . . . He was growing old; his joints were stiffer, not so quick and nimble after a day's fighting as they used to be. And the sun was sinking lower in the west. Somewhere far off the sky was red and the waters around were veined with red; blue twilight was fallen over the ford and the land; only in those eyes did there seem to be light anywhere in the world.

There was power in those eyes. He struck at them with his sword, but could not reach them. There was something about them that had outdone him before, that made him feel helpless. But how could a man be helpless when his arms and legs were free?

Now it was his turn to be pressed back, still flailing out with his sword, but if sometimes it touched flesh that was not what he wanted. Those eyes were still before him, shining in the red and bluish mist of the twilight that seemed to be thickening into a very cloud. Before and on either side of him, three pairs of eyes; and it flashed upon him with sudden sickening horror that there might be another pair behind him!

He turned quickly, mopping the sweat from his eyes, to guard against that possible blow from behind, and as he turned there was a rending crash, a tearing agony in his side and breast, that sent him hurtling down, down, through immeasurable black abysses roaring with sound and flaming with many-colored. . . .

Gwydion looked down upon the body of his foe where it lay on the trampled mud and sands at the ford's edge. He sank on his knees beside it, and that was easy to do, for nigh all his strength was gone. But from the other life had fled.

"You were a brave man, Pryderi," he whispered, when he had made sure that only a body was there, "and I doubt if a man so strong will be born again. For the men of this world grow weaker; brain will conquer brawn. As here today it has conquered. . . . You to your day and I to mine. Where shall we meet again, I wonder, and how will it go between us then? It would not have gone so well for me today had we stood before Arawn's judgment bar, face to face with him only and not our bodies between. . . .

"And I turned your own hate against you to strike you down. You scoffed at it, but you feared that power of the Old Tribes that you could not understand. Well, that fear has been your death, not mine. But Gwrgi Gwastra shall go back safely to the South, I promise you that, Pryderi. You may have loved him as I mean one day to love another. And this bargain I will keep."

8

How the Host Came Home

AND SOME SAY that the folk buried Pryderi at Maen Tyriawc above the Velenryd, and that it is there his grave is. But others say that it is in Abergenoli by the sea, as is told in the ancient *Englynion Beddau*:

> In Abergenoli is the grave of Pryderi,
> Where the shore is washed by the sea.

But nobody truly knows, and it does not matter anyhow. For he will not wake the sooner whether the grey wash of the vast waves sings his age-old lullaby, or whether only the little inland waters of the Cynvael murmur of him to the sun that gleams upon them. It may be that he has already waked, and that deeds that we hear of as some other man's are truly his. But wherever he is it is well with him, for he was a brave and true man; and natures are slower than names to change.

The men of the South went home slow-footed and weary-eyed, like horses with over-heavy riders. And weighty indeed were those riders. Woe for the loss of their Lord, and of the best of their men, and of the most of their mounts and weapons also. For there was no more hope for Dyved, and no escape from the guests whose names were all Grief.

But the men of Gwynedd turned homeward in glee and triumph, with jests and shouting. Before they had gone more than a day's march Gwydion made good the word he had given to dead Pryderi beside the ford.

"Lord," he said to his uncle, "now that the men of Dyved are safely gone, would it not be right for us to free the hostages that they gave us for peace? For now there can be no more fear of war, and it would be ill done of us to make prisoners of these boys."

"Let them be freed, then," said Mâth. And so it was done. Gwrgi Gwastra and his fellows rode free to follow their comrades back to the South. Back to the depleted host and the depleted sty of Dyved, where women wailed and children, learning for the first time of death, conceived of it as a dim and horrible precipice at the world's edge, over which some fell out of sight and sound, down into the dark forever, yet which others evaded: little dreaming that it is at last the common lot of all.

Bitter indeed must have been the first taste of that freedom that was the alms-gift of a triumphant foe. And however many years he may have lived or reigned thereafter, it is likely that Gwrgi Gwastra never traded with bards from Gwynedd, or forgot that sad homecoming, or forgave the wizardries of the North.

In Gwynedd two of the sons of Dôn absented themselves from the victory feast at Caer Dathyl. They made simple and reasonable excuses. Gilvaethwy said that there would be more to do when he made the rounds of the land to keep peace in it than he was wont to find; and that there would be the greater need for him to do it if Eveyd, whose custom it was to share that work with him, stayed at the feast.

"And Eveyd should have the feast," he explained, with great enthusiasm for justice, "for I was in the South with Gwydion while he was only here at home. And I have had that adventure besides the battle."

"It is truly the first time that ever I have known you to take so much thought to the rights of others where your own were concerned," said Govannon, "or not to try to get out of work, either. I have never seen such virtue oozing out of you except when you had broken something in the forge and had no chance to lay it on to somebody else. One would think you were afraid of something," he growled.

"Are you an old woman to be forever harping on things that happened years ago?" demanded Gilvaethwy, nervousness showing in his anger, for he generally treated the smith with respect. "I am now grown up—"

Here Gwydion intervened, for Govannon's blunt tongue could shear the delicate webs of guile as easily as his sharp axe could

cleave the intricate organisms of the body. And one thought of
Goewyn in the boy's mind might disclose and ruin all.

"Indeed you are, youngster. For once you are even right," he said.
"And I am of one mind with you. For I have been too long away from
Caer Seon. I would lead my men home and put all there in order,
and come back to you again when my wounds are white, my uncle."

Mâth looked upon him then, but with the eyes of the body alone.
For there was a delicacy in Mâth that respected the privacy of others, which he of all men was best able to violate, and left unread the
thoughts of his heir and pupil save when in some wise there was
need; or when their very intensity spread them before him in whatever colors the world of thought may know. But that intensity was
growing ever rarer as Gwydion learned the calm that is alone concealment. And today Mâth saw no need for the reading of thought.
The war was over and all danger to Gwynedd done.

"Go then," he said, "and see to whatever should be seen to, and
my blessing upon you and it. Gilvaethwy is right. For war is a great
breeder of disorders, nor do we yet know how much damage Pryderi
may have done in the land. And you, Gwydion, may your wounds
find swift healing. You have spoken like chieftains both, and it is
well."

So they went their ways, and their uncle and their brothers and
the host went on to Caer Dathyl. There was great merriment and
bustle there, much kissing and squealing and squeezing, as the
women welcomed home their men; and tales told and trophies
shown to round eyes that gleamed and goggled in delighted wonder,
and pricked-up ears that stretched and strained for more.

Only Mâth the King did not tarry in that happy din. He left
Govannon and Amaethon and Eveyd, each with a girl on either knee,
tickling and hugging and being hugged; and went on alone to the
peace and quiet of his chamber.

He was old, and it may be that he was a little wearied, as common men are wearied; that he yearned for that quiet. He had carried
within him through camp and battle his monumental calm that was
one with earth and great trees and the silence of night. In life he had
already found the peace of death; for he had outstripped death and
knew that he lived in eternity, and that time might discommode, but
could never hinder him for more than a moment out of all the endless ages of his being: that knowledge alone is freedom from the slavery and terror of time.

Yet his bones were aged and paid the moment's toll, and were glad of
this hour of rest and the chance to lay down sword and judgment staff.

He answered the greetings of the maidens and lay down upon his couch at the foot of which Goewyn sat. He would have put his feet in her lap; but she shrank back, very pale. Her eyes were dark and staring.

"Lord," she said, and her voice was no more than the whisper that leaves might make, falling on a forest pool, "only a virgin may hold your feet; and I am now a woman."

. . . Silence like night come at noon. Silence and all the immeasurable weight of silence. "What is this?" he had said; and the listening girls never knew whether he had spoken it aloud, or whether it was only in their own minds that they had heard the force of his thought, echoing and re-echoing, loud as thunder in that soundlessness, crashing and reverberating from wall to wall. . . .

The King had not risen, even on an elbow. He had not moved. But he looked at Goewyn. He looked at her and into her as though she had been glass.

But she did not fall to her knees as another might have done. She rose from her place and faced him levelly and unafraid, as though there were no thought or feeling within her that she dared not challenge those all-seeing eyes to read. Her silvery voice rang through the silence like a sword.

"Lord, I was seized upon and taken unawares. Yet I made such a clamor that there is none here in the court who cannot bear you witness that I am no cheap woman, to be lured to an hour's cuddling while you and every true man are away on the field of war. Look into their hearts, Lord, as well I know you can, and into mine. And this deed was done by your nephews, Lord, by Gwydion the son of Dôn and Gilvaethwy the son of Dôn. They have dishonored your chamber and you."

She was silent then. None had eyes for her any longer. For the King's face had become bleak and awful as an ice-bound sea that is yet stirred to its depths by the titanic powers of storm. He was looking past her and beyond her as though his eyes would seek and find those two that rode away from Caer Dathyl and drag them back by the very force of that gaze to face the crime that they had fled from, and the doom from which there could be no flight.

And something in the still awfulness of that face, terrible and inexorable in its passionless might, froze the heat of her outraged pride and her longing for vengeance, so that she sank, shivering, beside the couch and hid her face. . . . His hand touched her head after a time, fondly, as though it had been a child's.

"In truth," he said, "I will deal mightily in this matter, and I shall leave nothing undone that lies within my power. First I shall have reparation made to you, and then I shall see to it that atonement is made to me also. You shall be my own wife and Queen of Gwynedd."

And that was the first time that ever a king of Gwynedd had married. . . .

In that same hour of the evening, as the brothers rode toward Caer Seon, Gilvaethwy stopped suddenly, shivered, and turned toward Gwydion.

"How cold the wind is," he said with a shudder, "cold as though it blew straight up from Annwn in the Underworld. I did not know that it was there, and then of a sudden it was going through me like a spear, cold, colder than anything in the world. . . ." He shook himself. "I felt for a moment as if my blood were freezing into ice. Could that be the way a wind feels that carries messages to Mâth, brother?"

"To or from him?" said Gwydion. His tone was light, but his face was very pale. There was sweat about his lips. "But it may not have had to do with him, so what of it? There are many newly dead to ride the winds to Annwn, little brother. We have killed our share of them, you and I. . . . Baby, will you shiver at a wind?"

9

The Judgment of Mâth

MÂTH DID NOT send messengers to summon his two nephews. He may have thought that they would not come. Neither did he send out men-at-arms to hale them before him. He may have been sure that Gwydion had too much of his own magic to let himself be taken thus easily. He merely sat at Caer Dathyl and waited until all proper time for their return was past. Then he still sat and waited, having first given certain orders.

What those orders were the brothers probably learned in some such fashion as this:

Returning to Caer Seon tired and hungry after a day's riding through the land and eager for a drink and a warm supper, they would have been met by no sight or smell of a meal, and their angry comments upon this improper and amazing fact would have been encountered by an equally strange and unaccountable behavior on the part of Gwydion's steward and servants. By paleness and an incredible dumbness, and an unwonted waggishness of feet, as each man looked at and wriggled his own, and nudged his neighbor's. Each seemed to be thus telling the other to answer, but that other was always as frantically eager to pass that responsibility on to the next, who was as little minded to accept it. All of them seemed suddenly to have found something very interesting on the floor. They would not look at their Lord.

Gilvaethwy lost patience. "Will some of you stop looking at the ground and speak?" he demanded, seizing the man nearest him by the throat, "or must I lay a few of you there?"

His hand was on his sword, but Gwydion slapped it off again. "Do not be hasty, youngster," he said. "This is my house." He looked at all his servants and smiled and they took a step backwards. "What is the meaning of this? If you have lost the use of your tongues you surely have not lost the use of your hands also, so that you cannot cook. If you have, some way must be found of curing you. I would not be hard on bewitched men; unless I do the bewitching myself." And his smile grew sweeter than before.

They looked at one another. They moistened their lips.

"Lord," said one, "it is not our fault."

"Ah, whose is it then?" said Gwydion, and his smile seemed to grow a little stiff, as though all the chill of winter had suddenly passed over his face, freezing it to ice.

They looked at one another and at their feet again. Then they looked wary-eyed at him and licked their pale lips.

"Mâth the King has forbidden that you be given to eat or drink," said they.

Stillness then. A horrid final stillness as of a heart that has ceased beating. Gilvaethwy started and blanched and his lips parted as if for a cry that did not come. But Gwydion still stood moveless, the blood draining from his face, his greying lips still set in that smile that seemed frozen there as if carved in stone below eyes that smiled not.

The servants stared and shivered and shrank back. They glanced at roof and walls and ground, anywhere save in the one direction that drew their eyes as a magnet draws: at their master's face. There were terror and pity strangely mingled in those glances. Awe of sin and disaster and doom beyond their ken.

Gwydion spoke at last. "Was there no other message?" he said.

"None," they answered, and the low, muted word was like the rustle of dead leaves in the wind at evening before darkness and the snows of winter come.

Gwydion moistened his lips.

"Very well. There is nothing more to be said then." His voice was crisp and clear, calm as though he spoke of some little thing. "Get a torch, one of you, and show me to my chamber."

And a man scurried away for a torch and scurried back with it again. Gwydion took an arm of Gilvaethwy who still stood staring dumbly like one who no longer either thinks or hears.

"Come," he said, and the two went out together, following the man with the torch.

. . . When the man had gone, closing the chamber-door behind him, Gilvaethwy ran towards it with the swiftness of a released spring, then stopped short, staring at the blank wood as though at an impassable wall that shut him off from all warmth and life and sustenance.

"What are you going to do?" he whispered, and his lips worked, and his writhing fingers fidgeted with his sword. "Brother, what shall we do?"

"What indeed?" said Gwydion. He had dropped upon his bed, limply, wearily, and his face was very pale.

They looked at each other then, peering fixedly into the strained whiteness of each other's face. And the shadows cast by the torch seemed to grow more numerous, blacker and thicker, like grisly watchers dancing ever nearer. . . .

"She has told him," whispered Gilvaethwy, wetting his dry lips with his tongue.

They thought of the wind that had blown upon them that night as they rode away from Caer Dathyl. They could see again the twilight and feel that piercing unearthly chill. . . .

"It was then that she told him," murmured Gwydion. "It was his thoughts turning towards us that chilled us, not the wind. . . ."

And he stared into the realization of those fears that had haunted him ever since that night when he and Gilvaethwy had stolen away from the camp of the men of Gwynedd. Into the face of power that not even he could combat or measure, power that even now was arrayed against him. . . .

He had told himself that that wind need not have been any emanation from the mind of Mâth. With labor and determination he had convinced himself. Yet its shadow had lain cold upon his spirits whenever he had thought of return to Caer Dathyl. And now it blew again, chill and unfathomable, through his naked soul. . . .

"Why do we not lie?" Gilvaethwy demanded violently. "Would he take her word against ours, and you the greatest man in his kingdom after himself?"

"It would be of no use to lie," said Gwydion.

The boy shuddered and licked his lips.

"Will he take our heads off?" he whispered.

"Probably he will not do anything so crude," said Gwydion.

Gilvaethwy peered at him intently in the half-light.

"You know him better than any of us, Gwydion," he said softly. "Can you think what he will do?"

"I know him too well to be able to think," said Gwydion. Yet he did see, dimly and awfully, like the shape of a strange world, all the things that Mâth might do, though what doom Mâth might choose from out the awful vagueness of those unknown lands and seas he could not guess.

In silence they digested all the implications of that reply, having nothing else to digest. Then Gilvaethwy stirred.

"Magic?" he whispered, shuddering.

But Gwydion made no answer at all.

Gilvaethwy sprang for the door. His voice rose suddenly to a scream.

"Will you let him starve you to death in your own house? Who is to stop us if we go where the food is and eat? Those servants will not dare. You have magic too!"

"Even they could dare at the bidding of Mâth," said Gwydion. "We could overcome them. But then something worse might happen."

Gilvaethwy stopped with his hand upon the door, his eyes terrified questions.

"He has not yet laid force upon us," said his brother. "He only waits."

They looked at each other again. And even the air seemed black and cold. It lay like a weight upon their souls. . . . Gilvaethwy thought with sudden sick longing of the great hall outside, the firelight and the thronging people who could eat. He felt a rush of violent animosity toward all people who could eat. He felt a sudden great desire to get drunk. He opened the door.

"At least, if I cannot have any supper I will have some wine!" he exclaimed. "I can get drunk anyhow."

He was about to call for a servant, but Gwydion's eyes met his and his tongue refused to do its office. The unwise might sometimes refuse to obey the commands that Gwydion spoke, but few could disobey the lightning commands that he only thought.

"You cannot," he said. "Did you not hear? 'Mâth the King forbids that you be given to eat or drink.' Will you give them another chance to refuse you?"

They were silent. They were staring again at the black besetting shadows, that were dancing ever more weirdly, ever closing in. . . .

"He cannot destroy us utterly," Gwydion whispered. "That is a thing that cannot be done to anyone. But he can remove us for always. He can change us. . . ." And he shivered.

"Into what?" Gilvaethwy demanded, his teeth chattering. "How would he remove us?"

"Have I not said that I do not know?" his brother answered. "But I hope that he will not do that. And he would not be serving himself well if he did. You he could easily replace, but it would not be so easy to fill my seat. Govannon would not do well for the next king of Gwynedd. He would rule it from his forge, and his only way of judging a litigation would be to melt the contestants up or polish them off with his sword. He knows everything that metal can do, but very little about what goes on inside a man. And Amaethon* would only go wandering through the fields listening to the grain grow and telling the farmers how to bring it up in the way that it should go. He would leave the people to see to themselves while he saw to the crops. . . . Eveyd is clever at tricks; he will do well at magic, but he has no turn for statecraft, and he has never perceived wisdom. Only I have been trained for a king."

"But Mâth may not feel now that his training has done you much good," suggested Gilvaethwy reassuringly.

"That is true," said Gwydion. And he stared long and thoughtfully into the shadows. . . .

Gilvaethwy tried again to moisten his dry lips with his tongue, but this time it too was dry. And he remembered with a sudden cold sinking that he could get nothing more heartening than spring water to wet it with again. He could get nothing more solid either. . . .

He stood silent, fingering his sword futilely. The worst he had ever feared was the coming of soldiers, rough hands dragging him to Mâth the King and doom. But here was no foe to fight against. Only silence. Silence that by its very enigmatic coldness whispered of terrors greater than could be told or dreamed. A deprivation so simple and yet so great that it seemed to swing the world out from under his feet; might do so literally if it kept on long enough. . . . He swallowed.

"Can you not turn leaves or grass or something into food, brother," he asked eagerly, "as you turned the fungus into beasts at Pryderi's? Then we could have something to eat."

Gwydion sighed. "It might look and taste and smell like food," he said, "but it would turn to leaves and grass again within us. And that would be disagreeable. I can create only illusions, and it is easy to deceive a man's eyes or mind with illusions, but it is not so easy to deceive his stomach. That requires reality, little brother."

Gilvaethwy's jaw dropped.

"But then what shall we do for food?" he asked.

"Do without," said Gwydion.

And they did without.

In the morning they rose early and dressed. They drew their belts tight, but they could not draw them tight enough. Then they called for horses and left hurriedly, before any smell of surreptitious break-

*Amaethon seems to signify farmer or husbandman in Welsh. He may have been the pagan tutelary patron of agriculture.

fasting could reach the morning air. They rode on all day, stopping to ask for food at big houses and little houses, at houses set blatantly near the road and houses set well back from the road. At all kinds of houses. But they found none that Mâth's messengers had overlooked.

While man is well-fed he does not realize the importance of food. Eating, like breathing, is a necessity so basic as to be taken for granted: the means to an end. But if we do not breathe we die, and if we do not eat we die also. Yet a man would never admit that he lives to breathe, and seldom that he lives to eat: his opinion of his own happiness or unhappiness, his hopes and desires and ambitions, are centered upon other things.

But for these two food soon became their sole hope and ambition and desire. It became an obsession and a frenzy and a madness that devoured them as utterly as they would have devoured it. They dreamed of it sleeping, and ached for it waking; and even in their dreams, just as their teeth were about to sink into some succulent and delicious morsel, invisible hands suddenly whisked it from under their noses or a voice was heard crying: *"Mâth the King forbids that you be given to eat or drink!"* What had been the means to an end was becoming the end itself, and one for which before many days Gilvaethwy would have traded a yet virgin Goewyn or indeed all the women in the world. And Gwydion would have given all the pigs that ever came out of Annwn for a crust of bread.

No doubt they hunted and fished, but in Mâth's realm fish and game may not have been very plentiful for offenders. They may have stuffed themselves on half-ripe berries, and have unceremoniously un-stuffed themselves again, without real respite from famine. Their insulted stomachs may have had to leap up and spew forth old and odorous meats that had been too long dead. Berries may have seemed to turn green and beasts have suddenly developed an invincible swiftness and cunning at the King's will.

None, not even their dearest friends and nearest kin, could have dared to transgress the commands of so all-hearing a monarch. And when Gilvaethwy, growing frantic, would have resorted to battle and robbery to get food, Gwydion restrained him.

"For we have done enough already," he said. "We dare not do any more. It would be all the worse for us in the end, and I would not bring more scathe upon the people of Gwynedd if it would not," he ended, his gaunt face grown dark with memory. "Besides, youngster, do you want Mâth himself to leave Caer Dathyl and come after us?"

But Gilvaethwy was silent and his brother groaned and added: "If I had known that food was so much the chiefest of your passions, I would not have had to go to so much trouble. I should have starved you awhile and cured that lovesickness."

"Do not blame it all on to me," said Gilvaethwy sulkily. "It was you who wanted Pryderi's pigs. I wanted Goewyn, but I was not doing anything about it, was I? I never dreamed of starting wars and killing and cheating kings. But you would have pigs," he growled, "and now you have got pigs, but you have not got even a taste of half a curl of the tail of one of them."

"I got them for Gwynedd, not for myself. And if my uncle, as Lord of Gwynedd, thinks their price too high, he has the right to ask atonement of me; but not to call me traitor. But by helping you I have brought that reproach on both of us. And there is no escape from punishment, which we dare not take."

"I cannot think of any punishment that I would like less than being starved to death," Gilvaethwy grumbled.

"Go to Mâth and find one," suggested Gwydion.

But Gilvaethwy was not yet ready to do that.

Yet the time came when they reached the end of endurance, and they were ready to lose their heads if they could only fill their mouths first.

They entered Caer Dathyl quietly, like people who do not wish to be noticed. Yet they were noticed. Men who had been eating and men who had been talking and men who had been ogling women stopped and looked at them—and looked away again and went back to their former businesses a shade too casually. On the faces of their enemies moved the shadow of a satisfied smirk and those of their friends showed pale and troubled. Yet on these faces, one and all, was stamped a scared whiteness, a wondering and commiserating awe that transcended both malice and love.

None spoke to them. They were ignored as if they had not been living men. Yet all drew aside to make way for them. And there was something spidery in that silence, that cheerless, indrawing welcome. They felt like flies tangling themselves ever deeper in the silken, iron-fast meshes of a web. There was something unnatural and unearthly in that hush. Even the voices that still broke it with pretense of casual talk sounded futile, hollow, an empty buzz pitted against silence.

The guards made no move to touch them. They moved aside with ominous quietness to let them pass. And the Princes slunk by like the shadows they had begun to feel themselves, and might soon be, aware that every step brought them nearer to the spider waiting at the heart of the web. They had been glad at first that there was no sign of Govannon or Amaethon or Eveyd there to witness their downfall. But now it would have been good to see an intimate, familiar face, even with derision upon it, good to feel the warmth of wrath within or without.

Yet before they passed from that once-familiar world from which they seemed already barred forever, they were to look upon one well-known face. Goewyn the Queen was sitting with her maids near the high-seat, and when they saw their new aunt there they drew together and shrank themselves into the smallest possible compass and tried to melt into the walls like true shadows. But she saw them pass for all that, and smiled. And they got no comfort from that smile. . . .

10

Back to the Forge

MÂTH THE KING was sitting alone in his chamber when his nephews came in at last. He looked up at them and they looked across at him. They were paler and thinner than they had been. They were gaunt, and their bones had grown conspicuous and ridgy, and stuck out through their loosely-hanging clothes. They were meek; they were very meek.

"Lord," they said, "good day to you."

He looked at them a while longer, and his eyes gleamed cold as ice under the grey, knotted surf of his brows.

"Well," he said at last, "have you come to offer me atonement?"

Gwydion glanced at his uncle and away again. Gilvaethwy nudged Gwydion. They spoke at one moment, almost in one voice.

"We are at your will, Lord."

"By my will I should not have lost so many of my fighting men or of their weapons. Nor would so many women and children have been left unprotected in my realm." He rose and stood upright, towering over them, and there was something dreadful and unnatural in that rising, like a great sunken mountain heaving up from the sea. Not often did Mâth the King stand upright in his palace. His face was set like a stone, implacable as a stone, as void of malice or of mercy. "You have traded the lives of the men of Gwynedd for a few beasts' sake, and for a misnamed desire. You have violated love and loyalty and the symbol of that which gave you birth, and thrown away the lives of the men they led and the welfare of your people to serve your own whims.

"For the safety of the realm, for the safety of the womanhood of Gwynedd that brought you forth, can I spare you now? You cannot repair the shame you have brought upon me, apart from the death of Pryderi. Yet, since you have come hither to place yourselves at my will, I shall commence your punishment."

He reached out and took up his wand that had lain beside him, and struck Gilvaethwy with it. And then a strange thing happened. For Gilvaethwy's body seemed to melt as a cloud melts, to shake and fly apart, to twist and curl and swirl downwards until in a moment it vanished as if the stroke had dissolved it into thin air. In the place where Gilvaethwy had been a brown doe of the woods stood starting and trembling.

Mâth's hand shot out and grasped Gwydion's shoulder. Again the wand rose and fell, and Gwydion's form too wavered and grew vaporous and winked out. He disappeared and another deer started and trembled beside the first. . . .

It was done. They cowered before Mâth in their strange brute forms and whimpered with tongues that had forgotten language and the pride of men. And the son of Mathonwy looked down upon them, and his face was sad and inexorable.

"You have been slaves to your passions," he said. "Now shall your bodies too be enslaved. Nor shall you be parted in your punishment who were together in your sin. For it is my will that you go hence in comradeship and do according to the natures of the beasts in whose shapes you dwell. And a year from this day come hither to me."

They fled before his face then; and all the court drew back with frightened eyes and stiff white faces as those hurrying hoofs clicked on the stones and thudded on the rushes. Only Goewyn the Queen still sat smiling and unchanged. The deer ran through the great hall and the great doorway, across the cleared spaces outside the palace, and down into the forest. . . .

Long the old King stood in his chamber. He had not moved; yet with inner eyes he had seen that flight and that vanishing. . . .

"The flawed blade must back to the forge," he said.

And he lay down upon his couch again, and his face was calm as ever it had been in all the decades of his repose there. But on his lashes that were frosted with the winters of the generations gleamed a sparkle as of dew. . . .

So the heir of Gwynedd and his brother passed from the sight of men. They went down into the green world of the wildwood; and little is known of what they did there. They had received the doom they had earned. They had been sent back to that stage of being which their conduct best befitted, to that particular step on the stairway of life where creatures can follow their own desires heedless of right or wrong or the rights of others, and yet remain sinless.

They must have fed and drunk and mated, have hunted and been hunted, like those breeds of beasts whose shapes were on them. They must have worn through all their changes, and the wearing of the seasons, as the beasts about them wore. They were lost in the eventful eventlessness of the forest where nothing ends save to begin again, and only stiffening limbs and waning vigor mark the passage of time.

There is snow and there is heat; there are storms and days of sunshine; there are this year's young growing up and going their ways, and next year's to be conceived and born: but only to the brains of men do these things reckon time. So like is a beast's brief span to that of a whole race of men, each generation of which rears but one litter of young, for among them individuals change, but not the Great Plan, nor the order of its shaping.

And in this life those two who had been Princes of Gwynedd mingled, found it now their sphere. They must have suffered and enjoyed and feared as beasts enjoy and fear and suffer; have known hunger and thirst and satisfaction, weariness and vigor, desire and fulfillment. Their bodies must have forgotten that they had once been men.

Yet sometimes, in the dark, still watches of the night, one, lying wakeful and lonely beside the other, must have remembered. . . . The torches and the song and merriment around Mâth's banquet board in Caer Dathyl . . . scenes from camp and court and ladies' bowers drifting by like dreams. . . . dim bright images of the life that they two had known and lost. And the cramped soul would have whimpered in the strange limitations of its prison, helpless and longing.

But even if the other woke these recollections and regrets could not be clearly shared. For their beasts' tongues could not shape converse, only yelp noises of pain or pleasure, fear or tenderness or yearning. They were not instruments subtle enough for the exchange of thought. Yet in their whinings may have been some comfort, and in that simpler flesh a surer perception of what was in each other's hearts than the more separate, self-absorbed brains of men may know.

Thrice only do the green mists of the woodland lift to let us glimpse them across the centuries:

A year from the day when they had stood before Mâth to be judged a great din arose of a sudden beside the outer wall of the King's chamber: a stamping as of hoofs and a belling of strange voices all blended with the barking of dogs that have seen something new and noteworthy.

"Go, one of you," said Mâth to them that were with him, "and see what it is that the dogs are barking at."

"Lord," said a man, "I have seen. There are a stag and a doe and a fawn there, and it is at them the dogs are barking."

Then Mâth arose again from his ancient rest and went forth from the palace. Outside he saw two deer and a fine fawn with them, and the dogs keeping a respectful circle about all three and barking as loudly as seemed possible. But when these last saw the Lord of Gwynedd they all ran towards him, as if for advice and encouragement, barking louder than ever.

For they were shocked and offended. Deer were something that should be hunted out and discovered, and that, being discovered, should run from one and be chased. But how was one to chase deer that ran towards and not away from one; that overturned all propriety by seeking, instead of avoiding, the houses of men? There was something abnormal and improper about such deer. The dogs said so with big, imploring eyes and wagging tails and asked for instructions.

But Mâth waved them aside and went up to the three creatures from the wild. Only the fawn had been properly frightened by the barking of the dogs. One of the deer was muzzling and licking its shoulder constantly to keep it from running away. The two grown beasts did not shrink as the King raised his wand, but they looked up at him with wide, begging eyes.

"That one of you who last year was a doe, let him be a wild boar this year. And he that was a stag, let him become a sow."

So he spoke, and struck them with the wand. . . .

They were gone; they had wavered and winked out; and where they had been stood two great wild hogs of the wood, quivering.

And Gwydion, who had craved pigs, stood in the form of that which would give birth to pigs.

The fawn shrank back from these strangers, startled and scared-eyed, looking everywhere for its parents. But the King's wand caught it in turn. It too grew fluid and cloudlike, whirling and un-shaping and re-shaping, until in its place stood a handsome boy with gaping mouth and bewildered eyes.

The two swine still stood staring, a little anxiously.

"I will take this young one and have him baptized," said the King, "for he has no part or blame in your sin. And the name I shall give him is Hydwn. But go you and live as wild swine live, and do according to the nature of the beasts in whose likeness you are fashioned. And a year from today come hither to me."

He raised his wand and pointed to the forest, and they fled whither he pointed as arrows fly from a bow. . . .

And that was the birth into our world of Hydwn the Fawn. . . .

So another year went by. And in her castle in the sea lovely Arianrhod may have wept for her brothers banished from the world of men. And Dôn the King's sister may have wept likewise in her court that was called Llys Dôn, and has still its namesake among the stars,* though none knows now where the earthly palace stood.

If she lived she must have wept for her sons, but the ancient books that tell us of their doings say nothing of her, save that Taliessin, the many-lived poet and shape-changer, relates that in one of his countless incarnations he was at the court of Dôn, before ever Gwydion was born. So we know that she kept royal state as a queen. But her name and being are among the Mysteries, perhaps a dim shadow of the All-Mother's own. It may be that when she had brought those children into the world her work there was for that time done, and that she never knew her sons' crime and their doom.

. . . And to a sow heavy with pig, crouching comfortless in the muddy fens, it may have seemed strange indeed to remember the battle triumph, and men shouting for Gwydion heir of Gwynedd, and women's lifted, adoring eyes. . . .

But winter came and summer, and outside the walls of Mâth's chamber the barking of dogs was heard again, and high, squealing cries that were like swines' voices, yet rang with a weird, wailing note of tragedy such as dwells not in the throats of any common swine of earth.

Then Mâth the King arose again and went forth, while all the court watched him with white, wondering faces and kept as carefully clear of his wand as did the dogs from those beasts that broke the ordained rules of beasthood.

There were three creatures beside the wall: two great wild hogs, and a big, young pig with them. Mâth looked at the pig in silence. He rubbed his chin.

"Well," he said, "I will take this one and baptize him."

Then he struck the pig with his wand, and the animal shook and whirled and dissolved and disappeared. A fine stalwart boy with auburn hair stood there blinking and feeling of himself with wondering hands, as if to explore his changed form. It was he that was later called Hychdwn the Tall.

*The Welsh call the constellation of Cassiopeia, Llys Dôn.

. . . There had been three hogs, there were still two. The King turned and looked at them. They were staring up at him and panting; their great bodies on their short legs quivered with something more than fear. Above their bristling snouts the fierce little red eyes were misty and pleading: four fixed depths of mute appeal.

He looked back at them, and in his face, that was high above them as roofs are above the heads of men, there was no wrath and no yielding, only a pity great and far-off as the stars. . . .

He raised his wand.

"That one of you that was a wild boar through the year that has been, let him be a she-wolf through the year that is to come. He that was a sow last year, let him now be a wolf. . . . And do according to the natures of the beasts whose forms are on you. And a year from this day be you here under this wall."

. . . And so they went back to the forest, loping, two gaunt grey shapes of dread; and it may have seemed to them, as to later men who dreamed the nightmare of hell, that punishment was eternal, and hope a candle put out by the sweep of great winds.

It is not known where they wandered. Nor in what lonely fens they howled beneath the moon. Nor what bones they gnawed and in which cave of the forest they laired. Or whether they fed only on things of the wild or their padded feet left tracks in the snow as they slunk round the cattle-filled pastures of men, so that the belated farmer fled from them, two gaunt shadows with green eyes and frost-stiffened coats gleaming under the moon.

. . . Lonely those days were and bitter. They are lost in the grey dusks of unremembered time.

They had been beasts that ate only the sweet green coverings of the earth, and that all men hunt but do not hate. They had been beasts that had lost that grace of habit and also grace of body; and the green unthinking things were still their right food, but they would guzzle, when they could get it, something more. Now they were beasts that craved the scent and taste of blood, and in that grew more like again to men.

They had been hunters and takers before they forfeited their places in evolution, and went from the world of men. Now they were hunters again. But they still knew what it was to be hunted—the tremble and the chase and the fear, the tired, frantic heart that pounds as if it would tear itself out of the body wherein it may soon be stilled, and the knowledge that if one is taken there will be no escape and no mercy: only the crushing, murderous wrath of superior strength.

Men may have hunted them with fire and spears in the night when they had come too close to houses, houses in which perhaps they had once been guests. They may have taken hurts and have licked each other's wounds for healing and in silent sympathy. For being more like to men they were now the most hated foes of man. . . .

They may have preyed on the deer and the wild swine whose fellows they had once been. And in some moment of triumph, white fangs dripping red, that which had once been Gwydion may have remembered: *I too was one of these. I too dreamed in horror and dread of this end.* And have wondered at the strange laws of the cycles that make the destroyed the destroyer and the destroyer the destroyed, until the stupid fumbling beast's brain washed away the vision of the soul and sent the wolf back, ravening, to his raw, bleeding feast.

But the end of that time came at last, as the end of all things comes.

The dogs barked and the wolves howled outside the chamber of Mâth the King. And that howling was more eerie and mysterious than the howls that wolves give looking up at the moon on still white nights. Those howls that have more than hunger or loneliness and longing in them; some cosmic mystery uncomprehended, perhaps some far-off grief of the moon which neither the wailing throat nor the blurred brain knows, yet feels across the leagues of chartless space.

Only the woe in this cry was deeper, worse than that. . . .

And Mâth the King arose again and came forth from the palace. Where the dogs barked around their brothers he saw two grey wolves of the wildwood, and a strong whelp. And it was to the whelp that he turned.

He struck it with his wand, and it flew apart, and disappeared. Another fair boy stood there staring and startled, casting swift glances about him as if he were not yet sure that he was all there and looked to see if some part of himself had been lost in the change.

"I will take this one and baptize him," said Mâth. "There is a name awaiting him, and it is Bleiddwn the Wolfling. And such is the style of these three brothers:

> The three sons of Gilvaethwy the faithless,
> The three faithful fighters,
> Bleiddwn, Hydwn, and Hychdwn the High."

Then he turned to his nephews and looked upon them. They did not move; but their big eyes were sadder and more pleading than the eyes of dogs. Their tongues hung out and their bushy tails twitched between their legs.

Long he looked down at them where they cowered like creatures that pant for very eagerness, yet dare no longer hope. And his own eyes were sad also, sad as the illimitable sea. So a god might look down upon the groaning world of his creation, filled with pity for all that had been and might be, yet unswerving as the fates he had fashioned. . . .

He lifted up his wand and struck. . . .

Again there was whirling and twisting and unshaping and re-shaping, swifter than eyes might follow. They had been wolves; they became clouds; they vanished like clouds; and became shapes again. Two men knelt before Mâth the King.

He looked down at them with his great calm that had the serenity of ages. His eyes were gentle and at peace.

"Men," he said, "enough is the shame and the punishment that has been on you for the wrong that you have wrought. Let now priceless ointment be fetched for these men, and bathe their heads, and bring them clothing. What is done is done."

BOOK TWO

LLEW

I have been with learned men,
With Mâth the Ancient, with Govannon,
With Eveyd, with Elestron,
In the fellowship of Achwyson,
For a year in Caer Govannon.
I am ancient; I am young.
I am universal; I am endowed with piercing wits.

(Book of Taliessin I. Red Book of Hergest XXIII)

1

Mâth Seeks a New Footholder

SO WHAT HAD been was finished, and what was to be begun. There had been crime and discovery; there had been punishment and pardon. Gwydion and Gilvaethwy had been exiled from their world and now they were back again; and the only change that remained was in themselves. And only time could show the greatness or the littleness of that.

It is not likely that they found that much had altered during the years of their absence. A few people had died and a few had been born, and a few had got married or unmarried: that was all. The marriages and—by natural corollary—the divorces, may have increased a little in number as the customs of Dyved made ever steadier inroads upon the ways of the Old Tribes.

Gilvaethwy, noting some pretty girls that had flowered out of squealing, lanky youngsters while he was away, may himself have contemplated the safe and steady enjoyments of marriage—the disadvantages of both rape and celibacy being still very fresh in his mind, and the fashion of virginity being on the increase. There was only one drawback: it would have taken a good deal of time to have married them all. Nor is what he finally did recorded. For the ancient books say nothing of his doings after his disenchantment.

The only real change apparent to the eyes of the two brothers must have been that Goewyn the Queen now sat by the side of Mâth the King, instead of holding his feet in her lap: something that Gilvaethwy had disqualified her for doing—as all three, Queen and Princes, well remembered. Nor is it likely that there was ever more than lip-friendliness between them and her. For none of them yet breathed that rare air wherein Mâth moved, forgetting nothing and forgiving everything, weighing expiation against wrong and cancelling both. For wrongs that are forgotten are generally remembered again at a fresh irritation, and forgiveness is incomplete, a weak and cowardly evasion, if it cannot face fully the memory of what has been.

But the Queen had the memory of her vengeance to weigh against the memory of her outrage. And the brothers had to content them the blessed fact that the former was over. And both sides were now too comfortable to be much disturbed. For there was no reproach or humiliation on the Princes: no strings attached to their freedom. What was done, was done: the people knew it was not the will of the King that what had happened should be kept alive.

And it is probable anyway that most of them very secretly sympathized with their young Lords and thought that Mâth had been unduly severe. Gwydion's pig-stealing was then and for ages after regarded as a glorious feat, and chastity was a new fad which it seemed silly to make such a great fuss about, though it was a deplorable impropriety that the girl raped should have been the King's footholder. Before the innovation of chastity rape had been almost unheard of.

Only three days after their disenchanting Mâth the King summoned his nephews before him.

"What does he want with us now?" groaned Gilvaethwy, who had listened without much show of happiness to that summons. He put his hands to his head, which was aching, for those three days had been passed in jollity and celebration. "I am sure that I do not want to go," he said.

"I am sure that you will go," said Gwydion. "He will say nothing of what has happened. He never digs up an old bone and chews it again. But it may be that he has something for us to do, since he has given us time enough to celebrate our return with our friends. Too much time, judging by the looks of you," he added critically. "I could have done with less."

"You could indeed; you always could. You do not know how to let go and really enjoy yourself," said Gilvaethwy, with a plagued and aggrieved air.

"I do not not-enjoy myself in the way you are doing now, at any rate," said Gwydion. "And I have my own ways of relaxing and taking my pleasure, but you are too dull-witted to understand them," he explained kindly. "They require more power than can be put into guzzling food and swilling beer at a feast."

"Magic?" said Gilvaethwy, and groaned again. "I do not see much fun in that. Or women?" And he looked interested. "I have seen that you have noticed none since we got back to court, and there were many that I was glad to see again. You do not really act so differently from the rest of us on the sly, though nobody could ever catch you at it, unless it was uncle," said he.

"Be quiet and come along to him now," said Gwydion sharply, "for we have kept him waiting long enough."

So they went to Mâth who greeted them as one that was glad to see them again; for not even his ancient heart had outgrown the burdens of human love and longing, nor the fatal vulnerability that prizes one being above others. All men were dear to the son of Mathonwy, but Gwydion his nephew was dearest.

And in Gwydion's mind he saw nothing but genuine response to that welcome; as indeed there was at that moment little else for him to see. But he read the fears in Gilvaethwy's and smiled.

"You have won peace, my nephews," he said, "and friendship is yours also. But there is a matter concerning which I would take counsel with you. And that is, where I shall find a virgin to hold my feet."

Gwydion considered.

"There are young girls growing up constantly, Lord; and we who have been away these three years are now inexperienced among them. There is not one who was at court when I was here last that I could recommend. But some of the younger ones may still be virgins," said he.

"It would take time to tell about that," observed Gilvaethwy, and licked his chops like a cat that has smelled cream. "With a new crop of girls! . . ." said he.

"I am not asking you to make personal investigations," said Mâth. "You would be likely to spoil the article if you found it. There are not many girls who would deny a comely young man and a prince of Gwynedd. Yet I thought there might have been one."

"There has not—!" Gilvaethwy began in the pride of stung vanity, then stopped short, embarrassed, remembering to whom he spoke.

"I am afraid that the excitement of Gilvaethwy's homecoming has been too much for any chastity that he may have tested out, my uncle," said Gwydion suavely. His eyes laughed into Mâth's as no

other's would have dared. "The fashions of Dyved have not yet
become fixed among our women, it seems. And there is the matter
of taste: one of them who would refuse one man might not refuse
another. I have not yet made any experiments, but if I do and fail I
will not be ashamed to tell you of it, Lord."

"No, you would not," said Mâth. "And that is one of the reasons why you would not fail. You have all Gilvaethwy's advantages and your own besides. For women love a man who is not
altogether absorbed in his body but keeps a part of his mind
free and beyond them, above the need of them; though they may
not always be willing to grant him that freedom peaceably. For
his love is then a favor and a compliment, not a fruit to be
plucked from every bough. And moreover, in all human nature
there is that which yearns to explore what is higher and therefore mysterious; and it is that sexless craving, expressed even
through sex, that will one day lead humanity back to the godship
it has lost.

"No, this is not a good plan for finding me a footholder," said he.

Gwydion thought.

"It is true that you would not have much time for the duties of a
king if you had to examine the memories of all the girls in Gwynedd
to learn which had known a man and which had not. We, who have
cost you one footholder, should undertake the labor of finding you
another."

After that he was silent. All three were silent, sitting there in
Mâth's chamber, and their quandary was like a river that their minds
could not cross.

Mâth sat impassive, immobile, waiting for his nephews to breast
that flood; but it seemed that their thoughts halted, as though they
could not swim. . . .

Gilvaethwy was annoyed because he could not understand all
that his uncle had said, and sensed in some of it disparagement
of himself, whom he still prized highly, though not quite so
exclusively as of yore. Also because he could not think of anything to say. He remembered with uncomfortable clearness that
it was his fault that his uncle had a queen now instead of a
footholder.

But Gwydion's mind was moving swiftly, heavy with a plan that
here before his uncle he would not name, even in thought. . . .

"Lord," he said at last, lifting his head, "I am a fool that I did not
think of it before. Arianrhod the daughter of Dôn, your niece, makes
a boast of her virginity. Or has that changed while I was away?"

"It has not," said Mâth, "that I have heard of. But it has never been my business to set the winds to spy upon the doings of Arianrhod. Whether she loves or does not love a man has never concerned the good of my people or my realm."

"It might," said Gwydion, "for it concerns the succession to the throne. But if she will not have a child and do her duty by the race of Dôn, at least she can serve as a footholder. And after so long an absence there must be much for me to attend to at Caer Seon. Shall I go there now and bring her back with me when I return, if she still declares herself a virgin, Lord?"

"Do so, if it is according to her desire," said Mâth. "And do not plague her over-much about this virginity of hers, though it has always annoyed you. For these matters lie in her own choice. You have four sisters. It is not necessary, except because you love her most, that a son of Arianrhod's should be your heir."

"Neither Arianrhod nor Gwydion has ever wanted the one not to plague the other," said Gilvaethwy. "They could not leave each other in peace if they would. They may fight between themselves or be leagued against us others, but it is always each other's attention they must be having, and they are always friends against the rest of us: and they are a hard combination to get ahead of."

"You never did," murmured Gwydion, "yet I have shielded you against her wrath a time or two, baby."

He stood up, and his air was gay and careless. "Lord, I will remember what you have said. Yet you need have no fear for Arianrhod. I am no man of the South to go choosing a husband for my sister. If I were, I could not lay force upon her; for she is a mistress of magic. Dôn our mother instructed her well in all manner of women's sorceries. If she does not come to you a virgin it will be her own fault."

"So be it," said Mâth. "Go home now to Caer Seon. You will find your possessions and your lordship in good order, for I have had Govannon keep an eye to them. And when you choose to come back to this court there will be a welcome before you."

"I will be glad when the time comes to claim it," said Gwydion. "May I take Gilvaethwy with me, or have you a use for him here? Arianrhod might be glad to see him again."

"She would not," said Gilvaethwy, "not particularly, when she has you."

"Be quiet," said Gwydion; and Mâth said: "You can take him."

. . . When his nephews had left his presence Mâth the King sat long looking after them. He stroked his beard.

"He has an intention again. . . ." said he. "What will it be this time?"

He must have wondered as he sat and waited, pondering the years that had been and the years that were to be. To him the past was ever the womb of the future: not a creator of prejudices or feuds, but the field of development, the soil from which the flower was budding or the roots through which the lost acorn builds a tree. He knew that his nephew was still too clever to be straightforward, not having yet dissociated cleverness from guile, though he had lately learned the dangers of too much guile. What form his new intention would take, and how far-reaching would be its effects, it was impossible to tell. But this time cleverness would, of its own nature, reject any marriage with lawlessness and force.

"Yet has he learned the lesson? Have I taught him to prize only prudence, not worthiness? The letter, not the law? It is not me that he has gone to serve, but that is of no matter so long as he serves Gwynedd well. So long as his wish is noble and not base."

It is not likely that Mâth had worried over-much about his nephews' physical safety during their years of absence. No great harm could have come to them, even had they died or been killed in their beast-forms. For death is only a change; and they could not have changed beyond his power to discover and restore them to their proper forms. Over his own he was lord of life and death, at least until that inevitable fated moment of transference when a man's work on this plane is done, and he is called elsewhere for a time.

We do not know what the full extent of his power was, but it seems likely that it extended on both sides of the grave and regulated the conditions of birth and death and of the earthly life that lies between, though not the unearthly years that lie on the other side, beyond time, and between death and birth.

He was master of evolution, awarding to each the tests that he was ready for, and the lessons that he most needed to learn; and thus, with meaning forgotten now in these days when the divine appointment of kings has become a legend and an absurdity, had both the bodies and the souls of the folk of Gwynedd under his hand.

How to cure his nephews of those inner ills revealed by their trespasses must have cost him the greatest thought. For he could not have blotted them out of life and being even had he wished.

To have killed them would only have been to transfer them unaltered to another sphere, from which they would presently have returned the same as when they went forth, for him or another to deal with.

His task was to enlighten, not to punish; for punishment is vengeance, and vengeance is at best a wasteful degradation of strength. The delicacy of the work had lain in the framing of conditions of expiation that would be oppressive enough to provoke thought without blurring it with resentment at personally inflicted torment.

Gilvaethwy's sin had been one of animal grossness, conceived and executed with animal simplicity. But that of Gwydion, Mâth's trained successor, to whom the King had taught his own magic and thus given of his own power, was another and graver matter. For Gwydion had used the knowledge that was meant for the safeguard of Gwynedd to her hurt; had made it a tool to serve his own ends and indulge the desires of a lust-crazy boy. He could not again have been trusted with power until he understood the responsibility of power; nor with freedom until he had learned how to use freedom.

He had seen but had not clearly grasped wisdom. He had been too clever and had become drunk with his own cleverness, which state is a disease far more dangerous and wide-reaching than the cravings of Gilvaethwy's body. For cleverness and wisdom are as different as are the circuitous passages of a labyrinth and the straight, upward flight of a bird. And a master of evolution who showed favoritisms and dealt with his mysterious might so lightly and unscrupulously, using it as a toy to gratify his own whims and others', might well block the paths of evolution and disorder the course of the cycles.

Not to such hands could Mâth have passed on the sacred trust of his kingship; and he had done his best to steady them to fitness for their foreordained and inescapable task. That process was over and done. What it had conceived was shaping in the womb of the present towards the birth of the future.

Of the result of Gilvaethwy's penance there could be no doubt. That young man would walk a bit more warily and less selfishly in future, having learned that there were inescapable and not unjust laws above his own desires, and that was all that was to be expected of him in this round of life. But the doings of Gwydion, who was many times more alive than Gilvaethwy, because he was aware of many more dimensions, and his energies were sent in many more directions, were never altogether predictable.

Might he still think himself clever enough to set aside justice and the rights of another without telling out a price?

He who was to be the next king of Gwynedd rode merrily enough to Caer Seon, and then towards Caer Arianrhod, in the sea. There Arianrhod welcomed him, and there were weeks of feasting in that sea-girt fortress of a princess lovelier than dawn.

She may have been glad to see her brothers again, as common girls are glad, who have no sorcery but their girlhood, and whose faces have not a beauty that is the most glorious gift of gods. She may have yearned for Gwydion long, and have found lonely and bitter those years when Caer Seon stood lordless and he was a fanged or hoofed wanderer of the wildwood.

She may have rejoiced at his homecoming: perhaps too much. . . .

Gilvaethwy must have been with them in those days, and most likely their sisters also, Elen and Gwennan and Maelan, the other daughters of Dôn. They too would seem to have lived in the castle of Arianrhod, for in Anglesey even until recent days old tales were told of how these three escaped on that unknown day when Caer Arianrhod finally sank beneath the sea. The very places of their refuges were pointed out: Tyddyn Elen and the Moor of Maelan and Gwennan's Grave.*

There may have been a sacred well on that isle, as in other parts of Britain, and if so the daughters of Dôn would have been its priestesses and guardians, set to guard that closed Eye of the Deep through which otherwise the greedy water-gods might have risen to swallow more of earth's surface as once they had swallowed the lost lands of the west that were now Caer Sidi, the Country Undersea.

Such are the fears and fantasies of a people whose ancestors have seen a deluge, and in whose bones is bred the terror of the hungry sea.

Arianrhod herself, whose name meant Silver Wheel, perhaps was worshiped by the common folk as incarnation as well as priestess of the moon, the benevolent silver sky-lady herself, come down from her pale bright chariot in the heavens to watch more closely over the tides she ruled, and make them gentle to the coasts of men. Such mystic, mighty song and incantation to control or invoke the elements may have been the rites practices by all the dwellers on those sacred isles around Britain of which Plutarch tells us; on one of which, he says, the Dethroned Father of the Gods sleeps among his men, since sleep is the fetter forged for Him.

*See Sir John Rhys' *Celtic Folklore*, Vol. I. p. 108.

But those are things lost in mystery, and sages and historians quarrel over the fringes of them, happy in the seemingly barren strife.

And then and for long after none ever dreamed that the Castle of the Silver Wheel did not stand firm in its place forever. Nor did Gwydion and Arianrhod think of gods or deluges when they strolled on the white shores at evening, or dreamed under the shade of great trees by noon, looking out towards the green isle of Mona of the Druids, or back towards the mouth of the Menai and the shore where loomed Gwydion's fortress that a later day was to call Dinas Dinllev.

When night came with her frosts and her chill darkness and the pale moon shining over the grey-black sea, they would go indoors and seek the warm friendship of the red fire crackling in the hall. And Gwydion would sing and tell tales, as he had once in Pryderi's court, while his sisters listened, dreamy-lipped and starry-eyed.

He must have told Arianrhod soon of their uncle's lack of a footholder, and of her own candidacy. But he did not ask as to her qualifications, nor did she mention them. She laughed and flung her arms about his neck and kissed him.

"Ah, Gwydion, you were the good brother to think of me! Where better should the King look for a footholder than in his own family and among the daughters of Dôn?"

"Then it is your will?" said Gwydion. "I proposed it, but the matter lies in your own free choice, and I had thought that you might not be willing to leave this place where you are mistress and queen to go to Caer Dathyl and sit all day holding an old man's feet. And I warn you that there will be many eyes to watch you there," said he.

"I have eyes of my own to watch with," said Arianrhod. "Those others will not see more than I choose to have seen. And I have been here a long while. I have done everything that can be done here over and over until I am sick of it. There is nothing left but to listen to Elen and Maelan and Gwennan chatter and to watch my sorcerers do their tricks; and the gods know it has been long since they invented any new ones!"

Elen the Demure who always kept her eyes on the ground was sitting near them and weaving; and she smiled anything but demurely then, though she did not lift the blue modesty of her eyes.

"You had something else to do, Arianrhod, that night in the spring when you went down to the seashore at moonrise. It may have been a sorcerer that did his tricks for you then, but he was not one of those here."

"You are angry because I call you what you are, chatterbox," said

Arianrhod. She turned again to Gwydion. "Do not heed her, brother.
She was always a liar and spiteful. My own sister to tell such a tale
of me! I did go down to the sea that night. I was lonely and grieving
for you and the crystal was clouded. I thought that if I looked long
enough into the water I might see there what you were doing in the
wildwood. But I take the gods to witness that no man of earth met
me there."

"Perhaps he came from Caer Sidi undersea then," said Elen still
demurely. But Arianrhod did not look at her.

"You see what I have to put up with, brother," she said, and harps
never vibrated to more sweetness and sorrow than rang in the soft
dignity of her voice. "Is it any wonder that I am weary of it? Of this
endless tittle-tattle and small jealousies and tongues that stick like
pins? Or that I am not afraid of being peeped at, who have been
worn out with it already?

"But now I shall go to court and hear new things and see what
other women wear and whether my own raiment is still beautiful, or
has become absurd. I shall be the desire of all eyes, and outshine all
women, and seem more precious than any—even Goewyn the
Queen, for she is no longer a virgin."

"I have good cause to remember that," said Gwydion.

She turned to him swiftly. "Ah, my dear one, should I not have
spoken? Indeed, it must have been horrible, pent up in a beast's
body in the wood all these years!"

She caught his arm with both hands and fondled it. Her white
fingers looked delicate as flowers against his brown skin.

So they went away together and Elen the Demure looked after
them with her secret smile. . . .

They went to that place outside the castle where the last trees
grew before the white beaches sloped down to yield to the embrac-
ing sea. The sun was near setting, and all the sky bloomed like a
rose. And that wonder of color, roseate and radiant as only sky-col-
ors are, made the pale sands blossom pink as mayflowers, and tinged
with purple the singing sweep of the vast waters. The earth glowed
like a jewel.

And as they went they passed beneath a tree that was still gold-
decked despite the waxing of winter; and Gwydion raised his arm
and shook down a shower of leaves upon them. But as he did so he
murmured a charm and made a small wonder. So what fell about
them was not golden leaves but a shower of golden stars: not the
great true stars, those worlds of virgin fire or titanic barren balls of
stone that roll ever apart through the heavens, but the little stars we

know, the tiny shining sky-jewels that men think they see, gleaming
as no true gold ever gleamed, far off above the fields of earth.

Arianrhod laughed with delight at that little miracle and dropped
to her knees to gather up stars in her cupped hands. "They are beautiful, Gwydion. They are like beads of light! I wish that I had a necklace of them."

"That is like a woman," said her brother. "Must you be hanging
even the stars about your neck?"

"They are not real stars," said Arianrhod. "It is a woman's good
sense that tells her to do no more than toy with toys."

"A fair hit," said Gwydion, and laughed. "How many things do you
esteem as toys, Arianrhod? But you shall have your necklace for as
long as it will last."

He plucked a blade of grass, tossed it upon the stars she held, and
muttered a charm under his breath. It became a chain of fine gold
upon which the stars strung themselves in her hands; and she
laughed to watch them doing it, then hung them round her neck.

She gave him three kisses for that and he gave them back again.

"You are generous, sister," he said, "for that gaud will not outlast
the hour."

"Nor did the kisses last that long," she said. "What matter? It is
beautiful while it is here. You need not have whispered the spells so
low; I too know that kind of work. I have made such things with my
sorcerers, but we never thought of shaping stars."

"Each shapes his own dream," said Gwydion. "But have you never
wanted to shape something more lasting, Arianrhod? Women can do
that; men cannot."

She drew back a pace and looked at him. The stars of his making
still sparkled like a circle of golden fire around her white throat. The
paler sheen of her hair reflected it. But her eyes shone silver as
sword blades.

"Must you begin that old quarrel again, brother? I am not so lucky
as the girls of Dyved; their brothers care for the honor of their houses. There is not one of them that would berate me for barrenness or
propose such shame to me, a maid unwed."

"Must you pretend even with me, Arianrhod?" Gwydion's smile
was both steely and silken. "Have three years made you forget how
well I know the worth of your claims to maidenhood? Nor would you
be so well off in Dyved. For there you would get more than berating
from a brother who had heard that tale that Elen told."

She stamped a slender foot. "You have let that she-snake foul your
mind! You are jealous! . . . Would you believe her against me?"

"I would never believe either of you when it might be to your advantage to lie to me, my heart," said Gwydion reasonably. "I know you very well. And you would likewise be mistaken to believe me under such circumstances."

"That I too know," said Arianrhod.

"—But jealousy is an art I leave to the men of Dyved, who regard their sisters and wives and sweethearts as property. A thing that you women forget when you will go foolishly chasing after their fashions."

"But the women of Gwynedd have always been free. One can take what one pleases of new customs and leave the rest," said Arianrhod.

"So I thought . . ." said her brother.

He stepped nearer to her. "You and I alone of the children of Dôn have ever sought new things, and never feared them, Arianrhod. We alone have not been too proud or too custom-ridden to study the ways of the New Tribes. Govannon and Eveyd and Amaethon have been too cautious, but we have not been cautious enough; and it may be that that will be the fault forever of the bringers of the new. . . . It is seldom that the seer of a vision sees beyond that vision. . . .

"We have been so clever that we thought we could loot the New Folk of all we desired and pay nothing. But I have learned that whatever we get we must pay for in one coin or another. And what have I won through those three years in beast's shape in the wild-wood, or you with that barren name of virginity, that you are not willing to buy with fact?"

"I have it," she said, "and I keep it. That is enough for me. You lose courage, Gwydion."

"No; I merely begin to see that there are better ways of buying. Not that guile too is without its uses. . . . I will always get what I desire. But a desire should be worth buying. . . . And mine is fatherhood." He used a word from the language of the folk of the South; it did not exist in the tongue of the Prydyn. "And what is yours, Arianrhod?"

"What you know well," she said, "since you are forever urging me to forego it. You choose your time ill, Gwydion, since it is yourself who are now offering me a prize I cannot grasp except by means of it."

He shrugged. "I know that it is pleasing to you to call yourself a virgin, Arianrhod. It builds you up before all men's eyes as the image of an unattainable desire: this dream of the beauty of a virgin princess surrounded by sorcerers and maidens on an island in the sea, and cold as the waves about her. You think there is magic in it that may help you to new power and new glory. But if there is mystic might in virginity, it lies in the fact, not the name. And you have traded lovely things for that barren lie, Arianrhod: a child at your breast and the miracle that is greater than magic."

He spoke truth as he saw it. He thought there was no woman in the world that once the fancy was made fact would not rejoice in the glory of having given birth, or treasure the weight in her arms. But his sister looked at him and curved her sweet lips into a smile whose scorn was as cold as the ice that sparkles on springs and still pools in winter. The same chill radiance shimmered in the blue, sky-like depths of her eyes.

"It is a miracle that has grown stale through overmuch happening. It is a thing that almost any woman can do. And I would do new things; I would have magic and power and splendor. Why should I suffer to bring forth a child when there are so many new spells to be learned and so much in the world to be enjoyed? In my own mind I will marry the knowledge of the women of Dyved to the knowledge of the women of Gwynedd; and who knows what may be born of that?"

"No good thing in the end," said Gwydion. "Bondage for the women of Gwynedd such as already lies on those of Dyved. To be bound to one man and from looking at all others, forever; and to have your body always at your lord's pleasure whether love burns in you at that hour or not. That is what they call morality," said he.

"It is not natural," said Arianrhod. "It would be a foolishness indeed to keep the name of virgin so as to achieve that. But the women of Gwynedd will never let themselves be so yoked. And there is something precious and rare in the idea of a virgin. It gives a woman a prestige and a glamour—and a value that she never had before. To the people it is a mystery. They think it makes me stronger in magic."

"Do you think that you are better than Dôn our mother," asked Gwydion, "than the wise sister of Mâth the Ancient, her who was proud to give us birth? She was never married. Yet she rejoiced and felt the pride of a creator each time that she embodied a soul; and the people rejoiced with her. That is a might greater than any spell."

"What is 'better'?" said Arianrhod. "I do not know. I only know that I am different from the daughter of Mathonwy; that my desires are not her desires, and that I live in my time, not hers. And the gods know that I have no desire for marriage; I would keep my value, not lose it. I would not wish to tie myself to a man who might amuse me for an hour, and then eat stale fruit forever. I have never seen any whose face I could bear to look at every day of my life except my brothers'."

"Then would you doom women to barrenness forever?" asked Gwydion. "You are fighting against the laws of the tides, Arianrhod; and in the end they may sweep you whither you would not go. The old or the new: they blend ill; and for a time one or the other must surely conquer. I would lay no yoke or constraint on you. I only ask you to follow old custom and give the realm of Gwynedd an heir."

Arianrhod yawned behind a delicate hand.

"I thought it was a child of your own you wanted. So why plague me for a nephew? Go take a wife and get a son."

"I have thought of it," acknowledged her brother, "but I do not want a wife. Moreover, it would not satisfy the people. No man could sit securely on the throne unless he were born of a woman of the royal house of Gwynedd.

"There is but one arrangement that the people would accept if you cling to the customs of Dyved. . . . Will you marry me, Arianrhod?"

"Women never marry their brothers," said Arianrhod. "It is not done. It is against the custom of the New Tribes, the inventors of marriage: though why I do not know."

"Our own people would not know the difference," said Gwydion.

"You would be queen of Gwynedd some day," he urged her, "and that would please you. Nor would you be bound in any way. For I should not care how many men you opened your arms to, once you had given me my heir. Our love is too old and too deep within us to be disturbed by your passing fancies, Arianrhod. Or by mine. We would still be comrades and sometimes lovers, and I would teach you all the magical secrets that I dare reveal."

"'All that you dare.' If go to Mâth I might learn more. You have always been jealous of your secrets, Gwydion."

He laughed.

"I thought it. That is why you are so eager to go to Caer Dathyl: to worm out of Mâth some of the secrets of his power. But you would be disappointed, sister. The wisdom of Mâth is not to be won by tricks, but only by hard labor and the building and cleansing of character. It would be free to you if you could reach it; you cannot steal it. A blind man must get eyes before he can see the sun, and so must you before you can share the wisdom of Mâth."

"So say you," said Arianrhod.

And he saw at last that he could not move her from following the fashions of Dyved, any more than a woman of these days could be

moved to wear a dress of fifty years ago to a king's ball. So fast eti-
quette, not ethics, bound her mind.

"I will find you a quiet, biddable woman who will know her place
and not try to come between us," she promised. "One for whom it
will be enough to be a great lord's wife, and when you are king you
can change the law of heirship in Gwynedd."

"I would not get my son so tamely as with her you describe," said
Gwydion, "who must surely be ill-favored or feeble-minded, or you
would never be willing for her to have me. A child should be got in
ecstasy, not in weariness or distaste, or in a bought woman's arms."

"Then use one of your beast-cubs," suggested Arianrhod. "The
sow's whelp, for instance. . . . None could deny that he was born of
flesh of the royal house of Gwynedd."

She caught her breath a little as she said it. She did not know how
he would answer that taunt. But he stood still and only smiled at her,
and his smile had lost neither its silk nor its steel.

"You need not draw so far back out of reach, Arianrhod. I could
get at you without touching you, if I chose. . . . Did you think I was
Gwennan or Elen or Maelan to sharpen your tongue on, little sister?
I have been away too long; you will remember better next time."

And though he had done nothing she suddenly knew that she
would. He had learned his magic from Mâth himself, and his strength
blew through her like a cold wind, setting her own a-shiver. . . .

"I will not use the beast-born," he said, "a human birth is needed.
. . . But you shall ride with me to Caer Dathyl, since it is your ambition to hold feet, not to give birth."

She was playing with the stars that gleamed at her throat. She was
smiling. She was lovelier than the moon at moonrise: slender as the
young crescent, and as palely shining, with her white skin and gold-
en hair.

"I must go to Caer Dathyl, Gwydion. I could not give up that. But
I am not a bad sister to you. There is nothing else that you could ask
of me that I would not give you. I will not have children and be no
longer called a virgin. Let us be friends, Gwydion."

She stepped up to him. She had been frightened for a moment
and desired to repair her ego by seeing his will melt before her own
power.

The sun was nearer setting now. The rosy blossom of the sky had
deepened into flaming crimson. From the far red heights of the west
a golden path stretched over the sea, like the beaming road of light
down which a soul might come to earth. . . . And her white face
glowed against that shining loveliness of sea and sky and sand as

suddenly and startlingly beautiful as the pale moon shining out against the black immensity of night.

She laid her hand on his arm, and put up her lips for the kiss of peace. He gave it, and they forgot awhile heirs and footholders and all their troubling dreams. But in Gwydion, however he might whelm himself in joy or grief or visions, one thread of his being was always likely to remain cold and temperate, unforgetful of his purpose. . . .

2

Mâth Tests Arianrhod

IT WAS WINTER and nearing the time of the solstice, that has been sacred everywhere and in all lands since before man can remember, when Arianrhod at last made herself ready for a journey, and fared eastward with her brothers to the court of Mâth the King.

Many an instruction she must have left with Elen and Gwennan and Maelan as to the care of her house and goods and gear, though she may have locked up or hidden away all truly precious things first. Now she herself rode with her brothers through a world that shone white with the first snow of winter, the trees and the bushes all touched with silver lace; for the autumn had lingered long and been mild and sweet as the ripe fruit that hides late in lonely dells, unfound by bird or beast.

So they came to the palace and were welcomed by Goewyn the Queen. And all was lip-friendliness between her and Arianrhod, though there was not one true greeting in the heart of either. For however much she may have loved and revered her Lord, Goewyn had scant reason to love the children of Dôn; and all her instincts may have bade her not to trust this maid who boasted virtue so proudly, yet was ever hand in glove with a brother who had not respect for virtue at all.

Arianrhod had sent no wedding-greeting when her uncle was married and her brothers outlawed; and Mâth had dismissed that with gentleness, as he would have the petulant grief of a child, saying that his niece loved her brothers and grieved for them. But the bride may have seen it as the declaration of war.

Indeed it is not likely that Goewyn would have got much sympathy from Gwydion's sister, apart from the bias of kinship. For to

Arianrhod nothing was sin unless it was found out. Gwydion himself had sometimes envied her that peculiarity of mind to which guilt was but the singularly constant spouse of discovery—the blithe serenity to which any deed weighed light as thistledown so long as it did not threaten her with consequences. Within her there seemed to sit no judge, implacable and inescapable, weighing and naming a deed. Gwydion had that unwelcome magistrate, though at times he could still drug him into sleep for long whiles.

In that way his sister was stronger than he because she was lesser than he.

The truth is that the weakness of both of them was to think cleverness supreme above all laws, which were only made for it to outwit. And that tameless mental activity was the secret of their endless attraction for each other, and also of their endless skirmishing; for they could rest nowhere and in nothing, but must forever be trying to outwit even each other.

Gwydion had begun to recognize the eventual futility of lawlessness, even the justice of that futility, but to Arianrhod, in whom such consciousness had never been born. Goewyn was an enigma too good to be true, and of whom the worst must therefore be imagined.

For why should any girl throw away name and place to confess that which was in no danger of being found out? Such behavior was inconceivable, and there must have been a reason for it. "She must have made certain that she could trap the King our uncle into marrying her. Probably she did not mind Gilvaethwy's attentions at all, but only betrayed my brothers to make herself a queen. And by so doing she deprived me of Gwydion for three years, which is an offense I have every right never to forgive her for."

For Arianrhod did have one clear and not uncommon conception of what sin was: the inconveniencing or annoying of herself. "But hereafter I shall be at hand to keep an eye on her. Who knows but that the wily wench might even plot to cheat my brother and set her own son, if she can contrive to have one, upon the throne after Mâth?"

Thus Arianrhod, unaware of the web the destinies were weaving, and of what that day itself was to bring forth. . . .

But she greeted not only her young aunt, but with her Govannon, who was likewise then at court, and went on with her three brothers into the chamber of Mâth the King, who greeted them all from the place where he lay in his ancient vast repose, guiding and searching the thoughts of a people. . . .

He looked up at her from his couch. He looked up at her over the wintry forest of his beard. His grey eyes pierced her, and it seemed to her suddenly that they were not eyes, but a grey sea that flowed through every crevice and cranny of her being, exploring all. . . . She was not uninstructed. She held her mind blank as a cloudless sky is blank, void yet covering unfathomable depths; but stiff, as the sky is never stiff, with human fear.

In this strange transparency of her being, which he was reading as a book is read, there was no refuge but in cessation of every thought and feeling. And she made them cease. She became a rigid, unfeeling thoughtlessness. Yet she was terrified lest that very cessation seem to him a necessity and hence a concealment. . . .

"Ha, girl," he said, "are you a virgin?"

She bowed her head with all of Elen's modest demureness. She willed herself into concentrated forgetfulness as utter as though memory had been drowned in the wash of mighty seas: setting aside all the days and years of her life, and every consciousness save of this single moment. . . . She lifted her head again, and the clear beauty of her eyes of empty sky-blue met the grey depths of his.

"Lord, I know not otherwise than that I am."

Mâth took up his wand.

Gilvaethwy started and looked in horror towards Gwydion, but he saw nothing but the faintest shadow of a smile on his brother's face. It passed so quickly that he was not even sure that it had been there; and indeed he considered its presence unlikely enough.

Mâth heaved himself up from his couch and stood upright. Arianrhod's lips whitened and she recoiled a step, but his eyes caught her again and held her. Govannon looked keenly from her pale face to the set faces of his brothers, then back again, with some awe in even his iron regard, upon his uncle.

"Come hither," said Mâth. And like one that walks in sleep, her tranced limbs no longer obeying her will but his, Arianrhod came and stood before him.

Mâth bent the wand into a strange shape. He laid it on the ground.

"Step over that," said he, "and I will know whether you are a virgin."

It was the taking of an oath upon the High Druid's wand of office: the oath that their people regarded as sacred, perhaps also as a test and trial invoking the judgment of the gods themselves.

She shrank, yet now it was her own will that held her, set in the stubborn mold of her desire. She could not turn back.

Her slender foot rose in air, hovered there above the white wand that lay sinister and enigmatic, seeming to wait like a sentient thing.

Her foot fell. . . .

Then, according to *The Mabinogi*, extraordinary things befell. : . .

Her brothers saw her start and shudder as if in the grip of a sudden convulsion; saw her writhe and sway. . . . She screamed. . . .

It seemed to her that her own body was tearing itself to pieces. The broken connection between it and her brain was mended; her body was hers again. Yet she could not stop that frightful inner movement, that awful rending that seemed to be splitting her apart. . . . Something happened. Something gave way. She was relieved and staggered free.

Another cry went up, but not from her. A fat, golden-haired baby boy, sitting on the wand upon which he had fallen with too much force to please him, was yelling out his sense of insult and at the same time vigorously testing the power of his new-found lungs.

Gwydion frowned down upon him in discomfited amazement. . . .

Gilvaethwy and Govannon gaped.

But Arianrhod showed no impulse to pick up the newcomer and comfort those shrieks. For a moment she stared at him, stunned; then as his yells, piercing her eardrums, startled her brain into fuller consciousness of all that this meant to her, she turned and ran towards the door. There another convulsion overtook her. She swayed a second and shuddered. Then she rushed on and was gone.

But she had left something behind her on the floor. What, none had a chance to see, save that it was small. For Gwydion sprang forward, and snatching up the object before anyone could get a second look at it, wrapped it in a piece of satin he had had about his neck, and made off with it through the door.

Mâth looked after his fleeing niece and nephew, and noticed that they fled in opposite directions. . . .

Then he looked down again at what it was at that moment unpleasantly impossible not to hear: at the small stranger sprawled upon his wand.

"Well," said he, "I will have this one baptized, and his name shall be Dylan."

Govannon went over and picked up the dimpled howling mite. "This one has missed his calling," he growled. "He should have been a battle-trumpet.

"What does this mean?" he said next.

"Ask your sister," said Mâth; and rubbed his chin.

"I have a mind to," Govannon growled. "What does she mean by disgracing us all like this, trying to trick you into making her your footholder? Why, the girl is no more a virgin than I am, or this could not have happened! If she had loved some youth and lain with him, well enough. But to go about afterwards with her nose in the air pretending to be cold as a fish—! Having the impudence to try to foist herself into places where she had no right to be, and to look down on honest, warm-hearted women that do not pretend to be different from what they are. She is a shameless, sneaking little liar. She is a disgrace to the children of Dôn. I have a mind to go after her indeed," said he, "and I shall ask her some very sharp questions. Here—take this!" He tried to thrust the baby into the arms of Gilvaethwy, who retreated in lively alarm and refused to take it.

"Let her be," said Mâth. "She has lost the stake she has played for. And her deceits have hurt no one but herself. At least not you." And he looked at the baby in his nephew's arms. "It is ill to start without a mother," said he.

"He has one indeed," said Govannon. "Let me take him to her," he pleaded grimly.

"That would be to wrong them both," said his uncle. "I have no magic that can put love into a woman's heart; that only her own evolution can bring."

They took the boy down to the sea and baptized him. Mâth presided in his office of High Druid, but what those rites of druidical baptism were none on earth now rightly knows; or if once upon a time any did know, they have now forgotten. They held the baby carefully so that he should but touch the sea, but as soon as he came against it he seemed to recognize it as his own familiar and proper world; for the helplessness of babyhood dropped from him. He turned over and squirmed out of their hands and swam off.

Govannon stared after him and scratched his head.

"Well—!" said he.

Mâth stroked his chin again.

"That is that," said he.

"You should have seen that brat swimming off like a little fish, brother," said Govannon to Gwydion. "I thought at first that my own eyes were liars."

"They are not set as crookedly as that," said Gilvaethwy. "It would have been more likely that you had had too much to drink; that is a thing that sometimes happens. But if you had told me at the time that you doubted what you saw, I could have told you that it was really there, brother."

"Be quiet," snapped Govannon, "or I will quiet you! And it would take more than your word to confirm anything to me. There are plenty of liars in this family," he growled, "without my eyes getting the habit."

Gilvaethwy was quiet. He would never have dared to tease the smith at all had Gwydion not been present. It was evening, and the three brothers were alone in the chamber that the heir of Mâth always occupied when at Caer Dathyl. Arianrhod was not with them. She had left hastily that afternoon, carefully not taking time to say farewell to her brothers or her uncle.

"There are times to tell the truth and times not to tell anything," said Gwydion.

"If you can get away with that!" said Govannon. "There are times when somebody else tells it for you."

But both his brothers ignored this allusion.

"This must have been an interesting baptism," said Gwydion.

Govannon chuckled. "It was a sight indeed," he said. "All of us standing there on the shore like old hens staring after a duckling! Even Mâth the Omniscient, our uncle! I will wager that even he had never seen anything like that in all the generations that he has lived. You missed something, brother. I cannot think what you ran away for, anyhow. You acted as guilty as Arianrhod," said he.

"I had my own reasons," said Gwydion.

"You generally do," said his brother. "I thought I saw you pick up one of them by the door as you went out. What was it? You wrapped it up carefully enough, for all the hurry you were in."

But Gwydion only picked up his harp and ran his fingers over the strings, and the soft notes rang through the room like subtle voices from lovelier, wilder worlds than this. . . .

Govannon eyed the harp distrustfully.

"I am not Pryderi to be magicked with your music," he said. "Well, this is one of your times for not telling anything, I suppose. All the same, there are several things I should like well to know about today's goings-on: how and why the King put that charm on Arianrhod; and why she had this little fish instead of an ordinary baby. Is there nothing that it is the time for you to tell us?"

"Mâth did not charm her," said Gwydion. "She charmed herself with her own fear; because she knew that she had that which must be hid from him. So herself helped to betray herself."

"But if she knew that she was with child, how dared she come here to be footholder?" demanded Govannon. "It is disgrace enough to us that she did so," he growled. "Mâth has been a good lord to us, but we are not always good to him. I should have thought that you would have been made furious, indeed, Gwydion, when Arianrhod played him such a trick after it was you that had proposed her to him!"

"Would you?" said Gwydion. And his lips were grave but the eye that he turned upon his brother seemed to shine again with that secret smile. He was bland and blissful now; that discomfiture which had seemed to take him for a moment in Mâth's chamber, when Dylan was born, had vanished like a mist.

"Besides, she did not play a trick on him," he added. "He saw to that."

"Did you know that he would?" Gilvaethwy said, with a sudden interest that made Govannon glance sharply at him.

But Gwydion only smiled.

"I knew certainly that he would never take any footholder untested," said he. "And she was not already with child, Govannon. She would have been too clever for that. But it is not well to take false oath upon a druid's rod. That was the charm of the wand and of the form into which Mâth bent it: that if she who called herself a virgin had ever held within her man's seed and most of us believe nowadays that there is such a thing as that—it should come forth from her in that state of fruition which it would naturally have reached during the time that it had lain within her; or should so have lain."

"But you did not tell Arianrhod that before she came?" Govannon chuckled. He sobered. "But still this rule must apply only to recent doings, brother; or Arianrhod might have had quite a family."

"Mâth has judged recent doings enough," answered his brother.

Govannon scratched his head. "Well, there is nothing like magic," said he. "But still you have not told me why our nephew should be so like a fish. It does not run in our family," said he.

"It may run in his father's," said Gwydion.

". . . If you can be sure about such things as that," said his brother doubtfully. "After all, a child does not happen every time that a man and a woman lie together. If it did, the world would be so full of them that some would fall off of it. Virgins never have them; that grows certain now that we have a few virgins. Yet there must be something more to it than that. Something that even you magicians do not know, of if you do, you will not tell the rest of us."

". . . Idiots!" said Gwydion. "You can grasp the fact that virgins do not have children, and yet you can still doubt your own part in it! How can the world ever progress? I am beginning to be sorry that I have caused the deaths of so many of the men of Dyved, for at least they had more sense than this. Get out of here and let me sleep," said he.

"I have not said anything," said Gilvaethwy with a wronged air. "Why did you say 'idiots,' brother? Govannon has been doing all the talking."

"And he will continue to do it when he is where you are," Govannon grunted, "or would if it were humanly possible." He took his younger brother's arm. "Come along now. We are not wanted here."

"After all you cannot help it," said Gwydion graciously and forgivingly. "I did wrong to reproach you for being no cleverer than the degree of your development."

Govannon snorted and dragged Gilvaethwy out with him. . . .

Left alone, Gwydion smiled to himself. Then he went to a chest that stood by his bed, and touched it with his hand, tenderly, as if the wood had been living flesh. There was no mockery in his eyes now. They were grave and deep and shining, like a river under the clear radiance of dawn.

"Here at last is my desire, shaping under my hand," he whispered. And he thought with a pang of pity of Arianrhod fleeing back through the night to the Castle of the Silver Wheel, alone in her disappointment and chagrin and grief.

"But you will feel well repaid for all when you see what my guile has gained us, Arianrhod. And there was no other way, for you were too much of a fool to be brought to give us both this good gift otherwise. Why must you be so foolish, Arianrhod, and make me hurt you when I do not wish to? . . . But Dylan gave me a start." He chuckled. "What mer-man met you, sweet sister, that spring night that Elen told of, when you went down to the sea to grieve for me? Well, let him find some lordship for Dylan in Caer Sidi. Here on earth I will care for that which is mine."

3

Gwydion's Wish Come True

AND GWYDION THE King's heir took that chest back with him
to Caer Seon, and kept it at the foot of his bed. And winter howled
through the world, driving snow and storm before it, with cold
winds that were like whips of ice; and under the white, shrouding
snows and the grey-brown blanket of decay and deathliness the
earth brooded, hiding down nearer the fires of her ancient heart
all that she would presently bring forth in blossom and bloom
and birth.

That which would make the flowers upon the fruit trees slept,
unguessed at, under branches that were hung with the white lace
the clouds weave, and that we call snow, and were jewelled with
sparkling ice. The fields shivered under the wind and the stubble,
hiding the emerald treasures that were to be. In the caves the bears
laired, and there was no movement in those caverns except where
the cubs waxed within the sleeping mother.

And the servants at Caer Seon talked of magic, and told that they
had seen their Lord standing awake and alone at dead of night, murmuring spells over a chest. With a fever of curiosity and expectancy
they wondered why, yet shrank with the dread men have of magic.

And spring came over the Western sea, gentle as some shy girl for
the first time coming to her lover's arms. The lash of the winds
turned to the sweet-scented, silken blowing of her hair; snow and ice
melted from the earth.

Breathing became a delight and movement a joy, so full was the air
of the wine of growing and awakening life. The sun burnt through the
veils that had barred him from the world and glowed upon it like a
golden smile. The sap ran in the trees; the stags in the forest lifted

their heads to sniff the strange glory upon the breezes; and the earth sang her rising-song.

It was the time of the world's rebirth . . . .

And one morning as Gwydion lay awake in his bed, watching the chamber fill with the pink creeping twilight of dawn, he suddenly heard a thin, feeble yapping. It was not loud, it was muffled as though by heavy swathings, and the weakness of something that does not quite know how to cry, but gives its first stumbling orders to muscles that have never been used before.

It was a cry of impatience, of discomfort and demand, laying claims upon an unknown world. It came from the chest at the foot of the bed.

Gwydion sprang up when he heard it. He opened the chest with hands that shook a little for all the steadiness that they had gained from Mâth's training in magic. For the secret of magic is that it is a science that requires marvelous control and concentration of mind, just as the intricate metal machinery with which men of today work their miracles requires marvelous planning and shaping and fitting. And that is why magic is now denied and discredited by many who, lacking the mental vigor to carry out or envision the process, dismiss it as children's tales and phantasy; and clumsily substitute telephones and radios for the all-penetrating thought of Mâth.

For the man who is so average that we call him normal is driven this way or that by all the haphazard thoughts and moods at whose mercy we live, as sheep are driven by a dog. But the magician has gained mastery over his thoughts and moods, and they obey him as dogs do men.

But not quite always, for Gwydion was yet a young magician, and his heart beat faster as he looked to see the achievement of its desire. For it was a very human heart. That is to say, he loved with human weakness, not with the high, far wisdom of the gods, that is surely not less deep and tender in the end. Otherwise he would never have sinned for Gilvaethwy's sake.

When the lid of the chest fell back the satin bundle inside was wriggling and whimpering, still making those amateurish noises of discontent and of desire for it knew not what. But as the inrushing air invigorated the bundle and eased some of its discomforts, its resentment of these waxed correspondingly stronger, and its noises rose to a yell. It squirmed out of the satin and held up its arms.

It was a child.

Not red from the rough ejection of birth as are children who make a more orthodox first appearance; but pink as a rose or as the dawn itself, and fat as a little ball of butter. On its shapely small head gleamed here and there downy bits of fuzz moon-gold as Arianrhod's own oft-sung locks.

It was a boy.

Gwydion snatched it up and wrapped the satin about it again. "Good morning and be quiet," said he, "for we have a journey to make this day, you and I, the first of many journeys we shall make together; and your voice would get us over-much attention on the way. And we must make haste; for though you are too inexperienced to know it, it is probable that you are hungry."

And the magic in the soft tones of his voice soothed the baby's nerves, and carried his will to its throat muscles that had but just learned to obey its own, and imposed it there. So the baby, thus mastered by this transmission of thought, which later men would call mesmerism, was still.

Gwydion cloaked himself in a mantle that was great enough to conceal the child on his arm, and the two set off.

Behind them, in the vacated chamber, the chest stood open, the sun dissipating its magic and mystery. A warm dark nest despoiled alike of treasure and darkness, a cocoon emptied of the butterfly, a tool that had served its end. . . . And what charms Gwydion had put upon that chest to make it complete the incomplete and give the sexless and unshapen, shape and sex, remains a mystery to this day.

He is the first historical inventor of the incubator, and by far the most successful. Perhaps the art was brought by the forebears of the Prydyn from Caer Sidi, in the days when that lost land was above water, and the home of earthly men.

It is not recorded by what ways they journeyed, Gwydion and the child, not exactly whiter. Hasty that journey must have been, for Gwydion could take no risks with his precious achievement; and yet he must have yearned, with delighted and marveling curiosity, to examine every fraction of an inch, and every finger and toe of his masterpiece. Indeed, he may have designed all these in the course of the spells muttered over the chest.

Most men come by a child by chance; it is an accident in the pursuit of their desire for woman; and never greatly labored for and not always highly welcome. But for Gwydion the matter had not been so easy. He had not got a child save by dint of wishing and willing and plotting and laboring. This child was perhaps more intimately his than any other child has ever been any other man's.

But it was to a woman's house they came at last; for it would seem that magic could serve Gwydion no further, and that now the human aid of woman was required. This one had generous breasts, and nursed for hire the children of mothers whose milk was scanty or unwholesome, or who were flighty with the spirit of unrest that comes with times of change or new ideas such as Arianrhod and her kind were bringing in from Dyved.

Gwydion looked at this mother for hire, whose profession was then still a new one in Gwynedd; and she looked at him.

"Well," said she, "it is generally a woman that brings me the kind of burden you have there on your arm."

"It was brought forth by a woman of my kin," said Gwydion. "She had two or three at the birth, and not enough milk for this one. So I brought it since she could not come herself, though that is an unwonted kind of work for a man and a warrior," he grumbled with beautiful naturalness.

It was not beautiful enough. The woman surveyed him with a keen eye.

"She is of your own kin, and yet you do not seem sure how many she had at the birth; though you have one of them new-born in your hands there. This is strange."

"The women were not yet sure that she was through when I left the house," said Gwydion. "She was still making a good deal of fuss. But this was the second, and she has never had milk for more than one. Moreover, she was peevish about this gift of the gods. Blasphemous ingratitude, I call it."

"Maybe she thought it was the gift of a man," said the woman, and giggled. "Has she often had them before that you know so much about her supply of milk?" she asked.

"Three or four times before," said Gwydion, mentally cursing the haste that had denied him time to put another shape on himself. For he did not wish tales of his care for a child to get abroad in the land yet. Arianrhod might hear them too soon; and he knew his lovely sister far too well to trust her.

"But you will be well paid for caring for this one," said he.

That changed the direction of the keenness of the woman's eye; and they haggled over terms awhile; for Gwydion was too wily to foster her suspicions by letting her drive too easy a bargain. But she had the grace to take the irritated mite to her breast and show him where to begin a meal there while the proper and expected wrangling went on.

"For though you may be tight-fisted and a skinflint," she told Gwydion, "the poor child is too young yet not to be innocent of your mean nature, and I cannot see him die of hunger before my eyes.

It is his misfortune, not his fault, that he was born into your kin," said she.

Gwydion, remembering the might of the royal House of Mâth and its ancient glory and the lordship of Gwynedd, could have laughed at that last saying then, but in an after year he was to remember it with sorrow and bitterness.

"His misfortune is that I must leave him to be nursed by an out-rageous old she-goat," said he. "And if he did not come of sturdy stock I should be afraid that your base, boughten milk would poison him. I hope he is tough."

"Maybe his mother could squeeze out enough for him after all," said she, "for it is certainly not worth my while to let myself be sucked dry by every stranger's brat for charity."

"Indeed, if you keep on asking more for his keep than any child was ever worth, I shall have to carry him back and let him take his chance with her," said Gwydion.

But at last they made a bargain, and Gwydion gave her gold, though she said it was nothing, and not one tenth so much as she had a right to expect, or as the quality of her milk was worth.

"Indeed, you talk as if you were the prize cow of Gwynedd," said he when all arrangements were concluded.

"And who are you to say that I am not?" she retorted with spirit.

But that gave him a thought, and he looked at her with eyes that were keen as steel under his long veiling lashes.

"And do you know who I am?" said he.

"No, how should I know the name and kindred of every miserly rascal that comes traipsing to my door with an unwanted brat?" was the vigorous answer.

But he read the lie in her mind. Not for nothing had he been trained by Mâth.

"You know who I am indeed," he said softly; and his sweet bard's voice purred, and his grey eyes grew narrow and glittering as the edges of a sword. "You know that I am Gwydion the Magician, the King's nephew. And why did you hide that knowledge from me?" said he.

The woman turned pale. She shrank back. "Lord," she stam-mered, "I thought it was your wish not to be recognized—to pass as a common man. Otherwise I would never have made so free. And indeed I did not know at first who you were, though I was sure that I had seen you somewhere before."

"Indeed I did not wish to be recognized at all," said Gwydion, and sighed. "However, since you had seen me, you could not help doing so; and I will forgive you that fault. As to the freedoms you have taken in addressing me, they are no matter; they were all in the game. No enchanter who was so easily insulted could ever hope to work more than childish charms; and you would doubtless admit that I am gifted at paying gibes back in kind.

"So long as the child thrives and you keep silence about my having brought him here, you shall be paid as we have bargained and your house and your goods and all that is yours shall thrive. For my protection will be with them." And she knew that it was not of ordinary human protection, and of wordy injunctions to be laid on the men of Gwynedd, that he spoke: but of something far more powerful and mysterious. "But if you breathe a word of me, even to a tree or a bush; or if the child has an ache or a pain that you could have prevented, all that you have will be blighted and there will be misfortune and ruin on everything you do, and each of your joints will be extremely rheumatic to the day of your death," said he, and the silky purr of his voice was deadlier than the green gaze of a stalking cat.

She turned whiter than ever.

"I have heard that women cannot keep a secret," he said, and now he smiled; and his face was merry and friendly again. "But I have noticed that they can when it is to their own advantage to do so. (Except one," he thought, remembering Goewyn, "and in the end it turned out that it had been to her advantage to confess. Perhaps even to mine. Who knows?) And while I do not wish to threaten you, I am making it to your advantage to prove that women can keep secrets."

"That they can," she said. "None will ever know from me that you have been here, Lord, and the child will be well seen to, for indeed I know how to do it."

And though it seems absurd to us, it may be that Gwydion did well to pledge her never to speak of him even to a bush or a tree. For a tale is told of another Lord, March ap Meirchion, perhaps that same who was uncle to Tristan and husband to Iseult, that he had the strange blemish of horse's ears. Only his barber, who dared not tell it on pain of death, knew this; and he fell ill of keeping the secret, as many folk would now were there a fear great enough to lay such silence on them; and his cure was that his physician bade him tell the secret to the earth. But that earth grew reeds, and pipers cut them to make pipes. And when these were played before King March they would play no tune but *"March has horse's ears! March has horse's ears!"* And I do not know what happened to pipes or pipers after that.

But all this has not very much to do with Gwydion. . . .

4

The Warning of the Stars

ITS LORD returned to Caer Seon; and it is not told that his servants
knew that he had been away. Perhaps he had left a garment transformed into his own likeness in the bed in his stead; and nobody had
dared to wake him up.

But one wonders how many had had the courage to peep into the
open chest. . . .

At night he went forth again, when all the world was asleep
except for the wild things in the wood, and the fox that creeps
through the field on his way to seek the hens of men. In that lonely
hour of midnight gloom and stillness, so like so many nights now
happily bygone, did Gwydion remember that he too had once
roamed the wildwood and worn fangs and fur?

He came to a wide, still field where there were no trees even to
hide from him the heavens. The stars twinkled high above him, little
golden jewels that seemed eternal, watching through the aeons from
out the void of space; and yet shone no lovelier or brighter than those
that had once twinkled around Arianrhod's lovely neck in that rosy
twilight on the white beaches outside the Castle of the Silver Wheel.

One by one those stars had melted there, and she had taken her
hands from about her brother's neck to try to catch them, laughing,
as they flickered and flashed into nothingness. . . . That at least he
must have remembered as he set about the calculations ordained by
his druid's art. . . .

For great though his haste had been at dawn, after he had heard
the cry in the chest, we may be sure that he had marked well the
height of the sun and where each of the fading fleeing stars was, that
he might calculate now with a nice exactitude.

For he knew that already the infinite shining host of the heavens
had included in its cosmic, ordered movements and in the gleaming
cryptograms which through all the ages it has drawn upon the black
primeval vastness we call sky, that great dark formlessness which is
the mother of all form, the destinies of that young life which the last
dawn had seen begin.

And it was this rede of the stars that Gwydion had come forth to
seek. He must have been well-fitted for the task, for the Triads name
only two who were as skilled in the study of these floating torches of
the heavens as he: Idris, and Gwyn ap Nudd, the White One, a King
of the Underworld.

Long Gwydion read and pondered; and sometimes his face was
happy and sometimes it was troubled. He made a map of those
gleaming designs of fate and destiny and pored over that; and when
he had printed it upon his brain as indelibly as the men of his day
are said to have printed pictures on their skins, he built a fire and
burnt it. For there was no spot on earth that he would have considered safe enough to be its hiding-place. . . .

His eyes brooded awhile on those smoking embers. Something
darker and colder than night shrouded his soul. Then his gaze rose
again, as if for comfort, to the silent stars. He shrugged like one who
casts off the gloom of a cloaking chill.

"You have warned me of a great peril," he said to the quiet stars,
"but there is only the one. Many have dangers far more numerous to
face. And it should be small trouble for him to escape this doom,
being warned; for he will know of it and no others in the world will,
save myself and perhaps Mâth."

But the stars kept silence, unwinking, and the sleeping world lay
around him, dark and tranquil in its peace.

So he comforted himself, and the courage that had worn through
all the changes of his being and the dread mystery of exile not only
from his home but from humanity, came back and warmed him. He
felt once again that his wit was invincible, a sword sharp enough to
cut the web of all predestined perils. He forgot that the danger of
another is also the property of that other, to be dealt with in his own
turn; and that only for a few years may a man answer for the actions
or discretion of another, even of one who is his very creation.

Gwydion, who had always been well aware of his own separateness from Mâth, could not yet conceive of his own heir's separateness from him: and that has been the unwisdom of age throughout
the ages. For a child is not long to be reckoned as a doll or a pet, but
as a man who must stand or fall by his own efforts.

A year passed.

Nothing is known of what happened during that time except that the child who had been in the chest grew.

Indeed, it is said in *The Red Book of Hergest* that he grew so much that it would have been surprising to see a youngster twice his age as big as he. But due allowances must be made for poetic exaggeration.

Gwydion must often have visited the nurse's house by stealth that year; although *The Mabinogi* does not say whether he did or no. But he would surely have wished to see how his heir was doing, and how his instructions were being obeyed.

No doubt he gave her no warning of his comings; that omission would have suited both his policy and his mischief; and she may never have known at what hour of day or night she might be startled to see that tall figure with its long cloak and druid's wand beside her, taking in all with keen mysterious eyes. And she may not always have felt sure that he was not there when she did not see him. It would be somewhat of a strain to be nurse to a magician's child.

The two may have differed at times over details of the baby's care. For men and women have differed over these since Eve bore Cain; as indeed it is the nature of men's and women's minds to be oftenest at war over most things, though sometimes their bodies patch up an hour's truce. There is no suspicion and no feud so old as that between the sexes, so ancient in its beginning or more remote in the time of its end.

The nurse must have wanted to use old simple charms and old customs, in which the son of Dôn saw no sense. And he may have wanted to try innovations that seemed to her heresy and craziness, and for which she would take no responsibility. One wonders what commotions there may have been over the getting of a tooth, or the proper way to treat a spell of colic, and which won: druid's art, and man's experimental, brain-born magic, which was the first source of science, or the ancient rules laid down by the hard-won, hoarded experience of women.

But on the great point, the importance of the child's welfare, the two would have been at one, since their relationship was merely that of partners working together for this common end. There was no complicating love and jealousy between them, as between a father and a mother; they simply served the child whose being Gwydion had willed.

Yet Gwydion could not have spent a great deal of his time in the woman's house, for he might have been seen there or his protracted absences have caused curiosity. Besides, he had his duties at Caer Seon, in the judgment hall, and among the feasts and the fields and the folk; and whatever sway it was that he exercised over the beasts as Tribe-Herdsman of Gwynedd. That sway must have extended to pigs now as well as to the cattle through whose customs he had once worked out a definition of paternity. It is easy to imagine with what eager interest he must have supervised and planned the increase of those dearly-bought, grunting protegés of his, from whose overseeing he had been so forcibly removed during the three years of his own beast-shape and exile.

The habits of swine he had no need to study. He knew them. . . .

Also, it is probable that he visited Arianrhod often, where she sat in her sea-girt castle in boredom far worse than of old now that it was embittered by disappointment and wrath, and by the tales that were being told in the land, echoes of those happenings in the presence of Mâth. And her brother may have made many little charms and wonders to console her; yet have felt no tinge of guilt in his pity, thinking as a man might who deems that he has deprived a child of a light pleasure, yet only in order to give it a greater and more precious at an early day.

Neither had anything to fear from Mâth; for it would seem that he did not concern himself with affairs of sex unless, by involving rape, they violated the primeval law of mutual passion and the Ancient Harmonies he served.

His niece had tried to deceive him but had failed; so there was no more to be said of that. He was not a vain man, to feel his self-admiration or his self-importance outraged by her implied belief that he could be deceived. The basis of all such prideful swellings and glorifications of personality is self-aggrandizement, born of self-doubt, and neither was in the son of Mathonwy. He knew his own worth too well to hold that it could be damaged by the thoughts or deeds of others; and he saw no glory in suspicion. Arianrhod had learned that she could not deceive him; and penalties would not have improved on that lesson, or have altered her nature.

Nor was he a vengeful man, to pursue Gwydion with malice because he had, to serve his own ends, subjected his uncle to the disappointment of awaiting and receiving an unfit footholder.

But Arianrhod was not grateful to the King for his magnanimity. Had she dared, she would have raged at him for having had such foul-minded suspicions as to test her virginity. Fear of his all-reading thoughts restrained her from so venting herself, even in her own mind. Yet her aggrieved fury had to be loosed in some direction, and Gwydion heard some of its bubblings and frothings.

"Why could you not have warned me, brother, that Mâth would not take a girl's word for her honor, but must make trial of it in such hideous and embarrassing ways? The horror of that moment! And the terror of it! Not knowing what else he would do to me, for having dared to come before him at all. . . . And now the name of maidenhood has gone from me. . . . I am wrecked; I am wrecked forever! After the shock and the fear and those birth pangs I shall never again be the same. . . ."

And she wept, for she felt that indeed she would never be the same again; nor would the world be the same for her. She was ashamed, not of having lied, but of having been caught in the lie. She was likewise intolerably disgraced in her own mind because she had given birth, though doing that which had made it possible for her to give birth had never caused her one slightest twinge of guilt. The guilt was that of those others who had caused her deeds to come to light. Her offenses thereby became their offenses against herself; and she hated them proportionately. She had been subjected to pain and fright; and that was a great crime, for which someone should have paid. But she did not know of anyone who could be made to pay.

Presently she was to know. . . .

In the meantime Gwydion stood watching her weeping loveliness as a man watches a child weeping for some broken and trifling toy. And he said the thing that he thought would soonest soothe her. "You do not look wrecked! . . ." said he.

Then she lifted her dripping eyes to his that were become her mirrors; and saw in them all the joy of her own beauty: the line of her cheek that was fine and delicate as any poem, with the tears lying upon it like crystal beads, or dewdrops that might have mistaken her face for a flower—how sweetly her mouth was set between those twin poems of her cheeks, red as a rose, and more luscious than any honey that a bee ever made from a rose's heart's blood.

She gazed entranced by her own loveliness, cooling her hurt pride at the fountain of the wonder, which must surely still set her above all others.

Then she remembered again that it was her duty to grieve for her wrongs. "But you should have warned me, brother—"

"Am I to foretell all that Mâth will do?" said Gwydion. "If I could have done so, I would not have passed three years in beasts' shapes. I gave you a chance, Arianrhod, and you took the risk of it, and lost. Be glad that, if unmasked, you are unpunished."

"I would be glad that that wretched brat had swum off, if I were sure that he had drowned, and I will never be glad of anything else," said Arianrhod. "It is well for him that he did not stay ashore," she added vindictively, "for I could have reached him there, and I would have put him out of this world far wore gladly than I put him into it. Yet it is best that he went as, he did, for my vengeance might have come too late to save what is left of my good name, had either you or Govannon so lacked regard for me as to take him and try to rear him."

"If I had been trying to rear him it would not have been well for you had you tried to put him out of the world, Arianrhod," said her brother; and his voice was as soft as velvet.

She knew that velvety tone and mistrusted it. She glanced up at him swiftly. "Ah, yes, you always loved children, Gwydion; as I do not. But I think you would not hurt me, whatever I did. I was afraid at first—afraid that you might want Dylan. You had besought me so for an heir. I was glad when I heard that you had not even gone to his baptizing; that you had cared so much for my sorrow, brother. . . ."

And she let him take her in his arms and console her. But while he did so his thoughts were far off, with the real reason why he had laid no claim to Dylan.

His boy had another danger besides that doom whose menace was written in the stars, unless indeed she too had her part in that doom: Arianrhod, his mother.

5

The Dawning of the Mind

ANOTHER YEAR passed, and the child was big enough to come to the court by himself. So at least it is said in *The Mabinogi*. But if such little legs could make the journey, the nurse's house must have been very close to Caer Seon; or Gwydion must have had her and the child removed to a place near at hand.

The child may have seen great folk riding by on their way to Gwydion's court, and may have followed them, drawn by the lure of their gay clothes and bright faces and the prancing of their swift horses, until he saw where they went to: the great round house with its moat. And wonder and curiosity about the place that could be these bright beings' destination may have mounted within him until the fear and shyness that are common to children and all wild things were overcome, and he went within.

Or another brain than his may have stimulated that wonder, all unknown to him, and another will than his have guided those little feet. For no doubt Gwydion could at times read thought from afar, and, playing upon whatever vein of it best served his ends, shape the doings of the thinker. And what material could he find more plastic and impressionable than a child's mind, which is at once unbelievably intricate and unbelievably simple, all confused with the birth pangs of its own uncomprehended powers?

Be that as it may, the child from the chest did enter the court at last; and there were other children there, the offspring of courtiers and servants; so none marked him. None but one. . . .

It may be that for a time Gwydion had not gone to the nurse's house—at least not visibly, or when the child was awake. So that now his face was not known to the child or clearly placed, yet here among all these strangers shone out with a look that was dimly haloed by memory, friendly and trustworthy among all that was utterly unknown and strange. For it may not have been Gwydion's wish to reappear before the child as a recognized part of the old life, lived in the hired woman's house, or to transplant him abruptly, so that he might long for her and be afraid, but to become a magnet drawing him away from the past, fading the old and creating the new.

And who would have known better how to charm a child than he, with the brilliance of his bard's gifts and his mesmeric will, and the love that gleamed sincere and uncalculated in voice and look and touch, through all the calculation that his cleverness could never lay aside, even with a child? What a fund of inexhaustible and enrapturing tales he could have told, what dreamy depths of sleep and peace must have flowed to the call of his singing, or the touch of his cool, magnetic hands!

The ancient books say simply that Gwydion took heed of the child, and that it came to love him more than it did anybody else. . . .

So the boy was brought from his nurse's house to Caer Seon; and no doubt that woman, whom the old manuscript ever leaves nameless, wetted him with many tears and kisses at parting, and gave Gwydion countless instructions and advice—to half of which he may have listened, thinking that one fourth of them might be valuable. Perhaps it is proof that he was wiser than most men that he listened at all.

So now he had got all his wish, and had the child to himself at last. . . .

And that autumn, when he went after the harvest to a feast at Caer Dathyl, on that one of the four quarter-days of the year which marks the beginning of the winter, and is now called Hallowe'en, he carried the child along with him and showed him to the kindred, though he told no others what woman had done the bearing.

Govannon ap Dôn was the first that saw the young one. He looked at him and scratched his head and looked at his brother again. "Where did you get that from?" said he.

"From Arianrhod," said Gwydion.

Govannon scratched his head again. "I thought it was something she had dropped that you picked up by the door that day. But I did not think that it was any good. Let me lift him," said he.

And he did.

"He seems quite real," Govannon said, weighing him in his arms and appraising him with approval. "He is heavier than a full-sized axe already. How did you manage it, brother? But I know that it is no use to ask. . . . He is as good as the one that swam off."

"He is better," said Gwydion. "There never was one like this before."

Govannon handed their nephew back to him then, and that was not so easily done, for the child had got a fistful of Govannon's whiskers, and would have liked to keep it, though he preferred returning to Gwydion's arms, for he was not yet quite sure what he thought of his uncle the smith.

"He has a better grip at any rate," said Govannon "but then he is older too." He chuckled. "It is luck that Arianrhod has not had the face to show her face at this feast, brother. There will be war again in Gwynedd when she learns of this."

Gwydion sighed. "There would be a welcome before her if she did come; Mâth holds no grudge. There is no disgrace on her except in her own mind. What must she be always making such a fuss about?"

"She was born to make a fuss," said Govannon.

"Well, she will be a madwoman if she is not pleased when she sees what she has produced in spite of herself," said his brother. "But let her be or not be. I can deal with Arianrhod."

"So it would seem." And Govannon glanced again at the child and chuckled.

"What seems what?" inquired that young one.

"Nothing that anybody could tell you about," answered Govannon. But Gwydion's brows were furrowed and his eyes were dark with thought. His voice cut across the child's prompt demand of "Why?" with a question of his own:

"Is Elen here or Maelan or Gwennan? I would not have Arianrhod hear of the youngster before she has seen him."

"All the sons but none of the daughters of Dôn are here," said Govannon. "If one of those girls does not go to a place, the others stay away too. They are loyal in their way; they will all stay at home and keep busy annoying one another rather than that one should be left out. That you should know, Gwydion."

"I do indeed," said the elder brother, "but it is well to be sure. . . ."

Later Mâth saw the child.

He looked long at him and stroked his beard as he looked.

"Who is that one?" said he.

"He is the one who will be king of Gwynedd after me," said Gwydion. "He is Arianrhod's second son."

Mâth went on stroking his beard.

"He is also the intention that you had in your mind nearly three years agone when you set out for Caer Arianrhod to fetch me your sister," said he.

Gwydion had the grace to look ashamed. "There was no other way to get him," he said. "Arianrhod would never have had a child of her own will. I sorrow that I had to make use of your need for a foothold-er. But I did not leave you unwarned; I knew that you would know I had some plan in mind. That much my thoughts could not have hid from you. And I have served Gwynedd well, Lord; for where could we find a fairer to come after us?"

"We could not indeed," said Mâth. And he looked again at the child, who stared back at him unwinking and wondering, as a child might stare at a mountain, vast and venerable beyond all under-standing, and older than the ages. And in the King's look there was all the high tenderness and sorrow of the infinite, that sees in what paths the wheels of destiny are set, yet cannot turn them but must let them thunder on to do the will of the fates that man, their crea-ture, has shaped.

"You and Arianrhod between you—!" he said. "You are fast forcing in the ways of Dyved, and doing away with all that I have ruled over, and all that has been through the ages. And even as you do it, you thwart each other, as the wont of men and women is. Nor do you clearly see whither you are going, or the nature of the times you bring in, you who seek only your own desires! . . . But change is the way of the world and its progress; and who am I who still wear a body to say that the laws of the cycles have let a change come too soon?

. . . "You have your heart's desire, Gwydion; and you have set aside the ancient laws and used guile and trickery to obtain it, as your way is when your wish is strong; and once again you will tell out the price, but this time not to me."

"To what then?" said Gwydion.

"Did you not read the stars the night after you took him from the chest?" said Mâth.

So the child was received into the circle of his kindred, and all went according to Gwydion's will, and there was none but admired and praised the small heir of Gwydion heir of Gwynedd.

It must have been a strange world that the child who was later to be called Llew grew up in: a world of big houses full of big people who were always busy with myriad mysterious businesses that one knew well enough were only temporarily interrupted to feed and wash and dress one, or to play with one.

There were other children, but none of them were nearly so important as oneself. There was not such a fuss made over them;

and they were different. They nearly all had mothers. These were women who were fond of them and intruded into all their most private affairs very arbitrarily and seemed sometimes to be a comfort and sometimes a nuisance. In the main they were fussy and easily disturbed and clucked like hens. Gwydion was never fussy; nothing seemed ever to have been invented that could disturb him.

There were ladies, who cooed and bothered one with too much kissing. There were servants, who waited on one. There were men, who grinned down at a person, and said jovial things loudly, and then left him to mind his own business, as was proper.

There was Mâth, a vast remote being, rather benevolent, but wholly awesome. There was Gwydion, likewise a wonderful and marvelous being, but always humanly warm and near. One belonged to Gwydion and therefore owned him, as possessions have a way of owning their possessor. For what a man owns, he must tend and keep; and thus he ends by existing to serve it, instead of its existing for him.

Gwydion was his uncle; the child knew that. Also that therefore Gwydion must be his mother's brother, for nephews were sisters' sons: a confusing thought for one who had no mother, but evidently must once have had. The relationship of uncle and nephew was the most intimate that could exist between a man and a boy. The child had heard of fathers, but understood that there was a certain dubiety attached to them—something to make jokes about. He could not quite understand what they were supposed to be.

It was proper, therefore, that Gwydion, being his uncle, should bring him up. So far family relationships and obligations were clear. One could even understand that Gwydion himself might once have been a little boy being brought up by Mâth, just as oneself was now being brought up by Gwydion.

But if that were true, then Mâth too must once have been a little boy being brought up by somebody; and it was impossible to envision that. The mind reeled and imagination failed before the effort. Even as a baby the son of Mathonwy must surely have had a great dignity and a long white beard. He pictured a miniature Mâth, enlarging, but unchanging.

And what Somebody could ever have been ancient and venerable enough to have brought up Mâth? The child thought that the gods themselves sounded too young.

But then, ask as many questions as you might, you could never trace anything back to a clear beginning. For instance: if a god made the world and all that was in it, who made that god? Surely he must have had a mother. Surely, he could not have made himself too, out of nothing? He could not have just happened.

That question may have vexed him profoundly, as sometimes today it still vexes children; and it is unlikely that even Gwydion could have answered it.

Life would have been a very complicated business for the youngster, for life is always very complicated for children. It is only in maturity, when we are weary with the strain of responsibility for making our own livelihood and our own decisions, that we look back upon childhood as a time of peace.

To children the freedom of grown-ups seems godlike, and they have no doubt at all of their ability to use it if they could only get it. They know what a strain it is to be constantly governed; to have to submit blindly to decisions whose wisdom their brains are not yet sufficiently developed to see; always to have to ask whether one can do this or that; and to be called "bad" for growing impatient under any of these innumerable, incomprehensible restrictions.

It is less easy for a child, in whom energy and initiative are ever bubbling up fresh and undiminished from the very fountains of life, buds flowering, however boisterously, towards the development that shall enable it to stand alone, to bow to this inevitable, constant dictation, than it would be for many an adult, worn out with the grind of constantly exercising initiative, and of driving failing energies into action.

And when one goes ahead and acts on impulse, without thinking to consult anyone, there is always the probability of having to face the shock of being suddenly and grimly accused of a crime where none was intended, and whose very nature is a mystery until it is explained; yet which one should evidently, by some divine revelation, have known better than to commit.

There are so many things to learn to do and not to do, so much knowledge to be acquired whether one is interested in it or not, so many puzzles and surprises—for why, for instance, should one's desire to make a noise be wrong, and someone elses desire for one not to make it be right? Apparently, since the other person is larger, simply on the principle of might.

In even the happiest of homes small brains sometimes grow dizzy and therefore obstreperous from coping with these problems, and must—so long as there are grown-ups and children in the world, and eternal war between these two opposites as there is between men and women.

For it is a strange thing that the most intimate relations of our lives, those which hold our holiest and deepest loves, should also always be innate antagonisms, individual combats in the universal war that is as old as sex and consciousness and the reproduction of life. Yet so it shall be until the day when the world is healed and the sundered halves are welded, and consciousness is more clearly and truly conscious than ever, yet has fused and melted into the One.

And by this child all would have had to be learned and unlearned and vainly puzzled over and forgotten, which is all that children can do with their great riddles, twice as fast as by other youngsters, if it is true that he grew twice as fast. Yet it seems unlikely that Gwydion would have wished for, and therefore have magically fostered, such a rush of development with the scrambling haste to learn and lack of thoroughness that would have been its inescapable partners.

And it is likely, granted his wily cleverness in all things, that he would have been the most careful and subtle of teachers. He would even have been guileful enough to be always straight-forward, since guile would have alarmed the child and wakened its distrust. He would have been gentle, for violence was not his element, and was the one in which it paid him least to meddle, as his dealings with Goewyn and Pryderi bear witness. His province was ever the brain.

And that developing young minds must have been as lovely a delight to Gwydion as the growing garden is to the gardener; as the poem is to the poet or the painting to the artist. But perhaps the simile of the garden is best, for only the flower or the child can grow of themselves, into shapes of their own, doing their own work in the wonder.

Gwydion would have watched over and guided that development, pruning one thought and watering another, tending it carefully till the bud was ready to flower of itself. He would have planted seeds and have tried to dig up the shoots of others, though that is a hard task, for nothing can wipe out knowledge once obtained, though sometimes new knowledge may transform and transmute it.

His watchfulness would have been as tender and all-pervasive as air; but it would have been watchfulness. Not an experience, not a thought, could have escaped those faculties trained by Mâth. And exquisite art would have been used in hiding from the child what a thoroughly read and open book he was; for nothing is ever so feared and resented by the human brain as pressing inquiry into the privacy of its thought. Gwydion's long-coveted and now treasured little heir, if seemingly less interfered with than most children, would actually have been enfolded by a vigilance not much less omniscient than a god's.

Yet the time always comes when all vigilance must fail. . . .

Gwydion rode one day to a feast at a vassal's house, and the child, left behind, was set by some chance to pondering the dimness that surrounded his own beginnings. All children had mothers; they had to have. The few he knew that did not had had mothers, but they had died. Was his dead?

The child felt no need of one, so his interest in the question was purely mental, but this does not say that it lacked intensity. He had a naturally bright and active mind, which was being well trained to activity.

The servants were at his service: a fact he had always known and made as much use of as was safe. They would do anything for him so long as Gwydion had not forbidden it. This was partly because they were fond of him, and partly because they feared their Lord his uncle. He knew that, too. So he put a question to one of them, a round-eyed, red-checked girl, who was young enough to seem a little like a contemporary.

"Where is my mother?"

(He would not give her a lead, by asking whether his mother was dead. Grown people sometimes hid things from children, or confirmed suggested solutions sooner than disclose or go to the trouble to propound true ones.)

The girl grinned. She was young and liked her joke. Besides, she was new to Caer Seon and its master's ways.

"In the Lord your uncle's sleeping-chamber, at the foot of his bed," she said.

The child trotted off to look. He had his doubts; but it was possible that a strange lady might recently have entered the palace without his knowledge.

Presently he came back and stood looking up accusingly at the girl. "You told a lie," he said. "There is nobody there; nothing but a box."

"I said that you would find your mother there," she answered. "I did not say what she was."

"That is another lie," said the boy. "Children do not come out of chests, they come out of women." For he knew the fact of birth. The age was not one which had developed the finicking foul-mindedness that stimulates curiosity and an overgrowth of the sense of indecency by hiding natural necessities of life under a cloak of shaming mystery.

"It is all the mother you ever came out of," the girl said, and giggled.

The child stared at her and saw that, incredible though it seemed, she was not lying. The knowledge seemed to take a large piece of the ground out from under him—to suspend him over a bottomless gulf of fear. . . .

"But that is not true! My mother would have to be my uncle's sister!" he cried, and his voice had grown suddenly shrill. "You are an ignorant, silly girl and do not know what you are talking about."

She laughed. "I may be ignorant and silly," said she, "but I know well enough how people are born. And you were never born at all. Your uncle got you out of that chest, and people say that he made you there, by magic. Some who have been here longer than I have told me that they used to hear him muttering incantations over it by night; and then one morning they heard you cry when you were being taken out of it. That is why you have never been named. Because it is mothers that name children, and you never had a mother. They think he made you to get an heir, because none of his sisters have any children.

. . . "Though some do tell queer tales of the Lady Arianrhod," she added reminiscently, "that she did have a baby that swam off like a fish and was never seen again. But there is nothing fishy about you; I myself have seen the Lord Gwydion teaching you to swim. Unless you were that baby and were drowned, and he had to bring you to life again in the box."

She had enjoyed the wonder and agitation that she saw increasing with every word of her tale. Those marvelous events had awakened wonder and excitement in her too; and she was anxious to pass these on, especially to a principal, if involuntary, actor in those doings whose drama she could not otherwise share.

But to the child they were a tragedy. He stamped his foot and shrieked. "You are a fool and a liar and a bad girl, and every word you have said is a lie. It *must* be a lie! And when my uncle comes home I will ask him to turn you into a toad!"

Then he ran off, leaving her with her light malice shriveled and chilled to a rising fear that she had indeed gone too far and might even get some such fate as he had named. She shivered as she remembered the powers of her mysterious Lord. . . .

But the child was in the grip of worse fears. He had speedily forgotten both his threat and her, but he could not forget the things she had said. They hunted him as dogs hunt a deer; there was no psychic water in which he could make them lose the smell of him; no inner forest of himself in which he could twist and double and throw them off. They buzzed about his ears like wasps, as persistent and as stinging. They were nightmares that chased his panting brain and quaking imagination up hill and down dale.

For if he had not been born, if he had come out of a box, then he was no right child. Real children were always born of women. He was only a magical illusion; and he knew Gwydion's illusions. He had seen a pebble or a blade of grass turn into a golden ball or into a puppy-dog with a beautiful bark and a tail that wagged as naturally as other tails; and how, in an hour or two, these lovely things always disappeared and became inanimate pebbles and grassblades again. Their going had never deeply grieved him; Gwydion could always make some more.

But could Gwydion make him again? Would he disappear presently and become something else, something that did not know or feel anything at all? If he did, and Gwydion re-enchanted the thing that had been he, would it still be himself, or another little boy, not himself at all? Gwydion would surely not let him disappear while he was at home; he was too fond of him for that. But Gwydion was away. What if before he came back—? The child shuddered. . . .

Neither was it much comfort to think that he might have been the Lady Arianrhod's baby who swam off. That would be a grisly thing: to have been drowned and then brought to life again. He felt a little terrified of himself at the idea, as if he had been a ghost.

And he thought, with a shivering horror, of night. . . .

Night came; but he would not go to sleep. He was afraid of sleep. For what better time could there be than then, when he did not think or feel, when his mind seemed for a little while to have ceased to be, for his body too to go back to the feelingless, thoughtless state of a stick or a stone or a bunch of straw?

They put him to bed, but he got out again and began to play with his toys to keep himself awake. He continued to get out again as fast as they could put him in. They tried to sing him to sleep, but he shouted at them to leave and threw things at them. They coaxed and begged and threatened; but he knew that they dared to make no threats good for fear of Gwydion. And in any case he would not have told them what the matter was. It was as if to speak of it as reality would make it the more surely real. And besides, he felt ashamed of his lack of secure place in the common brotherhood of humanity.

Eventually he tired and pretended to go to sleep in order to get rid of them. But when they were gone it was a horror to lie there alone in the dark, wondering miserably what thing he might have been before he was transformed into a boy; and even worse, when, with a start of terror, he found himself dozing off to sleep. . . .

Whenever that happened he got up again and threw something across the floor so that the noise and exertion might wake him up. It woke up the servants also. But coming in again to remonstrate did them no good.

When he had thrown all the things that could be thrown and was sick of doing that, but still felt the dreadful demon of sleep creeping up on him, lying in ambush and stealthily waiting, lynx-eyed, to pounce in his first unguarded moment, he took to dancing up and down like a small fury, to keep awake.

But that too was dangerous. It brought exhaustion that lay like weights of lead upon his eyelids and tried to force them shut. And when he relaxed for a moment, feeling himself enfolded in a dimness that seemed friendly and not menacing, he heard one of the servants whisper: "Well, thank the gods he's settling down quietly and going off at last."

And that reminded him that he might indeed go off and out as well, and seemed so heartless a taunt that he sat up and hurled such abuse at that luckless yet ordinarily and safely born individual as he had never dreamed that his lips could utter.

This woke him up again, but that was a great grief to the servants.

When Gwydion rode home in the morning he found a tired and blear-eyed household that looked as if it had all got out of bed on the wrong side, and had gone there after getting the worst of a fight, at that. Gwydion looked all the servants over and singled one man out with his eye. That man stepped forward.

"What is it that is on all of you?" asked his master. "There is nothing wrong with the child . . . ?" And his eyes were sharp as Govannon's knives.

"There has something got into him," said the man. "He refuses to go to sleep. Last night if any of the women would try to sing him to sleep he would throw something at her, and if others of us folk were in the room he would throw things at all of us, and if we went out of the room he would throw them at nothing. He did not have one wink of sleep all night, and nobody else had many."

"This is a new thing. . . !" said Gwydion. And he drew his hand over his lips and chin in the gesture that was Mâth's. "Does he say why he objects to sleeping?" he inquired.

"He does not," said the servant.

"He was asked?"

"Yes. It only made him have a tantrum. Lord, we have done our best—"

But Gwydion was considering: "He has never had bad dreams. For I have been away only this one night, and I have always sorted out all his dreams before he dreamed them."

"He did not use any of them last night," said the servant, and sighed.

"You say he did not sleep at all? . . . Well, at any rate it is a great victory for a young child to have managed such a feat as that."

"It is indeed," sighed the servant, "if that is the way you look at it."

"What did he have for supper?" Gwydion asked with a very straight look.

"Nothing that was not wholesome, Lord. Nothing that he has not had many a time before."

"I hope that nobody has been putting notions into his head about the dark. I hope it for that person's sake," said Gwydion, and smiled in his soft, sweet way. . . .

The man took a step or two backwards. "Not that I have heard of, Lord!" he stammered. "It is not to be thought of, Lord, that any here would dare—"

"Yet there must be a reason somewhere," said Gwydion.

"We thought that perhaps it was an imp or a demon of the air that had entered into him," the man explained eagerly.

"It is more probably an idea than an imp," said Gwydion, "but one learns nothing without investigating the subject. Well, bring the child to me," said he.

They brought the child, and Gwydion looked at him and he looked at Gwydion. One of them had to speak first, and it was not Gwydion that spoke.

"I do not want to go to sleep," explained the child.

"You will," said Gwydion, "and you shall. But what are your objections to sleep? You have been sleeping off and on all your life, and it has never done you any harm yet."

But the child did not answer. He hated to tell the reason even to Gwydion, who might admit that it was true. And he was very tired and very cross.

"Well?" said Gwydion.

The child looked at him.

"Are you the brother of a box?" he asked.

"That would not be a good question if it were not gravely put," Gwydion said. "It is a strange one now. Explain it."

But the pause was so long and so troubled that Gwydion put out an arm and drew the child to him.

"If it is something that is too hard to put into speech, think it out clearly and I will know it and answer," he suggested, and his voice was as tender and luring as the thrush's when he calls to his mate.

The child clung to him and shivered. He was past clear thinking.

"Are you the brother of my mother?" he asked.

"Yes," said Gwydion, holding him close. "I have told you so before, and it is not the kind of fact that changes."

"But then my mother would be your sister, and is your sister a box?" the child inquired and wept. "I thought that sisters were always women. And Eigr told me yesterday that I was never born at all, that I came out of a box, that one at the foot of your bed, where you made me by magic. And if that is so, I am not real, and some day I will stop being me and turn back into something else. And I feel so very real" He wept again. "I do not want to stop being me."

"You will not," said Gwydion. "There is nothing you could turn back into. For you have never been anything but a child. You came out of that box indeed, but first you came out of a mother, my sister Arianrhod."

"Arianrhod?" repeated the child and shrank. "I have never been dead, have I?" he asked in fear, and shivered.

"Doubtless you have died and been born many times," said Gwydion matter-of-factly. "We all have. Having been dead is nothing to worry about."

"Eigr said that folk said that the Lady Arianrhod had had a baby who swam off. And that if I were your real nephew I must have been that baby and have drowned and been brought to life again by you," said the child.

But he no longer waited with bated breath and pounding heart for the answer. With Gwydion's arm about him, and Gwydion's calm, untroubled voice in his ears, night and fear seemed unreal as the dark shapes that the mists sometimes took on the moors at night, monstrous and threatening visions that were never there if you touched them, and that Gwydion said were only the illusions that the night made, playing with itself.

"You were not that baby," said Gwydion. "You were another. You were born before you were ready for birth, and you would have died if I had not kept you in the chest until you were as old as you should have been when you were born. It was not a good start, but you have got over it. There is nothing the matter with you now," said he, "and nothing for you to be afraid of."

"But Eigr said that I had never had a mother; that that is why I have never been named," the child made his last complaint.

"Is there anything that Eigr did not say? She would have been wiser if she had said nothing at all." Gwydion's voice was so gentle that it was almost a purr.

"Your mother has not named you because she does not yet know that you did not die of being born too soon. I have been saving you as a surprise for her. . . . It is time indeed that you had a name," he murmured reflectively.

The child lay quiet against his shoulder. Peace was flowing over him, warm and gentle as summer waves after the storm . . . peace and safety. The weights on his eyelids were no longer of lead; they felt light and sweet as a kiss . . He *was* a boy; he had always been a boy. He was human and had been born like other people. And his tired small heart sang with the knowledge . . . . Yet he pulled himself up once more out of that exquisite, billowy peace. A thought had caught him, flashing across his mind like a shooting star.

"That baby that swam away, it must have been a boy if Eigr thought it could have been me. Have I a brother then? I wish I could see him."

"He never swam back," said Gwydion. "Go to sleep." He rose, crooning a bar of the sleepiest song in the world, and carried the child off to bed.

Gwydion himself had slept little the night before. The feast had lasted long. Now he lay down by the child and kept his arm about him. But even while exquisite healing peace and oblivion stole over the tired little body from that hold, and his lips caressed the tumbled curls of gold, they murmured another kind of charm also. So that all that day the girl Eigr kept her face tied up in a cloth; and it seemed to her, so violent was the pain she had, that there was a coal of fire in her mouth in place of one of her teeth.

Gwydion had yet to attain Mâth's freedom from malice. . . .

6

At the Castle of the
Silver Wheel

YET WHETHER he slept beforehand or no, and whatever spells he cast, Gwydion must have done some grave pondering as well. He had had a time of peace, watching a seed blossom and a child grow; and now that time was past. His truce with life was over, and he must again pit his will and wiles against destiny and the will of another.

That will was Arianrhod's. . . .

"For this business has made it plain that the boy is now old enough to question. And it is the nature of a question never to rest until it has got an answer. And the young will find a wrong answer, if they are denied a right. Though he did not say so, he has gone hunting with a question or this girl Eigr would never have talked so much. That she did so is something she is already regretting or soon will be. . . ." And he smiled. "Hereafter I must keep all questions and answers in my own hands. I have watched closely, but I shall watch more closely still.

". . . Moreover, I have waited long enough. It is high time that Arianrhod named him, and do so she must and shall."

For according to the custom of the times, the child's position as Gwydion's heir and a son of the royal house of Gwynedd could never be secure unless Arianrhod herself named and thereby acknowledged him. A baby-name was a light matter; Gwydion's boy may have had one, though we have no record on this point. But the permanent name must be conferred by the mother and ceremoniously confirmed by the druid,* even as long ago the small Gwydion had

*See suggestion in *The Welsh People,* by Rhys.

had the name of Dôn's giving formally put on him by Mâth. So the scheme so guilefully conceived and executed at her expense now lay at Arianrhod's mercy; and her child's rights hung in the balance.

But Gwydion, appraising him with proud eyes under the morning light, could not believe that Arianrhod might actually choose to thwart her brother and disown her son. *The Mabinogi* says that the child was then four, and that it would have been a marvel to find a boy of eight so large. He may have been or have looked six. He was still round with the roundness of babyhood, but he had begun to lengthen and shape. He had a nose now instead of a button. His shoulders were still chubby and dimpled, but he was getting leggy, and those long little legs had the straightness of young pine trees. His crisp curls shone like gold, and the lashes of his closed eyes were as long as his lovely mother's. In any way and all ways he was perfect, and Gwydion could not imagine the heart that would not have swelled with pride and joy in ownership of him.

And could such an unnatural heart dwell in Arianrhod, sister and dearest of comrades, who all his life had been his own most intimate ally?

"It is the best time indeed for her to see him," he reflected, looking at the child. "Now when he begins to show what he will be and yet still has about him that look of the baby that women love. She would be more than human if she could resist him. Dylan she never saw, or got but a glimpse of as she fled, so that perhaps it is no wonder her instincts were not awakened. And who knows—may it not have been thwarted instinct, as well as disappointment over the loss of her chance to be footholder, that made her mind pursue him with such malice?

"But this one she shall see, and her own folly at the same time, if the gods have made her as other women."

The child slept until that day's end. Then, when the sky was red with the little death of day, and the crimson pyre of sunset was sinking into the ashes of twilight, he woke. And Gwydion had a servant girl—not the luckless Eigr—bring him hot milk and food. After that Gwydion told him a tale, not of the high marvels that excite, but all filled with the magical sleepy wonder and glamorous dimness of dreams, and wandering like a dream. So that presently the little boy's mind was washed away by that tale as gently as though it had drifted off on the soft-singing waves of some rainbow river.

And ever, as the tale was told, Gwydion's compelling eyes were on him, deepening his burden of sleep. . . .

For it was always so with Gwydion's tales. They could be a torch to the mind, or a lullaby. They could instill the lesson he chose to teach, or bring the forgetfulness he wished, or, rather, that over-lay-ing of consciousness which men so name; for forgetfulness is in truth an illusion, since nothing is ever lost, though it may be buried deep.

But they were ever beautiful, for it is by beauty alone that the mind is refined and the soul grows.

And having thus put the child to sleep again, that he might look his freshest and fairest on the morrow, when all his beauty would be needed, Gwydion went to his own meal and rest, and perhaps to his own thoughts. . . .

Day came again and its duties: breakfast to be eaten and digested, a bright new world to be inspected and enjoyed. And still the child did not know that today was to be different from other days.

He remembered his tempest of two nights ago clearly and vividly as blazing lightnings and roaring thunders are remembered; but he did not brood over it any more than people brood over the great storms of the elements. For that was over and this was now. He had a child's art of living in the present, the eternal shield of those small beings who must remember longer and forget sooner than any oth-ers in the world. If nothing can be truly lost, everything can be put away out of sight. And that is the secret of children's easy forgive-ness, which is not really forgiveness at all. Its lack is also what wears out grown men and women, bowing them more than the years.

But Gwydion did not forget. By which it is meant that he did not lay aside consciousness of what had passed. He had his own plans. . . .

He put on a cloak and made a great show of preparing to walk, and when the child looked at him expectantly, he moved his hand in the desired sign that he could follow. Man and boy went out together.

I do not know what distance may have lain between Caer Seon and Caer Arianrhod, but it was not far. Or else Gwydion transport-ed himself and the boy thither by some means swifter than that earthly, God-given magic of feet, to which we are so accustomed that we forget this, our own bodies' true and intricate miracle. For only that which is strange seems miraculous, though greater mysteries may surround us every day.

But before the sun had more than half finished his flaming. climb of the heavens, the two were before the round buildings of the Castle of the Silver Wheel And Arianrhod, having seen her brother's approach either with her own eyes or with some subtler vision learned from her sorcerers or from her mother's lore, came to greet him and give him welcome.

They met in the great hall and put their arms about each other. Joy and gladness were with her for that meeting; and the light of them was on her face. Her greeting smile was lovely as an unfolding rose at dawn. The boy, watching her in wonder, thought that he had never seen anyone or anything so shiningly beautiful. She looked like a lady fallen from the bright world of the sky.

"Ah, Gwydion," she said. "Welcome to you, and the gods be with you, brother."

"The gods give you good," he answered, and kissed her. And that was the first time that the child had ever seen him kiss a woman. . . . His mind was to hold the picture forever: her gold hair and white arms draping Gwydion; her upturned face that had no match in Gwynedd save perhaps Goewyn's, that the child forgot and would never see so vividly; and Gwydion's dark head lowered to hers, all that was known and safe and dear bending to the unknown, glamorous mystery of woman. . . .

The picture did not last long. She looked over her brother's shoulder and saw the clear young eyes fixed in wonder upon her. Her delicate brows knitted and darkened. "What boy is this that you have along with you?" she asked.

Gwydion gave her the straightest of answers. He did not undervalue the effects of surprise, for he always saw a lapse in his sister's control or in anyone's as an opportunity to be used for his own ends. Nor did he wish to break the news with a delicacy that could be construed as apologetic, and so admit her right to take offense.

"It is your boy," said he.

Silence fell as swiftly as a blow. She stared at the boy, and the boy stared at her: neither more amazed than the other. For Gwydion had in no way prepared the child. He had wished him to appear before Arianrhod unhampered by shyness or speculation, and not overwrought with expectation.

The child thought with a little thrill of awed yet triumphant wonder: "She is my mother! This lovely lady, and not a wooden box, is my mother!" And his heart gave a queer little skip inside him.

But Arianrhod stared at him amazedly, as the moon might stare at some outrageous, strayed little star that had somehow left its right, distant place in the heavens and intruded into her own orbit. Stared until the stunned blank of amazement gave way to something else, but not to tenderness. Her bright face lost all its glow and sweetness, blazed like some beautiful, fierce flame rising to leap forth in the hissing hunger to destroy.

Her hands did not clench, but they rose from her sides, every muscle in them tensed, rigid. Their delicate, long-fingered whiteness looked claw-like, cruel.

She gazed on her little boy as though the light in her eyes could have burnt him to a cinder, and she would have joyed in so obliterating him.

But Gwydion's eyes had measured the distance between the child and her; and now Gwydion's gaze turned hers and held it, that blue baleful stare meeting the grey sea-deeps that had never fallen before any look but Mâth's. So for a space they battled in silence. The child felt released and shrank back as though those blue fiery eyes had been hands that could grip him.

Arianrhod's gaze did not fall, but presently it was veiled in tears. Pain marred its anger—something deeper than the old, overgrown, spoiled child's malice for a thwarted whim—the pain of a woman who has been tricked where she most trusted. . . . She flung out her hands in a gesture whose fury of anguish was also an anguish of fury.

"My sorrow!" she cried. "What has come on you to shame me, and to cherish my shame and keep it by you so long as this? You to betray me, my brother, you of all men on earth!"

"If there be no greater disgrace on you than my rearing a boy like this one, slight will be your shame," he answered. Nor did his eyes turn from hers.

At that she looked from him to the boy again; and a dangerous smile played about the corners of her mouth.

"What is your boy's name?" she asked.

Gwydion may have been glad indeed at that moment that the boy had never been named. For knowledge of a name gives the knower, if trained in magic, power over the known. And nothing was more apparent now than that Arianrhod could never be trusted with any power over her son. Her brother's hope and plans were crashing about him.

"Indeed," he answered, with the proper degree of cool reproach for her oversight, "he has not been named yet."

The smile she gave them both had the sweetness of poisoned fruit.

"Well," she said, "I vow this destiny upon him: he shall never get a name until I give him one."

Clear in her smile was her meaning: that that would be never.

Gwydion took a step forward, but her eyes stayed him.

"You waste your time, dear my brother. I swear it by the magician's oath with fate, and not you or I or Mâth himself can break it. Nor can you take vengeance on me. I have power enough to guard myself against even you, when I will to use it. And from now on I shall will it. Woe to me that I did not so in the past!"

A tremor shook her and she wrung her hands in a sudden fresh spasm of anger.

"You have played well, brother. I see it all now. You knew that Mâth would never accept me as a footholder without first making sure. . . . You took me to him that I might be forced to bear a child. . . . The child you wanted, the child you would have if you had to draw down the stars in the sky to pay for him. . . . You have tricked and betrayed me from first to last. And you have got your wish, but you will never have your way; my brother. A nameless child cannot inherit Gwynedd after you. There at least I can thwart you. And never fear but that I will."

He stared back at her, hot with a white fury. Silence was the one weapon he could still cling to, and even that had grown slippery in his grasp.

"The gods bear me witness," he said at last, "that you are the worst of women. Yet the boy shall be named, howsoever your gorge may rise at it. And as to you, the complaint that is on you is that you are no longer named a virgin."

Then he snatched up the child and went out with him. The wind of his cloak brushed her in passing, where she stood looking after them both, her beautiful venomed eyes burning like bale fires, with the glare of the malice that lit her like a torch.

It is told in *The Mabinogi* that Gwydion passed that night at Caer Dathyl, but this is probably a mistake, for the journey thither from Caer Arianrhod would have been too long to be made by natural means within so short a time. Nor is it clear why Gwydion should have gone there by magic, since it is likely that Mâth's help was given only to those who had already used every vestige of their own powers. For only by using all that we have do we grow, and Gwydion had not yet used all that he had. Moreover, to have asked help would have been an admission that he himself could do nothing with his sister; and it would have been intolerable to a person of Gwydion's temperament to grant her that victory. Their special bond too may have made him feel that their feud was between themselves, and wish to protect her from any displeasure except his own. Mâth might have agreed with him that this was right.

Besides, he was probably not in a temper to have found congenial his uncle's great unshakable calm. Just then a hotter atmosphere would have suited him better. At Caer Seon he could create his own atmosphere, and he did, but he quickly put the child to sleep again to get him out of it. The servants sought safety in distance.

But Gwydion could not run away from himself, and he cannot have enjoyed his own company that evening. His plans had been knocked helter-skelter. He had meant to take Arianrhod by surprise and she in turn had dealt him a surprise that had robbed him of all advantage. Hitherto he had assured himself that her stubbornness and spite were all in her head and not in her heart, which would speak normally when it beheld the actual fruit of her body.

But her aversion to maternity was sincere and unalterable, and he could not get around it however much he might rage against those fashions of Dyved which had rotted all the sap and milk out of her, and made willing to violate all the primeval decent laws of nature and motherhood in order to keep a name she was not willing to live up to. A name she had already lost, if the tale of Dylan's birth was as widespread as Eigr's gossip to the child would seen to indicate.

Yet there was a paradox in raging against the ways of Dyved, for if these were now flinging obstacles in the childs' way, they had yet been the source of Gwydion's own wish and plan that had brought about his birth. Without them he would never have existed at all. . . .

To establish the child's rights unless Arianrhod named him was impossible. If she were forced to admit that she had left a sexless little object on the floor of Mâth's chamber, she could still maintain that the child her brother had taken from the chest had been made by magic or got somewhere else, from another woman. And there would be no proof.

The child could not only never be king of Gwynedd, but he would have to suffer the embarrassment of having to go through life without any name at all. For the oath with which Arianrhod had invoked destiny was twin brother to Death himself in terror, and was to be the dread of the Welsh folk for ages after.* What its exact nature and meaning were, learned men have never been able to discover, but its dark power was such that many upon whom it has been inflicted have lost their health and died of the sheer contact with such virulence, without ever having broken the taboos it laid upon them. Gwydion's magic could fend off this blight from his boy, but no power of his, or even Mâth's, could have averted the doom that would have followed his naming.

Only Arianrhod herself could have named him; for in mockery she had left herself freedom to do so. But she would never use it.

Yet mockery is generally unwise. And when Gwydion remembered that, his temper began to cool and he began to smile. . . . He lay down and composed himself to think; and when he had thought enough he went to sleep.

---

*Even so late as a hundred years ago. See Rhys' *Celtic Folklore,* pp. 647-49.

In the morning he rose early and woke the child, who was glad of a chance to be awake. For he had not been allowed to spend much time in that condition for two days, and he was as full of questions concerning the events of the day before as a well-watered and fertile field is of the growing stalks of grain. He was very full of questions.

He looked at Gwydion now and tried to see if the weather of his humors was at present good for them. Last night it had not seemed so, for the best that could be got out of him then had been, "Be quiet. I must think." And the child had kept quiet. For though he could not think of anything that he had done, it was somehow on account of him that the lovely lady had been angry, so it might be better not to draw too much attention to oneself and one's possible unknown guilt.

But curiosity works like yeast in whatever it enters, and by now the questions pent within him had so swelled that they were ready to burst him. He raised to Gwydion wistful eyes that were the inter-rogation points his lips desired to be. "Was that lovely lady really my mother?" he asked.

"She was. She is," said Gwydion.

The child considered that, and his lip quivered. "She did not seem to like me," he said. "Was she not satisfied with me? Did she think I had not turned out well in the box? I did not do anything," he said with a child's air of virtue that is aggrieved and yet pleading, "I did not do anything at all."

"The matter has nothing to do with what you did or were," said Gwydion. "She never wanted children; that is what is on her. It is why you were born too soon and I had to put you in the box. I thought she would come to her senses when she saw you and how well you had turned out. But she has none to come to."

The child thought that over.

"I wish she had wanted children," he said and sighed. "She is very pretty. She is prettier than any of the other boys' mothers."

"She is indeed," replied Gwydion. "If the inside of her had matched the outside she would have been perfection. There would never have been her like in the world."

"There would not?" said the child with eager pride.

Then his mind veered again, back to that heavy mass of informa-tion that he could never digest without help. "But why did she have children at all if she did not want them? Did she want me first and then change her mind later? And how did she make me be born too soon? I did not know that mothers could push babies out before they were ready."

"It was by accident that you were born at all," answered Gwydion. "She never expected you."

"What kind of an accident?" asked the child.

"That is too long a story to tell you now," said Gwydion. "We must make haste, for we are making another journey today."

"Where to?" said the child. And for a moment his mind nibbled like a little bright fish at the shining bait of that journey, for children love changes and travel. But it was still well-hooked in the earlier matter, and to that it swung back.

"Is it such a very long story?" he coaxed. "I had rather hear it now."

"It is in today's journey that you should be interested," said Gwydion, "for it has to do with getting you a name."

"But she said nobody but her could name me," the child objected, "and she did not act as if she intended to."

"I will make an intention for her," said Gwydion. And the child stared at him in silence and wonder, marveling over what he would do. For it had always seemed inconceivable that anyone should dare to oppose Gwydion. Only Mâth could be more powerful than he, and the son of Mathonwy was not anyone: he was like a god or a mountain, beyond the little pale of people—so old and so great that he was no longer a man.

Yet yesterday for the first time the child had seen someone dare to be angry with his uncle: that lovely lady the very thought of whom was at once a shudder and a magnet. As those two quarreled it had seemed to the child that the world was swaying, and he would not have been surprised to see them tear the sun and moon from their places and hurl them at each other's heads, so great and all-overturning had that strife appeared. And Gwydion had not seemed to defeat her; yet somehow he was now going to outwit her. How?

"What will you do?" he whispered at last.

"What you will soon see," said Gwydion mysteriously. "But it is time that we should be setting off. Eat your breakfast."

And the child ate it, but between bites he managed to squeeze out a final question or two. "Was it because she did not want him that my brother swam off? Was he afraid to stay?"

"No," said Gwydion. "It was his nature to swim, and that was well for him."

The child looked through the open door at the cold sea, beating against the rocks near Caer Seon—beating the rocks as though it hated them and would attack them forever, though of themselves they never came down to the sea.

He shivered. . . .

"I am glad that I did not have to swim off," he said. "I should not have liked to live all alone in the sea. I am glad that you kept me, Lord."

"Probably Dylan does not live all alone either. . . ." said Gwydion. But he did not explain that.

"Why did you not keep him too?" the child asked presently.

"I should have kept him if there had been no you," said Gwydion. "I did not need both of you."

The child pondered. He felt of a sudden very lonely. It was a lonely business to have been born by accident, against one's mother's will. Other mothers loved their children, who were sure of them. But his had never loved him; that was a strange thing, the like of which he had never heard before. And he saw for the first time how shaky the always firm-seeming foundations of his world had been. His mind hung dizzily over the abysses into which he might have fallen. Suppose Gwydion had not wanted him either?

"But you did have need of me?" he questioned, eager for reassurance. "You did want me? You never would have let her make me swim off?"

And Gwydion smiled, and the light of his smile seemed to close the dizzying abysses and make the sun shine warm over a solid world. "I wanted you indeed," he said. "Otherwise I would not have been saving you in a box while your much more promising-looking brother was swimming off. The accident that made her give you birth was my doing, and an awkward enough business, but the best I could do, for it is not easy to deal with an unreasonable woman. You were my plan and my contriving. You are my own, more than you ever have been or can be anyone else's."

"How?" the child asked eagerly.

"You have heard enough for the present," said Gwydion, and rose from the table where they took their food.

They walked down that morning to the seashore. And in a place between Caer Seon and Aber Menei, Gwydion found seaweed and sedges. He gathered them together and told the child to run and play while he said a charm over them.

The child went without protest, for though he would have liked to see the spell, and looked forward to the days when he would be bigger and could work magic with Gwydion, as had been promised him, at present he was still in awe of it. He knew that magic was a queer business and liked privacy and stillness. And it is very hard for a little boy to be still.

He ran races with the waves, that were soft and gurgling here, laughing like babies, so that sometimes he could imagine that perhaps he heard his brother's laugh. He would mark with his eye a place on the beach where the waves came, and then he would run to see if he could reach it and get back again before they caught him. Sometimes he won but sometimes he lost, and then the wave would slosh all over him, a big, cool, good-humored comrade whose only fault was its resemblance to a bath. He got very wet and very happy at this process.

But all things end, and finally Gwydion called him. There were no sedges and seaweed on the beach when he ran back, laughing and dripping. A boat waited there instead, slim and solid-looking and brightly painted; dry sticks and what was left of the sedges were piled in a little heap on its decks.

7

The Adventure of the Gold-Shoemakers

THEY SAILED in that boat to the port of Caer Arianrhod. There they stopped and Gwydion touched the sticks and sedges with his wand so that they turned, or seemed to turn, into the finest leather of Cordova. And he colored it so beautifully that there was no lovelier leather in the world. Then he sat down and began to cut shoes out of it and the boy stitched them. But he did not know how to stitch, so it was Gwydion's brain instead of his own that had to think the orders that his hands obeyed. And that is a way in which any unskilled person might still do any kind of work, if we had many such masters of telepathy today.

This was the shoemaking for which the Triads name Gwydion the Third Gold-Shoemaker. The first of these was Caswallawn the son of Beli of the Deep, when he went to Gaul to save Flur the daughter of Mynach Gorr from Imperial Caesar and her abductor, King Mwrchan the Thief. And the second was the royal Manawyddan, the son of Llyr Llediaith and brother of Bran the Blessed, in the days when he and his were exiles from Dyved through the charms of Llwyd. It was he whose stepson Pryderi Gwydion had later killed.

When Gwydion saw that the boat had been sighted from the castle he made his last preparations. He took up his wand again and rose. "Now look well," he told the child, "and do not be frightened, for I am going to take another shape."

"But you will be the same inside?" the child questioned rather anxiously. For he did not altogether like these magical changes in such well-known and important things, entertaining as they were when they only made boats of seaweed and lovely toys of trash. That Gwydion, who was the very center and axis of the earth, should change his form, was an idea that made the whole world seem shaky, as if the sun itself had threatened to turn into something else.

"Of course," said Gwydion. "For the inside of a man, which cannot be seen or touched, takes many years to change even a little; while the outside of him that can be seen and touched, and which most people therefore think the more important, can be very easily changed or even destroyed altogether. You must remember that."

"I will indeed," said the child. But he did not understand more than half of it.

Then Gwydion touched himself with the wand and instantly he seemed to whirl and waver and spread out cloudily, as if his form had been fluid. He grew lower and spread out wider on both sides, thus making up in width what he lost in height. His skin darkened and his nose grew bigger and his eyes turned black. His mouth had changed its shape and some of his teeth did not seem to be set in it in the same way.

The child stared in wonder and shrank back.

"You have seen that it is nothing at all," said Gwydion. "Now you too must be changed; for the whole plan would fail if anyone recognized either of us."

The child waited bravely and obediently where he stood and tried to look unconcerned, but he shivered a little. For he did not feel quite sure that the change was nothing at all. Nor did he greatly like the sight of this strange-looking man coming towards him with upraised rod. A little boy does not like to be hit with anything, even a magic wand. But it had to be, and it would look very babyish to act afraid of something that one had been told was nothing to fear at all.

"It does not hurt." Gwydion laid a hand on his shoulder, and the smile in his eyes was his own and no one else's in the world. It had not changed. It was warm as a fire on a cold night in winter. And the child looked at it as the wand fell. . . .

He felt dizzy for a moment then. He felt as if every part of him were in motion, moving all together and all at once, as he had never dreamed that anything could move—separately and yet in the same direction, as a cloud of snowflakes moves before a storm-wind. . . .

When it was all over and all the different parts of him had settled down again, he shook himself and went over to the side of the boat to look at his new face in the water. He saw a dark-eyed, dark-haired boy with a nose and mouth like those of the shape Gwydion had put on himself. He was evidently some years older than he had been; he looked about ten.

"Do you like it?" asked Gwydion. He was smiling a little, as if something amused him.

"I like myself better," said the child.

"You may be yourself again in an hour or two," said Gwydion. "But meanwhile I am a shoemaker from Dyved and you are my son to whom I am teaching my trade. And you must say nothing to give anyone an idea that either of us has ever been anyone else. If you do, you will never get a name in this world."

Her people brought Arianrhod word of the shoemaker's coming in his boat. They were glad to bring her some news that might distract her, for since the day before her mood had been black. A smoky blackness that was prone to shoot out tongues of flame and burn anybody who was so incautious as to get near her.

"There is a shoemaker from Dyved and his son in a boat outside," they told her. "And he is making shoes from the loveliest leather of Cordova that ever was seen."

She looked up at first with interest and then she remembered her mood and her eyes flashed. "It is a lie," she said. "Either you are all forked-tongued liars, and you generally are, or the man is a liar and you are all such brainless stupid oafs that you have believed him: and you are generally that too! It is not often that leather comes all the way from Spain to the Isles of the Mighty. And there is not one of you that is not too ignorant and lacking in taste to know it if you saw it."

"Yet he has the loveliest leather of the world, Lady," they answered, "and he is gilding some of the shoes he is making, so that they shine like the sun, and look as they were fashioned from pure gold. Govannon your brother could not forge any more metal-like."

But that last was not a wise speech.

"May the demons of the air fly away with all my brothers!" said Arianrhod, and flung a bowl at the head of the nearest speaker so quickly that he was not able to dodge it entirely, although he had been watching for it. They carried him out, and Arianrhod sat and grieved because his head had not been Gwydion's.

She had been sorely beaten in her pride; for she had been outwitted, and nothing is so galling as that to a clever person who is not wise. She had been used as a tool to bring forth a child she did not want, and whose existence was the gravest menace her reputation had yet known.

For by Dylan who had swum off nothing could be proved. Folk might accept him as a possibility, but he could never be a demonstrated fact. And sicknesses and great ills were likely to come upon people who gossiped about him too openly.

But this child would be present and incontrovertible proof if Gwydion could establish her motherhood of him. The beliefs of Dyved that she had invoked would condemn her. Virgins had no children.

But Gwydion could not prove her motherhood. That was her one comfort and also her one pleasure. She had left herself the power to name the child in order that she might plague and torment her imperturbable brother, whose serenity she had always envied with a fascinated rage, until he was ready to beg her on his knees to fulfill that vain hope. And then she could laugh at and scorn him. She had done so in fancy a hundred times since his visit. But phantom pictures of a vengeance that one's hands and brain are not actually working to materialize are as maddening as the mirages of crystal pools prove to thirsty lost ones in the desert.

She could have sent a sickness upon her brother's cattle or his people, or upon himself or the hated child; but his own powers would have enabled him to throw this off in a second, and perhaps even to hurl it back upon her.

She could have complained to Mâth her uncle. But he might have answered that if she was not willing to be a virgin, she had no right to lament if she was not called one; and had she told him lies about what had passed between herself and Gwydion, he would have read them in her mind.

And she would not waste her dignity in futile efforts. There was nothing for her to do but sit and wait for her brother's next move. Meanwhile she fumed and fretted in a fever of the brain that burned her more deeply than any fever of the body. Her hurt vanity smarted every moment, and her heart also. For it was Gwydion who had done this thing to her—Gwydion, whom she loved better than any man alive.

She loved him, and therefore it was torment to her to hate him. But the child she could hate happily; him she loathed with a very ecstasy and rapture of loathing. He was the wrong her brother had done her, personified in living flesh and blood. He was not the bond, but the barrier, between herself and her loved one: that which Gwydion had prized more than herself, and therefore the object of her raging jealousy.

Yet not even her hate was as devoted as another mother's love, for to it too her son was not an individual, but only the symbol of her loss of fame and Gwydion. Moreover, his ills were the one means by which she could strike at her brother's heart and yet not harm himself, a thing that even now she would have been loath to do.

But presently a new image began to dance among the murky flames that filled her mind and writhed there. A pair of golden shoes, slender and shapely as her own feet, shining as the sun. Their glitter began to draw her thought from the flame and dim them; and perhaps it was not altogether in her own mind that that tempting image was formed. Gwydion may have turned his own thought to the shaping of his sister's, that in that hour her passion left unguarded.

"Even if those scared fools do not know the leather of Spain from a Gwynedd cows' hide," she reflected, "they could hardly mistake gilt. Golden shoes would be a great treasure and very beautiful. And if I am not the first woman in Gwynedd to have them, some other woman will be; and I shall be following the fashions instead of setting them, as is my right. I will be the first," she said.

So she called a servant and bade him bear word to the shoemaker to make her a pair of golden shoes.

But when they were brought to her, all gleaming and sparkling in the sun, the exact delicate shape of her own foot, and she tried them on, there was half an inch's space between each side of her foot and each side of the shoe.

"This is strange," said she, "since he had the measure of my foot to work by. But in all except their largeness they are perfectly fashioned and very beautiful. Pay him for these; but bid him make some more that are smaller."

So the servants went back to the shoemaker and told him their Lady's word.

"Indeed," said he, "I will make her shoes that are small enough." And he set to work again.

But when they brought her the second pair of shoes they were so small that she could not get her feet inside them. Her toes would not go in at one end nor her heels at the other.

The servants looked for an outbreak then. But the glitter of those golden shoes had fascinated her as once the glitter of golden shields had fascinated Pryderi of Dyved and his chiefs. And she who was a mistress of magic had self-control enough when she cared to use it; it must have been gracious calm indeed that Taliessin called her "dawn of serenity." She only said: "Go tell that man that this pair of shoes will not go on." But this time she did not say anything about paying him for them.

They carried her words to the shoemaker, and he shook his head like one that is bewildered and sore amazed. "Well," said he, "I shall not make her any more shoes unless she lets me measure her foot myself."

When they told her that she rose up. "Indeed," she said, "I will go to him!"

She wrapped herself in a crimson cloak above which her fair head shone as the moon shines above flames, and went down to the seashore.

She saw the stout dark man and the boy in the boat, and it seemed to her for a second that the former's eyes twinkled at sight of her, as a spider's small eyes might twinkle when he saw his winged meal entering the soft, steel-strong meshes of his web. But she quickly put that fancy by. For what shoemaker of Dyved would dare lay any design against her, the royal sorceress and the King of Gwynedd's niece? But he should have looked frightened and apologetic and she stared at him until he did.

"Lady," he said meekly, "good day to you."

"The gods give you good," she answered. "But it is a wonder indeed that you have not wit enough to make shoes by a measure."

He bent low and rubbed his hands. "I have not been able to," he said, "but now I will be."

So she came aboard; and he piled the skins of wild beasts, tanned sleek and soft, and Eastern stuffs such as might have been in a trader's wares, upon the rough boards of the boat to make a seat for her. She took it, and an icicle might have been as beautiful as she, and as cold and hard in the sparkle of its frosty fire.

She noticed that the boy could not keep his eyes off her, but stared at her constantly with a fearful and fascinated wonder. Yet she made nothing of that; for she was used to stares. Indeed, this one put her in a better humor.

Then a wren flew by with a little whir of wings and lit upon the boat's deck. And as if obedient to a signal the boy turned his eyes from the lady to the bird. He picked up a sling that lay by him and shot a stone at the wren, striking it in the leg, squarely between bone and sinew.

Arianrhod laughed aloud and clapped her hands. "That was a good shot!" she cried. "By the gods, it is with a steady hand that the *lleu* hit the bird."

Then the shoemaker smiled, and that smile reminded Arianrhod of the dark opening maw of a spider. Before her eyes his figure trembled and spread out cloud-wise and whirled into another shape. Both the wounded wren and the gilded leather disappeared, and where they had been was a crumbling heap of seaweed and sedges, over which her brother stood, smiling scornfully down at her.

"The gods' curse upon you for making this trick needful," said he. "But now he is named; and good enough is his name. From this day men shall call him Llew Llaw Gyffes."

Llaw Gyffes means "Sure Hand." But the use of *lleu* is a mystery today. For the word is a dead, ancient one that meant light; and the later scribes rewrote it *llew* or lion. Yet nobody can say why Arianrhod should have called her little boy either a lion or a light (unless what she really said was that his hand was sure as light); and perhaps the Irish word *lu*, "little," was meant; though there is no such form of that word in Welsh today.

But for a moment Arianrhod shrank in panic, overwhelmed by the suddenness of those changes. Then her white face flamed, and her blue eyes flashed hard and bright as the sapphires in a swordhilt.

"By all the gods," she said, "you will not thrive the more for working this harm to me."

Gwydion looked at her. "I have not worked you any harm yet," he answered. And the child Llew thought that if he had been his lovely mother he would have shivered at the silkiness of that "yet."

But Arianrhod did not shiver. She drew herself to her fullest height and her whole figure sparkled as with fire.

"Well," she said slowly, "I will swear this boy a destiny: never shall he have arms or armor until I myself with my own hands fit them upon him."

She smiled a smile that was like a little curling flame the while her eyes pierced them both like triumphant spears.

Gwydion's hands clenched.

"By the Greatest of all the gods," he said, "good luck to your wickedness, but he shall be armed!"

"Did I not do well?" said the child gleefully on their way home. "I threw at the magic wren as soon as it came, just as you told me to, and I threw very straight." And with the last words he stuck out his little chest.

"Yes," said Gwydion, but he spoke abstractedly, like a man that thinks of other things.

The child looked at him, and his face sobered, and his spirit caught that contagious gloom. "Is it true that I can never have arms and kill people with an axe like Uncle Govannon unless she puts them on me?" he asked with the suggestion of a whimper in his voice. For he did not think that Arianrhod would ever put arms on him, and would have been afraid to get near enough to her to let her try.

"The arms or the people?" said Gwydion. "Child, when you speak you must always make clear what you mean, and that is an important thing to remember."

"Yes, but will she? said Llew.

"She will have to," said Gwydion. "But it is years yet until you will need arms, and then I will think of a way. Be satisfied now with your name. Yesterday it looked as if you might never get one."

And the child sat and thought of his name, hugging it to him as a dog might a coveted bone. Not with that lack at least would he have to face the world of men.

That winter Gwydion took him to Caer Dathyl again for the Feast of the Solstice, as he was wont to do. And he told the kindred that Arianrhod had named the child, and what his name was. Why Arianrhod did not deny this can only be conjectured. But the folk of those times believed that there was mystic virtue in a name; and it may be that she did not dare to lie in a matter involved with one. Especially when the words of that naming might have been carried by the all-hearing winds to Mâth.

. . . "It is as good a name as any," said Gwydion to his uncle.

The King looked at the boy who was playing ball with others and rubbed his white-fleeced chin again.

"It is indeed," said he, "but Arianrhod thought that no name at all was good."

"Arianrhod's thoughts—!" said Gwydion. "I am sick of her thoughts and her!" he added vehemently. "There was never such an unreasonable woman born."

"So what would have been said to bring you closer together has driven you apart and made you unfriends?" The King looked keenly at him from under his frosty brows. "Hers are ill deeds; and an unloving mother violates the Ancient Harmonies. Yet you have made her a mother against her will. And that is a thing that has seldom happened in the world before, but will happen often again in the ages that begin. You have done it for love's sake, in pure longing for a child. But many of those men who are to come will do it for pride's sake and lust's; and this breeding of her like a beast will lower the rank and degrade the ancient dignity of woman. Nor will the world go well while that fades, my nephew."

"Is not woman's ancient dignity already lost in such tricks and pretences as Arianrhod's, my uncle?" said Gwydion.

"That is so," said Mâth. He brooded, staring out across the snowy fields. . . . "And both ways the loss springs from the same source. Men are learning that they have their own share in the reproduction of life, and they will presume unwisely upon that knowledge. And each will seek the virgin upon whom he may set the first and single seal."

"Must not the world learn and change?" said Gwydion.

"It must. I grow old," said Mâth. "When I look ahead I only dread for the folk that are and will be the confusion and agonies of that forging of the future. Woman's power wanes, but nothing ever passes except to wax again. . . . And if men become tyrants, they shape for themselves the doom of tyrants, who are always betrayed. . . .

"For the recognition of fatherhood will enslave woman. It will no longer leave her absolute ownership of her own body, that it will place at one man's pleasure, this to demand rather than hers to give or withhold as her heart bids. It will likewise make it a crime for that body of hers to be aware of any but the one man, while his still retains its ancient freedom. And the end of it all will be that there will be no free women left in the world, to love for love alone as women did aforetime. All women will either submit their flesh to the yoke of marriage, or hire it out for gold and silver in base barter; and both alike will be the bondmaids of men."

"Not through all the ages," said Gwydion.

"Yet for long and too long," said Mâth. Again he brooded.

"But these ills on the road to the true marriage are inevitable, the millennium-long birth pangs of progress.

"Go you forward, my nephew, for you are young and do not fear change. But remember if you can to look back upon what was good in the past; or the future that you build may fall in worse ruin."

But Gwydion, remembering lovely, perverse Arianrhod and her menace to her son, thought that he could well endure some waning of the power of women.

Nor had Mâth mentioned that trouble which from time to time vexed his heir: How was Arianrhod, who would now be on her guard, to be tricked a second time, and made to give those weapons without which her son would stand shamed and helpless, like one without arms or legs, in a world of war-like men?

8

The Last Curse of Arianrhod

IT IS SAID in *The Mabinogi* that after the naming of Llew Llaw Gyffes, Gwydion took him to the place later known as Dinas Dinllev, or Llew's Town, which the poems call the Fortress of Llew and Gwydion. What name was on it then is unknown.

There Gwydion brought him up.

His education must have proceeded with his growing. If one old manuscript is right in stating that Gwydion first introduced books and the art of reading to the Gaels of Mona and Anglesey, it is likely that Llew was the first boy in Britain to learn his letters; and one wonders if he always appreciated the honor.

But it is more likely that Gwydion, a poet, who has been named as the very inventor of poetry and would have wished his poems to live, was only the first man to break through the rule of the druids and give their secret knowledge of letters to the people—true to his character of Opener of Doors—and that Llew, being born of a race of druids, would have had to learn this anyhow.

Doubtless he was too young during this period to be initiated into the mysteries of magic, but he must have been instructed in the mental discipline which is the first essential to their practice: that power of concentration which enables the mind, that in most people floats helpless as a rudderless boat upon the ocean of differing thoughts and feelings, at the mercy of fair weather or foul, to reject all other thoughts for one thought, and cling to it with the fixed, unshakable persistence of a leech, until every littlest detail of that thought's anatomy is known, and its very blood and bones sucked up. But such a power would have taken years to develop, and can be acquired only by great and willing effort. For a long time Llew would still have been a child, imagining oftener than thinking, feeling more than knowing.

Others of the clan of Dôn may have visited them at Dinas Dinllev; and they may have made visits to Caer Govannon and Caer Dathyl and elsewhere—everywhere but to Caer Arianrhod.

The child probably never met his aunts Gwennan and men and Maelan; they would have sided with Arianrhod, or at least have found it too much trouble to defy her. His mother herself he never saw again throughout his childhood. But sometimes he thought of her and wondered what it would have been like if she had loved him. Gwydion loved him; nothing could have been better than that close and ancient bond. Yet her love would have been somehow different . . . an unknown, unimaginable thing. How would it have felt if she had taken him in her white arms and kissed him, if he had seen her eyes and heard her voice grow soft and eager for his sake, as other mothers' did for other boys?

Yet, after all, one could get too much of mothers. His friends frequently did of theirs. Their fond pawing could become embarrassing because they never knew when to stop; and they were so full of bothersome admonitions and injunctions and precautions that they were forever boiling over, like soup pots on a fire. They were always afraid that something would happen to one (a defect certainly not shared by Arianrhod, who, Llew knew too well, was only afraid that something would not happen to him); and they had very unreasonable prejudices against muddy feet, and the climbing of too tall trees, and torn clothes. Sometimes they were even known, in irritable moments, to smack boys for such things.

So perhaps he was better off without one. . . . Only he could not help wondering. . . .

A child should be loved by two persons of opposite sex, and his development is likely to be lopsided if he is loved by only one. Goewyn, at Caer Dathyl, might have made friends with the boy, but between her and Gwydion were piled the ashes of an ancient grudge, which the son of Dôn, having been at fault would remember if she did not. Besides, it is unlikely that Gwydion's possessive love would have been able to tolerate the presence of any woman but Arianrhod in the boy's heart: her right there he would have had to concede. His half-feminine intuitions, those of the artist, may have been coupled with a kind of maternal jealousy. . . .

So Llew would have learned life only from men.

And from what men!

He may have known his grandmother Dôn, but certainly his

uncles Gilvaethwy and Govannon, Eveyd and Amaethon—he who was later to steal a bitch, a hind, and a lapwing from Arawn, King of the Underworld, and so bring about the fabulous, mysterious battle of the Cad Goddeu, when Gwydion turned trees to men and marshaled them against the Forces of Faery, though how he finally got the victory was by guessing in a song the name of that Champion of Faery, Bran of the Glittering Branches, whose side could never know defeat until his name was known.

Part of that song is still preserved:

> Sure-hoofed is my steed in the day of battle:
> The high sprigs of alder are on thy hand:
> Bran . . . by the branch thou bearest,
> Has Amathaon the Good prevailed.*

That must have been a great battle, when the troops of the dead poured up from the Underworld to fight with the living on earth; and perhaps that Bran was the ghost of Bran the Blessed, him who got his death-wound in the slaughter of Morddwydtyllyon. One wonders if Gwydion and Pryderi met again on that field. All this must have taken place in the days of Gwydion's own kingship; for the great son of Mathonwy is not named as figuring in that battle; and it may be that the sons of Dôn stole no more beasts during his lifetime.

Was it perhaps because of the memory of that great loss of life in the war with Dyved, caused by his own youthful theft to the pigs of Pryderi, that Gwydion turned trees into warriors to protect the men of Gwynedd? Who knows? But the venturesome blood of the son of Dôn was surely not much cooled, or he would never have dared to let his brother challenge the very powers of the Underworld. And the saga of all these doings is lost. Only a paragraph or two in the *Myvyrian Archaiology* leaves a clue to it, and the broken fragments of a song. . . . Evidently there was no disciplining of the thief, after the army that had been a forest was disbanded to settle down and grow leaves again; or Gwydion's victory-Englyns would not have called Amaethon "the Good."

But doubtless Llew was less interested in his fabulous uncles than in his younger kinsmen, the three beast-born ones, Long Hydwn and Tall Hychdwn and Bleiddwn the Wolfling. These would still have been young enough to play with; would have made up somewhat for the watery tastes of that aquatic brother who had swum off. . . .

*See Lady Guest's *Mabinogion*, Vol. II.

He must have been surprised when he first heard the story of these three comrades' birth, of the doom that had once fallen upon Gwydion and Gilvaethwy. . . . In the day-time this may not have sounded so bad. A small boy can imagine far worse things than absolute freedom to run about in the woods all day, with no lessons and no work or washing to do. No need, either, to ask for food when one was hungry, but only to run and catch it if it were an animal, or to eat it off the ground if it were grass or a plant. But at night, when the owls hooted, and the wolves howled in the forest, and the wind wailed in the treetops, he may have shivered in his warm seat by the fire as he thought of that strange exile: of being shut out in the dark and the cold and that weird, eerie realm into which the woodland turned after dark. Lonely and hideous it would have seemed then to sleep, not in a warm bed, but out on the misty moors or m the gloom of a cave—to be a beast prowling outcast about the comfortable, lighted houses of men. . . . And he must have hoped with all his small soul that he would never do anything bad enough to made Gwydion punish him in such a way.

One night, when he was in age or growth about ten, these thoughts weighed on him so that they became an ailment and a sickness of the imagination. They became a stone around the neck of his mind, dragging it down into the river of depression.

Gwydion observed this. "What is on you?" asked he.

"I was wondering," said the child, and looked embarrassed, "I was wondering how bad one had to be to get turned into an animal."

But Gwydion was not embarrassed. To him the past was never a dark prison-room in which he could find himself shut with an old humiliation, but a road whose landmarks he could use for guidance in the present and the future. Those sciences of the mind which he studied taught that there was no real humiliation except in error; and an error acknowledged and digested is over and has no more power to shame.

"It is necessary to do something much worse than you are yet able to do," he answered, "a variety of things for which I hope that you have no aptitude."

"I hope not too," said Llew, "for I should not like you to turn me into an animal. It would not be much fun to take another shape if you could not get out of it when you wanted to, but must stay shut up in it. I should not mind being loose in the woods all day. That might be fun. But I should hate having to think all the time that you were angry with me. It would be very uncomfortable."

"Probably I should be missing you instead of being angry with you," said Gwydion. "Do you think that Mâth was angry with me during those three years that I passed in beast form? Anger is weakness and impurity above which Mâth has risen. But he had to leave me a beast until I realized the value of manhood, and that cleverness is in the end never stronger than justice, and that a man's brain and strength and knowledge are responsibilities, not merely tools to serve his ends. It was education, not punishment; but I think that you will not require so much education; for I, who know my own mistakes, have watched and armed you against them."

"But what if I make my own mistakes," the child objected, "and not yours?"

Gwydion frowned and thought for a moment of the writing in the stars. . . .

"You cannot," he said, and thus cheered himself. "For I have taught you the folly of malice, and the folly of too much guile, and the inevitability of paying for all that you get. What way is there left for you to get into trouble?" said he.

Yet there was a way that neither of them dreamed of, though the form its peril would come in was not the form of Llew's childish fears. For Gwydion still forgot that Llew's being was not a mere reproduction of his; and that in training him to withstand the dangers that he knew, he might have overlooked, even fostered, other dangers of which his own quick and subtle mind, armed by its very faults, would never have needed warning. For that is the way of parents and guardians the world over: to attribute to the children of their love their own nature and their own problems and never to see until too late that these may be different. Nor would Gwydion the Golden-Tongued, the guileful, ever have dreamed that a boy of his, howsoever trained, could lack for guile. . . .

But penitential transformations had no part in Llew's education then or in later days. Though at times he may have been transformed. For how better could a boy learn the ways of beasts and birds than by taking on their shapes for a little while?

In strange forms he and Gwydion may have made strange journeys. They may have studied the depths of the sea, roaming in fish form through the illimitable lower layers of the waters. They may have explored the air and the shining lower reaches of the sky as birds, though their wings could not carry them high enough to investigate the stars.

As moles or mice they may have examined the queer, tiny little underground world of burrows; and as larger beasts have spied out all the secrets of the forest.

As ants or bees they may have entered stealthily into the hills and hives, and have studied the intricate, wonderfully organized civilizations of these tiny peoples. And Llew may have marveled at this perfection of order which is found nowhere else in the world.

"How can they do it?" he would ask Gwydion in the evening, when these strange and fascinating lessons in geography and natural science were over. "Why don't the workers get tired of supporting the queens and the drones, and have a revolution and make the drones work?"

(It was bees they had studied that day, Gwydion bewitching the sentinels that guard the hives so that they might not follow their custom of slaying stranger bees that tried to enter.)

"Yes, and why do the drones let themselves be killed or driven out as soon as the queen is tired of her lover and sure that her eggs will hatch? They're men, and all the other bees are women. Why can't they band together and fight?"

"Because their system does not allow them to do or desire these things," said Gwydion. "And none are yet conscious of themselves as individuals, only as members of the community, whose law arranges their death or their toil. It is only in man that consciousness burns with so fierce a flame that he is shut into himself altogether, separate from his kind: the individual.

"Where the individual is, no system can work perfectly or prove lasting; for in all systems there is injustice, and one class profiting at the expense of another; and since individuals will always work for their own gain and not the system's, the suffering class will always end by turning and preying upon the other.

"And so it will be till the individual, though his own consciousness flame as high as ever, wins back to that lost consciousness of the Whole which ants and bees still possess; and on that day the purposes of evolution and destiny will be accomplished, and there will be no more need for this world."

Llew was silent awhile, digesting the wonder of that vision, though he found that his mental stomach could never hold all of it. "Then we lost consciousness of the Whole in order to get to be individuals?" he asked. "And now that we are individuals it is our business to get back the consciousness of the Whole? That seems like going around in a circle."

"Eternity is a circle," replied Gwydion, "for only a circle has no end. . . . But before we were conscious only of our own species; that was all we could grasp of the Whole. And when we recover that wider consciousness it too will have widened; and we shall be one with all species, and know all creatures alike for our fellow beings. But mil-

lions of ages will pass before all the world has attained to consciousness of the Whole. And it is very likely that we men of now will by then
have outgrown this earth; and the men of that time will be those who
are yet so undeveloped as to be fish-worms and maggots today."

"Indeed! . . ." said Llew. "Where will we be?"

"You will know that when the time comes," said Gwydion.
"Nobody rightly understands, unless it be Mâth."

"And he will not tell?" asked the child.

"He cannot," said Gwydion.

. . . "But things will be wrong a long time then," sighed Llew, "if
all systems are unjust, and we cannot have justice until we get back
to the Whole. Is it impossible to govern rightly then? I thought that
everything that you and Mâth did was always right."

"It is as nearly right as we can make it," said Gwydion. "But no
government is ever entirely right, since true government can come
only from within, not from without. And therefore it is well for rulers
not to meddle too much, but to strive to protect the weaker and the
stronger from one another—for he who takes sides fosters feuds and
breeds the ruin of all—and otherwise leave this world to the individual, to whom it belongs, and who can learn only by making his
own mistakes."

When Llew was approximately sixteen a thing that is not told of
in any of the ancient books happened to him.

On a summer evening, when there was still a blush of rose in the
west, he went down to the sea to bathe; and that same sky-color lay
pink and purple on the waters and made them bloom like a field of
strange, shining flowers swaying faintly in a breeze.

The boy ducked himself in those blossomy waves. Sometimes he
attacked them and sent them flying before him with great sweeps of
a strong young arm. Sometimes he floated on their purple breasts as
quietly as he might have lain against his mother's in babyhood—but
never had—his white, boy's body still, quiescent, upborne by the
light, rubbery element which has yet been heavy enough to drown a
multitude of men. The roselit waves sloshed and sang about him like
a lullaby, though farther out he could hear their thunderous, angry
beat against the rocks. . . .

When he turned to swim ashore he saw that there was a girl sitting on the sands watching him. This did not disturb him, for his
century had not yet learned the foul-mindedness which sees in the
human body only the instrument for serving lust. It is that which

drove Adam out of paradise when he first looked upon his nakedness
with obscene eyes and covered it with fig-leaves as though it had
been a shameful thing. And thus, if the ancient parable of Genesis
were rightly understood, Shame and Self-consciousness are the
names of the Angel whose Flaming Sword bars humanity from the
happy peace of its primeval innocence.

But in Mâth's realm the mind still retained something of its primitive purity, and Llew would not have been ashamed to show his body
unless it had had blemishes: which it had not. He was tall by then, and
handsome. There was not in Gwynedd another youth so beautiful.

The girl sitting on the sand was beautiful also. She flamed gold
and brown against the sunset. Her bright head, the fluffy hair raying
out from it, gleamed star-like against the gold-washed background of
beach and sky. Her sun-tanned skin had over it a golden gloss.

When he came ashore, she smiled, friendly and yet a little shyly.
"Good evening to you, young Lord," she said.

"Good evening to yourself," he replied.

They looked at each other awhile, and then he sat down because
she seemed to be waiting for him to do something; he did not know
what. He kept on looking at her. He had never looked closely at a girl
before. And this one seemed well worth looking at: frank and simple,
like a comrade of one's own age, yet with the deliciousness of womanhood upon her. Lovely and soundly, sweetly human, not beautiful
and terrifying as a flame, like Arianrhod his mother.

He had never given much thought to girls. Magic had absorbed
him, and those other branches of education, of all of which Gwydion
had made such a fascinating and obsessing game. There had been so
much to do, so much to learn that he had not had time for other pre-
occupations. When he did have an hour to himself he had only wanted to wander off and spend it in the wood or on the seashore, watching and dreaming.

Girls might have their points of interest; he had grasped the possibility of that. But they were full of giggles and intent looks and
sidelong looks and chatter whose sense he could not make out. They
were beings of uncertain temper too, whose actions and reactions
not even Gwydion could accurately foretell. (Arianrhod had
impressed this mystified wariness of woman upon her son.)

It had not seemed worth while to bother with them while there
were so many other studies that could be followed up with profit and
interest and reduced to a logical and understandable basis. Llew,
having been reared on reason and nourished on deduction, was profoundly wary of all that did not conform to some rule of logic.

Yet now he saw that this girl was interesting; and knew that deal-ing with her was a science of which he was ignorant.

"Do you often come out to the beach?" he said at last, weakly. "I have not seen you here before."

"I have not been here before," said she. And that shy, ingratiating smile scurried again, nervously, across one corner of her mouth. "I came because I had watched and learned that you came here often. And it is a great compliment to yourself that I have come," she ended more decidedly, "for I have never gone to meet a man before."

"Then you have come to meet me?" asked Llew.

"Yes," she said, and looked at him expectantly, a sudden light in her eyes, the trembling smile running first to one corner of her mouth and then to the other.

But he only sat still and looked perplexed. He made a hundred wild speculations, but the situation still remained a riddle which had caught him unprepared.

She began to look white and troubled. She stirred uneasily under his blank gaze, and her little laugh had an unhappy sound. "Don't you like girls?" she said.

"I have never either liked or disliked them," said Llew. He smiled with swift eagerness. "But I believe I am beginning to like you."

Her face kindled at that like a re-lit torch, and for one moment the smile flashed like a star. "Are you indeed?" said she.

But after that the heavy waiting silence fell upon them again, thick as a storm cloud filled with lightning that yet cannot strike. They looked at each other like lost children, trembling and groping for one another under its shadow.

Had she known his inexperience and unease she could have relieved him. But she was too young and too absorbed in her own shyness and emotion for such discernment. Every moment only made her more conscious of failure and humiliation and the death pangs of her hope.

And he was thinking of her, not her thoughts. Somewhere in him there was dawn, in his mind and in his body, radiance like a rising sun. The world turned. His body, that like many of the intellectually reared had never been an instrument for either great pain or great pleasure, felt as though it were being turned, like a harp, for some unknown rhapsody. . . .

He hesitated, doubtful, uncertain, in the dimness of that light. . . . What was it that he should say first? Do first?

Moreover, though this he did not realize, he was unaccustomed to embarking upon enterprises on his own initiative. Gwydion had often left him to develop his wits by solving a problem within their range, but those problems had always been of the man's setting. All their enterprises had been made through doors that Gwydion had opened, or seeds that he had found and brought to flower in Llew's own mind. That master of thoughts may not always have been able to resist the temptation of thinking the boy's thoughts for him more quickly and better than he could think them for himself.

Llew's mind was not entirely his own possession to make up. He was still of an age to wait for Gwydion's decisions, unused to making his own. The almost perfect peace that had always been between them made his mind less swift to break free than if it had ever been fired with resentment and rebellion against the son of Dôn.

He sat there locked into himself, and the girl sat locked into herself, less happily. A tone, a lightest finger-touch, even a look from her, would have turned him from boy to man. Understanding would have delighted her. She would have been exalted by the sense of her own queenship, her ability to bestow unknown rapture—reassured, too, by the sense of their equality.

For she felt timidity, knew that she was giving more than he. The thing that she was doing was no longer done by every girl though still by most, whether they always admitted it or not.

But she was too dizzy with his beauty to be able to conceive of him as less than a young god, as partner to her own uncertainties. Every moment her shy daring was seeping out of her; there was sickness in her heart, a swelling in her throat. She had not pleased him. . . .

Finally she lifted her bright little head proudly. "Shall I go?" she asked.

"Why?" said Llew. "I like having you here well enough."

There was shy friendliness in the words, but to her they rang with mockery. She sprang to her feet in sudden passion.

"What then? Why don't you do something about it? Is all you want to make a mock and a jest of me?"

He stared at her, silent, startled. Here again was the wrathful, unreasonable perversity of woman.

"Make a what of you?" he said at last.

She stamped her foot. "You are not a right man at all! It is not so my brothers would speak to any girl that came to meet them, and they with time on their hands, unless she were as ill-favored as a mule or an old she-goat! But my brothers carry arms and bring home heads when there is trouble on the borders. And they say that you never carry arms, that if you could be got to go where you might get a finger cut, you would show nothing but your back in a battle, and you have never even shown that! I would never have offered myself to such a poor, slinking craven except as a jest."

Then she was off, running like a deer down the white beaches, hoping with all her hot, hurt heart that he would run after her. But he sat still where she had left him, aghast at the repute she had given him. Were people saying, thinking, *that?* The taunts which she had thought would be less or no more than a bee-sting to one so highly placed as he throbbed within him like a spearwound; and his sensitive young pride lay bleeding and quivering within him.

This hurt also had Arianrhod his mother and the nature of woman dealt him. . . .

When he returned to Gwydion's fortress all were at meat. Govannon was there as his brother's guest, chewing heartily and arguing as lustily with those about him concerning the comparative virtues of a sword or dagger blade affixed to the handle with rivets, in the ancient British style, or fitted into a socket after the fashion of Gaul: which was the more to be depended upon not to come apart in your hand while you were slicing your man?

One thought that only old ways could be good.

"For it stands to reason that a blade that is only screwed into a hole will not be as likely to stay there as if it were stuck fast with rivets. And if he were not already well carved when hilt and blade came apart, the person you were slicing might slice you."

"Rivets can wear loose," said Govannon, "and they will not stay in the same place so long as a good shapely hole will. That is, if you have the right man to do the work." And his great, hairy chest swelled out a little. "Moreover, if you poke your blade into your man deep enough, it will stick there even if the hilt does come off. And he will not feel much like slicing back at you until he has got it out again—if he does then.

". . . But I think iron, not bronze, is going to be the one war-metal of the future," said he.

But Llew, who could have weapons neither of iron nor of bronze, with rivets or without, went past him without speaking, and wished his uncle the smith back in his forge again, or with lost Dylan at the bottom of the sea. Anywhere out of sight and sound, he and his blades, and his talk of blades.

This was a woe that Llew could not bear to tell, even to Gwydion.

There was trouble on Llew after that. He walked silently and gloomily as his own shadow, and when he talked at all it was emptily and without zest, as a man talks to cover silence. For he had turned another corner of the road; as he had ceased to be truly a baby when the girl Eigr had told him that he had never been born, so had he stepped out of boyhood when he met the girl on the beach. He was now the beginning of a man.

Yet the boy always lurks within the man and there was youth in the very depth and width of his unhappiness. All things in the world had ceased to interest or please him. If he fixed his wits upon a study, the knowledge that went in at the front of his head one minute came out again at the back of it the next, as if his brain had been open there. Even the sunlight seemed to him to be of a dark blue color, and the earth a stinking sink of woes. For he was suffering in both his heart and his pride. Already behind his back folk were beginning to call him coward and effeminate idler; and there was no way to show them otherwise. For he could not get arms.

He had thought himself a prince and a crown's heir and a learner of magic and the Mysteries; and now he had discovered that he was less than a man. No farm boy in Gwynedd but could have a sword and use it. None but he had a mother whose curse would have kept them weaponless and doomed them to the helplessness of a cripple. And all might know that a cripple had once been a brave man; his misfortune would not have been a fault or a reproach. But a strong youth who never carried arms or went into battle must be a strange and shameful mock, a craven-like freak who could never hold up his head in any assembly—stuff unfit for either chief or king.

And his heart ached because this taunt of his blemish had first been flung at him by one of whom he had expected some lovely thing; he knew not what. But he had felt great beauty beating its wings above them there in the loneliness of that golden twilight; had heard in the rustle of those wings, faint and unclear but unmistakable, the sound of a song of wonder such as some mighty wave of rosy fire might sing, sweeping earthward from the sun's heart to wash the world in its glowing tide.

He tried to think in what way he had offended her, blighted and spoiled their rapture unborn. But he could not. He knew what often happened between men and women in such lonely meetings on the shore or in the quiet woodlands; he had heard the talk of men and boys. But all that had sounded hot and uncouth and boisterous, never awing and lovely, different from this.

Had she expected him to grab her and roll her over on the sand, as those men would have done? Was that what she had wanted? But all had seemed too special, too dear, too much their own, to be fitted into the rough forms men jested of. He had been shy before this strange new loveliness that had encircled them—reverent, as he would have been before the exquisite opening of a flower, or the first spreading and expanding of a butterfly's bright-hued wings. So delicate and rainbow-like had that dawn of passion seemed to him. He would have been afraid to lay demanding hands upon her beauty. . . .

And evidently she had thought that he had not wanted her; or else, more likely, she had been as disgusted by the sickly mawkish quality of his love as by his abstinence from war. She had left him in wrath. . . .

In his own eyes he was discredited and dishonored, and that is not a healthy sight for any man. Shame, eaten daily, gives the soul jaundice and dyspepsia, though a single square meal of it may sometimes purge well a system grown puffy with conceit. But Llew had not been much conceited, and his deflation left him at once flatter than a sheet of parchment, and heavier than a stone.

Gwydion soon saw his state, and set about sifting his mind, thought by thought, for its causes; but he found there only the lack of arms; for some queer reserve deeper than shyness made Llew hide that meeting on the sands, and he in turn was not without some of that defensive skill with which Gwydion himself had once been able to veil a thought from Mâth by ceasing to think it.

The boy may have left the lack of arms in his thoughts not only as a shield for the girl, but also to remind Gwydion of his duty. For the time had come for Arianrhod's brother to make good his threat to force her to arm her son—if he were able.

Gwydion seems to have thought likewise. For one day he called the youth to him. "Boy," he said, "tomorrow we shall go on a journey together. So be more cheerful than you are."

"I will indeed," said the boy.

And at dawn, when the sun was lighting his first red signal fires in the east, they rose quietly and left the castle. They went along the seashore towards Bryn Aryen.

Atop Cevn Clydno they stopped, and Gwydion turned two boulders into horses. If they did anything else there it is not told, but when the sun was westering, two youths with harps rode up to Caer Arianrhod and asked admittance of the porter there.

"Tell your Lady that two bards from Glamorgan are here," said that one who looked to be the elder. Yet why he looked older no man could have told, unless it was that his grey eyes and determined chin had some look that was deeper, more settled in purpose and power. . . .

So the porter went in and told Arianrhod: "Two minstrels of Glamorgan are without, two entertainers of the folk."

That pleased her, and she answered: "Let them in. The welcome of the gods be with them."

For it seemed good to her that there should be some new thing in Caer Arianrhod, where the quiet sometimes seemed to her like that of a becalmed sea that only her own moods could stir and trouble, as storms shake the sea, and where there was nothing that did not come from herself alone. . . . Though she valued that sovereignty, times come when the creator wearies of creation and would lose himself in the self of another—when all of us long not to stir, but to be stirred, to be refreshed by the energy of others instead of expending our own. . . .

Moreover, in the amusements of those days the bards were almighty. There were no theaters save the altars and the ancient oaks where the druids performed the symbolic rites of their Mysteries; and no song nor saga save what dwelt on the lips of the bards. And this woman of the magic-loving race of Mâth must have been an artist, a lover of story and song.

A feast was made, and the bards were set by Arianrhod herself, and all made merry. But none asked for a tale, for courtesy demanded that the poets be let eat in peace and given all the dues of hospitality before they were asked to show their skill.

Yet from time to time Arianrhod searched the elder bard with liquid eyes; for there was that in him that drew her and acted as a magnet upon her gaze. "Have I seen you elsewhere?" she asked, "for there is that in your look which should be known to me."

The younger bard had some kind of accident then and dropped his wine-cup, but the elder turned and withered him with a look.

"I think not, Lady," he answered his hostess courteously, "for I do not remember you, and you are a sight no man could forget. Look well, and perhaps you will think of some other face mine resembles." And he turned and looked into her eyes, and she searched his face inch by inch, yet found no feature there that was known to her, only strangeness, growing ever stranger. . . .

"It was a fancy," she said. "Yet"—and her eyes narrowed—"there was never a fancy but had a source, either in the deeps of ourselves, in some uncaptured wisdom, or elsewhere when it was sent upon us for our confusion and vexation."

"I have heard that your Ladyship is a druidess and a mistress of spells," he said respectfully. "Would it weary you to tell me your meaning, if it be not one of the secrets that are hid from all but the initiate?"

"It is no great matter," she answered, "yet it could be truly understood only by the instructed; and tonight I would have you instruct me. I have gone long without learning. I would hear of some new thing."

"My sorrow then! For I shall weary you that way also," he sighed. "For what is my poor art to amuse a lady whose brother is the first of storytellers, and chief of all bards of the world?"

A shadow crossed her bright face then, murky as a smoldering flame. "My brother is the last bard in the world I would care to listen to," she said. "For the prices that he sets for his songs are too high and, having heard them, there is no way but to pay. They are a web and he is a spider—as dead Pryderi, Dyved's King, could bear witness could he come back from the halls of Annwn and speak. For he too was caught in my brother's web. And I have heard say that he left a curse that flesh of the swine he was robbed of should feed on my brother's flesh. . . . But these affairs are none of yours. Sing me a song, and I will judge your art."

The man looked surprised and puzzled, as one might when hearing a great lady speak against her kin, but he took up his harp. "You speak well, Lady, when you say that these affairs are none of mine, for indeed they are beyond me. Yet I have heard that the Lord your brother has power to turn aside curses, such, at least, as come from Dyved. And now will I do for you the best that I can."

So Llew took the harp and Gwydion sang, and his voice was like a river of gold bearing them all away. And who knows what were the boats in which they drifted on that glittering tide, what rainbow bubbles of dream and fantasy and wonder, what fables of the fabulous and legends old even to them who now are legendary: glories lost under the lowest layers of time? Old things that he made new, dim relics of time's twilights, over which he threw the bright colors of sunrise.

For there is nothing that is not old, and there is nothing that is not new, since all are parts of the vast order of What Must Be, in which only the poet, whose work it is to try to utter the dreams in the deep unchanging heart of man, sometimes hears, fainter and farther off than any echo, the rhythm of some ancient, mighty song. . . .

All sat and listened like creatures becalmed by magic. Wide-eyed, Arianrhod sat and listened, the blue of her eyes like that of the heavens when they first shone wondering above the world. And the gaze of the younger bard was twin with hers, in color and wonder and joy. They might have been the same eyes, set in two faces.

When the song was ended, Arianrhod laughed and clapped her hands, and gave the singer the gold chain from about her own throat. Then she asked him questions about that tale and history and others, and they debated together. Their thoughts embraced and chased and fired each other. But she never succeeded in asking him a question he could not answer; for if he did not know the answer, he made one up. And the company marked that on their two faces was such glow and excitement and intensity of life as come to most only when they are a little drunken, or when their bodies are lost in the ecstasy of love.

But Arianrhod rose at last, and bade them all a gracious farewell for the night, and servants showed the bards to the chamber appointed for their sleep.

But they did not sleep at once. The younger lay down but his body was still tense as a spring coiled for action. He looked up with bright eyes at the elder. "What are you going to do?" he whispered. "I thought that you would ask her to arm me there when her mind was all blurred with the songs."

"Your own was as blurred," replied the elder, "or you would not have thought of such a witlessness. What pretext could I have given? She would have roused in a moment, and all would have been undone. But keep quiet; for it is not safe to speak here."

The boy lifted his head, swiftly alert as a fawn, and glanced about the chamber. "I do not see where anyone could be hiding," he whispered. And then, in a tone still lower. "Do you mean—?"

"I mean that Arianrhod's sorcerers have long ears," said the other. "Nor are her own short, though I think I have lulled them for this night. But I could not answer for our safety if we slept and she learned who we were."

And as he spoke his face was dark with thought, and older. For what life has written in a man's countenance is not easily wiped away though he have power to mold and remold his features as though they were potter's clay. Moreover, in that room alone with Llew, the mask of illusion may have dropped away, leaving his own face bare.

"She would not dare to harm us," said the boy, "she would be afraid of Mâth."

"She would," said Gwydion, "but perhaps not so soon as we could wish. Arianrhod does not know her limitations well enough. And will you be quiet?"

Llew became quiet.

But his uncle did not lie down beside him at once. He sat for a while in the quiet darkness listening to that deep stillness which was yet murmurous with sound, and playing with the golden chain Arianrhod had given him.

"I gave you that once, sister, and now it comes back to me as the gift you toss a strolling singer. But still it was to my genius that you gave it, and you are again in the spider's web. . . . There is a long account between us, Arianrhod. You are guilty against the boy. Am I also guilty against you? It may be. They are very tangled, our rights and wrongs. . . ."

He listened to the whispering hush of that dark, sleeping house until it seemed to him that, by his magician's sixth or seventh sense, he could pick out his sister's breathing from among all the rest, where she lay white and gold in her bed.

"Do you sleep too deep to dream that I am near, Arianrhod? . . . Almost you knew me there at the feast; I had to be quick to lay the illusion strongly enough upon your eyes to blind you. . . . You have grown in magic, Arianrhod, and therefore in power to carry out your malice. Yet shall it be futile. Let the gods and the future reckon up the debts between us as they will; the boy is here, and I am unrepentant for his coming. You shall pay the price of my song."

Then, having opened his mind wide enough to take in all the thoughts and feelings in that house, and to explore all the dreams of its inmates, he made sure that nothing there was a menace or conscious of him, and that it was safe to sleep. . . .

He woke in that grey hour of twilight when it would seem easiest for unearthly wanderers to stray between the worlds, and the sickly light, struggling to pierce the veils of night, gives all the earth a wan and distorted strangeness, like a dead face seen through fog. That charmed hour when neither light nor darkness has power, and the creatures of both seem to scurry, mist-shrouded and unhuman, through the unsettled spheres. The gates of both Underworld and Overworld stood open. The skies brooded, flame and iron, above the mists of the clouded earth.

Llew was still asleep. He lay like a child, the cover thrown off and one arm crooked above his curls. As he rose, Gwydion looked down tenderly upon that bright head. He touched it with a hand that deepened its sleep, then turned to his work.

Yet had there been a watcher, he would have thought that Gwydion did nothing. He sat quiet, still as the wall itself, with closed eyes and folded hands. Yet never had he been more fully and intensely active. From the inmost deeps of himself he was calling up knowledge and energy and power. His mind, like molten metal, seethed and flamed under the force of his will. . . .

Day came up over the edge of the world. The sun strode forward, a red, wizened infant no longer, shivering new-born in a pale sky, but a golden bridegroom coming open-armed to earth.

Sound shattered that shining stillness—sound sudden and appalling as the coming thunder from the clear blue and gold of that smiling sky. From Caer Arianrhod and from the shores beyond trumpets rang, and the screams of women and the cries of men.

Llew sat up in bed, startled. He opened his mouth to speak, but shut it again at sight of the white, rigid concentration of Gwydion's face. He sat tense, his eyes fixed upon the older man, his ears upon the rising din outside.

There was a rush of feet outside the chamber, a knocking as if someone beat upon the door with clenched hands; and the boy heard a voice whose clear, rich tones always thrilled him: his mother's.

"Open! Open!"

Gwydion, hearing, relaxed. He stretched his arms and smiled. . . .

Llew cast a swift glance at him, read permission in his mind—those two were too well trained in the transmission of thought to have to speak aloud—and sprang to the door and opened it. Arianrhod entered with one of her maidens. She was very pale.

"Men," she said, "we are in evil case."

"Is it so?" said Gwydion. "We have heard shouting and trumpets. What think you they mean?"

Mute and wide-eyed she signed to them to follow her. In the next chamber was a window that faced westward, upon the outer ocean. They looked and saw that all the sea seemed packed with white sails more closely than ever the sky with storm clouds. These came on arrow-swift, like a flock of giant birds come down to eat up all the earth. The decks were dark with swarming warriors and the sun gleamed like fire on helms and on the wicked, barbed heads of spears. . . .

"You see," she said, and her voice shook, though she was quick to steady it. "By the gods, we cannot see the blue of the ocean for them. And they are coming landward as fast as they can. What shall we do?"

She laid her hand on Gwydion's arm. Her eyes were dark with dread, sorceress' no longer, but woman's, lifted to his in mute appeal. As though she recognized in him, wandering bard though he seemed, some power that could help her. And Llew, wondering, saw a swift, softening spasm cross Gwydion's face, like the shadow of an ancient tenderness. . . .

Always in his mind he was to set that moment beside that other long ago when he had first glimpsed the mystery of man and woman, when Arianrhod had put her arms round Gwydion in her hall, and he had kissed her lips. . . .

But the change swiftly passed from Gwydion's face. It set like that of a man with his back to the wall, grimly preparing himself to face desperate odds.

"Lady, there is but one course left to us. We must close the castle and stand against the invaders as best we may."

Her swift smile flashed upon him, bright as the moon. "The gods reward you. None of my men here are fit for leaders. They have lived soft too long in a woman's service, and their hearts have become sheep's. Do you take charge of the defense. I will bring you arms in plenty."

She left them; and Llew watched the shore where the first of the ships was beaching and the warriors were leaping ashore, waving spears and axes above their heads in a grisly, spiky dance. . . .

When she came back two maidens were with her, bearing arms for two men. Arianrhod turned to Gwydion, in her eyes the glorying pride that women take in the desperate, almost hopeless courage with which some men can combat doom. She would have helped him don his weapons, but he waved her back.

"Lady, do you arm this lad, for he is new to war and weapons, and will be slow at getting them on. And there is no time to lose, for already I hear the clamor of men drawing near. I will manage with the help of your maids."

She obeyed him; she had no pride left to spare in resenting his command. Through the window she could see the dark strangers swarming like ants toward her castle; and she had no wish to be carried to a foreign land, a slave.

"Gladly," she said; and bent her proud head before Llew to buckle the arms upon him.

She had risen in haste, startled from her sleep by the trumpets and the shouting, and there was only one robe upon her. He could see the white sweet path between her breasts that had never nursed him. He could feel her hands, swift and light and cool, steady for all her fear. It was the first time that she had ever touched him. . . . A tremor went through him and he closed his eyes.

Never since his birth had they been so near each other; never again were they to be. . . .

"Have you finished?" asked Gwydion.

"I have finished," she answered. "He is armed."

"I too have finished," Gwydion said and smiled. . . . "Now let us take off these arms for there is no further need of them."

She looked up at him blankly, as if at once suddenly gone mad. Her lovely mouth fell open. "What do you mean? Do you not see the army around the house?"

Gwydion looked straight at her, grave and unsmiling.

"Lady, do you?"

She looked; and the slopes and the beaches, that a moment before had been dark with swarming men, shone vacant, bare of all life, under the sun. The sea gleamed blue and tranquil; not a sail blotted its billows. Ships and warriors were gone as though dissolved into thin air.

She stared. She rubbed her eyes and stared again. But there was nothing there. . . .

Now she looked at Gwydion with the eyes of one who doubted her own sanity instead of his.

"Oh," she gasped, "what then was the cause of all this uproar?"

And now he smiled at her, and the lines of his face seemed to change with that smiling so that she knew him, and no false shape hid her brother from her longer.

"It was caused to make you carry out the terms of your oath and arm your son," he answered, "and he has now got arms, but no thanks to you."

She went red. She went white. Then such flame blazed in her face as it seemed would burn her up and leap out of her and reduce them to ashes also. Yet her set features did not change. They seemed every moment to grow more hard and baleful, like a white-hot stone.

She glanced once and once only at Llew, in her eyes the hate deepened by the long years of hoarding: no mother's look, one such as a woman gives the rival who has triumphed over her in love. . . .

Gwydion watched her closely, for he mistrusted this inspiration that enabled her to control her agony of rage.

She slashed him with a smile that was bright and cruel as a sword. At her son she would not look again.

"By all the gods," she said softly, and the very softness of her voice held a venom too great to be expressed by any cry of rage: "You are an evil man Gwydion my brother. Many youths might have got their deaths in the commotion and the uproar that you have made in this Cantrev today. And as for this one with you, I will swear a destiny upon him."

She paused and waited, her eyes watching their suddenly whitened faces as a cat's might watch the mouse she holds fast in her claws. When they heard her voice again it was a soft gloating purr. It rang with a triumph that this time could never be cheated or evaded:

"Never shall his side touch a woman's of the race that now dwells upon this earth."

BOOK THREE

THE LOVES OF BLODEUWEDD

Not of mother and father,
When I was made
Did my creator create me.
Of nine-formed faculties,
Of the fruit of fruits,
Of the fruit of the primordial God,
Of primroses and blossoms of the hill,
Of the flowers of trees and shrubs.
Of earth, of an earthly course,
When I was formed.
Of the flower of nettles,
Of the water of the ninth wave.
I was enchanted by Mâth,
Before I became immortal;
I was enchanted by Gwydion
The great Purifier of the Brython. . . .
I was enchanted by the sage
Of sages, in the primitive world.

(Book of Taliessin VIII, Skene's Four
Ancient Books of Wales.)

1

The Counsel of Mâth

GWYDION AND LLEW did not return to Dinas Dinllev. They went instead to Mâth at Caer Dathyl.

For this time the son of Dôn was helpless, and not even his wits could devise a way to outwit his sister's curse. Rage and tell Arianrhod that she was a malicious woman to whom none should lend countenance or support, and that, in spite of her the boy should have a mate—this he could and had done; yet he had no least idea how this was to be achieved. And his sister had known that he had not, and had smiled on his wrath and his going. . . .

Arianrhod had barred her son from the joys of love. Llew could lie by the side of no woman of earth. That was as certain as that the sun would never set in the east. So then he must lie by one that was not human. But Gwydion owned to himself that there was none such to be found.

He had come at last to the place where he must ask Mâth's help, and he doubted if even Mâth could give it.

This time, too, he may not have been averse to drawing their uncle's wrath down upon his sister if he could. . . .

The old King made them welcome. They bowed before him, nephew and grandnephew, where he lay in his long repose. Never since the war with Dyved had he ridden forth from his palace, and he never would again. Yet above the vast wintry thickets of his beard his eyes still shone keen and deep as of old, and power and majesty still lay about him like a cloak. For in his ancient, grave-like repose that seemed inactive as death, he yet was more truly active than aught that moves under the slow, cumbering weight of the body, hearing and cleansing and uplifting, through his own thought, the thoughts of men.

For a man might not know how or why, lightning-like, the solution of his troubles flashed across his brain; or whence the peace came that moved down from the hills at evening, blowing like a white wind through his vexed and troubled soul, though his might be eyes that commonly saw, but never looked at, the hills. Yet these were the sendings of Mâth.

So he who had grown too old and near his Change to rule his people through the body still ruled them through the mind. And into the hearts of the wrathful he would send a stream of pity from the springs of his own inexhaustible store. And on the screen of the mind of the self-absorbed, he would suddenly cast the picture of another, and all the forgotten feelings of that other, and all the harm that might be done him.

Many were so warned. From the minds of many the pictures faded too quickly. Yet, if ignored; their light left behind a secret fiery spark that smoldered sullenly, stirring the first seeds of evolution: vision and remorse.

This was the wisdom whose help Gwydion and Llew sought.

They poured out their wrath and their woes before him, and he listened, his great calm untroubled yet not unsympathetic, and as uncontaminated by kindred passion as that of the timeless hills. And his very lack of alarm or anger made them feel that this strait could not be so desperate, or freedom from it so unattainable. Yet they did not see how these things could be.

"Well," he said at last, and rubbed his chin, "do you go out now and eat with the folk of the court, Llew, for if you must fast from love you will not help yourself by fasting from food. Your uncle and I will consider this matter."

But for a long time after the boy had gone he still sat in silence, rubbing his chin, while Gwydion paced back and forth through the chamber, flame-restless as of old.

"Are you going to let Arianrhod do this crime against her own son and yet go unscathed?" he burst at last. "She is laughing now because she has got the victory over me, and for that I care not, but the boy's life she shall not ruin! There was never such monstrousness heard of: that she should punish her son for being born, and not herself for unchastity, if unchastity she must name it! He did not ask for birth."

"You did. . . ," said Mâth. And there was silence between them while the wind and the swallows whispered in the eaves.

"What right has she to complain of that?" said Gwydion then. "I laid no force upon her."

"No; you would not have dared to violate the Ancient Harmonies a second time. You have not laid force upon her, yet you did lay force upon her when your plots compelled her to bear an unwanted child. And her fame, not yours, has paid the price of that birth. You were clever enough to keep within the law that she has trespassed by her open hate. . . .

"You too are not guiltless of the boy's misfortunes; for you would have him born before the time came for the men of Gwynedd to know fatherhood. And he whose birth violates the established order of things must always pay. . . . And it is not vengeance that will help him now."

"What will help him?" asked Gwydion. While his uncle spoke he had stood silent, his brow furrowed in thought. But now he took up his pacing again.

"If I have no right to ask vengeance upon Arianrhod, what then? . . . Is there no way to undo the oath? In all your years and all your wisdom, Lord, have you not heard of one? Howsoever hard or troublous, I would take it, for I love him. . . . Too great a responsibility is it to give life if one must let that life be made a burden to him who gets the gift."

"There is none," said Mâth. "That oath is beyond retracting or loosing. Always you have been able to outwit your sister when she left herself power to evade the oath, and now, learning by that the unwisdom of mockery, she has placed this curse beyond her own power. . . . So she misapplies what wisdom she wins. . . ."

"She does indeed," said her brother. "I should take pleasure in teaching her another kind of wisdom," he added grimly.

"You cannot fight her with her own weapon," said Mâth, "for she serves hate with a singleness of mind that you who love could never attain; and it is to the single-minded fighter that the victory goes. You can conquer her only by keeping to and cleansing your own weapon that you named a while ago; for love is a mightier force than hate. You would spare yourself for Llew's sake no more than you have spared her. Is not that a strength that is greater than any of hers?"

"It seems not," said Gwydion, "since I have failed to protect him from her. For he must have a woman. I remember well to what a pass it brought Gilvaethwy to do without one woman, though he could have had all the others in sight. And now must I see Llew brought to a worse plight than that? For to him all women will be as footholders."

"He is not like Gilvaethwy," said Mâth. "You yourself have seen that."

"Yet is he human," sighed Gwydion.

Mâth brooded awhile, rubbing his chin again. It was dusk, and in the darkening chamber his head shone with a frosty light. His great beard looked infinite, so white and so vast was it, like the essence of all snows.

"Has he ever known a woman?" he asked. "I thought I saw the face of one in his mind a while ago when he stood beside you here."

"He has not," said Gwydion. "He has never had any kind of passage with a woman at all, or I would have known of it. I would have seen it in his mind even if he had tried to hide it; and why would he try to do that?"

"Are you so sure of this?" asked Mâth. And it may be that he spoke only out of the stored knowledge of years of watching the hearts of men. Or, in his measureless omniscience, he may have heard that talk on the beach at sunset, and the voice of the girl who taunted the weaponless. . . .

But Gwydion shook his head. "The young can keep their own counsel. I remember that. But not Llew. Not from me. It must have been some girl that he had looked at, and whose beauty he remembered when he knew that it was beyond his reach forever."

"Perhaps," said Mâth. "He has now come to man's height, and he is the fairest stripling that ever was seen. It is time that he would begin to think of women."

"He has not been thinking about them," said Gwydion with a sigh, "not in the past when he could have had them. But he will be thinking of them now," he groaned.

"That is true indeed," said Mâth, "for what is most desirable is that which we cannot have; and nothing is ever so fascinating as the forbidden."

Gwydion sighed again. "He will think about them," said he. "They did not interest him before, but now they will obsess him. His eyes will drink in every move and look and turn and every kind of shape and complexion. They will be books that he cannot read and fruit he cannot eat. They will haunt him sleeping and waking, and they will become his torture.

"And youth and passion can weave a flaming snare. What if in some hour they should burn so high that he should forget all things, even Arianrhod and the oath, and be blasted?"

And his lips whitened at the thought.

"You must guard against that," said Mâth.

His nephew brooded.

"I could stay him with threats and with force, but that course must inevitably build a wall between us. And, besides, if he could forget Arianrhod's oath, what dread of me would he remember? I must find another way. I could convey him an endless variety of phantom women, who would be solid enough to his kiss and clasp for an hour. But he would not be satisfied, for love demands reality. It will not be sated with mere kissing and clasping, but seeks the self behind—though only the gods know why. You would think that a phantom love would be a man's ideal, since he seeks always a mirror of himself; and we are ever made angry when we prick ourselves on the difference between the mind of our beloved and ours."

"That is so," said Mâth, "and yet it is not so. Or rather, it is not all. The difference is the magnet as well as the sting. For men and women are incomplete, and, knowing this in their secret hearts, ever seek completion in each other. And so it has been since the Ancient Day when sex first severed humanity with walls of fire, and made halves of what had been a whole. And so it will be until the end when the halves shall be made whole again, and the lover shall have passed that barrier of flame and be at one again with his beloved, and eternally at peace."

Gwydion glanced at him keenly. For nothing—worry or pain or pleasure—could ever long quench the joy of the chase after knowledge in the son of Dôn.

"You have lived long enough to have heard tales of how the world was before that day, uncle, when men and women were not yet divided into two forms. Were there not some who could still tell them when you were young?"

Mâth went on, ignoring the interruption:

"—And men and women ever yearn unknowing after that lost wholeness, and strive to devour each other to obtain it, not knowing that union can be obtained only through peace and never through war—by the give and take of exchange, not by destruction. And through the brief moments when their flesh achieves it, life goes on and the endless round renews itself, and more souls are embodied in the world to carry on the old ceaseless quest and strife."

Gwydion thought awhile.

"Is it true that the difference is a magnet," he said. "It was always so with Arianrhod and me. For I wished to explore her and she me, and we each hid our own secrets and sought the other's, and there was joy but no victory in the strife. Yes, there was great joy; for there is not in the world another woman so clever and beautiful as she, though her heart has no wisdom and her temper is that of a balky mule possessed of seven demons into the bargain," he ended with sudden vigor. And that recalled him to thought of more practical and immediate matters.

"But how does all this help Llew?" asked he.

Mâth looked at him.

"You have spoken of phantom women. You say that you can create flesh that will be solid for an hour. But there are like creations that do not fade. Have I never taught you that?" said he.

Gwydion stared at him. "You mean that you can make a woman—?"

"Once we were all phantoms in the mind of a God," said Mâth. "He thought us into being. . . . Our bodies can call souls into the world. Can our minds do less? Now will we test our magic, you and I."

For three days after that the Lord of Gwynedd and his heir were shut into his chamber, and none saw their faces or knew what work they did there. Only Llew knew that in some fashion it concerned him and his plight; but how it could help him he knew not; he busied himself with his new-won arms and tried to think that their brightness was brighter than eyes seen all aglow on a seashore at sunset; and that sword-blades were stauncher than women, the weavers of trouble.

But the servants carried food and drink to the closed door of Mâth's chamber, and scuttered away in haste, even while their curious eyes clung to its thick slab of oak as though to spy out the mystery beyond. But that door was shut as tightly as the doors between earth and the worlds beyond, those hazy portals of twilight that most of us can open with but one key: death.

But during those three days not even death could have unlocked Mâth's door. . . .

Flowers the servants carried there also, at every noontide. Great heaps of the blossoms of oak and broom and meadow-sweet, the finest and fairest to be gathered in the woods and the fields. But what use Mâth and Gwydion made of those flowers, like all else they did in those three days, is one of the mysteries that lie dead with the druids—though perhaps yellow men, fashioning their thought into palpable images in lonely monasteries in the snowy mountains of Tibet, retain fragments of that strange science that may once have travelled from Stonehenge to the menhirs on far southern isles in an ocean of whose existence the folk of Gwynedd never knew.

But they may have needed those flowers to form the link of substance wherewith to anchor the immaterial to the fleshly world we know. And what stuff could be tenderer than flowers, more fragile and akin to fancy, and yet more full of all the promise and powers of life—the strength of the oak and the sweet springing vigor of plants, and the soft beauty of the little flowers that grow in the meadows? What better material could there be to shape life than blossoms, the frail blooming beginnings of life?

Did Arianrhod and her sorcerers learn of that work where she sat hugging her victory at Caer Arianrhod? Did they labor, with muttered and chanted charms and curses, to stay it, or alter the nature of the being it formed?

But at the third day's end Gwydion and Mâth opened the chamber doors and came forth; and they looked weary, but they smiled like men whose work is done.

Mâth looked at Goewyn his wife where she sat among her ladies and he said:

"Go you to my chamber, for there is one within who has need of your care. Show her all honor, for tonight she is a stranger and a guest among us; and in a day to come when my time is past, she too, in her turn, shall be Lady over Gwynedd."

The Queen stood up. Her breath caught a little, as if in awe. Her face shone white in the light of the torches, not untouched by dread.

"A stranger here and everywhere," she said, "a guest to the whole race of men. Is she as other women, Lord, this who awaits me yonder? By what name shall I greet her—my young kinswoman that is to be?"

And all there felt with her the strangeness of that hour and shrank from it, since within that chamber waited a woman who had not been fashioned from mother's flesh, or born of the race of men.

"She sleeps," said Mâth, "but on the morrow she will wake as other women wake. Then will I give her name and place before the folk. Do not fear her, for we are all strangers, as unknown as she, when first the winds of Annwn blow our souls into the world. Though this is unrealized, for those whose flesh we are fancy that our inner selves too are at least partly fashioned from theirs. And she will have no woman kin but you to look to, since Arianrhod forswears her son."

The Queen's form quivered. A sudden gust of passion blew across her face. "Ill done was this of Arianrhod!" she cried. "Llew is a fair lad, and she did better when she bore him than when she cursed him. Well would she be served for this if the sea swallowed up her and all that she owns as hers! Why must she make this thing to be?"

"Out of the unwisdom of her heart she did it," answered Mâth, "and out of what I deem my wisdom I have wrought what remedy I could. . . ."

"It is as you will, Lord," said Goewyn. "I will have her borne to my chamber and a couch spread for her there."

And she went out with her maidens.

But Gwydion went to the chamber where Llew was. He found him lying down, arms crossed beneath his bright head, staring out into the purple night.

"We have a wife ready for you," said Gwydion.

Llew sprang up with awe-widened eyes and gaping jaw. "You mean that you have *made* a woman!" he gasped. "You have been able to do that?

"But she is an illusion!" he cried. "She could not be real."

And loneliness and a sudden cold grue came on him, a longing for warm and human things, realities as indisputable as himself: even for a taunting voice on a beach at sunset and brown eyes sparkling with the warm, earthy anger of things that do not seem, but are.

"Not now," said Gwydion. "She is a reality. Whatever she was when first we shaped her semblance, she has her own life now. She is no longer an illusion; she is a maid for you to woo."

"But how can that be," the boy asked, "when she is not human?"

"Once she may have been of the race of men," Gwydion answered. "Who knows?"

And for a strange solemn moment he himself wondered whence it had come and what manner of being it might be, the soul that he and Mâth had drawn down from the upper winds to inhabit the form they had fashioned. . . .

But Llew was considering. "You said that she was a wife for me. Then I am to marry?"

"You are," said Gwydion. "There is nothing else you can do. It has been trouble enough to get one woman for you. . . ." He stretched himself and sighed wearily. "It is hard business for men, doing the work of gods."

And as he spoke he thought in wonder: "It is true as Mâth has said. My wish for a son has riveted the custom of marriage upon Gwynedd, though I myself did not marry. For now he who is mine must wed or go loveless. . . . It is my doing too that Mâth himself married Goewyn; and where we of the kings lead, the folk will follow. Marriage, that I have never wanted, is the end that all my plans and doings shape to. Is it so with us all, that we never know what end we truly work towards, any more than the mother knows the face or deeds of the unborn child?"

But he laid his hand on the boy's arm and said aloud the words calculated to kindle dreams and desire: "Child, we have done well for you. There is not in Gwynedd a girl so beautiful. She is as fair as ever Goewyn or Arianrhod your mother was."

And the rest of that night he slept. . . .

But Llew did not sleep. A flame of restlessness possessed him, a whirl of anticipation and dread. He was filled to overflowing with speculations and doubts and wonder. Both his brain and his body were stirred in ways that were new to him, and hard to comprehend.

For he stood upon the threshold of an unknown world, of mysteries that before that meeting on the shore had not often figured even in his dreams. A day before they had seemed barred from him forever; now they were close upon him, to be learned as soon as Mâth could call the kindred together for a wedding feast. And he half-craved that learning, and half-shrank from the intimacy and permanence it involved.

He was not overly eager to be married. He had always viewed marriage with suspicion, for youth, which has lived all its life in bonds, has a wary eye out for new ones. And he had noticed that the few married men he knew seemed less free than the others. Either they walked warily, like warriors scouting about an enemy encampment, or they grew discourteous and belligerent, as the ungentlemanly sometimes do to a bound foe. If they so much as looked another woman's way their wives fussed and scolded and screeched, or else dissolved into watery wails. Either phenomenon looked singularly unattractive.

But it would be too great an insult to ask the girl not to marry him, for people who lived together permanently always married. The old-fashioned, unmarried conservatives only lived together a little while. Besides, he had wit enough to see that a wedding feast would make no difference. If he lived with her all his life he would be married to her, whether he said so or not.

That was what marriage was.

It looked like an awkward and irksome business, and he had always been inclined to dispassionate agreement with his uncles, who said that it would never work. After all, was it sense to suppose that two people would have minds pleasing enough to each other to live happily together all their days, simply because one night they had had a desire to kiss and clasp?

Yet now his heart whispered: Why not, if both were courteous and loving and well matched in all things? Why should not one fair woman be enough, if she were kind and noble-minded? . . . And he wondered what it was like, that beauty of which Gwydion had spoken. He tried to think, and could not. His imagination pranced and curvetted and reared back again before the picturing, nervous as a skittish horse. And when he thought how closely it would soon be given to explore that unknown and mysterious loveliness, his heart bounded queerly with a quivering delight, yet his mind fled backward from that thought, with a timid, virgin shyness . . ..

In the morning he saw her. She was led down to the sea to be baptized, and Mâth gave her the name of Blodeuwedd or Flower-Like, though some have said that it was Blodeuedd, "Flowers," instead.

Then he laid her hand in Llew's before the folk, and all cheered at word of the wedding that was to be. For before her living presence all dread of her strange origin melted like mist before the sun. She was sweet as honey. She was warm and lovely as the dawn that comes up from far sky-places to light the dark and shivering earth. Her every movement was music and a fresh revealment of beauty; the touch of her hand or the turn of her head was a song.

And the lords of the Cantrevs and Cymwds and the chiefs of kindreds began riding in to the wedding feast to which Mâth had bidden them. All day they rode in, by ones and twos; and Govannon and Gilvaethwy and Eveyd and Amaethon were among them, and all those other unnamed nobles who were not sons of Dôn.

All day Llew's nervousness mounted until by the time evening began to veil the land it was a very fever of impatience and yet of shrinking. First it seemed to him that night would never come, and then it was coming with all the appalling speed of an arrow; and he would have been glad to dodge. For he had had no practice in the wooing of women. He had not pleased that girl on the beach. It would be a sad thing if he did not please his own wife either. And he was in awe of her. The dazzling flash of her beauty had awed him in the one instant that his eyes had met hers when Mâth joined their hands—the feel of her hand as it had lain, soft as velvet, yet vivid and thrilling as a flame, in his. . . .

He got advice in plenty, though he did not ask for any. His uncle Gilvaethwy gave him detailed and enthusiastic admonitions and his uncle Govannon slapped him on the back and told him to cheer up: she would not cut his head off. "Though she may feel like it if you get as sleepy early in the evening as you look like doing now," said he.

"She will wake him up; no fear," Gilvaethwy chuckled. "She is an awakening-looking piece. . . .

Llew blushed, and wished that he had not, for his cousin Bleiddwn, Gilvaethwy's youngest son, who was older and more experienced, was looking on. But he seemed sympathetic.

"It is a pity to have so much publicity the first time," he whispered aside. "You are being put through your paces like a stallion that has to get colts. Now it would be a pleasanter adventure if you could slip out by yourself and stop some girl behind a hedge . . .

But Gwydion thought there had been more than enough of this baiting, and he shooed them all out.

"Yes, we had better let him sleep now," said Bleiddwn, giggling, "for he will not have much time for sleep tonight. . . ."

But Gwydion gave him a look that made his mouth fall wider open and then shut again with a snap.

"I would not say that any of your heads are thick," said he, when they were all outside the chamber where Llew sat, "for they are all solid from the front of the skull to the back; and always were. There is no room for even thickness there."

"And yours and Llew's have nice hollows in them, I suppose?" said one of his brothers, laughing.

"They have activity in them," said Gwydion, "which is more than yours ever contained. But that does not matter. Do not spoil this business for the boy. He has lived less in the body than have any of you; and for him there is strangeness and newness in this, and the learning of a mystery. Do not take the bloom off the fruit."

"It would be hard to take the bloom off that fruit," said Govannon. "She is the downiest peach that ever grew in Gwynedd, and I would like to see the boy that could find her a sour taste in his mouth. My nephew Llew is too well-forged a blade for that, I am sure. Yet it is a pity indeed that Mâth never takes he-youngsters for footholders, Gwydion, for I think that darling of yours would serve him well. Why did you never let him run loose for a bit?"

"All of us ran loose," said Gwydion, "and the end of that was that Gilvaethwy and I ran in close confines indeed for a time. I would not have liked to have to do that to him."

Govannon scratched his head. "Well, you are right," said he, "but there is such a thing as being too right. . . . What if he does not know enough to watch for sound footing when you turn him loose to run at last?"

Gwydion digested that a moment.

"It is well put," he said. "Wisdom may sometimes come out of unlikely places," and he glanced at his brother's mouth. "But the end I have trained him for is to run well and surely. And he is clever. Never in his life has he failed to profit by a lesson."

"Well," said Govannon, "it is your business."

Llew bathed in the river Conwy at twilight, but he chose a wooded spot. He was glad not to have to bathe by the open sands. For some reason it would have seemed a queer sort of unfaithfulness, and a groping for the dead and fading past.

As he came up out of the shining waters he remembered that nameless girl by the sea, and wondered if she had since met another man on that beach where they had met. She was the mother of all these happenings, she, not less than Arianrhod. For it was she who had made him mope for arms.

Once, but a few days since, though now it seemed long ago, he had dreamed of showing himself to her in all the glory of his arms, when he should have won them. Yes, and of refusing her when she threw herself at his feet in admiration, though still he might have forgiven her. . . . But she soon passed from his mind now, like the outworn things of childhood, little old dreams and purposes long outgrown and forgotten. She was something that had happened very long ago.

Blodeuwedd was here and now, where she glowed in the place beside his at the right hand of Mâth. For tonight all honor was to be done the bride and bridegroom; the sons of Dôn sat on the King's left.

And Llew blushed again, embarrassed at the height of that honor, as he took his place between his grand-uncle's ancient, mystic might and that shining beauty who was his present and his future. Beauty and wisdom: one was on either side of him. And the imperturbable starry heights of the one, that it would take years or ages of toil to win, seemed no more mysterious to him than the glowing softness of the other, that lay ready to his hand. . . .

Through all his after-life he remembered that evening only as a haze of torchlight and song and shouting. Healths had been drunk and good wishes wished, and he had answered with the due courtesy of a prince. But he thought it must have been Gwydion's brain that had worded those answers and sent them to his lips, and had kept the wine in his raised cup from spilling on her, shining there beside him. So lost were all details in the warmth and shimmer of that haze. . . .

But at last the women led Blodeuwedd away. She touched his hand and smiled and went, her fair, flower-crowned head lowered modestly as she walked among the ladies.

"What does she hang her head like that for?" muttered a man farther down the table.

An old lady, who had been young before there were wives in Gwynedd, answered him: "She does it because some of the girls in Dyved do it at their weddings, fool. The poor young things are made shy by all this indecent fuss over their pairing off when they have never had a man before. And now the fashion is catching hold here, and this one does it because she thinks it is seemly. She learns the meanings of seemly and unseemly fast for one who is only a day old."

"Well, it is good for Llew Llaw Gyffes that she is well developed for that age," said the man, laughing, "or he might have had to wait a while. . . ."

"In my day no honest woman bothered about what was seemly or unseemly," the old woman remarked, "for there were no foul minds and nothing to be ashamed of." And she went on chewing the sliced meat off a sow's haunch, but she had trouble with even that, for most of her teeth were gone. . . .

Then Llew in his turn was led from the banquet hall.

He was the first heir of Gwynedd for whom a wedding feast had ever been held at Caer Dathyl.

At last he stood alone in the chamber of his wife. The moon had filled it with a clear and gleaming twilight that shone like deep, translucent waters. He could see her clearly where she lay awaiting him.

She was beautiful enough for a god. She was too beautiful for a man. And for the last time he thought of that girl on the beach. She had been solid and warm and human, and, like himself, very recently a child; she might have been a comrade. He had already forgotten that her beauty had ever awed him. . . .

But his wife lay there in magic youth that had known no childhood, and perhaps would know no age. Her yellow hair was spread on the pillows, golden as broom. Her arms and breast shone rose and white against the embroidered covers, as though molded from a drift of apple blossoms. Her flesh looked lovely as flowers, tender as flowers. He felt afraid that it would crumble into petals again if he should touch it. . . .

. . . She was smiling: "My Lord," she said, and held out her arms. . . .

He went to her; he put his arms around her. Her body felt so light in his arms, so warm and silken-soft, that he was still almost afraid that it lacked solidity. Yet the touch of it thrilled through him like a wine that only gods might drink. It had a glorious, enrapturing sweetness sharp as pain. . . .

He kissed her lips. He buried his face against the whiteness of her neck. For the first time he spoke to her. His voice stumbled with marvel and delight:

"Blodeuwedd. . . . Blodeuwedd. . . ."

Outside the feasting had ceased. The bards were silent. The women had gone to their quarters, and the men who were not able to get to theirs lay quiet, sprawled before the table or the dying embers of the fire. They lived, but they were not there. Over the great hall was spread the little death of sleep, the quiet of departed souls. . . .

Only Gwydion sat erect and bright-eyed, staring at Mâth where he sat in his high seat. Vast and more than human he looked there in the dullness of the dawn, like some grey, guardian world-spirit bringing day back to men, watching with quiet, fadeless eyes the miracle that he had worked through all the ages.

And his nephew wondered if for all his wakefulness he were nearer than those vacated sleepers. For Mâth did not need sleep to bridge the gulfs between the worlds. He could rest without sleep, so perfect was the freedom he had attained even in this body from the troubles and blindness and earthy heats of flesh, that the spirits of common men flee from, wearied by one day's sojourn, back to the purer, lighter worlds that lie on the other side of memory: realms that all of us visit nightly—though, waking, our brains are too gross to retain their loveliness.

Gwydion began to think a thought. He thought it so clearly and steadily there in the dawning that he knew that at last its intensity must ring through Mâth's consciousness loud as any spoken word. His uncle turned his face to him and waited, his grey eyes calm questions above the wan vastness of his beard.

"It is hard for a man to support himself without property," said Gwydion.

Mâth understood. "Well," said he, "I will give the young man the lordship of the best of the Cantrevs."

"Lord," said Gwydion, "which of the Cantrevs is that?"

"The Cantrev of Dinodig," answered Mâth. And this comprised the districts which in later times were called Eivionydd and Ardudwy; and this time Gwydion was satisfied. . . .

The tenth day after that Llew took Blodeuwedd the Flower-Faced to her new home in Ardudwy. Before they went, Mâth may have given Llew some advice as to the governing of a province, and Gwydion probably gave him much more, and so did all others who were high enough in rank to dare to. For good advice is the one commodity with which even the most niggardly person in the world will be lavishly generous. And it is likewise the least used of all gifts: which is perhaps well.

Goewyn counseled Blodeuwedd as to the duties and difficulties of a mistress of a house and of a lady of a Cantrev; and the girl listened with seemly interest, and asked the whole meaning of this, or the details of that. Her sense of seemliness seemed strange in one so young, and Goewyn thought of another woman who had set it above honor or motherhood. "It is she, more easily than Llew, who might have been Arianrhod's child."

But in Blodeuwedd's mind there was no quickening, no initiative and guile. She listened calmly, without wonder, or fear, or shyness, as she had done on the first day of her being, when Goewyn had instructed her in the duties of a wife.

And it seemed to the Queen that this very passive acceptance of all that came to her proved her still but a puppet to do Gwydion's will and Mâth's, animated only by instincts they had planted within her; that there were blanks in her mind and feelings as though she had never been completely ensouled and was no individual, only one of those fair images that poets weave, whose hearts and minds move only at their creators' will. And for such a one seemliness should be the inevitable, the only guide. Perhaps the one more-than-animal consciousness of self. . . .

But Queen Goewyn saw that Llew was happy, and of that she was glad, for she loved the fair, gentle boy who, though nearest kin to those who had once done her the worst wrong, was yet himself and no other, and doubly of her husband's blood.

Only she wondered what would happen if ever a will should waken within that fair, half-human thing that enchantments had evoked from the unknown void.

2

The Coming of Goronwy Pevr

THE YOUNG PAIR settled down in a palace at Mur y Castell, in
Ardudwy, and they were happy there.

It is a small word, "happy." For one it may mean a kind of pleasant quiet under a lukewarm sun, untroubled by many waspish
thoughts or by the ache of great griefs, and never fired by ecstasies.
That is a good state, and better than most of us get, but no great
thing grows out of it.

Or to be happy may mean to eat life healthily and with gusto, as
a hungry man eats a good meal, heedless of the depth or shape of the
dishes or of how they were invented, not complaining overmuch if
occasionally the meat is tough or over-dry or over-juicy, because the
most of it is good, solid nourishment.

Or again, happiness may be a rhythm that sets all the days to
music, and makes a dance of movement, a brighter brightness of the
sun, a wine in the air and a wonder in the world. As of a veil of glamour thrown suddenly over all things, or the lifting of a curtain that
has hid beauty. . . .

It was so with Llew. He was happy and he was busy. His nights
and days were brimming. The welfare of the people of a province
was on his shoulders, and beauty and delight were beside him; and
he was young and strong enough to embrace both with eager joy.

By day he sat in the judgment seat and judged as he had seen
Gwydion do at Caer Seon and Dinas Dinllev, and Mâth himself at
Caer Dathyl. He weighed quarrels over inheritance or over boundaries, wrongs that had been done and wrongs that were trying to be
done: all the evidence of people who were none of them trying to tell
him the bare truth, but only what they wanted him to believe.

Sometimes his head whirled before the twisty knots their words tied him into, and his brain shrank from the labor of sifting out those lies fast interwoven into the truth—and above all from the knowledge that his decision would not end the problem. Its consequences would go on happening, perhaps for a lifetime or longer, and the responsibility would be upon himself.

Always before he had had Gwydion to take counsel of, Gwydion to appeal to. Whenever a thicket of the mind had become too dense, the son of Dôn could speak a word that showed a path for one to cut free and cleave to. His own brain had seldom carried one out of the maze; but it had lit the light by which one could carve one's own freedom. . . . But now Llew had to light his own torch as well as hew his own path. And this challenged all his manhood, and called upon all his strength.

He must have met the need well, for it is written in the ancient book that all loved him and his rule. He was learning how to be a king, and he had also become a lover. For he who had been cherished all his life, now cherished Blodeuwedd, and found a new and strange delight in it, apart from her delightfulness.

For to him she was the song in the throat of the thrush. She was the sunlight that colored the world. She was as delicate as a rainbow and as gay. She was the peace that he had made with Woman, the strange foe that had pursued him with unrelenting malice through all his days in the world into which she had brought him.

His wife was the healing of all wounds and all wars. Her fragility was the treasure that he guarded. And her beauty was the wine that intoxicated him, and the shrine before which he bowed in reverence. She was his sweetheart and his friend and a garden where he alone could walk. She was the mysterious beauty that he had worshiped ever since that day when Arianrhod had refused to name him, made soft and kind at last—hostile no longer.

Nor did it occur to him that he had learned no secret by possessing this mystery, so absorbed was he in adoring it.

(Perhaps a son was born to them during this time, for Taliessin speaks of a "Minawg ap Lleu of courteous life," one whose "push was ardent in combats"; and that would seem to mean a son of Llew's. But *The Mabinogi* does not mention his birth.)

Prosperity was with the land during those years, and with the children of Dôn. Amaethon watched over crops that never failed, and in Caer Seon, Gwydion studied the stars. At Caer Dathyl, Mâth sank ever deeper into his ancient reverie, so that bodies became ever farther and farther from him, and the things of the soul ever nearer,

brighter than the fading earth. . . . And in her Castle of the Silver
Wheel, Arianrhod abode quietly, like one who has done her utmost
for vengeance and failed, or waits for its sown seeds to grow. . . .

We do not know whether any tidings of Dylan the Son of the
Wave were heard in Gwynedd in those days, he who was later to
make so strange and fateful a return to the shores of his birth. But
there is no record that Llew and his brother met ever again after that
little time that they were together in Arianrhod's womb. . . .

Nor do we know how, long the happiness of Llew and Blodeuwedd
lasted. But change comes to all things, and soonest of all to happiness.

It came to theirs on a day when Llew rode forth to Caer Dathyl
to visit Mâth the King.

He did not take the Flower-Faced with him, so perhaps there was
indeed a baby Minawg at home for her to see to. Or perhaps for this
little while he may have wished to be alone with his kin again, as in
his boyhood. He may have felt that this was due them, after the time
apart.

But after his going his wife walked alone in the court, and was
lonely. For so it was with her always; she did not like to be alone.
Perhaps her thin being drew in life and warmth through seeing its
beauty mirrored in a lover's eyes. Perhaps otherwise reality was hard
to hold to. The air may have seemed too vast, space a gaping maw.
It is hard, across the gap of the ages and the mazes of magic, to read
the mysteries of her being.

But she missed Llew, and she walked in the place where he had
kissed her good-by.

The sun was faring westward, spreading a golden heat-haze over
the windless world. The shadows of the trees were lengthening, waxing into the black giants that at night would seize the earth. No bird
sang and no breeze rustled in the leaves. The day lay quiet as a body
on its funeral pyre.

Then suddenly, through the soundlessness, came sound.

Far and clear it rang through the lands outside the castle.
Questing, and alive with the fierce lust of the quest. And something
within her leapt and tingled at that fierce eagerness that seemed to
come bodiless out of the air. She heard it not only with her ears, but
in her blood. More vivid than all that had ever come her way in flesh
or substance it seemed to her, quick with a springing, fiery joy. Her
hand rose to her heart. She stood listening, stone-still. . . .

Again the horn rang, sharper, nearer now, like a tocsin-call of
destiny.

There was a rise in the ground there, where she stood. She looked

over the castle walls, out into the fields beyond. There was something moving there, something brown against the green. It drew
nearer, and she saw that it was a stag running wearily, swaying as it
ran. Almost she could feel its tired, helpless terror and need, the
agony of its pounding heart. . . . Her own heart pounded too as she
watched, but with a strange, tense excitement void of pity . . ..
Behind the deer came dogs, speeding like red-tongued, gleaming-
eyed arrows over the green, and behind them hunters on horses, at
their heels a troop of men on foot.

"It must be some great chief that rides to the hunt," Blodeuwedd
said to herself. "He is no man of this land, or I would have seen his
train before. He is no man of Llew's."

And this thought thrilled her: that there should be lands and
powers outside the lands and powers she knew. It seemed to open a
door in the far horizon. . . .

She called aloud to the men by the wall, "Go, one of you, and ask
whose men are those outside."

A youth was sent and he caught up with the men on foot and
spoke to them. Then he came and stood before Blodeuwedd, and the
belling of the dogs, though faint and farther off, was still in their ears
as he spoke: "It is Goronwy Pevr," he said, "the Lord of Penllyn."

"Penllyn," she said slowly, and knit her brows in wonder. "That
lies beyond our boundaries. What like is Penllyn?"

The hunt passed on, and that strange gallantry with which, even
in the face of hopelessness, some creatures still cling to a life that is
already lost, carried the stage on. But at sunset, by the banks of the
river Cynvael, the dogs got him at last, and killed him. And by the
time Goronwy Pew and his men had stripped the sleek brown hide
from the red, quivering carcass and let the dogs lap their fill of the
blood, earth was passing between the dark arms of night, and day
was only a red memory in the west.

When the last gleam was gone from the sky and blue twilight was
deepening into the darker shades, Goronwy Pew and his men came
back towards the gates of Mur y Castell. Their shadows came long and
black before them, like outstretched, clutching fingers of night. . . .

Blodeuwedd saw them coming. All through the hours her
thoughts had hovered like fascinated moths about that one torchlike
moment that had lit the dullness of her day.

But her cunning sense of seemliness still ruled her. She turned to
the palace folk lips that were diffident, and delicate brows that were
knit with thought.

"My Lord is away," she said, "but indeed this chieftain will speak

ill words of us and of the hospitality of my Lord if we let him ride
back through the night to his own land."

"In truth, Lady," they answered, "it would be only fitting to let
him in."

So messengers went to Goronwy and bade him enter. He came
swiftly and gladly. Blodeuwedd greeted him before the court, her
hair gleaming gold in the light of the torches.

In their red flare he stood before her. He was a tall, dark man with
eyes bright as flames, brighter than the eyes of most men. His hands
were still red from the hunt and the kill.

"Lady, may the gods repay you your graciousness," he said. "But
for your kindness my men and I would have had to sleep on the fens
tonight or else travel until moonset."

"Lord, it was not so great a matter," she answered, but her voice
shook suddenly like a dizzy thing, and she had to steady it with a
greater effort than any ever made with hands. "There is a welcome
before you, Lord. Come in—"

She gave him the hostess' kiss of greeting, and he gave it back
again. And it seemed to her in that moment that a lightning flash had
cleft the world in twain and welded it together again in another shape.
As though the lightning had stayed on, ablaze in her heart. . . .

And she knew in that hour that she loved Goronwy Pevr. That for
good or ill that fire for him burned within her and would not die. And
by good or ill she meant happiness or unhappiness. The words had
no deeper meaning for her; they had had little more for Arianrhod,
who was a woman of woman born.

That night there were feasting and revelry in Mur y Castell. The
bards sang and fine meats steamed and the wine-cup passed from hand
to hand. The palace folk admired the horns of the stag, and heard the
tale of the hunt, and how well the quarry had fought for its life.

But two there were who did not hear the talk or the songs, or taste
what they ate and drank: the strange chief where he stared at
Blodeuwedd, and Blodeuwedd where she stared at the stranger. But
she did not see his stare, only his face. For the first time since she
had lived, events were stirring within her, not coming upon her from
without; so that she was unconscious of all else. And it seemed to
her an agony that would end the world that this man should leave on
the morrow, and she would never see him any more.

He would leave and never know that she loved him. Tonight
would be to him only a little incident among many nights, and he
would never know that for her it had been the beginning and the end
of the world.

How many women had already loved him? How many had he already loved?

She went to her chamber presently, but she could not sleep. She lay alone in her bed in the darkness, and she had never been so alive before. She felt like hot metal being smelted and hammered in Govannon's forge. She could feel the hammering in her heart.

Goronwy Pevr. Goronwy, Lord of Penllyn!

He had come to her a stranger from a strange land; and such lure the hearts of women. He had come to her with the glamour of the chase upon him, the savage thrill of flight and pursuit, and of the thirsty baying of dogs and the ringing of horns.

He had come to her with hands bloodstained from his triumph. . . .

He was dark where her young husband was fair. Llew's beauty was as known and accepted and familiar a thing as her lap dog's, but this man's was new, mysterious, compelling. . . . What mysteries there were in Llew lay on heights beyond her seeing, so that she never dreamed that they were there at all. And nothing in him had ever thrilled her as had this being of the hounds at evening, and the sight of that tall conquering figure with reddened hands.

She knew now that she had never loved Llew. She had merely enjoyed his beauty as she had enjoyed all good things that life had given her. She felt as though she had never been awake before, but had only dozed through a dull pleasant world of shadows. And now she must go back, waking, to the world of sleep; she must live on in that greyness with a shadow called Llew, among other shadows.

And all that unspent force of life and ecstasy flamed within her so that it seemed that it would burn her up, and she wept softly there, shivering before the lightless bleakness of the years that marched upon her. . . .

She heard a step outside the door.

It was soft, it was stealthy, like a thief's or a murderer's—the step of someone who above all things dares not be seen creeping about his darker business in the dark of the night. It was so faint that she could not have been sure that she heard it, had not all her being vibrated to its secrecy as to a trumpet call.

She sat bolt-upright in bed.

It came again, more and more stealthy. And then there was a faint scraping. The door moved inward, slowly, letting an advancing square of blackness into the moonlit silvery twilight of her chamber. . . .

She watched it with fascinated eyes, rigid as stone, her breath caught in her throat. . . .

It was wide open. It was a rectangle of blackness, taller than a man.

He stepped through it. His face shone white and ghost-like for an instant against the darkness, but his eyes were brighter than ever, more eager. . . . Her heart cried, though her lips would not part: *"Goronwy! Goronwy! Goronwy Pevr! . . ."*

For a long time they stayed looking at each other, where she sat golden in the silvery twilight, and he stood dark and still in the dusk of the doorway.

They thought of all who slept but might wake and hear them. They thought of the din that it seemed to them might follow their voices and shatter the quiet, refilling the palace that was now emptied of all souls save only theirs that were submerged in fire.

But at last he drew nearer.

"You are the Light of the World," he said in a whisper. "You are all my hope and all my desire. Having seen you I do not see how I can live on without seeing you; and yet I will go mad if I stay within sight of you without touching you. . . .

"I cannot go and I cannot stay. Lady, will you have mercy upon me?"

Joy bloomed in her then. She glowed like a garden of flowers opening at dawn, all tender and radiant beneath the sun. She clasped her white hands like a child at the promise of some great treat, and looked up at him, eyes shining with a delight she dared not yet wholly believe in.

"You love me?" she breathed. "You love me indeed?"

"I love you indeed," he answered, "but you are another Lord's wife."

At that she paled and faded; the light went out of her face. "Yet he is away," she said.

He licked his lips. "His kin are great magicians—!" said he.

They were silent on that. They stared on each other as two souls of the newly-dead might stare, dazed and alone in the grey windy spaces between the worlds. . . . But they could not tear their eyes apart. . . .

He came close. He stroked her arm, and his strong brown fingers seemed to touch her naked heart, come out of her breast for him. . . . Half she turned to him, and then she thought of Mâth's thoughts that might be upon them, more still and more vigilant than the mice in the timbers, or the air they breathed. . . . She thought of Gwydion's grey piercing eyes. But even her fears never made her think of her young Lord's face.

"My husband will come back," she said.

"He will not come back tonight," the man answered.

But she was still silent, and the dark chill passed from her spirit to his.

"I can go . . . ." he said. And he moved a little away from her, towards the door.

But then she raised herself from the bed. Her arms rose to his shoulders. Her face shone pale and hungry as a white flame.

"Not if Mâth and Gwydion were to tear my soul from my body, and sent it to whistle on the winds for ten thousand generations," she said, "not for that would I forego this night."

3

Weavers of Darkness

AT DAWN HE woke in her arms and was afraid. He tried to rise, but she clung to him, first in sleep and then in waking, and he could not get free.

"You will not go from me?" Her wide eyes begged his.

"We must not let the house folk see us here together," he said. "It would be an ill thing if they learned that you had not slept alone."

"But you will not leave the palace," she pleaded, "you will come back to me tonight?"

He was silent. All the wisdom he had was urging him to fly, as a bee flies from the flower that it has despoiled; not to measure his knowledge and his power against the fabled mysterious might of the House of Mâth. But in this flower there was still nectar, sweetness that it seemed to him could never end. And her rosy lips and white clasping arms worked as strongly on his unslaked greed as on the night before.

"I will stay tonight," he said at last. "But longer than that I cannot stay."

And she laughed and kissed him and was well content. For there would be one more night before the end of the world. . . .

That day she was his hostess, showing honor to her guest. He sat at Llew's table and ate and drank and jested with Llew's wife. And ever it seemed to him that all things there were better and goodlier than in his halls at home. The gold and silver and bronze vessels on the table and the lovely Lady at its head gleamed ever more brilliantly, fairer than anything he had or could ever hope to have.

Even the sun seemed to shine brighter on the fields of Ardudwy than ever on the fields of Penllyn. The riches of the court, too, seemed more rare than anything that he had ever seen: the fine and curious things that had been wedding gifts from Mâth and the sons of Dôn.

Envy of the Lord of Dinodig waxed stronger within him every hour. Old resentment of the glories of the House of Mâth grew also, putting forth darker, venomed shoots. . . . And he thought within himself: "If I had been Lord of all this, and of her, how happy we should have been!"

That happiness which had not been and could not be was a misery to him. It became a wrong also; and in due time a betrayal worked him by the fates, and personal injury done him by the man who had all this that he did not have.

He thought: "What better right has he to it than I? I am the better man. His wife knows me for the better man. What is he but a slow-witted, watery-blooded boy that could keep nothing and gain nothing if he were not the pet of his wizard-kin, a bastard that they got out of his deceitful mother by magic tricks? A bastard!"

And though it had as yet no weight and little meaning in Gwynedd, he mouthed over and over to himself the ugly new word that the New Tribes had brought into the Isle of Prydain. Some vent he got from that, but little solace, and he raged at its futility. . . .

But night came, and the dusk that to these two was dawn. The dark that was their shield and their hidden lair. The world whose grave-like gloom their own fire lit. He crept to her again by stealth, and again her open arms received him. . . .

The night marched on, and grey began to show in the raven tresses of its gloom. They lay in each other's arms spent and surfeited, the cold tides of thought already beginning to creep in and blight their happiness. The world that had rolled away to leave them together in glowing loneliness, apart from all the universe, had begun its inexorable return. It towered over them, a vast and monstrous shadow blacker than night. . . .

She clung to him and her hands that were weak with spent desire fondled his arms and chest. She whispered with lips that touched his cheek: "Can you not take me with you when you go?"

"I cannot," he answered. "For your husband would come after you, and all the forces of Gwynedd with him. And I cannot stand against the magic of Mâth and his nephew. My sorrow that it should be so."

At thought of vengeance from Llew she would have laughed, but at mention of the dread power of her creators, she shivered and wept. All her pleas and artifices dried upon her tongue. For how could any power, even that hot, savage strength of Goronwy's, in which she had exulted since the day of the hunt, stand against that mysterious, measureless might?

"It is a hard case," he said, "but it is ours. It is not now as it was in the old days when a woman was free to choose her loves."

She wept more loudly, and beat her hands on her breast. "Then I am his, and there is no escape. I am the toy they made for his pleasure. I am bound to him like a slave, and my life is not my own, but his chattel. Why was I created for such unhappiness as this? But I was created for his sake, and not for mine. And I must stay with him always, always, because even if they made him another he would not have her, so dearly does he love me."

And of a sudden she hated and could have cursed him for that love, for his very existence that barred her from happiness. She hated Mâth and Gwydion who had made her. She hated all things and all the world save only Goronwy Pevr.

Soul was growing in her, and malice. . . .

He let her weep awhile and then he laid his lips against her ear: "Are you sure we are not overheard," he whispered, "that the ears of Mâth do not listen to us from afar?"

She lay surprised and still, lifting her wide eyes to his. "What matter? What is there we could say that would make it worse than it is already, if he were listening?"

"There is one thing. . . . ," he said, and had to moisten his lips to speak. "There is one way by which we might always be together. . . ."

And he shuddered and peered about him in the grey gloom of the chamber, as though somewhere deep within its shadows he might spy a white-bearded, watching face, as knowing as God's and as awful in its passionless power. . . .

But she clutched at him with eager fingers. Her white face bloomed again. "What way? Tell me! tell me! He will not hear you, for he and Gwydion will have been too taken up with Llew to hear or see aught else. We have been safe and are safe. Besides, silence will not help you, for it is thoughts they hear, not speech: that is a fable the common folk believe who could not understand how their minds could be spied on, and might be made afraid. Llew told me how it really was."

A moment mere Goronwy pondered, measuring the depths of the abyss into which he was about to leap. . . . He looked down upon her where she lay in the half-light that was less light than a grey shadow forcing its way among the black. She was fair. She was sweet as the apples that once grew on a forbidden tree in a garden in the east of the world. She was a prize worth all risks, even those shadowy destructions more dreadful than common death that lay within the powers of the House of Mâth.

"There is but one way that we can come together," he said, "and that is by killing your husband."

At the words the grey dawn seemed to grow colder about them. The shadows became blacker and filled with menace. The pale light piercing the chamber clutched at them like ghostly hands.

She shrank back, her mind shivering before the greatness of that step, its risks and the penalties that might be, yet carried along, like driftwood floating on the strong stream of her desire.

"It would not be easy," she whispered. "The lords of the race of Mâth are hard to slay. They do not die like common men. Only in certain ways can they get their deaths before their time comes, and these are kept secret."

"Yet must you worm out of him the way he can get his," her lover answered. "He will tell you. Any man would do anything for you if you asked him in bed. Anything, my fairest, except abstain from you." And he kissed her mouth.

Her eyes shone. She held out her white arms. "Would you do anything for me there?" she coaxed.

"Indeed I would," said he and flung his arms around her. . . .

Later she said: "I will do what you wish. I will make Llew tell me how he can be killed."

He stayed yet another night, though he feared that Llew might come home.

Now indeed, if never before, was Blodeuwedd alive and awake. For her the earth was covered with the colors of the rainbow, and filled with fiery fountains. The flow of the blood in her veins was a burning ecstasy of song and flame. Gone was the old easy, basking content in which she had let herself be tended and cherished like a pet animal, accepting with gratitude and caresses every gift that was made her. Now will and desire were aroused within her, and set inexorably and unalterably upon one man.

So had she made her first step upon the ladder of evolution. And yet within her narrow, self-focused, puppet's mind there was no room for consideration of anything save her own desires.

On the third night she discussed with her lover some final details of their plan. She had wondered how he meant to escape the vengeance that Mâth and Gwydion would take for Llew. But he was confident and at ease.

"I too have some knowledge and power," he said, his flame-bright eyes shining gloatingly, "even if I was not trained by Mâth. I will take Llew's shape when he is done away with, and I will be your husband and Lord here in his stead. And if Mâth and Gwydion notice that I rule somewhat differently from his wont, they may be disappointed, but they will hardly move against their darling. Even should their magic enable them to learn the truth, will the old bulls have heart and strength enough left to come against him who has slain the young? Their day will pass with him they have held dearest. Kill Llew your Lord, and we are safe."

Llew enjoyed his visit to Caer Dathyl.

Mâth was there and Gwydion also. In these latter days Gwydion may have been oftener at Caer Dathyl than at Dinas Dinllev or Caer Seon, those lonely nests from which the bird had flown. Now that Llew was gone and he himself went no more to the Castle of the Silver Wheel, the son of Dôn may have pursued knowledge with even more avidity than before. For there is often an ache in emptied hands that have long been full.

For all three there must have been joy in that meeting. Good it must have been to Llew to feel again Gwydion's hand on his shoulder, happy for Gwydion to look once more into those young, bright eyes. . . .

Yet when the time came for return, though Llew was sorry to leave his kinsmen, he was not sorry to go. For the thought of Blodeuwedd called him, and anxiety over things that might be going amiss in his Cantrev while he was gone.

He rode away, and Mâth and Gwydion sat in silence and watched him out of sight. And then they sat awhile longer, watching the silver stream of the Conwy, where it gleamed like a naked sword between its banks.

Not long ago—though it was all of Llew's lifetime ago—they two had been youth and age, with Gwydion the young man to be guarded and guarded against. And now they were both elders, watching youth ride away from them, freed by the stream of time. So had the years washed away their strife and brought them into alliance: the years that will always move youth to the opposite side of the ancient battle, among the ranks of age.

They sat and watched the Conwy, flowing to the sea. . . .

"He does well," said Gwydion at last, and in his voice there was pride that was also the pain of renunciation, of the artist who sees the masterpiece that he has long labored over and cherished, at last complete and separate, and therefore no longer his.

"He does indeed," said Mâth. "He is a fit chieftain and ruler of men, and he can stand alone. Time was when I feared it might be otherwise. That his mind that you had always molded might still be over-plastic to molding from those around him, and his judgments be thus biased and his deeds prompted."

"I do not understand you," said Gwydion, "for you speak as though I had tyrannized over him, and that was never so."

"Never indeed," said Mâth. "Though the manner of his birth has laid misfortunes on him, he has never suffered directly at your hands. For fear and the desire for escape are seldom divorced, and you could never bear for him to have even a moment-long wish to escape from you. Furthermore, you have progressed far enough to know the needlessness of tyranny.

"Yet not often before his marriage did he know his will from your will. It was your voice that spoke secretly in his thoughts many a time when he did your wish, thinking it his own. You ruled him by your magic as well as by your love, and he who has yielded to one person's magic is likely to yield to another's. And he has never learned caution; for he has never had to watch for pitfalls since you have always guided him to where the road was firm beneath his feet."

"Pitfalls—!" said Gwydion, his brows knitting. "Sound footing! Govannon too spoke of that once. Yet I am far more fitted for fatherhood than Govannon. He would think he could smelt and hammer human thoughts and feelings into shape as he does the metals in his forge."

"In truth you are," said Mâth. "It will be long and long before the guardians of youth learn how to give enough freedom and not too much. Each step upward brings its own difficulties, though that is no excuse, as folk generally take it to be, for stepping back again.

"I know that it has sometimes been in your mind that I did not bind you to me closely enough, or you would not have sought to satisfy Gilvaethwy and snatch the pigs of Pryderi. But I had given you freedom and such instruction as I could. No man can be taught more than he is at that time capable of learning."

"You had never to fear that my mind was over-plastic!" Gwydion said, and laughed. "Rather to keep a vigilant eye out for what it might be evolving. But I too saw those dangers you speak of. When the time came for the fledgling to fly I let him go free to make his own nest."

"That also you did," said Mâth, "and he has proved that you had taught him to fly, nephew. I grow old. I speak of dead thoughts and fears that there is no need to speak of. Yet as he passed from our sight it seemed that for a moment a cold wind blew upon my soul. As though he passed from us for longer than we dreamed."

"You think some danger waits for him there in Dinodig—?" Gwydion's eyes were suddenly keen as sword-points, and his lips whitened.

"It lasted but a moment, nephew. I know nothing. It may have been but one of those fancies that love and watchfulness breed in the aged, we who grow more and more to be watchers, and less and less doers. But before night I will search the minds of his nobles and make sure that there is no plot against him."

"And if there is one, it should not be hard to put a stop to, by putting a stop to the plotters." There was an edge on Gwydion's smile.

"It is well, perhaps," he added presently, "that wife we made him is not likely to seek sway over his mind, for to her he might yield unduly. But the soul we got her is too light a thing, too easily contented to seek for power."

"I would he might have had a more substantial being for his mate," said Mâth. And for a moment his face shadowed, as white mountain peaks, high and serene in their still majesty, shadow in evening.

"I too," said Gwydion. "Yet if there is not great good in her, there is not great ill either. Among the many women born of women he might have done worse as well as better. My own dealings with Arianrhod have led me to believe that Blodeuwedd's is perhaps the most comfortable kind of mind for a woman to have, so long as one does not know the difference. And Llew never can." And he sighed at thought of all the experience, beautiful as well as exasperating, that Llew must be spared.

"Yet it is not evolution," said Mâth.

That night he searched the minds of all the nobles and men of substance in Dinodig, and of all such restless and wayward men as might fancy themselves oppressed, or plot against their Lord for the thrill's own sake. He sifted their walking thoughts and their dreams in sleep, pouring them through his own mind as through a sieve, all that great mass of little things, of pains and pleasures, loves and hates; here a toothache and there a disappointed love; the woe for a girl's face that would not smile, or the satisfaction of a good dinner. But never once did he find Llew there save in the colors that always surround a ruler: hope or fear of his judgments;

loyalty to or admiration of him; or idle irritation. Nowhere the tooth or nail of a plot.

So he and Gwydion satisfied themselves and were content.

On the third morning, when Blodeuwedd dared no longer hold Goronwy back, but let him depart, he said as he took his leave of her: "Remember what I have told you, and question Llew Llaw Gyffes fully, and when he is soft with love, so as to learn how I may slay him."

That evening, when the sunset haloed the palace at Mur y Castell, and the royal dwelling loomed like a shadow made substance, the dark heart of the blazing gold, Llew Llaw Gyffes came home. Glad his folk were to see him, and Blodeuwedd his wife came in swift greeting to his arms. She welcomed him in the red of the sunset, that made the great hail glow like blood, and her hair and eyes to gleam with reflected fires.

But it seemed to him as he kissed her that life that had been a song before his going burst now into fuller music, sweeter tones: that the sweetness of return was cause enough for absence. He had longed for her beauty and tenderness, as the snow-bound earth longs for the blossomy and fragrant wine of spring; and he found her fairer than in dreams or memory.

For she was too lovely for a thing so prosaic and earthly as memory to hold all her loveliness. It dimmed her in the mirroring and made her living presence a miracle as great as dawn.

But she was spring that had been chilled by blight, and upon her dawn had come a shadow.

He saw these things soon. He saw them all through the night's merry-making, while they feasted and the bards sang and she sat beside him. She ate little, and her face was white as a drooping snowdrop, frowned down upon in some lonely vale by dark gigantic grasses.

He could not make her smile, though ever his hand sought hers or his arm went about her waist. She would not drink until he drank from her cup and made her drink from his. Their lips met for a moment above the cups. He thought that she would laugh then, with the old little flower-like flush and shining look. But she did not. For a second it seemed to him that a strange spark flashed in her eyes, almost a baleful gleam.

When the night had reached its blackest depths they went to their chamber and lay down. The moon was shining faintly. Blodeuwedd glittered in the silver shade it cast upon the bed. True light had passed from the world. Only this glimmering dusk was left to war with blackness. But she lay with her face turned from it, to the dark. . . .

Llew looked at her and thought of that wedding night long ago in Caer Dathyl, when he had come to her a stranger and she had made him welcome in her gentle arms. He ached with tenderness for her, and rapturous, longing delight. He longed to share her trouble and dissolve it, to free her and comfort her.

He put his arm around her; pressed his face against the soft, sweet-smelling gold of her hair. He spoke her name. She did not answer.

"Blodeuwedd," he said again, "Blodeuwedd—"

He kissed the tip of an ear that he found unexpectedly in that shower of hair, but still she did not answer. Only from the darkness there came a strangled sob.

"What is it?" he asked. "Are you not well?"

"I have been thinking," she said, and her voice was thick with another sob, yet she held it pitifully steady, "of a thing that you have never thought of concerning me. For while you were happy with your kin at Caer Dathyl and forgot me, I was lonely and grieving for you. And it came to me then: How should I feel if you were gone never to come back? If you were to die, and leave me living without you? And sometime it may happen. For one of us must die first, and what if it should be you?" And she wept.

Llew drew her as close to him as might be. He strained her to him and kissed her face and her weeping eyes many times, and with delight as well as pity.

"I have no intention of dying," said he. "It is a long time before either of us will die."

"But it is a time that must come," she wept.

"Beloved, if it does come, since I am a great strong man and you a woman tender as a flower, which of us do you think would be like-liest to go? I beg you, save your pity for me." And he laughed a little, tenderly, into her hair.

"But it might not be so!" she wailed. "A woman sits at home in safety. But a man goes forth to war, and a boar may kill him in the hunt, or outlaws may lurk in wait for him in a wood!"

He laughed again. "May the gods reward your tenderness of me!" he said. "But unless the gods kill me, that killing will not be easy."

She wound her arms about him and kissed him many times. "For the gods' sake and for my sake," she begged, with her lips touching his, "tell me how you might be killed. For my memory for precautions is better than yours."

He hesitated then. Gwydion had strictly enjoined him never to speak of that secret hidden in the stars.

But she was lovely and he loved her. He could not deny her trouble this comfort that would ease it. He may have been a little glad of that trouble, deeply though he pitied it. For in earlier days he had watched her closely, lest thought of her magical origin bring her dread of dissolution, such as he had felt once in childhood. But he had never been able to see that she thought of beginnings or endings. She had basked in the pleasant things of the present as a kitten basks in the sun. The gold and the green and the bloom of today had sufficed her, heedless of yesterday or tomorrow. And he had not loved her the less for her childlikeness. Perhaps he had loved her more. But sometimes it had made him feel a little alone.

And now her solicitude was sweet. It made her lovelier, nearer, than she had ever been before. He kissed her and laughed, rubbing his cheek against her shoulder.

"I am glad enough to tell you," lie said. "I cannot be easily killed, save by a wound. And it would take a year to make the spear that could pierce me. It would have no power if it were worked upon at any time except when the druids were performing their sacrifices."

"Are you sure of this?" she said, and it did not seem strange to him that her voice should be eager. Naturally she would be pleased because nothing could be more unlikely than that a spear should ever be so made.

"It is indeed," he replied. "And I cannot be killed inside a house nor outside. I cannot be killed on horseback or on foot."

She gasped at that. He thought it was with wonder. But the tone of her voice sounded flat and lifeless when she said: "Indeed, how can you be killed then?"

"I shall tell you," he answered. "If a bath were built beside a river, with the cauldron covered by a tightly thatched roof, and a goat standing beside it; and I were to stand with one foot on the cauldron's edge and the other on the goat's back, any man who had the spear could deal me my death."

She kissed him in a passion of joy and gratitude. "I thank the gods," she said, "that it will be easy to escape this. And that you have put my mind at rest."

. . . Later he slept, but she did not sleep. She lay wide-eyed, unwinking, beside him, her blossomy breast and arms gleaming in the silvery moon-twilight, wonders shadowy as dreams. Her eyes that looked into darkness and nothingness saw Goronwy Pevr. Her heart whispered his name over and over until it became a rhythm to which her blood flowed and her thoughts moved and her breath was drawn. The wind outside seemed to rustle it, and the dogs to howl it in the night, and the mice in the walls to keep time to it with their little scurrying feet.

She rose at last.

She rose silently as a ghost, stealthily withdrawing herself from the sleeper's lax arms. She looked down upon him, and thought with disgust that she would have to stay with him a whole year more.

"But it might have been worse," she thought. "I might never have learned the way that he could be slain. I feared I would not. But it was easy, easy. No woman could ever so fool Goronwy. He would never blab his life away against a woman's breast. He would kill her with his hands if she tried to make him, kill her as quickly as he would a deed. . . . But then no woman would ever try to fool Goronwy. . . . Goronwy. . . !"

And she pressed her hands to her heart that beat so hard at his name that it seemed as though it might leap out of her. She thought of the might and strength and eagerness of Goronwy, the eagerness that was like fire from under the earth, from the place where the primeval demons of fire lived, beneath the dark. . . .

She thought of last night and of this.

She looked again at her husband.

Once the exulting reverence with which he joyed in her beauty had been her pride and pleasure. Now it seemed half-hearted, an exasperation, a thin milk-and-water love at whose sickening luke-warmness she could have railed. She had warmed herself at fiercer fires that made her consciousness glow more intensely, anchored her flimsy being more firmly to the earth, dispelling the cold of those unknown spaces whence she had come. And her spirit, that was almost too light to be held to our element by its own weight, clung desperately to this grosser heat.

"He will be easily killed," she whispered, looking down at Llew, "now that we know the way."

She said it without hate. For she did not hate him. He was no longer a person to her. He was only a weariness and a wall between her and happiness. She did not think of his death as murder: only as the shoving of an obstacle from her path. Hate requires as single-hearted a devotion as love, and her flickering flares of malice, even in this new activity of her passions that was lifting her above the level of the half-ensouled, could not claim so mighty a name. They were anger, not hate.

She turned from Llew and left him. She crept through the darkness of the hail to the door where the door-keeper slept, drunken with the wine in which he had celebrated his Lord's return.

It was hard for her to open the door alone, but she did it. Then she rested spent and panting against the great slab of wood which had swung her outward with it, her terrified eyes turning back to the sleeper. It seemed to her that the noise of that opening door had been loud enough to waken all the world: that the sky must echo it in thunder, and cries come from every throat in Mur y Castell. But the door-keeper still sprawled and snored, safely oblivious. Though had he been awake he would scarce have dared question openly the doings of his Queen.

She looked forward again.

She was beyond the threshold now. She was in a grey and monstrous world, where the sickly light warred feebly with weird hordes of shadows, all lost in a nebulous, uncanny dimness. In the east the stars were paling, winking out. The dawn came slowly, as though afraid of what it might reveal should some dark beings of the night still linger upon earth.

A bat flew by, a dark shape, silent and sinister, in that ghastly twilight. . . . She thought of demons of the air. . . .

For a moment she stayed where she was, shivering. She felt as though she, too, should she advance into that wan and grisly gloom, might be lost and become a creature of night forever, bound eternally in this ghost-grey world where black shadows stalked like fiends. Then she thought again of Goronwy. The fires of his queerly blazing eyes seemed like magnetic torches, drawing her on. . . .

She went to a hut near the palace, where was a man of whom she had already told Goronwy. He had no love for his Lord, because Llew had once given judgment against him for a cruel deed, though leaving him life and liberty.

She talked long with that man in the spectral greyness. She urged him and he shrank back afraid. Then she took a golden chain from her throat and showed it to him, and his eyes glittered with a greed that rose to battle with his fear. His mind too began to gloat over the satisfactions that this mysterious errand promised to his hate.

So in the end she gave him the message and half the chain. "The other half shall be yours," she said, "when you bring back a token I shall know to have come from the Lord Goronwy's hand."

And before the first red spears of dawn had pierced the east, she was back in Llew's bed, smiling to herself as her soul drifted away in sleep. . . . But her messenger was hastening away as speedily as the shadows, hastening to Goronwy Pevr's land. . . .

4

The Sentence of the Stars

THAT DAY BECAME a night, and other days became nights. Thrice a hundred times and more the sun retreated and advanced, hot and golden above the world. Twelve times the moon thinned to the narrowness of a blade and then swelled again to fullness, round as with a wonder of which she is never delivered.

During that time Llew must have ruled his land and loved his wife as of yore. And in peace and satisfaction Mâth and Gwydion must have watched his content, all their fears lulled to sleep and their hearts sure that it had been only a deceitful fancy roving on the wind that had warned Mâth that day of the boy's going from Caer Dathyl.

Dinodig bloomed with a golden peace that seemed changeless. Life seemed to have stopped save for the movements of the seasons, and to linger content in the fair place it had found. Only Blodeuwedd knew otherwise, where she waited, like some rare golden spider in her web, safely entrenched behind the blank sweetness of her flower-face.

Goronwy Pevr knew too, where he toiled in a secret place, while the druids of Penllyn conducted the sacrifices beneath the ancient oaks. Among the flames and the darkness of his hidden forge he gloated over the broad lands of Ardudwy and the beauty of the woman that this spear he wrought should win him; and his eyes glowed even brighter.

He too was waiting. . . .

But there came a day when he no longer toiled. When the spear gleamed hard and hungry beneath the sun, all its sharp slenderness barbed and waiting. . . .

That day he sent a messenger to Blodeuwedd of the Blossoms. . . .
The Mabinogi tells that she went to Llew Llaw Gyffes then and
spoke with him.

"Lord," she said, "I have been puzzling over that matter you told
me of last year. For I cannot see how it could be. If I have the bath
made ready for you, will you show me how it could be possible for
you to stand with one foot on a cauldron's edge and one on a goat's
back?"

He smiled as we smile when we humor a child. She looked so fair
in her coaxing, with her blue eyes and rose lips eager, and the sun
shining on her gold hair.

"I will show you," he said.

She smiled and kissed him for thanks, clapping her hands like a
pleasured child, and then went off to give the needed orders to the
serving-folk.

They built a bath by the river Cynvael, that same stream by which
Pryderi had got his death. They placed a cauldron there, and covered
it with a tightly thatched roof. Also all the goats in the Cantrev were
gathered together and brought to a place across the river, opposite
Bryn Kyvergyr.

And the messenger sped back again to bear that word to Goronwy
Pevr. . . .

But Blodeuwedd said to Llew: "Lord, the bath and the roof are
ready."

"Well," he answered, "I shall gladly go to look at them."

The day after that they walked down to the side of the river
Cynvael and looked at the great cauldron under the little roof.
Blodeuwedd gazed on her husband and she gazed on the dark, looming bulk of the hill Bryn Kyvergyr, where Goronwy was even now
waiting in ambush; and it was the man her eyes did not see that she
saw. . . .

She made haste to speak, afraid that in the silence Llew might
hear the violent beating of her heart: "Will you not go into the bath,
Lord?"

"Gladly," he answered. He stripped himself and entered the cauldron and bathed there.

Blodeuwedd stood watching him as he splashed in its waters.
There was about her as she waited something of the dreadful innocence of the spider, that works its subtle and elaborate cruelties
automatically to satisfy its hunger, without one thought of the feelings of its prey: conscious only of its own desire. . . . That splendid,
white young body splashing in the cauldron was less to her than is

the fly to the spider. It was not food, it was only a door to be battered down, a stone to be kicked out of her way.

After today she would never stumble over him again; he would be gone, utterly and completely gone—a trouble that was finished. She would be alone, alone with Goronwy, in their chosen world of flesh and fire. The sun would rise over the earth never to set again.

A shiver took her, a thrill of anticipation. Her spirit reeled with eagerness, leaping towards the arms of the freedom that awaited it. . . .

Her thoughts buzzed and whirled like frightened bees: "Goronwy. My Goronwy! In a little while now he will be dead, a little, little while! And you and I shall be together always. . . ." Could it be true that this day had really come at last? What if Goronwy should have worked on the spear for one second after the sacrifice was over, and it should lack the power to slay?

"He would suspect. He would look for the thrower. He might even kill *you!*"

And it took all the power of her will to keep her from wringing her hands at that thought.

Llew put a hand on the cauldron's edge, as though to climb out.

She called to him, barely keeping the fear out of her voice: "Lord, what of the animals you spoke of?"

His hand dropped from the cauldron's edge. "Well," he said, "let one of them be caught and fetched."

She went away eagerly to see that his bidding was done, and he stayed where he was, resting in the water.

The sun was sinking into the west; a hosting of shadows was gathering over the world. . . . In that red light he may have had a glancing thought that this deed was imprudence, a tempting of the fates. Had not Gwydion once laid bonds upon him never to set one foot upon a cauldron's edge, and the other upon a goat's back, and thus risk doom? . . . It was by this river that Pryderi had died, he remembered: Gwydion's great foe, slain in that mighty single combat that was already legend. Here if anywhere the Dark Forces might have power over the seed of the son of Dôn—here where that blood cried murkily from the waters. . . .

But he was no longer a child for whom it was wrong not to do Gwydion's bidding. He was a man now to judge of his own safety. Sometimes they made a man over-cautious, these druid warnings of death and disaster, of dark magical wounds that would not heal, even in another world. . . .

What harm could there be in inviting even death to your feast, if

you left no door open for him to enter? No enemy knew the secret
that was Llew's peril; nobody in the world had a weapon so wrought
that it could give him his bane, had any person who wished to harm
him seen him there.

Llew smiled at the phantasy of danger. . . . Besides, he would
make a fool of himself in Blodeuwedd's eyes if he showed belated
caution and disappointed her. He did not wish her to think him
afraid. . . .

His wife came back with a manservant who was leading a goat.
The fellow tied it beside the cauldron, his face that of one who wondered much at his Lord's and Lady's whims, then turned back toward
the palace.

Blodeuwedd remained close at hand, watching. . . .

Llew rose in the cauldron. The shadows were assembled now,
massed and waiting. Every moment they grew blacker, longer,
stretching forth their dark arms to cover the world. A red glow began
to gather in the west. The hill Bryn Kyvergyr cast a black and massive shadow, like the first watchtower of night, over the earth. . . .

Llew put one foot upon the edge of the cauldron, thus fulfilling
half the mystic conditions. He groped with the other for the goat's
back, and saw, somewhat to his surprise, that Blodeuwedd, who had
been so eager for this sight, was not looking at him, but towards the
hill. . . .

On Bryn Kyvergyr Goronwy had risen on one knee, and his arm
was raised for the throw. . . .

Llew's foot found the goat's back.

There was a whizzing flash of blue light in the air—something
that gleamed cold even under the sweltering gold of the sunset. It
met Llew's body in mid-air and passed into him. It passed through
him, but the spearhead still remained in his side as he fell.

It shone in the flesh of an eagle that fluttered up from where he
had fallen, uttering a wild, unearthly scream. . . .

Goronwy came to Blodeuwedd where she knelt, white hands covering her face. She had not had strength to look upon that last
moment which must spell either victory or defeat.

He stood tall and dark above her, and his lips smiled and his eyes
gleamed. . . .

She looked up, still shuddering, but with eyes widening and
lips curving into incredulous joy. "Is it over—?" she whispered. "Is
he dead?"

And for answer he showed her the red shaft of the headless spear. . . .

She rose. Her eyes were starry. They did not look towards the cauldron for what might lie beneath it. . . . They were fixed, glorying and exultant, upon Goronwy's face.

"Now it is to you I belong," she said. "To you!"

"To me indeed!" he answered. He crushed her to him. His hand that clasped her shoulder stained it red with the blood he had got on his fingers from the spear.

When they drew apart, "Night is coming. . . ," he said, and looked at her.

She smiled, her face like an opening flower. . . .

They turned and went back to the palace together, their arms about each other.

And Llew Llaw Gyffes was seen no more. . . .

The sun set, turning the waters of the river Cynvael blood-red, and in the west there was a mighty blaze like a funeral pyre. Light died out of the world. Night came down, with her black veils, soft and dark and ineffably mysterious, swathing the earth. A blackness that was sightlessness was on the world, and the silence of death.

The hosting of the stars came forth, myriad tiny, bright armies, marching up into the sky: the stars that Gwydion had once read in a field on a night long ago. Had read and read in vain. . . . They looked down now, impassive as ever, too high and far off to give help or pity to the earth, upon their warning unheeded and their doom fulfilled. They watched the night through, from their ancient places in the heavens, and gleamed down coldly upon that vacant bath of death beside the Cynvael. And the night was lonely, such an infinite, black void as a newly disembodied soul might flee through, lost and stunned and helpless, as though swept back into primeval nothingness. . . .

In the morning Goronwy Pevr arose from Llew's bed, and he took Llew's shape and ruled over Llew's land.

And soon it seemed to the folk of Dinodig that their Lord no longer gave judgment as justly as of yore, but favored all times the men whose friendship would be of most help to him. That is the wont of most rulers now, but was not the deed of a good lord in those days of Mâth. Likewise he laid new taxes on the land, fattening himself and his henchmen, and the love of gold grew ever bigger within him. His temper too grew shorter, and at times a thing to fear. Folk began to whisper that there was a new gleam in his eyes, as though another face peered out from behind his own, and that a changeling from Annwn was in him.

And on a day in autumn, when the leaves were red as blood and the footsteps of approaching winter chilled the sea, Gwydion the son of Dôn rode in haste to Caer Dathyl and the palace of Mâth the King. He had spared neither himself nor his beast in that coming, and the thing that greeted him was silence. A shadow lay over Caer Dathyl even there in the noonday sun.

He dismounted, and the man he gave his reins to was whitefaced and glum. Over all the faces in the court lay gloom and puzzlement and white, stricken wonder, as of folk who see the power of the sun fail, and the courses of nature thrust aside.

Goewyn met him with fair words of kinswoman's greeting, and in her eyes that had always been cold to him, he saw pity. That smote him like a spear, for in it he saw his blackest fears incarnate, and knew that that had come at last which it was beyond even the power of Mâth to amend. He saw that the court knew it also, that this was what had laid fear on them: their King whose power had always seemed as invincible as that of the stars or the tides to be helpless, doing no deed.

He could feel the fear and wonder that lashed at their hearts, cold as waves from the sea: "Is this foe so strong that he can withstand even our Lord who has had dealings with the gods themselves? Will his war-shout sound even here, in the halls of Caer Dathyl? Will we share the fate of the folk of Dinodig? Is the day of Mâth's power done, and himself a failing man unable to protect us any longer? Have the good gods been conquered, and is the night of the ancient prophecies coming down upon the world?"

It rustled through the brain of every man there as swallows rustle through the eaves: *Goronwy: Goronwy, the foe of the gods.*

Yet some hope must have lingered with Gwydion as he went into Mâth's chamber and closed the door behind him.

The old King sat alone. His head was bowed, and his great, jutting nose and the grey eyes, that were dull as a wintry sea spent by the lashing fury of a storm, were almost drowned in the white flow of his beard. He looked like some ancient, snow-covered rock beaten upon by tempests; and there was about him too the touch of more human woe, like the pitiful grief of helpless old men by common firesides.

Gwydion stood before him amazed and dumfounded, like one who hears that the sun will no longer rise.

The King looked up, and his grey eyes were lightless, older and sadder than the ages.

"So you have come at last, nephew. I wondered that you did not come before."

"I rested too long secure," said Gwydion. "When I first heard ill tales from Llew's land I thought them idle lies: froth whose slander was beneath the dignity of punishment. But they came and came till I grew worried and sent my mind through the night to search his thoughts. And I could not find him. . . . So I looked in the crystal and saw his chamber in Mur y Castell and the shape of another man sleeping beside Blodeuwedd there."

"I too heard," said Mâth. "Not the tales that lying tongues might tell, but the groans and discontent in the hearts of my people oppressed. But we who have seen him grow know that such deeds could never be Llew's, you and I. I was amazed as I have not been in all the centuries. And I tried to look into his brain from afar, but I could not find it, only another's there in his stead. . . . I saw that one who had some knowledge of the lower and darker forms of magic had taken his form and his place, and thought by his shape-shifting to deceive us, little knowing that there are surer ways to recognize a man than by his face. So he thinks himself secure."

"He will learn better!" said Gwydion, and the savagery of the wolf whose shape had once been on him flared for an instant in his face. "If Llew is gone forever he shall die by fire, and I will lay the worst bonds that I can compass upon his lives to be and set torments for him in every world that I can reach."

Mâth looked at him in silence until the wolf-red passed from his face and it wore again only the white woe that blanched the son of Mathonwy's own.

"You cannot do so much," he said. "You cannot tear him out of Arawn's hand. We are the lords of earth, and there are laws that bar us from meddling with the affairs of Annwn, or those who have become Arawn's subjects. Else we could win back Llew. You might send this slayer out of the world and arrange him an ill return to it, but between life and life Arawn would be his King. And justice, not vengeance, is ever the word, my nephew."

Gwydion laughed: a short and bitter sound, like crackling ice. "Justice should be enough," he said, "for him and for her. I explored their minds well as they lay there guzzling each other up like swine. There is one heart, and only one, that is joyous for the change of lords in Dinodig. She led Llew like a pig to the slaughter: Blodeuwedd, whom you and I created."

Mâth's hoary head sank lower on his chest.

"She was ill-fashioned, ill-destined. Is that her fault, or ours that mis-shaped her? It was too great a risk to draw down such a wanderer from the winds as would be content to enter so light a makeshift form. Such could not have been fit to mate with Llew. Would that the gods had withered my brain before I thought of her fashioning."

Gwydion laughed again. "Would rather that they had withered Arianrhod before her soured vanity and spite made her lay that doom on the boy! What else could we do, when she had barred all other roads to us? And Arianrhod has not the excuse that it is only some poor imp from space that dwells within her. Women have been Llew's curse from the beginning of his life. There must have been bane indeed in those flowers from which we fashioned him a wife!"

"Arianrhod will pay her own price for the deeds she has done," said Mâth. "This is the twilight of an age, and ill things draw on. We have not yet drunk out the cup, my nephew. And soon it will be at her lips."

He stared through the window, out towards where the shadows lengthened about the flowing Conwy. His face looked as if he saw a mightier and vaster river, limitless as life itself, flowing down to a colder sea. . . .

Gwydion turned from the hate that was barbed with poisoned love to those other two hates that could burn fierce and free. But even in the turn there was ill luck, for thought of those two brought upon him such a rush of longing for the one they had robbed him of that for a space he could only stand silent, with twisting hands and working face, wrestling with sheer, incarnate torment, such pain as he had never dreamed could be in the world.

It seemed to him that his heart was being ground and rent upon sharp stones, and he could have screamed aloud in his agony. Not until now had he stopped to measure it and taste its full horror. He had ridden post-haste, with it lashing like winds about him, to seek the help of Mâth. And now there was no help in the world. Llew was gone, and no man could say whither. This was the end . . . .

Yet once again his heart rose against the cold tide of that saying. Not by despair do men win to his power and Mâth's.

"What have they done with him?" he whispered. "He could not be destroyed; he could only pass elsewhere. Where is he?"

"I do not even know where is the body that he wore," said Mâth. "I have searched, but wherever Llew was I find only Goronwy Pew. By day he sits in the lord's seat and judges and punishes and awards.

But by night he goes to the bed of Blodeuwedd, and his own shape comes on him with the darkness, the shape she loves."

"Goronwy Pew, Lord of Penllyn and murderer of Llew," Gwydion said, and licked his lips as though an evil taste was on them. "But Llew too had both soul and body. Where are they now?"

Mâth rose from his seat. Again he towered upright, the great grey bulk of him seeming to fill the chamber, awesome and majestic as the cliffs stepping from their age-old places. His voice rang through the place as though the fire in the younger man strengthened it, as dying volcanoes are reawakened by the quenchless fires of earth.

"I have tried all ways, and in vain. Yet will we try again, and once again. Come, nephew, add your strength to mine."

Night came, and day again. Another night passed, and after it, its shining twin.

On the third noon Gwydion and Mâth sat alone in the chamber of the son of Mathonwy; and their hands and minds were idle and their faces grey and spent. A bleak gloom hung around them, a dulling shadow that the sun's gold could not warm or dispel. They looked old as they sat there, tired men who had failed. Sometimes the eyes of one would turn and search the deeps of the other's, as though seeking in them for some means yet untried, some art that had not yet been defeated.

They sat in greyness, like beaten warriors on a lost field.

"We have searched for him in earth and fire and water," said Gwydion. "In the air and undersea. We have sifted the minds of Goronwy and Blodeuwedd while they slept. And we have sifted the winds that blow from Annwn, but not one of them bore him to the Underworld. He is invisible in the crystal and in the pool. If he had had one thought of us, we should have found him. And he could turn to none but us. It is as if he were not thinking," said he.

And both were silent, appalled by that thought of an annihilation utterly beyond the bounds of nature.

"He is somewhere," said Mâth at last, "and he must be thinking there. But where is 'there'? . . . I grow old, my nephew. Once I should have found him. My mind would have pierced heaven and earth as swiftly and surely as a spear flies, and it would have found him as a spear finds, its mark. But now I cannot. . . . I draw near to my Change . . .

And he looked old indeed, not as of yore with the ancient rugged strength of mountains, but old as worn, wearied men are old, bowed beneath the woes as well as the wisdom of years. The loss of Llew bowed him, and the weight—as great, or greater—of Gwydion's mute agony.

And his nephew, looking at him, felt sorrow that that high, measureless might that had overshadowed all his days, now dreaded and
now depended on, should ever know fading or shadow. "He loves me
as I love Llew. Or almost as I love Llew. There could not in the world
be quite such another love. For I am of Mâth's blood, but I am not
of his own body: at least not to my knowledge. . . .

"Yet how much does possession matter in love? When I thought
Llew was happy in Dinodig, I too could be happy, though I was lonely; when I knew that he walked the world with his strong limbs and
his bright hair and his bright smile, even though I could not see him.
It is only now when I know he no longer walks so anywhere that
there is this pain in my heart.

He bowed his head upon his hands; sat silent, brooding.
"Somewhere he is. Somewhere he must be. I shall find him again if
I search long enough, though he may have gone too far for me to follow in the body." Could the god in a man make his will iron enough
to burrow through the inexorable walls of fate?

Somewhere, like white light gleaming faintly on far hills, dawned
the assurance that it could: grey dawn, wizened and puny, above the
wreckage of a storm-racked, sunless world, a glimmer that might as
easily have been dusk as morn. He knew that the light came from
within himself. But he did not for that reason regard it as an illusion;
rather as surer truth. He believed in himself and thus in God.

For the first time Mâth's strength had failed him. Therefore he
must put forth all of, and more than, his own.

He lifted his head at last.

Not of his own will alone could he undertake this journey: leave
alone the King his uncle who was old and sore-stricken, even if not
so bitterly pierced as he was—the King who might need him. Many
would have said that the heir of Gwynedd should be by his uncle's
side now, his help and mainstay.

"Lord," he said, "I can never know rest until I have news of my
nephew."

There was silence, silence in which even the beating of a heart
would have rung loud as hammer strokes.

"Go then," answered Mâth, "and the gods give you strength."

They parted at evening. Gwydion had again put on the garments
of a bard. The disguise that had served the hot ambitions of his
youth would now serve the bitter, it might be life-long, quest of his
manhood. Goronwy and Blodeuwedd must be given no hint that
they were suspected. There must be no eager eyes and ears upon his
search. Later, when palace and court were well behind him, he

would change the fashion of his face. But now when he bowed before his uncle it was as yet unmasked by magic. The old King looked for what might be the last time upon the face he loved.

They said due words of blessing and farewell, and parted. But at the door Gwydion turned again, touched by something in that somber, mountainous majesty in which Mâth sat there all alone.

"Are you sure that you will not need me, Lord?" he asked, "that you give me heart-leave to go?"

"While I live I can guard my own," said Mâth, "now that I am awake to do it. I may have dreamed too long and too lazily in the peace and happiness of these latter days. An old dog will sleep in the sun. So the wolf gets his chance to creep on the flock. But my teeth are still strong. Only remember, nephew, the duty that will be yours when my Change comes. The memory of me will not hold Goronwy from Caer Dathyl; and your brothers are straightforward and strong, but no match in guile for such as he. And guile more and more, and strength less and less, rules the world. So yourself proved when you conquered Pryderi."

"Like him, Goronwy will not live until you are a memory," Gwydion answered. "Since it would seem that he has not gone to Annwn, Llew must still be somewhere in this world, and if he is I shall find him. So have I ceased to think of vengeance. That I will leave for his hand to take."

"Then have you made yourself pure for the quest," said Mâth. "Go."

But he sat looking after his nephew long after he had ceased to see him with the eyes of the body. He had not grieved for Llew as Gwydion had, and yet the gods knew that he had known grief enough. He had still his heir beside him, and the greatest hope of his life-days secure. Not for him could a world that held Gwydion turn black as it had for Gwydion now.

But he knew that his nephew was drowned in the ocean of woe above which his wisdom still gleamed like white rocks of eternal promise. However long the storm may blow, the sun will shine again at last. Yet how long will the storm clouds endure? Oh, Lords of the Stars, how long?

Hard, even to wisdom, in the fading-time of life, when strife has seemed over and peace earned and won, to see the fair future blackened, and the young garden torn and trampled, and one's dearest writhing in agonies that one cannot spare them. He had thought that to him could come no time bitterer than those years when in their beast-shapes Gwydion and Gilvaethwy had roamed the forests. He knew better now.

The King covered his face with his mantle and sat in silence. . . .

But Gwydion walked on down a sunless road toward Powys. The red and gold leaves had fallen before the blast of an early frost. A thin wind wailed through their withered and faded heaps, and set the stripped and naked trees to shivering. The cloudy sky grew darker as night came on.

He went alone, on a quest for whose achieving a mortal man must rob and conquer even the conqueror of men: death.

The sky turned black, and one by one, rank on rank, the stars that he had studied the night after Llew's birth came out and watched him, silent, as he walked his lonely road.

5

The Death of Dylan

THEY BORE the word of Llew's death to Arianrhod the daughter of Dôn, where she sat in her sea-girt hall. She laughed to hear it, yet with malice, little mirth.

"So now has my brother lost the stake he has played for: that prize he was willing to lose even me to gain. Better for him had it been had he never played that game at all."

She said again: "My uncle and my brother are great magicians, yet they worked ill the time they fashioned this wife for Llew. Or perhaps for once another's charm worked better than theirs. . . .

"What has Gwydion done? Has he taken vengeance on this man and woman as was right?"

"He has not, Lady," the messengers answered. "He has vanished, and it is said that he has gone forth through the land to seek the soul of Llew."

Arianrhod laughed again, a harsh and nervous sound, like the shattering of crystal. "He is a fool then," she said. "The dead are not so swift to come back. Will he waste his strength in vain dreams and wanderings while Goronwy enjoys Blodeuwedd and the lands that my uncle granted to Llew as his right? When we have lost what we prized most, should we weep, cuddling childish hopes, and spend ourselves for will-o'-the-wisps? Or rise and take what good is left us: the making of bane for them we have a right to hate? The latter is the wise man's way."

"Yet is it an ill thing, Lady, and the sign that our own lives are ended, when we can get no joy but that," one of her sorcerers said. "Then are we truly dead, and nothing but our own avengers."

Arianrhod shivered and whitened at that; for a second it was as if a cold wind had shriveled her. But then her head rose the higher and her lovely lips curved in their scornfullest smile.

"Yet this I know: that Gwydion's love has little worth. Had I loved my son I would have avenged him."

And that was the first time that she had ever said those words, "my son."

But Elen the Demure looked up from her weaving. "Perhaps it is well for you that Gwydion does not seek vengeance, Arianrhod. For he might seek it here."

Arianrhod blazed like a flame in her passion. "Little good it would do him if he did! But he has not the right to! He challenged me. This game was of his choosing and beginning, not mine; and am I to blame if I would not let myself be utterly worsted? Let him look to his heir since he would have him; I will look to myself!"

"Can you?" said Elen, and smiled. . . .

But her sister had fled from the hall.

Yet restlessness was on Arianrhod throughout that autumn, and she walked often and alone on those white beaches around the Castle of the Silver Wheel. Only on one spot she never walked: there beneath the trees where Gwydion had turned the leaves to stars for her, long ago.

It may have seemed to her as an injury done herself that any but herself should have dared to harm her son. He had been her flesh and of the blood of Dôn. His death may have seemed to her but a sterile gain, for it could not re-establish her claims to virginity. Had she been a virgin, Llew would never have been in this world to get his death there. Nor could she rejoice in that for its own sake, because she had never hated him for his own sake. She had not even known him.

In the past it had pleasured her to think that Gwydion might even now be writhing under the thought that she hated him. They had always been dear to each other; was it likely that he could be entirely happy without her, even though he had Llew, just as she could not be happy without him? It could not be that he did not miss her, that even the child he had desired—oh! unutterable wrong and humiliation!—even more than herself could make him utterly forget. . . .

But now he no longer had the detested child, and it might be he that was hating her. And something in her writhed under the thought of that. . . .

She had wanted vengeance on him. But vengeance on those we love is apt to cost us dear. . . .

The days passed and shortened. The nights came sooner and sooner as winter laid his chill upon the world.

She walked abroad on an evening when the west lay red as a bloodstain upon a bleak, iron-grey horizon. Sky and sea seemed alike drained of color. She was saying to herself that she had got her revenge and was happy. But under the satisfaction in her brain there was a dull ache in her heart. She had to warm herself, shivering, at the stubborn fires of wrath of which her soul had long been the shrine.

Then it was that she saw a change in the waters. To the west, where the dying sun still gave them a glimmer of gold, they were foaming up white and sparkling. They rose higher, catching the fading light, glowing with rose and purple and gold, throwing their white spray towards the sky as heralds might lift the banners of their oncoming king.

She leaned forward, tense and wondering. In all her years by the sea she had never seen the like of this. Or—how long had it been since she had remembered that hour?—had she once, one moonlit night when she wandered the beaches, seen a wave of the sea rise up so, in foaming, whirling whiteness, sweeping landward?

But that had been spring, and this was autumn. Summer had lain ahead then, and now was only the approach of winter. No, for winter was there already. Had she forgotten what it was that made the earth and sky so grey? That had been the time of awakening and giving life, and this was the time for dying and decay.

But she watched that rainbow growing and glowing in the west. Saw the waves that made it rise to a man's height from the seafloor, shimmering like flames, all gathering and gleaming under a single crown of foam. Saw them sweep forward, a sparkling, whirling wonder, towards Caer Arianrhod.

Straight on they came, straight to the beach; and the little waves by the shore laughed to hear them coming, and danced for joy.

. . . They had reached the shore. They parted: that flaming flower of foam opened and fell back into the sea in a shower of glittering spray as a young man swam out of it, bounded lightly ashore. Tall and golden-haired and laughing he stood there, smiling down at her with sea-blue eyes.

She knew him. In that instant that the waves had opened for his passing she had known him. He reminded her all too much of the boy on whom she had laid the curse of lovelessness years ago. Only he looked less like Gwydion.

A horrible wave of sickness went over her, and she closed her eyes. She thought, the words like a cold spear in her dizzy brain: "Is there nothing that I have done in all my life that is not to return upon me now?"

"Dylan," she whispered, "Dylan, Son of the Waves." He mistook the reason for her sickness and her swaying. He laughed and reached for her hands.

"Yes, I am Dylan, mother. Are you so glad to see me? I had not known it was such a sorrow to you that I swam away.

She seemed to waken then. Her face flushed as though it had caught some of the red light that still gleamed in the iron sky above them. She put her white arms around him and clung to him and her face changed. Her mouth worked oddly.

"A sorrow!" She laughed unsteadily. "A sorrow—oh, my son!"

He held her close. He laughed and kissed her. "I will wager not many a man has swum away from you! I have always heard tales of your loveliness, yet I never thought to find so beautiful a mother."

She laughed and pushed the gold hair back from his brow. "I see that you have already learned the sayings that please women, my son. Yet not likely would they have been to let you go long without that lessoning, fair as you are. . . . Good is your homecoming, my son. There is need of you here."

"What is that?" he questioned. But she would not tell him then. . . .

They went back to her castle together, and that night she feasted and made merry with him at Caer Arianrhod until the serving folk said among themselves that their Lady's heart must have been softened by the loss of one son, so that now she was wise enough to be glad of him that was left. They spoke together and she asked him of the palaces undersea and of his childhood there. And her blue eyes that dwelt upon him shone with that light that the quest for knowledge ever called forth in the sons and daughters of Dôn.

Her smile was as soft as the moon in springtime and all the restlessness and discontent seemed to have gone out of her face, blown away by the tranquil radiance of dawn.

But at last it darkened again when the night grew aged and most of the feasters slept, and he asked of her as they sat facing each other in the light of the failing torches: "Mother, what was that need you said you had of me? Why is it that at this time my coming should be in especial good?"

She looked at him and said tonelessly: "Your brother has been murdered."

"My brother!" he said amazed. "Indeed, and I did not know that I had one."

"But you had. He used to be sorry that you had swum off; he would have liked to know you and play with you." She closed her eyes as she said it. How she had known it none may tell. "He was as young as you, and younger, and now he has been murdered."

"How was that?" said Dylan, and his face too darkened.

She told him the tale of Goronwy's love for Blodeuwedd, and of how Llew Llaw Gyffes had died. Dylan's fair face looked dark indeed at the end. "Well," he said, "what would you have me do?"

"You must kill him who killed your brother," said she.

"I will do that gladly," he answered. "Small task it will be for me, and a happy one."

"It will not be easy," she said. "There is only one kind of spear that can kill him, as there was only one kind that could kill your brother. And only my brother, Govannon the Smith, can make the one that will be Goronwy's bane."

"Well, I will go to my uncle Govannon then and ask him to make it for me," Dylan said. "But it seems to me that you land folk here are most unreasonably hard to kill."

"We have our own ways of guarding against death," she answered, "and when they fail we are undone. As Llew is. As Goronwy will be when you have pierced him with the spear. Now he laughs at all of us in the pride of his victory. For my uncle Mâth is in his dotage, and my brother Gwydion, the King that will come after him, reared Llew and has been a man without his wits since he heard of his death. He roams the land searching the winds for his nephew's soul. And lacking his first claim, none of my other brothers will take vengeance. But your right is as good as his."

"It is indeed," said Dylan, "and I will certainly use it."

She kissed him for that. "There spoke my son indeed," she said.

On the morrow she made him ready for the journey to Govannon and she gave him certain counsels. First she would have told him of the roads.

But he laughed and shook his curly head.

"Only tell me where the sea comes nearest to it, mother. I have never walked in all my life until last night—I did well at it then for one so unpracticed, did you not think?—but I would not care to do much of it. And I certainly would not know how to ride a land horse. My steeds have always been the waves. I will swim to my uncle's forge, if it is so placed that I can."

"It is at the mouth of the river Conwy," she answered. "But the waves look cold today, my son. Are you sure that you will not get chilled?"

"A child could as easily get chilled from drinking its mother's milk," he chuckled. "The waves are my oldest friends. You need have no fear for me, mother."

"I have not," she said. "Yet is there one thing." And she laid her hand on his arm. "Your uncle Govannon is a man of choleric temper. He himself saw you swim away as a babe, and he may think you are making game of him if you, a stranger, come to him and claim to be that drowned Dylan, his sister's son. Ask him for the spear before you tell him who you are. He will be amicable with anyone who asks him about weapons, so mad is he over his precious spears and swords."

Dylan frowned. "You should know him better than anyone else, yet I do not like behaving towards my uncle Govannon as if he were a dog that was likely to bite. I have never been afraid of dogs, or anything else," said he, "and my uncle will not think the better of my courage for this, when he does know. I would have your kin be glad of me not ashamed."

"They will never be ashamed of you," she said. "And it is well to approach Govannon with caution. Promise me," she begged.

For a moment the boy looked doubtful. Then he patted her hand that was on his arm, and smiled. "Well," he said, "as you will, mother."

She walked down with him to the sea and saw him enter it. She blessed him and sent him on his journey. When he looked back from the waves she was still standing there on the white shore, the wind blowing her golden hair. And she waved her hand to him in farewell.

He laughed. He called back to her: "I will bring you home Goronwy's head as a gift, mother!"

. . . Even after he had passed out of sight on the breast of the billows, she lingered, watching the sea. She glowed like a tongue of flame as she stood there, as beautiful and as fell.

"Should I deprive Gwydion of what he prized above all and yet let him who was never more to me than a night's pastime keep his son?" she asked herself. "Shall I let one of them live and not the other?"

Govannon the son of Dôn was working in his forge by the mouth of the Conwy, when a messenger came to him. He knew the fellow for a man of his sister Arianrhod's, though not for years had he seen him. There was no amiability in Govannon. His heart was sore for Llew's death, and for Goronwy's safety. Now least of all times did he wish to think of his sister, the first cause of all these woes. When he saw her servant he only growled like a great bear and worked on.

The messenger stood back and waited, white-faced, afraid to interrupt, while the smith's blows raised showers of red sparks that gleamed fitfully as lightnings on his great arms and grim face. He handled the metal as though it had been human flesh that he hated. And the messenger stepped back and back, until the wall stopped his stepping altogether.

He braced himself there and, keeping a wary eye on Govannon's hammer, spoke.

"Your sister sends you a message, Lord."

"Well," said Govannon, "what does she want?"

His hammer-arm was still above his head, and his eyes glared unpleasantly in the red light.

The man licked his lips. "She sends you a message—" he said.

"Well, what for?" growled Govannon.

"I will tell it if you will let me," the man stammered.

"I will let you die if you do not!" snapped Govannon. "Am I to waste the whole day waiting for you to mouth Arianrhod's nothings?"

Again the man moistened his lips. "She bids me tell you that she has learned by arts whereof your House knows that Goronwy Pevr, who killed Llew Llaw Gyffes, your nephew and her son, is on his way here today to get a spear from you. He will be tall and blue-eyed and golden-haired, and, as always now by day, much of the likeness of Llew will be on him. He will wear a sea-green mantle fastened with two brooches of red gold, joined by a chain of the same—"

He got no further. The smith's voice hit him with a great bellow that knocked the words off his lips. Govannon's clenched hands rose above his head and his hammer struck the forge roof.

"He will come here?" he bellowed. "He will dare to come to *me?*"

"He will indeed," said the servant, "and my mistress prays you for old love's sake, in the days when you were little ones together, and by the sacred bonds of kinship, to give him that spear as soon as he asks for it, and through the heart."

"It is the first decent, womanly thing that I have known her to say for a long time," said Govannon, "and you can tell her that it will be a joy to me to do her will."

Govannon ap Dôn had the helper who was with him in the forge fetch him his sharpest spear and poison it. "For I would not have the murderer of my nephew die too swift a death," he said.

The man obeyed. He dipped the slender bronze shaft with its gleaming, barbed head in the bubbling venom.

And Govannon smiled. . . .

"He has earned better than that at the hands of the children of

Dôn," said he. "It is Gwydion that should have done this," he mused. "But I am not infringing upon his rights greatly. None could expect me to let the murderer come to my forge and leave it again alive. And I have the bidding of Arianrhod, that was, after all, the boy's mother, and therefore the person that had most rights in him. Though it is a pity that she could not have been brought to her senses except by his dying.

"A pity, too, that my brother so spoiled the boy that he never learned sense enough to be afraid of anything, but must think the whole world his friend, and go spilling his dearest secrets in a whore's bed. It is Arianrhod that has had the most sense in the end, for while Gwydion wanders like a man moonstruck on a mad quest, she has plotted a right and proper vengeance for her son."

But the helper was not listening. He was gazing out through the low doorway toward the grey restlessness of the ocean. And his eyes began to pop, and to stick forward out of his head.

"Lord, there is something moving on the waters," he whispered. "See, yonder on the sea—. It is like a chariot of foam on the waves, it catches the light a hundred ways and with a hundred colors, like a jewel."

But Govannon's eyes were fast to the spear-head, and he thought of how another spear must have gleamed as if flew from the hill Bryn Kyvergyr. . . . That venomous, still steaming barb held all his soul in a waiting hot and deadly as its own. It ringed his consciousness like a wall of fire.

"What do I care for the sea?" he said roughly. "Let it belch up what it will. Look down the road, and see if there is anyone coming there."

The man looked, and Govannon looked, but they could see nobody there. Yet when they turned to step back into the forge again they did see someone at last: a figure, coming up, not from the road, but from the shore. He had appeared while their faces were turned away. His cloak gleamed green against the grey rocks. They saw how bright the sun shone on his yellow hair.

Govannon saw that two red gold brooches clasped the cloak upon the stranger's breast. The smith trembled, and his fingers shook with eagerness. His eyes gleamed as hungrily as a wolf's. But he went back to his anvil and worked there, like a man going about his daily business. Only he kept the spear ready by him, in the black shadow on the far side of the anvil, where one in the doorway could not see it.

The stranger came to the door. The red forge-light played ominously over his straight young form and gold hair. He did not speak for a second. His eyes were unused to that flame-shot darkness, and the smith in the shadows looked to him like the very bulk of night, looming up in that smoky gloom.

Then he took a step forward. He smiled, and his young voice rang clear and buoyant. "Are you Govannon the Smith, the son of Dôn? I have come to get me a spear."

Those words were the signal. . . .

Govannon picked up the spear and hurled it at him, and the sea roared and reared, rising in white jets to the heavens, as the blow went home. . . . That was the cast that has come down to us at one of the Three Nefarious Blows of the Isle of Britain. Taliessin says that

> The Waves of Erinn and Mann, and of the North,
> And of Britain, comely of hosts, the Fourth,

saw and mourned it, and that ever since the wild waves have beaten against the shore, longing for vengeance for that stroke.

It struck Dylan in the chest. He reeled, and the blood came spurting out around the imbedded spear like a kind of horrible red flower opening into bloom.

Yet he came on. He came forward, straight to the man who had killed him. Only as he reached him did he stagger and fall to the forge-floor; and then Govannon was upon him, one hand fast in his hair, the other raising a sword for the beheading stroke.

But Dylan looked up into his eyes and laughed: a strange. choking sound that covered his lips and chin with red. "You give me an over-warm welcome, uncle," he said.

The smith's face blanched, and his eyes started in his face. Slow perceptions did not run in the race of Mâth. "Who are you that calls me uncle?" he demanded. "Are you not Goronwy Pevr?"

"I am not Goronwy; I came to get the spear that would kill Goronwy. . . ." The sea-blue eyes were dulling; over them was spreading the film of death. "My mother Arianrhod sent me to you to get the spear to avenge my brother with."

Govannon had dropped the sword. His hands were on the boy's shoulders. They tightened there. His face was white with fear. "Arianrhod your mother! Who are you then? Speak!"

But Dylan only heard him dimly. There was a roaring in his head, a singing, as of great waters. "I am—" he whispered. "Do you not— hear them, as they come for me—singing? I am Dylan—of the Waves. A—ah!" For the anguish of the poison had come upon him, and he writhed so it seared his veins.

With set face Govannon lifted the sword again. "That at least I can spare you," he said. . . .

Later the smith looked down upon him. He was fair as ever, now that his uncle had washed the blood from his face. His gay mantle hid the marks of the mercy-stroke. He smiled like a boy that sleeps and dreams of new adventures. But there was no smile on the face of Govannon ap Dôn. The watching helper shivered.

"This is an ugly deed," his master said, "and my name must bear the stench of it, for I will never have it known that my mother's daughter could do so foul a deed. And I will chop you into as many pieces as there are stars in the sky if ever you breathe a word of it.

"Go you now to my sister and give her my message and see that you speak it in her ear alone."

He spoke the message and the man repeated it after him, trembling and stammering.

"I am afraid, Lord," he said, "afraid. Your sister is a sorceress, and she will not like that message. There is no wish on me to come back a mouse or a creeping or crawling or flying thing."

"She will like the message better than I like the deed she has tricked me into," said Govannon, "and she will not wish to provoke me further. Besides, you are the only man who can carry that message, because only you know the thing it speaks of. . . . Listen, how the waves roar, as if they were trying to batter down the world. We have done a deed that all mankind will pay for, Arianrhod and I. We have made the People of the Sea the foes of land folk, and for that there will be a bitter price."

The man trembled and said more, but Govannon swept him aside and looked down once more upon Dylan. He looked long upon that quiet, boyish face.

"So you were the little brat I carried to his baptizing long ago," he said, "when Gwydion hid Llew in the chest. . . . We did not look then for matters between us to come to this end, nephew. . . . And you were like Llew, and I hated you the more for that. It maddened me that Goronwy the murderer should wear that face. I did not know you had a right to it, that you were my young kinsman that I would have held dear. . . . Ah! Gwydion chose the better part, after all; he has not this pain on his heart.

"And through the ages men will remember that I murdered you, but why they will never know."

He sat down and covered Dylan's face, and he stayed there by the dead. His man crept quietly away.

Outside the sea raged, lashing the shore. It bellowed like a vast grey monster, hurling itself upon the earth. Never since has it been quiet as before that day. Ships have sunk and men have died to pay for that wrath of the waters. And it may be that it is the wrath of a lord of Caer Sidi that has lost his son. . . .

And for ages after, in the Vale of the Conwy, men called the sound of the sea-waves where they met the river, the Death-Groans of Dylan.

Govannon ap Dôn's man came at dusk to the castle of Arianrhod. They brought him before his Lord's sister, and he looked strangely and shrinkingly upon her as she stood there in the glow of the torchlight.

"Lady," he stammered, "may I speak with you alone?"

Arianrhod put her slim hands to her throat. Her face was white with terror, but of what neither she nor any knew. At her sign, her people withdrew.

Govannon's man made obeisance before her, but she cried out sharply: "Do not wait for that! Tell me—tell me what you have come to tell!"

"Lady," he said, "Govannon your brother sends you this word: that he has done your will, and that if you were not a woman and his sister, he would come and take your head off. And if ever he sets eyes on you again he will take it off anyhow. For that you have made him slay his own nephew without cause, and done such a foulness as no woman born of woman was ever guilty of before."

6

The Last Spell of Arianrhod

ARIANRHOD WALKED on the shore that evening, and she was
not happy.

She did not remember Govannon. His scorn did not companion
her there in the deepening dusk. It had retreated far off, a tiny spot
of flame in the farthest background of her mind.

She was alone with herself and therefore with many selves. For
her being, that was far more highly evolved than Blodeuwedd's, was
also far more complex. It was too wide to be filled by the simplicity
of one feeling, one desire, except for the space of time that was necessary to make that desire, that feeling, fact.

And now all her plans were carried out, all her wishes fulfilled.
She had no hates left to satisfy. She had no purpose. She had nothing. She had undone all others and had not repaired herself.

And she looked with terror into the depths of that nothingness,
upon which she must henceforth float aimless, chewing the dry
bones of a finished revenge.

She thought, "What am I to do now?" She wrung her hands and
whispered it aloud: "What shall I do?"

But only the oncoming night answered, terribly and loudly with
its very silence and emptiness. Worse than any human sound of
doom or accusation—for even doomsmen would have companioned
her in her misery—awful as the blank of the uncreated void.

And she saw that she too was ended: that the structure of her life
had fallen to pieces when those two young lives to whose obliterating she had devoted herself had been destroyed.

She thought in panic: "I have hated them so much that it is the
same as if I had loved them."

She wondered: "Would it not have been better if I had been as Gwydion would have had me be? Proud of my children because they were fair and strong? If from the beginning I had been like other girls of Gwynedd, caring nothing for the name of virginity?"

But the vision of how easily and happily life might have flowed onward then, with the children growing beside her, her darlings and not her banes, was one that she found she dared not face. Her heart winced away from it, shuddering. Besides, she knew that it could never have been so. Change had laid its grip on both her and Gwydion. They could never be still and follow old established ways. They must forever move and explore and discover, and somehow in that moving she had become confused and lost direction and firm footing—had stranded herself upon this rock of nothingness.

How had it happened? Why had it happened? She did not know. She refused to know. Yet it blew over the walls of her mighty vanity like a storm wind: Had she not lost substance and grasped at shadows when she had seized upon the name of that which she would not consent to be—a virgin?

Be it how it might, she had gone too far to turn back. Now she was fast bound on the rock, and could not move; bound fast in the coil of her own deeds. She had shut herself out of the warm pale of humanity, and barred its doors against her. She was the mother that had slain her own sons: the woman that henceforth would be apart from all women.

And all her wrath against Gwydion, that had lain in ashes during these long months when she had been haunted by thought of his dreadful and weary quest, and had striven to gloat over it and could not, flamed anew and swept over her in a searing, scorching tide. All these things would never have happened had Gwydion let her be. It was he who had driven her to all these crimes, he who had tricked her into motherhood and set before her eyes these two living insults that she had to wipe out as best she could. He was responsible for all, and guilty of all.

She raged against the whole race of men, that would not be content with the gifts she gave them, but must beguile her into making more, and then seem righteously horrified at her resentment of the trick. She thought with joy of the snare in which she had trapped Govannon. He had been her arm to strike Dylan with as her own body had once been the egg for Gwydion to hatch his chick out of. Now tonight a man too knew how it felt to be a dupe and a tool.

She had had a right to take revenge on Gwydion. It was only another of the wrongs he had done her that her vengeance had violated Llew's right to live.

For her brain, that was so much keener than Blodeuwedd's, could not deny this now that he was no longer in the world to vex her: Llew had had the right to live. Not consciously had he wronged her. Gwydion, not he, had willed his birth.

And even this last deed had been done, in a measure, for her brother's sake. Her contriving of the death of Dylan had been her atonement to Gwydion, though she had known that it would neither please nor help him. She had thought that she would not spare Dylan when she had not spared Llew; that she would not be kinder to others than she had been to her brother.

Or was it herself that she had wished to justify to herself?

Or Llew that she had wished, in some thwart way, to avenge?

Her head was whirling with a strange madness. She could not work anything out clearly. All was twisted and tangled irretrievably, like yards and yards of spider-web behind and about and over her, never to be escaped from.

And Gwydion was the spider that had woven the web.

Her fury boiled against him until she thought of using her darkest charms to slay him. But she knew that he had knowledge enough to take warning and defend himself. Yet she felt that she would not care if he struck back at her: if they two should engage in last and deadliest conflict, this time in their own persons, with no third between them, to be wrecked or saved. If he killed her and ended all, it would be well.

Yet she knew that she could not face the risk that she might win and kill him. She wrung her hands in thwarted fury and moaned to herself: "That would be the last thing—the one thing that I could not bear!"

She ran down the beach as a fawn runs when dogs pursue her, and she came to the place where Gwydion had turned the leaves to stars. She flung herself down in the sands and burrowed there, and cried out wild phrases to the unheeding sky. She beat her breast and wept.

But soon she rose again. Pictures haunted her, moving before her in the dimness that was settling down upon the earth. She thought of Dylan falling with the spear through him, there in Govannon's forge. She thought of another young form, poising straight and supple on the cauldron's edge, as the spear flashed through the air from Bryn Kyvergyr. . . . She shut her eyes and still saw them, clear against the dark screen of her eyelids.

Her breasts that had never given suck burned as though filled with bitter fire. All the love that she had never let herself feel curdled within her, soured and perverted: a demon that she must fly from.

Dylan and Llew! Llew and Dylan! Nowhere on earth was there escape for her from those names. They sounded in her breathing. They beat in her heart. The surf spelled them, where it beat the cliffs. The surf. . . .

She looked about her and saw that the twilight was fast deepening. The sky was turning black, and shadows were trooping up from the sea. It seemed to her that there was something hostile and angry in the muttering of the waves tonight, that they beat against the shore with a new malice, like enemies, though she could feel no wind. . . .

In all nature there was unfriendliness towards her. . . . That oppressed her, and she grew nervous and angry, feeling as though she were watched.

She had thought that Dylan's death would set her at rest, secure at last from sons. A fair reparation, too, to Llew and Gwydion, for deep in her sore heart, during one moment, while his gay, friendly young eyes first laughed down into hers, she may not have wished her elder son to die. . . . Of him she had never had to be jealous, never had to feel that Gwydion loved him better than her. . . .

Yet she had been loyal to Gwydion.

And now that death seemed only like the breaking of another loyalty, another wrong for her to avenge.

But who was there to avenge it on, save only herself? Not Govannon. She laughed at the idea. He was less responsible than if he had been his own spear.

On whom else then? She caught her breath at a sudden idea.

She had been in the mood to sacrifice Dylan for Llew. And now that that was done, she was ready to sacrifice Llew for Dylan. The actual possibility of this did not greatly concern her. Action and life were indivisible to her; and now she must act or go mad.

Besides—the possibility seared her mind like lightning—was *it altogether certain that Gwydion's quest would fail?* He had won altogether too often when his case seemed hopeless. Her brother could accomplish many things. And if he should succeed in bringing Llew back to life, after she had killed Dylan—! She sobbed with rage, perhaps for Dylan's sake, at the thought.

She ran back towards the castle. But at one side of it she paused, and crept along the cliff walls, feeling her way with her hands, until she came to a cleft so low and cunningly placed as to be almost invisible in that light. She entered there, and descended, through a narrow, sloping passage, into a crypt. There was a passage there that led on and on into the labyrinth of caves that lay beneath the castle, and she followed it down, down, into depths where she was forced to grope her way through the black sightlessness.

She was below the sea level now, and in her ears the angry murmur of the sea waxed ever louder as it beat upon the great barriers of stone that made the island-wall.

The sound seemed eerie there in the bowels of the earth. It made her quicken her pace, a nervous catch in her breath.

But she came at last to the chamber that was her goal. She stopped there, her hands digging into the walls that were wet with a green and slimy ooze. She tore at them, trembling as much with the frantic energy of her determination as with the strain of her physical effort. A stone yielded, loosened in her hands. She tugged it out, and after it other stones. She groped in the void thus formed until she felt something metallic—pulled and hauled until the thing was in her hands and then in her arms.

She turned and fled back towards the earth's surface, reeling, strong woman though she was, under the weight of what she carried. And it seemed to her as she ran that the sound of the waters had changed. That there was laughter in it now, a satisfied, gloating laughter that yet was somehow eager. . . .

Night had fallen completely when she reached the beach again. Clouds swirled about her namesake and mistress, the moon, and seemed about to cover her. Arianrhod was glad of the lights of her castle as she ran up to it, and called to the doorkeeper.

Elen and Gwennan and Maelan sprang up from their seats in the torchlight when they saw their sister, wild-eyed and with loosened hair, the ooze-covered casket dripping slime over her muddied hands and arms. The sorcerers one and all rose from their places also, their eyes glued in a kind of scared yet magnetized fascination to the box in her arms.

"Will you all stand there gaping like fools?" Arianrhod said, and her panting made the words a savage whisper. "Quick, sisters! Help me cleanse myself for the rites. Up, and get you to the caverns, you my sorcerers, and make all ready! We must perform an incantation there."

They still stood staring, their faces whitening in the deepening silence. Elen broke it, pointing to the coffer in Arianrhod's arms and putting out a hand that trembled, though her face darkened with a certain anger.

"Arianrhod, what is that?"

The coffer, green and unsightly now, had originally been made of gold. No other metal would have so resisted rust in that damp and slimy place where it had lain hidden.

Arianrhod laughed. "It is the casket of ancient spells that Hu the Mighty once killed a man for bringing from overseas with him when our forefathers escaped from the sinking land, and whose magic no wizard has dared to use from that time to this. The casket that my mother Dôn entrusted to my keeping when she told me, and me alone, of its hiding place. And now at last I have brought it out."

Elen drew back. "Have you gone mad, Arianrhod? Would you bring the wrath of the King our uncle down upon us? Or things that may be even worse? Well you know that what that casket holds is not safe for man or woman to meddle with."

"It is a pity that so much power should be wasted," said Arianrhod. "Besides, I need strong spells tonight. I will not have Gwydion thwart me a fourth time. I must make a spell that will drive Llew's soul beyond his reach forever. I must call upon all powers for that."

Silence fell then, tense and blanching. Eyes protruded and whitened, the scared pupils shrunk and rolling. There was none that dared hold another's gaze.

At last Maelan wrung her hands and gave a little, moaning cry. "Arianrhod, you will not—not dare not—open the closed Eye of the Deep, that we four were set to guard?"

"I will indeed," said Arianrhod. "I must call on water as well as on earth and fire and air. Stop your sniveling, fool."

Maelan shrieked and covered her face with her hands.

Gwennan put an arm about her and faced Arianrhod. "Is this your set will, sister? Is there no turning you from it?"

"There has never been any turning her from anything that she thought she wanted," said Elen, "even when she did not really want it. It is not really Gwydion or Llew that she wants to harm now. It is only that she is in a rage to be doing something lest she have time to stop and think and repent that she has murdered Dylan."

She got no further, for with a shriek Arianrhod whirled, lifting the casket, and would have struck her down with it had she not been quick to retreat. Gwennan and the sobbing Maelan flung themselves between.

Arianrhod quieted herself and stood smiling scornfully at her sisters. The daughters of Dôn surveyed each other, and Gwennan's eyes grew very cold.

"This is the end, Arianrhod," she said. "Long have we four labored here together, watching over the coasts of Gwynedd and controlling the tides in the name of our Lady, the moon. But now have you broken all the laws that were ever laid on women, and you will break the greatest that were ever laid on magicians also. And in that we dare have no share. It is not our doom. You have lit a fire in yourself that it will take all the waters of the sea to put out. Farewell, sister, and the gods give you peace. We go."

"Farewell and good riddance!" answered Arianrhod. "Why should I want you here, a pack of hare-hearted bitches forever wailing and whining? Get outside and take a boat to the mainland, and be quick about it, for I will not delay these rites that you fear so much a second longer than needs must be to prepare for them."

Gwennan gave her a long, wistful look, as though to paint her portrait upon the walls of memory. Then she turned without another word, and went off to fetch her belongings. Elen and Maelan followed her. As they passed Arianrhod they too looked at her long.

"Farewell, sister," they said. "We were not partners in your crimes; we may not be your partners in this."

But Arianrhod answered never a word. . . .

After they had gone, and their boat had passed from sight on the face of the waters, Arianrhod still stood silent. Under the torchlight her hair seemed to run like a yellow flame, eating at her face and shoulders. Her face looked small and wan in its fiery shadow, like a shriveled thing. She stood alone, as she knew that she must forevermore stand alone.

The sorcerers came trooping back into the hall they had left. But for a while she did not notice them. She turned at last. "Is all ready?" she asked.

"It is," they answered.

The eldest sorcerer came forward, a scared and troubled look in his rheumy eyes. "Niece of Mâth the Ancient, is this wise? These are mighty charms. They are those that the sorcerers of Caer Sidi were using in those last days when it sank beneath the sea. The fleeing wizard that brought them to the new lands with him died for the deed. Dôn your mother preserved them, though her brother the son of Mathonwy would have cast them back into the sea to go down and lie with all the other dark magic that brought the Lost Land of the West to its doom. But she never dared to use them."

"I dare," said Arianrhod.

But as she said it her eyes widened and her face whitened, for a strange thing had happened. The hall seemed to be whirling around her, and the man before her had grown bigger, whiter of hair and beard. His eyes were rheumy no longer, but deeper and clearer, the sea-grey eyes of her uncle Mâth: that all-piercing, god-like gaze that she had never met since the day of her children's birth. . . . She could have cried out at the illusion, but in an instant it passed. The hall stood still, and only her old sorcerer was there, looking at her in frightened puzzlement.

She grasped his arm and shook it fiercely. "Whence got you those words? Who bade you speak them?"

"I do not know," the old man mumbled, and his eyes looked doubtful and bewildered. "They seemed to come into my head from far off . . . a great way off. . . ."

He straightened and looked down at her. "Lady, must you do this thing?"

"I must," said Arianrhod, "for Gwydion my brother has degraded me by using my body for a tool to work his will with, as men who own them nowadays breed cows and mares. And for that indignity I have a right to vengeance, and I will not forego it, though my life were its price."

It was dark in the caves beneath the castle. The smoky glow of the ritual fire could not dispel the shadows. It merely set them dancing like triumphing madmen.

Arianrhod looked about her and she looked at a great stone that lay there in the center of that chamber in the island's bowels. "Open the Well," she said.

That was the sacred Well that she and her sisters had always guarded, the salty well that was called the Eye of the Deep because it had no bottom but the sea.

They pulled and hauled at the sealing stone at her bidding, but it was hard to get it up.

"It is as if something were holding it down from the inside," they said.

"It is the island itself that does not want the stone lifted," the old druid whispered. "It is afraid. . . ."

"Why should it be afraid?" his Queen asked in scorn.

Her sorcerer looked at her. "You know well," he said. "You know what has happened to other women who were false to their trusts and opened other wells. The lords in the waters are always greedy, always seeking new realms to rule over. . . . Once you might have done it. There is one down below who loved you once, but he will not be loving you tonight. Is it wise to trouble his waters further, when they already boil with his wrath against you?"

"Let him try to strive against me," said Arianrhod. "I can best him, as I have bested all other men I have dealt with. This is my land, my realm and my element, and not his."

The stone began to move: seemed almost to rise of itself in the sorcerers' hands.

The old druid looked again at his Princess, put out an appealing hand.

"Lady, it is not yet too late. Will you not bid put down the stone again?"

"It is too late," said Arianrhod. "What would I be but a fool and a coward if I turned back for fear now, when I would not turn back for love or honor before? If I thought that all the sea was waiting there, ready to spring up when that stone was lifted, I should still have it raised. For I have locked and barred all doors behind me. I have cast my lot with what the folk call wickedness, so I must be successful in wickedness: not a failure in all. I must make utterly sure of my revenge."

"It is true," the sorcerer said. "She who cannot go back must go forward. . . ."

But she did not answer him. She had opened the casket and was reading aloud the words on a golden tablet she had taken from it. She intoned them, half-singing, words in a language no longer spoken in any land visible beneath the sun, words written in a script that could not have been read by any under the sun, save those of the House of Mâth. Drawn up to her full height, straight and slender, she stood there, her arms outstretched above the flames, herself gleaming like the very spirit of the fire, as she chanted those words of mysterious power, and the stone rolled back. . . .

The sorcerers retreated quickly from that black, opened void. They made a circle about the fire and their Queen, and chanted her words after her. They began to sway in a dance; widdershins, about the flames.

The chanting grew louder, the dancing wilder, the flames leaped higher.

Far, far down, in the distant deeps of the opened pit, the water began to churn and bubble. It too sprang higher, in a hissing spray.

Arianrhod raised her arms above her head. The flames seemed to rise after them, like wings, above which the marvelous beauty of her face floated, aureoled in the gold fire of her streaming hair. She spoke in the language of the Prydyn.

"I call upon earth and fire and air and water. I call upon the Four Elements: I command them, I the sorceress, that they give no refuge to the soul of Llew, my son. From the deeps of the ocean let him be barred. From the cloudy heavens let him be barred. From the warmth of fire, from the fields of earth, and from the wombs of women let him be barred. Let a wind arise, mighty enough to blow his soul beyond the world, to lose it in the vast infinity of outer spaces—"

The hissing water rose in a silvery jet from the pit beyond the fire-glow. It gleamed there like a sword.

The stone floor trembled. The island shook and quivered, as though giant hands were twisting and squeezing it from below. There were noises of cracking and rending: a crashing of fallen stones.

The chanters stopped. They looked at one another with white faces, eyes distended above the breathless lips on which the chant was stilled.

The crashing grew louder, mightier. The roaring behind it swelled, as though the sea and the splitting rocks were joining each other in a vast song of downfall and destruction, the terrible music of a breaking and ending world.

The great jet of water in the pit shrieked and writhed as it forced its way up, like some monstrous birth, through the rock walls of the island's breaking heart.

The earth twisted in its agony as the rending sea pierced its vitals tearing them apart.

In that small place the humans' eardrums reeled under the sounds as under heavy blows. They put their hands to their ears to shut them out, but their hands were not large or thick enough. They rushed, like one body, toward the stair.

The stone cracked above them. Part of the roof fell, a great slab, crushing half the sorcerers beneath it. They lay there, only the feet and legs of some still protruding from beneath the heavy stone, over which the water from the Well began to boil, a vast white wave.

Arianrhod screamed. The men who were still alive screamed also, those cracked, horrible screams of men that are worse than any woman's shriek. . . .

They fled up the stone steps that led to the castle above. But, quick though they were, the water was quicker. It foamed about their feet, it rose to their ankles, their knees, their waists.

Arianrhod was first, above them all on the steps. She saw that churning tide reach their armpits, their shoulders, their necks. Saw it frame the agonized faces of the topmost in white aureoles as it covered the heads of those lower on the steps. Saw them, one by one, sucked down. . . .

She reached the top of the steps. There were women running back into the great hall as though from a foe outside, but at sight of her and the streaming crest of water that followed her, they stopped where they were and lifted their arms and shrieking lips to heaven.

Their posture told her that it was no use to fly; yet she tried to fly. She rushed through the doorway and stopped, aghast.

She could feel the island tottering beneath her, sinking like a broken-backed horse. But the sea had risen higher. It loomed above the island, a vast wall of waters, blotting out the horizon, the white foam of its crest curling out across the sky, ready to fall and cover the island as the floor of a bath is covered.

She saw. She sank to her knees, threw up her arm to shield her face from the sight of that vast, grey-green infinity of waters that had already crushed out her courage as it would soon crush out her soul.

She knew her doom and the cause of her doom. She had broken the first of laws, that ancient law upon which the being of the race depends: that a woman shall guard, not take, the lives of the children she has borne.

She had taken death for her servant, and in the end he had made her *his* servant, and claimed her own death as well as others'. It was Dylan's avenger that loomed above her, ready to fall. . . .

Only in the last moment, as that green stifling immensity rolled forward and blotted out the sky from her sight forever, she whispered, against her trembling fingers, the thing that she herself may have thought the whole truth:

"Gwydion, it was for you I did it! Oh, Gwydion! Oh, my brother!"

And then the wall of waves fell, and where Caer Arianrhod had once been, there was only a boiling and churning of the waters.

7

Gwydion Goes Upon
a Strange Quest

GWYDION AP DÔN wandered long through Gwynedd and Powys.

Far and wide he wandered, while the autumn winds played dirges in the brown leafless trees that writhed like shuddering many-armed things in the blast, and the pale mornings found the fields frost-silvered, grey as tired and aging heads.

Far and wide he wandered, yet Llew he never found.

Slow that journey must have been. A mile a day may well have been a good distance for him to cover. For no bush, no clod of earth was too small to be searched, and searched minutely, for his quarry, no treetop too high and no thicket's shadows too dense or inaccessible. For he believed in the teachings of his Order, that would seem to have held that the departed soul of man might most easily pass into the light and winged things of the air. And that teaching may be evidence of the kinship of the druids with the builders of the pyramids, for the folk of the pharaohs were wont to picture the soul as passing into the form and shape of a bird. So no bird, no bee, no moth, or winged insect of any race, but might hold the soul that Gwydion was seeking. It is told in the tales of Erinn that she who was to be the great Cuchulain's mother drank her son's soul down as a mayfly, given her in a cup of wine.

But the butterflies had passed with summer, and in the red glow of the evenings, watching the birds fly southward, speckling the bloody sky with black, Gwydion may have wondered if any of those high, remote forms in the heavens was his boy, flying away from him, away to those warmer lands beyond the sea.

How he hoped to know the soul of Llew if he found it is a riddle that only his druid mysteries could have solved. But he and Mâth had senses, knew planes of consciousness and vision beyond what we possess, who stumble along by the crude lantern of material science; and would accept it as a fact that the head does not think because we cannot see it think, had we ourselves not thought. Such are the logic and penetration of the science that we know.

But Gwydion and Mâth had surer ways of knowing a man than by his face, as they themselves had said. And the cry of every bird, the buzz of every fly, the sight of every white moth-miller fluttering before him in the dark, must have been to Gwydion a hope and a trumpet-call, to be followed up at whatever pains, and thoroughly explored.

But a vain hope.

Men may have wondered at the sight of him, a greying man with a harp, pursuing birds across the fields, or springing up suddenly to chase a fly and then not killing it, only peering at it. They must have thought him moonstruck, or possessed by bardic frenzy.

Many a time his quarry must have escaped him, and left him wondering, tormented by uncertainty and regret. "If I had caught up with this one, if I had caught up with that one, would I have had Llew again, my darling, by my side?"

Many a time he may have found a soul, but not the one he sought. Some of them may have been souls he knew, men who had died because of him in the great war with Pryderi long ago. And others may have been old women that had told him tales when he was little, before he left Dôn's court to go to Caer Dathyl and be taught by Mâth. Or girls that he had laughed with in his young days when he had still believed that his cleverness alone was great enough to mold the world as Govannon shaped the metals in his forge. We do not know what old friends or old enemies he may have met so, or whether sometimes he may have wished that he was with them, and the task of living done.

So the last heaped treasures of golden autumn leaves were beaten by the rain into muddy brown. And all the birds were flown. And the flies no longer buzzed, but were to be found floating wrong side upwards in puddles, loathsome bits of black between their stilled wings. Snow came and dressed the shivering trees in festal garb again, bepearling every poor, thin, arm-like bough with sparkling white. The puddles in the roads and fields froze to ice.

Gwydion still went on.

The laws of hospitality that ensured the livelihood of the bard protected him. Wherever he went the people gave him food and drink, and such sleeping-space as they had. And in return he told them tales, spinning like the old spider of wonders he had always been. Maybe he was a little glad to give joy so, easing the world's old, old pain whose weight he himself now had learned to fullest measure: warming a little the bleak of his desolation at the brief fire of their pleasure.

And to the poet and creator the joy of creation can never wholly dim, unless the time has come when it would be well for soul and body to be apart, and longer union is a danger to the one and sterility to the other.

Often, in the smoky gloom of the crofter's hut or of the shepherd's shack, he must have lain wakeful in the black night watches, listening to the howl of the winds that are said to be the steeds of the dead, and wondering if any wail in all that eerie tumult was the voice of his son.

He came again to his own dominions around Dinas Dinllev, and none of the folk knew their Lord in the shape of illusion that his skill had put upon him. They welcomed him only as a bard is welcomed, and his own steward gave him a gift and asked him for a song.

Gwydion gave it.

But he never entered the castle that had been his and where he had reared Llew from child to youth.

Yet one evening he went out to the shore beside the fortress. Llew had loved the place, and his spirit, drawn like a homing bird, might hover about there where his body had so often bathed in the days that were gone. It was not yet true evening, or perhaps it was truer evening than the later, darker hour would be. It was the brief twilight of winter, dull and bleak as death.

The pale beaches lay blanched before an iron sea. The dying sun made a bloodstain in the harsh grey sky. And under those hard and cheerless heavens there was no sound but sobbing, a bitterer human sobbing mingling with the ancient keening of the sea.

It was the sobbing of a woman.

Gwydion stopped. It flashed to his mind with electrical vividness from hers who wept there: they two mourned the same grief! And he wondered: what woman was this that wept for Llew?

He went on again. He came to where he could see her, kneeling, half-hidden by a great rock, her face buried in her hands. In that bleak light her hair gleamed dull as unpolished copper, like the soul of an extinguished flame. He looked at her until she felt the spears of his eyes, dropped her hands, and lifted her affrighted face to meet that piercing gaze.

"For whom do you weep, maiden?" he asked.

She looked in his eyes and saw the druid-power there. She said with a touch of defiance in her voice:

"For Llew Llaw Gyffes."

"Why should you weep for him?"

She laughed. "Perhaps because he was once my love for a little while on this very beach, stranger, before his accursed mother put the curse of lovelessness on him. And now he is dead."

"That is not true," said Gwydion. "Llew never had any love but Blodeuwedd. Moreover, what makes you so certain that he is dead?"

She laughed again, more bitterly, and this time with clear scorn. "All Gwynedd is saying it. All Gwynedd is telling that Goronwy Pevr slew him for their wife's sake, and took his lands and form. You know well enough that that at least is true, you who are druid."

"Maybe it is not true that I was his love. Yet I came to meet him here on this beach long ago. But I did not please him. He did not take me. But I wanted him then and I never wanted any other man before or after, though I have taken others since. It was no use. I could only lie in their arms and think of him . . . . I do not know why I did not please him. I tried. I thought that I had. And then he would only sit there and do nothing. . . . And I grew angry and ran off, crying that he was a coward who never went to the fight like my brothers and had not even courage to embrace a woman.

"And now that he is dead, it hurts me to think that my words may have hurt him, though I was nothing and had lost him, and he was everything."

She cried again, her tears running slowly from between her concealing fingers, like the ceaseless dripping that makes stalactites in dark caverns beneath the earth.

Gwydion watched her, coldly and calmly, and as he watched, he changed his shape. Perhaps she felt the metamorphosis. Suddenly she lowered her hands again and looked up. And as she looked she gave a shriek.

"You—*you*—are the Lord Gwydion—Gwydion the son of Dôn?"

"I am Gwydion ap Dôn," he answered. "Do you fear me then?"

She shrank a moment, peering at him wide-eyed, then, of a sudden, threw her head back like an upward-shooting flame. "No, I do not! What is there left for me to fear from your anger, or any other thing? Blast me if you will because I mocked him. Kill me, and send my soul out to seek his. I could find him, if I were dead and free, no matter how far he had been blown! There is that in me that would know and be drawn to him, though all the worlds were between!"

Gwydion said slowly, ponderingly, more to himself than to her: "You think that this desire of yours for him would last when you were out of the body then? That it goes so deep as that?"

"I know it!" she flamed. "I could not get him while he was alive, but now he is mine to weep for, since she will not weep, who killed him. I am flesh, not flowers!"

"You are woman," said Gwydion, "and it is right that some woman should weep for a man. I thought awhile of harming you, but I cannot harm faithfulness to him. I will save my vengeance for her who was less than woman."

She was looking up at him eagerly from out the bright shower of her hair. "Do you not think it might be a good idea," she breathed hopefully, "to kill me and send me out to find him?"

But Gwydion was changing. His form was wavering and quivering there in the dimness of the advancing twilight. It seemed to melt and spread and toss itself upwards like spray, then to darken and condense and swirl downwards again, as another shape quivered into being. He stood before her once more in the guise of the bard who had first looked down upon her.

He answered her. "No," he said, "I do not. Some day I may find a better use for you, child. Who knows?"

And he was gone, striding away into the twilight.

She looked after him until blackness rose and covered sea and sky.

The time of Y Calan, in mid-winter, found Gwydion in Arvon. Not far from him were the usurped lands of Eivionydd, part of Llew's Cantrev, where Goronwy still reigned in gloating peace, and enjoyed Blodeuwedd, and perhaps laughed to think of his victim dead and those great magicians, his dreaded kin, befooled.

But Gwydion was untroubled by the thought of Goronwy's laughter. Goronwy could wait. There was no longer room in the heir of Mâth but for one longing, one purpose. In his desire to save he had risen above revenge; though the time might yet come when he would turn back and deliberately bathe himself in those fumes of malice that his wisdom now forswore.

Only for a little had their red stream touched his soul when that weeping girl had told how she had taunted Llew. Yet they had died away as quickly before the sense of kinship. She, and she alone, shared the fullness of his grief. Even Mâth could not, for Mâth's love for Gwydion was a barrier between himself and the full desolateness that Gwydion knew.

He had only his quest, and it a quest without guide, without road.

Hardest of all it must have been for him there in Arvon, where once he had counseled Mâth and his chiefs to await Pryderi and the Southern hosts. He walked in a memoried land whose men had died and whose fields had been blood-soaked for his sake. And it seemed to him that a shadow and a stench still hung over them, a boding omen of ill. In the red dusks of winter sunsets, and in the later darkness, he could sense again the hate of Pryderi, hear again, like faint, far echoes, those screams of men whose flesh swords and spears had torn. . . .

He wandered through that scene of his ancient crimes, as much a ghost as any of those floating shells of men that drifted about their death-places, robbed now himself of what he had treasured far more than ever Pryderi had the stolen swine of Annwn. And he thought: *"Is this somehow fitting? Was it to be?"*

He thought: "Something will happen here. Something. I know not what. Will it be for good or ill? Is it Pryderi's malice that he left behind him, like a fire still burning on a lonely hearth, that guides it, breaking out at last? For I can feel it, this happening, shaping in the womb of destiny."

He drew near Maenor Penardd, one of those two Maenors between which the host of Mâth had taken its stand to wait for Pryderi. He came to a house near Maenor Penardd, and stopped.

The woman of the house made him welcome, and perhaps not only because he was a bard. For in women there was always a welcome for Gwydion. Goewyn is the one woman we have record of that ever misliked a son of Dôn. There was magic in Gwydion and sorrow on him, and both of these qualities are irresistible to women. This one may have fallen into a waking dream of him, and may even have dared inquire what the matter was.

"Good poet," she said, "is it a woman that has caused you woe?"

Gwydion had not looked at her. He had only seen that she was there. Her voice in his ears meant no more to him than the buzzing of a fly. Less, for a fly might have been Llew. Yet courtesy made him look and answer now:

A woman indeed," he said; "two."

"Oh," she said, "two at the one time?" And she looked at him with admiration for such virility.

He thought of Arianrhod and Blodeuwedd, and laughed bitterly.

"Two indeed," he said.

"I would like well to be the third," she said, "and it is not woe I would give you either."

"Are you free to do this?" asked Gwydion.

"I am married to the man of the house here," she answered, "but I am a decent, old-fashioned body with no great nose to smell harm."

"That much is plain," Gwydion said courteously, "or, rather, handsome. You have a very shapely nose. And I thank you, but I have journeyed far, and I do not feel well enough for love today."

He was glad of the excuse, for he had no mind to spare any energy from his quest, though it was a great lapse of courtesy to reject one's hostess' offer of her bed. And he thought besides of Goronwy and Blodeuwedd. But the lady seemed to eye him coldly after that, and he would have gone on again to pass the night at some other house, but that something seemed to warn him to stay.

That evening the man of the house and his men came home for their meal. Last of all came the swineherd, and Gwydion heard his master question him.

"Well, lad, has the sow come home tonight?"

"She has," the youth answered. "The pigs have this moment begun sucking."

Gwydion had a sudden strange feeling: as though an ear within him rose and pointed, as dogs' ears point when they scent game. Perhaps what had come to him was some blurred picture from the dim little mind of the sow, evoked by her master's and keeper's talk of her. Perhaps it was only another will-o'-the-wisp, one more wild hope among the many that pain and longing give birth to, and each of which is twin with two fears.

But for months will-o'-the-wisps had been his only stars in the trackless night that would know no dawn till the dead came back from death.

And when the man of the house had gone on, satisfied, to his meal, Gwydion stopped by the swineherd and spoke to him. "Where is it that this sow of yours goes?" he asked.

"I do not know," replied the youth, "nor does anybody. Every day she runs out as soon as the sty is opened, and after that none gets a glimpse of her, or knows where she goes, any more than if the earth had opened under her. She does not feed much when or where the other swine do, yet she gets food enough, for she is fat and her pigs are always full."

"Well," said Gwydion, "this is somewhat of a wonder. A disappearing sow. Will you grant me this: to keep the sty shut tomorrow morning until I too am beside it?"

"I will grant it gladly enough," the boy said.

The night deepened and they lay down to sleep, but for all his training in the mastery of the mind, sleep came slowly to Gwydion.

Long he lay listening to the black, noisy silence of the house about him, to the myriad scurryings and creakings and crawlings and rustlings, almost to the light ethereal sound the shadows made, on another plane than this, as the moon set them dancing on the walls.

He heard the breathing of all the people in the house, and he counted these sleepers by the different tunes played by their breathing: here a man with a snore that made a noise like a saw, and there a young girl that snored as daintily as a mouse nibbling bread, and yonder a woman that buzzed like a bee in her sleep. Some breathed quietly but heavily, and others lightly and evenly, and one or two moaned and muttered sometimes, struggling with those troubled fragments of consciousness that we name dreams. Those were the unlucky ones that had not reached whatever place it is that the sound asleep go to: that mystery-world which consciousness shuts from our sight like an iron wall.

He lay there long and he thought. But mostly he felt. Half he longed for the morrow and half he dreaded it. Now horror crept in his veins and now anticipation. And ever that strange sense of an event in labor, in the womb of fate.

He thought: "It is not far from Dinodig here. And Goronwy might not wish what was left of Llew to rest in his own fields, lest the gods or Mâth might smell it, and find out the crime. But where is the rest of Llew? Where?

"Blodeuwedd hid her face when he was murdered; she saw nothing. If Goronwy saw anything that might prove a clew, he is instructed, and has skill enough not to think about it even in his sleep.

"Am I on the track at last? Or is this another failure? Oh gods, let me not fail this time too!"

He lay and listened to the wind howling about the house. It seemed to him that there was strange strength in the wind tonight: that it was rising. It cried as though all the warriors that had died between the Maenors were riding in it, the dead mocking him with Llew's death and his own loss.

And then, suddenly, he fell asleep. . . .

In the dawn, when the first grey gleams of light were beginning to blanch the grimy sky, and the grudging shadows still clung with black arms to the misty earth, the swineherd awoke Gwydion.

He roused slowly. He felt as if he were coming back from faroff, from nebulous darkness and turmoil and storm, up out of deep waters. And the roar of those waters was still in his ears. He had dreamed, and in the dream Arianrhod's voice had been crying to him, and a wall of waves had risen from earth to heaven.

Whence and why had she called him? What had been on her?

But all that passed from him, as mists and darkness pass from a river at morning, as he woke and his mind leaped up flame-like, ablaze for his quest.

He dressed himself and followed the swineherd. They went out into a grey world that was thick with mist, dark with the last reflections of night. Only in the farthest east the dawn showed a livid face, like a sickly woman peering down at the darkness and chill of earth, afraid of what her light might find there.

Gwydion too felt that fear and yet knew it for his hope. . . .

They came to the sty.

Gwydion moved back. He stood silent, draped in his long cloak, that in that half-light left him hardly the semblance of a human figure. A shadow among shadows. Waiting, unmoving, except for the fire in his brain. He had the look of an unnatural thing, of one whose whole thought and goal has for so long been the dead that something of the awfulness of their dim company has come upon him, the cold breath of another world.

The boy glanced at him and shivered, vaguely awed. . . . He remembered suddenly that bards were druids, servants of the goddess Ceridwen, the Dark Queen of the Lake. And might not this man be a magician also? Could it be that the sow was involved in uncanny matters, strange to man? Swine had come originally from Annwn. Could it be there, to Arawn's realm, that she went back each day?

With shaking hands he opened the sty.

The sow ran out swiftly, all but knocking him down with the speed of her emerging. She ran on, with an un-swine-like swiftness, grotesque yet terrible there in the clammy dawn: a great belly with empty teats shaking jelly-like upon four short, tiny legs, her cask-shaped snout thrust forward eagerly, her little red eyes greedy and gleaming above it. . . .

So swiftly was she gone that the swineherd cried out an alarmed warning to the waiter in the shadows. But there was no answer, and, looking, he saw that the man was not there. Rubbing his eyes, he went back, shivering, into the house. . . .

Through the grey mists of the morning the two went silently, the man who had brought swine to Gwynedd following where the sow led.

She ran on without stop or grunt, silent and sure with purpose. Gwydion ap Dôn kept well behind her, so that she should not see him, but he clung to her tracks like her shadow. In his mind there may have moved memories of the time when he had been her counterpart, not her shadow: of the days when Mâth had put that shape upon him, and he too had foraged in the frosty mornings, while the hungry little pig waited in the warm lair.

By that experience he read her small, set mind more surely, its naturalness lessening the horror of what he might see. . . .

The mists dissolved. The sun came up, marching redly through the sky, above the bare brown trees and the frozen fields that lay hard packed as stone.

And still the man and the sow went on, bound on their lonely quest. . . .

They were against the course of a river, and Gwydion gave the sow a greater lead now that the sun was up. Yet ever he kept his eyes glued upon her, unswerving. . . . She did not know that she was followed. She turned at last, and went towards a brook. She stopped there under an oak, and bent her head, in a gesture hideously eloquent. . . .

Gwydion knew that she was feeding. He came forward boldly now, and she paid no attention to him, absorbed in her greed.

Gwydion looked, and saw what it was that the sow fed on: knew that Pryderi was at last avenged. . . .

He looked and leaned against the tree, and for a little space there swung inside his head a blackness through which the bell was tolling: *"May swine eat your flesh, and vermin help them!"*

Not his own body, but his own flesh. . . .

The curse of Pryderi was fulfilled at last.

"Yet I spared your son, Pryderi. I gave no death to him that had not striven against me. Though I risked his malice, and that the fire within him might break out and burn Gwynedd, I let him go. I sent him back to Dyved of the South in peace. I showed you that much mercy, Pryderi. Could you not have shown as much to me?"

He leaned against the great oak, and at his feet the sow guzzled, gnawing her grisly meal. The hard bright winter morning shone about them; the sky gleamed pale and pitiless as steel. Beside the icy brook, on an earth of snow and iron, man and beast seemed like specks, lost on the harsh wastes of destiny.

Through the man's mind horror and weakness moved slowly, dull tides like the colorless mists of morning, gradually unveiling the eternal peaks: a point of white light above the grey bleakness of the universe.

The old fire of movement stirred in him—that which had always characterized the heir of Mâth.

"It is not you that have done this, Pryderi. You have gone on, far on, beyond both Gwynedd and the South. It is the blind hate you have left behind you, to roam the world like a wind. But I who still walk this world a living man, shall I not be stronger than an emptied and soulless hate? Shall I let my quest end where it should begin?"

He looked up slowly, his eyes seeking that point of white light as though it had been a physical thing. Up and up, through height upon height of the oak, through great branches and branches that grew even lighter, smaller, towards that faded sky. . . .

And on the topmost bough he saw an eagle sitting, huddled among its draggled plumage, there beneath the sun.

He had been long among the treetops. So long that he had forgotten what the face of the earth looked like.

He had sat there when the trees were leafy, a quivering infinity of leaves, vast as the sea and rippling like the sea. Wave upon wave of leaves. . . .

He had sat there when the gales blew and the leaves fell; and the stripped, naked boughs had shivered, and he had shivered with them, cold, cold as if he would never be warm again, except for the one spot of ceaseless fire in his side where the Thing was.

He had forgotten that its name was spear-head. He knew it only as the Hurting Thing.

Vaguely he knew that he had not always lived in the treetops. Once he had lived somewhere else, in a place altogether different, where there was laughter and noise and happiness. There had been others with him there; he had not been alone. But he could remember nothing more. He did not care to try.

He had been long alone now. There was nothing with him except pain and the Hurting Thing. He could not remember what it was like not to feel pain, to be well and strong. First it had been fierce pain, as though the Thing had been a tooth gnawing him: as the beasts of the forest would gnaw him some day when he finally grew too weak to fly or cling to the bough with his claws, and fell. . . .

Sometimes it had been an agony that crept through his veins like fire, and filled all of him with that raging, racking anguish. . . . And now it had subsided into a dull burning ache that never gave him rest and never flamed: an apathy that robbed him of all ambition—even the wish to die.

Pain, pain. For long it had filled the whole compass of his shrunken, blurred mind. And now weariness was greater even than pain. He could not even wish to be out of his pain. Only to sit there without moving forever. . . .

He was sick, so sick that his flesh sloughed off him and fell to the bottom of the tree. But he never looked at the ground below or at the sky above him. He did not look at anything. All the world was a dimness in which nothing mattered but the solid branch he could feel beneath him. He would have been frightened by any swaying of that, by any need to exert his will to move his feeble wings and fly to another branch.

There was something under the tree.

There was a sound. A voice was singing there, rolling up wild and sweet, even to where he perched.

It had words, and he understood them, in some vague way that he could not understand.

> Between two lakes an oak grows-
> Dark it spreads over sky and glen.
> If I speak not untruth,
> Here lie the members of Llew.

Llew! Llew! The name rang through his consciousness strangely. It meant himself. It was himself. It was calling him. And when it called him he should come. That was, somehow, the Law.

Must he move? Must he lift his wings and stir from his one poor uncomfortable bit of peace? Was it wise to? Bird-nature whispered: Is this somehow a peril, a snare?

He came down slowly, very slowly, to the middle of the tree. Surely no harm could come to him there.

The stop, the rest, was blessed after the agony of movement, an unutterable relief. . . .

He saw the singer now. It was a man at the foot of the tree, and the man had never been there before, yet he was not strange. He was somehow as familiar as the treetops, as anciently known.

And the sound was not frightening, not a noise. It was gentler than dew, it had the wailing softness of great waters, it ached with a tender, piercing beauty like the understanding of all pain.

> In high ground an oak grows—
> Rain cannot melt it nor heat blast it.
> Ninescore the pangs, ninescore the throes,
> Borne in its branches by Llew Llaw Gyffes.

Llaw Gyffes! Llaw Gyffes! That too was himself. It had been he, long ago, before he was hurt. And it was the man down there that was calling him, calling him down to him. . . .

A rush of unremembered memories surged through him. His poor, dim bird's brain reeled before all these memories that it could never grasp or understand.

This man was someone who loved him. Yet there could be no friendship between birds and men. His tired feathered head battled with these two irreconcilable and indisputable facts. Each seemed to make the other impossible, and neither could.

There were bonds upon him, and they fought each other: the man below laid them on him; and nature, that told him he must beware of men.

He fluttered down to the lowest branch of the tree; stopped there. He could fly up again before any hand could touch him.

Gwydion threw back his head and sang again. His voice coaxed as calmly, as unanxiously as the spring sun calling forth the flower seeds from their dark frozen sleep within the earth, as intimately as a mother calling a scared child.

> Below the slope an oak grows—
> A fair hit it was for me to see him—
> If I speak not untruth,
> Llew will come to my lap.

That was the last of the three Englyns that Gwydion sang at Nant y Llew.

On the bough the eagle had listened, his yellow eyes never wavering from the man.

He seemed to shiver in his plumage.

All his bird's wildness cried out against the thought of human hands upon him. And deep within something whispered that many a time before he had gone to those hands. And he had been glad of their touch and unafraid.

He could not, yet he must. He would not, yet, with all his weary being, he longed to.

A voice that he had been wont to obey was calling him. The old love and the old authority were streaming out towards him, enfolding and warm and strong. The one support that in all his life had never failed him; the one safe, fair island, blooming steadily and faithfully in treacherous, shifting seas. . . .

He flew downward; he lit on Gwydion's knee. And in that moment, when his heart leaped at the terror of relinquishing the trees forever, an arm went round him. He saw a wand rise and, before he could flop free, felt it fall. . . . He was whirling, whirling.

. . . All his being swirled apart, into pieces and back together again, re-forming as they swirled. His brain, shaking and expanding, was rocked by a convulsion no less fearful than that which held his body.

He and something on the ground were merging into one: they were a man. He was a man. He felt inexpressibly weak. He felt ill and sore, and as if all things were strangely amiss with him.

But Gwydion's arms were strong and warm around him. Gwydion's eyes were looking down, with anxious tenderness, into his. And he knew them and smiled. . . . Then something whirled him off into the dark. . . .

8

The Hosting of Gwynedd

NIGHT LAY LIKE death upon the world. From her seat in the clouds the moon smiled wanly down, silvering the earth.

. . . The sense of movement, of swaying. Something was swaying beneath him, as sometimes his bough in the treetop did, only more softly, more gently. There was no sound of wind or storm. He lay still and for a while was conscious of nothing but that swaying. His mind floated in dark mists: a hazy passive thing alighting nowhere. There was pain in the background, but there was always pain.

Yet he became aware at last that tonight was somehow different from all other nights. He did not know how; he did not wish to make the effort to think how. Yet slowly, as the night wore, wonder began to sharpen his dim consciousness as a man might sharpen a rusty blade.

The moon and the sky were farther off than they had been; they seemed to have risen higher. Walls, heights, of vague dark shapes, loomed between them and him. Why did not his claws still clutch the bough? Why and on what did he rest here, holding to nothing, supported by no kind of support he knew of in the world? He reached out involuntarily, and it was no claws that obeyed him, but utterly unknown members. . . . It dawned upon him then, a sudden great shock: he had no claws; he was not a bird.

He was a man.

And the naturalness of that rushed over him, and at the same time, strangely and vividly, all the memories of his days as a wounded eagle in the treetops. He felt as if he were two beings; and he struggled frantically to gather all of himself together, to pour himself into the one mold, lest he be dismembered forever.

He remembered his life as Llew. He remembered Gwydion and white-bearded, stately Mâth the Ancient in his halls at Caer Dathyl. He remembered the three curses of Arianrhod. He remembered Blodeuwedd, as one remembers the perfume and brightness of an old garden, seen on a summer day long ago.

He was Llew and he had been a bird. How could that be?

He lay puzzling and there drifted through his mind the old tale of Gwydion and Gilvaethwy: of how they had wandered for three years as beasts of the forests. He lay and tried to remember; but he could not weave his thoughts together any more than he could have plucked floating thistledown from the air and have woven it into a web. Only, in and out of his efforts to remember, there flashed dimly, yet in a dreadful light, the memory of a bath built near the hill Bryn Kyvergyr. . . .

There was a quicker sound of horse's hoofs. A man on horseback rode up, stopped to look down at him. He saw the moonblanched face of Gwydion, tense and anxious, a sharp white outline against the night. Llew tried to stir, but his hand was too great a weight for him to lift. He spoke, but the words stumbled in his mouth as though it were not yet entirely his again.

"Lord," he whispered, "Lord, I cannot remember. . . . I know that the form of a bird was put on me, but not . . . how or why. Was it you who put it on me, Lord? Had I done some . . . evil . . . that I . . . do not . . . remember? Tell me . . . what has happened. All is dim around me. I cannot think; I cannot . . . remember."

"Lie you still," said Gwydion. His eyes were looking into Llew's. His hand, that was laid on Llew's, was light and tender as a woman's, yet heavy as though all the weight of the world were in it, pressing him back into the sweet, dark cloudlands, the vast, unmeasured sea of sleep. . . .

"Lie you still, and do not try to think. I did not transform you, though there are others that it may be I will transform. There has been a black enchantment practiced against you, and that largely through your own foolishness. Now is no time for the telling; we ride now to Caer Dathyl. Sleep, and do not try to remember."

Sleep. . . . Gwydion's eyes were strangely bright in the night. They were bright as two torches. They were brighter than the far-off moon. They crept into him like the warmth of a hearthfire, making him drowsy, bidding him sleep. He had a feeling that somewhere near, waiting for his attention, was a calamity, a monstrous shadow yawning. But it could not come here, under Gwydion's eyes and Gwydion's hand. All was well with the world again, as it had been in his childhood, when terrors and night dreams passed, and he was safe under the shadow of Gwydion's might, Gwydion's love. . . .

Llew slept, and Gwydion rode beside him, under the unwinking stars. He thought: "Not now can I let him learn of Blodeuwedd. It might raise a fever that would blow him forth and drive him beyond the ken of men again; and all the quest would be to do over, and all that is gained lost. I have found him and I will keep him."

He looked at the stars and thought of that night when he had read them long ago, and of the weary nights when he had searched them, all in vain, during the quest.

"He has suffered that which was written, and I have redeemed him from your doom. Write well for him now, oh stars. He has one more thing to bear. Let him not learn it too soon."

Day came and darkness: dreams that now were bright and now seemed to float, unrealities among the unreal, upon the black breast of night. . . . Llew had been carried upon a litter of plaited twigs, covered with rushes and hung between two horses' backs, and now he lay upon a bed, but he did not heed the change. Sometimes he heard voices, and sometimes he saw faces, drifting through the mists of his consciousness as the white shapes of fog float through the misty moors.

All the druids and leeches of Gwynedd were gathered about his bedside. In the palace was the sound of chanting and prayer. Women wept and men strode about with lowering gloomy faces. And sometimes they shook knotted, weaponed fists toward Ardudwy, where Goronwy dwelt with Blodeuwedd.

For frightful were the wounds of Llew. He who had been the comeliest among the men of Gwynedd was now the most miserable-looking in the world; and it is said that there was no flesh left on his bones. They let no maidens see him, nor any but the doctors and druids; and these may have shaken their heads despairingly over that mangled and decayed body in which only Gwydion's will and magic still held the soul and flame of life.

There may have been days when hope wavered, fluttering into nothingness like a torch before the wind. Days when it seemed that miracle had been wrought in vain, and the dead brought back to a body too wrecked to be habitable.

Days when all but Gwydion would have given up. . . .

Nor do we know what charms they used to make new flesh grow where earlier flesh had rotted, what spells of unknown power and might may have gone into Llew's reshaping, as Mâth and Gwydion helped the leeches.

Llew's death and return, and what happened to him between, are alike mysteries, beyond our logic's solving.

But the day came when the body that lay upon the bed was a whole, if wasted one, when all the gaping wounds were closed and the blood of life flowed through the quickening flesh that was no longer festered, no longer poisoned.

Llew woke, and no longer slept or dreamed. He looked at the sun where its light entered the window, and he relished the food that was brought him. For a few days that contented him. Then he asked of his realm and of Blodeuwedd.

"Goronwy Pevr holds your lands," Gwydion told him, "the man that thinks himself your slayer. He has some knowledge of a low kind. He learned the means to effect your death and he thought to rule in your stead."

"But how could he learn them?" Llew burst out. "I told no one. None save—" He stopped, and his jaw fell. He remembered with horror that Blodeuwedd had asked him to go to the bath. Yet between her innocent curiosity and this plotting enemy there could be no link. It was sacrilege to think it.

"You told what should never have been uttered, even in thought," said Gwydion. "Once, and once only, since I must, did I ever speak of it to you—the secret that you should have guarded with your life, because it was your life. Did you not think that other ears than hers might hear it?"

And he waited, wincing, for the look that he thought would come upon the boy's face. But Llew raised himself in the bed. Fear blanched his face, sweeping over it like a wintry gale. But not the fear that Gwydion had thought to see: not unwilling understanding.

"But Blodeuwedd, my wife?" there was agonized solicitude in the cry— "where is she? If this man has seized my land and my folk, what has become of her? Has he got her also—my wife? Have you let him keep *her* there with him—suffered this—that he should force her—" Gwydion turned his face away.

"He did not have to force her. . . ." he said.

Llew said little for days after that. He lay and stared at the blank walls as though he saw pictures there and on his face there was a white brooding, bleak as wintry mountains, though now all earth was dressed for the festival of spring.

Again he had been betrayed by a woman, and for the last time. For now he was cut off from all women forever.

And he wondered if there was something in himself that made him hateful to women. He had never found favor in the eyes of any, even of the woman who had borne him, though through all his boyhood he dreamed of her, shyly, secretly. And Blodeuwedd had loved better than him the first stranger that came to their gates in his absence. All their days together that to him had been the glory of the world had been to her as nothing. For that other's sake she had led him out, as one leads out a beast to the butcher.

Blodeuwedd! Blodeuwedd! The name of her cried itself through all his being, fierce as the wound in his side had been, intolerable in its ache of loss and longing.

Yet aloud he named it never again.

He wished that she had died before Goronwy came to Dinodig. Not because he would have been spared Goronwy's spear, but because he would never truly have known her. Hardest of all to know that one's love has never lived, has been but a dream one's own heart built around a fair, empty face.

Not empty; for she had loved Goronwy.

And a flame leaped up within him. "Her I do not wish to see again, in this world or another, but him I will see. Him I long to see. Goronwy! Goronwy Pevr!"

His heart cried that name as ardently as once Blodeuwedd's had cried it: *"Goronwy! Goronwy Pevr!"*

Spring bloomed into summer and flowers trooped over the fields. The green corn grew tall, rippling like pleasant, stormless seas beneath the breezes. Plenty smiled on the land of the sons of Dôn.

And Llew grew stronger, and the fire within him waxed as flesh and sinews knit more firmly and the muscles swelled and hardened again on his chest and arms. But his face was carved in different lines than it had been in the old days when he was the young Lord of Dinodig, or when he had first awakened in this bed at Caer Dathyl. His eyes looked older, and his sensitive lips had a grimness that was the end of youth. Stern they had been sometimes of old in the judgment seat at Dinodig, but sorry to be so, if unswerving. Now they had no wish to swerve. They were like metal forged in the heat of a mighty fire.

His return was not noised abroad in the land. Mâth and Gwydion had kept it secret, but there was a restlessness among the folk: a stirring. Men sharpened and polished their weapons, and Govannon toiled day and night in his forge. And some said that the sons of Dôn meant at last to march in vengeance against Goronwy.

But the harvest ripened and was gathered. The forests flamed with red and gold, summer's funeral pyre. Frost nipped and whitened the brown fields. The winds of winter began to blow in coldly, like airy spears, from the grey sea.

Llew had left his bed. Sometimes towards sunset he walked abroad, covering his face with a fold of his cloak if any that might know him drew near. He waited with a strange patience, that in no wise suggested apathy, for his body's full mending.

And Gwydion stayed at Caer Dathyl and exercised his office of Controller of the Household there. Not yet had he gone, even for a day's length, to Dinas Dinllev and his own coasts, where at tide's ebb showed the grey rock that had once been Caer Arianrhod, proud and beautiful between sky and sea.

Once, and once only, he spoke of his sister to Mâth. "You who know all things, could you not have saved her, Lord? Have kept her from unleashing the forces of the sea?"

"I tried," said Mâth the son of Mathonwy, "but none can save a man or woman until he or she wishes to be saved. That is the law with all things: that none can kindle wet wood to flame till the day when the drying sun shall reach it."

"Then you could not reach her, Lord?"

"Arianrhod had chosen," said Mâth, "and she would not turn from her choice. She had come to the end of that road: she had done more evil than she could endure and she would not do good. She had become the slave of her own will that in turn was enslaved by her malice. For her the death of Dylan was the end, however many years she might have lived after it. And it was better for her to pass elsewhere awhile than to do more ills, incurring more debts, in the frenzy that consumed her."

"Yet you tried to warn her?" asked Gwydion.

"I did warn her," answered Mâth. "I gave her the chance to save herself if she still could take it. She died the death her life cried out for, because no lesser medicine could have purged it."

". . . And her servants and sorcerers, too?" Gwydion asked at last. "Was it not incurring another debt to make them share that fate?"

"They had their chance to go with Elen and Maelan and Gwennan," said Mâth. "They stayed behind to do the will of Arianrhod. On them too had fallen the pride and lure of her sorceries, and the shock of death freed them quickly and simply from that snare, before they had time to become more deeply entangled, as she is and will be, through her lust of forbidden power."

Gwydion thought of his sister, who had held herself too high to fashion life, and had fashioned death for herself and many, and beside that lost face of beauty there drifted the faces of Llew, and of golden Dylan, and, last of all, bearded Govannon's.

Mâth spoke as though he too had seen.

"Malice is a two-edged sword," he said, "as Govannon learned when he let it blind him so that he would not look at Dylan rising from the sea. Had he looked he would have known that it was not Goronwy who came so."

Gwydion said: "Is it your thought that I need warning against malice now, uncle?"

"Do you not ever need it?" said the son of Mathonwy. "You who are forever swinging between the upper and the lower roads?"

And at that time they said no more. . . .

Winter whitened the world.

The time of Y Calan drew near and Llew came before Mâth the son of Mathonwy, where he lay as of old on his couch-throne. Straight and splendid the Prince looked as he stood before his granduncle. A cloak red as blood was on him, and a great sword of the new moon-bright metal called steel, that Govannon had sent him from the forge at the mouth of the Conwy. A collar of red gold with the ends fashioned into the shape of little shields was about his neck, under the yellow flame of his hair. And his face was set with a new resolve.

"Lord," he said, "the time is come for me to have atonement of him that wrought me all this woe."

Mâth looked long at him.

"Indeed," he said, "never will Goronwy be able to keep that to which you have a right."

Llew flinched at that, as though some hidden meaning had barbed it, then flushed. He looked like heat lightning, ready to burst through the black clouds of storm. "Well," he said, "the quicker I get my rights, the better I shall like it."

So the word of hosting went forth, and trumpets sounded it through the land. Like swarming bees or homing birds flying northward in spring the men of Gwynedd answered. From every Cymwd and every Cantrev they came. The earth was black with them, hastening toward Caer Dathyl.

Never since before the birth of Llew Llaw Gyffes had there been so great a hosting in the land.

And on the eve of Y Calan, when all the host was gathered, and the druids lit fires and chanted songs to keep off the Dark Powers that roam loosed upon our world on the nights of the changes of the seasons, Llew showed himself in the doorway of the palace, with

Mâth and Gwydion on either side of him. And the host rejoiced with a mighty shouting as they saw their Prince come back from the dead.

There was feasting that night, and mirth, and all praised the mightiness of Gwydion, that had been able to make even death disgorge his swallowed prey.

"We will make another bath for you, Lord," they said to Llew, "and the water in it will be the blood of Goronwy Pevr."

Llew laughed and thanked them. He laughed and jested through all that night. But in the grey of dawn, when he went to his chamber, there was no sleep with him, as there was with the others. He lay and watched the moon and the stars die and the cold earth pale and shiver in the cheerless morning of winter, and on his face there was the pain of one wound still unhealed.

Land and folk he could win back from Goronwy, but never her. She was not his, she was Goronwy's. She had given her love to Goronwy, and not to him.

And that thought was colder than ice; it was colder than the blasts from the winter sea. He felt lonely and lost as though in an infinite wilderness of ice that nothing could ever thaw or break. More chilled than ever he had been in those dim days in the treetops when winter storms had battered a forlorn bird with sleet and snow.

His heart cried: *Blodeuwedd! Blodeuwedd!*

And knew that that cry must go forever unanswered. That of her nothing was left that was his. . . .

He became aware of a tall shape beside him in the dawn. Gwydion was looking down at him. Llew looked up, not altogether with welcome. He felt the wounded beast's instinct to be alone. "Why do you not sleep?" he demanded. "Is it needful that we both lose our rest?"

"I cannot sleep," said Gwydion gently, "and you in this torment."

Llew pulled at the bearskin he lay on. He gave a short and bitter laugh. "Then will you have to do without sleep long and long," he said.

There was silence for a time.

"Must you sorrow so?" said Gwydion at last. "Mâth and I can make another as fair as she."

"—Who would not be she, or, rather, what I thought her." Llew laughed again, more bitterly than before. "I do not want another. If I did, if I could love again, what would be the use, my uncle? What should I take another wife for? To watch and spy on lest she prefer another man to me? To wonder, each time I came home, what man she had had while I was gone? Would that be love?"

702   EVANGELINE WALTON

"If you distrust phantom women," said Gwydion, "it might be that a mortal one could be found who would have courage enough to leave her own body and dwell in one that we had fashioned, thus fulfilling the terms of the bond laid upon you, yet bringing you a warm and human heart. There are many women that would be glad to love you."

"Have I found flesh-and-blood women's hearts so warm?" Bitterness was fading in the pain of Llew's laughter now. "Did I so move my own mother's? Or. . ." But he stopped there, for he thought that that alone was yet his one secret that Gwydion did not share. Besides, he remembered that he had never known her name. . . .

And he thought of the beauty and sweetness of women as of a garden whose gates were barred against him forever. Blodeuwedd had been his one and his last chance, and she had failed him utterly. And he had no longer the heart to stake it on the throw again. . . .

Nor could he. There was but one woman he thought of, one woman he longed for.

Gwydion, watching him, thought: "This is marriage: This yearning after one woman, or one man, so that all others are like dry bones after meat, and being unable to escape from him or her. So that though one flee in the body the mind and heart will carry along the image of the other howsoever far one goes. . . . The wedding feast or lack of one does not change it. How many people will ever be really married, even when all seem to marry?

"Marriage—this grieving because of another's dearness to one's own beloved. Perhaps it has been growing in the world for ages, fashioning itself through something in the nature of men and women, and was not, as we thought, merely a device necessary to men's getting of sons. . . . Was I too then married to Arianrhod? Was that the beginning of all this woe?"

He remembered how fixed had been his resolve to make her the mother of his son. With Elen or Gwennan or Maelan he could have dealt; there was no great malice in them. But he had wanted Llew to be hers—hers alone.

He looked at his boy again. And he wondered if, in all the ages, humanity would ever find an answer to the crucifying riddle: how to make painless the love between man and woman when love must die in one heart at a time.

Llew thought: "Will she weep and plead and try to soften me when we meet? How am I to bear it? How deal with her? I am eager to meet Goronwy, but it will be bitter as death to meet her. That the gods know."

A qualm of fear stirred within Gwydion as he read those thoughts. He said aloud: "This is your business, nephew. Yet little of it except Goronwy Pevr will be sweet to your taste. Will you give me leave to go on ahead of you to Mur y Castell, and deal there as I see fit?"

"With . . . her?" Llew rose on one elbow, staring at Gwydion, his face suddenly white in the growing rose of dawn.

"It is too late for her to die," he said presently. "What can her death change now?"

Gwydion's voice rang cold and inexorable through the still chamber: *"Yet has she written her own doom."*

The bearskin tore in Llew's fingers. "So be it. Yet let her not suffer as I did, Lord. Let there be no after-horrors. She was always so beautiful, so tender, so little fit to bear pain. . . . I pray it of you, Lord. Let her not be burned, as the law is, or tortured."

The morning wore and Gwydion came to Mâth.

The old King looked up. "What errand is it you go on, nephew, before the host sets forth?"

"I think that you know," said Gwydion. "It is Blodeuwedd."

Mâth bent his white head and brooded long.

"She has done murder," he said, "and that not for hate or fear, but only to serve her own desires. And that is such a sin as has seldom been known in this land aforetime. Never before has a woman of Gwynedd slain so lightly a man she has loved. But never before have the women of Gwynedd been bound. They have given their love when and where they pleased, as their right was, and there was no need on them to slay yesterday's lover in order to go to today's. For they had granted him their favor, not rendered him his due.

"But now this woman who was bound to one man, yet had not a faithful nature, has contrived his death that she might be free to follow her own instincts. And these are the crimes that shall be the fruit of marriage for ages after we are forgotten. Human nature changes more slowly than human customs." And he sighed. . . .

"What cannot be changed can be destroyed," said Gwydion, thinking only of Blodeuwedd. For that thistledown thing Llew grieved and would not be comforted. For her sake Gwydion had had to leave him, white and brooding in the dawning, to learn at last the bitter lesson of age: his own helplessness to help. From death and wounds he had saved the body; from this pain he could not save the soul. His darling was a man now, no longer a child for whom he could devise a new toy.

Mâth sighed again.

"So men will say too often in ages to come, my nephew. Would you destroy all women? For they are ill property, but sweet comrades. And guile is always their answer to force. You, who lay bonds on them that you do not lay on yourselves, will never get from them the honesty that we of the old time knew. Nor have we been altogether fair to her to whom we gave life for Llew's pleasure, not her own."

"Would not Llew have been any decent woman's pleasure, fair as he is?" Gwydion demanded savagely.

But Mâth was silent, and presently Gwydion answered that silence. "I will not cast her utterly from the stair of evolution," he said, "not if I find in her one sincerity, one truth. But if I do not, then may the hounds of Annwn, that hunt the souls of the dead, be more merciful to her than I!"

He rode forth at noon. From the palace doorway Llew watched him go, this man who had given him life and then dragged him back to life, that in this moment seemed a heavy weariness. Much as he loved Gwydion, in that hour he almost resented those encircling battlements of love that would not let him go when happiness was spoiled and hope dead and the future a mighty loneliness, grey at dusk. . . .

A loneliness in which he could depend on Gwydion alone . . . .

He turned back into the palace, called to men to make his weapons, that were already shining, bright.

Gwydion rode on alone toward Dinodig, going forth, after the fashion of all orthodox gods, to damn the creature that he had fashioned ill. . . .

9

Doom

GORONWY PEVR was out hunting and Blodeuwedd sat alone in her bower. She was embroidering with her maidens, and she may have sung as she worked. She was happy. For over a year now she had been happy, a dweller under a cloudless sky.

Llew was dead and forgotten. At first fears of vengeance may have haunted her, but time had lulled them. Day after day had brightened and faded and still Mâth and Gwydion had learned nothing, done nothing. So had her child's brain come to feel secure, and to laugh in secret at the dread mysterious might that had made her. As the small will laugh, gleefully, in their petty vengeance, when they have fooled those whom they resent for being greater than they. She thought that as today was, so would tomorrow be, and all the days after tomorrow.

To her as she sat there came the palace bard. He was a man of Goronwy's, from Penllyn. Goronwy had not liked Llew's bard, and the man had met with an accident.

It was not customary for this one to enter her bower when she sat with her maidens. But now he did so. He stopped there and looked at her, but he did not greet her. His face was white, even to the lips, and them he licked.

"Lady," he said, "Lady, the son of Dôn is riding hither."

She dropped her embroidery. She had no need to ask him which of the sons of Dôn, yet she did ask, with scared and stumbling lips:

"Gwydion?" she whispered, and that name seemed to her to fall into the room like a shadow, dark and cold. "Gwydion? . . . In what state does he travel? How many are with him? Is it as on a visit of pleasure that he comes?"

And her mind raced and rocked dizzily, trying to think and yet not to think, of all that a visit of Gwydion's might mean, of all that might come of it.

It was a visit. It must be a visit. It must not be anything else. Her mind cried that with stubborn terror, as though by the very force of her wish she could turn back destiny.

She had felt so safe, so sure and happy. There could not be disaster now. She said within herself, louder than she had spoken aloud: *"Does he suspect? Is it to find out that he comes?"*

Her mind flew to the palace cooks, to poisons. They had all learned to fear Goronwy too much by now not to do her bidding, however their hearts might cling to the House of Mâth. The malice that had flared briefly after she first desired Goronwy, had grown under his tutelage, flamed now, fear-kindled. Needful, or unneedful, she would have liked to see Gwydion's death.

All these thoughts in the space of a second, before the man with her had time to open his lips and speak.

"He comes alone, Lady," he said. "There is none with him. But there is a great dust far behind him, as of a whole host. And he is coming very fast."

She caught his arm with fierce, shaking fingers, and shook it. Her teeth chattered. "A host!" she gasped. "You are sure of these things? You are sure that there is a host?"

He looked somberly at the floor. "All Gwynedd has risen," he said. "All Gwynedd is marching against us."

She loosed his arm. She put her hands to her heart that felt as if an arrow of ice had pierced it.

"But how would he know?" she demanded. "Llew my Lord is dead, has been long dead. And only he could have told. They could not know. It must be that they still think it is Llew here—that Mâth is angry and Gwydion brings the army only to frighten Llew, who, he thinks, has been behaving badly, but whom he would never hurt. That is why he rides ahead: to make peace and persuade his nephew to submit and promise betterment. Do you not see?"

But the bard did not look at her. His eyes seemed to have sunk deep into his head, and they were rolling in those recesses, gleaming with fright, as though they would have liked to get behind his skull and hide there. A kind of dreadful awe was in them. Again he licked his pale lips.

"Your Lord is not dead," he said. "He is with the host, and Gwydion ap Dôn rides on before."

She laughed then—laughed wildly and madly, sweet, jeering peal upon peal.

"You are mad," she said. "When Goronwy comes home he shall take off your head for that madness. To frighten me with such a fool's tale!"

But he looked at her, and her laughter was slowly strangled by that look.

"Gwydion ap Dôn brought him back from the dead," he said. "He found the bird into which Llew had passed, and he gave him the form of a man again. Long and long he sought until he found him. He and Mâth have known from the beginning what you have done."

She stared at him, and her face was white as though she looked into an open grave. She shrank back, her hands grasping at the wooden seat.

"They know . . ." she whispered. "Have you learned this by your arts? All bards are druids; I was forgetting that. You know this surely?"

He nodded darkly. "When I heard of the rider and the dust, I used my arts," he said. "I saw. . . ."

"You learned what was in their minds," she whispered. "Did you see . . . aught else?"

"I saw earth and heaven running red with blood," he answered, licking his lips. "Lady, do not ask me more. I cannot tell you more. I cannot remember what I saw. But I will not wait here until the Lord Gwydion comes."

He turned and went out; and she knew that he would not tell her what else it was that he had seen. . . . She heard the sound of his retreating footsteps, and she thought of the sound of horse's hoofs clicking, clicking, swift and purposeful and inexorable, on the way from Caer Dathyl. . . .

Then her scream rent the stillness as flesh is riven by a spear, and all the servants heard it and shuddered, even the grooms outside among the horses. They shuddered and thought it a death scream, or the cry of a witch of the air. . . .

She sprang up and called to her maidens to follow her. She ran to the palace doors, and there they tried to stay her, clinging to her hands and garments.

"What of your Lord, Lady? Would it not be better to send a messenger to warn him, and bide here under his protection, than to run through the land alone?"

But she struggled with them, fought them off. "Let another warn Goronwy! Do you think I will stay here and let Gwydion find me? There is no power on earth that can stop the son of Dôn, now that he knows!"

She ran through the court and out into the fields where once she had seen the stag run, that day when she had first looked upon Goronwy Pew. And all her maidens ran with her, like a herd of frightened deer pursued by invisible dogs. . . .

They came to the river Cynvael, and they forded it. They passed through it without pausing, and ran on. Their wet clothes clung to them, and the wind whipped their dripping hair.

The sun was westering. The mountain beyond the Cynvael loomed up before them, black against the brilliant sky. A shadow, whose darkness might be protection, seemed to beckon Blodeuwedd home. . . .

On that mountain there was a fortress that a few men could hold against hundreds: the greatest stronghold of Dinodig. Goronwy had garrisoned it with men brought, in the role of hired mercenaries, from Penllyn. Men he thought that he could trust. Some of them may have been druids, his own instructors in the black art.

Blodeuwedd thought: "If I can only reach there, I shall be hidden, I shall be safe for a little while. Those there can protect me. Not even with his magic can Gwydion easily pass those walls. And if Goronwy comes with his men we will be able to stand a long siege."

But it was not Goronwy that she wanted, only the protection of his fighting-arm.

They were climbing the mountain. They were struggling along steep, rocky slopes under the dark and frowning cliffs.

Blodeuwedd said pantingly to a girl that ran beside her: "It would be hard for a horse to come this way. But it may not be a mortal horse he rides, but one of his creatures of magic. . . ." And she shivered at the thought.

"Or he may dismount from his horse," the girl whispered back, "and make himself invisible, and come up behind us unseen. . . ."

Blodeuwedd shrieked at that and turned and struck her, so that she fell and tumbled down among her comrades.

But after that they all ran faster.

They thought of all the mysterious horrors that a magician might inflict as punishment: of their souls wandering lost and helpless on the bleak spaces of the upper winds, perhaps pursued by the slavering white hounds of Annwn, whose teeth tear the souls of the wicked dead. They thought of transformations, and strange and uncomfortable shapes, of creeping insects and hopping toads. Could he even blow their spirits off the world itself, off the wheel of life forever, into the dark . . .?

They fled the faster, but such fear was on them that they could not watch for their destination and kept continually peering backward into the gathering shadows. . . . The shoulders of the mountain hid the setting sun. It grew even darker where they were. The looming cliffs scowled down more ominously, in their strange, impersonal hate of human life.

The women on the mountain side were no longer women. They were only so many terrors, scrambling and scrabbling up the steep way, each one a quivering, quaking fear.

One of them cried out, "I see him!" and the others, looking, could not be sure whether it was a shadow or a man that moved below them, in the shelter of the rock. . . .

They went on, but now they were so afraid that they walked as though their heads were screwed on backwards, their faces glued to the shadows behind them.

Later they saw him in a patch of late sunlight beneath them, the tall shape in the green cloak, in its hand the awful wand of wonder. . . . They knew him, recognized his face beyond all mistaking: the dread that drove them made visible, their fear given flesh and form.

Then the rocks swallowed him up. But from time to time after that they saw him. . . .

They climbed the mountain, and he climbed the mountain, advancing steadily, inexorably as fate.

He gained upon them very slowly, yet ever, inch by inch, that little gain was constantly increasing. Each time they saw him, he was a little nearer.

Blodeuwedd cried: "It is his phantom that he sends on before him to frighten us! It may not be himself at all!"

But she redoubled her speed that she might reach the fortress sooner, and the others did likewise.

The way was hard and they needed their eyes as well as their hands and feet. But they could not look before them. They still stared backwards as they climbed, their eyes searching for their pursuer.

A lake gleamed somewhere below them, like a dark jewel in the lavender light of dusk.

One of the women slipped and fell into it. Her companions did not notice her fall. Their eyes were not for what lay beside or ahead of them.

Another lost her footing and rolled down the mountain side, whirling like a dropped stone until the lake engulfed her. . . . But she had shrieked and the others had heard her. After that the scramble was madder, wilder than before, but still they could not tear their eyes away from the way they had come.

One by one they fell and the dark waters closed over them. . . .

And that is the lake that is called LLyn y Morwynion, Lake of the Maidens.

Blodeuwedd looked about her. The last of her companions was gone. She was alone.

Not until now had those scattered deaths disturbed her. All her thought had been for her own steps, her own peril. Yet entire loneliness, entire isolation, filled her with a kind of horror. So blank and vast, so unfriendly, was the world about her: the redstained sky that peered down at her, the shafts of red light that speared the thickening purple gloom among the rocks through which she toiled, the high cliffs that frowned down upon her struggle.

In all that bleak unhelping world there was nothing animate save herself and that silent figure far below, yet drawing ever nearer. . . .

She spurred her tired feet, her laboring lungs, to fresh effort. But she could not shake him off. . . .

She was growing very weary. The red light and the black shadows mingled oddly, flashing and blurring before her sight. The dusk grew ever deeper. She felt as though she were walking into the very arms of darkness, out of the world of light and joy and human warmth forever. Never again would she see Goronwy. Never again would a friendly voice speak to her, or a lover's hand touch her.

How much farther could it be to the fortress? How much farther?

Night was closing down upon her. Soon she would be alone in the dark and the cold, and all her life she had feared aloneness above all else. She could have wept and wrung her hands for pity of herself, but that she had not strength left to spare.

Never would Llew have doomed her to this. He had loved her. She could have wept and groveled before him, and he would never have been able to hurt her. But Gwydion had come on alone and ahead to forestall that: Gwydion, who would be merciless.

To Mâth's high calm or Llew's love she might have appealed. But with Gwydion there could be no appeal. His love for Llew would make him terrible. And what might not his powers to deal out terror be?

He was not a man, who pursued her up the mountain. He was the God who had made her, and Whose design in shaping her she had thwarted: her angry Maker, who could perhaps un-make her. . . .

And he was there behind her, coming nearer.

How much farther? Ah, gods, how long?

Why had Goronwy ever had to come to Dinodig? Why could he

not have left her in peace, satisfied with Llew? Then she would still have been safe and happy, not here exhausted on a mountain side, with the cold and the dark and Gwydion closing in upon her.

She did not wonder where Goronwy was, or what was happening to him now. All her desire for him was dead: drowned in the tide of anxiety for herself.

Would she ever see the fortress, looming near the mountain's crest? Would darkness fall and make her unable to see it when she reached it? Or could Gwydion be making illusions of cliffs, veiling it from her eyes?

The thought clutched her like an icy hand, and a thin wail rang between the mountain walls.

But she dared not give up to despair. She ran on, stumbling, every breath a sob.

. . . He was only twelve feet behind her. She dared not look back lest his eyes seize hers and chain her. Her straining gaze searched the gloom before her for the place of her refuge, but it was not there.

He was only a man's length behind her now—a short man's length—a woman's length—a child's. . . .

He was beside her.

She dropped to her knees then; they could no longer uphold her. She covered her face with her hands to shut out those piercing grey eyes she dared not meet, but their brilliance seemed to burn through hands and face, into her brain. . . . Her tongue was stiff within her mouth. It could not shape the frantic lies and excuses that she tried to pour out, yet knew would never be believed.

She dared not look at what was in his hand. Was it already poised above her, the weapon that would end her world? The lightning-flash of a remembered blow. . . . Her soul moaned in sickness: *"Bryn Kyvergyr! . . . Bryn Kyvergyr. . . ."*

She could only crouch there, waiting. . . .

Long Gwydion looked down upon the fair form he had fashioned. His face was set and stern as a head carved in stone, but his eyes were sad and weary. Not happily can an artist destroy his own masterpiece or a poet burn his own poem, though the lovely thought he meant to mirror there may have escaped it.

Clear as glass her mind lay before him, the light, empty thing void of thought or meaning, all the regret without repentance, the lust extinguished by the chill of fear. Even that one tie that bound her to the race of women had not endured. Even Goronwy was forgotten, lost in her fear for herself.

And he knew that she too was a child he had got with

Arianrhod—the offspring of Arianrhod's curse as surely as Llew was the offspring of her body. Defeated, Arianrhod had defeated both Mâth and him. It was the mirror of her malice, not of his own love, that bowed here, before the stroke he would never have dealt herself. . . .

He looked down at Blodeuwedd where she crouched shivering like a creature sinking into shadows from which there was no return.

He raised his arm.

"I will not deal you an ordinary death," he said. "I will do to you that which is worse. For I shall send you forth in the shape of a bird. And for the sake of the shame that you have wrought Llew Llaw Gyffes you shall never again show your face under the sun. It shall be the nature of all other birds to hate you and drive you from wherever they find you. And you shall not lose your name, but shall be called Blodeuwedd* forever."

His arm fell. . . .

So she became an owl, and flew away to hide in the dark. And she will hide there till the world ends.

*The Mabinogi states that the owl has ever since been called Blodeuwedd, or the Flower-Like, in Wales.

10

Llech Goronwy

GORONWY PEVR retreated to Penllyn. Nor did he stand upon the order of his going.

From there he sent ambassadors that asked Llew Llaw Gyffes would he take land or lordship, gold or silver, in atonement for the wrong that he had suffered.

Llew listened to them where he sat his war-horse, Melyngan Gamre, "the Steed of the Yellow-white Footsteps"; and his face while he listened was unchanging, hard and bright and beautiful as a sword.

"I will take none of them, by all the gods," he said. "Not one of these nothings that you have named. These are the gentlest terms on which I will make peace with him: that he come and stand where I stood when he threw the spear at me, while I stand where he stood and cast a spear at him. And this is the least atonement that I will accept from him."

They took that word to Goronwy Pevr, where he waited upon the borders of Penllyn. He sat among his men, with a naked sword on his knees, but his face grew grey and his eyes dull as burnt-out coals while he listened.

He thought of battle; but he knew that his men were not many enough to stand against the whole host of Gwynedd, that Gwydion could reinforce at need by turning trees and sedges into men.

He thought of flight; but he knew that nowhere on earth could he hide beyond the power of Mâth and Gwydion to track him down.

He must take the terms of Llew or whatever worse things the magic and the malice of the mighty could devise. And his imagination could not face what these might be. . . .

He moistened his lips and looked around upon the faces that ringed him in, waiting. They were all waiting. Like so many live question marks hung on his word. They not only hung upon it, they were weights, actual physical weights, trying to drag it out of him. He felt the tense stare of each one of them, heavy as a stone, upon his soul. There was no sympathy or solicitude behind those gazes. All of them were thinking of their lands, their lives, and their homes that would be at the mercy of the men of Gwynedd if he refused.

He moistened his lips again. Never before had he needed loyalty that could not be got by force, or seen the value of things so ethereal and incalculable as friendship and affection.

He looked around upon all the circle.

"Is it necessary that I should do this thing?" he asked. "You my faithful fighting-men, and my foster-brothers, and my house folk, is there not one among all of you that will take the blow in my place?"

And he thought of all his tribe as of members of his own body. It seemed incredible that there should not be one that would sacrifice itself, realizing its own relative unimportance, to let the head live. But the circle of white faces did not open to let a man through or to let him pass. It drew back a little, as if from some cold presence that suddenly stood beside him, but it did not part. It still enclosed him.

"There is not indeed," they said.

And he looked, and felt or saw what that Cold Presence was, that they had left him alone with, in the middle of the circle. It was Death.

He licked his lips.

"I will take the blow," he said.

In the grey of dawn he came to the banks of the river Cynvael, opposite the hill Bryn Kyvergr. The bath that Blodeuwedd had had built for Llew still stood there. He saw that there was a goat tethered beside it, and shivered. . . .

The black of night was fading before a harsh grey pallor in the heavens. A red spear of light thrust its fiery tip up over the eastern rim of the world. He could see Bryn Kyvergyr only as a tall dark shadow looming up through the river mists, but he strained his eyes trying and dreading to catch the gleam of armor there.

Silence brooded over the world. Heavy, grey silence that seemed to be waiting as he was waiting. . . .

He felt very cold. He shivered and wrapped his cloak closer around him. He thought: "It is unfair. It is worse than what I did to him. He did not know that I was there, waiting. . . ." And he remem-

bered that today it would be another who waited, and he who would
be the prey. . . .

Red light streamed like an opened vein, far to the east. The mists
over the river whitened, grew feathery and half-transparent.

He saw the sheen of armor moving on Bryn Kyvergy. . . .

He stood and stared as long as he thought that he might stare.
Then he went slowly to the cauldron and climbed upon it. He turned
there and stood with one foot upon its edge and the other stretched
out towards the goat's back.

Then, of a sudden, he screamed. His voice rang out desperately,
calling upon the man on the farther bank of the river.

"Since it was because of a woman's beguilings that I did to you
what I have done, I beg you by all the gods to let me take up the slab
of stone that is yonder on the river bank, and hold it between me and
the blow!"

There was silence across the water.

Llew remembered all the beauty of Blodeuwedd, the lost fragrance and the thousand sweetnesses of her who now was a gloomy
bird of the night, doomed to pay for her nights of love through countless ages in the dark, without respite till the world's end. . . . Memory
rushed over him in a tide so vivid that it was rapture as well as pain.
He thought: "In his place, might not I too have wished to kill to win
her, I who will kill now for the barren prize of vengeance, for her that
can never be restored to me?"

For a moment he felt a strange sense of brotherhood with the man
he meant to kill. They both had loved her; both had longed for her.

A window seemed to open far above him, on the grey-white light
of another world. . . . It closed again. Yet he answered: "Indeed, I will
not deny you that."

"May the gods reward you and love you for that," said Goronwy.

He went down to the river and took up the great slab from beside
it. They were mighty men in those days.

He came back and climbed upon the cauldron again, hugging the
stone to him lightly, as though it had been a woman he loved. It covered him from head to foot like a gigantic shield.

He put his foot upon the goat's back. . . .

The sky streamed red as with the fiery blood of giants slain in
combat in the heavens. It flamed like a funeral pyre. The sun rose
blood-red over the right side of the world. The river mists scattered
before it like flying feathers, dissolving under its burning light.

Llew crossed the river. He came to where lay the pierced slab of stone that for ages after was to be called Llech Goronwy. He drew his spear out of the hole within it. . . . The red shaft, as he lifted it, blazed back, dripping and crimson, to the sun. . . .

Then he turned and went back toward Mur y Castell, where Gwydion and the men of Gwynedd waited.

Notes

MÂTH'S POWERS OF HEARING. *The Mabinogi* says that whatever word was spoken, if the wind caught it, it was carried to Mâth. A power too unwieldy for even legend to deal with, since he apparently neglects to have the winds report to him a number of conversations which it was vitally important for him to know about.

But in Central Asia telepathy is called "sending messages on the wind."* May not the original idea of the druids have been the same before popular superstition and the extinction of their cult brought about the simpler and even more miraculous explanation of omniscience, an explanation which seems more primitive, but may really be decadent? Nicholas Roerich, the great Russian artist and traveler, has recorded, in his *Altai-Himalaya,* his desire to investigate the Central Asian temples of Bon-Po, where he thought he might find connections with druidism.

DEATH OF DYLAN AND SUBMERGENCE OF CAER ARIANRHOD. No account of the death of Dylan has survived. We know that a Triad said that he got his death-blow from his uncle, Govannon, and Taliessin speaks vaguely of poison and of Dylan's being pierced by some weapon, but does not mention Govannon, whose motive remains lost in darkness. Neither is the cause or manner of the sinking of Caer Arianrhod known, but this disaster to the mother of a sea-god whose slaying by her brother is still fiercely resented by the waves of the sea, makes it easy to imagine a connection. And a woman's unwise uncovering of a sacred well is a commonplace of the inundation stories in *Celtic Folklore, Welsh and Manx,* where Rhys discusses the possibilities (1) that the well was regarded as the eye of a water deity, (2) that the woman was either its priestess or forbidden to approach it.

*See Mme. Alexandra David-Neel's *Magic and Mystery in Tibet.*

THE MAKING OF THE FATAL SPEAR. According to *The Mabinogi* this spear could only be worked on during mass on Sundays. But I have carefully removed all Christian references and interpolations, because *The Mabinogi* is held to be really a story of the ancient tribal gods euphemerized into mortal kings and princes. See *The Mythology of all Races,* Vol. III.

PRYDYN is a Welsh name for the Picts. My depiction of the origin and philosophy of this race is some more of my housebuilding—too Atlantean and Pythagorean in flavor to be backed up by Celtic scholars. But the classical authorities did believe druid teachings to be similar to those of Pythagoras; and, after all, theirs is the only contemporary evidence.